Praise for Tracy Wolff's *Crave*

An Amazon Best YA Book of 2020
Glitter magazine's #1 Pick for Best YA of 2020

★ "The generation that missed *Twilight* will be bitten by this one.
Recommended first purchase."
—*SLJ*, starred review

"*Crave* is about to become fandom's new favorite
vampire romance obsession."
—Hypable

"Throw in some deadly intrigue to mingle with the dark secret
Jaxon bears, and you've got a recipe for
YA vampire success in *Crave*."
—*Bustle*

"Wolff has a masterpiece on her hands. It's as simple as that."
—Vocal.Media

"My favorite February read...it's full of suspense and interesting
characters that keep you turning until the last page!"
—Aurora Dominguez, Frolic's YA expert

"[C]raving something fun to read, slightly dark
and romantic...couldn't put it down!"
—Natalie Morales, NBC

"Brings gripping tension teeming with a blend of action and
teenage angst. *Crave* is beautifully descriptive with amazing
pacing and wonderfully sinister settings."
—#1 *New York Times* bestselling author Christine Feehan

covet

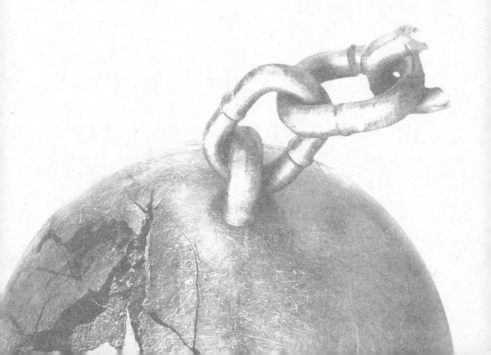

covet

NEW YORK TIMES BESTSELLING AUTHOR

TRACY WOLFF

Copyright © 2021 by Tracy Deebs-Elkenaney. All rights reserved, including the right to reproduce, distribute, or transmit in any form or by any means. For information regarding subsidiary rights, please contact the Publisher. Preview of *Ember of Night* copyright © 2021 by Molly E Lee

Entangled Publishing, LLC
10940 S Parker Road
Suite 327
Parker, CO 80134
rights@entangledpublishing.com

Entangled Teen is an imprint of Entangled Publishing, LLC.

Visit our website at www.entangledpublishing.com.

Edited by Liz Pelletier
Cover design by Bree Archer
Cover artwork by
allanswart/gettyimages,
Nadezhda Kharitonova/Gettyimages,
LarisaBozhikova/GettyImages
Interior Endpaper Design by Elizabeth Turner Stokes
Interior design by Toni Kerr

ISBN 978-1-68281-581-6 (Hardcover) ISBN 978-1-64937-105-8 (B&N)
ISBN 978-1-64937-106-5 (BAM) ISBN 978-1-64937-107-2 (TARGET)
ISBN 978-1-68281-615-8 (Ebook)

Manufactured in the United States of America

First Edition March 2021

10 9 8 7 6 5 4 3 2 1

an imprint of Entangled Publishing LLC

*To my dad, for nurturing my imagination and
making me believe I could do anything.*

*And for my mother, for supporting and
loving me through everything.*

Author's Note: This book depicts issues of panic attacks, death and violence, emotional torture and incarceration, and some sexual content. It is my hope that these elements have been handled sensitively, but if these issues could be considered triggering to you, please take note.

Life After Death

This isn't how it was supposed to happen.

This isn't how *anything* was supposed to happen. Then again, when has my life gone according to plan this year? From the moment I first got to Katmere Academy, so much has been out of my control. Why should today, why should this moment, be any different?

I finish pulling up my tights and straighten my skirt. Then I slide my feet into my favorite pair of black boots and grab my black uniform blazer from the closet.

My hands are shaking a little—to be honest, my whole body is shaking a little—as I ease my arms into the sleeves. But I feel like that's fair. This is the third funeral I've gone to in twelve months. And it hasn't gotten any easier. Nothing has.

It's been five days since I beat the challenge.

Five days since Cole broke the mating bond between Jaxon and me and almost destroyed us both.

Five days since I nearly died...and five days since Xavier actually did.

My stomach pitches and rolls and for a second, I feel like I'm going to throw up.

I take several deep breaths—in through my nose, out through my mouth—to quell the nausea and the panic rising inside me. It takes a minute or three, but eventually both feelings subside enough that it's no longer like I've got a fully loaded 18-wheeler parked on my chest.

It's a small victory, but I'll take it.

I pull in one more deep breath as I fasten the brass buttons on the front of my blazer, then glance in the mirror to make sure I look presentable. I do...as long as you play fast and loose with the definition of "presentable."

My brown eyes are dull, my skin sallow. And my ridiculous curls are fighting the bun I've wrestled them into. Of course, grief has never been my best look.

At least the bruises from the Ludares challenge have started to fade, turning from their original violent black and purple into that mottled yellow/ lavender color that happens just before they disappear completely. And it helps slightly to know that Cole finally hit my uncle's too-many-strikes-and- you're-out limit and got expelled. Part of me wishes that he'll meet an even bigger bully at that school for paranormal delinquents and misfits he was sent to in Texas...just to see how it feels for once.

The bathroom door opens, and my cousin, Macy, walks out, robe on and towel wrapped around her head. I want to hurry her along—we've only got twenty minutes before we're supposed to be in the assembly hall for the memorial—but I can't. Not when she looks like her every breath is an agony.

I know, too well, how that feels.

Instead, I wait for Macy to say something, anything, but she doesn't make a sound as she heads toward her bed and the dress uniform I've laid out for her. It hurts to see her like this, her bruises no less painful than mine for being on the inside.

From my first day at Katmere, Macy has been this irrepressible presence. Light to Jaxon's dark, enthusiasm to Hudson's sarcasm, joy to my sorrow. But now...now it's like every single speck of glitter has disappeared from her life. And from mine.

"Do you need help?" I finally ask as she continues to stare down at her uniform like she's never seen it before.

The blue eyes she turns my way are haunted, empty. "I don't know why I'm being so..." Her voice drifts off as she clears her throat in an attempt to force away the hoarseness of misuse—and the sadness that is causing it. "I barely knew—"

This time she stops, because her voice breaks completely. Her fists clench, and tears swim in her eyes.

"Don't," I say, moving to hug her, because I know what it's like to beat yourself up over something you can't change. Over surviving when someone you love hasn't. "Don't discount your feelings for him just because you didn't know him forever. It's about *how* you know a person, not how long."

She shudders a little, a sob catching in her chest, so I just hug her harder, trying to take away a little bit of her pain and sadness. Trying to do for her what she did for me when I first got to Katmere.

She holds me just as tightly, tears rolling down her face for so many tortured seconds. "I miss him," she finally chokes out. "I just miss him so much."

"I know," I soothe, rubbing her back in slow circles. "I know."

She cries in earnest now, shoulders shuddering, body shaking, breath breaking, for minutes that seem to last forever. My heart crumbles in my chest—for Macy, for Xavier, for everything that's brought us to this moment—and it's all I can do not to cry with her. But it's Macy's turn right now...and my turn to take care of her.

Eventually, she pulls away. Wipes her wet cheeks. Gives me a fragile smile that doesn't reach her eyes. "We need to go," she whispers with one last pass of her hands over her face. "I don't want to be late to the memorial."

"Okay." I return her smile with one of my own, then walk away to give her some privacy to get dressed.

When I turn back a few minutes later, I can't help but gasp. Not because Macy has done a glamour to dry and style her hair—I'm used to that—but because her hot-pink hair is now pitch-black.

"It didn't feel right," she murmurs as she combs her fingers through a few strands. "Hot pink isn't exactly a mourning color."

I know she's right, and still *I* mourn for the last vestiges of my bright and shiny cousin. We've all lost so much recently, and I'm not sure how much more we can take.

"It looks good," I tell her, because it does. But that's no surprise—Macy would look good bald or with her hair on fire, and this is a far cry from either of those. It does make her look even more delicate, though. Even more fragile.

"It doesn't feel good," she answers. But she's sliding her feet into a stylish pair of flats, adding earrings to the myriad holes in her ears. Doing another glamour—this one to get rid of her red and puffy eyes.

Her shoulders back, her jaw locked, her eyes are sad but clear as they meet mine. "Let's do this." Even her voice is resolved, steely, and it's that determination that gets me moving toward the door.

I grab my phone to text the others that we're on our way, but the second I pull open the door, I figure out it's unnecessary. Because they're all right here in the hall, waiting for us. Flint, Eden, Mekhi, Luca. Jaxon...and Hudson. Some are more banged up than others, but they're all a little worse for wear—

just like Macy and me—and my heart swells as I look them over.

Things are a mess right now—oh my God, are they a mess—but one thing hasn't changed. These seven people have my back and I have theirs... and I always will.

But as my eyes meet Jaxon's cold, dark ones, I can't help acknowledging that while one thing hasn't changed, everything else has.

And I have no idea what to do about any of it.

Check Your Mate

Three weeks later...

"**I**'m begging you." Macy throws herself across her rainbow-comforter-covered bed and stares at me with imploring eyes. It's so good to see her finally almost smiling again since Xavier's funeral that I can't help myself from smiling back. It's not a full smile yet, but I'll take it. "For the love of God, please, please, pleeeeeeease put those boys out of their misery."

"That's going to be hard," I answer as I drop my backpack next to my desk before flopping down on my own bed. "Considering I haven't put them *into* their misery."

"That is the biggest lie you have ever told." My cousin snorts, then lifts her head just enough to make sure that I can see her rolling her eyes. "You are one hundred and fifty percent responsible for the way Jaxon and Hudson have been moping around school for the last three weeks."

"I feel like there are a lot of reasons Jaxon and Hudson are moping around school, and I'm only to blame for about half of them," I shoot back...then immediately regret the words.

Not because they aren't true but because I now have to watch as the little bit of color Macy had in her cheeks slowly drains away. She looks so different from the girl I met in November that it's hard to believe she's the same person. Her wildly colored hair still hasn't made a reappearance, and while the deep raven black she dyed it for Xavier's funeral suits her coloring, it doesn't suit anything else about her. Except her sadness...it suits that just fine.

I start to apologize, but Macy rolls over to face me and plows ahead. "I know exactly what a miserable vampire looks like, and you've got two of them on your hands. And just an FYI, deadly and pathetic make for a really dangerous combination, in case you haven't noticed."

"Oh, I've noticed." It's a combination I've been dealing with for weeks, a combination that makes my every breath feel like a bomb about to go off, my every move like I'm playing Russian roulette with everyone's happiness.

And since the universe just isn't done screwing with me...apparently, Macy was wrong when she first told me that Hudson had graduated before Jaxon killed him. Turns out: nope, so close and yet not quite there. Something about him lacking enough credits because he'd had private tutors instead of attending Katmere for all four years. Macy was several years his junior, so she'd shrugged—what did she know? No one spoke his name after his death. Either way, it means that everywhere I turn, there he is. Just like Jaxon. Both of them in our friendship circle but not. Both of them watching me with eyes that appear blank on the surface but hold a multitude of emotions underneath. Waiting on me to do or say...*something*.

"I still don't know how I ended up mated to Hudson," I say dully. "I thought you had to be interested in being mated, or at least 'open' to it, for it to happen in the first place?"

Macy grins at me. "Clearly you feel *something* for him."

I roll my eyes. "Gratitude. I feel gratitude for him. And I'm pretty sure that's a terrible reason to hook up."

"So..." Macy's eyes are positively sparkling with humor now. "You've thought about 'hooking up' with Hudson, eh?"

I throw a small decorative pillow at my cousin, who easily dodges its path and laughs. "Well, all I know is, most everyone at school would kill to find even *one* mate. You having had two since arriving is so not allowed."

Macy's teasing me, trying to lighten the moment, but it doesn't help.

Hudson often sits with us at meals or in classes we share. Although most of the Order and Flint watch him warily, he's somehow managed to woo my cousin with no more than a teasing half smile and a French vanilla latte.

In fact, she's actually one of the few people who blames Jaxon for our mating bond being severed, and she's let it be known she is firmly Team Hudson. I can't help but wonder if she's on Hudson's side because she really thinks he's best for me—or just that he isn't Jaxon, the boy who insisted we challenge the Unkillable Beast, a move that ended up getting Xavier killed.

Either way, she's right about one thing: eventually I'm going to have to deal with this mess.

I've been doing my best to ignore the situation a while longer, though...at least until I have a plan. I've spent nearly all my time since Xavier's funeral trying to figure out what to do, how to fix things—between Jaxon and me, and Jaxon and Hudson, and Hudson and me—but I can't. The ground has turned to quicksand beneath me, and my wings aren't nearly as much help as you'd expect them to be... I mean, I have to land sometime, and every time I do, I start to sink.

Macy must sense my inner anguish, since she sits up on the end of her bed, her amusement fading as quickly as mine. "I know things are rough right now," she continues. "I was just teasing about the boys. You're doing your best."

"What if I don't know what to do?" The words explode out of me like I'm a bottle under pressure and Macy's just caused the first leak. "I had barely begun to deal with being a gargoyle, and now I have to deal with winning a seat on the Circle of Doom and Desperation and being coronated right after graduation."

"Circle of *Doom and Desperation*?" Macy repeats with a startled laugh.

"After which I'm sure I'll be locked in a tower or beheaded or something else equally fatalistic." I say it like it's a joke, but I'm not kidding. There isn't one ounce of optimism in me about being a member of the paranormal council Jaxon and Hudson's parents head up...or anything else that comes with it. Including politics, survival, *and* being mated to Hudson instead of my *actual* boyfriend in this brave new world I've found myself in.

"I'm still in love with Jaxon. I can't change how I feel." I groan. "But I can't stand hurting Hudson, either—or the look in his eyes when we're sitting at the lunch table and he's watching me with his brother."

The whole thing is a nightmare beyond comprehension, and the fact that I haven't been able to sleep pretty much at all since I nearly died only makes everything worse. But how can I relax when every time I close my eyes, I feel Cyrus's teeth sinking into my neck and the agony of his eternal bite spreading through me? Or I remember Hudson placing me in a shallow grave and burying me alive (still not ready to ask how he knew to do that)? Or worse—and yes, this is actually worse—I see the look on Jaxon's face when Hudson told him I am his mate?

Memories so devastating, all I want to do is run away and hide.

"Hey, everything is going to be okay," Macy says, voice tentative but eyes concerned.

"'Okay' might be a stretch." I roll over so that I'm staring at the ceiling, but I barely see it. Instead, all I see are *their* eyes.

One dark pair, one light.

Both tormented.

Both waiting for something I don't know how to give them and an answer I don't even know how to begin to find.

I know what I feel. I love Jaxon.

And Hudson, well, that's more complicated. Not love, which I'm worried is not what he wants to hear. Yes, my pulse races when he's near, but objectively, the guy is next-level gorgeous. Any person in their right mind would be attracted to him. Plus, there's now this mating bond between us that is causing me to feel things that aren't really there as well. At least not that I want them to be.

After everything he did for me, after the bond I realize we built over those weeks trapped together, I don't want to disappoint him and tell him I don't feel more than friendship for him.

I groan again. There I go, assuming Hudson even wants to be mated to me. He might be as mad at the universe as I am for putting us in this awkward situation.

Macy lets out a long sigh, then climbs off her bed and settles onto the end of mine. "I'm sorry. I didn't mean to push."

"Your pushing isn't what upset me. It's just…" I trail off, not sure how to vocalize the confusion roiling around inside me.

"Everything?" She fills in the blank I left, and I nod, because yeah, everything is a hell of a lot.

Silence stretches between us, long and uncomfortable. I wait for Macy to give up, to go back to her own bed and forget about this dumpster fire of a conversation, but she doesn't move. Instead, she leans back against the wall and watches me with a calm patience that isn't exactly her normal modus operandi.

I'm not sure if it's the silence or the way she's watching me or the need to spill my guts that's been building all day, but the tension ratchets higher and higher until finally I blurt out the truth I've been trying to hide from everyone, even myself. "I really, really don't think I'm strong enough to do this."

I don't know exactly what reaction I expect Macy to have to my confession—in a split second I imagine everything from her lavishing sympathy on me to her telling me to *suck it up, buttercup* with a hard edge that has nothing to do with me and everything to do with how things are going pretty awful for her, too.

In the end, though, she does the one thing I don't expect. The one thing I've never even *considered*. She bursts out laughing. "Well, no shit, Sherlock. I'd be worried if you actually thought you *could* deal with all of this on your own."

"Really?" I'm flummoxed. And maybe a little insulted—does she really think I'm so incompetent? Just because *I* know I'm a mess doesn't mean I want everyone else to know, too. "Why?"

"Because you're *not* alone, and you don't have to go it alone. That's what I'm here for. That's what all of us are here for—especially your boyfriend*s*."

I narrow my eyes at her plural use of the word—and the emphasis she put on it. "Boyfriend," I correct, stressing the hard *d* on the end. "One, not two." I hold up my index finger just to make sure she gets it. "One boyfriend."

"Oh, right. One. Of course." Macy shoots me a sly look. "Sooooo, just to be clear. Which vampire is that exactly?"

My Achy Breaky Bond

"You're obnoxious," I tease. "But would you mind if we focus on what really matters? Graduating high school?"

Between losing my parents, transferring schools, and missing four months while I did my best impression of a waterspout, I'm about as behind as I can get and still be a senior. Which means if I don't finish the extra projects I've been assigned and pass all my finals, I'm going to be a senior again next year, too. And that is *not* acceptable, no matter how much Macy would like me to stick around another year. I mean, if Hudson can make up classes after being *dead*, for God's sake, I can make them up, too.

"You know that's the real reason I'm burying my head, don't you?" I finally admit. "Because there's no way I can deal with the ridiculous amount of work I have to make up *and* try to figure out what to do about Cyrus or the Circle or—"

"Your mate?" Macy smiles ruefully and holds up a hand before I can protest. "Sorry, couldn't resist. But you're right, as much as I'd wish it otherwise, you seem to really want to graduate." She walks over and grabs her laptop off her desk. "So, as your self-appointed best friend, it's up to me to make sure that happens. You've got a presentation due for Dr. Veracruz's class on magical history, right? I heard some other seniors talking about it."

"Yeah." I nod. "Everyone had to pick a subject discussed in class this year, then write and present a ten-page paper about some aspect of that topic we didn't have time to go over. She says it's so that we all get a more well-rounded knowledge of the different parts of history, but I think she's just trying to torture us."

Macy climbs back on her bed and types something on her laptop. "I know just the topic for you to research!"

"Oh yeah?" I ask, rolling over and sitting up.

"Yes," she says. "You guys discussed mating bonds, right? I've been dying to take this class just for that reason. Well, you're a walking example of something not discussed in class."

I shake my head. "Unfortunately, I missed that lecture, but Flint told me it's possible to be mated to more than one person in your lifetime. I'm not the only person to ever have more than one mate."

Macy pauses her typing and looks up at me, one brow arched. "Yes, but you're the only one to ever have a mating bond severed by something other than death."

"It's never happened to anyone else?" I repeat, my heart pounding in my chest. "Really?" It seems so hard to believe, but also too terrible to believe. If no one has ever experienced this before, how are we going to fix it? What are we going to do? And why, why, *why* did it happen to Jaxon and me?

"No one," Macy reiterates. "Mating bonds never break, Grace. They just don't. They can't. It's a law of nature or something." She pauses and looks down at her hands resting on her keyboard. "Except, somehow, yours did."

Like I really need to be reminded of that.

Like I wasn't there.

Like I didn't feel it snap with a force that nearly tore me in half, a force that nearly destroyed me...and Jaxon.

"Never?" I must have misheard that part. Surely I'm not the only one.

"Never," Macy insists, deliberately enunciating each syllable even as she looks at me like I've suddenly grown three heads. "Not kind of never, Grace. Not almost never. *Never* never. Like *never in the history of our species* never. Mating bonds can*not* be broken while mates are alive. Ever." She shakes her head for emphasis. "I mean never. Ever. Nev—"

"Okay, okay. I get it." I shake my head in surrender. "Mating bonds never break. Except Jaxon's and mine *did* break and neither of us is dead, so..."

"Yeah," she agrees with a frown. "We're in totally uncharted territory here. It's no wonder you feel so messed up. You *are* messed up."

"Wow. Thanks for that." I pretend to pull a dagger out of my heart.

But Macy just makes a face at me. "You know what I mean."

"I do," I agree. "But there's one part of this whole thing I just can't figure out. I've been thinking about it for days, and it's why I'm so skeptical about the whole *this never happens* thing. I—"

"Never," she interrupts, waving her hands around for emphasis. "It literally *never* happens."

I hold up a hand again to get her to pause, because I'm really trying to work toward a point here. "But if that's true, and mating bonds *never* break, why exactly was there a spell to break mine? And how did the Bloodletter just happen to know it?"

Keep Calm and Wingo On

"**H**ey, do you know what's for dinner tonight?" I ask as Macy and I make our way down the dragon-sconce-lit hallways to the cafeteria. We both worked up a massive appetite researching mating bonds for the last three hours—although no closer to discovering someone else whose bond had been severed or any mention of a spell to do it. "I forgot to check."

"Whatever it is, it will be terrible." She makes a disgusted face and sighs. "It's one of the bad Wednesdays."

"Bad Wednesdays?" I should probably know what she means, considering I've been eating in the dining hall nearly every day for the last three weeks, but I've been more than a little preoccupied. Most days, I'm lucky if I can remember to wear my uniform, let alone what the cafeteria is serving...well, except for waffle Thursdays. Those are indelibly imprinted in my brain.

Macy gives me the side-eye as we head down the stairs. "Let's just say I suggest the frozen yogurt—and maybe a dinner roll, *if* you're feeling brave."

"Frozen yogurt? Seriously? How bad could it be? The kitchen witches are awesome." I mean, what could they possibly serve to engender this kind of disgust in my cousin? Eye of newt? Toe of frog?

"The witches *are* awesome," she agrees. "But one Wednesday a month, the witches take off early for Wingo nights. And tonight is one of those nights."

"Wingo nights?" I repeat, completely mystified even as my imagination conjures up images of witches with giant raven wings flying around the top of the castle. Then again, how would I have missed that?

Macy looks shocked that I haven't heard of whatever this ritual is. "It's a witchy version of bingo. I can't wait till I'm old enough to play."

"Old enough to play?" I rack my brain trying to figure out what sort of bingo the kitchen witches might play that would be adults only.

"Yes!" Macy's face lights up. "It's like bingo, but every time they call a number on your card, you have to do a shot from whatever potions they're serving that night. Some make you dance like a chicken, others turn your clothes inside out… Last month, they even had one that made them walk the entire room roaring like a T. rex."

She laughs. "Let's just say, when you finally score a bingo and win, you've totally earned it. The kitchen witches are addicted, even though Marjorie always wins, since she's such a drama queen. Which then becomes a whole thing on its own because Serafina and Felicity accuse her of charming the balls—"

"Exactly whose balls are you charming?" Flint asks as all six-foot-whatever of him pops up behind us. As per usual, he's got a huge grin on his handsome face and mischief in his amber eyes. "I'm only asking because I'm pretty sure it's against the rules."

"Don't you start, too," Macy says with a grin and a shake of her head. "I was *talking* about Wingo and how the kitchen witches get their wands in a twist over—"

"Wingo?" He stops dead at the bottom of the stairs, his easy smile replaced by a look of horror. "Tell me it's not Wingo night already?"

Macy sighs. "I wish I could."

"You know what? I'm really not that hungry." Flint starts to back away. "I think I'll—"

"Oh, no. You're not getting out of it that easily." Macy loops her arm through his and starts tugging him forward. "If the rest of us have to suffer, so do you."

Flint grumbles, but Macy just propels him along even as she agrees with him.

The two of them whine the whole rest of the way, until finally I say, "Nothing can be this bad. Heck, I survived public school cafeterias, where frozen yogurt wasn't an option even on the good days."

"Oh, it's that bad," Macy answers.

"Actually, it's worse," Flint warns me.

"How? How could it actually be worse? I mean, who's doing the cooking?"

They give me identical looks of horror as they both answer at the same time. "The vampires."

Wednesday,
Bloody Wednesday

"The vampires?" Not going to lie. I recoil a little as I think about what Jaxon—and Hudson—eat.

"Exactly," Flint tells me with a disgusted face. "Why Foster decided to put the vampires in charge on the kitchen witches' day off, I'll never know."

"Who should have been in charge?" Mekhi asks as he walks up behind Macy. "The dragons? Roasted marshmallows only get most of the student body so far."

"At least marshmallows are food," Flint tells him as he pulls open one of the dining hall doors with a flourish, then gestures for me to go inside.

"Blood cake is food," Mekhi shoots back. "Or so I've been told."

"Blood cake?" My stomach turns over nervously. I have no idea what that is, but it sounds scary.

Flint shoots Mekhi a smug look. "How are those dragon-roasted marshmallows sounding now, Grace?"

"Like dinner, if I can add a pack of cherry Pop-Tarts." I glance around the dining hall, checking to see if the à la carte snack table from breakfast and lunch is still out. But, typical of all the other dinnertimes, it's nowhere to be seen.

"It won't be that bad, I swear," Mekhi says as he starts shepherding us toward the food line.

"How can I have been at Katmere this long and not known about Wingo night?" I wonder, even as a part of my brain is cataloging every dish I've ever heard of with blood in it—which, to be honest, isn't that many. The other part of my brain is busy checking out the cafeteria, trying to spot Jaxon... or Hudson.

I don't know if I'm worried or relieved when I can't find either of them.

"Because you've never been around this many weeks in a row before,"

Macy answers. "And I think the last time one of these rolled around, Jaxon was feeding you tacos in the library."

My mind boggles a little at the thought that that night in the library was only a month ago. So much has changed since then that it feels like it happened several months ago. Maybe even years.

"I wish I was eating tacos in the library right now," Flint grumbles as he grabs a couple of trays and holds them out for Macy and me.

Macy takes the offering with a sigh. "Yeah, me too."

"Don't listen to them," Mekhi tells me. "It's not that bad."

"You don't eat, so you don't get a vote," Flint says.

Mekhi just laughs. "Fair point. I'm going to grab a drink, and then I'll find us a table." He winks at Macy, then heads toward the big orange sports coolers against the back wall of the dining hall.

The line is shorter than usual—I wonder why—and moves pretty fast, so it only takes a couple of minutes before we're standing in front of Katmere's elegant buffet tables. Usually they are overflowing with food, but tonight the offerings are pretty slim. And none of them is particularly tempting to me.

Even the salad bar is gone, in its place a giant cauldron of soup that has vegetables floating in it, along with a bunch of dark-brown cubes I don't recognize. "What are those things?" I whisper to Macy as we pass by several adult vampires—including Marise, who smiles at me and waves.

I wave back but keep moving down the line as Macy whispers, "Coagulated blood."

We pass a black sausage that I don't even have to ask about—I've seen enough British cooking shows to know what gives the sausage its distinctive coloring. And to be fair, a lot of people love it. But I don't know...the whole vampire thing makes it feel really weird. Like, how do we know for sure that they're using animal blood and not human blood, since at least some of the vamp teachers here are totally old-school?

Just the thought has my stomach turning queasy. But up ahead is a huge pile of pancakes, and I've never been more relieved in my life to have breakfast for dinner. At least until I get closer and realize that these aren't ordinary pancakes. They're a really deep, dark reddish-purple.

"Tell me they didn't actually put blood in the pancakes," I say.

"They totally put blood in the pancakes," Macy answers.

"It's a Swedish recipe," Flint tells me "Blodplättar. And they're actually pretty good." He reaches over and puts several on his plate.

The vamps are watching the line closely, so I grab one of the pancakes. They obviously worked hard on dinner, and the last thing I want to do is hurt anyone's feelings. Besides, the frozen yogurt station is on the way to the table…

After dousing my pancake in syrup and filling up a bowl with a mix of vanilla and chocolate yogurt and all the toppings it can hold, I follow Flint and Macy through the crowded dining hall to the table Mekhi chose. Eden and Gwen have already joined him, and I can't help grinning when I read the front of Eden's newest purple hoodie: *For The Hoard.*

She sees me smiling and winks, right before she reaches over and snags the cherry off the top of Macy's frozen yogurt sundae.

Macy just laughs. "I knew you were going to do that." She reaches in and grabs another cherry. "That's why I got two."

Quick as lightning, Eden snatches that one as well. "You should know by now never to trust a dragon with your treasure."

"Hey!" Macy pouts while the rest of us laugh. But once we're settled, I spoon a couple of the half dozen cherries from my bowl into hers. If being at Katmere has taught me nothing else, it's the value of being prepared for anything.

"Best. Cousin. Ever." Macy beams at me, and I realize it's the first real smile I've seen from her since Xavier died. It makes me breathe a tiny bit easier, makes me think that, while happy is a stretch, maybe she's beginning to find her way back to being at least okay.

Conversation flows around me, talk of senior projects and finals and gossip about classmates I don't know, as I dig into my frozen yogurt. I'm trying to pay attention, but it's hard when I keep looking around for Jaxon and Hudson. Which is ridiculous, I know. Half an hour ago in my room, I was all *I don't have time to worry about them,* and now I can't stop scanning the dining hall for one, or both.

But I can't help it. No matter how out of control things are today, I can't just turn my feelings on and off. I love Jaxon. I'm friends with Hudson. I'm worried about them both, and I need to know they're fine, especially since I haven't had the chance to talk to either of them about everything going on.

I'm halfway through my frozen yogurt when a hush comes over the dining hall, right about the time the hairs on the back of my neck stand up. I look to see everyone staring at something behind me and I know—even before I turn around—who I'm going to find.

5

Macy, who has already turned around to see what all the fuss is about, elbows me in the side and hisses Jaxon's name out of the corner of her mouth.

I nod to let her know I've heard her, but I don't move. I hold my breath, though, as the shivers running up and down my spine warn me that he's getting closer...and his attention is focused entirely on me.

Macy squeaks, which tells me everything I need to know about what mood he's in. She's relaxed around him a lot in the last few weeks—friendship will do that—but it doesn't mean she's forgotten how dangerous he is. And neither has anyone else, apparently. It's reflected in the faces of every single person around me, in the way they all seem frozen, like they're just waiting for Jaxon to strike...and want to make damn sure that they aren't the one he goes after.

Even Flint is sitting back in his chair, both his pancakes and his conversation with Eden about their physics final forgotten, as he looks right past me. The look in his gaze is a combination of wary and reckless, and it's worry over Flint—over what he's feeling and what he might do—that has me turning around before things go to absolute shit around me.

I'm not the least bit surprised to find Jaxon behind me. I am, however, surprised at just how close he really is. A few weeks ago, there's no way he'd have been able to get within a few inches of me without my entire body going haywire. All I've got now is this shiver down my spine, and it's not exactly a good feeling.

After dinner last night, he'd invited me back to his tower to study, but I couldn't go, since Hudson had already asked me to study with him. I get frustrated just thinking of the mess that ensued, since neither of the Vega brothers could be adults about the situation and let us all study together.

I'd ended up studying in my room, alone. And not learning a damn thing because I was too busy being pissed at them.

But then I texted Jaxon twice today, and he hasn't so much as acknowledged I exist. I get that he doesn't like my friendship with Hudson—but he has to know that's all it is. Friendship. I apparently have no choice in who I'm mated to, but I've shown Jaxon in a thousand different ways that he's who I choose to love.

Which is why I'm so annoyed by the cold shoulder he's given me all day.

He must feel the same way, because his dark eyes are as cold as midnight.

As cold as Denali's summit in January.

As cold as they were the very first time we met. No. Colder.

For what feels like forever, he doesn't say anything and neither do I. Instead, the silence stretches thin as ice—between us and around us—until Luca finally steps out from behind him and asks, "Mind if we sit with you guys?"

For the first time, I realize the entire Order is here. I've grown used to eating with Jaxon and Mekhi a few times a week, obviously, but it's rare for all of Jaxon's friends to join us. Yet here they are—Luca, Byron, Rafael, Liam, all lined up behind Jaxon like they're expecting an attack.

"Of course." I gesture to the empty seats scattered around the table, but Luca isn't asking me. His gaze is laser focused on Flint. Who, it turns out, is looking right back, a slight flush on his brown cheeks.

And wow, this is a development I did not see coming. But one I am absolutely here for.

A glance at Eden tells me she's watching the whole thing as intently as I am, and the smile on her face makes me wonder if maybe I was wrong about who Flint has been in love with. I thought he meant Jaxon that day on the Ludares field, but maybe he meant Luca all along? Or maybe Luca was the new guy he was referring to? Since our talk, Flint hasn't mentioned his love life again, and I didn't feel it was fair to question him about it, either.

But whatever he was getting at that day, it's obvious—right now at least—he is definitely interested in Luca. Who, apparently, is interested right back.

Flint nods, and Luca crosses over to sit next to him. Before I can even think about where Jaxon is going to sit, Macy has scooted her chair closer to Eden's, creating an obviously empty space for someone to sit beside me. Jaxon nods his thanks, and seconds later, he's pulled a chair from another table and is sliding in right next to me.

My heart jumps as his thigh grazes mine, and he grins just a little. Shoots me a look out of the corner of his eye I'd recognize anywhere. Then very slowly, very deliberately, does it again.

This time, my breath catches in my throat, because this is Jaxon. My Jaxon. And though our relationship hasn't felt the same since the challenge, and though I'm so confused I can barely think, I still want him. I still love him.

"How was your day?" he asks softly.

I shake my head as the state of my grades, and the precariousness of my graduating, comes back to me. "So bad that I don't want to talk about it."

I don't mention that him not answering my texts only made the day worse. I can tell from the look in his eyes that he already knows it. And that he doesn't like this mess any more than I do.

"How—" My voice breaks, so I clear my throat and try again. "How about you? How was your day?"

He makes a face, shoves his hand through his silky black hair hard enough to reveal the jagged scar on his left cheek. The scar the vampire queen Delilah—his mother—gave him for murdering her firstborn son. Who is now back. And is now my mate, even though I am still in love with my old mate whose bond with me should never have been able to be broken.

Just thinking about it makes my head hurt.

Talk about a soap opera. I couldn't make this stuff up if I tried.

"Pretty much the same," he finally answers.

"Yeah, I figured."

He doesn't offer anything else, and neither do I. Around us, the conversation ebbs and flows, but I can't think of a single thing to say to break his stony silence. It feels strange to be this awkward with Jaxon, when we used to talk for hours about anything. About everything.

I hate it so much, especially watching how easy everyone else is with one another. Eden and Mekhi are laughing together, and so are Macy and Rafael. Byron and Liam are talking intensely about something, and Flint and Luca… Well, Flint and Luca are definitely flirting, while Jaxon and I can barely look at each other.

I start to take another bite of my frozen yogurt but realize I've lost my appetite before I so much as get the spoon to my mouth. I drop it back in the bowl and decide: fuck it. If things are so weird that I can't eat, I might as well go to the library.

Jaxon must sense my unease, though, because just as I'm about to get up, he slides his hand over mine. It feels so familiar, so good, that I automatically turn mine over to lace our fingers together even though I'm still annoyed with him.

He kisses my fingers before placing our joined hands onto his leg under the table, and a shiver of awareness runs through me. It's moments like these, when we're touching, that I think maybe we still have a chance. Maybe everything isn't as screwed up as it seems. Maybe there really is hope.

I'm pretty sure he feels the same way, judging by the grip he has on my hand. And the fact that he doesn't say anything to break the comfortable silence between us, almost as if he's as afraid as I am to ruin this moment. So we just sit there, soaking in the conversations going on around us. It works, too, at least for a little while.

And then it happens—every nerve in my body goes on red alert.

I don't need to turn around to know Hudson has just walked into the cafeteria, but the way Jaxon's hand tightens on mine gives me all the added confirmation I need.

6

A Tale of Two Vegas

A second later, it's like everyone notices him at once. Each person at the table stills as if holding their collective breath even as their eyes dart everywhere—except toward Jaxon and me. Well, everyone except Macy, who's waving like she's trying to flag down a bush plane in a snowstorm. And that's *before* she slides her chair down to make room for him to join us, moving so far that she's practically in Eden's lap.

Hudson murmurs a quick "thanks" even as he grabs a chair and plops his tray down next to Macy. There are four slices of cheesecake on it, along with his usual tumbler of blood.

Macy grins even wider, grabbing one of the plates. "Awww, you shouldn't have."

"I heard it was Wingo night. Thought you might appreciate some of the leftovers," Hudson says to Macy, but his eyes never leave mine, except for the one brief moment where he tracks the fact that both Jaxon and I have a hand under the table. And even though I know he can't see us touching, I feel like I've been caught doing something wrong. Jaxon must sense my sudden discomfort because he pulls his hand from mine and folds both of his on top of the table.

Hudson doesn't say anything to either of us. Instead, he turns to my cousin like he didn't even notice us holding hands and asks, "Anyone up for chess later?"

The two of them have been playing chess a couple of times a week. I think Hudson asked her to play with him the first time to take her mind off Xavier, and she accepted because she felt bad that everyone gave him such a wide berth. But lately, I've caught her googling chess moves when she thinks I'm not looking, and I know she's started to really enjoy their friendship.

"You better believe it," she replies around a mouthful of cheesecake.

"One of these days, I'm going to kick your ass."

"Pretty sure you're going to have to remember how to move your knight first," he shoots back.

"Hey, it's complicated," she tells him.

"Waaaaay harder than checkers," Eden teases her even as she steals a bite of Macy's cheesecake.

"It is!" Macy pouts. "Every piece does something different."

"I'll play with you, Macy," Mekhi calls from his spot at the end of the table. "Hudson's not the only master strategist at the table."

"No, but I am the only one with my own chess table," Hudson tells him.

Eden snorts. "Not sure that's something to brag about, Destructo Boy."

"You're just jealous, Lightning Girl."

"Damn straight." She grins. "I want to be able to blow shit up with just a wave of my hand."

He lifts a brow. "You mean you can't?"

She just laughs and rolls her eyes.

"Hey, Hudson, hit me up, man," Flint calls from the other end of the table.

Hudson glances at Macy, who shrugs, before he slides a piece of cheesecake down the table to Flint.

Flint nods his thanks before shoving a huge bite in his mouth. Luca smiles fondly at him before gesturing to the book Hudson put down next to his tray. "What are you reading now?" he asks.

Hudson holds up the book. "*A Lesson Before Dying*."

"A little late for that, isn't it?" Flint asks, and after a shocked pause, everyone cracks up. Especially Hudson.

I want to say something to him—I read that book junior year and loved it—but it feels weird to join in a conversation I'm obviously not included in. Hudson has talked to everyone at the table—everyone—except Jaxon and me. Which isn't awkward at all.

Especially not when the conversation continues to go on around us. Every time Flint says something funny, Hudson's eyes meet mine like he wants to share the joke...then they dart away like he thinks we aren't supposed to do that anymore. I hate it, just like I hate the weirdness that keeps growing between us. Hudson has done nothing to make me feel guilty for being in love with his brother—in fact, just the opposite. But us being mates (and that Jaxon and I used to be) hangs in the air between us like a bomb about to go off.

Add in the way Rafael and Liam keep staring him down because they can't seem to let go of the past and the way Flint blows hot and cold depending on his mood, and I can't help thinking Hudson would rather be anywhere but here. But he comes back, every day. He keeps trying, every day, because he wants things *not* to be awkward between us.

Unlike me, who won't even talk to him when Jaxon is nearby.

Suddenly, it's all too much, and I tell no one in particular that I need to go study.

God knows I've got more than enough work these days to keep me busy.

But when I push away from the table, Jaxon pushes away, too. "Can I talk to you?" he asks.

I want to laugh, want to ask what he could possibly have to say to me when he's spent the last ten minutes doing anything *but* speaking to me.

I don't, though.

Instead, I nod and avoid making eye contact with Hudson while I send the group what I know is a really fake-looking smile. Jaxon doesn't even bother doing that before he turns and heads for the door.

I follow him—of course I do. Because I'd follow Jaxon anywhere. And I can't deny the tiny part of me that hopes he's finally ready to discuss how we can make this work.

7

I Think I Missed the Punch Line

I expect Jaxon to stop right outside the cafeteria doors and say whatever it is that he wants to say. But I should have known better—he's not exactly into public displays of anything. So when he starts down the hall after holding the door for me, I figure we're going to his tower.

But he turns at the last second, and instead of going up the staircase that leads to his room, he takes me up the one that leads to mine.

The lump in my throat is beginning to feel like a bad B movie, except instead of *The Tomato That Ate Cleveland*, it's *The Sadness That Swallowed a Girl, a Gargoyle, and an Entire Fucking Mountain*. We always go to his room—for serious talks, to hang out, to *make* out. That he isn't taking me there now tells me everything I need to know about how this conversation is going to go.

Once we get to my room, I open the door and walk in, expecting Jaxon to follow me. Instead, he stands on the other side of Macy's beaded curtain, a look of uncertainty on his haggard but beautiful face for the first time in who knows how long.

"You know you're always welcome in my room." I force the words out of my too-tight throat and try to pretend like I'm not choking on them. On everything. "Nothing's changed."

"Everything's changed," he counters.

"Yeah," I admit even though everything inside me wants to deny it. "I guess it has."

My breathing turns ragged as a giant stone starts pressing down on my chest—one that has nothing to do with me being a gargoyle and everything to do with the panic churning inside me—and I turn away from him, try to gasp for breath without being too obvious.

But Jaxon knows me better than I want him to, and suddenly he's standing in front of me, his big, steady hands holding my own as he tells me, "Breathe with me, Grace."

I can't. I can't inhale. I can't talk. I can't do anything but stand here and feel like I'm suffocating.

Like the floor is moving beneath my feet and the walls around me are caving in.

Like my own body has turned against me, bent on destroying me as surely as the outside forces I'm growing so tired of struggling against.

"In—" He sucks in a long, deep breath and holds it for a second. "And out." He breathes out, slow and steady. When I do nothing but stare at him with wild eyes, his grip on my hands gets firmer. "Come on, Grace. In—" He takes another breath.

The breath I take in response is nowhere as deep, nowhere as steady—I'm actually pretty sure I sound like I'm choking on a blood pancake—but it's still a breath. Oxygen rushes into my lungs.

"That's it," he says, and now his hands are rubbing up and down my arms, my shoulders. It's meant to be comforting—and it is—but it's also devastating, because it doesn't feel like it's supposed to. It doesn't feel like Jaxon, my Jaxon, is touching me, at least not like it used to.

It's not fast and it's not easy, but eventually I get the panic attack under control. When it's over, when I can finally breathe again, I drop my forehead onto Jaxon's chest. His arms go around me automatically, and it isn't long before my arms slide around his waist as well.

I don't know how long we stand like that, holding each other but also letting each other go. It hurts more than I ever imagined it would.

"I'm sorry," he says as he finally releases me. "I'm so sorry, Grace."

I fight the urge to cling to him, to keep my body pressed against his for as long as I can. "It's not your fault," I tell him softly.

"Not about the panic attack—though I'm sorry about that, too." He thrusts a hand into his hair, and for the first time tonight, I can see his whole face in stark definition. He looks terrible—lost and tormented and in as much pain as I am. Maybe even more. "I'm sorry about all of this. If I could take back that one careless act, that one moment of utter selfishness and naivete, I would do it in a heartbeat. But I can't, and now…" This time it's his breath that sounds shaky. "And now, we're here, and I can't do a fucking thing about any of it."

"We'll get through it. It's just going to take some time—"

"It's not that easy." He shakes his head even as his jaw works furiously. "Maybe we'll get through it; maybe we won't. But look at you, Grace. It's hurting you being like this, giving you panic attacks."

He pauses, swallows convulsively. "*I'm* hurting you, and that's the last thing I ever wanted to do."

"So don't." It's my turn to reach out and grab on to him. "Don't do this. Please."

"It's already been done. That's what I'm trying to tell you. This, what we're feeling now...it's just the phantom pain after you've lost a limb. It still hurts, but there's nothing there. And there never will be again...at least not if we keep on like this."

"That's all we are to you?" I ask, pain slamming through me like a sledgehammer. "Just something that used to matter?"

"You're everything to me, Grace. You have been from the moment I first laid eyes on you. But this isn't working. It hurts too much. For all of us."

"It hurts now, but it doesn't have to be like this. Our mating bond broke. But that just means mine with Hudson can break, too—"

"Do you think that's what I want?" he demands. "I've lived two hundred years, and this is the worst pain I've ever felt in my life. Do you think I would wish that on you? On Hudson?"

His voice thickens, but he shakes his head. Clears his throat. Takes a deep breath and blows it out slowly before continuing. "Every time he sees us together...I know he's hurting."

I shake my head. "You're wrong, Jaxon. I told you. We're just friends, and Hudson is fine with that."

"You don't see him when you walk away," Jaxon insists. "I killed my brother once, because I was arrogant and childish and thought it was the right thing—the only thing—to do. I won't do it again, not like this. I won't hurt him, and I won't hurt you."

"What about you?" I ask, even as the pain radiates through me. "What happens to you in all this?"

"It doesn't matter—"

"It *does* matter!" I shoot back. "It matters to me."

"This is my fault, Grace. All of it. I'm the asshole who loaded the gun, and I'm the asshole who threw the loaded gun in the trash. The fact that I got shot is no one's fault but my own."

"So that's it?" I ask him on a shaky breath. "We're breaking up, and I don't even get a vote?"

"You had a vote, Grace, and you chose—" His voice gives out, leaving the ghost of what he was going to say hanging between us.

"But I didn't!" I try to explain, the words coming out on broken sobs. "I don't love him, Jaxon. Not like I love you."

"You will," he says, and I know it costs him dearly. "Mating bonds can snap into place when two people first meet, before they even know each other's names. Look at how it happened between us. But the magic knows. You just have to have faith. Something I should have done."

I look away, look down—look anywhere but at Jaxon as my heart cracks wide open—but he's not having it. Instead of backing away like I'm desperate for him to do, he slides a finger under my chin and tilts my head up until I can't do anything but look into his dark and heartbroken eyes.

"I am sorry that I didn't hold on to us with every ounce of strength I had," he tells me in a voice so hoarse, I barely recognize it as his. "I'd do anything to spare you this. Do anything to have my mate back."

I want to tell him that I'm right here—that I'll always be right here—but we'd both know it's a lie. The chasm between us keeps growing, and I'm terrified that one day, neither of us will be able to find a way to jump across it.

Tears bloom in my eyes at the thought, and I blink furiously, determined not to let him see me cry. Determined not to make this any worse—for either of us. So instead of sobbing like I want to, I do the only thing I can think of to make this okay…or at least better.

I whisper, "You never did tell me the punch line to that joke."

He looks at me, baffled. Or maybe like he can't believe that I'm bringing up something so ridiculous at a time like this. But Jaxon's and my relationship has been fraught with so many emotions, good and bad, that I don't want it to end like this.

So I force myself to smile just a little bit wider and continue. "What did the pirate say when he turned eighty?"

"Oh, right." Jaxon's laugh is a little watery, but it's still a laugh so I count it as a win. Especially when he answers, "He says, 'Aye matey.'"

I stare at him for a second, openmouthed, before shaking my head. "Wow."

"Doesn't seem worth the wait, does it?"

There's so much to unpack in that statement, but right now I'm out of energy, so I just concentrate on the joke. "That's really bad."

"I know, right?"

His smile is small but there, and I find myself wanting to hold on to it a little longer. Maybe that's why I shake my head and say, "So, so, sooooooo bad."

He lifts a brow, and not going to lie, my knees tremble just a little, even though they don't have the right to anymore. "You think you can do better?" he asks.

"I know I can do better. Why is Cinderella bad at sports?"

He shakes his head. "I don't know. Why?"

I start to answer, "Because she always—" but Jaxon cuts me off before I can deliver the punch line, his mouth slamming down on mine with all the power of the pent-up sorrow and frustration and need that still seethes between us.

I gasp and reach for him, my fingers aching to bury themselves in his hair one last time. But he's already gone, the sound of the door slamming behind him the only sign that he was here at all.

At least until the tears start to roll—silent and steady—down my cheeks.

8

Ghosts Don't Need
Moving Vans and
Neither Does My Baggage

I spend the week after Jaxon breaks up with me making every excuse I can think of not to leave my room except for class and food. I don't want to chance running into him, can't stand the way I'm blindsided by pain every time I so much as catch a glimpse of him in the halls.

The Order has pretty much given up being in the cafeteria lately, which I think is Jaxon's way of giving me space. I appreciate it even as it hurts.

I've also taken to avoiding Hudson, which I know is cowardly of me when he's done nothing but try to be a friend to me. But I can't shake that comment Jaxon made about the look on Hudson's face when I turn to walk away.

I don't know if it's true or not, but I know I'm not ready to deal with it either way. Better to hide until I can think about either of the Vega brothers without wanting to curl into a ball and cry.

On the plus side, today is the first morning in a week that I haven't sobbed in the shower. I don't think that means I'm okay, but it does give me the strength to do something I should have done days ago—leave the safety of my room and brave the library. My Physics of Flight makeup project is due in a few days, and I still need to get it done.

I wait until after ten at night to go to the library, in the hopes of getting the shelves all to myself. By now, everyone in the school is well aware of the drama surrounding the Vega brothers and me, but I don't think the news of my breakup with Jaxon has made the rounds yet.

He obviously hasn't said a word and neither have I.

For a second, I think about shifting to my gargoyle form—I even go so far as to reach for the shiny platinum string deep inside me. But flying around the Alaskan wilderness isn't going to make this hurt any less, especially since turning my body to stone doesn't mean that my heart turns to stone, too.

I change into a pair of sweats and my most comfortable and faded One

Direction T-shirt, then scoop my backpack up from the floor and head out the door.

But the universe has obviously given up passively fucking with me and is now actively gunning for me, because the second I walk into the library, I can't miss that Hudson is sitting next to the window, his face buried in a copy of Helen Prejean's *Dead Man Walking*.

It's a little too on the nose for me, but Hudson's always been a bit of a drama queen when it comes to his reading choices. For a second, I think about going over to talk to him, but I'm not exactly up for trading wits tonight. Plus, he's basically wearing an invisible NO TRESPASSING sign, so interrupting him feels...rude. Especially when he makes absolutely no attempt to so much as look at me.

With someone else, I might just think they hadn't seen me. But Hudson's a vampire, with the most acute senses on the planet. No way he doesn't know I'm here. Especially considering we're mated. Already, I can feel the invisible string stretching between us, connecting us to each other on a soul-deep level.

Again, I think about going over to say hello to him. He did save my life, after all, even though it meant taking on his evil father to do it...not to mention getting "cuffed" until graduation—which I've since learned means being forced to wear a charmed wrist cuff that prevents the use of any of his powers.

But in the end, I chicken out before I can take more than a couple of steps in his direction. I mean, yeah, we've seen each other around school and sat at the same table in the cafeteria since we were mated, but there's always been a buffer between us. We haven't actually been alone together since those minutes before the challenge when I did the spell to get him out of my head. And judging by the way he always gives me a wide berth even when our friends are around, I'm pretty sure he doesn't want alone time with me any more than I want it with me.

I end up going to sit at a table all the way at the other side of the library. Avoidance *is* my middle name...

Determined to ignore both him and my bruised and battered heart, I slip into a chair and pull out my laptop. Then I connect to the library's wifi so that I can log in to one of the databases that can only be accessed in this room. Less than five minutes of setup, and I'm working on my project on aerodynamics and the mechanics of flight—with an emphasis on the difference between gargoyle and dragon wings/methods of suspension.

There is almost no research on gargoyles—considering the Unkillable Beast has been chained for centuries and I'm the only other one in existence for a thousand years, at least as far as anyone knows. Then again, I do have myself for a test subject, so there is that.

It doesn't take long before I find my groove, and I spend nearly two hours immersed in both my research and a random playlist on Spotify. But when James Bay's "Bad" comes on, it jerks me straight out of the article I'm reading and back into my own personal hell.

My hands shake as the lyrics slam through me like grenades. As he sings about a relationship being so broken that it can't ever unbreak again, I can't help but feel each word burn my soul.

I drag my earbuds out of my ears like they've caught fire and shove back from the table so hard that I nearly go over backward in my chair. It takes me a second to right myself, but when I do, I can't help noticing Hudson staring at me from across the library.

Our eyes meet and, even though the damn earbuds are halfway across the table, I can still hear the song. My breath catches in my throat, my hands tremble, and those damn tears are back in my eyes.

I tap at the screen erratically, desperate to make it stop, but I must have accidentally hit the output source button instead because now the song is playing from my phone speaker, the lyrics echoing off the walls of the otherwise silent space.

I freeze. *Shit, shit, shit.*

Suddenly, Hudson's long, elegant fingers close over mine, and everything goes still...except the stupid song. And my even stupider heart.

9

Me and My Unmentionables

Hudson doesn't say anything as he eases my phone out of my death grip. He doesn't say anything as he turns off the song and blessed silence finally fills the library again.

And he *still* doesn't say anything when he slides the phone back into my trembling hands. But his cold fingers brush against my own, and my already fucked-up heart starts to beat all fast and hard.

His blue eyes, bright and brilliant and bold—so bold—stay locked on mine for the length of several painful heartbeats. His lips move just a little, and I'm certain he's going to say something, certain he will finally break the silence that's been echoing between us for days.

But he doesn't. Instead, he turns away, heads back to his own table without so much as a word to me. And I can't take it for one more second—the silence that throbs between us like a pounding heart that suddenly forgets how to beat. "Hudson!" Like the song, my too-loud voice echoes through the thankfully nearly empty room.

He turns back with a regal lift of his brow, his hands shoved deep into the pockets of his black Armani dress pants, and I can't help but smile. Only Hudson Vega—with his perfect Brit boy pompadour and even more perfect smirk—would be wearing dress pants and a dress shirt to a late-night reading sesh at the library.

His only concession to the growing lateness of the hour is the sleeves of his probably very expensive, very designer shirt, which are rolled up to the middle of his perfect forearms—which, I have to grudgingly admit, only makes him look better. Because he's Hudson and of course it does.

I realize I'm staring at him about the same time I realize he's staring back at me, that endless gaze of his burrowing into my bones. I swallow in an effort to push back the sudden nerves blooming inside me. I don't even know why they're there.

This is Hudson, who spent weeks living inside my head.

Hudson, who saved my life and nearly destroyed our whole world to do it.

Hudson, who has somehow—despite everything—become my friend… and now my mate.

It's that word, "mate," that hangs between us. And it's that word that has nerves bubbling up inside me even as I give a small smile and say, "Thank you."

His look turns slightly mocking, but he doesn't say any of the things I can see brewing right behind his gaze. Instead, he just inclines his head in a kind of you're-welcome gesture before turning and walking away.

And just like that, my blood boils. Because seriously? Seriously? Jaxon doesn't want to be with me because he thinks Hudson is in pain, but Hudson can't even talk to me when I'm clearly upset about a damn song? I know their relationship is complicated—know this whole thing is complicated—but I'm tired of being collateral damage. I mean, who lets their friend avoid them for a week without even trying to find out why?

And just as quickly, I'm over it. Completely, 100 percent over it. Throwing my phone onto the table, I shoot after him. "Really?" I say to his broad shoulders as I chase him across the library. His long, rolling stride eats up more distance than my short-legged one does, but my annoyance gives me speed, and I catch up to him before he can sit back down.

"Really what?" he answers, and this time his gaze is watchful.

"You're not going to say anything to me?" My hands are on my hips in challenge, and I just barely fight the urge to stamp my foot. I know what I'm doing—deep down, I know. I'm angry with the world, with the universe, for doing this to all of us. For taking Jaxon from me and then taking my friendship with Hudson, too. I've been working through my grief since it happened, but last week Jaxon forced me to give up the denial I've been clinging to since our bond was broken. Now I guess I'm fully embracing stage two: anger. And I'm not even a little sad I'm misdirecting it at Hudson.

"What would you like me to say?" His crisp British accent makes the words, and the look that accompanies them, even colder.

I throw up my hands in exasperation. "I don't know. Something. Anything."

He holds my gaze for so long, I think he's going to refuse to speak. But then his mouth curves in that obnoxious smirk that's driven me wild from the first time he showed up in my head, and he says, "You have a hole in your sweats."

"What? I don't—" I break off as I glance down and realize not only do I indeed have a sizable hole, but also that it's in a pretty embarrassing area, providing a decent glimpse of my very upper thigh. And my underwear. "Did you just do that?"

Now both brows are up. "Did I just do what?"

I gesture to my pants. "Make this hole. Obviously."

"Yes, yes I did," he answers, his expression completely deadpan. "I absolutely used my fabric-ripping superpowers to disintegrate a hole over your crotch. How did you guess?" He lifts his wrist, and the magical handcuff around it, and waves it in front of my face.

"I'm sorry." Heat floods my cheeks. "I didn't mean—"

"Sure you did." His gaze is locked on mine now. "But on the plus side, at least now I know you're wearing my favorite pair."

My blush gets about a thousand times worse as it registers what he's referring to, that I'm wearing the black lace underwear that he'd dangled from his shoe in the laundry room what feels like a year ago. "Are you seriously looking at my panties right now?"

"I'm looking at you," he answers. "That my doing so means I can also see your *panties* seems like that's more on you than me."

"I can't believe this." Annoyance skitters through my embarrassment. "You ignore me for days, and now that I finally have your attention, this is what you want to talk about?"

"First of all, I believe it is *you* who has been ignoring *me*, wouldn't you say? Secondly, I'm sorry, did you have a different topic in mind? Oh, wait! Let me guess." He pretends to examine his nails. "How's dear old Jaxon doing today?"

With anyone else, I would be apologizing for avoiding them. I'd be making a joke about the panties mishap and explaining that I'm not mad at them; I'm just mad. But Hudson makes it so hard sometimes, especially when it feels like he's deliberately pushing my buttons. "Maybe you should ask him. I mean, if you can get over feeling sorry for yourself."

He stills. "Is that what you think I'm doing? Feeling sorry for myself?" Insult—and injury—drip from his words.

But that's fine with me, because I'm feeling pretty damn insulted myself.

"Oh, I don't know. Should we talk about your choice in reading material?" I glare at the book he left open on the table when he came over to help me.

For a second—just a moment—his blue eyes turn molten. Then, as quickly as it came, the heat fades away. In its place is his old too-weary-for-words, you're-a-trial-to-my-very-existence expression, and I think I'm going to scream.

Yes, I know it's his defense mechanism, know he uses it to keep anyone from getting too close. But I thought, after what happened the day of the challenge, that we were past all this.

"I was just doing a little bit of light reading."

"With a book about a guy in prison? One who's been sentenced to death for his crimes? What, was Dostoevsky a little too over-the-top for you?"

"A little too cheerful, actually."

I snort-laugh, because how can I not? It's the *most* Hudson response *ever* to what may be the most depressing book ever written. And my anger drains away, my shoulders sagging.

He doesn't laugh with me, though. In fact, he doesn't even smile. But there's a gleam in his eyes that wasn't there before when he glances over my shoulder at the table I've been sitting at for the last two hours. "What have you been working on so furiously over there?"

"My makeup physics project." I pull a face. "I need to get at least a B on it, and a B on the final, if I want to have a chance of passing the class."

"I'll let you get back to it, then," Hudson says with a dismissive nod that hurts more than I want to admit, even to myself.

"You really can't even talk to me for ten minutes?" I ask, and I hate the plaintive note in my voice, but I can't seem to do anything about it. Not today, not here, and most definitely not with him.

For long seconds, Hudson doesn't say anything. He doesn't even breathe. But eventually he sighs and tells me, "Honestly, Grace. What is there to talk about? You've obviously been avoiding me for a reason." His voice is low, and for the first time, I see the weariness on his face...as well as the hurt.

But he's not the only one who's tired, and he's definitely not the only one who is hurting. Maybe that's why my own sarcasm is on full display when I answer, "Oh, I don't know. What about that we're—"

"What?" he interrupts, even as he stalks toward me with a sudden, predatory intent that has every hair on my body standing straight up in alarm. "What exactly are we, Grace?"

"Friends," I whisper.

"Is that what you're calling it these days?" He sneers. "Friends?"

"And—" I try to give him the answer he's looking for, but my mouth is as dry and frozen as the Alaskan tundra.

"You can't even say it, can you?"

I lick my lips, swallow. Then force out the word he's clearly been waiting for. The word that's been hanging in the air between us from the moment I walked into the library, even though he never so much as acknowledged my existence. "Mates," I whisper. "We're mates."

"Yeah, we are," he answers. "And isn't that just a clusterfuck of epic proportions?"

10

A New Bond Experience

I wince.

"I don't know what it is," I answer him as honestly as I'm able.

His eyes narrow, and for the second time tonight, I'm reminded that he's not just the guy who lived in my head for a few weeks, then saved my life. He's also a dangerous predator. Not that I'm scared of him, but...the danger is definitely there.

Especially when he growls, "Don't play with me, Grace. We both know you're in love with my brother."

It's true. I do love Jaxon. But I don't say that. I don't know why I don't say it—probably for the same reason I don't tell him that Jaxon broke up with me last week. Because he'll find out soon enough, and I don't want to look pathetic when he does.

Normally, I don't care what people think of me. But he isn't people. He's Hudson, and everything inside me rebels at the idea of him feeling sorry for me. Whatever relationship we have is based on a mutual toughness and respect. I can't stand, even for a second, the idea of him thinking I need his pity.

I don't know why it matters so much with him, and to be honest, I really don't have it in me to delve into my psyche to find out. This week's been rough enough without any deep psychological revelations about myself, thank you very much.

So instead of dealing with the Jaxon statement on the table—and all the baggage that comes with it—I nod toward the towering pile of books he's got stacked in his work area. "So what have *you* been doing these last few days, besides reading every 'light' and uplifting book you can get your hands on?" It's a blatant change of subject but one I'm praying he'll go along with.

At least until he smirks at me and answers, "Mating bonds."

Okay, so maybe Jaxon was the better subject here. Trust freaking Hudson to drop the two-ton purple elephant we'd just avoided right back in the room between us—and not even bother to stand back when it falls.

Of course, he did it on purpose—to scare me off. I know Hudson, and I know he expects that revelation to make me pack up shop and run. I can see it in his eyes. More, I know how he thinks—I didn't spend weeks with him in my head not to have figured out some things. But the fact that he's trying to scare me away only ratchets my determination to stick it out, no matter how uncomfortable the topic. And it definitely makes me more determined not to do what he expects.

So instead of running back to my safe little physics project on the other side of the library, I plop myself down at his table and ask, "What about them?"

And there it is in the depths of his eyes. Surprise, yes. But also the respect he's always had for me, the respect he's always treated me with, even when we bitterly disagreed about something.

"Mostly I've been trying to figure out how they work," he says as he settles into the chair farthest away from mine on the other side of the table.

Which is an interesting choice, considering he's a badass vampire and I'm "just" a gargoyle. But it's obvious that he's wary of me. I can see it in the twist of his lips, the way he's holding himself, and how he's awkwardly looking at anything and everything but me.

But he's not backing down, either, and I can't help wondering if it's for the same reasons as me.

"I thought everyone knows how mating bonds work," I tell him.

"Yeah, well, obviously not." He taps his fingers on the table in the first display of nervousness I've ever seen from him. "We know the basics, like that they snap into place the first time people physically touch, but obviously there's a lot more to it than that or we wouldn't be in the situation we're in now."

"That can't always be true, right? I mean, ours didn't snap into place the first time we touched."

"Yes, it did," he tells me quietly. "You just didn't feel it."

"You felt it?" I repeat as shock ricochets through me. "Really?"

"Yes." There's no sarcasm in the word—or the look he gives me as he waits to see how I'll react.

"How? When?" A terrible thought occurs to me. "Did we—were we mated during those months we spent together?" The months I'm growing more and more desperate to remember.

"No." He shakes his head. "While mating is a spiritual thing, it kicks in on the physical plane, and at that time, we weren't corporeal."

Right. Trapped together in spirit isn't enough to activate the bond. Okay, then. "So when *did* it happen?"

He's watching me closely now, and there's something in his gaze that makes my skin itch and my mouth go dry all over again.

"On the Ludares field. You were a little busy with the near-death thing, but I felt it right away."

My eyes go wide as things slide into place, including the way Hudson turned his father's bones to dust before destroying the entire Ludares arena with a thought. I'd overheard Macy ask him at lunch a few weeks ago why he'd destroyed the arena, and he said it was so that nothing like what happened to me there could happen to anyone else—and I still believe that played a part in it. But understanding now that he knew then that I was his mate, and he thought I was dying in his arms...I'm surprised there was anything left of the whole school when he was done.

"I'm sorry you had to find out that way," I tell him, because none of this is his fault—any more than it's my fault. Any more than it's Jaxon's, no matter what he thinks. It just is. And the sooner we accept that, the sooner we'll be able to figure out what we want. And what we're going to do to get it. "It must have been awful."

"It wasn't optimal," he admits with a twist of his mouth.

"Are you upset?" I ask, my voice barely a whisper now in the silent library.

At first, I don't think he's going to answer—he refuses to look at me, and the sudden silence between us grows more awkward with every second that passes.

Normally, I'd move on, gloss over the discomfort with easy words that defuse the situation. But instead, I force myself to ignore the awkwardness of this moment and push Hudson for an answer to the question that's been plaguing me for weeks. The question I've always been too afraid to ask.

"What exactly happened between us during the four months we were trapped together?"

11

Badass Boys Are
the Best Boys

H is eyes go dark, and something nameless moves in their indigo depths. Something perturbed. Something painful. Something…powerless. It's strange to think of Hudson that way. Even stranger to realize that I might somehow be responsible.

But before I can wrap my head around the pain I'm seeing, let alone think of something to say about it, an underclassman approaches. I'm not sure if he's a freshman or a sophomore, but he's definitely younger than sixteen. And he is also definitely a wolf.

Which doesn't necessarily make him bad. Just because Cole and his minions were assholes doesn't mean every wolf is—look at Xavier. But I'm not sure I'm up to finding out who this kid is or what his intentions are. Not when my heart is pounding like a thunderstorm and I'm already feeling far too vulnerable.

Hudson must feel the same way—or at least sense how I'm feeling— because he's out of his chair in the blink of an eye. More, his focus on the kid is absolute, unwavering, and 100 percent predatory, so much so that the wolf's eyes go wide, and he stops dead in his tracks. And that's before Hudson growls, "You're walking away now."

"I'm walking away now," the wolf repeats, nearly stumbling over his feet in his haste to get away from us. I expect him to turn around and flee, but I forget how finely developed survival instincts are in this place. The wolf moves past us, but he doesn't take his gaze off Hudson until he's at the library's main door. And even then, he only looks away long enough to find the door handle.

He shoves the door open and flees like a pack of hellhounds is hot on his heels. As I watch him go, I can't help wondering what he saw in Hudson's eyes that made him move so fast, without so much as an attempt to stand his ground.

But when Hudson turns back to me, there's nothing there. No threat, no anger, no promise of retribution. At the same time, whatever else I saw there a few moments ago is also gone, the anger and the pain slipping away as easily as they had come.

In their place is a blank slate, sheer as glass and about as deep.

"I thought you couldn't use your powers?" I comment as he settles back down in his chair.

The look he gives me is half amused and half affronted. "You do remember I'm a *vampire*, right?"

"What? That means your power can't be grounded? Or—" A new thought occurs to me. "Did you just persuade Uncle Finn into believing he grounded your powers?"

"And why would I do that exactly?"

"Why *wouldn't* you do that?" I shoot back. "I don't know very many people who would just hand over their abilities when they have an actual way to keep them."

"Yeah, well, I'm not most people. And in case you haven't noticed, my powers aren't exactly easy to live with. If I could get rid of them completely, I'd do it in a heartbeat."

"I don't believe you." Affront turns to indignation as he continues to stare at me, but I don't back down. Instead, I just shrug and continue. "I'm sorry, but I don't. You've got way too much power to just walk away from it. Don't forget, I know exactly how vast it is."

He lifts a brow. "Have you ever thought that it's *because* I have so much power that I'm so willing to give it up?"

"Honestly, no. You don't exactly seem the type."

He stills. "And what type is that?"

"You know, the self-sacrificing, do-gooder, save-the-world type." I widen my eyes in a deliberate *gotcha* kind of look. "Besides, if you've actually given up your ability to persuade people, how did you get that wolf to run away so quickly?"

"I already told you." His voice and expression are all smug satisfaction. "I'm a vampire."

"I have no idea what that means." Except my damp palms say otherwise.

"It means that baby wolf is quite aware this vampire could separate his arms from his body in a blink if I wanted, with or without my powers."

He looks so satisfied that I can't help taunting, "Oh yeah? You really think you're that big and scary, huh?"

His only response is to slowly blink at me, like he can't believe I'm actually making fun of him. Or worse, *flirting* with him. Not as shocked as I am, though, when I realize that's exactly what I'm doing.

I just wish I knew where it came from. I'd definitely be lying if I said there wasn't something about the way Hudson snarled at the wolf that sent shivers straight down my spine. And not necessarily in a bad way. I clearly have a type.

Still, it doesn't mean anything—except that both my human and gargoyle side recognize and appreciate strength when they see it. Right? Hudson is my *friend*. I'm *in love* with Jaxon, breakup or no breakup. Any chemistry that is showing up between Hudson and me has to be because of the mating bond and nothing else.

I know how powerful that chemistry was with Jaxon from the very beginning—before I even knew him, let alone had fallen in love with him. Is there any reason to suspect that it would be different between Hudson and me?

Just the thought has me freaking out a little bit.

Not to mention, Hudson still hasn't answered the question I asked him before the wolf showed up, which means I'm pretty much in the dark here. I have absolutely no idea what happened between us or how he feels about me, let alone how he feels about being *mated* to me. Not that all this uncertainty isn't scary or anything...

"Scary enough," Hudson says so suddenly that I think he must be reading my mind. At least until he flashes a bit of fang, and I realize that he's responding to my previous comment.

Since just seeing the tip of his fang sends another shiver along my spine, I realize I might have a serious problem on my hands, even before he asks, "What do you want to know about those four months?"

"Anything." I take a deep breath in the hopes of calming the wild beating of my heart. "Whatever you can remember."

"I remember everything, Grace."

12

Eternal Ambivalence of the Spotless Mind

"**E**verything?" I repeat, a little stunned at the admission.

He leans forward, and this time when he says, "Everything," it comes out as much growl as word.

And I nearly swallow my tongue *and* my tonsils in one fell swoop.

Deep inside me, my gargoyle stirs, raising its wary head, even as I feel its stillness washing through me. I force it back, settling it down with the reassurance that I really am okay, even if I currently feel anything but.

"I remember what it was like to wake up to your incessant cheer and unwavering optimism," he tells me hoarsely. "I was sure we were going to die locked in that place, but you were just as certain that we would survive. You refused to think any other way."

"Really?" That kind of unbridled optimism feels foreign to me these days.

"Oh yeah. You were always coming up with someplace you wanted to take me when we got free. Certain if I could just see all the things to love in the world, I wouldn't be evil anymore, I suppose."

"Like where?" It sounds like I'm challenging him more than I'm asking a question, and maybe I am. Because all I can think about is how hard it must have been for him after we finally *did* make it back. First, me not even knowing he was there and then, when I did find out about him, I treated him with every ounce of suspicion I could muster.

"That little strip of Coronado you like to haunt when you're in San Diego. You take the ferry over and then spend all afternoon checking out the art galleries before stopping at the little café on the corner to get a cup of tea and a couple of cookies the size of your palm."

Oh my God. I hadn't thought of that place in months, and with a handful of words, Hudson brings it back to me so clearly, I can almost taste the chocolate chips.

"What kind of cookies did I get?" I ask him, even though it's more than obvious he's telling the truth.

"One was chocolate chocolate chip," he answers with a grin, and it's the first real smile I've seen from him in ages. One of the only real smiles I've seen from him ever. It lights up his face—lights up the whole room, if I'm being honest. Even me...or maybe, especially me.

Because it's an uncomfortable thought—an uncomfortable feeling—I ask, "What about the second cookie?" I never tell anyone about this, so I figure I'm safe.

But Hudson's smile only gets wider. "Oatmeal raisin, which you don't even really like. But it's Miss Velma's favorite, and no one ever buys them from her. She always said she was going to stop baking them, but you could see it made her sad, so you started buying one every time you went just so she would have an excuse to keep making them."

I gasp. "I've never told anyone about Miss Velma's oatmeal cookies."

His eyes meet mine. "You told me."

I haven't thought of Miss Velma in months. I used to visit her at least once a week when I lived in San Diego, but then my parents died, and I just fell apart and never went back. Not even to say goodbye before I left for Alaska.

We were friends, which sounds silly considering she was just some lady who sold me cookies, but we were. Some days, I would hang around her little shop and talk to her for hours. She was the grandmother I never had, and I was a good stand-in for her grandkids, who lived halfway across the country. And then one day, I just disappeared. My stomach sinks thinking about it—thinking about her, wondering where I went.

Because I've had more than enough sadness lately, I force down my regrets and ask, "What else do you remember?"

For a second, I think he's going to push—or worse, start reciting some story I told him about my parents that I don't think I can handle tonight. But, typical of Hudson, he sees more than he should. Definitely more than I want him to.

And instead of bringing up something sentimental or sweet or sad, he rolls his eyes and says, "I remember the way you used to stand over me every morning at seven a.m. and demand that I wake up and get moving. You used to insist that we do *something* even when there was nothing to do."

I grin a little at the slight aggravation in his words.

"So what did we do? Besides swap stories, I mean."

There's a long pause, and then he says, "Jumping jacks."

So not the answer I was expecting. "Jumping jacks?" I ask. "Seriously?"

"Thousands upon thousands upon *thousands* of jumping jacks." If his expression got any more bored, he'd be comatose.

"But how is that even possible? I mean, we didn't actually have bodies, right?"

"You shook the whole realm when you jumped. It was completely embarrassing, but—"

"Oh my God, tell me I was not stone the whole time, was I?" I interrupt.

"You absolutely were. I tried to convince you to pick up a quieter hobby—skeet shooting, for example, or wooden clog dancing—but you were insistent. It was all about the jumping jacks." He gives a what-could-I-do? shrug before the laugh that had been trying to force its way out finally escapes. "No, you were in your normal human body, but the marathon jumping jacks..." He winks.

"But I hate jumping jacks."

"Yeah, me too. Now. But you know what they say about hate, right, Grace?" He leans back in his chair and gives me a look so hot that it curls my toes and straightens my hair at the same time. "It's just the other side of—"

"I don't believe that." I cut him off before he can finish the old saying about hate being only one side of a coin with love. Not because I don't actually believe it, like I told him, but because there's a part of me that does. And I can't deal with that right now.

Hudson doesn't call me on my bluff, for which I am intensely grateful. But he doesn't just move past it, either. Instead, he stays where he is—arm draped over the back of the chair beside him and long legs splayed in front of him under the table—and watches me as the seconds tick by.

I should go—I want to go—but there's something in his gaze that keeps me right where I am, pinned to my chair, with my stomach turning flips deep inside me.

I grow more and more uncomfortable with each second that passes, though, and finally I can't take it anymore. I'm not ready to deal with this. With any of it. I push my chair back from the table and say, "I need to get going—"

"You want to know what else I remember?" Hudson cuts me off.

Yes. I want to know everything he remembers, want to know everything I told him so I can make sure it wasn't too much, so I can make sure I didn't give him the power to destroy me. But even more than that, I want to know everything he told *me*.

I want to know about the little boy whose brother was ripped away from him. I want to know about the father who treated him like a trained seal and used him like a weapon. I want to know about the mother who looked the other way at all the terrible things that were done to her son, but who then so easily scarred Jaxon for destroying him.

"'Oh, what tangled webs we weave...'"

"Stay out of my head!" I command, glaring at him. "How can you—"

"It doesn't take mind-reading powers to know what you're thinking, Grace. It's written all over your face."

"Yeah, well, I need to go."

"And here I was, just getting warmed up." He stands when I do, and the mocking tone is back in his voice when he says, "Aww, come on, Grace. Don't you want to know what I thought of your red prom dress? Or that bathing suit you wore to Mission Beach that one time?"

"Bathing suit?" I squeak out, my cheeks on fire as I realize which one he's talking about. A teeny tiny little bikini. Heather had bought it on sale at a local surf shop, then dared me to wear it. Normally, I wouldn't have taken that dare for anything, but she'd also accused me of being staid, stuck in my comfort zone, *and* flat-out chicken.

"You remember," Hudson prompts. "The purple one with all the strings. It was very"—he draws a couple of tiny little triangles in the air—"geometric."

He's teasing me, I know he is, but there's something more than just a few laughs kindling in his eyes. Something dark and dangerous and just a little bit hot.

I lick my suddenly dry lips as I struggle to get words past the giant lump in my throat. "I really did tell you everything, didn't I?"

He raises a brow. "How exactly am I supposed to know the answer to that question?"

He makes a good point, but I'm too far gone to acknowledge it now. "If you saw the bathing suit, then you saw..."

He doesn't say anything else, and he certainly doesn't fill in the blanks for me. I don't know if that's a kindness, though, or just another way to torture me. Because there's no mistaking the heat in his eyes now, and all of a sudden, it feels like my blood is freezing and boiling at the same time. I don't know what to do, what to say—may even have forgotten how to breathe for a couple of oxygen-deprived moments—but then Hudson blinks, and the heat is gone as easily as it came.

So easily, in fact, that I wonder if I imagined it.

Especially when he smirks at me and says, "Don't worry, Grace. I'm sure you still have plenty of secrets left."

"Yeah, well, I'm not so sure about that." I force myself to answer his smirk with one of my own. "Which sucks, considering I can't remember if I've ever seen you in anything besides your little Armani safety blankets." I wave an airy hand toward his shirt and pants.

He glances down at himself, then demands, "What's wrong with how I dress?"

"There's nothing *wrong* with it," I answer, and it's the truth, because no one—and I mean no one—looks hotter in a pair of Armani trousers than the vampire standing across from me. Not that I'm going to say that to him. His head is big enough already. Plus, admitting it feels like turning the corner on something I'm still not sure I want any part of, mating bond or not.

His eyes narrow dangerously. "Yeah, well, you may say that, but the look on your face says something entirely different."

"Oh yeah?" It's my turn to lift a brow as I lean in a little closer. "What exactly does the look on my face say?"

At first, I don't think he's going to answer. But then I can see something inside him shift. See something dissolve until the caution he's been wearing like a shield for the last several weeks morphs into a recklessness I don't expect from Hudson.

"It says that it doesn't matter what happened between us during those four months. It says that you're always going to want Jaxon. It says—" He pauses and leans forward until our faces are mere inches apart and my heart is beating like a wild bird in my chest. "That you won't rest until you find a way to break our mating bond."

13

Antisocial Influencer

"**I**s that what you want?" I whisper over the sound of blood rushing in my ears. "To break the bond?"

He leans back again and asks, "Would that make you happy?"

His question stirs something inside me, something I'm not ready to face, so I turn to the anger that's always so much easier between us. "How can I be happy when so much of my life is still a mystery? How can I be happy when you won't even pretend to tell me the truth?"

"I have *always* told you the truth," he snaps back. "It's just that you're usually too obstinate to believe it."

"*I'm* the obstinate one?" I ask, incredulous. "Me? You're the one who won't give me a straight answer."

"I've given you plenty of answers. You just don't like them."

"You're right. I don't like them because I don't like getting the runaround from you. I asked you a simple question, and you can't even—"

"There is nothing simple about the question you just asked me, and if you weren't so busy hiding your head in the bloody sand, you would damn well know that." Fury crackles in the depths of his eyes, and this time, when he bares his fangs, it's scary as hell. Not scary because I would ever worry Hudson would hurt me, but scary because I realize just how much the uncertainty of our mating bond is really affecting him.

Add in his words hitting entirely too close to home, and the anger drains right out of me. Not because I don't have a point about Hudson's nonanswer, because I do. But because he's got a point, too. Which means the truth is probably somewhere in the middle between us.

It's that knowledge that has me taking a deep breath and blowing it out slowly.

That has me reaching for his hand and squeezing it tightly.

That has me whispering, "You're right."

His shoulders relax, his own rage draining as easily as mine. He squeezes my hand back, his long fingers sliding between mine and holding tight, even as his face remains wary. "Why do I feel like you're trying to lull me into a false sense of security?"

I give him a rueful look. "Probably for the same reason I keep thinking you're trying to pull one over on me."

"And what reason is that?"

There's a part of me that doesn't want to answer the question, but it's the same part that regrets ever starting this conversation. But I did start it, and I did accuse Hudson of not being straight with me. Which means I need to do better, even if telling him the truth is more than a little embarrassing.

"I'm scared," I finally admit, looking anywhere and everywhere but at his ridiculously handsome face.

"Scared?" he repeats, sounding stunned. "Of me?"

"Yes, of you!" I say, my eyes darting up to his. "Of course of you. And Jaxon. And this entire situation. How can I not be? It's a mess, and whichever way it turns out, someone is going to get hurt."

"Can't you see that's what I'm trying to avoid, Grace?" He shakes his head. "I don't want to hurt you."

"So don't," I tell him. "Just be honest with me, Hudson, and I'll be honest with you."

"Honesty doesn't guarantee that you won't get hurt," he says softly.

And that's when it hits me, really hits me. Hudson is just as confused as I am.

Just as confused as Jaxon is.

I don't know why I didn't register that before. Probably because he always sounds so smooth and confident and in control, like he always knows what's happening in any given situation.

Then again, this is a situation like no other, a situation that no one I've talked to has ever even heard of before. And can I just say, I'm getting a little sick of being the test case in all these situations.

The first human at Katmere.

The first gargoyle born in a thousand years.

The first person in forever to challenge for a seat on the Circle.

The first person to have a mating bond break...and then find another mate almost instantly.

Fantasy novels always describe finding your mate as this wondrous, glorious, amazing thing. But I figure the authors who write about those have obviously never been mated to anyone in their life. If they were, they'd know just how messy and terrifying and overwhelming the entire situation is.

They'd know that there is no magic wand that just makes a relationship work. Or easy. Or even what you want.

There's a piece of me that wants to run away, that wants to do exactly what Hudson accused me of and bury my head until this entire situation goes away or just doesn't matter anymore.

But Hudson is watching me, waiting for my response. And he and Jaxon are both immortal anyway—and I'm pretty damn close. Which means this situation isn't going anywhere until I deal with it.

So instead of running, instead of hiding away in a desperate attempt to protect myself, I look at Hudson and tell him the only truth I know.

"You're right. Honesty won't keep any of us from getting hurt," I say as I think back to my conversation with Jaxon earlier that week. Our talk was as open and honest and *devastating* as any conversation I've ever had in my life, and we both walked away hurting. "But it does guarantee that we're on the same page. And I think that's all any of us can hope for."

I see the words hit Hudson, see him absorb them like body blows. And that's when I know that I have to tell him the whole truth, no matter how vulnerable, how exposed, how *damaged* it makes me feel.

Which is why I take a deep breath, do a slow count to five, and then blurt out, "Jaxon and I broke up."

14

Talk to the Stone

Hudson's eyes go wide, his face colorless. "You broke up?" he repeats, like he can't believe what he's hearing.

I study his face, trying to figure out what he's thinking or feeling, but astonishment is the only emotion I can get from him before everything goes blank.

Which isn't exactly a surprise. I always thought Jaxon was good at hiding his emotions—if you discount the earthquakes, of course—but Hudson belongs in the World Series of Poker.

Even knowing that, I can't help but get nervous as he stares at me with deliberately empty eyes. Which is probably why I start tripping over my tongue trying to explain myself. "We decided to take a break so we could... well, he brought it up, so I guess you could say he decided...but we talked and thought a break might—"

The more I babble, the more stonelike Hudson's face becomes until I force myself to stop vomiting words and take an actual breath. As I do, I count backward from ten, and when I can finally think in some kind of coherent fashion, I start again. "He said it wasn't right... Everyone was in pain...and things, well, things just weren't..." I trail off, not sure what else to say.

"What they used to be?" He fills in the blanks. "Yeah, a rogue mating bond will do that to a couple."

"It isn't just the mating bond. We—"

"It's the mating bond," Hudson says, cutting me off. "Trying to pretend otherwise just makes us all look like children. You broke up because of me, which is what I've been trying to avoid."

"Is that why you've made sure you're never with me alone, at lunch or anywhere?"

He shrugs. "Yet here we are."

"Jaxon and I broke up because everything feels off between us lately," I contradict him. "Without the mating bond, nothing feels right. That's not because of you. That's because of Cole and the godawful spell from the Bloodletter." I squeeze his hand. "Honestly."

Hudson stares at me for a while but doesn't say anything. Instead, he drops my hand and just kind of shakes his head before he starts gathering up his pens and notebook off the table.

"What are you doing?" I ask. "Are you seriously just going to walk away without saying anything? Again?"

"The library's closing," he tells me, even as he nods to someone over my shoulder. "Go pack up your stuff, and I'll walk you to your room."

"You don't need to do that." I back away from him, confusion and hurt churning in my belly. I thought being honest was the way to go—we just agreed it was the right thing to do—and now he's treating me like gargoyle-itis is something he can catch if we have an actual conversation.

"I know I don't *need* to, but I'm going to." He steps out from behind the table for the first time since we started talking and begins shepherding me across the room toward my belongings.

"I'm perfectly capable of walking to my room on my own," I try, more forcefully this time.

"Grace." He sounds weary as he says my name, like everything about me, about this, is too much effort for him. It gets my back up, even before he continues. "Can we skip this fight if I acknowledge that I am aware that you are fully capable of doing anything you put your mind to? And I'm still going to walk you to your room."

"Why should I let you do that when it's obvious you don't want anything to do with me?"

His sigh is somehow both exaggerated and impatient. "What I want, at this exact moment, is to finish our conversation in private while I walk you to your room." His accent turns the words into sharp little arrows that hit with precision. "Is that obvious enough for you, or do I need to be more specific?"

I stop packing up my backpack to glare at him. He glares right back, mutters something under his breath that I can't quite catch but which I totally know was all about how tiring it is to put up with me. And I get it. I know my emotions have been all over the place tonight, but I'm trying to get that under control. And even though they are a mess, that doesn't mean he gets to talk to me like I'm a child. Unless he wants me to actually act like a child.

It's a tempting thought. Wrong, probably, but still so tempting that I can't resist.

I lean back on my heels, cross my arms over my chest, and turn to stone.

The cool thing about learning to control my gargoyle is that now I can turn to my statue form and still be sentient—which means I get to watch as Hudson's eyes go big and his mouth literally drops open. And can I just say, turning Hudson speechless is worth every second of not being able to slap back at him while I'm encased in stone.

Especially when he remembers to close his mouth with a snap but makes sure to leave his fangs on full display this time. Although I'm not sure what he plans on doing with them, considering he'll need some serious dental work if he tries to take a bite out of me now.

Amka, the librarian, approaches warily, as if she's not sure she wants to get involved in whatever this is. Not that I blame her. Of course, this isn't the first altercation between students with power that I've seen, and I've only been here a few months. I can't imagine what she's seen in her time here.

Hudson says something to her, but I have no idea what, as it sounds like it's coming through at least fifteen feet of water—maybe more. She answers him, and whatever she says must not be what he wants to hear, because the anger on his face slowly morphs into something that looks an awful lot like fear.

It's not a common emotion for him—the last time I remember seeing it was when his father bit me—so I can't be entirely sure, but as he steps forward and starts talking urgently to me, I figure it might be time to change back. I wanted to teach him a lesson about being condescending, not actually worry him.

I close my eyes and reach deep inside myself for the platinum string that lets me shift between gargoyle and human so fast that my fingers brush past another string. It's the emerald-green string I noticed first in the laundry room, the one something inside me said not to touch. But I don't have time to consider that accident because another string has all my attention. It's a brilliant blue that's glowing brightly. More, it's shooting off sparks in all directions.

It doesn't take a genius to figure out it's our mating bond. I've known it practically from the moment Hudson announced I was his mate—the first thing I did when I got over the shock was look for the string. It didn't take long to find it, as it was the only string that was glowing so brilliantly at that moment.

That was the last time it glowed. I've been checking it out every day, so I'm certain of it. But now it's glowing so brightly that it's practically iridescent, and the only thing I can think of is—

I gasp, my entire body going on red alert because in the blink of an eye, I can feel Hudson deep inside me.

It's not like before, when we could talk so clearly to each other. I don't know what he's saying now any more than I did a second ago, when he was all but shouting at me through the stone. But I can *feel* him, warm and strong and frantic. All the detachment he was projecting earlier is long gone.

It's that knowledge that has me grabbing on to the platinum string and shifting back as quickly as I can. Teaching him a lesson for being a jerk is one thing. Actually scaring him is something else entirely.

The moment I turn human again, Hudson grabs and pulls me against him in a hug that feels both incredibly relieved and incredibly intimate.

"What happened?" he asks as he moves away, his hands skimming up and down my arms like he can't quite believe I'm flesh and blood again—or like he's checking for injuries. "Why'd you shift?"

"Because you were being a jerk, and I was tired of listening to it, so I shifted to make sure I didn't have to listen anymore."

His mouth drops open for the second time in as many minutes, and behind us, Amka just shakes her head, chuckling. Hudson is too busy glaring at me to spare her so much as a glance, so she winks and gives me a thumbs-up sign. Apparently, I'm not the only one who thinks guys need to be put in their place when they act like overbearing jerks.

I have one moment to think to myself that I would never pull something like that on Jaxon, before Hudson is snarling, "Turning yourself to stone is the most immature use of powers I have ever heard of." Once again, his fangs are on full display, and I can't decide if he's trying to scare me or if it's just because he's that mad, he can't control them.

In the end, I decide it doesn't matter, that two can play this game. So I finish packing up my stuff, and then I lean forward until our faces are only about an inch apart. Then I tell him, "No, the most immature use of my powers would have been if I'd turned *you* to stone."

Then I pat him on the shoulder—half threat, half reassurance—and sweep right past him. I wave at Amka on my way out the door and leave Hudson to either stew in his own anger or swallow his pride and scramble after me.

I'd be lying if I said I didn't want him to pick the second choice.

15

A Little Thread-to-Thread Competition

I'm halfway to the staircase, just about convinced he's let his anger get the best of him, when Hudson catches me. And when I say he catches me, I mean exactly that.

I'm watching for him, listening for him, and still he moves so quickly and quietly that it's a shock when he wraps his hand around my wrist from behind and whirls me around. His hold is gentle despite the fact that the whole yank and spin happens so fast that I barely understand what's going on until I find myself face-to-face with a half-annoyed, half-amused vampire.

Hudson, however, knows exactly what's happening as he invades my space, backing me up until I can't go any farther, until my back is literally against the ancient tapestry–lined wall.

I think about pulling my wrist free, but he must sense it because his hold gets a little tighter—not tight enough to hurt but definitely tight enough that I feel the cold press of his fingers against the sensitive skin of my inner wrist.

"You don't think you're the only one who can use your powers irresponsibly, do you?" he asks, and there's just enough arrogance in the question to set my teeth on edge…and, conversely, to make my breath catch in my throat.

Which makes me feel like such a cliché. Come on.

Boy acts like jerk. Girl gets one up on boy. Boy beats his chest and girl falls under his spell?

Umm, no thank you. It's going to take more than some random chest beating to get me to fall into line—no matter how attractive and creative the guy doing the chest beating is.

Which is why I say, "I thought you told me that you didn't need to use your powers," in the most bored voice I can muster. "You *are* a vampire, after all."

"That was an observation, not a statement of intent," he answers, and now he's so close that I can feel his breath hot against my ear.

Shivers that have nothing to do with fear work their way down my spine, and I squirm a little, trying to put some more space between his mouth and my skin—not because I don't like the feel of him but because I'm afraid that I might like it too much.

"Bummer," I tell him when I've finally achieved a satisfactory distance from his face. "I was looking forward to you blowing stuff up again."

He turns serious, the mischievous glint fading from his eyes. "And here I've been working really hard to make sure that doesn't happen."

His voice is as sardonic as ever, but I know Hudson well enough by now to recognize the sincerity running just below the sarcasm.

It sneaks past the defenses I've had in place all night, and I answer, "Yeah, so have I," before I even realize I'm going to say it.

His shoulders slump, and for a second, he looks more defeated than I have ever seen him. "This is a huge mess, Grace."

"The hugest," I agree, right before he lowers his forehead to mine.

It feels like an intimate position—an intimate moment—and I think about pulling away. But intimate doesn't necessarily mean sexual. We've had plenty of intimate moments—he lived in my head for weeks. And so I tell myself this is just one more.

Besides, I think I need his comfort at least as much as he needs mine.

And so I do the only thing I can do in this situation, the only thing that feels right. I pull my wrist from his now loose hold and wrap my arms around him. The universe might have played one hell of a practical joke on us when it made us mates, but right now we're just two friends sharing a quiet moment in a fucked-up situation.

Or at least that's what I tell myself.

The embrace only lasts a minute, but it's enough for me to memorize the feel of his long, lithe body against my own.

Long enough for me to feel the super-fast beat of his heart beneath my hands.

More than long enough for me to...

"I felt you," I tell him when he finally takes a step back. "When I was stone. I felt you along the mating bond. You were trying to get to me."

And just that easily, annoyance and something else—something I don't quite recognize—flash back into his eyes. "I thought something had happened to you, that you'd managed to get yourself stuck as a statue again. Or maybe someone had done a kind of spell on you. It freaked me out." The look he gives me warns me not to do something like that again.

"Yeah, well, I really didn't like the way you were talking to me. I'm not a child, and I don't appreciate you treating me like one."

I think I can actually hear Hudson's teeth grind together, but in the end, all he does is incline his head and say, "You're right. I apologize."

His admission astonishes me, so much so that I say, "I'm sorry, I thought I was talking to Hudson Vega."

"Never mind," he mutters as he pulls away and starts walking again.

I fall into step behind him, appreciating the way he always keeps his stride short for me so that I don't have to scramble to keep up.

"So you used the mating bond to try to get to me?" I ask as we round a corner.

He looks uncomfortable with the subject, and maybe I should lay off, but how am I supposed to know how the mating bond works if I don't ask questions? These are the kinds of details they don't cover in my magic class, the kinds of things I don't think to ask until I experience them.

"I used it to send you energy, the same way you did to me after the Circle challenge." He shoots me a look. "You remember. When it nearly killed you."

"I'm pretty sure that was your father's bite," I shoot back. "And what was I supposed to do, die with your powers still inside me?"

"Oh, I don't know. Trust me not to let you die at all?" He sounds so exasperated that I nearly laugh. Only the knowledge that it will aggravate him even more keeps me from cracking up.

"I did trust you," I tell him as we finally reach the stairs. "I mean, I *do* trust you."

The look he gives me is searing, even before he reaches between us and takes my hand. He squeezes it softly before letting it go again.

"So you saw our mating bond?" he asks as we make it to the top of the stairs.

"I see it every day," I answer. "But it looked different today. Like it was all lit up and sparking with energy." I look at the strings again, and the sparks coming off it are gone, but it is still glowing.

"I'm pretty sure the sparks were me, trying to get to you."

"Yeah, that's what I figured, too."

"Did you notice anything else?" he asks as he steers me into the long hallway that leads to my room.

"Like what?"

He clears his throat a couple of times and keeps his eyes facing straight ahead as he says, "Like how different it looked from the bond you had with Jaxon?"

"Seriously, Hudson? You're comparing *bonds* now?" My tone suggests he's comparing something else.

"Not like that!" It's his turn to roll his eyes at me. "But I've been reading up on mating bonds, and every single thing I find about them comes to the same conclusion."

"And what's that?" I ask warily.

"That they can't be broken. Not with magic, not with will. The only thing that breaks them is death, and—"

"Sometimes not even then," I finish for him. "I know, I know. I got the same speech from Macy."

"Yeah, but Cole broke your bond with Jaxon—"

"I am aware of that," I tell him with just a hint of my own sarcasm. "I was there, in case you don't remember."

"I know, Grace." He sighs. "And I'm not trying to hurt you by talking about it. But every book ever written on the subject can't be wrong. Which got me thinking—"

"How did the Bloodletter even have a spell to break it?" I ask.

He looks surprised, whether that I've questioned this, too, or that I keep interrupting him, I don't know.

What I do know is that it bothers me hearing Hudson talk about mating bonds—and especially about breaking them. I don't know why, but it does, so I plow ahead, determined to finish the thought for him. "If they can't be broken, how did some old vampire in a cave just happen to have the spell lying around to do the one thing no one else in history has been able to do?"

"Exactly. Plus..." He pauses a moment, like he's got to prepare himself for whatever he's going to say next—or my reaction to it.

It's that thought that has me rolling my shoulders back and bracing for whatever blow is coming, even though I know it won't be physical.

"Do you remember what your bond with Jaxon looked like?" he asks. "I only saw it once, in the laundry room, and I didn't think anything of it at the time. I didn't realize then..."

"What?" I ask as my stomach twists itself into knots.

He sighs. "What a mating bond should look like."

"So what are you saying?" I ask in a voice so shrill, I can't believe it's coming out of my body.

"I'm not saying you weren't truly mated." Hudson places a soothing hand on my shoulder. "I'm saying something was wrong with your bond with Jaxon. I'm not sure if that was because the spell was already at work or if…"

"Or if there was always something wrong with it?" I finish.

"Yes," he answers reluctantly. "It was two colors, Grace. Green…and *black*."

Turns out I was right to brace for that body blow, because—just like that—my stomach bottoms out and I feel dizzy, one thought circling in my head over and over.

If something was always wrong with my bond with Jaxon…it might never be fixable.

16

You Can Run but
You Can't Hide

"**I** need to go," I mumble and take off down the hall, hoping Hudson will just let me go. The last thing I want to do today is more soul-searching detective work.

Up until this moment, I think I still believed this situation could be fixed. That Jaxon and I could be together again. All week, I'd been finally grieving the loss of the mating bond, but breakup or no, I still thought we'd find a way to work things out. Silly me.

I should have known the magical universe would have one more fuck-you up its sleeve.

I just hope Hudson lets me make it back to my room to mourn in privacy the loss of *everything* Jaxon and I had.

Hudson obviously doesn't get the memo, though, because he starts walking with me. Of course. Because why would he actually do what I want him to do, even this once?

My hands are shaking as I'm fighting the tears threatening to lay me bare, and I wait for him to ask me what's wrong or, worse, if I'm okay. But he doesn't. Instead, he just walks silently beside me until, finally, he says, "I understand that news was a bit of a shock, Grace. But really, are you that surprised Jaxy-Waxy couldn't even get a mating bond right?"

I stop walking and slowly turn to face him, fury quickly replacing the despair that had been swallowing me whole. "Are you serious right now? Do you even have an *ounce* of compassion in your *entire* body?"

He looks bored again. "I'm a vampire. Compassion isn't something we actually do."

I narrow my eyes at him. "Keep it up, and I'm going to turn you into a pile of rocks."

"Ooooh, I'm *so* scared." He waves his hands in mock panic. "Oh, wait.

Been there, done that, didn't want the T-shirt."

I don't know if it's the ridiculous hand gestures or the idea of Hudson in a *Vampires Rock* T-shirt, but my anger disappears as fast as it came on. This whole discussion is just so absurd.

Hudson must not think so, though, as he looks totally offended—at least until I look deep in his eyes and see the satisfaction there. And I realize another truth tonight.

Hudson picked a fight on purpose. He knew I was devastated, knew I was using every ounce of control I had not to burst into tears right in the middle of the hallway. All the badgering and sarcasm wasn't because he was being a dick. It was because he was being *nice*, though I'm sure he'd rather die than admit it.

It's not the first time he's done it, and it probably won't be the last. But maybe, one of these days, I'll stop falling for it. Maybe.

Then again, maybe not.

Because something about it, something about the snide comments (on both sides) and the bickering back and forth, sometimes it feels an awful lot like...foreplay.

Just the thought has my already queasy stomach flipping and knotting up at the same time. Because foreplay is a lot of things—fun, exciting, sexy—but it usually leads to something else, something important, and I don't have a clue how I feel about that. Not when it's barely been a week since Jaxon broke my heart all over again...and just a handful of minutes since I learned it can never be fixed again.

We finally make it to my room, but before I can dart inside and throw a *thanks for a weird evening* over my shoulder, Hudson reaches a hand out to stop me. "You okay?" he asks, brows raised and forearm resting against the doorframe.

"Yeah," I tell him, even though I'm not sure it's true, what with these strange kinds of things happening inside me, things I never imagined I'd feel in response to Hudson of all people. He may be my mate, but he's also my friend and this moment, this pose, feels distinctly un-friend-like.

"I should go in," I tell him, hating how breathless I sound. Hating even more the way his pupils dilate in response...except, also not.

"Okay." He steps back. "But let me know when you really want to get some answers."

"Answers to what?"

"To those questions we keep throwing around. You can't hide forever, Grace."

It's so close to what I'd been thinking earlier, what I'd sort of told Macy, that it gets my back up. "I'm not weak," I tell him. "I am capable of dealing with hard things, you know."

"You're capable of dealing with anything. No one doubts that—and if they do, they're daft, because you've proven it over and over again. You're the most incredible person I've ever met."

Hudson doesn't say things he doesn't mean, which is probably why his words touch me so much. But before I can think of how to respond, he continues. "But you have a tendency to avoid conflict whenever you can."

"There's nothing wrong with not wanting to fight," I tell him.

"No, there isn't. But there is something wrong with hiding from things until they get so big that you can't ignore them anymore. It's like people who shove bills in a drawer because they don't want to face them. They keep stuffing the drawer until no more bills fit—and by that time, their life has gone completely to hell. Yes, things might be bad, and it doesn't seem like there is an easy solution at first, but after a while, if you wait too long, there are only hard choices left to make."

His words hit home. And I can't help but feel he's talking about our mating bond. He never said what exactly he'd been researching in the library, but suddenly I have a clue. I haven't really let myself examine too closely how Hudson might be feeling being mated to me. I wasn't ready to face any answer he might give—that he wanted the bond *or* he regretted it. But while I was hiding my head in the sand, Hudson wasn't.

"You said you were researching mating bonds tonight," I say, my breath barely a whisper above the pounding of my heart. "Exactly what were you trying to discover?"

His gaze holds mine for several beats before he tells me, "How to break them."

17

Mixed Messages

Three hours later, I'm still staring at the ceiling over my bed as I consider what Hudson said about how I avoid conflict.

I want him to be wrong, I really do. But the longer I lay here on this hot-pink comforter that I don't want—that I've never wanted—I can't help wondering if he's right. Especially when I roll over and bury my face in a hot-pink throw pillow.

I take a deep breath.

And for the first time, I allow questions I've ignored for months to invade my head like a swarm of angry bees.

How did Lia know that I was Jaxon's mate before I'd ever heard of Katmere? Before Jaxon and I ever touched—since you supposedly only mate after you touch? For that matter, how did she even know where to find me?

How was I able to take Hudson and trap us on a different plane—for months? And why did my mating bond with Jaxon disappear while we were there?

Why was my mating bond with Jaxon two colors instead of just one, a twisted braid of green and black instead of one brilliant, solid color?

How did the Bloodletter know how to break it? How did she even know it *could* be broken if a mating bond has never been broken before?

How did I end up mated to Hudson? It's one thing to have a mating bond break—which is supposed to be impossible. It's another thing to have a new mating bond snap into place with a new person on the same afternoon—umm, impossible times a million, anyone?

As the familiar panic bubbles in my chest, I can't help but be angry with Hudson for basically daring me to do this. It wasn't fair. He has no idea what it's like to live with panic attacks.

It's not that I've never thought about these questions before. Of course

I have—and a zillion other ones, too. And then I lock them away in a box as quickly as they come. But can anyone blame me? I'd do almost anything to avoid a panic attack. To lose control of myself so much that I can't even regulate my own ability to breathe—it's terrifying. And yes, maybe my coping mechanism is a bad one. That doesn't mean anyone has the right to judge me on it, especially not Hudson, for whom sarcasm is an actual emotion... or twelve.

Besides, what am I supposed to do with the answers once I have them? Will they really change anything? Or will knowing just make things more difficult, one more painful thing to face? If I've learned anything in the last six months, it's that every time I think things are okay—every time I think I've solved a problem—a bigger one shows up to kick my butt.

Seriously. What does Hudson really know about my life? I start to work up a heady level of righteous indignation, and it's all aimed at Hudson's too-strong-for-his-own-good jaw.

It's barely been six months since my parents died—*six months*. Plus, I spent over half that time locked in stone with Hudson. And still, the number of things that have come at me would have been impossible to imagine if I hadn't actually lived through them all.

Not to be dramatic, but is it any wonder I'm having panic attacks on a semi-daily basis now?

Since my parents died, I've moved thousands of miles away from the only home I've ever known. I've met my mate, found out I was a gargoyle, gained a bunch of enemies, fought for my place on a council I didn't even know existed a few months ago, found the only other living one of my kind chained up in a cave where I also lost one of my friends, lost my mate, got bitten by one of my new enemies and almost died, *and* found my new mate—all while trying to graduate from high school.

Hudson can say I'm hiding from my problems all he wants, but from where I'm sitting? It looks like problems are doing a really good job of finding me whether I'm hiding from them or not.

But then I think about what Hudson said about the drawer getting filled up with bills until no more will even fit inside. And I think about Xavier dying, about Jaxon breaking up with me, about Cole hopefully rotting somewhere cold. About Hudson being mated to someone he wants to *not* be mated to so badly that he's spending his evenings researching ways to break our bond.

That last one makes me pause. And swallow my indignation in one bitter pill.

My fear has left Hudson to try and solve our problems all alone. I maybe can't deal with every question, but I can at least try to answer one.

But which one should I start with?

And then I think about the Bloodletter. I think about the Bloodletter a lot, along with the spell she somehow knew to give Jaxon to break our mating bond.

If someone went so far as to harm my bond with Jaxon...what else would they do to me? To Jaxon? To Hudson? And suddenly, it isn't the panic attack these questions bring that seizes me. It's the anger. If she knew how to tear Jaxon and me apart...then she owes us a spell to fix it, too. And some answers.

"You keep tossing and turning over there." Macy's voice is soft and sleepy. "What's up?"

"I'm sorry. I didn't mean to wake you."

"No worries. I don't sleep much anymore anyway." There's a rustling of sheets, and then the small multicolored light by Macy's bed clicks on. "What's going on? I notice Jaxon hasn't been around much lately... Nor has Hudson, come to think of it. You guys fighting?"

I take a deep breath and rip off the Band-Aid. "Jaxon broke up with me last week."

Macy doesn't say anything, just lays there in the semi-darkness, her steady breath going in and out for several minutes. She doesn't ask me why I didn't tell her, and I love her even more for that. Then she rolls over, holds my gaze, and just says, "I'm sorry."

I shake my head, fighting back tears. I cannot talk about this tonight. I'm too exhausted to have a heart-to-heart with my cousin. And she must sense this because she asks simply, "Anything you want to do about it?"

Yes, I do, and an idea begins to form in my head. "Do you think I could get an appointment with the Bloodletter?"

"The Bloodletter?" Macy sounds surprised but must clue in on what I'm thinking pretty quickly because she adds, "I don't know about an 'appointment,' but I'm pretty sure you could convince Jaxon to take you."

"What if he won't? I don't have a clue how to get there on my own."

"He'll take you." She sounds a lot more confident than I feel after the conversation Hudson and I had this evening. "Your mating bond is as important to him as it is to you."

"Last week, I would have agreed, but now..." I think about the coldness in his eyes when he told me we needed a break. "Now I'm not so sure."

"Well, I'm sure enough for the both of us," Macy says. "Text him and ask him to take you this weekend. If nothing else, she owes you both an explanation."

I tend to think she owes us more than that, since her spell destroyed my life. Then again, that could just be me...

I roll over and grab my phone. But instead of texting Jaxon, I text Hudson.

Me: Hey, want to go somewhere with me this weekend?

There's no response, and I realize it's late; he's probably already gone to bed. But then three dots appear, meaning he's texting a response, and I can't help that my heart picks up a beat.

Hudson: Define somewhere

I smile. Of course that's what Hudson would reply.

Me: Does it matter?

Hudson: If you're planning a coup d'état of a small country, yes. If you want to make snow angels, no.

Me: Sorry. No coup

Me: I want to go see the Bloodletter

No response. I force myself to stare at my phone until three dots appear again.

Hudson: I'm free now...

Of course he is. I mean, it's not insulting *at all* that he's so eager to break our bond that he's willing to drop everything to do it.

Me: Saturday

Hudson: Or now

I send him the eye roll emoji.

Me: I won't change my mind.

Me: And I'm inviting Jaxon, too

Hudson: Maybe I was too hasty about the snow angel thing...

I burst out laughing, because how can I not?

Me: I'll see you in class

Hudson: "Pain and suffering are always inevitable"

Me: I thought Crime and Punishment was too light for you

Hudson: Apparently I'm feeling optimistic

Me: Good night

Hudson: Good night, Grace

I hold my phone for a few more seconds, waiting to see if Hudson will text something else. When he doesn't, I think about texting Jaxon a heads-up about Saturday, then decide I can just talk to him in class tomorrow. Texting a boy the week after he breaks up with you reeks of desperation, especially when it's after midnight.

"From the size of the grin you're wearing, I'm guessing he said yes," Macy says.

She thinks I was texting Jaxon. I know I should correct her, but the truth is, I don't have it in me tonight to explain Hudson is just as eager to break up with me as Jaxon was.

18

Macy and I wake up ten minutes before the bell rings.

Which is no big deal for Macy, who does a little glamour and is ready to go. I, on the other hand, am pretty much completely screwed. Normally I love being a gargoyle, but I have to admit, this no-magic-works-on-me thing is a total drag sometimes...especially when it means splashing ice-cold water on my face because I don't have time to wait for it to warm up past forty degrees.

"Come on, Grace, let's go!" Macy calls from her spot next to the door, and I fight the urge to flip her off. It's not her fault she can't do a glamour on me, after all—she's tried numerous times. Any more than it's her fault that she looks perfectly put together while I look like a monster-movie reject after the fight scene.

"I'm coming, I'm coming," I tell her as I sling my backpack over my shoulder and grab a purple rabbit-ear scrunchie from my desk drawer. I fasten my hair into a ponytail as we walk out the door and am glad we left before I could look in the mirror. Especially since I'm pretty sure the purple polo I grabbed off my closet floor in a panic is the one I threw there last week after realizing a stain didn't come out in the laundry.

Fantastic.

Because the only thing worse than walking into a room full of monsters looking like you just rolled out of bed is walking into a room full of them looking like you never even *made* it to bed.

They sense weakness.

Macy and I race down the stairs together, then split off once we get to the first floor. She has drama in one of the outside cottages while I have Ethics of Power. It's a senior seminar taught for one six-week period, and it's required to graduate—I assume because Uncle Finn isn't okay with sending a bunch of powerful paranormals into the world without some grounding in right and wrong.

It's an interesting subject, and also the only one I'm taking that I'm currently doing well in, since I haven't missed any classes, but I dread it anyway. The teacher is brilliant, but she's also a real jerk. Plus, her classroom is, by far, the scariest room at Katmere—and that's saying something, considering the tunnels down below the castle are filled with human bones.

I've asked about a million times what this room was originally used for, but no one ever answers me. I think it's because they're trying to spare my delicate sensibilities, but all the not-knowing does is spur my imagination on...and not in a good way. How many reasons could there possibly be for soot stains and claw marks etched into stone? Especially when there are remnants of what look to be iron shackles at various heights and locations in the room...

A quick glance at my phone tells me I've got about a minute before the tardy chimes go off—and by chimes, I mean the chorus of Uncle Finn's new favorite song, Billie Eilish's "Bury a Friend." Because he really is all about the atmosphere. It drives Macy up the wall, but after spending the last twelve years of my life following a boring bell schedule, this makes a nice change.

The ethics classroom is separated from the rest of the castle by a long, winding, windowless hallway, and I move through it at a run—partly because I'm late and partly because I really hate being in this passageway alone.

There's nothing overtly scary about it, except every time I walk through here, I get a chill down my spine that has nothing to do with Alaska and everything to do with something being off in this part of the school. Really, really off.

Of course, the hallway leads to what I'm pretty sure is a centuries-old torture chamber, so is it any surprise it feels creepy?

Eventually the passageway ends, and even though I know I'll be late, I pause for just a second to get my wits about me *and* to smooth my hair. After all, its location isn't the only thing that makes this the scariest room at Katmere. It's what's inside that also stresses me out.

Which is why, even though the tardy chimes sound, I still take a couple of moments for a few deep breaths before opening the door and ducking inside the large, circular classroom. I keep my head down and aim for one of the empty desks in the back, but I've barely taken two steps before my teacher's voice booms across the classroom.

"Welcome, Miss Foster. So nice of you to join us for class today."

"I'm sorry I'm late, Ms. Virago." I start to tell her it won't happen again, but I've been at Katmere Academy long enough to know not to make promises like that. Especially to the most shrewish teacher in the school.

"As am I." She speaks slowly, biting off each word like it's the enemy. "See me after class for an assignment to make up what you missed."

What I missed? I glance around the room, trying to figure out what I could possibly have missed in ten seconds, but it doesn't even look like they've started taking notes yet. Ms. Virago must see me looking, though, because her eyes narrow right before she spins around and marches back up to the front of the classroom, her heels clapping out an angry staccato rhythm with each step that she takes.

"Is there a problem, Miss Foster?"

"No, not at all—"

"Then perhaps you should explain to us how Rawls's first principle can be applied—"

"I'm sorry to interrupt, ma'am." Hudson's voice rings through the class-room, his tone placating and...*angelic*? "But could you please go over what Kant's stand would be on magical torture one more time? I'm still a little confused by his categorical imperative—"

She sighs heavily. "CI is *not* that hard to understand, Mr. Vega. At least not if you pay attention."

"I know. I'm sorry. I'm just really struggling with Kant's entire philosophy, to be honest." There's not an ounce of sarcasm in his voice, and I swear he sounds sweeter than I have *ever* heard him.

"Well, then maybe you should see me after class, too. You and Miss Foster can spend your weekend working on an extra-credit project together."

"I would—"

A loud cracking sound fills the air, and half of Jaxon's pen goes flying across the room. It bounces off Ms. Virago's podium before rolling across the floor to land at her feet.

She turns her stink eye on Jaxon and Flint who, God bless him, cracks up. Just full-on starts laughing like a hyena in the middle of class.

And that, in a nutshell, is why I hate this damn class despite the interesting subject. Not only do we have the teacher from hell, but somehow I'm part of the most screwed-up testosterone-filled quadrangle—rectangle—square?—in history.

And that's before Ms. Virago announces we're going to spend the class working on different ethical problems as part of a group project—right before she gives a viperish smile and says, "Oh, and Miss Foster, Mr. Vega, the other Mr. Vega, and Mr. Montgomery, the four of you will be doing today's very first presentation."

19

Misery Hates Company

"**R**eally?" Jaxon is the first one to speak after we push our desks together. "You just couldn't keep your mouth shut, could you?"

"This coming from the child who threw his pen at the teacher?" Hudson snipes back.

"I didn't throw it. I—" He breaks off as he realizes his defense of what happened is going nowhere good.

"How are you, Grace?" Flint smiles.

"I'm fine." As long as you don't count having to spend the next ninety minutes in my own personal version of hell. "Why?"

"No reason." He shrugs. "Just thought you were…"

"Looking a little rough?" I fill in for him. "It was a long night."

Jaxon glares at him. "She looks fine."

"I never said she didn't," Flint responds.

"You okay?" Hudson asks softly. "Did something happen after I left?"

"You spent the night with him?" Jaxon's voice is emotionless, but the eyes he turns on me are anything but.

"Evening," I tell him. "We spent the evening in—"

"Wow." He swings his gaze back to Hudson. "Preying on upset girls is super classy."

"Wait a minute!" I interject. "Nobody was preying on anyone—"

"Maybe you shouldn't have upset her," Hudson interrupts me. "Then *you* could have spent the night with her."

"Evening!" I clarify again as Jaxon's fist clenches on his thigh.

"So how do you think Kant would feel about this whole thing you've got going on?" Flint interjects with a wave of his hand, his eyes bouncing back and forth between Hudson and Jaxon like he's watching a tennis match.

"Are you high right now or something?" I demand.

"Hey, someone's got to do the actual classwork," he shoots back. "I'm just trying to do my part."

"By exacerbating the situation?" I glare at him.

"By refocusing us on ethics philosophers," he answers with a look so deliberately pious, I'm surprised he hasn't pulled out a halo to plop right on top of his afro.

"You couldn't wait to go to him?" Jaxon asks.

"If by 'go to him,' you mean running into him in the library, then yes," I tell him, not even trying to hide how insulted I feel.

"You know," Hudson adds, "the big room with the books. Oh wait, do you even know what a book is?"

"I need a new group," I say to no one in particular.

"I'll be in your group," Flint volunteers.

"You're already in my group," I tell him through gritted teeth. "That's kind of the point of a new group."

"Hey!" He pulls a mock-wounded face. "I'm the only one in this group who's done any work."

"Oh, really?" I ask. "And what work have you done exactly?"

He scoots his notebook over to me. He's drawn a line down the center of the page and written *Kant* at the top of one side and *Hudson* at the top of the other. Underneath *Kant* is a sketch of Jaxon...with devil horns and a pointy tail.

Hudson leans over to check out Flint's work and grins. "It's a surprisingly good likeness," he tells Flint, who holds his hand out for a fist bump.

"What do you think Kant and Kierkegaard would say about bringing your personal issues into the classroom?" Ms. Virago's voice slices through the already thick tension surrounding our group.

Because what this conversation really needs is her butting her nose in and making everything worse. I don't want to make excuses to this woman, but since I can't trust any of my partners not to screw things up, I know I need to try.

But before I can come up with anything to say, Hudson replies, "I'm pretty sure Kierkegaard would think it was subjective." Which...come on.

Jaxon rolls his eyes, Flint ducks his head to hide his grin, and I can't help it—I let out a snort of laughter, then slap my hand over my mouth and nose in a desperate effort to hide the evidence.

But it's too late. Ms. Virago is fuming, and she doesn't care who knows it. "That's it!" she hisses at Hudson and me. "Both of you, up to my desk!"

Shit. There goes the one good grade I've currently got.

I'm sorry, Hudson mouths to me as I grab a pen and notebook.

I shrug back at him. It's not his fault I was ridiculous enough to laugh.

Hudson starts to follow the teacher, but Jaxon grabs my hand and asks softly, "You want me to get you out of it?"

His skin feels good against mine, so good, in fact, that it takes me a few seconds to register what he's saying. But once I do register it, I shake my head.

I mean, sure, I'd *like* him to get me out of it. I do not have time for whatever extra work Ms. Virago is about to heap on Hudson and me. But at the same time, I hate how scared people are of Jaxon again, how much they distance themselves from him. How much worse would that get if I just let him use his influence to get me out of trouble?

I smile my thanks at him for offering, but whatever brief glimpse of humanity he gave me is gone as he stares at me with those dark eyes that seem to get colder with every second that passes.

I drop my gaze, more hurt than I want to admit by the indifference written all over him. I know we're not together, but does that mean he can just turn off his feelings for me? Does it mean that he really doesn't care about me anymore?

But how can he just do that? I'm mated to someone else, for God's sake, and I still care about *him*. Yes, things feel different between us. Yes, I have confusing emotions zinging around inside me for Hudson. But that's the bond, not me.

I, Grace Foster, the girl inside the gargoyle, still love Jaxon. I can feel it when I look at him, feel it when he touches me. So how can it be possible that he doesn't feel the same way?

It isn't possible, I decide as Ms. Virago speaks firmly to Hudson and me and assigns us that extra project she promised at the beginning of class. Jaxon may be hiding his feelings behind that awful wall of coldness, but that doesn't mean the feelings aren't there.

And once we meet with the Bloodletter, once we figure out a way to break Hudson's and my mating bond, everything will go back to normal. It has to.

Because if it doesn't? I don't know what will happen...to any of us.

20

The Joke's on You

The rest of the day passes in a blur of classes and work, more classes and more work, until I want to say *screw it all*. So when a text comes in from Flint asking to go for a flight with him, I'm tempted. Really, really tempted. It's been more than a week since I've flown, and I'm so ready to stretch my wings.

But running out on the pile of homework I have would be completely irresponsible—not to mention only put me further behind. It's one thing to be drowning because of circumstances. It's another thing entirely to make bad decisions that only drag you down. I have a little less than two months until graduation. I can do anything for that short amount of time—even ridiculous amounts of philosophy homework.

Me: Sorry, can't go. Drowning in ethics project

In response, Flint sends me a GIF of a little boy crying—which makes me send him a GIF of a little girl crying even harder.

Flint: Study hard, New Girl

Me: Try not to fly into a mountain, Dragon Boy

He responds with a paper airplane crashing and burning, because of course he does.

While there's a part of me that would like nothing more than to stay here trading GIFs with Flint all afternoon, that's not going to get this project done. I drop my phone in the front pocket of my backpack, then do a quick change out of my uniform and into black sweats and the *Notorious RBG* T-shirt my mom gave me for my seventeenth birthday.

I grab an apple and a can of Dr Pepper on my way out, then head to the study room on the second floor where I'm supposed to meet Hudson. But I'm barely halfway down the hall when Mekhi comes barreling out of his room and straight into me.

"Oh, shit!" Mekhi grabs on to my shoulders and keeps me from flying into the nearest wall—just one of the hazards of getting in the way of a vampire on a mission. "Sorry, Grace. I didn't see you there."

"Here I thought you were trying to break a rib or two," I joke.

"And get myself on the Vega brothers' shit list?" He gives an exaggerated shudder even though his warm brown eyes are laughing as he teases, "My neck just got better, thank you very much."

I roll my eyes. "Yes, because you've got so much to worry about from Jaxon and Hudson."

"If I hurt you, I do," he says, and though he's still smiling, his tone is about a hundred times more solemn now. "And so do you. You need to be careful, Grace."

"I'm *trying* to be careful. But in case you haven't noticed, it's really hard to figure out what either of them is thinking at any given moment."

"Jaxon loves you," Mekhi tells me.

"Does he?" I shake my head. "Because these last few days, I haven't been so sure."

"He's hurt."

"Yeah, well, so am I. But every time I try to talk to him, it just makes things worse. He's treating me like I'm..." I drift off on a sigh, not sure what I want to say. Or more honestly, not sure I want to say it.

But clearly Mekhi has no such inhibitions. "Like you're already gone?"

My shoulders slump. "Yeah."

He looks away and doesn't say anything else for what feels like forever. But when his gaze finally meets mine again, it's deadly serious. "You might want to think about why that is."

I start to tell him that that's pretty much my point—*I don't know why.* But before I can, he wraps his arm around my shoulders in a hug and says, "Things will work out the way they're supposed to. You just need to give it time."

I start to call him on the biggest cop-out ever, but he shoots me a sympathetic look and takes off in the opposite direction from where I'm heading.

Freaking vampires. You never know exactly where you stand with them, do you?

I wouldn't trade being a gargoyle for anything—except maybe having my parents back—but I'd be lying if I said I didn't think about how much simpler my life was before I knew vampires existed. Certainly before I met two of the most attractive, contrary, *difficult* vampires in the entire world. Probably even the universe.

Still, I can't help thinking about what Mekhi told me about being careful—with Jaxon *and* Hudson. And I get it. I do. Because there's a tiny corner of me that's terrified we'll destroy one another before this is all over.

Maybe that's why I pull out my phone and text Jaxon.

Me: How does a mummy start a letter?

I wait a minute for him to answer, but he doesn't, so I finish making my way to the study room. To Hudson.

He isn't there, which I probably should have anticipated, since I'm ten minutes early. But I don't know. I guess I grew so used to him being in my head all the time that I just expect him to be wherever I need him to be. Which is ridiculous and a habit I definitely need to break.

I set up at the only open table, snacking on my apple as I pull up a bunch of information on the ethics of Plato, Socrates, and Aristotle. Ms. Virago assigned the philosophers—and apparently she's got a thing for the ancient Greeks—but we have to pick the ethical question we want to examine from all three philosophers' points of view before we decide which one we think is right.

I've got a couple of ideas, and I'm jotting them down when Hudson finally gets there. "Sorry," he says as he settles into the chair across from me. "I didn't expect you to be here yet."

"This is the time we agreed on, right?" I glance up with a smile, then refocus on my notes. I don't want to lose the idea that's brewing.

"True. It's just—" He breaks off.

"What?" I ask.

He shakes his head. "Never mind."

I glance up again, but he's looking at me strangely, so strangely that I put my pen down and hold his gaze. "Hey, what's going on?" I ask. "You feeling okay?"

"Yeah, of course." But he seems taken aback by the question, though I can't figure out why.

"You sure?" I ask after he doesn't say anything else—which is distinctly un-Hudson-like in and of itself. God knows he's never been one who's short of things to say. But after the day I've had, I'm really not in the mood to try and guess what's wrong with him, so I just raise my brows and ask again, "What's going on, Hudson?"

"Nothing." There's a bit more bite in his tone this time, and relief skitters through me. This Hudson I know what to do with. The other, softer one...I don't have a clue. "Why?"

"I don't know. You just seem...weird."

"Weird?" He lifts an imperious brow. "I am *never* weird."

And I giggle. That's the Hudson I know. "Never mind. Let's get to work."

"That is what we're here for." He pulls out his laptop and a notebook. "Any ideas on what question you want to discuss?"

I give him my ideas, and after a few minutes of debate, we settle on the butterfly effect—is it ethical to change something in time, for the right reasons, if you know that it will change other things later on, maybe in a not-so-okay way?

He takes Socrates, I take Aristotle, and we decide to meet in the middle with Plato.

I find an article about Aristotle's *On the Soul* and start taking notes on things we might be able to use. It's a pretty interesting article, and I get wrapped up in it, so much that I'm barely paying attention when Hudson clears his throat before saying out of the blue, "No one's ever asked me that before."

I'm in the middle of writing something down, so I don't look up as I ask, "Asked you what?"

"If I'm okay."

His answer doesn't register at first, but when it does, my brain shuts down. It just flat-out stops working for one second, two.

But then I'm jerking my eyes up, and Hudson is right there—his face open, his gaze oceanic—and for a moment, I forget how to breathe. Not just because of the way he's looking at me but because the full weight of his words finally sinks in. What they *mean*.

Awareness charges the air between us, has my heart beating way too fast and the hair on the back of my neck standing straight up. And still, I can't bring myself to tear my gaze away from his. Still, I can't do anything but lose myself in the bottomless depths of his eyes.

"No one?" I manage to force the words out of my too-tight throat.

He shakes his head, gives a little self-deprecating shrug, and just like that, he destroys me.

I've always known his life was awful. I've seen glimpses of it, figured things out by what he didn't say, even met the horrible people who call themselves his parents. But it's never registered before—at least not like this—that Hudson has never had anyone in his whole two-hundred-plus-year existence who cared about him. Who really, truly cared about him and not what he could do or what they could get from him.

It's an awful realization, and a heartbreaking one.

"Don't." His voice is hoarse.

"Don't what?" I ask, my throat somehow even tighter than it was just a minute ago.

"Don't feel sorry for me. That's not why I told you." It's obvious he's uncomfortable, but he doesn't look away. Neither do I.

I can't.

"This isn't pity," I finally whisper. "I could never pity you."

Something moves behind his eyes, something that looks an awful lot like grief. "Because I'm a monster?"

"Because you made it." I reach for his hand impulsively, and the second our skin touches, heat slams through me. "Because you're better than them. Because no matter what they did, they couldn't break you."

His hand tightens on mine, his fingers sliding between my own. And then we're holding hands.

It feels better than I expect it to, certainly better than it should, so I don't pull back. Neither does he. And for a minute, everything fades away.

The other students all around us.

The project neither one of us has time for.

That everything about this situation is messed up.

It all disappears, and for this one moment in time, it's just us and this connection that has nothing to do with the mating bond and everything to do with us.

At least until my phone, sitting on the table next to me, buzzes with a series of texts, shattering the fragile peace between us.

Hudson looks away first, his gaze going to my vibrating phone. And the moment is gone.

"I should get going," Hudson tells me, even as he pulls his hand from mine and pushes back from the table.

"But we haven't finished—"

"We have a week. We can work on it on Sunday." His tone is clipped as he shoves his stuff into his backpack.

"Yeah, but I cleared the whole evening. I thought—"

"The library closes in a few hours, and I have some more research I want to do on mating bonds. I read some interesting stuff last night, and I want to follow up on it while it's still fresh in my mind."

"What kind of stuff?" I ask, completely bewildered by his sudden curtness.

"About people who've tried to break them before." He turns and walks away without a backward glance.

My heart is pounding in my ears. Why does it hurt so much to see another example of how eager he is to break our bond?

Which...fine. Obviously he can do whatever he wants. I just wish I knew why he has to do it now, when we should be working on this ridiculous project.

Screw it. I stand and start to pack up my stuff as well. If Hudson can work on other things, then so can I. It's not like I don't have a million and one different projects due before the end of the school year.

It's only as I pick up my phone that I remember that someone texted me. I glance down at my lock screen, figuring it'll be Macy or Uncle Finn or maybe even Heather, who I haven't talked to in a couple of days. But it isn't any of them.

Instead, it's Jaxon. And he answered my joke.

21

I Hate What You've Done with the Place

Jaxon: I miss my heart
Jaxon: And all the other organs, too?

I fumble the phone in my haste to unlock it, which is ridiculous, I know. He's kept me waiting for more than an hour, but that doesn't matter. All that matters is that he answered me. Maybe he doesn't hate me after all.

Me: Tomb it may concern

I figure he won't answer me for another hour—if he even answers at all. But it turns out I'm wrong, because he texts back just as I'm zipping up my backpack.

Jaxon: You're getting worse at this

Me: Not every joke is gold

Jaxon: Apparently not

He's not exactly being forthcoming at the moment, but he isn't ignoring me, either. Figuring that's as good an indicator as any, I decide to press my luck.

Me: Can you meet me for a few minutes?

Me: I want to talk

Long seconds that feel like hours drag by before I finally get his answer.

Jaxon: Yeah. I'm in the tower. Come on up.

It's not a particularly enthusiastic response, but it's more than I was hoping for, so I count it a win. Then practically sprint for the door as I fire off one last text telling him that I'm on my way.

I race up the steps to the tower, taking them two and even three at a time. It leaves me breathless once I hit the top of the last flight of stairs, but I don't care. There has to be a way to make things right with Jaxon and not hurt Hudson in the process. There just has to be, and I am certain it centers around asking the Bloodletter some important questions. And demanding answers.

I take a second to catch my breath before stepping into the antechamber of the tower. Then stop dead as soon as I get my first real look at the room. It looks *nothing* like it usually does.

Normally, there's furniture arranged in an invitation and shelves upon shelves of books and candles and other small knickknacks. Art hangs on the walls, while more books are stacked in piles around the room, and there's a cabinet full of granola bars, Pop-Tarts, and chocolate just for me.

It's my favorite room in the castle, the place where I can just curl up with a snack and a book and the boy I love. What more does a girl need?

But that tower room I loved so much? It's gone now, replaced with doom and gloom to a degree I haven't seen since Lia tried to sacrifice me.

The books are gone, the furniture is gone, and the only art left—an original Monet—has a giant hole through the center of it. In place of furniture is workout equipment. Lots and lots and lots of workout equipment. The center of the room is dominated by a weight-lifting bench with a lot of really heavy weights on the bar. In the corner hangs a very large punching bag that Jaxon must use a lot, judging by how badly dented and crumbling the stone walls on either side of it are.

There's also a heavy-duty treadmill against the wall and an exercise bike near the window.

The room looks nothing like Jaxon—nothing at all like him—and everything inside me trembles in horror as I look over this new setup.

I mean, it's not the new workout equipment itself that is so bad—although Jaxon usually gets his workouts from long runs in the wilderness. It's that this room, which had always seemed like a window into Jaxon's *soul*, has been gutted. There's nothing left of the guy I fell in love with in here, nothing left of who he is or what matters to him. And I hate it.

I hate it, I hate it, I hate it.

I must make a sound, or maybe Jaxon just figures I should be here by now, but the door from his bedroom flies open. I get a quick glimpse through the open doorway before he shuts it again, and his bedroom looks as empty as this room does. No drum set in the corner, no stacks of books. Nothing but his bed, with its black sheets and duvet.

I start to ask him what happened here, but then I realize he's carrying a duffel bag, and everything else flies out of my mind.

"Where are you going?" I demand.

One of his brows goes up at the belligerence in my voice, but he doesn't answer. Just sets his black—of course it is—bag near the top of the stairs and asks, "What did you want to see me about?"

"You didn't answer my question."

Now both his brows are up as he leans back on his heels and crosses his arms over his chest. "You didn't answer mine."

I don't respond, my gaze glued to the bag at the top of the stairs. Maybe it's naive, considering we're on a break or whatever, but I still can't believe Jaxon was going to leave Katmere to go God only knows where—with a suitcase—and didn't even plan to tell me about it.

"Was I just going to wake up tomorrow and you were going to be gone?" I ask, hating how small my voice sounds all of a sudden.

"Don't be dramatic, Grace." His voice is ice-cold. "It's not like I'm leaving for good."

"Well, how would I know that?" I hold my arms out to encompass the room as I spin in a slow circle. "How am I supposed to know anything about you anymore?"

"I don't know." Anger flashes in his eyes. "Maybe if you spent less time with Hudson, you'd have a clue what's going on with somebody, *anybody*, else."

I gasp. "That's not fair. I'm trying to make up enough work to graduate. You know that."

"You're right. I do." He closes his eyes, and when he opens them again, the anger is gone, but so is every other emotion. For the second time today, I can't help thinking that it's like looking into his eyes that first moment we met, when there was absolutely nothing there. "I'm sorry."

He starts to gesture for me to sit down, and I watch as it dawns on him that he no longer has anywhere for me to sit. A weariness comes over him then, and he shoves a hand through his hair as he quietly asks, "What did you need?"

"I'm going to the Bloodletter tomorrow—"

"The Bloodletter?" Suddenly, he sounds alarmed. "Why are you going there?"

"Hudson and I are hoping she can break the mating bond between us. We want you to come with us."

He shoots me a skeptical look. "Hudson wants me to come with you?"

"*I* want you to come with me. I don't care what Hudson wants."

Jaxon stares at me, his gaze searching my face for I don't know what. But just when I start to think that I've gotten through, that he's going to agree to come with us, he says, "You really should just let this go, Grace. Let me go."

"I can't." There's nothing more for me to say, so I wait. Hope he feels the same way.

But he just shakes his head. "I've already got plans."

"Plans." I look toward the duffel bag that might as well be another elephant in the room.

He sighs. "I've got to go to the Vampire Court for the weekend."

"The Vampire Court?" It's the absolute last thing I expect him to say, especially after everything that happened during the Ludares challenge. "But why?"

"Someone has to keep an eye on Cyrus after that shit Hudson pulled. He may not have raised me, but my father is predictable enough for me to know that he's not going to let what happened on that Ludares field go."

"We all know that. What does that have to do with you going home?"

"I'm bringing the Order with me. We're hoping among all of us, we'll be able to figure out what he's got planned."

"I thought he had a war planned," I tell him. "That's what everyone is saying."

"You don't actually think Cyrus is just going to show up with his faithful army of wolves and made vampires, do you?"

I think about everything I've heard since the challenge—not just from Jaxon and Hudson but from Uncle Finn and Macy and Flint and...everyone, really. "I thought that was what we were preparing for."

"We are. But he won't come at us straight on. Not yet. Not when he has to face Hudson, you, and me, as well as Flint and a whole host of other powerful paranormals."

"So what do you think he's going to do?" I ask, even though I'm not sure I want to know the answer.

"Try to kill two birds with one stone." The look on his face has chills running up and down my spine of the very-not-good variety. "If you think he's going to let Hudson's performance on the challenge field go, you obviously don't know how a megalomaniac like Cyrus thinks. And what better way to hurt Hudson and even the odds for the coming fight than to destroy his mate?"

"Me?" I squeak. "You think he's coming after me?"

"I *know* he's coming after you," he tells me in a voice so deadly that it makes me take a step back, even though I know Jaxon would never hurt me. "I'm not going to let that happen."

This time, when our gazes meet, there's something in his eyes that wasn't there before. Something raw and real and powerful. And that's when I know. Jaxon still cares for me. At least a little.

He may not want to, but he does. More, he's determined to take care of me in his own way—whether that means stepping aside so I can be with Hudson or protecting me from his sociopathic father.

My heart breaks for him, for us—for what was and what could have been. For what still might be if we all play our cards exactly right.

Then, because I know there's no talking him out of his plan, I throw my arms around him and whisper, "Be careful."

He holds me close for the space of one, two, three breaths, then steps away. "I have to go. The Order is waiting for me."

He grabs his duffel bag and starts down the stairs.

I follow him. There are so many things I want to say. And so many things I no longer have the right to say. They all burn on the tip of my tongue, but in the end, I settle for, "Please, Jaxon. Don't do anything rash."

He turns to look at me, and in that moment, it's all there in his eyes. The love, the hate, the sorrow, the joy. And the pain. All the pain. But still, he gives me that crooked grin I fell in love with all those months ago. And whispers, "I'm pretty sure I already have."

I close my eyes as my heart breaks all over again, and when I open them, he's already gone.

As I head back down the stairs and to my room, I can't help a nagging feeling in the pit of my stomach that this was the last time Jaxon will ever look at me that way again—like I matter to him. Or worse, like anything does.

22

WanderLUST

My alarm goes off at four the next morning, but I'm already awake studying a topographical map of Alaska. Unfortunately, there's no X marks the spot when it comes to the Bloodletter's cave, which means I'm going to have to go from memory—something I'm not looking forward to, since Jaxon is the one who got us there last time, and I was just along for the ride.

I'd been counting on him directing us again this time, but that's not going to happen now, considering he's in London. And since Hudson has never been there corporeally, I need to figure out from memory and this map of the terrain how to find the Bloodletter's cave again. Easy-freaking-peasy.

I know it's several hundred miles away, and I know we started out going northeast, but we made a turn somewhere. I just wish I could remember where…or how long it took us to get there.

My phone vibrates, and I reach for it, ready to respond to Hudson with a text to go back to sleep because we aren't leaving until I can figure this out. But the text isn't from Hudson.

Jaxon: Text me if you get lost

He's also sent a series of shots from Google Earth and drawn a red path through the mountains and thawing snow. And, thank God, on the last shot, he put a giant red X over where the Bloodletter's cave should be as well as instructions for how to remove the wards.

Me: Thank you, thank you, THANK YOU

Jaxon: Don't do anything rash

Me: I already have

I take a couple of minutes to trace the path he gave me onto the map, just in case my phone dies while we're out traversing the wilderness. Then I get dressed, which is a production, as always.

It's April now, so temps are finally above freezing for the most part, thank

God—but just barely. Which means tights, leggings, ski pants, and several layers of shirts and socks, as well as my puffy hot-pink coat. I keep thinking about ordering a new one, but it doesn't seem worth it—not if it's going to hurt Macy's feelings. She's hurting more than enough as it is.

I grab my outdoor pack—also hot pink and also courtesy of Macy—and shove some bottles of water into it, along with some granola bars and a few packs of trail mix. Lastly, I pack a large thermos of blood I got last night from the cafeteria for Hudson.

I know he could probably drink once we get to the Bloodletter's, but the last time the two of them met, they didn't get along so well. I'm not sure that she'll offer him refreshments or that he would take them if she did. So a thermos of blood seems like the best move, unless I want to offer Hudson one of my veins.

A little shiver runs through me at the thought. I'm not sure if it's a good shiver or a bad shiver, but I'd be lying if I said I didn't remember that night by my bed when Hudson ran an imaginary fang down the side of my throat. At the time, I was horrified, but now...now it's a lot more intriguing than it used to be.

I'm sure it's just the mating bond, doing what mating bonds do. But I can't help but wonder what it would be like. It couldn't possibly be as intense as it was with Jaxon—I can't imagine anything being that intense—but that doesn't mean I'm not a teeny-tiny bit curious.

A quiet knock sounds on my door just as I zip up my pack, and the distraction of it yanks me out of my wildly inappropriate thoughts about Hudson. Macy knows where I'm going, so I don't bother to text her, and she's finally getting some real sleep, so I'm as quiet as I can possibly be as I let myself out of my room.

Hudson's standing in the hallway with a pack very similar to mine hanging over his shoulder—except it's navy blue and Armani. Big surprise there. Then again, everything he's wearing is Armani, except for the Alaska-weather-certified boots. And if Armani made them, I'm pretty sure he'd be wearing those, too.

"Something on your mind?" he asks as we start down the hall.

"No, why?"

"No reason," he answers. "Except your cheeks are currently the same color as your coat."

His words only make me blush harder—mostly because I'm afraid my earlier thoughts are written all over my face. It's a good thing reading minds isn't one of Hudson's powers...

"I don't— I can't— It doesn't—" I force myself to stop babbling, then take a deep breath and try again. "I was just...exercising. My cheeks always get red when I do."

He gives me a strange look. "Aren't we about to get a lot of exercise?"

"Oh, um, yeah." I resist the urge to bang my head against the nearest wall, mostly because I figure it will only make things worse. I always knew I was a bad liar, but apparently I'm a really, really bad liar. But I'm in it now, so I might as well own it. "I just wanted to do a little warm-up, that's all."

"A warm-up?" he repeats, totally deadpan. "Right. Wouldn't want you to strain anything. Like the truth, for instance?"

I've got nothing to say to that, so I don't. Instead, I start down the hall, tossing over my shoulder, "Are you coming or what?"

"Aren't we waiting for Prince Jaxon?" He looks in the direction of the tower.

"Be nice," I admonish him as he catches up to me. "And he had other plans for the weekend, so we're on our own."

"Other plans?" Hudson lifts a skeptical brow. "What could possibly be more important to him than this little excursion?"

"He's going to London—"

"Are you kidding me?" His accent is about a hundred times heavier than it was just a minute ago. "Are you fucking kidding me? What is he thinking? The bloody wanker—"

I lay a hand on his arm, wait until those furious indigo eyes meet mine. "He's worried about what Cyrus is planning. For both of us."

"Yeah, well, so am I, but you don't see me running off to Cyrus's lair like a bloody chump, do you?" He's so annoyed that for the first time ever, he walks ahead, leaving me to do a near jog to catch up to him.

"He thinks he's so bloody clever, thinks he's ten steps ahead of everyone else. But he doesn't get it. Cyrus knows he's a threat. Son or not, he'll bloody well kill him the second he gets the chance." Hudson's rummaging in his bag now, pulling out his phone.

"Of course he gets that. That's why he went—and why he brought the entire Order with him."

Hudson pauses with his thumbs over his phone. "He brought all of them? Mekhi? Luca? Liam? Byron and Rafael?"

"Yes, all of them." I rest a hand on Hudson's arm, shocked to realize he's trembling just a little. "I'm worried for him, too, but I talked to him. He knows what he's walking into."

"He doesn't have a bloody clue what he's walking into." Hudson's eyes have turned to ice. "But there's not an arsed thing I can do about it now, is there?"

Still, he fires off a couple of text messages in quick succession. I don't expect Jaxon to answer—he's not exactly in a good place—but, surprisingly, Hudson gets a response back right away.

"What did he say?" I ask.

"I didn't text him." He's back to typing again.

"What do you mean? I thought—"

"I wanted an answer, so I texted Mekhi." He sees the question in my eyes and nods. "You're right. He swears he's got Jaxon's back—and that they know exactly what they're doing."

"Do you believe him?" I ask, studying his face carefully.

"I don't *not* believe him." He puts his phone away and zips up his backpack.

I take a deep breath, blow it out slowly. "I guess that will have to be enough, then."

"It'll be something," he tells me, then heads down the stairs without another word.

We don't talk again until we're outside. "I forgot to ask. You do know where we're going, right?"

"Jaxon sent me the coordinates. I've got it mapped on my phone. And an actual map."

He grins. "Then what are we waiting for?"

"Absolutely nothing," I shoot back, then reach deep inside myself and grab my platinum string.

23

Live and Let Fly

Hudson lets out a very un-Hudson-like whoop as I finish shifting and take to the air. And can I just say? It's so much cooler doing this under my own power as a gargoyle, instead of being carried by Jaxon.

I shoot forward several feet, then call back to Hudson, "Hey, slowpoke. Are you coming?"

"Just giving you a head start," he answers with a grin that is entirely too sexy for my own good. "Figured you might need it."

"I might need it?" I shoot him a look of pure affront. As if. "Last one down the mountain loses."

"Oh yeah?" he asks, and I realize for the first time that he's given up on the so-called head start and is keeping pace with me. He's not fading as much as just running very, very fast. "What do they lose? Or, more specifically, what do *I* win?"

"Oh, really? You're mighty confident there, Mr. Vega," I call down to him. Then I put on a burst of speed to show him that I'm not quite the pushover he thinks I'm going to be.

But it only takes a second for him to catch up to me. "Just being honest, Miss Foster." He grins up at me right before he jumps over a giant boulder in a single leap. "So what am I going to win?"

I laugh as I do a somersault in midair before going straight into a deep, fast dive. I don't stop until I'm hovering a few feet in front and above him. "Loser has to do the entire ethics project on their own."

He lifts a brow. "Not quite what I had in mind, but it'll do." Just to be a show-off, he leapfrogs over me. "For now."

There's something about the way Hudson says *for now* that makes my stomach flip-flop more than a little bit. But before I can try to figure out what that means, he blows me a kiss...and then takes off in full-out fade mode. The cheater.

I take off after him, flying up at an angle until I'm above the trees. And then I lay on every ounce of speed my wings can muster.

Down below, Hudson is racing through the trees, jumping over snowbanks and racing down rocky, jagged cliffs. I mostly keep pace with him, but it's harder than I thought it would be. I know vampires are fast—I've seen Jaxon and Mekhi fade full-out—but Hudson is seriously fast.

Even though it's a struggle to keep up, I love every second of it. Spring is finally coming to Alaska, and though the temperature is still in the high thirties, the landscape is coming to life all around us. And it is gorgeous.

A lot of the trees are evergreen up here, but as we near the bottom of the mountain and the top layers of snow begin to melt, shoots of green are starting to poke through. Plus, I can see for miles up here, and in places where the snow has begun to melt—where lakes are coming to life—wildflowers are springing up.

Bold and beautiful, they cover the ground in shades of pink and yellow, purple and blue. Part of me wants to stop and smell the flowers—I haven't seen any just growing like this since I left San Diego in early November—but if I do that, I'll lose for sure. And I don't want to lose. Not just because I have zero interest in doing that damn ethics project alone but because the idea of losing to Hudson grates against my pride. It's not losing to a vampire I mind, though. It's losing to *him*. I haven't spent our entire relationship trying to one-up him just to let him beat me now, in our first real competition. No freaking way. The flowers will have to wait.

We're almost to the bottom of the mountain, and Hudson has disappeared into a clump of trees far below me. At first, I don't worry too much about it—it's hard to see someone through a forest of spruce trees, especially when you're flying above them.

But long minutes go by without so much as a glimpse of his bright-blue snow jacket peeking through the trees, and it starts to make me nervous. Really, really nervous.

Not because I think he's ahead of me and I'm worried about losing (although that is certainly a valid concern with Hudson) but because this is freaking Alaska. Anything can happen out here in the middle of the wilderness.

One second of inattention, and you can be lying at the bottom of a ravine with a concussion or a compound fracture while a bear or pack of wolves tries to eat you.

Or a pissed-off moose might decide to use you as target practice for his antlers.

Or you could be impaled by a giant icicle coming around a curve...the list goes on and on in my head, getting a little more irrational with each second that passes. Admittedly, Hudson is the most dangerous predator on this mountain, despite the very wild wildlife, and I'm sure he can handle himself with them just fine.

But I still want to see him. Still want to make sure he's okay—and that he hasn't taken a wrong turn somewhere. And if he *has* taken a wrong turn, he could be halfway to Canada or the North Pole by now, and that means we'll never get to the Bloodletter's cave.

It's that thought and not any worry for Hudson that spurs me to fly lower so I can get a better look in between the trees—or at least that's what I tell myself. But no matter how low I fly, I can't see any sign of him.

Worry settles into my stomach, as heavy and unignorable as one of those giant boulders he's been jumping over ever since we left Katmere, and I prepare to drop almost to the top of the trees. I could text him, see if he answers. Service isn't the best out here, but we aren't that far from Denali National Park, so maybe—

I scream as something broadsides me out of nowhere and sends me spinning straight toward the ground.

24

Beauty and
All the Beasts

I have a split second to think of bears and mountain lions, wolves and lynx, as my scream echoes across the snowy mountain, before it registers that I'm being held by a (very) strong pair of arms. And that the spin I'm currently in is definitely controlled.

Hudson. Not in trouble but deliberately hiding. The jerk.

"Let me go!" I screech, even as I reach out with a balled-up fist and punch him in the shoulder as hard as I can.

In my human form, I know he would just laugh at such a blow, but my gargoyle stone packs a lot more of a wallop than my human hand does, and Hudson actually grunts in pain. What he doesn't do, however, is loosen his grip on me. At all.

"What are you doing?" I cry out as we finally stop spinning.

"Hitching a ride," he answers with a wicked grin that is somehow both extremely charming and extremely suspicious.

"Don't you mean cheating?" I shoot back.

"I suppose it all depends on your perspective." His breath is hot against my ear, and it sends all kinds of sensations careening through me. Sensations I have no business feeling for the brother of the guy I love, even if we are broken up.

"Considering you're the one tagging along for the ride, I'm pretty sure my perspective is the only one that matters," I mutter. Still, I stop struggling against his ridiculously strong hold. Not because I've given up but because there's no other way to lull him into a false sense of security. The second our feet hit the ground, he's not going to have a clue what *hit* him.

Except we never actually touch down on the ground. Instead, Hudson drops us onto the top branch of one of the tallest cedar trees around.

"Stop fighting me," he says once he's got us balanced properly on the branch. "Or we're both going to end up falling out of this thing—and gargoyles are a hell of a lot more breakable than vampires."

"If you want me to stop, you should let go of me!" I answer as I struggle against him, preparing to rack him if I have to.

"Okay." He lets go abruptly, and sure enough, I start to tumble straight off the branch.

The fact that I squawk like a chicken and grab on to him for dear life is something neither of us is going to forget for a long time—him, because it means he was right, and me, because there's no way he'll let me forget.

We're face-to-face now, so close that we're pretty much breathing the same air—which is not okay on a whole bunch of levels. Hudson must feel the same way, because he takes a step back. But this time, he keeps one firm hand on me so that I don't do my best impression of a Weeble Wobble.

And can I just say that it's really hard to balance on a tree branch at the best of times, let alone when you are made of stone? Which is why I say to hell with the whole gargoyle thing at the moment and reach inside for my platinum string.

Seconds later, I'm human again, which is way better when it comes to being able to balance properly. It's so much easier, in fact, that I actually feel comfortable taking a couple of steps away from Hudson, until my back is resting against the tree trunk.

As I do, I get my first good look at Hudson since he grabbed me. And he looks...good. Really good, with the wind blowing through his silky brown hair and a touch of color from the sun and wind kissing his normally pale cheeks. The giant grin doesn't hurt, either, along with a lightness in his eyes that I've never seen before.

I don't know if the changes are just because we're outdoors and having a little bit of fun for what feels like the first time in forever or if it's because he's finally close to getting rid of me.

"Hey, where'd you go?" he asks, and the lightness in his eyes clouds over.

"Just thinking." I smile, even though it's a lot harder than it was just a few moments ago.

His brows draw together. "What about?"

I don't have an answer to that question, at least not one I want to share with him. So after I look him over, I say the only thing I can think of. "I guess I'm just wondering why you've got one of your hands behind your back when you had no trouble grabbing me with both of them when you dragged me out of the air."

"Oh, that." Even more color floods his cheeks.

I narrow my eyes suspiciously, preparing to shift into a gargoyle again at the first hint of another dirty trick. But then he pulls his hand out from behind his back, and I realize he's carrying a small bouquet of wildflowers in all the shades of the rainbow.

He holds it out to me with a small smile and watchful eyes. And I melt.

"You picked flowers for me?" I gasp, eagerly reaching out to take them.

"They reminded me of you." He puts his tongue firmly in his cheek. "Especially the bright-pink ones."

But I'm so overwhelmed by the gesture—no one has ever hand-picked a bouquet for me before—that I don't rise to the very obvious bait. Instead, I bury my face in the flowers and inhale the scent of spring after a long, long, long winter.

Nothing has ever smelled so good.

"They're amazing," I say and watch the uncertainty on his face fade away. Impulsively, I throw my arms around him in a hug.

"Thank you so much," I whisper in his ear. "I love them more than anything."

"Yeah?" he asks, pulling away just a little so he can see my face.

"Yeah," I answer.

He smiles. "Good." Suddenly, his eyes widen, and he pulls me closer to him, even as he turns me around.

"What—"

"Look!" he whispers and points out across the huge ravine we're on the precipice of.

I follow where he's pointing and gasp, because on the ground, barely thirty feet in front of us, is a giant brown mama bear and her two half-grown cubs. The mom is lying in the sun, watching as her cubs tussle and tumble over each other.

Ears get pulled and tails get nipped, but their claws stay firmly sheathed as they roll around the ground together. And, I realize with delight, bear hugs are absolutely a real thing.

Hudson laughs when one of the cubs trips over a fallen tree and goes rolling down the shallow edge of the ravine and her sibling goes tumbling after her. When they don't immediately climb out of the ravine—choosing instead to roughhouse up and down its slippery, craggy slopes, Mama Bear roars her annoyance and walks over to investigate.

The bears climb out pretty quickly once she growls at them from the edge of the ravine, and then the three of them lumber away.

"That was ..." Hudson breaks off with a shake of his head.

"Incredible? Awe-inspiring? Amazing?" I fill in the blanks for him.

I don't know how long we stand there, checking out the truly breathtaking view of snow-covered mountains meeting a canyon covered in wildflowers.

Long enough for the bears to finally wander fully out of sight.

Long enough for a bald eagle to swoop across the canyon on a powerful gust of wind.

More than long enough for me to become aware of the hardness of Hudson's long, lean body pressed against my back, his fingers resting lightly on my waist to steady me.

As the eagle, too, disappears from view, Hudson pulls slowly away from me. I want to protest, want to grab on to his hands and hold him in place for just a few more minutes. For just a little longer. There's something so peaceful about standing up here at what feels like the top of the world, looking over land that has been untouched by humans for centuries...maybe even forever.

It's awe-inspiring, but it's also humbling. And a reminder that no matter how grave my problems are, they're only a momentary blip in the grand scheme of things. The world turned for a long time before I was born, and it will keep turning no matter how long Hudson's and my immortality lasts... provided climate change doesn't destroy it all before then, of course.

"We should get going," he says, and I'd be lying if I said I didn't like that he sounds as reluctant as I feel.

"I know," I answer with a sigh. Then I hand him my flowers. "Will you tuck these in the side pocket of my backpack? I don't want them to fall out when I fly."

He doesn't say anything, but he seems pleased as he does what I asked, zipping the pocket snug around the flowers' stems so that only the blooms stick out. He holds on to one stem, however, with several clusters of white flowers in it.

I start to ask him what he's going to do with it, but the words turn to dust in my mouth as he leans forward and slowly, carefully weaves the flowers through the windswept curls that aren't tucked into my hat.

"How do they look?" I ask, tilting my head so he can get a better view of the flowers.

"Beautiful." But he's not looking at the flowers when he answers. He's looking at me...and somehow that makes everything better and worse, all at the same time.

25

Follow the
Blood-Soaked
Road

The rest of the trip to the Bloodletter's cave is uneventful. A storm is moving in—I can feel it in the damp air all around us—so we travel fast, without any more rest breaks.

I check Jaxon's directions on the fly, and as expected, they're right on. All of which means we get to the Bloodletter's faster than I thought we might, and as we stand on the icy ground directly above her cave, me downing a granola bar while Hudson drinks from his thermos of blood, I can't help wondering if we should wait a while before trying to enter. It's barely noon, and I don't know if she's napping...or maybe enjoying a particularly fresh lunch.

Just the thought turns my stomach a little as I search for the opening to the cave, but it is what it is. And since this is my world now—especially considering I've been mated to two vampires at this point—I need to get used to the whole drinking-blood thing. Or, if not used to it, at least comfortable to the point where it doesn't traumatize me every time I think about them feeding from humans.

"The entrance is over here," Hudson calls, pointing to a small opening at the base of the mountain. Since the snow is melting, it's thankfully no longer hidden behind a giant snowbank like it was when I came with Jaxon, which makes it a lot easier to find *and*, more importantly, to access.

I cross over to where he's standing, then crouch down and prepare to enter the cave. "Ready?" I ask over my shoulder.

But Hudson's hand snakes out to stop me. "You forgot the safeguards. If we don't disable them first, they'll fry us alive."

Horror sweeps through me as I realize that he's right. I hand him my phone and say, "Jaxon sent instructions to remove them here."

He does a few complicated moves with his hands, then reaches for mine and says, "Come on. Let's get this over with."

He tugs me to him and then walks with me straight through the entrance of the cave. He keeps my hand in his as we start down the steep, slippery path that will eventually lead us to the Bloodletter's antechamber. I'm expecting the same long, challenging, and slightly gruesome walk as before, but this time is different.

Because as soon as we make it around the first curve, she's right there waiting for us, with her green eyes blazing and a grumpy frown on her face.

26

Why Can't
You B Positive?

"**M**aybe I wasn't as smooth getting through those safeguards as I thought," Hudson tells me in an aside, even as he shifts to put his body in front of mine. It's a move that should piss me off—I am a gargoyle, after all, and more than capable of defending myself.

Then again, the Bloodletter is basically the oldest and most powerful vampire in existence. Something tells me she won't need to rely on her powers if she wants to make me bleed...or break me into pieces.

So, just this once, I don't complain about him stepping in front of me. Especially since this position means I get to watch his back—just in case, you know, she decides she wants to break *him* into pieces instead of me.

"You unraveled the safeguards perfectly and you know it," the Bloodletter snaps at him. "Which makes me wonder if Jaxon has been telling tales." Her tone says that there will be hell to pay if he has.

I start to jump in to defend Jaxon, but Hudson beats me to the punch... and lies. "Do you honestly think I need my little brother's help to get through a few measly protections?"

Her laser-green gaze locks with his, and she looks nothing like the sweet old grandmother I originally mistook her for and a lot more like the deadly predator she actually is. "Those *measly protections* are the strongest in existence."

Hudson never even blinks as he answers, "Oops."

My stomach climbs into my throat, but the Bloodletter doesn't move. For long seconds, I'm not even sure she breathes. She just tilts her head and studies him, like he's a bug under a microscope and she's contemplating pulling off his wings.

Or wondering how he'll look draining into her blood bucket.

"Interesting that you would lie to me, Mr. Vega." Her eyes narrow on Hudson. "Very interesting."

Just when I'm beginning to think *Dead Man Walking* refers to a lot more than a book title, her too-bright gaze flicks over to me. And my stomach goes from my throat to my toes.

"Grace, my dear. It's so nice to see *you* again." The subtle emphasis she puts on the word "you" doesn't go unnoticed by Hudson or me.

"It's nice to see you, too." I give her the best smile I can muster, considering I'm pretty sure there's no chance Hudson is getting out of this cave alive.

"Come here so I can see you, child. It's been too long." She holds out a hand to me.

And my mouth feels like it's full of cotton, my mind racing with how many times Jaxon has warned me over and over to never, ever touch her, that she hates to be touched.

"It's been six weeks," Hudson tells her flatly—right before he moves to block me as I start to come behind him.

"Like I said. Too long." She continues to smile, continues to hold out her hand. But there's a look in her eyes now that warns me disobedience won't be tolerated.

It's not a good start to the visit, especially since I'm hoping to convince her to help us. But why does she want to touch me now? Is this a trick? Is it a test? Well, if it's a test, I decide, I have every intention of passing. This visit is too important.

It's my turn to give a warning look. But mine is directed at Hudson as I shove his arm out of the way. He responds with a low growl, but he doesn't try to block me again.

I move past him, pull in a deep breath, and take the Bloodletter's hand.

I only have a second to register that her eyes are swirling green orbs as we touch; then I kind of freeze as she pulls me in for a hug, like I'm some long-lost relative or something. I'm so confused—this isn't the kind of relationship we had last time—until Hudson snarls, and I realize that this performance isn't for me. It's for him. Part boast and part threat, all payback.

"I thought I warned you that he was the dangerous brother," she murmurs to me. And though her voice is soft, I know very well that she means for Hudson to hear.

Also, she's not wrong.

"You did," I answer as she releases me. "But there have been some developments."

"Developments." Her eyes gleam with interest. "Do these developments have anything to do with my Jaxon not being with you?"

Hudson snorts—whether at my use of the word "developments" or her use of a possessive pronoun to describe Jaxon, I don't know. But I count my blessings when he doesn't say anything...and when she does nothing more than lift a brow at his rudeness. Not that I know exactly what she could do to him, but I wouldn't put it past her to smite him, or whatever it's called when a vampire as powerful as she is unleashes her power.

"Yes." I answer quickly, before Hudson can do anything else to upset her.

She looks between us, like she's weighing her options. Finally, with a sigh, she turns back toward the depths of the cave. "Well then, you'd better come in, shouldn't you?"

She starts down the steep, frozen path that leads into the antechamber and, after exchanging a look of our own, Hudson and I follow her.

As we do, I worry about the Bloodletter slipping and breaking a hip or something as she makes her way back toward her sitting room. I have a terrible time navigating this trail, and I'm a lot younger than she is. But she must do the walk more frequently than I give her credit for, because she never hesitates—even in the most dangerous spots.

Still, I breathe a sigh of relief when we finally make it down to the main level of the cave. We pass through the doorway I remember, and I brace myself for what I'll see. Not going to lie, the bucket of blood that was sitting there last time still shows up in my nightmares occasionally, and I'm not thrilled at the possibility of seeing it again.

I tell myself not to look as we start across the antechamber toward the door to her main quarters, but in the end, I can't help myself. And once I do... Oh. My. God.

I don't say anything, but I must make some kind of sound because both Hudson and the Bloodletter turn to look at me—Hudson with alarm, the Bloodletter with a strange kind of fascination that doesn't make sense at all.

"I wasn't expecting visitors," she says mildly as she parades us by the two human corpses currently hanging upside down from hooks in the corner. Their throats are slit, and they're draining into two large buckets.

Her words aren't an apology, and I get it. I do. I don't apologize to anyone when I walk into the grocery store and buy chicken breasts. Why should this be any different? Well, except for *two people* being *dead*. And I don't normally—and by normally, I mean ever—get to see my food in such a natural state.

My stomach rolls.

Hudson moves so he's between the corpses and me, his hand coming up to rest on the small of my back in what I'm pretty sure is supposed to be a gesture of comfort. But it only makes me nervous, considering the Bloodletter's scrutiny of both of us. I don't pull away, though.

We move past the large buckets—which I note with some horror are nearly overflowing at this point—and she waves a hand to unlock the door that leads to her main apartment.

"Sit, sit," she says as she gestures to the black couch facing an illusion of a roaring fire. "I'll be with you in just a second."

Hudson and I do as we're told, and I can't help noticing that she's redecorated from the last time I was here. Before, the couch was a warm harvest gold, facing two wingback chairs in deep red like the poppies in the painting over the fireplace. Now, everything in the room is black and gray with accents of white. Even the art on the wall is in shades of gray, with only a couple of bold slashes of red.

"I like what you've done with the place," Hudson tells her as we settle onto the couch. "It's very...serial-killer chic."

I kick him, hard, but he just makes a face at me, the picture of innocence—as long as you don't count the wicked glint in his eyes.

When she finally moves to sit in the black rocking chair opposite the couch, the Bloodletter is carrying an elegant crystal goblet filled with what I can only assume is blood. My stomach clenches, and I think I'm going to be sick. Which is bizarre—I see the vamps drink blood at school all the time. Why should this be any different?

Except the vamps at Katmere drink animal blood. And the animals it comes from aren't hanging in the corner of the dining hall as they partake...

For a while, she doesn't say anything. Instead, she just watches us over the rim of her goblet. I can't help feeling like that mouse in *The Lion King*—when Scar plays with it, letting it run through his claw, and everyone watching knows its life is completely in his hands.

But then she blinks, and she looks like a little old grandma again. Especially when she smiles and says, "Okay, dearies. Tell me everything."

27

Lies that Bind

"**G**race is my mate," Hudson blurts out, even as I'm racking my brain, trying to decide where to start.

"Is she now?" The Bloodletter doesn't seem particularly surprised by the statement, which alarms me—at least until she asks, "What makes you think that?" and I realize she doesn't believe him.

He lifts a brow. "The mating bond that's currently connecting us is a pretty good indicator."

Surprise flashes in her eyes, but it's gone as quickly as it came. As she continues to study us with an impassive gaze, I can't help wondering what it is that surprises her—the fact that Hudson and I are now mates? Or that he refuses to bow and scrape to her and instead meets her as an equal?

I'm pretty sure there aren't many people who do that—and by *not many*, I mean none. Even Jaxon, who she raised, treats her with deference and maybe even a little bit of fear. But Hudson doesn't. I don't know if that means he's reckless or if he really is just as powerful as she is.

"How exactly does that work?" the Bloodletter asks as she sips her blood. "Considering I know for a fact that there's a bond between Grace and Jaxon."

"A bond you gave him a spell to sever," Hudson tells her.

"Did I?" She takes a sip from her goblet. "I can't seem to recall—"

"At your age, I'm sure there's a lot you don't recall," Hudson comments. "But try to remember this, if you wouldn't—"

"Be careful how you speak to me," she snaps, as quick and biting as a cobra. But then she seems to catch herself and settles back with a demure smile. Even as she continues: "Or those two unfortunate hikers won't be the only ones I drain dry today."

Hudson yawns. He actually yawns, and now I'm thinking he's not so much brave as really, *really* reckless.

As for the Bloodletter, I'm pretty sure she's trying to decide whether to drain him or flambé him into a nice Hudson Jubilee.

"So if I actually gave him the spell like you say I did—"

"Oh, you gave it to him," Hudson tells her.

"If. I. Did," she repeats in a voice like steel, "shouldn't you just say *thank you*?" she asks with narrowed eyes. "Considering how you benefited from it?"

"You think I should thank you?" Hudson hisses. "For screwing up our lives this badly? For destroying my brother—"

"If he chose to use the spell, I can't imagine why he would be destroyed."

"He didn't use the spell," I tell her, trying to ignore the way Hudson's words make me feel. I know everything is screwed up, I know he doesn't want to be mated to me any more than I want to be mated to him, but hearing him say it like that—like being my mate is the worst thing to ever happen to him—hurts in a way I didn't expect it to.

"Someone else did," Hudson says. "But that's not really the point here, is it? What I want to know is how you knew the spell to break the bond in the first place."

"Why does it matter? Unless..." She studies us, cold calculation laid bare in her eyes. "Unless you're here because you want me to break your bond, too."

"That *is* what we want," I tell her before Hudson can say anything—partly because I don't want him to piss her off and screw this up and partly because I don't want to hear him talk any more about how awful our bond is. "And we also want to find a way to fix Jaxon's and my bond."

"Really?" The Bloodletter turns mocking eyes on Hudson. "Is that really what you want? To tie up Grace and Jaxon's mating bond in a nice little bow?"

Now I'm the one looking between them, as a million different undercurrents sweep through the room. I feel like a child because I can't figure out either of them.

"I want Grace and my brother to be happy," he tells her through gritted teeth.

"And you think repairing their bond will do that?" She takes another sip of blood, even as she contemplates him over the rim of her goblet.

"They were happy before," Hudson grinds out.

"They were," she agrees. "But if they really love each other, does it matter if there's a mating bond or not?"

"It does if the mating bond in question has her mated to me."

"I'm sorry," I interrupt in a voice that is anything but nice. "But can I be a part of this conversation? You know, considering it is literally about the rest of *my* life."

"Of course, Grace." The Bloodletter is all magnanimous sweetness as she looks at me. "What is it that you want, dear?"

It takes every ounce of self-control I have not to trip over my tongue in the face of that laser-eyed scrutiny. Be careful what you wish for and all that… But in the end, I manage to pull it together and say, "I want to be mated to Jaxon again." I make sure not to look at Hudson as I say it.

The Bloodletter studies me for a while, as if trying to assess the truth of my statement. In the end, though, she just gives me a sad smile as she shakes her head. "Well then, I'm sorry to say that your trip was for nothing. I can't break your and Hudson's bond, and I definitely, definitely can't fix the one between you and Jaxon."

"Why not?" I plead. "You did it once—"

"Because, Grace dear, once broken, some things can never unbreak." She gives a sympathetic little smile. "I only knew how to break yours with Jaxon because I'm the one who created it."

28

Today's Forecast:
A Deep Freeze

My heart is thundering in my chest. "What do you mean you *created* it?"

"*That*'s what was wrong with it," Hudson interrupts, a dawning horror invading his eyes. "I knew it didn't look right, green twisted with black. I just…" He shakes his head as if to clear it. "I never imagined that it was off because it should never have existed in the first place."

The Bloodletter shrugs. "Should or should not aren't concepts people with power tend to think about much."

"Yeah, well, they need to," I tell her as all the pain and fear and sadness of the last few weeks well up inside me until it feels like I'm about to be ripped to shreds.

"Come now, Grace." This time when she smiles, I can see the tips of her razor-sharp fangs. "You have quite a bit of power yourself. As does your…" She waves a dismissive hand. "Mate. Are you telling me you don't ever use it to benefit the people you care about?"

"How exactly do you think you bloody benefited anyone in this situation?" Hudson demands. "All you did was fuck everything up." His accent is so heavy that "fuck" comes out sounding like an entirely different word.

"I wasn't talking to you," she snaps in a voice more frigid than the ice all around us.

"Yeah, well, I was definitely talking to *you*. What kind of monster plays God with four people's lives—"

"Four?" I interrupt, confused.

He's so busy glaring at the Bloodletter that he doesn't even glance my way, still speaking directly to the Bloodletter. "Did it ever occur to you that Jaxon has a real mate out there somewhere? One he would never even look for because he was already mated to Grace?"

His words sink like stones into the air around us, and I forget how to breathe. How to think. How to be. Oh my God. This can't be happening. Oh my God.

For the first time, the Bloodletter looks furious. Pure, unadulterated rage pours out of her as she points a finger at Hudson. "Are you worried about Jaxon's imaginary mate?" she asks. "Or are you worried about yourself?"

"That's the problem with people who abuse their power," he snarls. "They don't like to think about what they've done. And they can't stand it when someone calls them on it."

"Don't you think you're being a little sanctimonious, considering you're Cyrus Vega's son?" she accuses, and now her fangs are completely bared.

As are Hudson's.

"It's because I am his son that I recognize abuse of power when I see it," he answers, and the way he raises his hands makes me wonder if he plans on strangling her.

The Bloodletter sighs and waves a dismissive hand at him again. But this time, Hudson freezes. Like full-on freezes, snarl on his face, eyes narrowed, hands still raised.

"What did you do?" I demand, the accusation coming out before I can think better of it. "What did you do to him?"

"He's fine," she assures me. "But he wouldn't be if he kept talking, so really, I did him a favor."

I don't even know what I'm supposed to say to that, so I just carefully ask, "Will you eventually unfreeze him?"

"Of course." She makes a face. "Believe me when I say that the last thing I want cluttering up my home is a statue of Hudson Vega."

"He's not a statue," I tell her. "He's—"

"I know exactly what he is. And I'm bored with it." She gestures to the chair next to hers. "You, however, I'd like to talk to for a while. So why don't you come sit by me?"

I'd rather sit next to hungry bears than sit next to her now—or ever—but it's not like I have much choice. Besides, sitting where I am doesn't make me any safer if she could freeze Hudson with nothing but a wave of her hand.

I don't want to risk setting her off and getting both of us frozen, so I settle gingerly into the rocking chair next to hers.

"What do you think about all this, Grace?" she asks as soon as I'm seated.

"I don't know what I think." I keep looking at Hudson, worrying about him, willing him to unfreeze. Is this what Jaxon and Macy and Uncle Finn felt when I was frozen in stone all those months? This helplessness and all-consuming fear? He's only been frozen about three and a half minutes, and I'm ready to crawl out of my skin. I can't imagine how they handled three and a half months.

"I remember seeing Jaxon's and my mating bond." I think back to that night in the laundry room, to the green-and-black string that looked so different from the others. "I didn't realize at the time that something was wrong with it, but looking back, I can tell that it wasn't like any other string I have. Especially now that I've seen the bond between Hudson and me."

"Seriously, Grace?" She sighs at the mention of Hudson's and my bond. "You couldn't have made a better choice?"

"I don't think I've had much choice in any of this," I tell her. "It seems like all the choices have been made for me."

"How do you feel about that?"

"Like I want to rip someone's head off." Again, the words come out before I think to censor them, so I end up backtracking. "Of course, not yours. I just—"

"Don't ever soften what you feel, Grace. Own it," she tells me. "Use it."

"Like you did?" I ask.

The Bloodletter doesn't answer right away. Instead, she studies me for what feels like forever before sighing. "I want to tell you a story."

"Okay," I say, like I have a choice.

"It starts before you were born," she tells me. "Long before you were born, actually, but for now we'll concentrate on the more recent past."

She takes a drawn-out sip from her goblet, then sets it on the coffee table in front of us. "Nineteen years ago, a coven of witches came to me in the middle of the worst snowstorm Alaska had seen for nearly fifty years. They were terrified, desperate. Worried for the fate of their coven and the world, both human and paranormal."

She's staring into the fire now, the look on her face more pained than I have ever seen it.

"What did they want?" I ask when she doesn't immediately offer any more information.

"They wanted help finding a way to bring gargoyles back. It had been more than a thousand years since one was born, nearly that long since one had roamed the earth, and without the balance gargoyles bring to us, the paranormal world was spinning rapidly out of control. It had gotten so bad that it was affecting the human world, and that was endangering us all. Or so they argued."

"But there was another gargoyle alive," I tell her. "The Unkillable Beast—"

"You figured that out, did you?" She smiles. "Smart girl."

"I can hear him in my head. When I'm in danger, he talks to me."

"He talks to you?" And just that quickly, she's focused back on me, her eyes glowing that eerie green again. "What does he say?"

"He warns me. Of course, he doesn't talk to me all the time—only when I'm in danger. He tells me not to do something or not to trust someone."

"Does he, now?" She crooks a brow. "You're a very lucky girl, Grace."

"I know," I tell her, even though I don't feel very lucky—haven't felt lucky in a long, long time.

"Several witches and warlocks came to me in that coven—including your father. I talked to them all, *and* I talked to your mother, who wasn't a witch but whom I could sense carried magic within her. And I knew, instantly, that you would be of the utmost importance to us later."

"Because I'm a gargoyle?" I ask through my suddenly too-tight throat. I don't know if it's because she's talking about my parents or if it's because she's finally telling me about myself—even though it feels a little like I'm being sold a bill of goods. Like I'm at one of those fake fortune-tellers who just give people what they want to hear.

She clicks her tongue at the interruption but continues anyway. "Because of who you really are."

29

Less Grandmother and More Grand Master

I wait for her to say more, and when she doesn't, I whisper, "I don't know what that means."

Her smile is placid. "Don't worry—you will."

"But what does this have to do with Jaxon? With my bond?"

"I agreed to help the witches, but I asked a favor in return." She sighs heavily.

A chill creeps through me. "I don't understand. What kind of favor?"

"That this child I promised them would come, this gargoyle who they so desperately wanted and who would have so much power in her own right, that she would be mated to my Jaxon…if she wanted."

"Before I found my real mate, you mean." I barely get the words out as horror sweeps through me and my gaze darts to Hudson.

"No, you would be destined to mate with Jaxon—until you touched and refused him." She smiles now. "But you didn't refuse the bond, did you?"

Her words swim in my head, looking for the nearest shore. "Does that mean Jaxon wouldn't mate with anyone else, either, until we met?"

Her eyebrows shoot up. "Well, of course, dear. How else could I insure you at least had a chance to become my Jaxon's mate if he was already mated before you met?"

Oh my God. I feel sick. If I was right and the guy Flint had been talking about, the one he'd been in love with his whole life, was Jaxon… That means, all this time, Flint's heart was breaking, thinking Jaxon wouldn't choose him—when all this time, he *couldn't*. Because of me.

I wrap my arms around my waist, the walls of the room closing in as I take a shallow breath. "So it was *all* fake? Nothing I felt for Jaxon was real?"

"Did it feel fake?" she asks and leans over to pat my hand.

I think of his eyes, of his smile. Of the way he touched me. And some of the pressure building in my chest starts to ease. "No. No, it didn't feel fake at all."

"Because it wasn't fake," she tells me with a shrug. "You know the mating bond rules—"

"You broke all the rules!"

"No." She holds up an emphatic finger. "I bent a few rules, but I didn't break any. I created a mating bond for you, but if you weren't open to it—if Jaxon wasn't open to it—you two never would have mated and would have been free to find your true mates. It's as simple as that."

It doesn't feel simple. None of this feels simple. Even before a new and horrible thought pierces the whirling kaleidoscope of my thoughts.

"What if we'd never met? Would Jaxon—would he have spent the rest of his immortal life alone?"

"That would never have happened. I used an ancient magic that calls like to like. It was inexorably drawing you to Katmere, to Jaxon, from the day you were born." Something close to kindness enters her green eyes.

I drop my head into my hands and fight the tears burning against the backs of my eyes. But I'm not going to do this. I'm not going to cry, not here and definitely not now. I won't give her that satisfaction.

"Grace." Her hand hovers over my arm like she wants to touch me again, and her eyes are softer than I've ever seen them.

Neither makes me feel better.

I push out of the chair and walk toward Hudson with some vague idea of convincing her to unfreeze him now that she seems to have mellowed out a little bit. But before I can, the one question I've had from the start—the one question that's been burning inside me from the moment she admitted she manufactured the bond—bursts out of me.

"I just don't understand why you did it. Not to me, because I get that. I was just a commodity to them, a bargaining chip to you. But what about Jaxon? You raised him. You trained him. He loves you. So why would you do something like this, something that had the potential to hurt him this much?"

"Do you remember what Jaxon was like when you met him?" the Bloodletter asks.

An image of his frozen black eyes flashes through my mind. "What does that have to do with anything?"

"He'd closed himself off a long time before you were born. Maybe I was too harsh in raising him or maybe it was just the product of having those two people as biological parents. I don't know. I thought giving him a mate might undo some of that, or at least make up for it.

"And it wasn't just for him, you know. You were supposed to be the last gargoyle in existence, that poor creature in the cave notwithstanding—" She stops for a second to clear her throat and to finish off her drink. "I knew that you would need his protection. That you would need Katmere and everything that Finn and he could give you."

Her eyes are steady on mine when she adds, "I did it for both of you, Grace. Because you needed each other."

There's a part of me that hears the truth in her words. That flashes back to that first day at Katmere, when I was so lost and hurting. When I realized Jaxon was the same.

She said I needed the protection of Katmere—does that mean that the Bloodletter told Lia about me, knowing that she would kill my parents, and I would end up at Katmere?

It's a terrible suspicion, one that makes my blood boil and my skin crawl, but then I realize she would have no need to do this. If the magic of our bond truly would have eventually drawn us together.

I turn away and see Hudson, his perfect face frozen in time. And wonder, just for a moment, if we were supposed to be mates all along. If, in a different world where millennia-old vampires didn't do whatever they wanted, would we have been meant for éach other after all?

I rub my chest as I swear I can feel a new crack slicing through my already bruised and abused heart.

I reach for Hudson, wanting the comfort—the solace—that comes from the feel of his skin against mine, even if it's just for a second. But the moment my fingers brush his, something miraculous happens.

His fingers grab on to mine and squeeze, even as he blinks away whatever spell has been holding him frozen and immobile for the last fifteen minutes.

30

Who Needs Plausible as Long as You've Got Deniability?

I gape at Hudson for a second—totally shocked that he's somehow come out of whatever trance the Bloodletter put him in. I glance behind me to see if she decided to let him go, but she looks as surprised as I am.

She covers it quickly, and that's when I start moving, putting myself between Hudson and her. I expect him to come out of whatever this was gunning for her, and the only chance I have of stopping him is putting myself directly in his path. Because I don't know much about anything, but I do know that Hudson will never, ever risk hurting me. Which means maybe, just maybe, I'll have a chance to save this mess before it goes completely off the rails.

Except Hudson isn't anywhere near as livid as I expect him to be. He's annoyed, sure, but he was annoyed right before she froze him, and I figured the whole forced-statue thing would ratchet that up about two hundred notches. Instead, he's just looking at us like he's expecting an answer to a question.

I look back at the Bloodletter again, and this time she gives me her most grandmotherly smile. "He can't remember, dear."

"Remember what?" Hudson asks as he looks back and forth between us.

I should tell him—he's got a right to know what just went on—but if I do, all hell will break loose. So I'm definitely operating on a *don't*-need-to-know basis.

"Nothing," I say.

I'll tell him what happened later, when we're safely away from this cave. He'll be mad at me, but he'll get over it. And I'll be relieved he didn't piss her off so much that she decided to use him as her own personal chew toy.

It's a win-win-nobody-dies situation.

And yes, I'm more than aware that my standards for win-win situations have deteriorated significantly since I got to Katmere Academy, but now isn't exactly the time to address that.

"I don't care what you have to do," Hudson tells the Bloodletter, "but you need to break Grace's and my mating bond."

She looks at him questioningly. "I thought you were just chastising me for playing God."

"And you were telling me that power demands to be abused," he shoots back. "So go ahead. Abuse it one more time and get us all out of this bloody damn clusterfuck."

For a minute, I think the Bloodletter is going to explode over being ordered around, which really, really makes me want to drag Hudson into the corner and insist that he stop pushing her. I mean, I know he wasn't privy to the conversation she and I just had, but still. He acts like he's wanting her to come after him.

Or like he really, really wants to destroy our mating bond.

That thought cascades through me like a boulder. I knew before we came here that Hudson didn't want to be mated to me, thought it was all a cosmic joke. But now that I know he was likely always meant to be my true mate, well, it feels like an even bigger kick to the gut.

"You need to learn a little respect," she tells him with a glare.

"Give me something to respect and I'll be happy to," he shoots back with a glare of his own.

Not going to lie, I almost ducked at that one. Because I'm still not convinced smiting isn't a thing.

But instead of ripping him limb from limb with her millennia-old power, the Bloodletter picks up her goblet and all but glides to the small bar made entirely of ice on the other side of the room. Once there, she very slowly, very carefully pours herself another cup of blood and takes a long sip.

When she turns around, the flames in her eyes are banked, though her mouth is still tight and her shoulders very, very stiff. "So," she murmurs, and now she's back to watching us like a dangerous cat with a very small mouse.

Which doesn't make me nervous at all.

"You really want to break your mating bond?"

I'm reconsidering, half based on what she told me and half on the survival instinct deep inside me that's screaming for us to get the hell out of here.

But Hudson is all in, saying, "That is why we came. Jaxon and Grace don't deserve this."

"What about what you deserve?" She makes the question sound like a threat.

"I know exactly what I deserve," he answers. "But thank you so much for your concern."

She gives a little shrug, makes a face that can roughly be translated to: *your inanity isn't my problem.* And says, "There is a way you can maybe, *maybe* break this bond."

"And that is?" Hudson prompts.

"The Crown."

"The what?" I ask, but Hudson must know exactly what she's talking about because his whole face has gone flat.

"It doesn't exist," he tells her.

"Sure it does." She looks down, checks out her nails. "It's just been missing for a bit."

"It doesn't exist," Hudson says again.

But I'm not so sure—the Bloodletter doesn't look like she's bluffing. At all.

"Is that what Cyrus told you?" she asks him. "More like he couldn't get his hands on it, so he doesn't want anyone else to even know it exists."

That sounds exactly like something Cyrus would do, and I can tell Hudson must think so, too, because he stops arguing. He's not ready to ask her any questions about it, but he isn't fighting anymore, either. Which is as close to surrender as he gets.

"What does the Crown do?" I ask, still very confused about the whole thing.

"The Crown is supposed to give whoever wears it infinite power," Hudson says flatly.

"That's it?" I ask. "Just more power?"

"There's no *just* about it," the Bloodletter tells me. "The power is unparalleled. Some even say that it grants its wearer the ability to rule the Seven Circles."

"Wait. Circles? As in the council we're supposed to be on now?" I gesture to Hudson.

"The council *you're* supposed to be on," he tells me.

"Yeah, with *my mate*."

He looks away. And damn, just damn. Somehow this situation keeps getting worse, and everything I say is the wrong thing.

"There are seven of them?" I ask.

"Of course, child. You didn't think there were only five paranormal creatures in the world, did you? You just happen to belong to this Circle."

I have no idea what I'm supposed to say to that. She's barely gotten started, and I already feel like that emoji with its mind blowing up. "Who's in the other Circles?"

"Does it matter?" Hudson snarks.

The Bloodletter ignores him. "Fairies, mermaids, elves, succubi, just to name a few."

"Succubi," I repeat. "Elves. Just walking around the world, minding their own business."

"Elves mind everyone's business," Hudson says. "They're a nosy lot."

Not what I was expecting him to say, but okay. "And this Crown rules them all?"

"The Crown brings balance to the universe. For a long time, paranormals held too much power, so the Crown was created to balance that out. But where there is that kind of power, there is always avarice. The desire to wield power over everything and everyone."

She takes a slow drink of blood. "A thousand years ago, the person who tried to claim the Crown was Cyrus."

"Of course it was," Hudson mutters.

"It disappeared, along with the person who was wearing it, and Cyrus has been searching for it ever since. Find the Crown and maybe, just maybe, you'll find a way to break your mating bond and *un*break your bond with Jaxon."

31

I've Got to See
a Man About
a Beast

"Let me get this straight," I tell her. "It's been missing for a thousand years, with people all over the world—including the vampire king himself—hunting for it, and you think Hudson and I can find it?"

"I never said I thought you could find it. I said it's possibly the only way to break the bond." She walks to her chair and settles back into it. "Sorry, these old bones of mine get tired if I stand too long."

I don't believe that for a second, and a quick glance at Hudson tells me he doesn't, either. But neither of us calls her on it, not when she's in the middle of this story.

"But if you were to decide that you wanted to look for it, I would start with the one person who might know where it is. And since you've already met him, you could actually have a chance to get him to talk to you."

"Who?" I ask, even as I rack my brain trying to figure out who she could be talking about. Even Hudson is leaning in, as invested in her answer as I am.

"You mean you don't know?" She crooks a brow. "The Unkillable Beast, of course. Some say it's why he was imprisoned to begin with...so no one would know where he hid the Crown."

"The Unkillable Beast?" I repeat, heart beating faster. "I already told you, he speaks to me. You think I could just ask him, and he would give me the answer?"

"I think he's too far gone to impart anything but the very basic things needed for survival. But you tell me. What do you think?"

I think back to his cave, to how he only talks to me in very short sentences. How he tried to give me his heart. "I don't think he remembers."

"Then you've only got one choice. You need to turn him human—he's been in his gargoyle form so long, it's likely driven him mad."

"Wait a minute, is that possible?" I ask, because it feels like something someone should have told me. Like, *stay a gargoyle too long and that could happen to you, too.* Yeah, it definitely feels like something I should know.

"Centuries, Grace." Hudson chimes in for the first time in a while. "You'd have to stay in your gargoyle form for centuries for it to happen to you."

"How do you know?" I ask.

"Because I've been researching gargoyles for weeks." He rolls his eyes at me. "Do you think I'd let you figure it out all by yourself if there's something out there that might hurt you?"

Of course not. Not Hudson, who is as crotchety as they come but who also would never, ever let someone he cares about face something awful alone.

I smile at him, and for a second I think he's going to smile in return. But he looks back to the Bloodletter at the last minute and demands, "So how exactly do we turn him human?"

Her green eyes sharpen on Hudson before she replies, "You free him. His chains keep him in his gargoyle form. Break those, and he'll become human again."

"We already tried to break them," I tell her. "We couldn't. Vampire, dragon, witch, gargoyle—" I gesture to myself. "None of us could do it."

"That's because they're enchanted."

"Enchanted?" Hudson throws his hands up in the air. "Are you fucking with us now? Sending us on some wild goose chase to get us out of your hair?"

"Hudson—" I lay a calming hand on his shoulder, but he shrugs it off.

"No! No way, Grace. She has all these bloody rules that just get more outlandish every second of the day. *You can't break the bond. Oh, yes you can, but you need the Crown. Oh, no one knows where the Crown is. Except, wait a minute, someone does. But you can't actually find out from him...* Come on. It's a bunch of shite and she knows it."

"Maybe it is," I whisper to him. "But maybe it isn't. Maybe we should try."

"Is it really that important to you?" he asks, and the anger is gone from his eyes—along with every other emotion.

I don't know how to answer that question, so I sidestep it for now. "We don't have to make a decision this minute. We can just hear what she has to say and then decide later."

He looks like he wants to argue some more, but in the end, he just sighs and waves a hand in a *whatever* gesture.

"How do we break the enchanted chains?" I ask, even though I'm feeling as overwhelmed as Hudson obviously is. Maybe even more.

The Bloodletter looks back and forth between us, like she's debating whether or not she's even going to tell us. But in the end, she heaves a little sigh and says, "All I know is that you need to find the Blacksmith, who made the chains. Actually," she adds with a small smile at Hudson, "he's the same Blacksmith who made that cuff you're wearing. Made a whole set of enchanted cuffs that were later gifted to Katmere. If you want to break the Unkillable Beast's chains, then you need to find him."

"And how exactly do we find the Blacksmith?" Hudson demands.

"Honestly?" She shakes her head. "I have absolutely no idea."

32

Hello, Is it Brie
You're Looking For?

We don't get much more out of the Bloodletter—either because she has nothing else to tell us or because she's holding out on us for God only knows what purpose. With her, you never can tell.

She offers to let us spend the night because it'll be super late before we get back to Katmere, but I'd rather face all the nocturnal wildlife Alaska has to offer than spend one more minute in her ice cave.

Thankfully, the trip back is uneventful. The storm that had been threatening seemed to head in the opposite direction instead. And the only wildlife we run into are a few wolves, but a snarl from Hudson sends them on their way pretty quickly. Besides, I can fly and they can't, and that makes everything better in my book.

At one point, we take a brief break, and I tell Hudson the Bloodletter froze him (which he was not a fan of, no surprise) and what the Bloodletter shared with me, about the coven and the mating bond and how Jaxon and I were drawn to each other. Hudson is silent through all of it, just gazing into the dark night as we quietly walk through the forest—which is better than I expected him to take it.

At least until the end, when he snarls, "Fucking bloodsucker," and that says it all. Especially since I know it's about a lot more than her being a vampire.

We take off again after that and head straight back.

I'm exhausted and starving by the time we make it to school and want nothing more than a hot shower, some food, and my bed. But at the same time, my mind is still racing with a million different thoughts. It's Saturday night, so I know Macy will be out with the witches, and I don't want to be alone. Not when I can't stop thinking about Jaxon and Hudson and Cyrus and the Unkillable Beast.

I think about the beast a lot as Hudson walks me down the hall to my room. I promised him I'd come back and free him and I want to—I need to. I just don't know if this Blacksmith guy, whoever he is, will actually know how to do it. Or if he'll even want to. If the Bloodletter is right, then he's the one who made the shackles to begin with, so why on earth would he want to help remove them?

And how evil does he have to be to have done such a thing in the first place?

I ask Hudson as much, but he just shakes his head. "I'll never figure out why people make the choices they make," he answers. "How they can be so indifferent to right and wrong, good and evil. Or how they can just go along with the evil when it benefits them, or because it's too hard to fight it."

I think of his father, of the things that Cyrus has done and all the people who still follow him. Then I think of everything Hudson did trying to stop his father—and the price he had to pay.

"There's no easy answer, is there?" I say with a sigh.

"I'm not sure there's an answer at all," he tells me.

We're standing awkwardly outside my door now, and I don't know what to do. I can tell Hudson doesn't, either, because his hands are in his pockets and his usually direct gaze is focused anywhere, everywhere, but on mine.

At least until my stomach growls. Loudly.

"Hungry?" he asks with a sudden grin.

"Hey, flying burns a lot of calories!" I make a face at him.

He nods toward my room. "Do you have something to eat in there?"

"Yeah, I'll grab a granola bar—"

"You've already had three granola bars today." He leans a shoulder against the wall next to my door. "Don't you think it's time to pump some actual nutrition into your body?"

"Yeah, well, the dining hall is closed, so what do you suggest?" I grimace. "And please don't say a thermos of blood."

At first, I don't think he's going to answer, but then he says, "I suggest that you go take a shower. You need it."

"Are you saying I smell?" I gasp in mock outrage.

"I'm saying you're shivering. A shower will warm you up." Then he grabs on to my hat and pulls it down hard and fast over my eyes.

"Hey!" It only takes a second for me to pull my hat back above my eyes, but by the time I do, he's almost at the other end of the hallway.

"Hudson—" I call but then stop myself. Because I have no idea what I want to say to him.

He must understand, because he gives me a grin and a little two-finger wave before disappearing down the stairs as I head into my room.

Sure enough, Macy isn't around, though she has left two chocolate chip cookies on a plate by my bed. I think about just grabbing them and diving under my covers, but Hudson is right. I'm shivering. Plus my shoulders are aching—probably from flying hundreds upon hundreds of miles today in thirty-degree weather.

Using their wings for long periods of time never seems to bother Flint or Eden—the only two dragons I know well enough to ask—but it always makes me sore. Likely because my upper back muscles were never meant to support wings, let along my entire weight, for as long as they do these days.

But surely that will change, right? Just like any other muscle—the more I use them, the more acclimated to it they'll become.

I take a quick shower, then grab a pair of pajamas and get dressed. Cookies, then an episode of *Buffy the Vampire Slayer*—what can I say, playing peacemaker to Hudson and the Bloodletter for most of the day has put me in the mood—and then bed.

I *should* do some schoolwork. Heck, I *should* do anything but lay on my bed and think about how getting me to Katmere, to Jaxon, might have gotten my parents killed. Were we nothing more than pawns on a chessboard for the Bloodletter? Or was there someone else playing games with them? I really need to figure this out, need to know who my enemies are, but I'm just too tired tonight.

Besides, if I were going to wrestle with anything, it would be how hard my heart was hammering when I learned Jaxon was never meant to be my mate—Hudson was. I've tried to keep Hudson firmly in a box marked "friend" because it didn't seem fair to Jaxon to even consider him any other way. But now, it doesn't seem fair to Hudson to think of Jaxon as anything more than an ex-boyfriend. Well, until I remind myself how badly Hudson doesn't want to be mated to me in the first place. I swallow. Hard.

And this is why I prefer to keep my shit in a drawer, thank you very much. My heart is hammering in my chest, my stomach is one twist away from heaving, and it takes me a full five minutes to calm my breathing again.

Eventually, I make it into bed, but I've barely pulled the covers up with my laptop before there's a knock on my door. I'm tempted to ignore it, but before I can decide, Hudson calls, "Come on, Grace. I know you're in there."

"What's wrong—" I start as I pull open the door seconds later.

I break off when I realize he's carrying a cafeteria tray loaded with a grilled cheese, some sliced fruit, and a Dr Pepper. "Where did you get all this?" I ask as I step back to let him in.

He gives me a look like he can't believe I just asked that. "I made it. Obviously." He puts the tray down on my bed, then settles himself at the end of it...like he belongs there.

Then again, when he was in my head, that and the spot near the window were his two favorite places from which to harangue me, so he probably feels like he does.

"*You* know how to make a grilled cheese?" I ask as I sit down on the other side of the tray. "How? Why?"

"What?" He looks offended. "You think because I'm a vampire, I don't know how to make a sandwich?"

"Well...it does seem part of a skill set you have no need for."

For long seconds, he doesn't say anything, just kind of watches me out of eyes that are unfathomable. But eventually he answers, "I do have a half-human mate, you know. And she needs to eat human food. Besides," he continues with a shrug, "YouTube is a thing."

An awkward silence descends between us, and I honestly don't know what to say to him. There's so much to unpack there that I don't have a clue where I'm supposed to start—and I'm too exhausted to try.

So, in what I'm coming to realize is typical bury-my-head fashion, I focus on the least-triggering comment. "You YouTubed how to make a grilled cheese sandwich?"

He lifts a brow. "Do you have a problem with that?"

"No. I just..." I trail off, not sure what I want to say.

"Just?" he prompts.

"Thank you." It's not quite what I mean—at least not completely—but for now, it will do. "I appreciate it."

"You're welcome." He leans toward me and for one bizarre second, I think he's going to kiss me. Every alarm bell I've got goes off inside me, and I tense up completely—though I'm not sure if it's from fear or desire.

I start to say something else, then kind of strangle—whether on the words or the breath that's suddenly caught in my throat, I don't know—as Hudson's shoulder brushes against my arm.

Oh. My. God. He's really going to—

But then he sinks back down to his spot on the bed...my laptop now in his hands. "Want to watch something?"

I am beyond ridiculous.

He wasn't trying to kiss me. He was reaching for the computer. Except... except the way he's looking at me tells me there was more to it than that. As does the fast and hard beating of my heart.

33

"Sure." I don't think I could sleep now anyway. Plus, I don't know, it just feels like maybe Hudson doesn't want to be alone, either.

"Any suggestions?" he asks, brows raised like he expected me to say something more than a quick affirmative.

I shrug. "I was about to turn on *Buffy*."

"*Buffy*?" He sounds clueless.

"The vampire slayer?" I'm shocked. I know it's an old show, but he's way older. How could he not have heard of it?

"Charming," he tells me with a roll of his eyes. "Mind if I veto that and pick something else?"

I wave a magnanimous hand at the screen. "Pick away."

He scans through the different streaming services we've got, then settles on Disney Plus—which is *not* what I was expecting.

"Let me guess," I tease. "*Monsters, Inc.*?"

He glances at me out of the corner of his eye. "Actually, I'm more of a *Beauty and the Beast* kind of guy."

I try to think of something flippant to say—or anything to say, for that matter—but before I can, Hudson hits Play. But instead of the old Disney fairy tale, Star Wars writing starts scrolling up the screen.

"*The Empire Strikes Back*?" I ask, surprised.

He shrugs. "It's a classic for a reason." Then he nods at the tray I haven't yet touched. "Eat. You need it."

As if to underscore his words, my stomach growls again. So I do as he suggests and take a bite of the grilled cheese. Then ask, "Which YouTube video did you watch anyway? One from Gordon Ramsay or something?"

"We Brits need to stick together." He eyes me warily. "Why? Is it not good?"

"It's amazing." I take another bite and nearly moan in pure joy. "This might be the best thing I've eaten since..." I break off as I realize what I was about to say. *Since my mother died.*

Hudson must get it, though, because he doesn't push me. Instead, he settles back against the wall and nods toward the laptop. "This is one of my favorite parts."

"The snow?" I ask, because it's been a really, really long time since I've seen this movie.

He gives me a dry look. "Yes, because snow is such a rare commodity in my life that I need to just bask in its glory on-screen."

"Wow." I make a face at him. "Who peed in your cup of blood?"

He just kind of stares at me for a while, then says, "I don't even know where to start figuring out what that means. And I'm pretty sure I don't want to know anyway."

"It's just a funny saying. About peeing in someone's cornflakes, but you don't eat cornflakes, so..." I sigh. "I'm just making it worse, aren't I?"

"Maybe a little bit, yeah." He shakes his head. "People are strange."

"Umm, excuse me, but so are vampires."

He gives me a mock-offended look. "Vampires are perfectly normal, thank you very much."

"Yeah, right. We did just come back from visiting a woman who had actual human beings draining into a *bucket*. And you're going to hassle *me* about some bizarre phrasing?"

"The draining thing is weird, right?" He shudders. "I much prefer to drink from—" He freezes, like he's suddenly realized what he's saying and who he's saying it to. Then he becomes very, very, *very* interested in what is happening on-screen.

But no way am I letting him off that easily, especially since it's really hard to even get a vampire to talk about what they eat...at least, it's always been for me. "So you like feeding from the...host?"

He looks at me like he's debating how much he wants to say, but in the end he shrugs and says, "You like it when your food's warm, right?"

"Oh, right. Of course." I don't even realize that I'm gently stroking the sensitive skin of my throat until I notice Hudson is staring at my fingers with a look in his eyes that has nothing to do with food and everything to do with a lot of things neither one of us is talking about. At all.

His look has me fidgeting, has me wondering, for just a second, what it would feel like to have his fangs scrape against my skin. Which basically gets me all flustered again and has me looking anywhere but at him as I try to banish the thought from my mind.

We watch the next few minutes of the movie in silence, but there's a tension in the air now that won't go away, and it's making me feel all kinds of shaken. Making me think of all kinds of things—including that Hudson and I are mates.

But also, that I used to be mated to Jaxon.

Just the thought has me squirming uncomfortably.

"What's wrong?" Hudson asks.

Since I'm in no way emotionally prepared to tell him that I just spent entirely too long thinking about his fangs on my skin, I admit to the other thing I haven't been able to get out of my mind, no matter how hard I try not to think about it.

"I can't believe my parents made a deal with the Bloodletter. Like, what did they say? 'Sure, absolutely, mate my unborn child to a vampire. As long as I get what I want, I'm in. No big deal.'" I give a little what-the-hell shrug. "How could that not have been a deal breaker? And then they didn't even bother to tell me about it. They just…"

I drift off, because the only way to finish that statement is with a comment about how they died before they ever told me…that is, if they were ever going to tell me.

"Are you angry?" Hudson asks softly.

"I don't know. I'm—" I sigh, then run a hand through my still-damp curls because it's all I can do at this point. "I'm just tired. Really, really tired. I mean, there's no point in being angry with them. They're dead, and nothing I feel now is going to change that fact, so…" I blow out a long breath. "I just really want to know what they were thinking. Why did they think it was okay to take away my choice like that?"

"That's the thing, though, right? They didn't actually take your choice." He grabs the laptop and pauses the movie before turning back to face me. "Or, at least, I'm pretty sure that's not how they thought about it."

"They chose my mate—"

"Yeah, but it wouldn't have worked if you weren't open to it. They could have done all the magic in the world, but if you didn't want Jaxon, it wouldn't have mattered. You chose him, and that's why he became your mate. They were part of this world. They know how it works. Worst-case scenario—or best case, depending on your point of view—you meet Jaxon, fall for him, and then realize he's your mate when you choose him. If you hadn't chosen him, neither of you would ever have known. They probably thought it was a win-win situation."

I think about what he said, turning his words over and around in my head until I decide he might be right. And if he isn't, I'm just going to pretend that he is because I really can't handle being angry with my parents now, not on top of everything else I'm feeling and going through at the moment. But as I play his words back in my head one more time, I can't help realizing something else. "Is that what happened with us?" I ask before I can think better of it. "Did you choose me?"

The second the words are out of my mouth, I kind of want to crawl under my bed. Instead, I stare straight ahead at the frozen screen as I wait, breath held, for his response—and to find out just how embarrassed I should be for asking him that question.

To make matters even worse, Hudson doesn't answer right away. He's not staring at the laptop, though. He's staring at me—I can feel the weight of his gaze even though I refuse to so much as glance at him.

The silence goes from unnoticeable to awkward to uncomfortable as fuck, and still he doesn't answer me. Still he continues to watch me. It's awful, terrible, and when I can't take it anymore, I turn my head and prepare to tell him to forget it.

Instead, the moment our eyes meet, he smiles just a little and says, "How could I not want to be mated to my best friend? I've known you were incredible from the first day we met."

Oh my God. The relief that rushes through me is so huge that it almost makes me light-headed. Which, to some degree, seems totally ridiculous. But I don't care because I'm not humiliated. And also because...

Hudson chose me on that field. He chose me in that clearing. And that matters.

Maybe he doesn't love me, maybe he'll never love me—maybe I'll never love him. But I'd be lying if I said we didn't have *something* between us. I've felt it a bunch of times—from that one weird moment when he was still in my head, when I swore I felt his fangs scraping along my neck, to just a few minutes ago, when he reached for the computer. He brought me flowers. He helped me figure out how to channel my magic. He stood up for me with the Bloodletter.

He's never once not believed in me.

Not to mention the obvious—he's seriously easy on the eyes.

Yeah, there's definitely something there. And this guy, this really great guy, has never had anyone love him before, has never had anyone choose *him*.

Don't I owe it to him—don't I owe it to us both—to at least try to make things work between us? Maybe they will, maybe they won't. But he matters to me. He matters to me a lot, and maybe I need to figure that out before I even think about doing anything else.

Maybe Jaxon was right, and I need to trust the magic.

I clear my throat, swallow, tuck a strand of hair behind my ear, fidget with the covers. Anything and everything to avoid making myself vulnerable. To avoid walking right into something else that's going to tear me to shreds.

So instead of just saying what's on my mind, I start a little more slowly, a little more carefully. "What if—" I blow out a breath and force the words from my too-tight throat. "What if we don't go after the Crown?"

Hudson's brows go way up. "You don't want the Crown?"

"I mean, I want to free the Unkillable Beast. I promised him we would, and we need to do that. But…maybe we don't need the Crown once we do it?"

For a second, it seems like Hudson has stopped breathing completely. His eyes are nearly black, his pupils blown out until I can see only a thin rim of blue around the edges. But then it's his turn to clear his throat as he asks, "Is that what you want to do?"

"I think so, yeah." I swallow. "Is it what *you* want to do?"

He grins just a little, and for the first time ever, I notice a tiny dimple in his left cheek. It makes him look more vulnerable, less armored, and I'd be lying if I said my heart didn't jump a bit in my chest at the idea that I'm seeing a side of him that no one else gets to.

Even before he says, "Oh yeah."

Then he leans forward, and it's definitely not for the laptop this time. His eyes are focused on mine, his lips open just a little as he slowly, slowly, slowly—

My heart is pounding so hard in my chest, I'm certain he can hear it. The first time Jaxon kissed me, I was dying for it. But right here, right now, the thought of Hudson's lips on mine is a lot. Maybe almost too much. "Umm, can I ask a question?"

Hudson pauses, only inches from my mouth now, his soft gaze holding mine. "Anything."

I swallow. So much trust in that one answer, it makes me want to lean forward the last bit and kiss him back. But a part of me knows that, with him, it's going to be much more than just a kiss. More than just physical. Probably more than either of us is ready for. So I take a deep breath—and pump the brakes. "Can we, umm...can we take it slow?"

He blinks. "Slow?"

"Yeah, I'm..." I blow out a breath. "I don't know what I am." More, I don't know what this is, except scary as fuck.

He smiles a little, strokes a finger down my cheek. Then whispers, "Sure, Grace."

But as he starts to move back away from me, I can't help but realize the mistake in my request. Because the only thing worse than a kiss I am not sure I'm emotionally ready to handle with Hudson is not kissing him at all. And just like that, I reach up and fist his shirt in my hands, tugging him toward me again.

Hudson growls, a predatory gleam replacing the softer look from before, and thrusts one of his hands in my curls, his other snaking around my back and yanking me against his hard chest. My hands slide up to tangle in his silky hair, and I think I'm going to die if he doesn't—

Suddenly, a knock sounds on the door—loud, hard, urgent—and we break apart so fast that Hudson has to grab me again to keep me from tumbling off the side of the bed.

34

And You Thought You Had Daddy Issues

Hudson glances at me in question, but I just shrug, so he gets up to answer the door. He hasn't taken more than a step before the door flies open, and I realize Jaxon is standing on the other side...along with the entire Order.

And none of them looks happy.

"Jaxon, what's wrong?" I ask, jumping off the bed.

Before I can reach him, he turns toward his brother. "We have a problem," he tells Hudson.

Hudson is watching him warily, and I don't blame him. The warmth I usually see in Jaxon's eyes is gone, and in its place is a distance I'm not used to. Not to mention a chill that has me looking for a sweater.

Which isn't exactly a good feeling—especially when I give them permission to enter and my little dorm room is stuffed to the gills with seven vampires. And not just any vampires. Seven very large, very disgruntled vampires, all of whom look like they're ready to draw blood at the slightest provocation.

"What's going on?" Hudson responds, even as it looks like he's bracing for a body blow—whether from the news or from Jaxon himself, I'm not sure.

"We just got back from Court," Mekhi tells him.

"And?" Hudson draws out the word.

All eyes turn to Jaxon, but he doesn't say anything else. Just walks to the window and stares out into the night.

I exchange a baffled glance with Mekhi, who looks like he wants to say something to Jaxon but then changes his mind at the last minute. Instead, he focuses on Hudson and says, "Cyrus convened a secret Circle meeting and has issued an order for your immediate arrest, presumably for the crimes committed against those students you persuaded to kill each other. And while he can't arrest you at Katmere, the second you step off campus, you're fair game for the Watch to take you."

"The Watch?" I interrupt as horror sweeps through me. We spent the whole day off campus. If someone had found us, would they have taken Hudson? Or at least tried to, as I can't imagine him going quietly? "Who are they?"

"No one," Hudson says with a dismissive wave of his hand.

"They're not no one." Jaxon's voice is colder than the Bloodletter's cave. "They're a sort of paranormal police force governed by the Circle that rose up in the absence of gargoyles to deliver justice by capturing those accused of crimes and delivering them to prison."

Well, that sounds absolutely awful. But, "Wait. Why straight to prison? There's no trial or anything?" I ask.

Again, the seven vamps exchange looks that very definitely leave me out. I'm about to call them on it when Hudson answers, "The Aethereum's not a normal prison."

Of course it isn't. When has anything in this world been anything as mundane as *normal*? I wait for him to elaborate, but when he doesn't, I turn to Jaxon and cut straight to the chase. "What makes this prison special?"

But he looks as reluctant to answer me as Hudson does, despite the coldness that continues to radiate from him.

"Mekhi?" I skewer him with a look that tells him he'd better start talking.

And while he might have laughed at such a look a few months ago, this time he jumps in right away. "The prison is cursed, Grace. There are nine levels of...hell...in an effort to prove innocence or redemption. They say the prison knows your sin and will let you go when you've been fully *rehabilitated*. But almost no one ever gets free. Like, ever."

"How—how are prisoners deemed...rehabilitated?" I can barely get the words out of my too-tight throat.

"It tortures you. In every way you can possibly imagine, befitting your sins. An eye for an eye and all that. Most people go insane if they stay long enough. It's considered a fate worse than death. Only the worst criminals are sent there."

Torture. Insanity. Fantastic. I blow out a long breath as the terrible truth slams through me. "And this is what his own father wants to do to Hudson?" The only thing surprising about that question is that I'm surprised I even had to ask. "But why wasn't I allowed a vote, if the Circle is who issued his arrest warrant? Why can Cyrus get away with this?"

"Because he's the vampire king," Luca says. "He's untouchable."

"Yeah, well, I'm the gargoyle queen, in case anyone's forgotten!" My voice snaps like a rubber band, and the already quiet room turns eerily silent.

They're all looking at me with varying degrees of surprise or respect, but I don't care what any of them thinks of me. Not when Hudson's life—and sanity—is on the line.

I shake my head and turn to hold Hudson's gaze, trying to figure out what he's thinking and feeling, but his face is stoic. "Surely as king and queen of the Gargoyle Court, we get a vote in what's going to happen, right?"

Jaxon very quietly answers, "You're not queen yet."

I turn startled eyes toward him. "What—"

"You're not technically the queen until the coronation. Which means Hudson, as your mate, isn't gargoyle king yet, either. He's fair game." His jaw works. "You both are."

"Me? I didn't do anything to Cyrus." Well, besides beat his ridiculous challenge.

"That's why the arrest warrant isn't for you," Mekhi says. "But Cyrus isn't naive, and he knows that it's usually too difficult for mates to be separated for any length of time. Which means…he's expecting you to choose to stay with Hudson and go to prison for his crimes, too."

My gaze seeks out Hudson's again, and I don't have to be a mind reader to know what he's thinking this time—no way would he ever allow me to pay for his crimes.

"So if we're imprisoned before coronation—no more gargoyle queen and king," I say. "And no shift of power on the Circle."

"Exactly," Hudson agrees.

Terror reverberates through me—partly because I don't want Hudson or me to go to prison or die (obviously) and partly because it's becoming clearer and clearer that we're not in control of anything. None of us is. Instead, Cyrus holds all the power here.

"So we need to think of something. You're safe for a few more weeks, until graduation, but after that, it's open season," Mekhi says. "There has to be a way to stop this before then."

"Of course there is," Hudson tells him with a sarcastic twist of his lips. "I'll do what I should have done on that field and end Cyrus once and for all."

"And spend the rest of your life in prison for his murder?" I demand, my hands on my hips. "You can't do that."

He doesn't answer, and that's when my fear ratchets straight up to full-blown terror. Because the look in his eyes says it all. One way or another, Hudson is going to put an end to his father's ability to threaten us...to threaten *me*...or die trying.

Just the thought of losing him makes my hands shake and my heart beat way too fast. There has to be another way. There has to be. We can't just—

And that's when it hits me.

"What about the Crown?" I whisper.

35

"The Crown?" Mekhi looks confused. "You won't get that until the coronation after graduation—"

"No, not the one I get for being gargoyle queen. The one the Bloodletter told us about today. It's been missing, but it can—" I break off when Rafael starts laughing.

"You think you can find *the* Crown?" he asks when he finally stops laughing. "Some of the most powerful creatures in existence have searched for that Crown for centuries, and you think we can just conjure it up?" He laughs again, even as he shakes his head. "It might have been true once, but at this point, it's just an old vampires' tale."

"It's not," Hudson tells him flatly. "The Crown is real."

"Because the Bloodletter told you so?" Rafael challenges him.

"Because I've spent the last two centuries listening to Cyrus obsess about it. My father is a lot of things, but he is no sucker. If it didn't exist—if he hadn't seen it with his own eyes—he wouldn't have cared so much about uncovering it."

"And you think you can find it?" Liam interjects. "As you say, the vampire king himself has been searching for it for centuries, and you think you're just going to walk right up to it?"

"I didn't say *that*," I tell him, smarting a little from being made fun of. "I know it won't be easy. But none of this is easy, and the Bloodletter pointed us in the right direction—"

"She told you where it is?" Jaxon asks, and forget cold. Now his voice is absolutely frigid, the look on his face as blank as any I've ever seen from him. "Why would she do that?"

I glance at Hudson before I can stop myself, and he subtly shakes his head at me. I understand where he's coming from—I'm not exactly up for airing all our baggage in front of the entire Order, either—but when I turn back to Jaxon, it's obvious he's seen the entire interaction. And he's not happy.

Still, he must not be all that excited about showing off our differences in front of everyone, either, because he doesn't call us on it. Instead, he glosses over his first question and moves on to, "So what did she tell you? Where's the Crown?"

"She doesn't know," I answer after a second. "But she told us who she thinks does. The Unkillable Beast."

"The Unkillable Beast?" Mekhi asks incredulously. He looks like he thinks it over for a second before shaking his head. "You don't think that sounds a little questionable? She *did* just send you there a few weeks ago to kill it. Why didn't she mention it before you went?"

"She didn't need to mention it then—" I start to explain.

"And she needed to mention it now?" He sounds so skeptical, and when he says it like that, I don't blame him. Like, yeah, last time we talked to her, none of us had any idea I'd end up mated to Hudson and want to break that bond. But still. It's a good point. Especially when I consider Hudson's mistrust of her.

It's hard to trust anyone who doles information out on a when-she-wants-to-tell-you basis.

"Why does the Bloodletter do anything?" Hudson snaps at him, and this time he's definitely showing some fang. "I don't think anyone is going to dispute that she has her own agenda, whether we know what that agenda is or not. Besides, the Crown isn't a faction artifact. It couldn't do anything for us last time, as it wouldn't have worked in the spell Grace performed. And I think we can all agree, there was never a chance we would actually kill the beast before, so she likely felt nothing risked." He shrugs.

"And you think the Crown can do something for us now? Really?" Luca sounds as skeptical as Mekhi.

"I don't know." I throw my hands up in defeat. "It was a bad idea. I panicked at the thought of Hudson getting arrested and—"

"Don't do that," Hudson growls, and for the first time since Jaxon and the Order got here, he steps forward to put himself just a little bit in front of me. "You don't need to make excuses to him," he continues with a searing look at the other vampires in the room.

I start to inch up, just in case I have to put myself between two aggressive vampires, but Jaxon moves forward at the same time. And Liam falls back immediately.

"Why the Unkillable Beast?" he asks, gaze once again moving between Hudson and me. "Why does she think he knows where the Crown is? And even if he once did, does she know what kind of shape he's in now? I know you can hear him in your head, Grace, but do you really think he's capable of having a full conversation with you, let alone able to tell you where the Crown is hidden?"

It's a good point, one I've thought about a lot since the Bloodletter warned us we'd have to find the Blacksmith first. "Once we break his shackles, he'll get better," I tell Jaxon. "She says it's the enchanted chains that have made him like this. They were never meant to be worn this long."

"We already tried to break those chains," he reminds me. "It didn't work."

"That's why we're supposed to find someone called the Blacksmith. He's the one who made the chains."

"And where is he?" Jaxon asks, both brows lifted.

"We start with the giants," Hudson replies.

"The giants?" I ask, totally surprised by his suggestion. If I've learned anything over the past few weeks, it's that Hudson always has a reason for what he says and does, but I have no idea what that reason might be here.

The Bloodletter never mentioned giants at all—and neither has he—which makes me wonder where he's coming from now. Though I have to admit the idea of getting to see where they live is both exhilarating and daunting. Like, are we talking huge beanstalks? And if so, how exactly do they hide them from passing airplanes and NASA satellites?

"They're known for their metalwork," Luca explains quietly. "And it's actually a pretty good idea to start with them." He sounds surprised.

I expect Hudson to be annoyed, but he just rolls his eyes and snarks, "Damned by faint praise."

Apparently, Jaxon isn't the only one who likes to misquote *Hamlet*...

"Is there a particular place to find great metalworking giants?" I ask, my gaze moving from vampire to vampire. But no one seems to want to answer me, so I huff. "Or should I just look for a giant beanstalk somewhere?"

Luca snickers, but Hudson looks clueless. "I'm not sure giants grow beans there but—"

"I don't mean actual beanstalks." I make a face at him. "I mean like *Jack and the Beanstalk*. You know. With the magic beans."

He still looks clueless.

"The beans grow into a huge beanstalk that goes all the way to the sky? And this boy climbs it, only to find a giant at the top?" He's still shaking his head like he has no idea what I'm talking about, and I'd be lying if I said I wasn't a little shocked. He's literally read just about everything, but he's somehow missed out on the most basic fairy tales? How is that possible?

"Never mind," I tell him with a shake of my head. "It's not important."

He looks like he wants to say more, but Jaxon says, "Let me get this straight." He looks between Hudson and me. "You want us to chase after a maybe mythical, maybe not *giant* in a *city* of giants in hopes of finding out how to break the chains on the Unkillable Beast in the hopes that *he* might know how to find this all-powerful Crown?"

Not going to lie, it sounds a little absurd when he puts it like that. "I don't know that that's what I want," I tell him after a second. "I do know that I *don't* want to be in a full-out war with your father—"

"Too late for that," Hudson interrupts with a snort.

"Then how about I don't want to watch you go to prison because your dad's an asshole? And I definitely don't want to go, either." I throw my arms up as I look around the room. "If someone has a better idea, please let me know. Because I've got a shit ton of work to do between now and graduation, and the last thing I want is to spend time chasing giants when I don't need to."

I wait for Jaxon to chime in, for Hudson or Mekhi or Luca to tell me there are a *million* better ideas. But it doesn't take very long for me to figure out—complaints or not, sarcasm or not—none of them has a better idea. At least not one that has a chance of stopping Hudson, and maybe me, from being arrested...or worse.

"Okay, then," I say after the silence has gone on way too long. "Where do we start?"

As far as I'm concerned, the sooner we find the Blacksmith, the sooner I can get Cyrus off his sons' asses—and my ass—for good.

But once again, no one answers.

"Seriously?" I ask. "You're not even going to try to help me come up with a plan?" Forget the others, I look between Hudson and Jaxon. Surely they'll help me.

"It's not that we don't want to help," Mekhi says in a soothing tone. "It's just that, to go against Cyrus, we should have more than a maybe-a-giant-can-help-us plan. What if we get to Giant City and no one will help us—but someone else is more than happy to tell Cyrus what we're doing?"

"Well, we'll just have to take that chance, right?" When no one agrees—not even Hudson—I don't bother to hide my annoyance. "Well, *I'm* going to try. The rest of you can do whatever you want...but you need to do it somewhere other than my room."

"Because we don't agree with you?" Mekhi challenges.

"Because I'm exhausted. I flew to the Bloodletter's and back today, and all I want is to get some sleep." I move to the door and open it. "Thanks for the warning. I'm all in about figuring out how to stop Cyrus from ruining Hudson's and my lives forever. But..." I blow out a long breath. "Tomorrow. Tonight, I just want to eat my cold grilled cheese, drink my Dr Pepper, and go to sleep."

For a moment, nobody moves. But then Jaxon lifts his chin in a little nod toward the door, and the rest of the Order files out.

Jaxon starts to follow them, but at the last second, he turns and gives me a warning look. "Pinning all your hopes on finding the Crown isn't going to end well for any of us. We need a better plan."

"I don't disagree," I tell him. "And as soon as you come up with something, you know where to find me. Until then, good night." I look at Hudson and nod toward the door myself. "To both of you."

Hudson doesn't say anything, but it's obvious he's as unhappy as Jaxon is as I close the door behind them. Which is just too bad, because right now... right now I need to have a full-blown panic attack, and the last thing I need is for Hudson to see it.

Because as sure as I know anything, I know Hudson will do something completely reckless—and most likely get himself killed if not locked in a prison meant to torture him for his immortal life—if it means protecting me.

I just hope I bought enough time to keep him safe until dawn.

36

Like a Monster
to a Flame

"So how much do you actually know about the Crown?" I ask Hudson the next afternoon as we work on finishing up our extra ethics project in the library.

He looks wary as he glances up from where he's reading *Symposium*—in Ancient Greek. The show-off. "What do you mean?"

"Well, you didn't seem to know anything about the Crown when the Bloodletter brought it up yesterday afternoon. But when we were discussing it with the Order last night, you acted like you knew everything."

"I don't know any more about it than anyone else," he answers before ducking his head and going back to reading.

"I don't believe that," I tell him. "You said your father is obsessed with it."

This time, he doesn't even bother looking up from his book when he says, "My father *is* obsessed with it. But, in case you haven't noticed, Cyrus and I aren't what most people would consider close."

I wait for him to say more, but of course he doesn't. This is Hudson, after all, and curt is his middle name when he's in a full-blown snit—which he currently is, though I don't know why.

"Are we seriously going to do this all day?" I ask, blowing out a frustrated breath.

He raises a brow. "Do what?"

"This." I gesture expansively between us. "Trying to talk to you when you're like this is like pulling fangs."

"Actually, removing their fangs kills vampires, so I'm guessing the struggle would be a lot more violent than this." He turns the page emphatically.

I'm not so sure, considering I'm going to lose my shit if he turns another page like that. Still, "I've never heard that before, about fangs."

"Shocking."

My eyebrows lift. "I thought a stake through the heart is what killed vampires, not—"

"Who *doesn't* that kill?" He rolls his eyes. "And of course you've never heard about our fangs before. Do you think we go around broadcasting our vulnerabilities to humans so they can stomp all over us?"

"Yeah, but..." I trail off as I realize I don't actually have anything to say to that. And Hudson has gone back to his reading anyway. Big surprise.

I look down at my own book—Aristotle's *On the Soul* (definitely not in the original Greek)—and try to focus on my part of the project. The sooner I get this read, the sooner I can answer the Aristotle portion of the ethics question. And the sooner I can get away from a very pissy Hudson.

Except I can't concentrate when he's sitting over there stewing silently. He might be able to comprehend what he's reading when he's annoyed, but I might as well be reading in Greek. Which means this project is never going to get finished if we don't find a way to clear the air between us.

Which is the only reason I finally ask, "Hey, what's wrong?" Or at least, that's what I tell myself.

Right up until he answers, "Nothing," anyway.

"That's bullshit and you know it," I tell him. "You're ignoring me, and I don't know why."

"*We* are sitting at a table in the library, working *together* on a project, and I have answered every single thing you've said to me," he says in a voice so primly British that it only stokes the flames of anger deeper inside me. "How, *exactly*, is that ignoring you?"

"I don't know, but it is. And I don't like it."

And yes, I am perfectly aware of how ridiculous I sound, but I don't actually care. I know when I'm being given the non-silent silent treatment, and that is definitely what's happening here. Which is unfair, considering all I wanted last night was to not freak him out while I had a complete meltdown.

"Yes, well, it's rough out there for a gargoyle." He flips the page just a little too emphatically, and that, combined with the way he bastardizes the title of that old song to make fun of me, makes me snap.

I lean forward and, without giving myself a chance to change my mind, I shove his book right off the table.

I expect him to get mad, maybe demand what the hell I think I'm doing. Instead, he just looks from me to the book and back again. And says, "Not a fan of Plato?"

I grit my teeth. "Not at the moment, no."

"Looks like you and Jaxon have more in common than I thought," he answers as he bends down to pick up the book. And then goes back to reading it.

"You know what? I'm not going to do this with you," I tell him, grabbing my stuff and shoving it into my backpack without so much as looking at what I'm doing. I hear paper rip, but I'm so mad that I don't even care.

"Now, there's a surprise," he answers, and this time when he flips a page, he does it with such force that I'm pretty sure he rips something, too. Not that I'm sticking around to figure out what. I'll go to my room and finish my half of the project, and then he's on his own.

"And you accuse *me* of being the one who doesn't deal with conflict," I say and then turn and leave.

I fume all the way up the stairs and all the way down the hallway. I have stuff to do today—a lot of stuff—and I don't have time for Hudson being petty. Sure, snarky is his default state, but not like this. Not to me.

I just wish I knew what set it off. Maybe then I could figure out how to fix it. But the longer we were at the library, the more annoyed he got, and I have no idea why. Any more than I know why he told me about the fangs thing, when he's so obviously mad at me.

I'm still trying to figure it out when I turn the last corner before I get to my room...and find him leaning against the wall near my door. Ugh. Vampires.

"I'm sorry I was an arse," he tells me in his perfect British accent.

"Don't you mean wanker?" I tell him as I open my door.

He moves his head in a back-and-forth, maybe kind of motion. "Seems a bit harsh if you ask me, but sure. If it makes you feel better. I was a tosser."

"A wanker," I repeat as I cross the threshold into my room. And can't help grinning as he tries to follow me in and gets stuck on the other side.

"Seriously?" he asks.

"You're not invited in. So not sorry." I move to close the door, but his hand flashes out and hits the door, stopping it from moving.

Which is surprising enough—I've always been under the impression that no part of a vampire could enter a room they're not permitted into, but that's obviously not true.

The fact that he's gotten the better of me makes me even more annoyed, and I shove against the door even though I know I'm not going to be able to budge him.

Except he does retreat a little, even as he makes an odd hissing sound in the back of his throat. "Stop," he says hoarsely.

"What's wr—" I break off as I glance at his hand and realize that welts are burning through his skin and flesh.

For one second, panic holds me immobile, and then I realize what's happening. "Come in," I tell him in a voice several notes higher than my regular tone. "Come in, come in, come in."

The burning must stop instantly, because he breathes a sigh of relief as he lets the door go and steps over the threshold.

"What's wrong with you?" I demand, even as I grab him by the forearm so I can get a better look at his hand and wrist—both of which look like he just thrust them into a raging fire. "Why would you do that?"

"I wanted to apologize."

"By setting yourself on fire?" I gasp, dragging him over to my bed. "Let me at least bandage you up."

"It's nothing," he tells me. "Don't worry about it."

"It's obviously something," I shoot back, because even though the burns have healed somewhat—the subcutaneous tissue is no longer exposed—they still look like they're at least second-degree. "It won't take long. I have a first aid kit in my backpack."

He smiles softly. "I know."

"How do you know?" I ask, but then I realize. "Another thing from when we were trapped together?"

"'Trapped' is such a harsh word," he answers, and his little smile has become more of a wicked grin. One that makes my stomach do a flip or two... hundred, not that I'm counting.

"Yeah, well, I'm feeling pretty harsh right now," I mutter, even though it's not quite the truth. And also, not quite *not* the truth, either. "I can't believe you did this to yourself."

He doesn't say anything else and neither do I as I put some antibiotic salve—I don't know if it works on vampires, but I figure it can't hurt—over what remains of the burns. And then, because I can't stand the idea of Hudson in pain because of me, I close my eyes and focus on sending healing energy into his burns, one by one. I'm careful to monitor my breathing so he doesn't realize that healing is in any way draining my energy, and it's really not. At least not much.

I'm on the last one when he clears his throat and says, "I didn't like getting kicked out of your room last night. I thought we'd just decided to try to make this work, almost even"—he looks away for a second, and I blush—"you know. And then you just tossed me out like one of the guys."

It's the last thing I expect him to say, and I fumble the antibiotic cream as I go to put it back in my kit. "I ..." I trail off as I realize I have absolutely no idea what I'm supposed to say to that.

"I know, it's silly. Obviously you have every right to kick me out anytime you want. I just got used to..." It's his turn to trail off.

"Being in my head all the time?" I ask him with a raised brow. Because I get it. I do.

I thought I'd be thrilled to be separated from Hudson and, for the most part, I am. But there are times when I go to share something with him, only to remember he's not there.

There are times I wish he *was* there, times it almost feels lonely without him.

And that was only after a couple of weeks—that I remember. How much harder must it be for him when he remembers us being together for four months? I can't even imagine.

"Maybe I miss it a little," he finally agrees. His reluctance only makes me feel worse, as does the way he refuses to look me in the eye.

"I'm sorry," I whisper as I glide my fingers along his smooth and healed skin. "I wasn't really kicking *you* out. I just couldn't handle being surrounded by all that vampire testosterone mansplaining to me for much longer. It was a lot."

"You make a fair point." His wicked little grin is back, which makes me smile, too.

"If it makes you feel better, the grilled cheese was delicious."

"Really?" He looks skeptical but also, maybe, just a bit hopeful.

"Absolutely." I smile. "So, so good."

His shoulders seem to relax. "I'm glad. I'll make you another one sometime."

I have absolutely no idea what I'm supposed to say to that, so I just smile and nod. This mate thing—even if we're just friends—is surprisingly hard work. But, also, not.

37

Charmed, I'm Shore

"Have a good day, Grace."

The voice of my art teacher, Dr. MacCleary, startles me out of the stupor I've been in all day, and I glance around only to realize that I'm the last person in the room. Everyone else has already packed up and left.

"Sorry." I shoot her an apologetic smile, then gather my things as quickly as I can. At least I have lunch next, so I don't have to worry about being late anywhere.

Because I do have an hour before my next class, I decide to skip the tunnels and take the long way back to the castle. It's a beautiful day, and I want to spend a few minutes in the sun if I can.

A frigid wind slaps me in the face the second I step outside the cottage, but I ignore it. This is Alaska, after all, and it's still cold out. But it's an okay kind of cold, the hoodie and scarf kind rather than the kind where I need a full abominable snowman outfit.

A storm is supposed to blow in tomorrow, though, so I might as well take advantage of the weather while I can. Instead of heading straight back to the castle, I wind my way around the art cottages to the path that takes me by the lake.

It's been frozen ever since I got here, but as I head down the path, I realize that the ice has finally melted. The lake is actually a lake again.

I stop for a minute and take a quick selfie or two with the water and the bright-blue sky in the background. Then I fire them off to Heather, along with the caption: Beach weather, Alaska style.

It only takes a few seconds before she texts back with a picture of herself in shorts and a T-shirt on the boardwalk at Mission Beach.

Heather: Beach weather, beach style

I shoot her back the eye roll emoji.

Heather: Bitter much?

She follows it with the laughing/crying emoji.

Me: So, so, sooooooo bitter

She sends me another pic, this one of her standing in line for the old wooden roller coaster we used to ride every time we went to Malibu Beach.

Heather: Wish you were here

Me: Me too

Heather: I'll be there soon enough

And fuck. I totally forgot about her coming to visit for graduation.

Angry tears burn in my eyes, because this is one more thing Cyrus has ruined for me. Heather had originally planned to come for Spring Break, but I'd pushed her off until graduation, But now I can't let Heather come then either—not when Cyrus and Delilah are going to be on campus. And not when I know they're gunning for me.

Cyrus would have no compunction about using a human girl to hurt me, and I can't stand the idea of something happening to Heather. My parents already died because of me—if Cyrus does something to Heather, I don't think I'll ever be able to forgive myself.

So, despite the fact that it kills me, I fire off a quick text that I know is going to piss her off.

Me: You can't come to graduation

Heather: Why not?

Me: We're not allowed visitors

It's a terrible excuse, but I don't know what else to say. Telling her I've got a homicidal vampire on my ass sounds like a very bad idea.

Heather: If you don't want me to come, all you have to do is say so

Heather: You don't have to lie

Me: I'm sorry. It's not a good time.

I wait for her to text back, but she doesn't, and I know it means she's pissed. Which she absolutely has a right to be, even though I'm just trying to save her life. I think about texting some more, but right now there really is nothing else to say. So I shove my phone back into the pocket of my hoodie and start the long trek to the castle. But I've only taken a few steps before I see a flash of black and purple in the gazebo across the lake.

I almost ignore it—it could be any one of the students at Katmere, after all—but when the hair stands up on the back of my neck, I change my mind and take a closer look. Only to find Jaxon staring straight at me from his perch on the gazebo railing.

I haven't talked to him since I kicked him out of my room Saturday night, but that doesn't mean I don't want to. So I smile and raise a hand in a wave as I wait to see whether he's going to ignore me or wave back.

In the end, he does neither. Instead, he hops off the railing.

But seconds later, he's made it all the way around the lake.

"Hey, you," I say as he comes to a stop inches away from me.

"Hi." He doesn't smile, but I'm getting used to that, even though I wish I wasn't.

Impulsively, I lean in for a hug—mainly because it feels awkward not to but also because I just really want to. This is Jaxon, after all, and though the look in his eyes gives me a chill, I'm not about to push him away. Not when he's made the effort to come to me.

I get the impression that he puts up with the hug for as long as he can—about ten seconds, really—before he pulls away. "What are you doing out here?" he asks.

"Enjoying the weather before I have to get to my next class." I look him over as we start to walk, startled that he looks skinnier than he did just a couple of days ago. "What about you?"

He shakes his head, gives a little shrug. And keeps walking so fast that I have to scramble to catch up.

I don't like the awkward silence between us, so I cast around for something to say. I settle on, "Did you have a good—" then break off, because I already know how his weekend went. He spent most of it at Court with his parents, so probably not all that well.

Without an ending to the sentence, though, the first half is just hanging there, waiting for me to finish it or for him to smooth it over.

But he hasn't smoothed things over in weeks, not since our mating bond broke, and I'm suddenly so nervous that I can't think of anything else to say. Not one single thing to say to this boy who was once my mate.

I hate it so much.

What's happened to us? Where have all the conversations about nothing and everything gone? Where have all the feelings gone?

They couldn't have just disappeared, right? Couldn't have existed only because of the mating bond. Some of them had to be real—for both of us.

I know mine were real. If they weren't, my heart wouldn't feel like it was breaking wide open at everything we've lost. I told Hudson I wanted to give our mating bond a chance, and I meant it. But that doesn't mean I can't mourn my relationship with Jaxon. Can't wish we could at least be friends now.

What happened to us? I think again, then freeze as I realize that this time, I've spoken out loud.

Jaxon's face closes up—a feat I didn't think was possible, considering what he's looked like since I saw him across the lake—and for a minute, I'm convinced that not only is he not going to answer, but that he's about to walk away as well.

Not that I blame him. We're going to great pains to pretend that everything is at least a little bit normal, so it really sucks that I just blew all that right out of the water.

But he doesn't walk away, and he doesn't ignore what I said. Instead, he looks down at me with those dark eyes of his, eyes that are anything but cold and removed, and answers, "Too fucking much."

38

Promises Made, Promises Broken

I hate to admit it, but he's not wrong. Too much has happened for things to feel normal between us now—or maybe ever again. It sucks, yeah, but there's a relief in hearing him admit it, a relief in having the words, and the sentiment, out in the open...no matter what happens next.

"What are we going to do?" I ask as we start walking again.

"The same thing as always," Jaxon answers. "Whatever we have to do to survive."

"Yeah, well, I'm not sure it's worth it." My mind whirls, trying to think of a non-"us" topic to discuss. Something bland. Something two exes who are friends would discuss. I settle on, "Well, with as much history class as I have to catch up on, surviving doesn't sound so easy."

Then I wait, breath held, to see if Jaxon will meet me halfway. To see if there's at least a chance that we can be friends.

He doesn't answer right away, and for a while the only sound is that of our boots crunching along the path. The silence stretches so long that eventually I have to let out my held breath, and as I do, my shoulders sag with the grief of it all. Of what we were and what we have become.

But then Jaxon glances at me out of the corner of his eye and asks, "Still having trouble?"

"I know. Believe me, I know how ridiculous it sounds to be drowning in a *history* class of all things. I just need to read and memorize, right? No big deal. But honestly, it's so much harder than that. There are all these case studies we're supposed to go over and then weigh in on, and I have no idea what I'm supposed to think about them, let alone what I'm supposed to write."

"I imagine it's hard coming into thousands of years of history for the first time," he adds.

"Right?" I throw up my hands in frustration. "I know the basic historical event—like the Salem Witch Trials—but the new version of events they're teaching me is so different from anything I've ever imagined that it's hard to get my mind around it."

Jaxon makes a sympathetic noise. "That sounds like a lot."

"It *is* a lot. Finding out that what I consider historical facts are really just one side's opinion..." I use my hand to show my mind blowing up. "It's worse than my Physics of Flight class, and that one is pretty much an unmitigated disaster."

"You know, Grace." Jaxon gives me the side eye. "You really don't have to hold things in so much. You should tell me how you really feel."

"Wow, someone's extra sarcastic this morning." I stick my tongue out at him. "Bite me."

"Don't mind if I do." He leans forward, fangs at the ready, and I laugh. Push him away.

Still, for a second, all the awfulness clears, and it's like it used to be.

Jaxon must feel the same way, because he asks, "What flavor of ice cream do vampires like best?"

It's my turn to side eye him. "Blood sherbet?"

He laughs. "Good guess, but no." He pauses, then says, "Vein-illa."

It's so bad—*so* bad—but for a moment it's like having the old Jaxon back, and he looks so proud of himself that I can't help cracking up. "That's awful. Like really, really awful. You know that, right?"

"It made you laugh."

"Apparently, I like awful."

He rolls his eyes. "Yeah, I've noticed that about you lately."

It's a swipe at Hudson, and normally I'd call him on it. But things are going so well that I just roll my eyes back at him and keep walking.

"You know, if you need help with your history class, I'm here," Jaxon says after we've walked about a quarter of a mile in silence. "Paranormal history is kind of a must-know for a prince."

"Oh, right. I bet." I start to think I should turn him down—I don't want to rock the boat. But the truth is, the end of the semester is closing in on me, and I'm freaking out. "That would be awesome. Thank you. A lot."

Jaxon looks a little uncomfortable—whether that he offered to help me or the enthusiasm with which I accepted it—but I'm too desperate to let him off the hook now.

Instead, I say, "When can we start?"

He shrugs. "Whenever you want."

"I'm free this afternoon if you are."

"I'm not," he tells me with a shake of his head, "but I can be. Let me clear things off, and I'll text you."

Now I feel bad. "You don't have to do that. I can wa—"

He cuts me off with a look. "You don't get to tell me what I can and can't do anymore."

"Yeah, right." I snort. "Because that's how things ever went with us."

He grins but doesn't say anything else until we come to the path that will take us to the castle door. "How is everything going?" he asks. "With you and Hudson, I mean."

It feels like a loaded question, one that will destroy the fragile peace that's sprung up between Jaxon and me. At the same time, he has the right to know—more so than anyone else in the school, save the two of us.

I sigh. "It's complicated."

"He's a complicated guy." Jaxon crooks a brow. "But I was talking about the whole arrest thing. Have you guys come up with a plan?"

"Beyond finding the Blacksmith, you mean?" I shake my head. "We've got nothing."

He nods, swallows. Then very quietly asks, "Do you need some help?"

"Finding the Crown?" I swing around so I can get a good look at his expression. "I thought you didn't like that idea."

"I don't." His mouth twists, making his scar stand out in stark definition. "But I like the idea of you and my brother going to prison less, so I guess we do what we can do."

"Even if it's a dead end?"

"What's this I'm hearing?" He pretends to be shocked. "Doom and gloom? From you?'

I elbow him lightly in the side. "It does happen on occasion, you know."

"Well, cut it out. It's my job to be the pessimist and your job to convince me otherwise. Besides, I had enough bad news this weekend to last me for a while, thank you very much."

That's not unexpected, considering he just spent a couple of days gathering intel at the Vampire Court, but that doesn't make it any easier to hear. "Was it really that bad?" I ask.

"It wasn't good," he answers grimly. "Cyrus is calling in favors left and right and getting angrier if those favors aren't delivered at the moment he demands them. The Circle is decimated—the witches and dragons have aligned against the vampires and wolves."

"I thought it's always been like that." The tensions were super high when they were here for the Ludares tournament and challenge. I just assumed it was normal.

"To a certain extent, it has. Our Circle definitely doesn't work with the ease and cohesiveness some of the others do, but it's never been this bad before. At least not in my lifetime. Cyrus is out for blood."

"Yeah, I know. Mine." I'm trying to lighten the mood, but the look Jaxon gives me tells me I didn't succeed. As does the coldness that is back to rolling off him in waves.

"We're not going to let that happen," he says. "You and Hudson have already suffered enough. But one way or another, war is coming. We just need to make sure we're ready for it."

"How are we supposed to do that?" I ask. "I'm a little busy trying to graduate from high school and sort out a mating bond. I don't have time to go to war."

If his expression is anything to go by, my second joke fell as flat as my first. Then again, Jaxon's never really found the topic of my safety to be very funny. I can't blame him, considering I've always felt the same way about his.

"What are we going to do?" I ask.

He shakes his head. "I don't know yet. But we'll figure it out. I promise."

"Wow. Is that optimism twice in one morning from Jaxon Vega? What will the universe think?"

"I won't tell it if you don't."

I laugh, even though I'm not sure he's joking. Still, I start to tease him a little more—anything to loosen up the bitter chill that is so much a part of him these days—but break off when I realize we're at the steps of the castle.

He starts to go up them, but I stop him with a hand on his arm. "Thank you," I whisper.

"For what?" The look he gives me is wary.

"For…everything," I say, unable to get anything else out as my throat closes up just a little, sorrow for what we've lost mingling with hope over what we just might have a chance to regain—our friendship.

Impulsively, I hug him again, this time pulling his face down so that our cold cheeks are mashed together. At first he's unyielding, but I don't care. "I miss you," I whisper to him as I hold on for an extra few seconds. There is no innuendo in the words, and I know he understands. The last thing I'd ever want to do is lead Jaxon on, but he deserves to know that his friendship means just as much as the mating bond did.

His arms tighten around me, but he doesn't say it back. In fact, he doesn't say anything at all. But he does hold me for several more seconds before he lets me go. I count that as a win—at least until I see his blank face and realize whatever gains I thought I made on the walk have been completely erased.

It's frustrating, infuriating, and I really want to yell at him. To ask him why he's doing this, why he's treating me like this when I haven't done anything to deserve it.

But he's already gone, so far away from me that I know it doesn't matter what I say. It won't get through to him.

So instead of humbling myself anymore, I give him the same parting smile and wave to say goodbye that I gave him to say hello at the gazebo a little while ago, then head up the stairs, telling myself I have enough to do without worrying over what's going on with a guy who has made it very obvious that he only wants me on an all-or-nothing basis—the "nothing" having won out.

But the moment I pull open Katmere Academy's front door, I realize that we've got a bigger problem than what's going on between Jaxon and me. Because every student in the entryway and common room is frozen in anticipation as three wolves move in on Hudson in an ever-tightening circle.

39

Not Every Dog
Has Its Day

"Stop!" I yell and start to wade into the fray, but Jaxon is right beside me again, and this time he's holding my arm in an iron grip.

"Let me go!" I cry out as I try to shake him off.

"I can't," he tells me. "If you get in the middle of this, it'll only make him look weak."

"He *is* weak!" I growl. "His powers are grounded." Which is beginning to look like a spectacularly bad idea on my uncle's part...

"That is exactly why they're pushing at him," Jaxon tells me matter-of-factly. "They figure this is the best chance they've got. He needs to knock them back himself, or this shit will just keep happening."

"What if he can't?" I cry out as one of his attackers shifts so that he's still mostly human but with a wolf's head—and teeth. "What if they hurt him?"

Jaxon gives me the same insulted look Hudson gave me the other day in the library, like it's sacrilege to imagine that a vampire can't take on three wolves—and win—with just sheer badassery alone.

I don't like the odds, though. Especially not when so many of the other students are crowding around, egging the wolves on even as Hudson doesn't back down.

He's not even ruffled, standing there in the middle of Marc (I should have destroyed the jerk on the Ludares field when I had the chance) and two other wolves I recognize from classes but whose names I don't know.

No, Hudson looks amused, which might be reassuring if it wasn't pissing the wolves off so badly. And if it seemed, even a little bit, like he took the threat of them seriously.

But it doesn't appear that way at all, despite the fact that all three of them are within arm's reach of Hudson now. I use every ounce of concentration I have to will him to end it now or to walk away, but he does neither. I think about trying to reach for him through the mating bond, to let him know that I'm here, but I'm afraid of distracting him.

I definitely don't want to give them a reason to stop toying with him and go for the jugular. But that doesn't mean I'm fine with being stuck way back here, out of range if he needs my help.

"You can let me go," I tell Jaxon quietly. "I won't try to get between them."

Jaxon hesitates, but he must decide that I mean it, because his grip loosens significantly. Even as my unspoken *yet* hangs in the air between us. I won't get between them yet.

With Jaxon's grip more supportive than restraining, I start easing my way through the ever-widening crowd until I'm almost at the front row. But when I move to make the final shift, Jaxon right behind me, the group of wolves in front of me deliberately closes the gap.

Unless we want to pick a fight of our own, Jaxon and I are effectively cut off from the front lines.

"It's fine," he whispers to me, even as the guy with the wolf's head leans in and snaps at Hudson, his teeth inches from my mate's face.

I swallow a little shriek as Hudson dodges, then raises a sardonic brow and asks, "You don't really think that's going to impress me, do you? I'm pretty sure the fleas you're carrying have a harsher bite."

"Does he have to taunt them like that?" I moan. The last time Jaxon got in a fight with the wolves, he just walked in and kicked their asses. It was terrifying to watch, but this…this is so much worse. The tension of worrying about Hudson going up against them without his powers is killing me.

Jaxon just snorts. "I'm sorry. Have you met my brother?"

It's a good point, but that doesn't make this any easier to watch. Especially when the wolf lunges again—and gets so close that I swear Hudson could smell his breath before he manages to fade a few steps away.

This time, both brows are up as he glances down at his shoulder. "Does mange run in your family?" he asks as he brushes a tuft of wolf fur off his shoulder. "Because if it doesn't, you might want to see someone about that."

All three wolves growl this time, so loud that the sound reverberates through the room. My stomach is basically doing somersaults now, and not in the good way. I can feel my heartbeat speeding up, can feel a weight pressing down on my chest as panic wells inside me.

"He needs to just finish this," I tell Jaxon, and my voice sounds thin even to my own ears.

"What he needs is to stop playing with his food and kick their sorry asses," Jaxon snarls, which means all this tension is getting to him, too.

"Maybe he can't," I whisper as Hudson dodges another attack, still without lashing out. "Maybe he needs his powers—"

"That's some serious faith you've got in your mate there, Grace." I jump a little at the sound of Mekhi's voice right over my shoulder.

"It's not a lack of faith in him," I shoot back without turning around. I'm terrified Hudson will be torn apart right in front of me if I so much as blink. "It's a total lack of trust that the wolves have so much as one ounce of honor among them all."

"Fair point," Mekhi agrees, shifting until he's on the other side of me, while Luca and Flint move in right behind me. I'm not sure if they're trying to protect me or if they're getting in a position to intervene if Hudson needs them. Either way, I'm grateful that they're here—even if their ridiculously big bodies do take up all the air around me.

"Hudson's got this, Grace," Flint murmurs quietly in my ear.

I swallow a scream as Wolf Head lunges at him again. Hudson, in the meantime, doesn't even seem fazed. He just glances out at the crowd and asks, "Why is there never a newspaper around when you need one?" even as he pretends to smack the wolf on the nose. "Bad doggy."

Half the crowd gasps (I'm part of that group) while the other half cracks up—including all my friends. Even Jaxon chuckles, and that's before Hudson continues in the most British voice imaginable.

"Sorry to interrupt your little...ambush? But with all the foaming at the mouth going on here, it seems prudent to ask if you've had your rabies shots?"

This time, it's Marc who lunges straight for him, his hand shifting into a claw as he goes right for Hudson's face. Hudson, on the other hand, must have decided that he's taunted the wolves enough, because instead of dodging this time, he stands right where he is and leans back just far enough that Marc rakes his claws down the side of his neck instead of his cheek.

I don't even try to stop the scream that explodes from my throat—not that I could have if I tried. Jaxon's hand clamps down on my right shoulder just as Flint's clamps down on my left.

Jaxon growls. "That was just about not getting into shit with Foster. He let them draw first blood."

"Well, he did a good job of it," I snarl back, because blood is flowing pretty freely from the claw marks.

Even worse, it's emboldened Marc and the others, who are now closing in on Hudson—Marc and Wolf Head from the front, the third wolf from the back—with the look of people intent on ripping their prey limb from limb.

I wait for Hudson to respond, wait for him to give some kind of clue as to how he plans to handle this latest attack. But for what feels like forever, he does nothing except watch them, his bright-blue eyes going back and forth between the two guys closing in on him from the front.

I'm most worried about the one from the back—who he can't see—but Hudson must sense him, because he shifts a little, making sure that his back is against the wall. But that's the only move he makes as everything seems to happen in slow motion.

Seconds feel like minutes as sweat rolls down my spine. Terror is a wild thing within me, and I'm positive if something doesn't happen soon, I'm going to end up screaming the castle down or throwing myself between Hudson and the wolves. Or both.

Probably both.

But just as Jaxon tenses beside me—probably with shades of the same thoughts running through his head—and I reach down deep to find my gargoyle string, Marc rushes Hudson, with the other two hot on his heels. And Hudson…Hudson does the absolute last thing I would ever expect him to do. Ever.

He grabs Marc by the shoulders and lifts him several feet off the ground. But instead of throwing him and moving on to the next threat, Hudson never lets him go. Instead, he pulls his arms up and to the side (while still holding Marc) and then swings the struggling, snarling wolf like he's a baseball bat straight at Wolf Head, like he's the ball.

And apparently, Hudson is one hell of a batter, because Wolf Head goes flying. Like, bases-loaded, home-run-ball flying, straight across the foyer and out the still-open castle doors. Then, instead of dropping Marc like most players do their bats, he keeps swinging until Marc's body meets the stone wall and the laws of physics go to work.

A collective gasp rises up from the crowd as the sounds of both bone and stone shattering fill the room.

Hudson drops him into a heap of broken limbs and ribs before whirling around to face the next threat. The third wolf obviously has a death wish or a God complex, because anyone with an ounce of self-preservation is backing away—including every other wolf in the room.

I'm not sure if this guy is worried about losing face or having his ass handed to him by the rest of his pack later, but whatever it is, it keeps him barreling straight at Hudson like a vampire-seeking missile. Hudson doesn't so much as blink. He just braces for the attack, feet grounded and arms loose by his sides until one second before the wolf shifter reaches him. Then he lashes out with his foot and kicks him as hard as he can in the kneecap.

The shifter goes down with a high-pitched whimper, but Hudson isn't done yet. He pulls back his hand and slaps him, hard, right across the face.

The entire room recoils, and I don't even have to ask why. I may be new to the paranormal world, but I don't need to be an expert to know that right there is the biggest insult any male of any species could deliver to another.

Even before Hudson leans down and says, "Next time you want to play, I suggest you bloody well make it worth my time. There's nothing I hate more than being bored."

And then, to add insult to a whole heap of injury, he pats the guy on the head and says, "Good doggy," before dusting his hands off and walking straight toward me.

40

Fight or Fright Club

All around me, the guys are whooping and hollering at Hudson's triumph, because testosterone is a thing, but I'm just kind of frozen in shock. I was so scared, so certain that they were going to rip him apart, that I'm having a hard time getting past the fear.

I jump on him as soon as he gets close, throwing my arms around him in a hug. "Don't ever do that again!" I tell him.

"Do what?" He pulls back to look at me, brows lifted, a slightly bemused grin on his face. "Kick some werewolf arse? Because I'm afraid I can't promise that."

I narrow my eyes at him as I pull away, place my hands on my hips. "You know exactly what I mean. I was terrified you were going to get hurt!"

"I tried to tell her you could handle a few dogs, no matter how bad their attitude problem, but she wasn't having it," Mekhi tells him.

"What *was* their problem anyway?" I demand, glancing among Hudson, Flint, Luca, Mekhi, and Jaxon, who is suddenly interested in looking at anyone and everyone but me.

"What do you mean?" Flint answers blankly.

"Why would they just start in on Hudson for no reason? It doesn't make any sense."

All five of them look at me with varying degrees of amusement. "Sure it does," Luca finally says. "With Cole gone, there's a power vacuum as they fight it out for the alpha position. It was a dominance display, pure and simple."

"Pretty sure you mean a *lack* of dominance display." Mekhi snickers. "Except for my man Hudson here."

Hudson just shakes his head, looking more bemused by the second. Once again, I realize just how strange it must feel to realize there are people in your life who have your back, who have faith in you and who genuinely want you to succeed.

At least until Uncle Finn comes tearing down the hallway, loaded for bear—or, in this case, vampire. "Vega brothers!" he snaps out, looking at Hudson and Jaxon both. "Go wait for me in my office." When they just kind of stare at him, he adds a "Now!" to the command in a voice that has every single person in the room standing at attention—*including* the two Vega brothers.

"What did *I* do?" Jaxon asks, an insulted look on his face.

But Uncle Finn gives it right back. "Something, I have no doubt." He points toward the hallway that leads to his office, then turns to Marise—the vampire who runs the infirmary—and directs, "Get all three of the wolves to the infirmary wing. Have a few of the other seniors help if you need it. I'll be by later to discuss punishments with them.

"In the meantime—" He turns to look at the still-overcrowded common rooms and orders, "Disperse."

For once, there's absolutely no hesitation. The second his eyes sweep the room, people start to scatter.

To be honest, I'm impressed. I didn't realize Uncle Finn had it in him. He's always seemed like the kind of headmaster who rules through love, not fear, but apparently he knows how to do the fear thing when he needs to.

I wait for the room to empty out before I approach him, but I've barely reached his side when he says, "You too, Grace."

His voice is a lot quieter with me than it was with the others, but there's no mistaking the order in it. Still, I'd like to try to explain to him what happened.

"But, Uncle Finn, this wasn't Hudson's fault—"

"That's not for you to decide, Grace." For the first time ever with me, his voice is cold. My lovable uncle Finn is gone, and in his place is a very pissed-off headmaster, one who apparently isn't going to take any shit from anyone. Including me. "Now, go to class. The bell's going to ring any minute."

As if on cue, the after-lunch chimes start to play the chorus of the old song, "I Put a Spell on You." Apparently, Billie Eilish's day at Katmere is done—at least for now.

I squeeze Hudson's hand, then head to class after stopping by the dining hall to grab an apple, but I can't concentrate the rest of the day—especially when neither Jaxon nor Hudson returns my texts. I know Hudson was already grounded or on probation or whatever you call it, but Uncle Finn can't actually kick him out for this, right? He was just defending himself.

Sure, yeah, he egged the wolves on, but it was obvious to anyone with eyes that they were going to attack him first. The fact that he didn't cower in a corner isn't his fault. From the moment I got to Katmere, the wolves have been horrible. If I knew then what I know now, there's no way I would have let Marc and Quinn get away with what they did to me my first night. No way I would have just let it go in the hopes that things wouldn't get worse.

But I did, and now Hudson may get kicked out because of me.

My breath catches. If Hudson gets kicked out of school, he'll not be under Katmere's protection anymore, which means he would be arrested and sent to that horrific prison.

By the time I run into Macy and Gwen later, I've gotten myself totally freaked out. It's been hours, and I haven't heard from either brother—which isn't unusual under normal circumstances these days. But I've texted them both several times that I'm worried and I want to make sure they're okay. And still nothing.

"They're fine," Macy tells me as we walk to our room, but she sounds strange, like something isn't quite right. "They're probably still in my dad's office, along with a bunch of other students. He'll spring them eventually."

"Why are there other students there? You mean the wolves?" I know I sound confused, but that's because I am. I have no idea what's happening here.

Gwen and Macy exchange a long look. "You didn't hear?"

"Hear about what?"

"During lunch. There was an incident before the whole Hudson/werewolf thing happened. In the dining hall."

My blood runs cold. "What kind of incident?"

"The vamps and the witches full-on got into it at the beginning of lunch."

"Vamps? You mean the Order?" I ask, trying to sort things in my mind. "But that doesn't make sense. I saw Luca and Mekhi during the fight Hudson had with the wolves. They didn't look like they'd been in any kind of fight."

"It wasn't the Order. It was a bunch of sophomore and junior vampires—I don't think you know most of them." Macy sounds more freaked out than I've ever heard her. "One grabbed Simone and just started drinking from her, right there in the middle of the dining hall. I think she wanted to kill her."

"Oh my God." My whole body recoils in horror. "Oh my God. Is Simone all right?" No wonder Uncle Finn was so furious over what had happened between Hudson and the wolves.

"She's fine," Gwen says, but there's something in her voice that has me leaning in, double-checking.

"Are you sure?"

"One of the other vamps grabbed Gwen," Macy says quietly. "She almost didn't get away before he could bite her."

"But I did get away," Gwen says forcefully. "Macy and Eden kicked his ass and then took on about six or seven other vampires."

"With help from several other witches and dragons."

"Oh my God," I say again, even though I know I'm beginning to sound like a broken record. "What is happening? Is it a full moon or something?"

I glance outside to where the sun is starting to set, but it's only a quarter moon. So the excuse the wolves use for everything just went out the window.

"It was the weirdest thing," Macy says as we drop Gwen at her door and then continue down the hall to ours. "Everything was fine and then bam, they just started attacking us. And not, like, one of us, like they did with Hudson. They went after, like, seven or eight witches. We couldn't fight them all off—that's how Simone got bit. And Cam."

"Cam? Your old boyfriend?" I ask, incredulous.

"Yeah. And after everything that happened during the challenge, I want to say what goes around comes around. But the vamps can't just do whatever they want to us."

"And neither can the wolves," I add, thinking back on the three who went after Hudson. And what might have happened if they'd gone after someone else.

"Do you think the wolves heard about what happened in the cafeteria and decided to just see what they could get away with while my dad was distracted?" Macy asks as we reach our room.

"That's as good a theory as any, I guess. They've been pretty freaking obnoxious to both Hudson and me since the Ludares challenge." Actually, I'm surprised it's taken Cole's former pack this long to start shit.

"Since you kicked their alpha's ass, you mean?" Macy drops her backpack next to her bed and goes straight for the fridge—and the Ben & Jerry's cookie dough.

"I wasn't going to put it like that, but yeah."

"Why wouldn't you say it like that?" she asks as she opens the bag and holds it out to me. "It's exactly what happened."

"I got my ass kicked on that field, too," I tell her. "A couple of times."

"You were on your own. It's a miracle you aren't dead, and we all know it." She sinks down onto her favorite spot at the end of my bed.

"Yeah, well, I may not be dead, but I'm going to lose my mind if I don't hear from Hudson or Jaxon soon." I pull out my phone and check it for the thousandth time in the last half hour. There are a couple of new messages from Mekhi and Flint, both of whom are checking on me and fishing for information at the same time. There's also a message from Eden telling me to watch my back.

I fire a commiserating text back at her, then tell the guys that I don't know anything more than they do—which is incredibly frustrating, since I'm eating chocolate chip cookie dough with the headmaster's daughter as he holds my current mate and my ex-mate hostage in his office.

Considering what happened to Cole the last time Uncle Finn was this furious, there's no way I'll be able to rest until I'm sure Hudson and Jaxon aren't currently falling through some portal to Texas to join him.

41

C'est La Vamp

My phone finally buzzes at three a.m. after a long, nerve-racking night. Normally, I wouldn't hear it, but it's not like I'm getting much sleep anyway.

Hudson: Sorry

Hudson: Foster had our phones

I sit up in bed, heart pounding and phone clutched in my hands. For a second, I can't breathe as relief swamps me, and I have to ask myself what's going on. I managed to stave off a panic attack all night, so why am I having one now that I know he's actually all right?

Tension release? Relief? Fear that there's something bigger going on here than anyone wants to think about, let alone acknowledge?

I sit up so that I can feel the cool wood floors beneath my feet. It's not grass, but here in Alaska, it will do. I take a few breaths, count backward from twenty, focus on the cold seeping through my arches and the balls of my feet.

And nearly cry with relief when the panic subsides almost as easily as it came. Either this wasn't a bad one or I'm finally getting the hang of these things. Either way, I'll take it.

Picking my phone up again, I text Hudson back.

Me: What happened?

Me: Are you all right?

Me: Did you just get out?

I can't believe Foster had students in his office until three in the morning. Surely that's not okay, even with paranormals?

Hudson: Jaxon and I got our arses chewed out.

Hudson: I'm fine. Got stuck on belfry duty, but I'm good.

Hudson: Yeah. Your uncle was on a roll tonight

I switch over to Google just to make sure my definition of belfry is the right one. Turns out it is.

Me: Belfry? Like bats in the belfry?

Hudson: More like vamps in the belfry

It's not the answer I'm expecting, and I can't help staring at my phone, wondering if warlocks are capable of performing lobotomies with their wands—and if that's what took him so long in my uncle Finn's office.

Me: Did you just make a corny joke?

Three dots appear.

Hudson: Maybe

Me: Stop before you hurt yourself

Hudson: You've got a real mean streak in you

Hudson: You know that, right?

Me: Know it? I cultivate it

Hudson: No you don't

Hudson: You're just pouting because I stole your belfry joke

Me: I don't pout

Hudson: Oh, right. Sorry

Hudson: You're deflecting

Hudson: Grumpily

Me: How do you know that?

Hudson: Because I know you

His words give me pause, have me staring at my phone for several seconds as I take in the simplicity and the assurance in those four words. As well as that after living in my head for four months, he does know me—better than almost anyone. Maybe even better than I know myself.

Maybe that's why my fingers are paralyzed over my phone, my mind completely blank as I try to figure out how I should answer him. In the end, I leave the sentiment hanging and revert back to our former conversation. I tell myself it's because I really don't have anything to say to his assertion, but the truth is, I have too much to say.

And I'm afraid to say any of it.

Me: So what exactly is belfry duty?

Hudson: I'm in charge of the bell tower for the next few weeks

Hudson: And the chimes

Me: The chimes?

Me: Oh, you mean the songs? You get to pick?

Hudson: Maybe. Why?

Me: Because I've been dying to see what people would do if the chimes started playing Monster Mash

Me: Can you do that?

Hudson doesn't reply.

Me: Can you?????

Still no reply.

Me: Helloooooo

Hudson: I think the question is, will I?

Hudson: Do you want me to play Five Little Pumpkins, too?

Me: Only if it's the Disney version

He sends me the eye roll emoji.

Several seconds pass, and I settle back into bed, wondering if he's done texting for a while. But just when I'm thinking about messaging Jaxon one more time to make sure he's okay, too, my phone buzzes again.

Hudson: How about you? You good?

Me: I'm not the one who had to fight three werewolves today

Hudson: That wasn't a fight. That was a bad day at the dog pound

Hudson: And that wasn't an answer

Of course he picked up on my nonanswer. Hudson picks up on everything when it comes to me. He always has. Most of the time, it's seriously inconvenient, but sometimes...sometimes it's nice.

Me: I'm fine

Me: Did you hear about the vampires in the dining hall?

Hudson: Just spent the last several hours with them

Hudson: Absolutely cracking it was

Me: I bet

Me: What was going on with them anyway? Who would do that?

Hudson: It is kind of a defining factor of the species

It's my turn to send him an eye roll emoji.

Me: You know what I mean

Hudson: Yeah

Hudson: Jaxon and I can't figure out what caused it

My stomach flips at the mention of Jaxon. He still hasn't texted me back.

Me: What's going to happen?

Hudson: One of the younger vamps got the boot

Hudson: And everyone else is grounded

Me: Except for you

Hudson: Can't take away what I don't have. Hence, belfry duty

Hudson: C'est la vie

Me: What about Jaxon? Is he grounded, too?

I hold my breath, waiting for him to answer. But he doesn't.

At first, I think he's just become distracted by something, but as seconds become minutes, I decide he must have fallen asleep. Which makes sense. It *is* almost four in the morning, and we've got class in a few hours.

I tell myself I should get some sleep, too, but that doesn't stop me from clutching my phone in my hand when I roll onto my side—just in case he decides to text back.

I'm almost asleep when my phone finally vibrates. It jolts me awake, and I nearly drop it on the floor in my rush to grab it. But this time, it's not Hudson.

Jaxon: Everything's fine

Oh, thank God. I clutch my phone and wait, heart pounding, for him to write more. But he doesn't.

Finally, I break down and text:

Me: I'm glad

Me: Are you grounded?

He doesn't answer.

A few minutes go by, and I'm starting to get annoyed. I know things are off between us, but he doesn't need to act like this. He definitely doesn't need to treat me like dirt when I've spent the last several hours worried about him.

Another text comes in, and my heart is pounding fast and hard as I swipe open my phone, only to realize that it's Hudson again.

Hudson: Good night, Grace

Hudson: Don't let the werewolves bite…

Me: Lol

Me: Never

Me: Good night, Hudson

It's only after I put my phone down and curl up beneath my hot-pink comforter that I realize he never answered my question about Jaxon—almost like he already knew I'd gotten an answer.

42

It's Not the Tower
That Makes
the Prince

The next couple of days pass in what feels like a kind of fugue state. Nothing feels right, everything is off, and tension in the halls—and classes—is off the charts.

The made vamps are pissed one of their own got kicked out. The born vamps are pissed they're getting blamed for what the made vamps did (rightfully so). The witches are pissed the vampires attacked them (even more rightfully so). And the wolves...well, the wolves are just pissed in general (big freaking surprise).

So far, the dragons are okay, but I've got a feeling that's about to change, since I saw a few of the freshman wolves starting something with one of the sophomore dragons on my way to class this morning. Mr. Damasen broke it up before things got too heated, but I don't know how long that will last.

Uncle Finn's got to be close to having the whole school grounded by now, which one would think would make a difference. But it's, like, 60 percent of Katmere has gone aggro and the rest of us are just trying to figure out what's happening—and how to stay out of the way and not get our own butts kicked by Uncle Finn, who is basically on the warpath hourly.

It's even harder than it sounds.

Plus, there's all the makeup work I still have to do *and* the fact that I might have ruined my relationship with Heather—who hasn't answered a single one of my texts in days.

So when Macy texts the group that we should meet in Jaxon's tower after school to study and strategize, I'm all in. At least until I remember what Jaxon has done to the tower. I don't think anyone wants to try to do homework around his handy-dandy workout machines.

In the end, we settle for meeting in Hudson's room—which turns out is in the castle's old undercroft—because it's bigger than any of the rest of our rooms. And also, it turns out, because it's a lot more isolated than anywhere else in the castle.

I don't think I had a clue just how isolated until I start to wind my way down to it. It's above the tunnels but below Katmere's official first floor, existing in a kind of no-man's-land that you totally miss if you don't know it's there.

I'm not sure how I feel about that—that Jaxon has a tower and Hudson is practically in the basement—at least until I head down the only staircase that leads to the undercroft and realize it is the coolest room in the entire castle—and that includes the library.

To begin with, it's huge. I mean, really, really huge—like runs-the-length-of-the-whole-castle huge. Sure, it's narrower than a lot of the rooms above it, but who cares when everything about this place is incredible?

I thought it would be dark, but it's at least partially aboveground, so there are a ton of windows lining three sides of the room. No wonder there are so many steps leading up to the front door of the castle if this is what's underneath the first floor.

Not to mention that the room itself is filled from one end to the other with the most incredible carved stone arches, which gives the room a seriously amazing gothic vibe. The arches are only about two-thirds as wide as the room, which leaves a long, narrow strip along one side of the undercroft separated from the rest of it. Hudson has apparently turned this part into his own private library.

There are thousands—literally thousands—of books lining the walls and the backside of the arches, and they all look like they've been read about a hundred times each. And in the middle of all those books is a very comfortable, very well-worn-looking chair and ottoman.

I kind of want nothing more than to just dive into his shelves and see what's there, but there's so much more of the room to explore, I don't know where to look first.

The arches themselves are elaborately carved, and each one is a little different. The first one is carved with scene after scene of dragons flying, while the second is filled with stars and moons and even full-on constellations. The third one goes back to dragons, but it's all scenes of home and hearth and family. I want to look at them all, but there are probably twenty-five or thirty, and I don't exactly have the time to examine each one. Or lust after the gorgeous jewels—some as big as a grapefruit—that are embedded in the arches and used to separate the different scenes.

I look for Hudson, but I must be the first one here. I know I'm fifteen minutes early, but I was hoping to talk to him for a few minutes before everyone else got here. Looks like that's not going to happen, though, since he's missing as well.

There's a seating area farther down the main part of the room, and I head toward it, figuring that's where we're going to be studying. But I can't help getting distracted by how cool this space is...not to mention how very cool the vampire who lives here is.

Besides the ridiculously cool library, which a quick trip through shows is mostly devoted to ancient philosophy, plays and poetry from all eras, and modern-day mystery-thrillers, there's also a whole section of the undercroft that Hudson has devoted to his very extensive, very eclectic vinyl collection. Next to that are shelves filled with photographic equipment, which surprises me, since I had no idea he even liked to take pictures beyond the requisite selfies all vampires take, since they can't see their reflection in mirrors. There's also a couple of top-of-the-line printers, including a 3-D one and some impressive-looking stereo equipment.

To be fair, I just listen to music on my phone or laptop, so I don't know for sure. But it definitely looks state of the art...and expensive.

Next is the small sitting area, which has a desk and an oversize couch, not to mention a couple of purple chairs that look like they were stolen from one of the lounges upstairs. Past that is a space about four arches long that is completely empty, if you discount the different-size targets attached to three sides of the arches. They're all banged up and gouged, and I have no idea what they're for—until I see the workbench against the wall and realize it's loaded with axes.

Hudson throws axes. And, judging from the number of knicks and gouges near the targets' bull's-eyes, he throws them pretty damn well—which, in its own way, is as unexpected as the photography equipment.

The final section of the room is obviously where he sleeps. It's dominated by a huge king-size bed that's so high off the ground, I'm not sure I could even climb onto it. Not that I'm thinking of climbing onto Hudson's bed, because I'm definitely not. But if I were, I don't think I could manage it without some help.

And its height isn't even the most spectacular thing about the bed. No, that belongs to the elaborate iron bed frame that pretty much screams *I'm a vampire* and the bloodred bedding that only underscores the point.

It's part hilarious—because Hudson really is the most sarcastically unapologetic vampire I've ever met—and part sexy as fuck, because I can't help but picture him lying half naked in the middle of this bed, his skin warm with sleep and his usually perfect hair all messed up.

It's a really good picture, so good, in fact, that my cheeks are burning even before I hear a *thud* sound behind me.

43

My Grace

I have about one second to register that I was right about Hudson stealing the chairs from one of the study rooms—the sound I heard was him putting another one down next to the couch.

"Oh, hey!" My voice is about three notes higher than usual as I try to pretend that he didn't just catch me imagining him half naked while staring at his I-can-fuck-you-senseless-several-times-in-a-row bed. "I know I'm early, but—"

My throat closes up completely as I realize he's more than noticed the color of my cheeks. Not to mention that he is currently looking between his bed and me with what can only be described as a desperate look in his eyes.

My whole body goes hot, then cold, then hot again, and for a second, there's nothing but Hudson and me and the inferno incinerating everything between us.

But then he blinks and he's just Hudson again, standing twenty feet in front of me with a sardonic look in his eyes and a second chair balanced against his hip. "But?" he asks, quirking one perfect, rich mahogany brow.

"Oh, umm. I, umm, wanted to…" I trail off as my brain stops working at the sight of his very nice muscles bunching just a little under his striped oxford shirt as he shifts to put the chair down.

"Wanted to…?" Now both brows are up.

And that's when it hits me. "You're wearing jeans." And not just any jeans—ripped and well-worn and so, so sexy jeans. At least on him. "You never wear jeans."

"I've been alive more than two hundred years, Grace. *Never* is a long time." He straightens up the chair he just put down, then ambles toward me with a slow, measured walk that gets me even more flustered. I swear, it should be illegal for anyone to look this good. I lick my suddenly too-dry lips.

Hudson stops a few feet in front of me, and the look on his face is so watchful, I can't help wondering what my face looks like. Which then makes me so nervous that I furiously rack my brain, looking for something to say that does not involve me wanting to climb on his...bed.

What I end up with is, "You have a turntable."

Oh my God. This boy lived in my brain for weeks, and we never shut up. All of a sudden, I can barely form a coherent sentence around him. What. The. Everlasting. Hell is going on?

From the way Hudson is slowly nodding, I figure he's probably wondering the same thing. But instead of calling me on my weirdness, he must decide to just roll with it, because he says, "Yeah. I've been collecting vinyl since it came out."

"Oh, right. 'Cause you were..."

The brow is back up. "I was..."

"Alive then." Jesus. Could I sound any more incoherent if I tried? I clear my throat. "Can you turn something on?"

"Now?"

"Yeah, my best friend in San Diego loves vinyl. Her name's Heather and—"

"I know who Heather is." He walks past me, and I nearly have a heart attack thinking he's going to get on the bed, but then he just walks to the nightstand and picks up a controller. "What do you want to listen to?"

"Oh, it doesn't matter. Whatever you've got on the table will be great."

For a moment, it looks like he's going to say something, but then he just shrugs and hits a button. Seconds later, dark, hard rock music comes through the small speakers he's got positioned all over the room. I don't recognize the music or the lyrics that suddenly flood the air. But that's nothing unusual, considering Hudson's and Jaxon's musical tastes likely span a century.

"What song is this?" I ask.

"Godsmack's 'Love-Hate-Sex-Pain,'" he answers.

"That's..." *Oh my God.* The universe is fucking with me. It's just...fucking with me. Or Hudson is; I don't know which at this point. Maybe both of them. "Interesting."

"You want me to put something else on?" he asks, and I swear he's laughing at me, even though he's totally keeping a straight face.

"No, it's fine. I like it." I release a long breath as I pull out my phone and text Macy to hurry the fuck up.

"I'll put something else on." He heads toward his music area. "I don't have any Harry Styles, but I'm sure I can find something you'll like."

"Hey, don't knock Harry Styles!" I tell him, then breathe a sigh of relief as I realize I'm back to normal. "He is very talented."

"I never said he wasn't." Hudson shoots me an amused glance. "Paranoid much?"

I narrow my eyes at him. "I know derision when I hear it."

"When it comes to Harry, I'm pretty sure you hear derision even when there is none," he counters as he puts another record on the turntable.

He has a point, but it's not like I'm about to admit it, so I just kind of shrug as the first notes of Lewis Capaldi's "Grace" start playing. I've heard the song once or twice before and loved it, but I don't know. Something about standing here with Hudson as the lyrics echo through his room has a whole lot of everything welling up inside me.

And when he turns around and looks straight at me just as Lewis sings basically my name over and over, my knees—and everything inside me—go weak. Because there's nothing sarcastic, nothing witty, nothing distant in Hudson's eyes.

There's just him and me and everything remembered and forgotten that stretches between us.

I take a step toward him before I even know I'm going to do it. Then another step and another, until I'm standing right in front of him.

I don't know what's happening, don't know why my heart feels like it's ricocheting around inside my chest. But the one thing I do know is that whatever it is, Hudson feels it, too.

He lifts one trembling hand toward me but stops inches from my face. I can see the indecision in his eyes, can see him wondering if he should touch me or not—if I want him to or not.

And while I don't have a clue about the first question, I've definitely got an answer to the second. Which is why I take one final shaky step toward him, closing the gap he left between us. I don't reach for him, but I do lean forward just enough that his fingertips brush against my cheek.

"My Grace," he whispers so softly that I'm not sure if I imagined it or not. Right before he cups my cheek in the palm of his hand and leans forward.

44

Even If It's Broke, Don't Fix It

I forget how to breathe, and as I stare into Hudson's shattered eyes, I'm half convinced oxygen isn't necessary anyway.

At least until Macy calls out, "I'm sorry, I'm sorry, I'm sorry," as she clomps down the stairs and to my rescue in a pair of chunky heels.

Hudson and I spring apart, and the next thing I know, there's a loud screech as he yanks the needle off the record so fast that I'm pretty sure he scratched what is fast becoming one of my favorite songs.

In the meantime, I all but throw myself onto the nearest chair—which happens to be a rolling desk chair—and end up sliding right off the other side of it and onto my ass just as Macy careens to a stop at the bottom of the stairs, a plate of cookies in her hand.

Her cheeks are flushed and her eyes wide as her gaze bounces between Hudson and me. "What'd I miss?"

"Not a thing," Flint says as he walks in right behind her, carrying a giant tray of tacos that he must have sweet-talked out of the kitchen witches. "The party just got here."

"Is that what you call it?" Hudson says as he flips through his phone and Nothing More's "Go to War" comes blasting through the speakers.

I glare at him. *Be nice*, I mouth.

He rolls his eyes but shrugs and turns the music down to a more reasonable decibel. He doesn't, however, change the song. But this is Hudson. He's only got so much compromise in him.

Flint plops the tacos down on the nearest surface—which happens to be Hudson's desk—then leans over me and asks, "What are you doing on the floor there, Grace?" even as he reaches down and pulls me straight into the air.

Normally, Flint can throw me around with abandon, but either I've turned to stone (I haven't) or something's wrong with him, because he winces as he sets me on my feet.

"What's wrong?" I ask.

He shakes his head, gives me his cockiest grin—the one that tells me something actually *is* wrong—and says, "Nothing fire-roasting a couple of vamps won't fix."

"Will any old vampire do?" Hudson asks, sounding only vaguely curious. "Or do you have a specific few in mind?"

"A very specific few," Luca says as he, Jaxon, and Mekhi walk in together. Luca heads straight to Flint, a look of concern on his face. "A bunch of the mades jumped him in the tunnels this morning."

"You too?" Macy asks as she pulls out her phone. "Does my dad know about this?"

"Yeah, I told him. Added five more people to his grounded list," Flint says glumly.

"Five? I thought there were only four of them?" Luca's gaze narrows.

"There were, but Foster took my powers, too. Said if I didn't get into any trouble between now and Friday, he'd give them back. He's afraid I'll go looking for retribution."

"Maybe I should go looking for you," Jaxon says, and his expression is seriously pissed.

"I held my own," Flint tells him. "Three of them ended up in the infirmary."

"And the fourth?" Luca asks, and for the first time since I've met him, I can sense the danger in him. Usually, he's one of the more easygoing members of the Order, but right now he's anything but. "What if he comes back?"

"The fourth has a sprained wrist and a black eye." Flint pretends to flex his muscles. "Don't worry about me. It'll take more than a few baby vamps to take down a dragon."

"Oh, right. I forgot." Macy rolls her eyes. "You're Iron Man and the Hulk all rolled into one."

"If the shoe fits." He tosses her a wink.

"If the shoe fits, you should shove it up their asses," Eden growls as she walks in with her head tilted back, a bloody cloth pressed against her nose.

"Oh my God!" Macy all but sprints across the room. "What happened?"

"I'm fine." Eden waves her off, but Macy refuses to stop fluttering around her. "More pissed at myself than anything else."

"Who did this to you?" Hudson asks, even as he escorts her over to the couch.

As I pull my first aid kit out of my backpack—again—I can't help thinking that when Heather's mom put the thing in there to ward off my panic attacks all those months ago, neither one of us ever thought it'd get this much use.

"Let me see," I order as I push my way through the wall of big male bodies currently gathered around Eden.

Macy does the same on the other side and settles herself on the couch beside the pissed-off dragon shifter. "Did the vamps come after you, too?"

Eden shakes her head. "The freaking wolves."

"What the hell is going on?" Mekhi demands. "We've been at Katmere for four years. And sure, the factions fight, and there's a power vacuum with the wolves since Cole got sent away, but we've never had this kind of violence before. Not even when…" He breaks off, looking anywhere and everywhere but at Hudson.

"Not even when I was killing off the born-vampire supremacists who planned on helping Cyrus burn down the world?" Hudson's acerbic tone cuts through the sudden quiet.

Flint tenses up, which makes Luca tense up—things have obviously progressed there more than I thought, and I smile softly.

As I watch the two of them make eyes at each other, I can't help being glad I didn't tell him what the Bloodletter did to him—what she did to all of us. It would have just messed with his head, and that wouldn't have been fair to him or to Luca. Not when they've got a good thing going now that he's finally over Jaxon. And not when he might be hurt all over again knowing that Jaxon didn't choose him this time, either, even after the fake mating bond magic wore off.

I turn back to Eden. "How's it feel?"

"I think the bleeding's stopped," Eden says as she lowers the balled-up shirt she's been holding over her nose. "What do you think?"

Macy gasps and jumps to her feet again. Eden's delicate nose is a whole different shape than it was when we had breakfast this morning, and Macy answers, "What I think is that your nose is broken. You need to go to the infirmary!"

Eden rolls her eyes. "Broken shmoken."

"I…have absolutely no idea what that means." I look from her to Macy, who just grimaces.

"It means we've got this." Flint steps forward.

"Whoa, whoa, whoa," Eden says, throwing both her hands up. "Slow your roll there, Fire Boy. You are not touching my nose."

"Damn right he isn't," I tell her, horrified. "Macy's right; I'm taking you to see Marise."

"We don't need to do anything that extreme," Eden assures me. Right before she reaches up and pops her own nose back into place.

"Oh my God!" I screech, the sound of cartilage and bone moving back still ringing in my ears as I stare at her in horror. "What did you just do?"

"She fixed her nose," Jaxon tells me calmly, but his eyes are laughing.

"I still think you need to at least see a nurse," Macy hisses at her. "What were you thinking?"

"I was thinking I wanted a taco. I'm starving." She gestures for me to clean off the cut on the bridge of her nose, but before I can, Macy holds out her hands for me to give her the kit.

She pops open the lid and grabs the small bottle of peroxide and a cotton ball. "This is going to hurt a little," she says gently.

"You don't have to worry about hurting me." Eden grins. "It's already starting to heal."

"It can't possibly—" I start, leaning over Macy's hand to look for myself.

"Shifters heal fast," Hudson reminds me quietly. He's less than a foot behind me now, and I shiver as his breath brushes against the back of my neck.

The shiver makes me feel guilty, and I glance at Jaxon out of the corner of my eye. It's one thing for Jaxon to say he's okay with Hudson and me being together and a whole other thing to watch it happen.

His face is so hard, it could be carved from granite, but he isn't looking at me anymore, so I don't think it's about us. To be honest, he isn't looking at anyone with that face, for what it's worth. Just kind of scowling into the distance. I don't know what to think.

"I don't heal fast," I whisper over my shoulder to Hudson.

His hands settle on my hips as he leans in closer and murmurs, "*Animal* shifters heal fast. You have other gifts, Grace."

His breath is warm against my ear, and he's so close now that I'm sure he can feel me trembling. I don't know what "gifts" he's referring to, but my face is burning just thinking about it.

He obviously notices, because his smile grows wicked as he teases, "You look a little flushed. Do you want me to turn the fire down?"

The jerk. He knows exactly why my cheeks are red.

Determined that two can play his game, I turn around to face him. His hands never leave my hips as I do, though, and now we're so close that we're breathing the same air. "I'm fine," I tell him with a deliberately provoking look, "but I know how sensitive you are to heat. Feel free to turn it down if you need to."

I was totally referring to the day he burned his hand in my doorway, but as his eyes turn to molten lava, it's clear he took my words to mean something else entirely.

"I'm all for seeing how much heat I can take, Grace. As long as you're the one dishing it out." A devilish grin lifts one side of his mouth and that damn elusive dimple of his appears. As it does, I'm a little shocked to realize just how much I want to lick it. To lick him. Even before his hands tighten on my hips and the last inch of space between his body and mine disappears.

My mouth turns desert dry at the first press of his body against mine. I swallow hard, lick my too-dry lips. And nearly forget how to breathe as Hudson watches the slow movement of my tongue with a predatory gaze. And just like every other time he looks at me like this—every other time he touches me like this—the rest of the room disappears. Everybody vanishes, and it feels like we're the only two people left in the world.

And as he leans closer, all I want, all I really, *really* want, is to see exactly how much heat we can both take...

"Good God, people. Get a room," Flint calls out, shattering the moment.

I only thought my face was warm earlier. Now it's practically on fire, because oh. My. God. Did I almost just climb Hudson like a tree? *In front of everyone?* I've never had Jaxon's issues with PDA, but I'm not an exhibitionist, either. At least I didn't think I was. But I'm quickly realizing that Hudson is capable of bringing out parts of me I didn't even know I had.

"We *are* in a room. *My* room in fact," Hudson tosses over my shoulder at Flint. It's a light-hearted response, but I can see his face shuttering, see him putting distance between us, as he takes in my embarrassment.

And I can't help it; I turn around, looking for Jaxon. We're not mates anymore, but almost making out with Hudson in front of him is so not fair, and I feel awful. Even before our gazes collide and I see stark, unadulterated pain in the depths of his. But then he blinks and it's gone. Replaced with the cold disinterest I'm growing to hate.

I sigh heavily, not because I want Jaxon to still be suffering at what we lost but because I can tell that with every day that passes, the Jaxon I once loved is slipping even further away—from me and from himself.

A coldness seeps into my bones, and it takes me a solid minute to realize Hudson is gone.

45

When the Going Gets Cuffed, the Cuffed Get Going

Macy finishes with Eden's nose pretty quickly, since she flat-out refuses to let her cover it up. Apparently, my unicorn bandages don't fit her badass reputation.

By the time I get my first aid kit packed back up, everyone else has drifted away toward the tacos and drinks. Turns out Hudson had darted out to grab a cooler of blood for the vamps after our *moment*, and now we all gather around the coffee table in Hudson's sitting area.

For the most part, we talk about finals and who has beaten the hell out of whom—as well as who's had the hell beaten out of them—this week. But as Macy is going over a not-so-pleasant encounter she had with a wolf this morning, Flint starts to frown, even though Macy's experience didn't end with bloodshed.

"What about you, Grace?" he asks.

"What about me?" I ask, surprised.

"Have you had any problems in the last few days?"

I shrug. "No more than usual."

"What does that mean?" Hudson asks, his voice sharp as a knife. "Is somebody messing with you?"

Everyone is staring at me now with concern—especially Hudson and Jaxon, both of whom look like they're ready to slaughter a small city or at least a moderately sized boarding school.

"No more than the usual Ludares stuff," I tell them firmly. "Some of the challenge team's still pissed, so they try to mess with me. It's no big deal."

My friends don't look convinced, especially Hudson. "Don't worry about it." I lean forward and rest a hand on his knee. "Seriously. I've got this."

"Do you really have it?" Hudson raises one brow. "Or are you just ignoring it and hoping it will go away?"

I don't know what to say to that—mostly because it's true—but thankfully, Flint saves me from having to come up with a response when he says, "Something you mentioned earlier has me thinking. You said you thought we had enough people trying to beat the hell out of us lately."

"Well, yeah." I gesture to Eden and him. "Obviously."

"So my question is this." He looks around the group. "How many of you have had someone mess with you in the last few days? It doesn't have to be as screwed up as Hudson and the wolves or what happened in the cafeteria with the vamps. It just needs to be out of the ordinary. Who else has had someone mess with them who normally wouldn't?"

I watch in shock as every single one of my friends raises their hands—and every single one, save Macy, is wearing an enchanted cuff binding their magic.

"Everybody?" I manage to choke out once they've lowered their hands again. "Everybody's been messed with?"

"Looks like it," Luca answers quietly. His hand goes to Flint's shoulder, whether for support or because he's trying to calm Flint down, I don't know. "I heard Finn mentioning that it was so bad, he was almost out of cuffs, and there's nowhere to get more."

Hudson and I exchange a look, but then I turn to Jaxon. "What happened to you?"

He shrugs. "Joaquin and Delphina thought they'd take a few potshots at me yesterday."

"Fucking lousy excuses for dragons," Flint snarls. "So what happened?"

"What do you think happened?" Jaxon shoots back. "They lost."

Hudson snorts, but he doesn't say anything to piss Jaxon off, which I appreciate. Jaxon already looks coldly furious.

Jaxon turns to Mekhi, who admits a few witches are regretting their life choices this week. He adds, "I'm fine, but you should check my man Luca out."

"What the hell?" Jaxon's voice cuts like a whip even as he skewers the Order member with a glare.

"Why didn't you tell me?" Flint asks, looking shaken.

"Because it wasn't nearly as bad as what happened to you," Luca tells him. "And I haven't seen you since the vamps got me coming out of my room."

"Vamps?" Hudson asks in a voice that's a lot more chill than Jaxon's. But the look in his eyes is anything but as he leans forward. "*Vampires* went after you?"

"Mades?" Eden asks, and even she sounds a little uneasy at this revelation. Luca shakes his head. "Borns."

"Who?" Hudson asks in a voice deadly with calm.

"Do they have a death wish?" Jaxon asks at the same time.

I watch the two of them as they grill Luca on the specifics of his attack before switching back to Mekhi and then finally to Flint and Macy, questioning every detail of what happened to them. Of what vamps did it, how they attacked, and what brought it on.

They're both regal. They're both determined. They're both focused, and they both have amazing depths of kindness if you get past the coldness of one and the sarcasm of the other. And yet, as I watch them ferret out all the details of the attacks, I can't help comparing them.

I swore I would never do that, but seeing them like this, it's impossible not to.

Both are clearly furious about what's been happening to their friends— particularly when the vampires are the aggressors—but the way they handle it is so different. Jaxon is ice-cold yet somehow looks like he's ready to burn the world to the ground. He's like a lightning strike—unexpected and thrilling but also dangerous as fuck.

Hudson, on the other hand, has a slow burn. He just kind of sits back and absorbs what's going on, looking at it from all angles. He asks very specific questions, none of which seems especially meaningful on its own. But by the time he's done, you realize he's like the sun—warm and inviting but more than capable of incinerating you with almost no effort at all.

And somehow, I've been lucky enough to be mated to both of them. Jaxon, through the machinations of the Bloodletter, and Hudson through...I don't know what. Fate? Destiny?

I just wish I knew what to do about it. I was so sure that I loved Jaxon, so sure that the boy with the tortured eyes and broken heart was everything I could ever want. But he wasn't mine to love, not really. Not when the Bloodletter controlled everything so that we would be mates.

Which is the exact opposite of how things happened with Hudson. I hated him at first. I thought he was evil and awful, and I was determined to have nothing to do with him. Then I realized the incredible depths of kindness and hurt under his prickly exterior and ended up friends with him. And now? Now I don't know what I feel, except confused as hell. That moment Flint interrupted, the look in his eyes, the way my entire body seemed to burn just from being around him?

Is that real chemistry or just the mating bond? Real emotion or just manufactured by the universe to make sure things go smoothly between mates?

As if.

"But why?" Macy complains, interrupting my thoughts with a voice loud and frustrated in a way I almost never hear from her. "What are they hoping to get by doing this?"

"That's why I asked how many of us had been hassled," Flint says quietly. "Because, like Grace said, it seems like it's happening to us more than anybody else."

"Yeah, but it also happened to Simone," Macy objects. "And Cam, and—"

"Misdirection," Hudson comments softly. "Look over here at all these things that are happening, and don't pay too much attention to this one big thing that's happening."

"Which is?" Eden asks intently.

"They're getting us out of the way," Jaxon and Flint say at the exact same time.

"Out of the way?" Luca asks, looking confused. "Of what?"

Eden appears grim as she answers, "I'm pretty sure that's the million-dollar question, isn't it?"

46

Cats Aren't the Only Ones with Nine Lives

"Who?" Mekhi demands. "Cyrus?"

"Of course Cyrus," Flint tells him. "Who else would it be?"

"Think about who's been doing the attacks. Mostly wolves and mades, with a few of the born vamps thrown in," Hudson comments.

"Don't forget the witches," Mekhi says with a glower.

"Or the dragons," Macy adds.

"Yeah, but the only witches and dragons who participated in the attacks are ones we already know are loyal to Cyrus," I say as what they're getting at finally becomes clear. "All of this has been masterminded by your father."

"Looks that way," Jaxon says, and there is absolutely no emotion in his voice as he says it.

"War is coming to Katmere—and the rest of the world. I've known it for two years," Hudson says pointedly, glancing briefly at Flint before continuing. "I think we all know it now."

My heart is pounding in my chest. "Cyrus is really planning to attack Katmere?" A thought occurs to me, and I ask Hudson, "Do you know what his plan was last year? What were those students about to do that made you"—I wave my hand—"do what you did?"

I can tell by Hudson's wide gaze that no one has bothered to ask him this before. Not the details, at least. But I want to know. And since all eyes are staring at Hudson expectantly, I'm clearly not the only one interested in his answer.

Hudson crosses his arms as he leans against the wall. "They were planning to take control of Katmere and hold the students hostage to force all the major ruling families, whose kids attend this school, to join his attack on humans." There's a collective gasp from everyone in the room, but Hudson continues. "As proof of his seriousness, he'd ordered those students to kill the firstborn of every family with more than one child at Katmere."

"My God," Luca whispers, and Flint pales. Luca has a little brother in the ninth grade, which would mean... I shudder. I can't even imagine Katmere, our friend group, without Luca in it.

I knew Katmere was an elite school for vampires, werewolves, witches, and dragons, but I had no idea every major ruling family had students here. It was a brilliant plan, honestly. How do you control powerful men and women all around the world? Threaten their children. And how easy to do so when they all happen to be in the same place at the same time.

"Your father's a real bastard," Eden growls.

"That's one way of putting it," Hudson says without an ounce of humor.

"Why didn't you tell someone? Instead of just killing them?" Flint asks, and it's hard not to realize this new information is difficult for the dragon to swallow. If true, it would mean his own brother was willing to do some pretty heinous things for Cyrus.

Hudson spears him with a hard gaze. "I did. No one believed me."

"You told Uncle Finn." It's a statement, not a question. I can see it in his gaze, the answer.

"I don't blame him. I probably wouldn't have believed me, either." He shrugs, but I can tell it bothers him. As our gazes collide, I note the stark pain swimming in his blue eyes before he quickly shutters them. And I know, as sure as I will take my next breath, Hudson is blaming himself. If he'd been a different guy, if he'd been anyone but Cyrus's kid, things might have ended differently.

"So what do we do?" Mekhi asks. "And do we think this is what's going on? Cyrus is going to try to take Katmere again?"

"I'm sorry my dad didn't believe you, Hudson," Macy says softly. "But he would listen now, and once he realizes Cyrus is behind putting his students in danger, he'll go after him—in the Circle first, and then if that doesn't work, he'll go straight to the source."

Tears fill her eyes, so she closes them and whispers, "And then Cyrus will kill him."

"We're not going to let that happen," Eden assures her.

"No way," Mekhi agrees as Flint nods along.

"We can't tell him," I say. It's the only thing that makes sense. "If we tell him, he will try to do something—all alone and without proof—and Cyrus will ensure he's removed from the chessboard. One way or another."

"You can say that, but how are we going to stop Cyrus without his help?" Macy asks. "Especially since Cyrus and Delilah are coming for graduation."

"They are?" Hudson asks sharply. "How do you know that? I haven't heard anything about it."

"They RSVP'd with Dad, as the graduation announcements requested." She spins her phone around and around in her hand. "He was unpleasantly surprised they were coming, too."

"I thought it would take that asshole longer to heal." Hudson doesn't sound pleased that it hasn't.

And suddenly I know what we have to do. The only thing we *can* do. We were already planning on finding the Crown anyway to thwart Hudson's arrest warrant—which makes even more sense why Cyrus wants the only guy who stopped him last time out of the way, but now...now the stakes are even higher. We'll need the Crown if we have any hope of saving the students at Katmere...and preventing a war. Maybe if we're lucky, Cyrus won't even make a move if he knows we have it.

I try to catch Hudson's gaze, to make sure we're on the same page with this plan, but he's staring at his phone, deep in thought.

So instead of waiting to see what he thinks, I take a deep breath and say, "We need to find the Crown before he gets here."

Hudson still doesn't meet my gaze but nods. "It's the only chance we've got."

I continue to try to get Hudson's attention as Mekhi explains to everyone else about the arrest warrant for Hudson, what the Bloodletter said about the Blacksmith, and Hudson's theory about the giants. But he won't look up. Instead, he stares silently at his phone, occasionally swiping his finger across the screen. I know he's feeling guilty right now. He killed all those students, and it didn't stop a damn thing. I can tell in the rigid way he's holding his shoulders, he's wrestling with his decisions. I briefly consider walking over to him, but if he's this uncomfortable about our *distraction* earlier, I feel like that would just make him even more uncomfortable.

Distraction. Ha. What an insignificant word to describe what happens every time we get close. It feels more like my senses are just so focused on taking in everything that is Hudson, not missing a single breath, a single twitch of his mouth, a single crinkle of his eyes, that I have no senses left to notice that we're not the only two people in the world.

"You know, that means we have to go to Giant City sooner rather than later," Luca says.

"Hell yeah." Flint grins. "Those giants really know how to party." He wraps an arm around Luca's shoulders and whispers something in his ear, and Luca blushes. Watching them makes me smile, despite all the shit that's about to come down on us. Flint deserves someone who is wild about him.

"How about Friday?" Mekhi suggests. "It's a staff workshop day, so we've got it off. I could use a break from all the studying anyway." Mekhi coughs, then adds, "I've always wanted to try the Gorbenschlam Challenge. Want to join me for one, Macy?"

"Mekhi!" Macy looks horrified, but underneath the horror, my cousin also looks...interested.

"I'll take that as a yes." Mekhi grins.

Macy groans. "Fine. But only one."

Mekhi winks at her. "I've heard that's all it takes."

And now my cousin's cheeks are positively on fire, but I notice she doesn't correct Mekhi, either. Next to her, Eden shifts her gaze between Macy and Mekhi, and I can't help but wonder if *she* was interested in Macy herself. Well, if she was, she better get to moving. Mekhi doesn't look like the type to wait around when he sees something he wants, and if the gleam in his gaze is any indication, the vampire is most definitely interested in Macy.

An awkward silence falls, so I ask to break the tension, "What's Gorbenschlam? Can I try it, too?"

Hudson looks up from his phone and arrows me with a sharp gaze. "It's only for couples, Grace."

"I thought—" I start to say I thought *we* were a couple, but then his meaning hits me in the chest, and I narrow my gaze on him, a clear message in its depths that we *will* be talking about this later.

Macy rushes in to explain. "It's a giant stein of beer that you race to see who can finish first. Loser buys the round—which is not cheap, considering I mean quite literally a *giant*-size mug. Legal drinking age in Giant City is fourteen, and they take their beer drinking very seriously." She grins at me.

"Ah, okay, well, I'm not a huge fan of beer, but I bet Eden and I could race you two," I suggest, and Eden lets out a whoop and we fist-bump. I send an arched look at Hudson, and he mouths back, *Touché.*

My shoulders sag a bit that he seems to be over his snit. I'll be the first to admit I love matching wits with Hudson. When we argue, I forget about my anxiety, about my problems, about everything. I feel alive in the moment. But this doesn't feel like one of our regular fights. This feels like a lot more is going on, and instead of freeing me from my panic attacks, a bubble of fear is growing in my belly.

"Okay, then," Flint says as he picks up a taco with his patented grin. "Let's do this thing."

47

With Enemies Like These, Who Needs Friends?

We study for a couple of hours more, but eventually we're all tired of schoolwork, and the gathering breaks up.

Hudson looks bemused as we help him clean up. And I get it. We're a little loud and a lot disorganized as we talk and move over and around one another.

For a guy who has lived such a solitary existence, this must feel like absolute chaos. But there's something in his eyes, something in the *very* slight upward tilt of his lips that tells me this is good for him. That it's past time Hudson Vega stopped being a loner and got himself a fun, loyal, and absolutely ridiculous group of friends. The fact that most of us were once his enemies doesn't matter. He's part of the group now, whether he likes it or not.

Maybe that's why I stop Flint and Luca as they start to pick up the purple chairs to carry back to the study lounge. "Leave them," I say, grinning at Hudson, who's now looking at me with wide eyes. "We've got lots to do in the next couple of weeks. I'm sure we'll be down here again."

"Good call, New Girl," Flint tells me, holding up a hand for a fist bump. "I didn't even get a chance to try out any of those sick axes over there."

"Maybe that's a good thing," Luca tells him as he herds him toward the exit. "None of us has time for an ax in the back tonight."

"Excuse you." Flint makes a face at him. "I have excellent aim, thank you very much."

"Oh yeah?" Luca wraps his arm around Flint's waist with a grin. "Maybe you could show me sometime."

Mekhi snorts at that, which makes Macy giggle as they, too, make their way toward the door. Jaxon doesn't say anything, but for just a moment, I can see amusement lurking in the depths of his eyes, too.

At least until Macy turns around and asks, "Are you coming, Grace?"

Everyone is looking at me—Jaxon and Hudson included—and my palms grow damp. I should say yes, should just walk right out of here with the rest of them, but the truth is I want to talk to Hudson. More, I want to figure out what happened between us earlier and if it means something or if it's just an aberration.

"I'll, um, I'll be up in a few minutes. I just need to talk to Hudson about something real fast."

"Is that what you kids are calling it these days?" Eden murmurs as she scoots past me, backpack over her shoulder and wide grin on her face.

She didn't say it loud enough for anyone else to hear, but as I watch them leave, I realize that doesn't matter. If my friends hadn't been thinking something was happening already, my bright-red cheeks would definitely convince them.

I glance at Jaxon as he nears, but his face is surprisingly warm. He leans down and whispers in my ear, "It's all good, Grace," before heading up the stairs. And I want to cry at what that must have cost him.

I love Jaxon. I do. He saved me when I got here, brought me out of the frozen depths of depression and numbness that had surrounded me since my parents died. I'll be grateful to him for that for the rest of my life. He was my first love. And those never go away, not really.

But then there's Hudson, who sees so much more than the weak, wounded girl I used to be. He sees who I really am and who I have the potential to be. Jaxon wanted to protect me, wanted to take care of me, but Hudson wants to help me learn how to take care of myself. And I know, if I were to give in to these mating bond feelings coursing through my body—and it doesn't work out...

Losing Jaxon was terrible, but our relationship was struggling before our bond was broken, if I'm being honest. Struggling between the girl he fell in love with and the girl I wanted to become. We hadn't known each other before we were mated, and there's a part of me that knows deep down, part of the reason I loved Jaxon with all my heart was because he loved me back just as much. We needed each other. We were both in pain, and we filled an emptiness we didn't know how to fill on our own.

But with Hudson, it will always be different. He knows me better than anyone, better than myself. And even though I can't remember those months we were trapped together, we've spent the last several weeks becoming real friends.

And that's what really terrifies me.

When Jaxon broke up with me, he walked away from only a piece of me, the piece he knew. The only piece the wounded girl I was could let him see. But if Hudson were to reject me? It wouldn't just be a piece of me—he would be rejecting *all* of me. And that...would be oh so much more devastating. That would break me in places I didn't even know I could break.

But after what happened with Hudson earlier tonight...I don't know. Suddenly, it feels like all the hiding, all the burying my head, all the pretending this isn't happening doesn't just have the ability to hurt me—but Hudson, too. Like if I don't do something soon, I'm going to destroy any chance we have, and that thought is more frightening, even, than making a decision is.

"Are you planning on just hiding out in here all night, or do you actually have something to say?" Hudson asks, and he's back in full sardonic mode.

48

Honesty Is the Most Uncomfortable Policy

Are you fucking kidding me? I'm standing here worried about trying to figure out how not to shatter us both, and he's going to come at me with that?

My nerves disappear in a second, and now I'm just pissed off. Doesn't he realize how hard it was for me to say I wanted to stay with him, to admit to what that implied, to *everyone*? And he's going to stand there and pick at me?

"Oh, you can bet I most definitely have *something* to say to you." I square my shoulders as I look him dead in the eyes. "But I don't think you deserve to hear it now."

I grab my backpack from its spot next to the couch, ignoring the tears that are burning in the backs of my eyes for no reason that I can understand. "Let me know when you're not in asshole mode, and maybe we can talk."

"Hey." I freeze as Hudson's hand rests lightly on my shoulder. "I'm sorry. That was uncalled for."

"You seem to be saying that a lot lately," I tell him with a shrug, but I still don't turn around to face him. I need a few more seconds to make sure all traces of those ridiculous tears are gone. And also I'm embarrassed—of the tears, of the situation, of my inability to deal with it properly—and now facing him feels all but impossible. "I'm just going to go."

I duck out from beneath his hand and make a beeline for the door. If I'm really fast and really lucky, maybe he'll just let me—

Or maybe he won't. I freeze when suddenly, he's right there, blocking my path. I stare at one of the holes in those too-sexy-for-my-own-good jeans and pray for the ground to open up and swallow me whole.

Is one of Jaxon's infamous earthquakes really too much to ask for in this situation? Or—and I'm just spitballing here—some giant, snow-dwelling leviathan to burrow through the stone floor in search of its next meal?

Turns out the paranormal world isn't with me here—big shock—because the jeans, and the legs they are encasing, don't move an inch. And neither does the guy they're attached to.

Because of course he doesn't. This is Hudson, and he's never made things easy for me. Maybe if he had, we wouldn't be in this situation. Milquetoast is so much easier to walk away from.

"Talk to me, Grace," he says. "You can't keep blowing hot and cold. It's not fair to either of us."

What the actual fu— "What did you just say to me?" My gaze zeroes in on his with the fury of a thousand suns. "You think *I* am the one blowing hot and cold? *Me?*" I laugh, but there isn't a sliver of humor in it. "Says the guy who flirts with me in front of everyone one second, then disappears the next. Who says he wants to see how much heat we can take, then tells *our friends* that we're not a couple."

I poke him in the chest, but he doesn't budge. Fucking vampires. But I'm just getting started. "I thought we were going to give this thing between us a chance, but you don't seem capable of deciding what you want. Do you have any idea how scared I am? And yet you don't see me pulling this shit on you!"

"No, you just keep checking Jaxon's reaction every time you touch me." His words land like a bomb at our feet.

And I roll my eyes. Hard. "Of course I'm checking Jaxon's reactions. He's innocent in all of this."

"You think I don't fucking know that? Why do you think I left to get the vamps' blood?" His jaw clenches so hard, I think he's going to crack a molar. "I love my brother more than you ever will. I *died* for him. But I'm not going to die for him again, and what you're doing to me, Grace—you're killing me slowly."

He sighs, running a hand through his hair in frustration, leaving the ends sticking up at odd angles. It should make him look ridiculous, but it just makes him seem...vulnerable. Maybe, just maybe, Hudson is as scared as I am at the intensity between us.

So I pull in a deep breath and take a chance. "Are you scared, Hudson?"

He holds my gaze so long, I'm not sure he's going to say anything. But then the weight of his answer seems to be too much for him to carry, and he sinks onto the stairs below me, his arms resting on his knees. And says with a ragged voice, "More than you'll ever know."

And now I see it. His scars.

This poor boy has had everyone he's ever loved taken from him. Why wouldn't he expect the same thing to happen with his mate? And he would let me go without a fight. I know it. If I told him I wanted Jaxon, he would sacrifice his happiness for mine. For Jaxon's.

I swallow as I realize he deserves to know that's not going to happen. On a soft breath, I tell him, "Jaxon gave us his blessing as he left tonight."

His eyebrows shoot up. "He did?"

"Yes." I nod. And because he deserves to know this, too, I add, "I only look at Jaxon after we touch because I don't want to hurt him—with my happiness."

I watch as my words sink in, watch as a slow smile gently lifts one corner of his mouth. And cocky Hudson comes back as quickly as he left as he says, "So you like it when I touch you, eh?"

I roll my eyes. "Leave it to you to only focus on that."

He grins back at me. "Hey, I can't help it if I've got game."

"It's just the mating bond, you goof," I tease, but he sobers.

"Is that what you think?"

I bite my lip. "How can I not?"

He seems to ponder my words for a moment before he stands and says, "We can take things slow, Grace. It's something to build on."

And I can't stop the tears of joy welling up in my eyes. "Thank you."

He pulls me into a hug, his large arms wrapping around my shoulders and pulling my head against his chest, and I try to ignore how good he smells up close like this.

Like sandalwood and warm ginger.

Like amber and an open flame.

Like safety, the voice deep inside me whispers.

"Want to watch the rest of *Empire Strikes Back*?" he asks.

"There's nothing I'd like to do more," I admit. Then I imagine us curled up on his huge, sexy-as-fuck red bed and add, "On the couch."

Hudson chuckles. "Of course."

But as he laces our hands together and leads me to his couch, I can't help wondering if going slow will take the pressure off...or if it will just make everything explode.

49

Bite the Big One

"So, umm...how did last night go with Hudson?" Macy asks as we pack up some things to take to Giant City with us early the next morning. "You know, if you want to help your cousin live vicariously and all."

I grab a shirt and fold it, placing it into my backpack. "Nothing happened. We watched a movie."

"Above or below the sheets?" She winks at me, and I snort-laugh.

"On the *couch*," I clarify. Although my cheeks heat as I remember how he tucked me snugly against his side, his large hand covering mine where it rested against his muscled thigh. True to his word, he didn't make a single move on me all night.

Well, until the end when we got into a fight about why Princess Leia couldn't admit she loved Han Solo until it was too late. One minute, we were just casually hanging out, and the next we were sniping at each other over a fictional character. One minute, we were in the friend zone, and the next all I could think about was ripping his clothes off and climbing with him under those oh-so-sexy sheets.

Instead, I made an excuse and hustled back to my room as fast as I could, his last taunt still echoing in my ears.

I'll be here when you change your mind.

If *I change my mind*, I shot back.

And he laughed. He actually laughed. The jerk.

I didn't run because I was scared—or at least, not just because I was scared.

I ran because if the heat in our arguments is any indication, I'm a little afraid of what we'll burn down if we actually get together.

Or maybe the better question is, what *won't* we burn down?

I don't know if I'm ready for that, don't know if I'm ready for any of this.

"You look exhausted," Macy says in a deliberately upbeat voice.

Yeah, well, that happens when you spend the night tossing and turning over relationship issues.

"Hudson just said something I didn't like at the end of the evening." I cross to my closet and reach for my black coat because it matches my mood.

But Macy is right there, taking it out of my hand and putting it back in the closet. "No brooding," she tells me. "I'm totally in that boy's corner… until he hurts you. Just say the word, and then I'll help bury the body."

"Nah, it wasn't that bad. I'm not brooding." It's a blatant lie, but apparently I'm doing a lot of that today, so what's one more?

"Oh, right. Is stewing better? Languishing? What verb would you like?"

"Ruminating," I tell her as I crack up, because it's impossible to be sad around Macy for long. Even when she's still a little sad herself. "I'm *ruminating* over the state of my affairs."

"Oh, well, ruminate away. But do it in your favorite color." She takes my hot-pink coat off the hanger and hands it to me. "It'll make you feel better."

I look from her to the coat as it occurs to me that now would be a perfect time to tell her that hot pink is very definitely not my favorite color. But she's smiling for the first time in quite a while, the prospect of this trip away from school making her happy in a way she hasn't been since Xavier. Telling her I don't like pink would be like kicking a puppy just to hear it cry. I can't do it.

Plus, the ridiculous color is growing on me. Of course, the comforter is definitely overkill, but the coat really isn't that bad.

"What time is it?" I ask as I slide the coat on, then double-check my backpack to make sure I have everything I might need. The plan is to travel down this morning and then back up tomorrow night, but I want to make sure I've brought enough work to do in case we stay until Sunday.

I mean, yeah, we're going to spend most of our time looking for the Blacksmith and, hopefully, talking to him once we find him, but still. There'll be some downtime, and I want to take advantage of it by finishing my makeup architecture project and my essay for history. If I'm lucky, Jaxon will be in a decent-enough mood to follow through on the help he offered the other day. And if he isn't, well, maybe one of my other friends could be persuaded.

"Nine fifteen," Macy answers as she pulls on her rainbow-colored jacket.

It's a change from the black she's been wearing lately, and when I raise a pleased brow at her, she just shrugs. "I think maybe I want to feel good while I ruminate, too."

Now I'm full-out grinning. "I think that sounds like a really great idea."

She nods and whispers, "Me too."

"You know, today is my mom's birthday," I say as we make our way to Macy's secret passageway—no need to tip off any of our new and unappreciated enemies that we're leaving school for a couple of days. The last thing we need is one of them clueing in that Hudson is no longer on Katmere Academy property. With how protected Giant City is with magic, we all feel fairly sure even if Cyrus discovered we were there, we'd be gone before he could marshal the Watch in the city walls anyway. Still, no sense taking a chance and advertising our adventure, either.

"Her birthday?" Macy's eyes go wide. "Oh, Grace, I'm sorry. I didn't know."

"Nothing to be sorry about," I tell her as I think of my free-spirited mother, with her love of flowers and poetry and midnight pancakes. "I mean, yeah, usually it makes me sad to think about her, but it's hard to be sad on her birthday. It was always one of my favorite days of the year."

"Really?" Macy looks charmed at the idea. "How come?"

"We always took the day off school and spent it together—you know she was a high school teacher, right?"

"I didn't remember that, no." She grins. "Was she always correcting your grammar?"

I laugh. "Not even close. She was, however, always giving me a book to read—and then making me talk about the books with her over brunch at our favorite restaurant. It was right on the water, and if it was the right time of year, we'd get to walk in the cove later and watch the seals that come up to the sand to give birth and take care of their babies."

Macy's eyes go huge. "Oh my gosh. That's amazing!"

"It was, yeah." I smile, remembering. "There was one weekend a month my dad had to work, and that was always our book brunch time. She was big on finding favorite passages to talk about—and memorize."

"That's why you're always quoting some book! I've wondered."

"Yeah, that's why."

"Hudson must love that. He's always quoting books, too."

I laugh. "Hudson is the only person I know who actually reads more than my mom did."

"No shit. And considering how long he's been alive, I'm pretty sure he's read almost everything."

"I don't know about everything, but the boy has read a lot."

We're walking down the section of the passage that has all my favorite stickers in it, and I grin as we pass one that says *Hex the Patriarchy* and another that's a crystal ball with the words *Looks Like You're Screwed* written inside it. It makes me laugh every time.

"So is that what you did on your mom's birthday? Go to brunch and talk about books?"

"It's where we started, yeah. Then we would go shopping and buy an outrageously expensive outfit just for fun. And we'd end up at home making the most fantastic birthday cake we could find. My mom was a great cook."

"Yeah, she was," Macy agrees. "Her cookies were legendary. She used to send them, even after you guys stopped visiting."

My smile fades. "I always hated that we stopped coming."

"Me too. The last time was that summer before I turned nine. Do you remember?"

"I do, yeah. We had picnics every day." I haven't thought about that summer in years.

"Every day," she says with a laugh. "With all the cookies from your mom."

"Yes." If I close my eyes, I can still smell her lemon cookies. "And your mom's tea."

Macy's smile fades. "Yeah."

"I'm sorry," I tell her as we start down a staircase to the first floor. "I didn't mean—"

"It's okay. My mom really did make the best tea blends," Macy says with a shrug. "Especially the hibiscus one."

"That was the red one, right?"

She nods.

She puts up the no-trespassing sign, and I don't ask anything else about her mom. Losing my mom was one of the worst things that ever happened to me, but I can't imagine how I would feel if she had just walked out one day. Just disappeared off the face of the earth after nine years of being Mom of the Year.

I was only ten when it happened, but I remember Uncle Finn freaking out. I remember dozens of late-night phone calls between him and my parents. My dad even flew up to Alaska for a few weeks when it happened to help my uncle talk to police. Eventually it was concluded that no foul play was involved, that Aunt Rowena had simply decided to not come home one day. Uncle Finn didn't believe it.

He'd searched for her for years, to no avail. I can't imagine what that must have been like—for him or for Macy.

I hug my cousin as we head down the passage to one of the exit doors on the first floor. She hugs me back and tells me I'm the best cousin ever. Then we push the final door open and step out into the slowly melting snow to find Hudson, Flint, Luca, Eden, Jaxon, and Mekhi already waiting on us.

"It's about time," Hudson says. They're the first words he's spoken to me since last night, and I barely keep my smile under control. Sure, they're surly and not exactly polite, but that doesn't bother me. Hudson is Hudson, after all, and I'm sure he slept about as well as I did.

"You're welcome to get there on your own," Macy says and gives him a sharp look, then walks toward the edge of the clearing, tugs open her magic bag, and pulls out her wand.

Hudson glances at me like, *what's that all about*, but I just shrug and look as innocent as I can. No need for him to know I was *ruminating* about him earlier.

Everyone stands back as Macy sets eight candles on the ground, evenly spaced in a circle around us. "Gwen helped me create a portal big enough for all of us to go at once, since she's visited Giant City before. These candles will keep this one available to us, and correct for the rotation of the Earth, too."

Macy's been practicing building portals all week with Gwen, and I am so proud of her when she creates this one on her first attempt. One minute, we're standing on a field, patches of grass visible beneath the melting snow, and the next we're sliding through the earth, the walls of the portal flying by so fast, it looks like we're inside a brilliant kaleidoscope.

I reach out with a hand and let my fingers flutter through the jeweled-tone lights, because of course Macy's portal sparkles like a rainbow. I turn to share my delight with Hudson, but he's already grinning. He knows how special this is, too.

Before I know it, the rainbows are gone, and we're standing in the middle of a forest of massive trees, sun-dappled light peeking between their branches.

Well, everyone else is standing. I'm kneeling on the mossy forest floor because apparently, I still can't figure out how to land on my feet.

Hudson helps me up as Macy grins at everyone. "Pretty kick-ass, right?"

"So kick-ass," Hudson tells her. "You made it look easy."

"Maybe it was easy," she tells him, still a little snooty because of our conversation earlier.

"Well then, that just makes you more kick-ass, doesn't it?" he counters. And she folds like a bad poker hand, because Hudson is just that charming when he wants to be.

The two of them high-five while the rest of us look around. And realize that no matter how awesome the portal is, we still have a problem.

Because there's no city—Giant or otherwise—anywhere around.

50

So Down-to-Earth

"So what do you think?" Flint asks Macy with a wide smile. "Getting any earth vibes?"

"I'm not a seismograph," she tells him with a roll of her eyes. "I can't just read the earth hundreds of miles in all directions."

"I thought that was the plan?" Luca asks, sliding a hand around Flint's waist as he joins us.

"The plan is for me to tap into the earth magic they use to keep themselves and their city hidden," she answers, rummaging in her magic pack around her waist and then inside her backpack. "Which I'm going to try to do."

"What can we do to help?" Eden asks as she comes up behind Macy.

"Stay out of my way," she says, even as she shoots Eden a grin over her shoulder. "I know it goes against the dragon superiority code, but this is one of those times when witches have to do the heavy lifting." She flexes her fingers together, like she's preparing for a workout at the gym.

"Why don't you try to help her, Grace?" Hudson says, and all eyes turn to me.

"I thought this was a witch thing," I tell him uneasily. "How can a gargoyle help?"

"Earth magic is what heals you. You probably have some kind of affinity for it."

Ugh. I hate even thinking about the day Hudson buried me alive to save my life. I know he had to do it, but it's still one of the most awful things that has ever happened to me. Maybe even the *most* awful, and I include the whole Lia human-sacrifice debacle in that. I've wanted to ask him dozens of times how he knew to do that, but I'm smart enough to know the panic attack doing so would unleash. I have enough panic attacks these days without deliberately courting another one. But that's the whole thing, isn't it? I drop my head and sigh, because no matter how much I want to deny it, Hudson's right. I have *got* to get better about dealing with conflict. And I guess there's no time like the present to start.

I turn back to Hudson, but he's not where I expect him to be. Instead, he's moved closer, and as our gazes meet, I can see the encouragement I need in his bright-blue eyes. He wants me to ask the question, needs me to trust him enough to take a leap of faith.

And he's right. I know he is. I've wanted to know the answer to this question for weeks—am I really going to let a little fear stop me from finding out more about my gargoyle? And about myself?

I take a deep breath, blow it out slowly. And ask, "So, umm... How *did* you know burying me in the earth would heal me?"

The smile on his face is enough to light up the entire forest as he answers, "I remembered reading in one of the books in the library that gargoyles were immune to all forms of elemental magic—earth, air, fire, and water. We already knew you could control water and we already knew you could channel magic, so I figured gargoyles weren't so much immune to the magic as they were able to deflect it—to channel it away from them in much the same way they could channel it into them.

"And if that was true, then you could manipulate it. You manipulated water, so why not all the other elements, too?"

I wait for my heart to start beating too fast, for my lungs to empty of air at the reminder of being buried alive. But it doesn't happen. Instead, all I can think about is finding out what else I might be able to do. "But how did you go from thinking about elemental magic in general to knowing earth magic could heal me?"

He lifts a brow even as he gives me a self-satisfied smile. "The Unkillable Beast, of course."

Macy leans against a tree as her eyebrows shoot up to her hairline. "What does *he* have to do with earth magic?"

"He was huge, remember?" Hudson glances at her before turning back to me. "He looked like he'd swallowed boulders for breakfast for the last hundred years."

"And?" Flint asks. He looks as fascinated with all this as I am.

Hudson winks at me. "Babe, if people kept coming to kill you and you couldn't run away but you *could* use earth magic, what would *you* do?"

My eyes widen, and not just because he called me babe, although that does make my heart skip a beat or two. "I'd make myself as big and badass as I possibly could."

He nods. "And use earth magic to *heal* your stone body, right? Otherwise, how is a gargoyle trapped in a stone cave *unkillable*?"

Mekhi whistles. "Being a gargoyle just got about a hundred times more badass than it already was."

"A thousand times," Macy contradicts. "Seriously, wow." She's grinning even wider than Hudson is.

Yeah, wow. Because in the middle of Hudson's explanation, something else hit me. This guy, this amazing guy knew I was afraid to ask questions, afraid of finding out something I couldn't handle. So he did it for me, just so he would have the answer when I was ready to ask.

I walk toward him, and I'm not thinking about PDA. I'm not worrying about what Mekhi or Luca will think, or even Jaxon. All I'm thinking about is Hudson as I wrap my arms around him and hold him as tightly as I can.

He hesitates for a second like he's surprised, but then his arms snake around my waist, and he hugs me back. He bends over enough to rest his cheek on my head, and I close my eyes, let his familiar ginger and sandalwood scents fill my senses and just breathe him in. It feels like coming home.

I don't know how long we stand like this, long enough for the others to drift away and give us a little privacy. Eventually, he murmurs, "You doing okay?"

I think of all the things I can answer to that question, all the feelings swimming in my eyes. Of how he pushed me to ask questions but also stood back and let me take my time to get here. Of how he knew I would eventually find a way to ask. And so—he waited for me. Like he's waiting for me now.

In the end, I say the only thing that I can. "Thank you."

He squeezes me against his chest again, crushes me against his warmth, and I know he heard everything I didn't say. He always does.

After a moment, he drops a soft kiss on the top of my head before leaning back and saying, "Not that I'm complaining about having you in my arms or anything, but if I'm not mistaken, your cousin is about to do something seriously badass. Or maim us all."

I pull away and follow where he's looking...and my eyes go wide. Holy hell. My cousin is testing the weight of four unbelievably large athames in her hand, bouncing them up and down like she's about to throw—

"Oh my God!"

51

A Cut Above the Rest

I gasp as she tosses the blades into the air as hard as she can.

We all look up in alarm, getting ready to dodge, but instead of falling back down and impaling one of us, they flatten out before arranging themselves into a kind of compass formation.

Hudson and I walk over to the clearing and marvel at the floating knives.

We wait for them to do something, anything, but for long seconds they just hang there—hilts facing inward, blades facing outward—and point to what I can only assume is north, south, east, and west.

"So what goes up *doesn't* come down?" Flint whispers loudly after the seconds stretch into first one minute and then another.

"Shhhh," Macy tells him as she lifts her wand above her head and starts swirling it around in a circle. "Gwen says the giants are constantly moving the entrance, and the entire city is protected by confusion spells so stray human hikers don't wander in. Gimme a minute to locate it."

Seconds later, the athames start to spin in a circle, too, faster and faster until they are whirling above our heads so quickly that it's nearly impossible to distinguish one from the other. Until, all of a sudden, one starts to glow so brightly that it almost looks like it's on fire.

The brighter it glows, the faster and jerkier Macy's movements become, until the other three knives drop like stones to the ground—amid yelps from the rest of us.

We barely have a chance to register what just happened before the fourth athame—which is glowing so brightly now that it's hard to look at—takes off, flying due south right into a huge clump of trees.

"Let's go!" Macy shouts excitedly.

I'm still a tiny bit shaken by the very close call I just had with an athame, but in the end I suck it up. This is what we're here for, right?

The others are already racing after Macy, so I join the chase with Hudson hot on my heels. I smile at him—then deliberately knock my shoulder into his. And because he's a vampire and more than capable of holding his own, I put just a bit of stone into it.

He shoots me an inscrutable look as he takes the hit, then speeds up a little. It makes me grin, because this is his version of my shoulder check. Hudson would never hit me even in jest, but he will challenge me. A lot.

Good thing that's the way I like it.

I increase my speed to match his, and then we're racing through the forest, getting into denser and denser populations of trees, skipping over creeks and jumping over narrow ravines.

It's more fun than I ever would have expected.

I can hear the others up ahead—Macy and Eden in the lead, with the guys right behind them. Flint is closest to us, whooping and hollering as we all wind our way through this forest that already feels a little magical, even without the giants.

We jump over another creek—this one complete with tiny frogs hopping along its banks—when Hudson cuts to the right and starts to pull ahead of me. Determined not to let him get any advantage, I use my power to channel the water and smack him right in the face with a giant ball of it—including a couple of frogs.

He looks so shocked that I crack up, then take the tiny advantage granted to me by his surprise and run for the tree cover as fast as I possibly can.

He catches up with me quickly—big surprise—but I zig when he zags and dart right when he darts left. And while there's no water for me to throw up at him this time, the move still surprises a growl out of him, which then surprises a laugh out of me.

I'm smart enough to know he's coming for me now, so I reach for the platinum string inside me. Moments later, my wings are out, and I fly straight up and over him.

I can see the others from up here, and they're still hot on the trail of the athame. It's moving fast, so Jaxon and Mekhi have moved up in front and Eden and Macy can drop back a little without worrying about losing sight of the knife. I'm at the very tops of the trees, but we're moving into denser, taller forest, so I start to fly up a little higher to get a look at the land out in front of us—and to make sure I don't hit any branches.

But before I can do much more than think about it, Hudson jumps straight through the tree branches to catch me.

I shriek a little as his arms come around me, but he just laughs and whispers, "Gotcha."

I start to laugh with him, but the sound sticks in my throat along with the breath I just took, because what started out as good-natured fun has turned into something completely different.

My wings made it impossible for him to grab me from the back, so we're face-to-face, his mouth inches from mine and the front of his body pressed flush against the front of mine as he holds on to me. It feels good, really good, to be held by him like this, especially when the look on his face says he feels the same way.

And when he leans in, adjusting his grip so that it feels more like he's holding me than simply holding on to me, heat explodes between us. My heart kicks up triple time, and whatever air I've managed to pull into my body leaves in a rush.

For a second, just a second, I think about winding myself around him, arms circling his shoulders, legs at his hips. But then I remember where we are...and who is right below us.

He smiles even as he pulls back from me and whispers, "See you on the ground."

Then he just lets go and falls straight through the treetops back to earth.

I hold my breath until I see him land safely in a crouch, before he takes off running through the trees again. I start to drop lower, planning on landing a little bit ahead of where he is so we can run together again. But then I look out over the world in front of me and am transfixed by what I see.

Trees in all directions, lush and green and majestic. It's one of the most beautiful sights I've ever seen.

I've always considered myself an ocean girl—growing up on San Diego's beautiful beaches will do that to a person—but this? This is breathtaking in a totally different way than the mountains of Alaska are.

I take a few spins, do a few loop-de-loops as I revel in the view—and that I'm not freezing my butt off for the first time in what feels like forever.

Down below me, there's lush greenery as far as the eye can see, from mossy trails to tangled undergrowth to towering pines and redwoods that have been here for centuries. We're not so far inland yet that I can't see the

Pacific Ocean to my right, but that only makes the whole experience feel more surreal.

Redwoods and the ocean and the big, beautiful sun shining so brightly over it all—after the freezing temperatures of the last several months of my life, this feels like paradise. It's still cold, of course, but not Alaskan winter cold. And that makes me feel at home for the first time in a very long time.

I totally understand why the giants picked this area in which to settle. If I had a choice, I think I'd settle here, too.

But I can't stay up here forever, no matter how tempting the view. We have a lot to accomplish and only a couple of days to do it in.

I land next to Hudson, who grins at me. "Took you long enough."

"Did you see the view up there?" I ask. "It's gorgeous."

"Yeah," he tells me softly. "It is."

There's something in his voice that tells me he's not talking about the view, and that makes me feel all kinds of things again. Instead of leaning into them the way I want to—this isn't the time or the place—I run faster. And revel in the way Hudson stays beside me the whole time.

I'm beginning to think we're going to run forever, which really isn't okay with me, no matter how good the view, when Jaxon shouts something from in front of us.

I can't hear what it is, but it sounds urgent, so we all lay on the speed. And break through the tree line just in time to see the athame embed itself into the trunk of what has to be the largest tree in the world.

52

AncesTREE

D irectly in front of us is the most beautiful grouping of sequoia redwoods that I have ever seen—and that's saying something, considering when I was ten, my parents took me to Muir Woods as part of our Northern California vacation, and I became obsessed with the redwood trees there. We ended up spending half of our ten-day vacation wandering through forests of giant sequoias and coastal redwoods, just because I couldn't get enough of them.

Because these trees we are standing in front of now are beautiful, perfect, *amazing.* All those years ago, I felt the magic in the Muir Woods redwoods. I remember standing among these majestic trees and spinning around and around, giggling with sheer joy, wildflowers of every imaginable color stretching up to tickle my outstretched arms.

I remember I never wanted to leave and begged my parents for us to stay forever.

They refused, of course—my parents' jobs and our life was in San Diego—but I still remember how bitterly disappointed I was. How I couldn't understand why they would choose not to feel this kind of magic every second of every day if they could.

But what I felt then is *nothing* compared to what I feel standing here now. The trees are all but glittering with the magic sparking off them, and I feel honored, overwhelmed, insignificant to be before them.

I walk up to the giant tree and pull the athame from its trunk, and I swear I hear it groan. I hand the knife to Macy and then lean forward and place both my hands on the tree's massive trunk. I rest my cheek against its rough bark, close my eyes, and feel the soft earth beneath my feet. I draw its magic up my body and then channel it out of my hands and straight into the tree.

Instantly, I feel an answering magic from the tree skim through my body and back out my feet and into the earth around me. An infinite loop of energy, of nature, and I'm a part of it, breathing with it and humbled by it.

After a moment, I step away from the tree and turn to face my friends. We still have to find the entrance to the city.

But they're all staring at me, jaws slack and wonderment in their eyes. Even Jaxon looks stunned.

"What—" I ask, looking around, then freeze as I realize—I'm surrounded by wildflowers where there were none a minute before, huge and tall and every imaginable color.

And the giant sequoia no longer has a gash where the athame lodged itself.

Hudson steps forward and snaps one of the flowers about three inches down its stalk, then pushes the brilliant blue flower's stem behind my ear. "You are amazing."

I duck my head as heat blooms in my cheeks, but Flint's shout of surprise snaps my head back up.

And now I'm the one standing, openmouthed in wonderment, as Giant City is finally revealed.

53

I blink several times, just to make sure my eyes aren't playing tricks on me. Because the wall of thick sequoias is gone now—as if they were just a magical wall hiding what lay beyond. And what has taken their place is... beyond description. I don't know where to look first, my gaze darting from structure to structure, some high in the trees, others almost hidden between massive tree trunks, and all of it bustling with giants.

Standing right in front of us, tucked up against the base of the first redwood, is what looks to be a guardhouse, just big enough for a giant or two.

Even more astonishing is what's going on behind the guardhouse—a busy, bustling town filled with giants, all of whom are going about their lives with absolutely no idea we exist, let alone that we are watching them.

"This is incredible," Luca whispers, walking closer to get a better view.

"Totally incredible," Macy echoes as she, too, moves closer. "And oh my gosh! There's another building!" she squeals. "It's huge, but you can barely see it because of the way it's designed. This is..."

"Magical," I tell her, stepping around Flint and Jaxon so I can see what she's seeing. "Oh, wow. It *is* huge."

The building she's talking about is hidden between three of the larger trees, so they give it incredible cover. The base of each tree has to be close to thirty feet wide, and I can't even begin to guess how tall each of them is, considering all I see when I look up is more tree.

The building, which is made from gorgeously polished wood, is probably close to fifty feet tall on its own, but it's dwarfed by the trees surrounding it on all sides.

"The design of the wood alone is incredible," Macy comments as we get closer. "How does anyone design a building to look like that?"

"I think it's kind of plain," Flint says.

"Plain? Are you kidding me?" I gasp. "It's gorgeous."

"Okay." He shrugs in an everyone's-allowed-their-own-opinion kind of way, but then I realize he's not looking at the same trees Macy and I are looking at. He's staring several feet to the left of us—which I don't understand, because there's nothing there.

"I don't think it's that big," Eden agrees with him. "It's cool the way they've done it, but—"

"Wait a minute. That's an entirely different building!" I exclaim, finally able to see what they're talking about now that I've walked closer to them.

And they're right. It is plain…and small. A little dollhouse of a building completely encapsulated by the ring of giant trees that surrounds it. They're a lot thinner—and obviously younger—than the ones I was looking at earlier, but the tiny building fits beautifully within them.

I move even closer to get a better look, then turn back to say something to Macy, only to realize that the building she and I were staring at just a few moments ago is gone. It's completely vanished.

"Oh my God." I know what's going on here. "You can't see it."

Flint looks at me like I'm very, very confused. "Sure I can. It's right there."

"No!" I grab his arm and start tugging him to where Macy is standing as I wave the others over.

"Holy shit!" Flint exclaims. "Where did that come from?"

"What do you mean?" Macy asks. "It's been here all along."

"No," Jaxon starts. "It wasn't—"

"Yes," I tell him excitedly. "It was."

I look around, trying to spot more buildings, but I can't see any others from where I'm standing. Except the giants are obviously coming in and out of somewhere, so the buildings must be here, hidden among the trees, like these two are.

"I've heard of this before," I tell them. "When I was thinking of going to UC Santa Cruz for college." It seems like a million years ago instead of months. "When we went to visit, they made a huge deal of talking about the architecture and how the whole campus is designed so that you can only see two buildings at any one time, so as not to mess with the landscape. They have redwoods, too."

And, admittedly, their architecture is a lot more utilitarian than these whimsical buildings, but the environmentalism behind the design is the same.

I'd fallen in love with the campus all those months ago, and now I've fallen in love with this Giant City just as completely.

"It's the sickest thing I've ever seen," Luca says as he paces from one edge of the clearing to the other. "Do you think the whole city's like that?"

"I would bet on it." Hudson walks a little more to the right and points out a third building none of us had noticed yet. It's a candy shop, I think, judging from the different-colored jelly beans painted on the roof. "This is all too carefully done for it to just be a whim."

"Yeah," I agree, tilting my head back as far as I can in an effort to see to the tops of the nearby trees.

"This is where the fairy tale really comes from," Hudson says, lightly resting a hand on my lower back as he, too, looks up.

"Oh my God, you're right. Not beanstalks. Redwoods."

He grins. "Exactly."

"Wait a minute." I narrow my eyes at him. "You said you didn't know that story when I mentioned it in my room."

He holds my gaze for a second, then deliberately glances away. "I looked it up afterward."

"You did? Really?"

He shrugs. "It seemed important to you."

"Not important, just…" I blow out a breath, then let it drop. Because what I want to say is that his parents suck. That it's not fair that he doesn't know something as simple as *Jack and the Beanstalk* because his parents are selfish assholes who probably never read him a bedtime story in his life. That tutors are great for the brain but maybe not so great for everything else.

Between Cyrus trying to get him to use his power to destroy his enemies and Delilah ignoring him unless she needed him to be an accessory, Hudson's childhood was a nightmare. He never uses it as an excuse, though. Never even talks about it at all, unless I ask him a direct question. But he thought the story meant something to me, so he made the time to read it.

I don't know what I'm supposed to do with that, except lean in to his side and lace our fingers together as I whisper, "Thank you."

At first he seems startled, and I think he's going to pull away. But then he sighs, and I feel his body relaxing—slowly, slowly, slowly—against mine. "You're welcome," he tells me, and his accent is super pronounced. "Now if only we can figure out why those pesky magic beans got added to the story."

"Only one way to find out," I say with a laugh.

He lifts a brow. "And how is that exactly?"

I look around at my friends, all of whom look as in awe of this city as I am. "We ask someone," I answer as I tug his hand and head straight for the guardhouse.

54

Knock-Knock,
Who's There?

"I thought they couldn't see us," Eden says as she follows close on my heels.

"Seems like a terrible defense, that we can see them and they can't see us," Flint adds, and I have to admit that I agree.

We approach the guardhouse gingerly, not because we're afraid so much as because we don't want to startle the guards.

Except as we move to walk up to the guardhouse's front window, it becomes apparent that they absolutely know we're here, even if they haven't said anything to us before now. The massive slingshot one of them has aimed directly at us—loaded with a boulder almost as big as I am—says that much. As does the sword the other has drawn.

"Who are you?" one of them demands in a voice so loud, it shakes the ground around us.

He's much taller (like five feet taller) and larger than Mr. Damasen—they both are—and has a bushy brown beard; a wide, burly chest covered by a black uniform shirt; and the most suspicious blue eyes I have ever run across—which is saying something, considering I'm mated to Hudson Vega. Suspicion is basically his first, last, and middle name.

"What is your business at the Firmament?" asks the second, who is smaller than the first but only by a little, which is to say that he only towers over me by about six feet.

He's also younger-looking, though I don't know if it's because he's actually younger or if it's because he doesn't have a beard covering two thirds of his face. His eyes are the same strange gold as Mr. Damasen's, but he wears his dark-blond hair pulled back in a man bun, and black tattoos decorate his forearms below the rolled-up sleeves of his uniform.

He's no less dangerous-looking, though, thanks to the giant saber he has braced over his shoulder.

"The Firmament?" I ask. "Is that the name of your city?"

His eyes narrow dangerously. "State your business with us or be on your way."

"We have no official business—"

"Then hit the forest," says the bearded one. "We have no use for a band of lost Lilliputians, even if you be a wee bit magical."

My eyes widen at the familiar term for the tiny, arrogant people in *Gulliver's Travels*.

"You know what we are?" Eden asks, her own face as suspicious as the giants'.

"I can smell ye, can't I?" interjects the blond one. "Now go, before we decide to call pest control to exterminate ye."

All right, so maybe walking right up and trying to talk to them without a cover story in place wasn't a great plan, but to be fair, what kind of cover story were we supposed to come up with?

We were lost and our magic just happened to expose your city?

We want to join the Firmament?

We fell down a rabbit hole with four vampires, two dragons, a witch, and a gargoyle? Sounds like the start to a very bad joke.

"We don't plan to stay long," Macy says sweetly. "We're looking for someone, and we were hoping one of you might be able to help us out."

"You want to find a giant?" Brown Beard says. "I don't think so. Now walk away, or I'll *make* you walk away."

I can feel Flint tensing next to me, can sense the way Jaxon is shifting his weight onto the balls of his feet, and I'm really worried this is about to go south fast. And then we'll be totally screwed, as this lead, unhelpful as it appears, is the only one we've currently got.

I'm pretty sure Hudson feels the same way, because he shifts so that he's directly in front of both Jaxon and Flint, even as he says, "Actually, we were trying to keep a low profile, as we're traveling in such a small group, but several of us are representatives from the Indigo Circle." He gestures to Flint, Jaxon, and myself. "Four of us are members of the ruling families, and we were hoping to pay our respects to the Colossor and Colossa while we are in the area."

If possible, Brown Beard's eyes narrow even more. "We weren't informed of any royal visit."

"It was an impromptu trip," I jump in hastily. "But when we found ourselves on your borders, it felt churlish not to stop and pay our respects to your own ruling family."

Mekhi chokes a little bit at my use of "churlish"—and yes, I admit it's a bit historical and over-the-top—but everything about these guys screams over-the-top. I feel like leaning into it is the way to go. And if it's not...well, they weren't going to let us in anyway, so no harm, no foul.

Both of the giants continue to look suspicious, but they also look concerned now, like they're afraid of the consequences of turning away members of other paranormal royal families without at least a consult with someone on their rulers' staffs.

Talk about a good call on Hudson's part. Using royal credentials to get in when we're actually here in search of a way to bring *down* the vampire king is more than a little ironic, but who am I to judge? At this point, I'm very much a whatever-works/any-port-in-a-storm kind of girl.

Besides, it's not like we're lying. We are who we say we are, and we mean absolutely no harm to the giants or anyone else...well, besides Cyrus.

And maybe Cole, the jerk. I wouldn't mind hurting him a little.

After demanding our names, Blond Man Bun orders us to "Wait right here," as he and Brown Beard move to the back of the guardhouse to try to decide what to do with us. The funny part is that they try to whisper, but their voice boxes aren't exactly cut out for that, so we hear everything they say—including the part about throwing us in the oubliette if they have to.

I have no idea what an oubliette is, but judging from the delight on their faces when they say it, I can't help thinking it has something to do with a jail cell...or worse, a dungeon. Which is not how I was hoping this would go.

To be fair, I never anticipated that there would be a guardhouse at all. I'm not sure what I thought, but whatever it was, it focused on convincing people to talk to us rather than trying to avoid a dungeon—excuse me, an oubliette—in our first ten minutes in the city.

We wait as phone calls are made, another discussion is had, more phone calls are made. The others are getting impatient—which doesn't exactly surprise me in regards to Flint or Eden, because if Katmere has taught me anything, it's that dragons shoot fire first and ask questions later.

But even Mekhi, Luca, and Macy are looking like they want to make a break for it. Jaxon looks ready to level the entire city at the first inkling of a threat. Only Hudson and I seem to be out for a casual stroll as we wait.

Eventually, the guards come back to us, and they don't look happy—though I'm not sure what we've done to set them off this time other than simply existing. Not that I'm about to ask.

"We haven't been able to get ahold of the Colossor or Colossa," Brown Beard tells us with a frown, "and their advisers aren't willing to let an unknown paranormal into the Firmament without strict permission."

"Unknown paranormal?" Hudson asks. "We've already identified ourselves—"

"You said you were from the Indigo Circle. That means dragons, wolves, vampires, and witches," Blond Man Bun interjects. "But she"—he glares at me—"is none of those things. So until we know what she is and have permission for her to enter, the whole group of you stays right here."

He starts to shut the window before his words even register, but as a few of us try to get a hand in to hold up the window closing and convince him to change his mind, I hear a tinkling laugh.

And turn to see one of the most gorgeous girls I have ever seen walking toward us. That she is also nearly twelve feet tall despite only being twelve or thirteen years old only makes her beauty more obvious and her excitement inescapable.

55

Forged in Fire

"Oh my gosh, it's true! Vampires here, at the Firmament! I couldn't believe it when Rygor told me." She holds out her enormous hands to us. "Come in, come in! It's been so long since we've had visitors. I can't wait to talk to all of you."

"Cala Erym." Brown Beard drops into a deep bow. "I'm sorry, but I don't think it's safe for you to meet with these people. They haven't been cleared by your parents—"

"Give me a break, Baldwin." She rolls her bright-purple eyes at him even as her sleek black ponytail shakes back and forth. "I don't think the Vampire Court is here to assassinate us. And if they were, they wouldn't announce their presence by showing up at the guardhouse first."

She turns to us. "I'm Erym, cala of the Giant Court. Welcome to our home."

"Thank you." Hudson steps forward with a practiced smile that is as unexpected as it is impressive and introduces himself. This is Hudson the diplomat, I realize as I watch him chat easily with Erym. This is the vampire raised at court who I've heard about but who I've never really seen before.

Flint steps forward, too, and does a half bow that is both rakish and charming as he takes Erym's hand, which is about twice the size of his. "I'm Flint Montgomery, first prince of the Dragon Court. It's good to meet you, Cala Erym."

She giggles, then gives him a half-curtsy back. "It's good to meet you, too, Prince Flint. Dragons have always been my favorite."

"And giants have always been mine," he answers with a wink.

She giggles again, maybe even blushes a little, and Luca chuckles behind me. I glance at him to see what he thinks is so funny, but he's smiling indulgently at Flint. When he catches me looking at him, he gives me a tiny eye roll and a shrug. It's totally his *Isn't Flint the most adorable thing in the entire world* look, and he's so right that I can't help grinning back at him.

After Flint is done charming Erym, Jaxon moves forward and introduces himself to her as well. He's not flirtatious like Flint or smooth like Hudson, but that doesn't seem to matter to Erym, whose eyes light up the second his palm touches hers.

Behind me, Mekhi snickers just a little, because it's so obvious that she's about to have a giant-size crush on Jaxon, and I elbow him softly in the ribs. Partly because it's rude and partly because I know exactly how Erym feels. It wasn't that long ago that I was falling for Jaxon nearly as fast.

Erym greets the others with a gracious smile, but when I step forward to introduce myself, she claps enthusiastically. "Oh my gosh! You're the gargoyle we've all heard so much about! Welcome, Grace! Welcome!"

And then she picks me up like I'm a rag doll and gives me a giant-size hug.

"It's so exciting to finally meet you!" she says, even as she shakes me around like I'm a favorite pet. "And to think you're really here, at the Firmament! I can't wait to introduce you to Xeno! He's always trying to leave because he says nothing exciting ever happens here, but look—" She gently sets me back down on the ground. "Look at all the fascinating people who have come to see us!"

I'm a little overwhelmed from having just been picked up and patted on the head like a puppy, but she's so sweetly innocent that it's impossible for me to be annoyed with her. A quick look around tells me everyone else is having the exact same reaction.

"Well, come on!" she says, waving an arm for us to follow her as she starts half walking, half skipping back into town. "I can't wait to show you *everything*!"

Blond Man Bun moves in to try to stop her one last time, but she just waves him away with a, "Stop worrying, Vikra! We'll be fine." She looks over at us. "Right, guys?"

We all nod enthusiastically, because what else are we supposed to do? Also, it's pretty obvious none of us wants to disappoint her.

"What do you want to see first?" she asks as she starts leading us through the center of town.

"Whatever you'd like to show us," Flint answers. "We've never been to the Firmament before, but it looks absolutely amazing."

She shrugs. "I don't know about amazing, but there are a bunch of fun things to do. And I instructed Rygor to prepare a banquet in your honor for tonight. Mama and Papa will be home by then, and they will be as excited to meet you as I am."

"Is there a hotel or an inn we can check into for the night?" Hudson asks as we wind our way through several small groupings of trees, each with some kind of house or building secure inside it.

"You don't actually think I'm going to let you stay in a hotel, do you, silly?" She gives him a light pat on the shoulder that nearly sends him flying. "You'll stay with us, of course."

"We wouldn't want to impose," Flint tries, but Erym just shakes her head.

"It's no imposition. We have plenty of room." She rubs her hands together. "Now, what do you say I give you a tour of the Firmament, and we can all have some fun along the way?"

It's not quite the investigation we had in mind for our first day here, but her enthusiasm is infectious. Besides, when will we ever have another chance to explore a city made by giants?

"I say, what's first? I've heard your Gorbenschlam Challenge is an experience not to be missed," Mekhi tells her with a grin, then winks at Macy.

"That's the spirit!" She holds up a hand for a fist bump, and Mekhi doesn't leave her hanging. But he does brace himself first—a lot—and she still manages to push him back a foot or three.

I can't help laughing, because walking through this beautiful city with Erym, surrounded by my friends and the most magical trees in existence, is the most fun I've had in a very long time. After months of feeling scared and sad and sometimes even downright awful, it's like I can finally breathe again.

Everywhere we go, giants stop to stare at us. Some are bold enough to come up and ask Cala Erym to introduce them, while others just watch or wave from afar. It feels strange being the center of attention like this, but then I try to imagine what it would be like at Katmere if eight giants just started walking through the halls. I'm pretty sure there would be a lot of staring then as well.

One of the first things I notice is that there are no vehicles of any sort in the Firmament. Everyone gets around on foot or on giant tricycles that are definitely bigger than we are. It seems odd that there is no other transportation here, but area wise, it's really not that big of a town, since they make the best use of the vertical space as well. Besides, when you're between ten and twenty feet tall, I'm guessing you can walk pretty fast when you want to.

"Let's go this way!" Erym says as she herds us around a redwood with a base that has to have a circumference of close to ninety feet. The thing is massive, and unlike so many of the other trees, it doesn't have a building nestled between it and some of the surrounding trees. Instead, down near the bottom, the trunk has been partially hollowed out so that people can actually walk straight inside the tree.

Above the twenty-foot triangular-shaped door is a sign that reads, GIANT CAULDRONS.

"Oh my God!" Macy shouts as understanding dawns. "All this time, I thought they were called 'giant cauldrons' because they're so huge! Seriously, you can easily fit three people into some of the bigger ones. But really they're *giant* cauldrons?" Macy asks, her voice dripping in awe as she moves closer to the tree door. "You make *witch's cauldrons*?"

"Of course." Erym grins indulgently. "Giants are the best metalworkers in the world because we can easily manipulate earth magic into everything we create. Come on. I'll see if I can talk Sumna into letting you observe the process."

She says the last part extra loud, even as she bats her big purple eyes at the older woman behind the very high counter near the entrance to the tree. She's got long brown hair, which she wears in a single braid down her back, and though her face is serious, her bright mocha-colored eyes are awash with mischief as she winks at Erym.

"Are you sure you want to give away all our secrets?" she asks, but she smiles at Erym before moving over to an area about thirty feet behind her where an easily ten-foot giant is working at a massive wooden bench. Behind him is a roaring fire in a pot-bellied stove. So strange that we couldn't feel the fire until we got closer, but I suppose if you're going to build a fire *inside* a tree, you need to protect it with serious magic.

His beefy hands are encased in orange leather gloves, his face covered by an apparatus similar to a welder's mask. Large metal tongs are clipped onto the side of a metal bowl, and he uses them to turn the bowl this way and that as he presses a long metal rod with a bright-orange metal ball on the end along the inside of the bowl, only pausing every few minutes to drop the cooled ball into the fire to reheat it before starting again.

The whole process doesn't look anything more special than how I'd imagine you'd make a cauldron, if I'd ever bothered to consider it before today, that is. But then the giant places the long metal rod with the ball back into the fire, lifts his mask, and then leans forward and whispers along the side of the cauldron, slowly turning it into his breath.

Runes of various shapes and sizes start to appear all over the outside of the cauldron, everywhere his breath meets the cooling metal. They flame a bright orange like the fire before fading to red and eventually disappear into the black metal as they cool.

"Are those magical runes?" Macy all but squeals, her eyes glued to the fading symbols.

"They are indeed," Sumna tells her, and this time she doesn't even bother to hide her smile. "Each cauldron is blessed with a special type of magic, depending on what the blacksmith's purpose in each creation is. Some cauldrons are meant to create healing spells, others to bring harmony and balance, and there are even those for war."

"I'd heard that, but I had no idea this is how you did it!" Macy grins at me. "My dad is going to *die* that I got to see how our cauldron was made."

A quick look at Flint and Eden and the vampires tells me they are just as fascinated by the entire process as Macy.

Macy's eyebrows hit her hairline as she gasps. "Does this mean each blacksmith has their own talent, their own spells, and that's what an Amweldonlis Cauldron is—it was made by the giant named Amweldonlis?"

Sumna's smile is as big as her face now. "Close. The first part is the blacksmith's name and the second is the name of the tree it was crafted within. An Amweldonlis Cauldron was made by Amweld in the Onlis tree."

She points to one of the giant redwoods not far from her shop. "Like, that's the Falgron tree. It helps infuse spells with strength and goodness. Which is why it's my favorite tree." She smiles at Macy. "And that is why the cauldron your family uses is a Sumnafalgron."

Macy's mouth drops open "How did you—"

"I know where all my cauldrons go, sweetheart. They are very near and dear to my heart, and I want to ensure they have a happy home. Your father is a very good man. I was honored for him to use one of my cauldrons."

"I can't—" Macy's voice breaks, and tears bloom in her eyes.

Eden wraps an arm around her and whispers, "Coolest thing ever, huh?"

My cousin nods. "The coolest."

"You see," Sumna continues, "the trees in the Firmament speak to us. They offer us their magic, to build our houses and our shops. We always use them for making our cauldrons, or really any of our metalwork. The tree's own magic where the metal was crafted brings something special to the item as well as the blacksmith. In fact, the tree's magic is so important, blacksmiths have been known to seek out a specific tree for a particular commission."

She puts a hand to one side of her mouth and leans toward us, as though she's about to share a trade secret she doesn't want anyone else to overhear. "I'm especially partial to jewelry made within the Manwa tree." Her eyes are positively twinkling now. "That tree is known to give the wearer a special glamour of beauty."

Macy glances at Eden with an awed look on her face, motions with one hand that her mind is blown, and Eden laughs.

And I have to say, it's all really, really cool. I'm so intrigued, I'd forgotten why we came until Hudson nudges me with his elbow. Sumna is suggesting Erym take the group over to another giant just starting his cauldron process, a hunk of metal six feet tall resting on his workbench.

Sumna starts to head back to her position at the front of the tree, and Hudson follows her.

"Excuse me, Sumna?" Hudson calls out, smooth as butter, and she stops and turns with a smile. "I'm sorry to bother you. But I was wondering if you have a blacksmith in town who makes magical cuffs?"

Sumna winks at him. "Honey, half the city are blacksmiths. And all of them dabble in crafting jewelry as well as cauldrons. What are you in need of?"

My stomach sinks. We'd just assumed the Blacksmith was his name, like with a capital B. How foolish I feel now as I realize that's not his name at all; it's just his profession. The Bloodletter told us to find the blacksmith who made the cuff—not *the Blacksmith*.

I turn to Hudson, my eyes asking how in the world we can find a man whose name we don't know in a city where half its inhabitants are similarly employed. He just winks at me and turns back to Sumna.

"Can you help me out, then? There's this girl I want to impress, but I kind of screwed up," he lies smoothly. "I got into some trouble at school, and now I'm grounded for a few weeks." He lifts his wrist to show her his cuff. "But if I don't get this cuff off, I'm not going to stand a chance. How can I convince her I'm the guy for her if I'm just a regular old vamp?"

Sumna studies the cuff for a second, then shakes her head and frowns. "I'm so sorry, son, but the blacksmith who made these original cuffs hasn't been seen in centuries."

Which is the last thing any of us wants to hear.

56

A Giant Little Crush

My shoulders sag. How are we ever going to free the Unkillable Beast and find the Crown without the right blacksmith? And if we don't find the Crown, how are we going to save Hudson from prison? Stop Cyrus from attacking Katmere?

But Hudson is determined. He turns up the charm and gives the giant a wink. "Now, come on, Sumna. I really love this girl. There's gotta be something I can do, someone who can help me."

Sumna holds his gaze for a beat before she chuckles. "Oh, I remember young love. So foolhardy and exciting." She pauses to look around for the others at the opposite end of the factory, then leans in to Hudson and whispers conspiratorially, "I hear his wife still does some repairs on his old work. She might be willing to help you. Maybe. She's not been the same since her husband left, but she's got a soft spot for young love. If she's working, it'll be in the Soli tree."

Hudson positively beams at her. "I won't forget this, Sumna! If you're ever in the Vampire Court, I'd be honored to show you around."

The older woman blushes like a schoolgirl as she swats him away. "Oh, you are a handful, aren't you?" Her eyes turn to mine. "Is this your girl?"

Hudson doesn't hesitate. "Yes, ma'am."

She studies me, her eyes going wide for a second before the brown orbs twinkle devilishly. "Yes, I can see why you want to impress this young lady. She's positively radiant with magic. It'll take a lot for you to keep up with her."

"You have no idea," Hudson agrees, his steady gaze holding mine. "But I'll spend the rest of my life trying."

Is this just part of his act, I wonder, or does he really mean what he's saying? It's probably the former, but that doesn't stop the heat from warming my cheeks or my heart from pounding fast and hard in my chest.

"I think he does pretty well," I tell her. "I'm still getting a handle on my gargoyle magic."

And then the old woman does something completely startling. She sniffs me. "Yes, I definitely smell the gargoyle in you, but…" She sniffs again. "I was referring to something else. Something much more ancient. What were your parents?"

I'm so surprised by her question, I answer without thinking. "My father was a warlock, but my mother was just a human."

Her eyes narrow. "Hmm. Was she now?" A few seconds pass, but then her features soften again, and she laughs. "Look at me, being fanciful. Now, go on, you two, get that cuff off, and don't do anything I wouldn't do."

She's still laughing to herself about that last comment as she walks away, and I stare at Hudson and mouth, *What the hell?*

He shrugs. "Giants."

I want to ask him what he thinks she meant, but Erym and the rest of our group are done with the other demonstration and join us again.

"Come on, you guys. I have so much more to show you." Erym ushers us around a corner and down a quiet street filled with little clumps of trees, each with its very own house inside it.

The Firmament's suburbs? I wonder as she rushes us past. *Or downtown condos?*

"You came on the best day of the week," she explains as we turn another corner, this time onto a street that's got a lot more buzz going on as people move back and forth between shops, carrying bags of everything from bread to books. "It's Market Day!"

"Market Day?" Eden asks as we wind our way down the lightly crowded street. "Do you mean like a farmers' market?"

When Erym gives her a blank look, she clarifies, "A market where you can get fresh food?"

"It's a market where you can get anything and everything," Erym answers as she herds us around one more corner.

And as I look at the gorgeous, colorful melee spilling out in all directions in front of us, I can't help but think that she's right. This market has everything.

We're obviously in the town square, or the closest thing to it that the Firmament has. Though a large, square-like area is outlined in redwoods, the whole center is completely clear. It's the most land I've seen without trees since we arrived in this area several hours ago, and it's filled to the brim with huge, colorful tents in shades of red, blue, and green.

Giants are wandering from tent to tent, large canvas bags in their hands as they scoop up one treasure or another. The air is redolent with the scents of fresh bread and beer and flowers, and it should be a nauseating combination, but it actually smells really good. Especially when you add the scent of buttered popcorn currently floating through the air and overlaying everything.

As we get closer, I can see inside the tents and what they're selling—everything from the aforementioned flowers to bubble bath to shoes I could hide in to cupcakes the size of a giant's fist (which in our world would simply be called triple-layer cakes). Artists and artisans are hawking their wares—paintings the size of my bedroom wall, gorgeous wooden furniture so tall that I can't see the tops of some of it, necklaces that look like belts.

It's the most fantastic thing I've ever seen.

My parents and I used to wander through craft fairs and farmers' markets all the time in San Diego, but none of them was this spectacular. And none of them had a party vibe like this one, with food that smells so amazing, my mouth is actually watering.

"Where do you want to start?" Macy asks, and she looks as excited as I feel.

But Hudson quickly jumps in. "Erym, do you know where I could find the Soli tree? I hear the blacksmiths there make the best jewelry."

Erym claps her hands. "Oh, they do, although you better be sure you really love your girl before you buy something for her there." She tosses me a wink. "The Soli tree lends immortal magic to its creations. Jewelry from this tree is the most sought-after in the whole world."

I swallow the lump in my throat that forms at the word "immortal." Would the tree's immortality make the beast's cuffs unbreakable? Hudson seems unfazed by this news and reaches down to hold my hand, tossing me a wicked grin before replying, "Oh, I think this one might be a keeper."

The giant laughs and gives Hudson directions to the tree, which is at the other end of the market area. Hudson nods and catches Jaxon's eye, some sort of silent communication passing between the two of them. They must reach an agreement, though, because Jaxon coughs and turns to Erym.

"I think perhaps we should split up," Jaxon suggests. "It'll help us get through more booths quicker."

Erym squeals and says, "That's a great idea!" She grabs on to Jaxon's hand. "*You* come with me. We'll meet the others back here in two hours."

She doesn't even wait to see if we agree with her suggestion, just starts hustling him toward the nearest tent. Jaxon, in the meantime, is throwing out every kind of *help me* vibe and expression he can, but I just smile and wave. Maybe we should be ashamed of ourselves—it's obvious that Erym has a gigantic crush on him—but the truth is, the panic on his face is the most emotion I've seen from him in days. Negotiating her hero worship without hurting her feelings will be good for him.

The others must feel the same way, because they don't make a move to help him, either. Except Macy who, when Jaxon gives us what can only be called a pleading expression, finally gives in. "I'll go with them," she says on a sigh. "Jaxon looks like he needs all the help he can get."

"That's the whole point," Mekhi tells her with a grin, but she just rolls her eyes and heads after them, shouting for the lovebirds to "hold on."

The rest of us divide up, too. Flint goes with Luca (of course), while Eden and Mekhi wander off to look at a display of giant weapons in a nearby tent. Which leaves Hudson and me.

"Shall we go find this Soli tree?" he asks, brows raised, when I just kind of stand on the grass staring at him instead of following the others.

My stomach flips a little at the British in his voice—I've learned that the heavier his accent, the more he's feeling, even if his blue eyes don't show any of it—and I have to clear my throat before answering, "Yeah, let's go."

For a second, I think Hudson is going to say something else, but in the end, he just nods and starts off in the direction Erym gave us. He doesn't move to release my hand and neither do I, so I have no choice but to keep up with him. He's leading and I don't mind following this time, as it gives me a chance to take in all the sights and sounds and smells spilling from the different tents without having to pay attention to where we're going.

I know we're in the middle of a forest, but something about this place reminds me of the boardwalk back at home on Saturday afternoons. People in whatever clothes they feel comfortable in, spilling out of stores loaded down with food and packages, laughing and talking and having a great time. It's colorful and beautiful and so fun that for a second, a jolt of homesickness rocks me to my core.

But then a little girl runs by in a flower crown, laughing as her parents chase after her, and the sadness passes as suddenly as it came.

I start looking inside all the tents and am so enthralled by one filled with beautiful leather belts and purses that I don't even realize Hudson has stopped walking until I run right into him. His hand goes around my waist to keep me from stumbling as he grins down at me. "Hey, you."

I blink. "Hey." I'm actually a little surprised I managed to get that word out, since my body is trembling so hard, pressed up against his, my gaze drowning in his deep-blue one.

He raises one brow as if to ask what's up, then adds, "We're here."

"Oh!" I push out of his arms as embarrassment swamps me and I glance around, looking everywhere but at him. He just laughs a little and presses a hand to the small of my back as he guides me to a giant redwood on the outskirts of the market, a huge wooden sign hanging from a branch that proudly proclaims: SOLI TREE.

57

When I Asked for a Ring, I Just Meant on the Phone

Hudson and I exchange a look as we push open the door and walk into a massive space. More than half the tree is a jewelry store filled with huge glassed cases with rows and rows of all different kinds of jewelry. Rings, bracelets, earrings, and yes, even cuffs.

The other half of the space is taken up by various giants working at tables, magical kilns running around the edges of the room. My heart is pounding at the thought that the blacksmith's wife might be one of the giants working at a table right now.

"These are beautiful," I tell the girl behind the first counter as I pause to investigate a display case of rings in human sizes.

"Thank you!" she answers, and though she's a few years older than Erym—and probably even me—her smile is just as open and friendly. "I have fun making them."

"I would, too," I tell her as I linger over one that's a flat silver band with delicate symbols etched all the way around. Something about the symbols feels like it's calling to me, and I have to fight the urge to beg to try it on. "They're amazing."

Hudson is walking the aisles, too, but he's more focused on the cases in the back with large bracelets and wrist cuffs. Most are too small to be made by the same blacksmith we're seeking, but they're certainly a good direction to start. "These are really cool," he tells the jeweler, whose name tag identifies her as Olya. "Who makes these?"

"One of the women in town," Olya answers. "She's super talented and can do the most amazing things with any metal she touches."

"Really?" He appears fascinated with a large cuff bracelet, symbols almost dancing around its edges, and my breath catches. The way the runes are etched looks very similar to the ones on the cuff around the beast's ankle.

"Does she take commissions?"

"I don't think so." Olya's face clouds over for a couple of brief seconds. "She doesn't like to deal with people very much—especially strangers. She's been very sad since losing her husband, and we're all just a bit protective of her."

"Are you sure?" Hudson asks, and he's doing an incredible job of pretending to be fascinated with that bracelet. "Because this is—"

He stops as I grab his hand and press gently in an effort to get him to back off a little. Olya has started to look uncomfortable, and we don't want to raise any red flags that will get people to clam up or, worse, tell Erym's parents about our agenda, which is growing more obvious by the second.

Hudson must get the message, because he stops pushing at her about the jewelry maker and instead comments on the ring I'd been admiring near the front of the shop.

Olya's smile comes back right away as she regales him with the names of all the different runes etched into the silver. Satisfied that Hudson isn't going to push too hard, I start to pull my hand from his, but instead he threads our fingers more tightly together, and that stolen moment above the treetops a few hours ago comes rushing back, his arms wrapped around me, his face inches from mine, his voice dark and a little flirtatious as he whispered, "Gotcha."

A thousand butterflies take flight in my stomach, and I pretend to focus on the ring and not our joined hands, oohing and aahing over it, though only vaguely paying attention to the explanation about the various runes and what they mean.

"Would you like to try it on?" she eventually asks.

"Oh, I would love to," I tell her honestly. "But I don't have any money." It's not strictly true—I have a couple hundred dollars in my backpack, but that's American money. I have no idea what giants use.

"I do," Hudson says, reaching into his pocket and pulling out a gold coin with a tree stamped on it.

Olya's smile beams at the potential sale. "I've never met a vampire or a gargoyle before." She turns back to the ring. "Besides, I can already tell, the ring has chosen you."

My eyebrows shoot up, and I turn to ask Hudson what she means, but he is full-on grinning at me. The little dimple in his cheek I so rarely see melts my heart, and I am powerless to resist him. I place the hand not caught in his death grip onto his chest, and my whole body melts into his with a sigh. I study his eyes, fascinated as his pupils grow so large that they swallow almost his entire iris, so that I can only see a rim of stormy blue along the edges. His lips are moving, but the words sound like I'm underwater. And that's when I realize I must have drowned in the endless depths of his oceanic eyes. It seems like a fitting way to die.

Olya pulls the case out of the display, but Hudson beats her to the punch, lifting our joined hands and slipping the ring gently on my finger as he murmurs something on a soft breath. His fingers brush against mine, sending shivers through my whole body as my breath catches in my throat.

Even Olya must sense what's passing between us because she sniffles and says, "That was beautiful."

It's just the mating bond, I tell myself as I clear my throat and try to find the breath I somehow lost. That's what's making me feel all these weird things toward Hudson. Just the mating bond.

My finger starts to itch, and I glance down as the tiny runes burn a bright orange for a second before fading back to their previous silver etchings.

My gaze searches out Hudson's again, and he says simply, "My gift to you, Grace."

Hudson bought me a ring? Why? What does this mean? My heart starts to pound in my chest as I become aware of where we are again, like waking up from a cozy nap.

Oh my God. I let Hudson buy me a ring.

He narrows his eyes on me and sighs. "You're about to make a thing about this, aren't you?"

I sputter. "Well, o-of course. You can't just go around buying people magical rings!"

"Well, she found her voice again." He winks at Olya. "I know, honey, what you really wanted was one of those cuffs over there." He dips his head toward the thick bracelets at the back of the store he'd been looking at before.

I want to argue, but he's staring at me hard, and realization dawns on me. "Yes, *honey*, you know I wanted a cuff today." I effect my best imitation of a spoiled girl pouting. "Pleeease?"

Like he's used to my tantrums, he turns pleading eyes on Olya. "If you care about my happiness at all, you will let my mate try on one of those amazing cuffs."

Olya just shakes her head, murmuring something about mates as she walks over to the display case holding the cuff at the back of the store.

"What are you doing?" I whisper.

He raises one brow. "Trust me?"

I don't even hesitate. "Yes."

His dimple appears again, and he squeezes my hand and says in an intentionally loud voice, "Anything for you, honey."

As we walk over to Olya, I can't help but feel like I've been getting hit by a Mack truck with Hudson's name stamped all over it from the second we walked into this store.

I just hope I don't end up with tire tracks on my heart.

58

Only Fools and
Vampires Rush In...

I have to admit, Hudson's idea was smart. After I tried on the cuff, he inspected it, turning it this way and that...until he found the word he'd been hoping to find etched inside it: FALIASOLI. If the jeweler refused to tell us more, at least we had the name of the blacksmith's wife now. Surely that was a good start.

I explained to the jeweler that I just didn't think this cuff was as flattering as the ring Hudson had already bought me, and she happily nodded (since, of course, she'd made the ring herself) and put the cuff back in its case.

"It's hard to compete with a Soli *promise* ring," she says. "Believe me, I get it."

My eyes go wide—I have absolutely no idea what I'm supposed to say to that, especially with all the undercurrents suddenly flowing between Hudson and me—but I'm saved from answering when a mother and daughter come into the shop, chattering brightly.

The mother stops and stares at us, but the little girl smiles and waves. At the prospect of having a new customer, Olya seems to give in and says, "If you really want a cuff like that one, Falia Bracka made it." She then tosses out some directions to her house (today is her day off) and wishes us luck before turning to the mother and daughter inspecting a case with lockets inside.

We wave and thank Olya one more time for the ring before making our way to the door. I share a smile with Hudson as we realize we've got the information we came for. We're one step closer to freeing the Unkillable Beast and finding the Crown.

As we wander back to the market to meet up with our friends, I can't help wondering what's going to happen next.

Especially since Hudson is still holding my hand. The one with a *promise* ring weighing it down.

I decide, as we exit the store, that Hudson can call me a coward all he wants, but no way am I going to ask what I might have promised to do when he placed that magical ring on my finger. Not today, Satan. Not today.

Thankfully, he seems perfectly comfortable not bringing it up, and we spend the next hour and a half wandering around, waiting on our group. And I, at least, also spend it eating all the food. Like, all the food.

Every food vendor we pass wants us to try their wares for free—guests of the royal colossor and all that—and since Hudson doesn't eat, I'm the one who has to try everything. And I mean everything.

Normally, it wouldn't be a chore. The food is delicious and I've been living on cherry Pop-Tarts and granola bars a little too much lately, but the portion sizes are enormous. No matter how many times I tell them "just a little bit," I end up with at least half of what a giant would eat...at every single food booth.

Which means by the time our two hours are up, I am beyond stuffed with beef pastries, forest falafel (which tastes a lot better than its woodland name suggests), boysenberry tarts, a smoked turkey leg (only because I refused the whole turkey), a giant skewer of roasted vegetables and fruit, and one barbecued rib from what had to be the largest cow in existence.

"We have to go," I whisper to Hudson after I manage to choke down a couple of bites of the rib. "I can't eat any more. I can't."

Hudson nods as he steers me away from the last part of the market.

The second we're out of sight, I trash the rib in the first garbage can I find. "I don't think I've ever eaten that much in my life."

"I have to admit, I'm impressed," Hudson jokes. "I didn't think you had it in you."

"That's the problem," I tease. "Everybody always underestimates me."

"A lot of people do," he says, and he sounds a lot more serious than I intended him to. "But I never have."

"What does that mean?" I ask, sending him an arched look.

"It means I've never met anyone like you before, Grace. I think you can do anything you want to do."

It's a really big compliment, especially coming from Hudson, and I have no idea what I'm supposed to say to that. At least until he smirks and continues. "Well, besides trying to eat an entire restaurant full of food in one day. Big fail on that one."

"You know what? I'm totally okay with failing there," I shoot back. "Especially since the person calling me on it basically subsists on a few glasses of blood a day."

"Are you blood shaming me now?" He gives me a mock-offended look.

I roll my eyes. "I'm pretty sure that's not a thing."

"It is *totally* a thing."

"Because you say so?" I arch a brow.

"Maybe." He narrows his eyes at me. "You got a problem with that?"

"Maybe I do. In fact—" I break off as Flint calls to me from across the square.

"Hey! There you are, New Girl."

It's Hudson's turn to roll his eyes. "Dragons really do have the worst timing, don't they?"

Mekhi, Eden, Luca, and Flint descend on us seconds later. "Oh my God," Eden says as she takes the last sip of a giant milkshake and tosses the cup in the nearest recycle bin. "That was so good, but I am so full."

"They got you, too, huh?" I ask sympathetically.

"They got us all," Flint answers. "When I saw Macy a little while ago, she was more than a little green around the gills."

"Nice people, though," Luca says with a grin. "Everyone has been so friendly."

Mekhi shrugs. "Yeah, but we got absolutely no info on the blacksmith."

"That's because you're all amateurs," Hudson gloats. "His wife's name is Falia, and she's a jewelry maker from the Soli tree." He winks at me. "We also got directions to her house."

"We're never going to live this down, are we, Eden?" Mekhi jokes.

"What can I say?" I tease. "Sometimes you got it—"

"And sometimes you don't," Hudson finishes.

Mekhi rolls his eyes, but Eden doesn't reply. She's too busy staring at my right hand. "She's a jewelry maker, you say? Is that why Grace is suddenly wearing a promise ring?"

All eyes turn to me, and I squirm. "It's just a ring." I shrug. "I thought it was pretty."

Flint whistles long and hard, then says, "Dude, you already got her a *promise* ring? I thought that was, like, a hundred-year anniversary gift or something. Da-yum." If I'm not mistaken, there is actual admiration in

Flint's green eyes for the vampire he normally only vaguely tolerates on the best of days.

Not to be left out of the fun, Mekhi adds, "Holy hell. What did you promise her? You know that shit's, like, forever, right?"

All the guys snicker at that, Flint fist-bumping Mekhi as he mentions something about Hudson being "bond whipped." For his part, Hudson takes the ribbing good-naturedly, but his gaze darts to mine a few times, probably to gauge if I'm going to ask what *he* promised *me* with the magical ring. Well, he'll have to wait for that, because all I feel is relief that I didn't actually make some lust-drunk promise to wash this guy's sheets for an eternity.

Only Eden seems to not find the humor in the ring, one eyebrow going up as she says to me pointedly, "I sure hope you know what you're doing."

"Almost never," I reply, and it's the truth.

She chuckles but doesn't add anything else.

After another five minutes of everyone trying to guess what Hudson promised me, Eden asks, "Do you think we should go talk to Falia now, while Macy and Jaxon are entertaining Erym?"

Luca adds, "Or do you think we should wait for them?"

"I think Jaxon will kill us if we leave him with a lovesick thirteen-year-old for much longer," I comment.

"More reason to bail, if you ask me," Flint says, and there's something in his voice that has me looking at him closely, wondering if he's really as happy as he's seemed lately.

But his eyes are clear, the smile on his face easy, and I decide I must be mistaken.

"I'll text him and Macy," Mekhi says, pulling out his phone. "Let him know where we're going and to keep Erym occupied for a little longer."

We head west as we were instructed, and it isn't long before the quaint, structured environmentalism of town gives way to wilderness and unstructured forest. Houses start looking more run-down and are coming further and further apart.

I'm stressing a little, afraid that *on the lake* isn't going to be enough directions to find Falia's house, but once the lake comes into view, I realize it isn't quite the problem I thought it would be.

To begin with, it's more of a pond than a lake, so there are only two structures on the whole north edge of it. One is a small shed that looks like a stiff wind would knock it down. The other is a house carved into and around one of the largest redwood trees I've ever seen.

The one I saw in town was nearly ninety feet across, with a shop carved into the first twenty feet or so of the trunk. This tree is easily that large in diameter, maybe even a little bigger. But instead of carving into the bottom of the tree, someone has built all the way around it—without carving into it at all. Considering redwoods don't have big branches like the trees that usually hold treehouses, it is one of the most amazing things I have ever seen.

There's a staircase that starts at the bottom of the tree and winds its way around and around it in a widely spaced diagonal pattern. I'm on the ground looking up, so I'm not really sure how high it goes, but it looks like it doesn't stop until close to 150 feet up the trunk. But the staircase isn't even the most interesting or magnificent part of the tree.

That goes to the platforms extending over the staircase, built snugly against the side of the tree in all directions, that wind their way up the trunk along with the staircase. The platforms, like the staircase, are built on all four sides of the tree, so one faces east, the next one north, and so on, all the way up the tree.

Whoever built the platforms didn't carve into the tree to secure them— they obviously wanted to make sure not to harm the tree in any way—but they fit the trunk so perfectly that they must be custom-built. Each platform has a roof over it, and most are even screened in.

"Each room is built onto a different part of the tree," Flint says in awe as we stand back and study it.

"I've never seen anything like it," Eden comments. "It's brilliant."

"And old," Mekhi agrees. "Who would have thought they would have had this kind of construction know-how hundreds of years ago? Or been so concerned about the tree that they made so much extra work for themselves? Most people didn't even think about the earth way back then."

I start to say something about generalizing, but then I remember who I'm talking to. People who have been alive a really long time—and who know exactly what life was like a couple hundred years ago...or more.

"Earth magic," I remind him. "It's hard to do something to hurt the earth when you're so intimately connected to it."

"Maybe so, but something is definitely hurting that tree," Luca says. "See how different it looks from the ones around it? All those strips and cankers on the bark mean it's really sick."

"Not the house," Hudson agrees. "But yeah, something is definitely making it sick."

We look all the way up to the thin branches that adorn the top quarter of the tree. And I realize that even the treetop looks sick with the way it's wilting forward.

"What do you think is wrong with it?" I ask as we finally get close enough to see it in the sunlight.

As we do, I'm struck by how it really was an engineering feat of incredible marvel.

The whole house—the whole property—looks like it was once well loved and beautiful. All the bones are here, from the cheerful carvings on the staircase and room railings to the large, fenced-off garden that I'm sure was a sight to see in its heyday. Even the roses, now growing wild throughout the land on this half of the pond, once had a place to belong: a circular area off to the side of the tree that looks like it was overgrown a hundred years ago, maybe even more.

As I look at this place, I'm reminded of one of the versions of *Sleeping Beauty* my mother read to me when I was a kid. After the girl pricked her finger and fell into a sleep for a hundred years, the entire castle fell asleep with her. All the plants continued to grow until the castle was overrun on all sides. Everything was dusty and in ill repair, simply waiting for Aurora to wake up. Waiting for her to return and make the place whole again.

This entire parcel of land has that same feel to me. Like everything about it has been waiting so long that it has given up. Waited so long that every piece of it is slowly dying.

It's one of the saddest things I've ever seen in my life.

"So how are we going to do this?" Luca asks. "Knock on the door and ask if she just happens to be married to the person who made an unbreakable pair of shackles for an Unkillable Beast? And if so, how do we break them, please and thank you?"

"Your optimism is heartwarming," Flint tells him as he gently knocks their shoulders together.

"Sorry. We probably should have talked about this before." I think for a minute. "If Falia is as sad as Olya says she is, I think honesty really is the best policy. She doesn't need more drama in her life."

"That's fair," Eden agrees "But maybe we all shouldn't knock on the door together. We don't want to scare her."

"She's a giant," Mekhi retorts. "I'm pretty sure she could rip us limb from limb if she wanted to."

"Good point," she answers. "On second thought, maybe we need Jaxon and Macy, too."

"You know, I totally wasn't prepared for how big these giants are," Flint says as we start down what was once a well-structured walkway and is now just pieces of broken cement overrun by weeds. "Admittedly, Damasen is the only giant I've ever met before, but he's a shrimp compared to most of these people."

"Right?" Luca agrees. "I was prepared for them to all be seven or eight feet, but these people are huge! I met a guy today who had to be close to twenty feet."

"No wonder they have to live out here," Eden comments. "We think we've got it bad, having to hide our existence from regular people. But so many of the giants we met today can't hide, even if they wanted to. It's so not fair to them."

"I hope she's nice," I whisper as we finally reach the stairs at the bottom of the tree. But before we can so much as begin to scale the first step—which is several feet off the ground—the very unmistakable sound of someone weeping drifts down the stairs right at us.

59

Leaf Me Alone

"**I**t sounds like her heart is breaking," Eden whispers, and for once, the very tough dragon sounds like she's choked up.

"No," I disagree. "It sounds like her heart is already broken. And has been for a very, very long time."

I recognize the sound.

"Is it coming from upstairs?" Mekhi asks as he vaults up the first step... or tries to.

The second his foot touches it, the staircase rolls several yards up the tree.

"Umm, what just happened?" Eden asks as we all kind of look at one another.

"I have no idea," Mekhi replies as the staircase rolls itself back down several seconds later.

Luca tries next, and it does the same thing. It just rolls itself up. Only this time, the guardrails move, too. Except, it's not the actual guardrails that move. It's the carvings inside them—pictures of a woman and two children doing all kinds of different things.

Swimming in the pond.

Tending the roses.

Digging up stones for the jewelry.

Baking cookies.

The list goes on and on...and the people in each of those carvings are literally scampering up the tree away from us.

"What. The. Actual. Hell?" Flint asks, and he sounds amazed.

"I don't know," I say, stepping up to put a hand on the tree trunk.

I'm prepared to tap into my earth magic to try and figure this out, but the second I touch the tree trunk, I realize I don't have to. The tree is literally screaming on the inside.

"It's tapped in to her," I whisper as sadness whispers through me. "It's drowning in her emotions."

"What's wrong with her?" Eden asks, and for the first time since I met her, she sounds reticent. Like she isn't sure she wants to know.

"She's been missing her mate for a long time," Hudson says quietly, and there's a somberness to him that sets off all the alarm bells inside me.

Is this what I'm dooming Jaxon to now that our mating bond is broken?

Or is this what will happen to me if Hudson is sent to prison and I don't join him?

Either way, the thought is horrifying. Devastating. Soul-crushing.

"Maybe we should go," I say, stepping away from the tree with an uneasy feeling in the pit of my stomach.

"Go?" Flint stares at me incredulously. "This is the whole reason we're even here."

"I know. I just..." Truthfully, I don't want to face what this feels like. It wasn't that long ago that Cole broke my mating bond with Jaxon, and I could barely get off the ground. I don't want to remember what that felt like. I sure as hell don't want to be immersed in the agony of it all.

Yes, I have Hudson now. But that only makes it all scarier. Because losing Jaxon nearly killed me. What happens if I lose the mate who was my destiny?

Just the thought has anxiety skating under my skin, and it takes every ounce of courage I have not to run away.

Just feeling the tree scream was enough to put cracks in my very fragile heart. I don't know if I've got it in me to take on Falia as well.

"Hey." Hudson puts a hand on my lower back and wraps himself halfway around me. He looks at the tree, grim-faced, and I know he knows what I'm thinking. What I'm feeling. He pulls me closer into the shelter of his body and whispers, "I've got you. I promise."

"I know," I answer as the warmth of him seeps into me. As the heat of our connection works its way past the cold and burrows into my very bones.

I just wish I knew how long it will last. Forever, like the mating bond lore says it should? Or is that just another pipe dream that can be snatched away from me whenever someone decides to do so?

But now isn't exactly the time for a crisis like this, so I shove the doubts back down and force a little half smile as I look up at Hudson. "I'm good."

He doesn't buy it—neither the words nor the smile. But he gives me one more tight squeeze, almost like he's trying to instill his own confidence within me, before he lets me go.

Once he does, I realize the others are busy trying to figure out how to climb a tree that very definitely doesn't want to be climbed.

And every time one of them attempts it, something more severe happens. Not only does the staircase move, but when Flint tries to climb the tree, very worn, very aged leather rolls down over the first two screened-in platforms, hiding the rooms from view.

When Hudson tries, the tree drops hundreds of small pine cones on our heads.

And when I finally try, well, the minute I touch the tree, all I hear is screaming so loud and anguished that I immediately let go.

Through it all, Falia continues to weep.

"What. The. Hell?" Flint exclaims again.

"I don't think she wants to see us," Luca says.

"But we still need to see her," Eden adds, frustration rife in her voice. She walks around the tree 180 degrees until she gets to the area where the crying is coming from. And there, three platforms up, is a woman in gray, sobbing her eyes out.

"Hey!" Eden calls, but she doesn't get an answer.

"Excuse me?" Flint cups his hands around his mouth and joins in the shouting.

Nothing.

"We're sorry to bother you," I shout up, "but can we have just a minute of your time?"

Still nothing.

Eventually, Luca gets tired of waiting and jumps straight to the platform. Except the second he lands on the wood, the floor swings up and sends him spiraling back to earth.

Even though it probably isn't necessary—vampires always land on their feet—Flint hustles and catches him. Luca grins and whispers, "My hero," just loudly enough for us to hear him.

Flint flushes a little with embarrassment, but his grin is huge.

"Well, that didn't work," Mekhi teases. "The way it slapped you back, I was sure you were going to end up doing your best impression of a vamp cannonball."

Luca laughs. "Yeah, me too."

"Now what?" I ask, because we really need to talk to Falia. And to do that, we're going to have to get past this tree's amazing security system.

Except as we circle the tree, trying to figure out how to breach its defenses, I finally realize that the crying has stopped. Right before I look up and see a tall woman in a gray sweatshirt and a long gray skirt walking slowly down the staircase.

Apparently, Falia has decided to come to us.

60

A Fate Worse than Death

She doesn't say anything until she gets to the bottom part of the staircase. And even then, it's only, "Can I help you?" in a voice so rusty with disuse, it's barely understandable.

No rebukes about the shouting, no queries about why we decided to jump into one of the rooms *in* her house, nothing but a polite smile and tragic gray eyes that make my heart ache just looking at her.

"We're so sorry to bother you," I say, stepping forward and holding out my hand. "My name is Grace, and these are my friends." I don't introduce all of them because it's fairly obvious she doesn't care.

She studies my hand for a while, then reaches out to shake it. But the house interferes again, raising the stair she's on until our hands are too far apart.

Falia watches with a small smile. "I'm sorry. The house is very protective of my girls and me."

"Very protective" is one way to put it. "I think it's amazing," I tell her, because I do. I've never even imagined a place like this could exist.

"My mate built it for me." Her eyes go shuttered, and her warm brown skin turns a little sickly looking. "Every part of the house can move to open up for more space or close down in protection, with pulleys and levers. My mate wanted this house to be a safe sanctuary for the kids and me, but now, well, the tree uses its earth magic to protect us. He's so much more than a blacksmith."

"Absolutely," Hudson agrees from where he's studying the elaborate carvings on the handrail. "His craftmanship is incredible."

"It is," she agrees. "But my mate didn't do those."

"Oh, I'm sorry." Hudson looks embarrassed by his assumption. "Did you—"

"The house did them," she tells him, and for the first time, there's a tiny twinkle in her eyes. "For my mate, so that when he returned, he would be able to see all the things that he missed."

And just like that, the carvings make a lot more sense. Two girls picking apples, learning to swim, dancing in the forest. These are records for their father, of his children growing up.

"That's so beautiful," I tell her. It's also sad, but I don't tell her that. Then again, I don't have to—it's written in every pore of her skin, every breath that she takes.

She nods her thanks. Then asks, "How may I help you?"

"Actually, we were hoping to talk to you." Flint gives her his signature grin. "We have some questions, if you don't mind?"

It doesn't seem to work, as her voice is as listless as the rest of her when she asks, "About what?"

I think about lying, about trying to get in the door with some bullshit story. But I'm a terrible liar at the best of times, and I don't think this woman would fall for it anyway. She's sad, not naive, and I don't think she has any stomach for bullshit.

So in the end, I tell her the truth and just hope for the best. "We want to talk to you about your mate, if you don't mind."

"Vander?" she asks, a trace of desperation in her tone. "Do you have news of him?"

"No." My heart breaks all over again. "No, I'm sorry. We were actually hoping you would be able to tell us about him."

"Oh." The painful flash of hope fades from her eyes as she turns around and starts back up the stairs.

When she doesn't say anything else, I don't know if she wants us to follow her or if she wants us to get lost. I'm guessing the latter...especially when the handrail slides across the stairs, barring us from even the option of following her.

Except Falia stops when she gets to the first platform and says, "You all had better come inside, then. Would you like some tea?"

Out of nowhere, the handrail springs back into place.

"We would love some tea," Flint tells her as he bounds up the stairs after her. "Thank you so much for asking."

And that's what I love about him. He's bold and brash and super funny most of the time. But he's also incredibly gentle when he needs to be, and as he follows Falia up to the second platform, he talks to her as softly and sweetly as I have ever heard him talk to anyone.

She doesn't really respond, but she doesn't recoil, either. And as we climb higher, the tree stalking us suspiciously with every step we take, I hear her ask him if he would like some of the cookies her daughter made for her.

He says yes—a dragon never turns down food—and I make it up to the second platform just in time to see him flop down into the chair closest to where she's standing.

"Please sit," she tells the rest of us as she fills a kettle with water from a pitcher.

Hudson starts to give me a boost up onto one of the giant-size couches, but before he can, the platform does it for me. The wood beneath my feet pushes upward and plops me right down on the couch before settling back into place.

The others wait for it to do the same for them, but it doesn't. It just lays there, and Hudson can't help laughing as he jumps up to sit beside me. "Even the house likes you more than the rest of us."

"More like it knows I've got less skills than the rest of you," I shoot back as everyone else settles down on the various other pieces of furniture.

I look around as Falia busies herself getting mugs out of a small—well, small for giants—outdoor buffet. I don't know what I thought when we followed her up here, but I didn't expect the platform to look so normal. Giant-size, yes, but still normal.

This one is apparently a sitting room, designed around the large firepit table in the center of the platform. It's beautifully wrought iron—obviously a giant design—with the fire in the middle and an iron-filigree tabletop all the way around it. Surrounding the firepit are two large sofas on two of the sides and two chairs on the other.

Falia walks over and puts the largest teakettle I have ever seen onto the firepit, then takes the lid off a large kitchen tin. Inside are homemade chocolate chip cookies the size of my head. "My daughter makes these for me. Usually they go to waste, but I'm sure she would be happy to hear I shared them with some people who might actually enjoy them."

As we pass the cookies around, she puts a quick tray together with cups the size of soup bowls, spoons, honey, and several different types of tea bags.

Hudson jumps up and offers to carry it over to the firepit table—even though it's almost as big as he is.

"Thank you," she says as she runs a nervous hand through her short, dark curls. "I'm sorry. I haven't had visitors in…" She shakes her head, sighs. "In a very long time."

"Thank *you*," Hudson tells her. "For inviting us in. We appreciate it very much."

She shrugs as she settles herself into the last unoccupied chair. "After a thousand years of him being gone, people are tired of hearing me talk about Vander. No one ever asks about him anymore."

"A thousand years?" Mekhi chokes out. "He's been gone a thousand years?"

She nods, and the hand she uses to pass the tin of tea bags around is shaking so badly that I want to reach out and hold it, just to help steady her. The only thing stopping me is fear that it will hurt her more than it helps her. She looks so fragile, so tired, so *broken* that I don't want to do anything that might make her feel worse.

We busy ourselves getting cups and tea bags as we wait for her to say something else—I don't think any of us wants to be pushy. But when she doesn't speak for several minutes, Flint quietly asks, "Can you tell us what happened to Vander? We really would like to help him, and you."

Behind us, the treehouse railing starts to move back and forth, as if agitated. But it doesn't do anything else, like try to silence us or toss us off the platform, so I decide to call it a win.

Again, Falia doesn't answer right away. In fact, the silence goes on so long that I almost decide this is a lost cause. At least until she whispers, "The vampire king did this. The vampire king betrayed us all."

61

With This Ring

"**V**ampire king," Hudson repeats, his whole body tensing. "You mean Cyrus?"

"He is cruel," she murmurs, and though she's talking to us, it's apparent that, at least in some part, she's locked in her head with memories no one should ever have. "Deceptive. Evil."

So far, that sounds exactly like Cyrus, so the rest of us just kind of nod to encourage her to keep going.

"He came to Vander almost a thousand years ago now, with a request for unbreakable chains. He didn't tell him who the chains were for, only that they needed to hold a monster of unprecedented strength, a monster who would bring destruction to the entire world if he was not stopped. A monster who would destroy everyone and everything Vander loved, if he couldn't find a way to forge chains strong enough to hold him.

"I didn't trust the vampire." She shakes her head, tightens the hold she has on herself as she starts to rock, just a little. "There was something not right about him, even then. I could see it in his eyes. Malice, greed, decay. It was all right there, if only Vander would look."

"I'm so sorry," I say softly, but she just shakes her head.

"It's not your fault my mate is a stubborn, stubborn man. We fought about it for days. But the evil king said the one thing Vander couldn't ignore, and he definitely couldn't let it go. We had just had twin girls, and he loved them—and me—more than all the stars in the sky.

"Cyrus played on that," she adds as she starts scratching her ring finger like it's on fire.

I follow her movement and realize there are long scratches in her skin—welts and scabs up and down the finger. I wonder if she has a bug bite or something, though I can't imagine what bug would leave a bite annoying enough to make someone as big as Falia scratch herself until she bleeds.

"Cyrus made Vander believe—*really* believe—that this monster would find a way to harm us if we left him unchecked. He pointed to some terrible destruction that the beast was supposedly responsible for, told Vander that he had the giants in his sights next, and if they didn't find a way to stop him, the beast would come for us first, because he knew we had the power to destroy him."

My stomach churns at the story she's telling, at the evil that has been coursing through Cyrus's veins forever. And at the fact that this monster had a hand in raising Hudson and, to a lesser extent, Jaxon. That these two vulnerable boys have had to suffer at the hands of this evil for two centuries. It breaks my heart even as it rekindles the rage inside me, rage that I'm growing more and more afraid will never truly die.

I glance at Hudson, who is looking at his feet, as if the mere act of raising his head is too much for him to bear. His face is blank, but his fists are clenched so tightly that I'm afraid he's going to break something. I want nothing more than to hug him, to smooth his hair back from his face and promise him that it's going to be okay.

That, when this is all said and done, *he's* going to be okay.

But I don't know if I believe that any more than he does...and he's not looking at me anyway. So instead of trying to reassure him, I turn back to the blacksmith's wife and will her to continue with her story. Because if she doesn't, any hopes I have of keeping Hudson safe go up in smoke.

"Vander believed him," she finally begins again, absently scratching at her finger. "Over me, over everyone, he believed him. And he worked like a man possessed, day after day, night after night, for months, until he finally created the chains that Cyrus was so desperate for."

She breathes out then, seems to sink into herself, but the story isn't done. What happens next is the most important part, and I'm on the edge of my seat. Except she seems in no hurry to tell us any more, and I am seconds away from screaming in frustration. I need to know what happened to Vander. If we can't get him to help free the Unkillable Beast so we can take the Crown...I can't even consider what might happen to Hudson next. Or Jaxon. Or Katmere.

"Please," I beg when she doesn't say anything else and I can't take the silence anymore. "Please tell me what Cyrus did to your husband."

"What does Cyrus ever do when he's done using someone? He discarded him," she finally whispers, and my stomach sinks.

Was Vander dead? We hadn't even considered that possibility, and now my chest feels like a vise is gripping it. My heart is pounding, and I can barely breathe, but I force myself to ask, "Did he kill Vander?"

The giant's soft eyes fill with tears. "That would have been a mercy. To us all." She shakes her head. "Since the king had no reason or justification for killing Vander, he did the next best thing—he accused him of treason against the Crown and had him sent to the Aethereum."

The tree is shaking all around us now, as if it is as enraged about what Cyrus did as we are. The branches sway, the trunk trembles, and the carvings on the handrails seem to turn in to themselves, like the story she is telling is too awful for the children carved into the handrail to hear.

"Prison?" It's the last thing I expect her to say, even though knowing it reveals that there really is a scary kind of parallel between what happened to the blacksmith and what Cyrus is threatening to do to his own son.

Of course, if it's not broke, why fix it? For all I know, Cyrus could have used this same method for dealing with his enemies a thousand times.

It's a sobering thought.

"How long was he sentenced for?" Mekhi asks.

"Forever?" She laughs, but there's no humor in it. "It's been a thousand years, and he hasn't returned."

"Has no one tried to break him out?" Eden asks.

"Break him out?" Her laugh is phlegmy and broken. "Cyrus would kill him before seeing that happen. And I hear tales that it's impossible anyway." She scratches at her ring finger yet again. "No, but one day I hope to join him there. When the grandkids are older."

"Join him?" Now I really don't understand. "Why would you want to do that?"

"Do you know what it's like to be without your mate, day in and day out, for a thousand years?" she whispers. "For an *eternity*? I should have gone with him then, when Cyrus had him taken away. But we had the babies, and Vander made me promise to stay with them, to take care of them until they could take care of themselves. I agreed, not knowing that I was damning us both. Not knowing it would be a fate worse than death."

This time when she looks at me, her eyes are way past haunted. They are desperate, devastated, *dying*, and the sight of them sends terror pouring down my spine in frozen rivers.

"I'm sorry," I whisper even as my stomach hollows. Desperate to give her any small modicum of comfort that I can, I reach over and rest my hand on hers. "I'm so sorry."

"Thank you," she tells me, and there are tears in her eyes as she starts to pat the back of my hand with hers. But she freezes the moment her fingers come into contact with mine.

"That ring. You have a mate, too?" she asks, low and urgent.

I glance at Hudson, who is looking between us with narrowed eyes.

"I bought it for her," he says before I can answer.

This time when she moves to scratch her finger, I realize that she is wearing a ring, too—one that is silver, with several symbols inscribed on it. One that looks an awful lot like mine.

She rubs her fingers over the ring, ends up wringing her hands. "I wish you more luck with yours than I've had with mine," she tells me, and it sounds like she's about to cry.

"What does that mean?" Hudson asks, his voice unusually strident. And he's so tense now that I fear one wrong move might shatter him. "What's wrong with your ring?"

"Nothing's wrong with it. It works just as intended."

"And that is how?" Eden asks urgently, and I can't help but remember how concerned she was when she saw the ring. And how disapproving.

"Vander gave me this ring nearly twelve hundred years ago, along with a promise that he hasn't been able to keep for a thousand years." She rubs at her finger again. "It itches and burns incessantly every day the promise goes unfulfilled. It's like it knows the promise can never be fulfilled and wants me to take it off. But I can't."

"Why not?" I ask, almost afraid to breathe.

"My poor, sweet child." She shakes her head. "Because if you remove the ring, the promise is forgiven."

"So why not take yours off?" There's a slight edge of hysteria in my voice now, but I'm not sure why. "If Vander can't fulfill the promise, why torture yourself and not remove the ring?"

"He promised he would come home to me," she says on a broken sob. "As long as I wear this ring, I know he's still alive—he will one day fulfill his promise."

"He has no choice?" Eden asks.

"The promise must be fulfilled. Forever...or until you remove the ring or the giver dies," Falia says. "Which is why, despite everything, I'm grateful for this small piece of silver. Because it tells me my Vander is still alive, even after all these years."

But she sighs and runs a finger over my ring one more time. "I'm very tired. Thank you for the visit, but I fear I must rest now."

Hudson leans forward, holds her gaze. "Cyrus is trying to send me to the Aethereum as well. I will go—and I will find your husband and bring him home to you."

My chest tightens as her face softens. Hudson doesn't even hesitate to offer his own safety and sanity to end her suffering. It's humbling.

But she shakes her head. "My dear, no one breaks out of the Aethereum. If they could, Vander would have found a way and fulfilled his promise." Then she turns her gaze on me, piercing me with its intensity. "When the time comes, go with your mate."

I swallow. "Is there no other option for you now?"

She lifts a hand and cups my cheek until the pressure makes my jaw ache. "When you must make a choice as horrible as mine, only death will free us both."

62

I'll Be Watching You

"**W**ell, that was fun," Flint jokes, but there's no humor in his voice at all. He looks as shaken as the rest of us at what Cyrus has done. The suffering this woman has endured for a thousand years.

The mood is hushed the entire walk back to Giant City, as though even the energy to speak is too much for any of us. No one is talking about what we plan to do tonight. No teasing about drinking challenges or excitement for more shopping. We're all weighted down by one simple truth: eventually Cyrus will get Hudson into that prison...and I will go with him. If we don't find a way to break out before then, Hudson and I have a fate worse than death ahead of us—for an eternity.

Hudson is staring off in the distance as we wind our way through the forest. And it doesn't take a genius to know what he's thinking. If we can't find a way to get in and get out, he will choose death and set me free.

He gives me a startled look as I reach for his hand and say, "Don't even think it."

His gaze widens, realizing that I've picked up on his thoughts so easily. "But—"

I interrupt him. "Never."

By the time we make it to the market, we've all kind of silently agreed we want to just head back to Katmere. We walk to where we agreed to meet back up with Jaxon and Macy and Erym, eager to grab our friends and go.

Macy's face lights up with a giant smile as soon as she sees us, and she comes bouncing over. She leans in to me and says, "Oh, the stories of today I have to share with you later. I smell a vampire-giant wedding one day in our futures." When I don't join in her humor, her gaze sharpens on my face, then bounces to the rest of our group. "Hell. Bad news?"

"I'll tell you later," is all I can manage to get out.

Jaxon has also caught on to the mood of our group, but Erym is blissfully unaware as she excitedly tells us about the banquet tonight and how excited she is for her parents to meet us.

"My mother says the Vampire Court used to throw the most beautiful balls!" And her adoring gaze falls upon Jaxon again.

I'm racking my brain, trying to come up with a polite way to skip the party, when Brown Beard comes running up to Erym and whispers in her ear loud enough for all of us to hear. "The Watch is here and demanding entrance into the city, Cala. They say they have an arrest warrant for Prince Vega."

My stomach sinks like a stone, my heart pounding in my throat. How did they find us so fast? My gaze meets Hudson's, fear skittering down my spine as I realize he's considering our options—one of which includes turning himself in to spare us all.

I shake my head at him, and his jaw clenches, but then he gives me a quick nod. I let out a ragged breath of relief that at least he's going to fight imprisonment. For now.

Erym, though, turns wide eyes to Jaxon. "You must leave quickly!" She's mistakenly assumed the Watch has come for Jaxon, and we don't correct her. Especially when she says she knows a secret exit out of the city that will give us a head start.

I just hope it's enough.

63

I'm Rooting for You

We race through the tunnel Erym directed us to and burst out into the forest floor outside the city. Once there, we run, after deciding the vampires should carry everyone but me.

I only have a second to wonder why the Watch hasn't caught us yet. Because they're definitely faster than we are with the extra weight, even though the vampires fade like hell was on their heels. My wings are burning keeping up with them, but I dig deep and put on a sudden burst of extra speed so I can flip around to check why the Watch hasn't caught up with us.

And it doesn't take long to figure it out.

They're not coming straight at us...they're surrounding us. Boxing us in.

Jaxon must realize their strategy at the same time, because he pulls us to a stop in the center of a small clearing, and we stand in horror as vampires step around massive trees—in every direction. I land with a thump, staying in my solid gargoyle form, using my large stone wings to protect my friends as much as I can.

"Macy," Jaxon says, not taking his gaze from the vampires circling us, "I'm going to need you to build the fastest portal in witch history."

Macy is on her knees, riffling through her pack and pulling out her wand. "Already ahead of you."

I swallow. Hard. There must be at least thirty of them...and everyone but Macy and me has their powers grounded.

"This looks bad. Very bad." Fear for my friends, for Hudson, is beating against my chest like a living thing. Even my palms are sweating—and I'm stone, so that's saying something. "Should Hudson and I surrender, give you guys at least a chance to get away?"

But Mekhi just turns and says, "Jesus, Grace. It's not an army."

Luca gives him a fist bump, and the rest join in that action.

Well, everyone except Jaxon, who steps forward and says in a loud, commanding voice, "I am Jaxon Vega, prince of the Vampire Court, and my friends are traveling under *my* protection. I suggest you rethink this before you suffer my wrath."

Several members of the Watch turn to look at the one member not dressed from head to toe in a solid-red uniform. His clothing is black as night, and it's clear he is the senior officer. "Don't try to bluff me, Vega. I happen to know for a fact everyone but your little gargoyle is cuffed right now."

"True, Re-gi-nald—" Hudson draws out each syllable of the vampire's name like a taunt. "But then I've never needed mine to teach you a lesson, now have I? How's that leg doing, by the way?"

Reginald definitely doesn't like that. His jaw clenches, and his eyes narrow. "You'll pay for that, asshole."

"I'll probably pay for a lot of things one day, but definitely not from you." Hudson glances around at the other Watch members. "Now, all, I know you're probably eager for a fight, but what do you say you hop on the winning team and we kick your commander's ass for fun? Whaddaya think? Any takers?"

"What are you doing?" I hiss at Hudson. Riling them up for a fight seems like a supremely bad idea.

But Hudson just winks at me—he *winks*!—then says under his breath to Macy, "How's that portal coming, Mace?"

"Almost there," she replies, biting her lip as she finishes a complicated symbol with her wand before beginning a new one.

"That's my girl," Hudson murmurs to her before shouting to Reginald again. "I dunno, Reggie. Looks like some of your boys might be thinking it over. What say you we save them the court martial and just you and I work out our differences? Maybe a little mano a mano?"

Reginald grabs a short baton from his waist and jerks it to the ground, three extra lengths popping out to make a large staff. That must have been a signal of some sort, because the entire Watch does the same with their own staffs and then begin to move forward, closing in on us.

"Wrong move, Reggie." Hudson shakes his head. "My brother there has been dying to kick someone's ass since I *stole* his mate. And you know who trained him, right? The Bloodletter."

Several members of the Watch hesitate long enough to check their commander's reaction and confirm it's true. But it's a small pause, and soon they're all moving forward again—only about a hundred feet from us now.

"You didn't *steal* my mate," Jaxon bites out, his gaze bouncing from Watch vampire to Watch vampire—and I'm shocked. Not because he wasn't affected by Hudson's words but that he didn't get that his brother was trying to send him a message. Hudson would never say something so callous to Jaxon. Ever. How could Jaxon not see that?

Hudson rolls his eyes and says with more emphasis, "You think you might want to *steal* something back, brother?"

"Yes, Jaxon," I chime in, "I really think you should *take* something back."

Jaxon's gaze meets mine, and I can see he finally understands.

"Of course, if the Bloodletter's training wasn't enough for you..." Hudson begins, but before he can even finish the sentence, Jaxon has faded around the clearing in a blink too fast to follow with my eyes.

"I think it was enough," Jaxon says and starts tossing six of the staffs he'd liberated from the Watch to everyone except Macy. I catch mine in midair, hovering over the group now so I can pivot more quickly to wherever I'm needed.

Jaxon's move stuns the Watch for a second, but they're trained soldiers, and they recover quickly. I can tell from my height as I slowly turn in a circle that they're about to rush us. Mekhi whispers to Macy, asking how much more time she needs, and my cousin pauses only long enough to hold up two fingers. Shit. Two minutes. We don't have two minutes.

My mind races with our options. It's too many to fight. If only we could slow them down. I glance around the clearing, looking for *something* to use to do just that. But all I see are grass and trees. And that's when an idea occurs to me.

I swiftly land on the ground again next to Hudson, slightly in front of him, actually.

"You got this, babe?" he asks, already knowing I'd have a plan before I'd land in front of him and block his attack.

"I got this," is all I say—and fall down into a crouch, my hands wide on the grass in front of me, my weight on one knee.

Hudson grins. "Reggie, do you have any idea what gargoyles can do that's really, really cool?"

I let my senses sink into the earth, down through my hands and back up through my feet. And I reach out. I open myself up to the magic of the earth, let it channel through me, until it feels like I'm as tall as the trees overlooking the clearing, staring down at my friends, staffs ready, Macy's wand swooshing through a series of almost poetic moves in the air...and the vampires heading straight for them. And just beneath their feet, I feel it...my enchanted forest.

"What are you about to do, little girl? Throw rocks at us?" Reginald taunts, and a few of the other members of the Watch chuckle with him.

"Not rocks," I say out loud, and with my magic, I ask the trees for help, and I feel their answer immediately. I take a deep breath. I'm only going to have one chance. And then I open my eyes and fix my gaze on the commander. "This."

Before the vampire can react, giant sequoia roots break out of the earth, soil raining down on the entire clearing, as the thick roots swing through the air like the legs of an octopus. The Watch fades left and right to avoid the wild swipes, but the roots are relentless. Vampires scream as bodies are thrown like rag dolls hundreds of yards away from us.

One Watch member gets through, but Jaxon has him down on the ground, one foot on his throat in a blink.

"Got it!" Macy shouts. "Go, go, go!"

And everyone except Jaxon and Hudson makes a dash for the portal. I can't leave yet. I've got to keep the roots holding the Watch back until everyone is safe.

"Get through!" Hudson shouts to Jaxon as another vampire makes it through the roots, and Hudson knocks him back. Jaxon says something; I don't know what because the trees are screaming in my head as one of the Watch rips a root in half.

Oh my God, the pain! It feels like I've been ripped in half myself, and tears stream down my face, but I grit my jaw. That vampire will die for harming my forest. My gaze pierces his, and a root bursts through the ground and spears his thigh. He screams in agony, but I have no mercy.

"Babe," Hudson is whispering in my ear, his hands on my shoulders, I realize, stroking up and down. "Babe, it's time to go. You did good. Let them go now, okay?"

I blink. And stare at the clearing in front of me. Blood is mixing into the earth, bodies lying at odd angles everywhere. Jesus.

I take a deep breath and exhale, slowly pulling the magic back, whispering a "thank you" to the trees as I do, and I hear a whispering answer in return. *Goodbye, daughter.*

Once I've pulled all the magic back, my vision starts to blur. I'm so tired. I just want to curl up in the earth. I want to feel the rocks cover my body…and sleep.

I can sense Hudson's arms reach under my body as he whispers, "I've got you."

And then everything goes black.

64

Pin the Tail
on the Dragon

It's been two days since we made it back to Katmere, and Hudson hasn't picked a single fight with me. It's really damn annoying.

But I get it. I probably scared ten years off his life when I passed out in the clearing. I had no idea channeling magic would be so draining. Hey, I chalk it up to learning something new about my gargoyle powers, and that's nothing but a win in my book. We're going to need every edge we can get, since, you know, turns out the blacksmith who made the beast's cuffs is in the one place we've been working so hard to avoid. Prison.

Still, I'm trying to have tunnel vision, to just focus on school and graduating and what I can do at this specific moment. It's difficult, though, especially with the specter of Cyrus breathing down Hudson's and my necks. And why he wants us off the chessboard so badly.

We all agreed our next best step was to check in with the Dragon Court. Flint claims a member of the Court went to this prison and was able to get out of it a day later—so it *is* possible. He said he'd ask his mom for more information and until then, we were in a wait-and-see state.

As much as I believe getting the Crown is our best chance to stop Cyrus, if we can't get the blacksmith out of the Aethereum—or ourselves... Well, going to prison isn't an option, then, and we need to start brainstorming a Plan B.

Which we are totally going to do...after finals.

I always thought this would be the easiest time of my academic career—coasting through the last couple of weeks, taking finals that don't really mean much, and hanging out with Heather as much as I can. Instead, I'm in a sudden-death kind of situation, where one screwup means I don't get to graduate.

So *not* my idea of a great way to spend my eighteenth birthday, especially with everything else that's going on.

But it's hard to focus on studying when I keep thinking about Falia and Vander and the Unkillable Beast and everything they've suffered. It's awful, and every time I close my eyes, I think about them and all the pain they've had to go through, all the pain that's still to come.

It's not fair. And I know life isn't fair, but this whole paranormals-can-live-for-millennia thing isn't nearly as cool when you realize it also means you can suffer just as long.

I sigh. There's nothing I can do about that right now.

I have an Ethics of Power final to study for (a class Cyrus obviously slept through) and a history study session later today. So, despite everything going on and the fact that it's my birthday, I'm trying not to think about anything but the differences between Jung and Kant. And yes, it's just as hard as it sounds.

Two hours later, I'm just finishing up the last of my notes on Kant when my alarm goes off, reminding me that I'm supposed to be in a study session in Hudson's room in ten minutes. There's a part of me that wants to cancel—I'm so tired that I'm not sure I'm going to be able to keep my eyes open for much longer.

Then again, I really need the session. History is still kicking my butt, even after Jaxon and I did a brief study session the other day, and I am not going to fail my senior year because I can't keep my paranormal history straight. So instead of running back to my room to eat a pint of Cherry Garcia, I pack up my stuff and head down to Hudson's room. And try really hard not to think of that ridiculous bed of his while I do.

I text Macy to see if she's coming tonight—when I talked to her this morning, she wasn't sure, since she's only a junior and this isn't one of her classes—but I hope she does. I haven't told anyone it's my birthday, more because it snuck up on me than because I deliberately omitted telling them, but it would still be nice to hang out with her tonight.

Especially since this is my first birthday without my parents...which is, honestly, the real reason I haven't told anyone. It feels so strange to be turning eighteen without my mother's cherry chocolate chip pancakes for breakfast or my favorite fish tacos for lunch with my dad or an all-night movie marathon with Heather, like we've been doing on our birthdays for years and years and years.

Heather still hasn't texted me since I told her not to come to Katmere for a visit, and that hurts even more today. I thought maybe she would break her silence to wish me a happy birthday, but she hasn't. She is really pissed.

And I don't blame her. I deserve it. But if this is what it takes to keep her safe—I'd do it all over again.

Macy doesn't answer, so I shove my phone in my back pocket and try not to pout as I turn down the staircase to Hudson's lair. It's no big deal. I'll have some ice cream with her later and call it a—

"Surprise!"

I scream, just full-on scream, as I walk through the doorway into Hudson's room and my friends jump out from every hiding place available.

"Happy birthday, New Girl!" Flint calls from across the room, where he's draped in so many streamers that he looks like a hot-pink mummy.

"Thanks!" I call back, then turn to Macy, who's standing right next to the door and currently showering me with glitter and confetti. "Okay, okay, enough! Hudson is going to be walking around with hot-pink glitter in his hair for the next two weeks."

"Haven't you noticed?" he asks with a lift of his brows. "I already am."

I laugh—I can't stop smiling even though I told myself this was the last thing I wanted—then look around at the rest of my friends.

Mekhi is sprawled on the couch with a grin and a giant HAPPY EIGHTEENTH BIRTHDAY banner.

Luca is standing next to Flint with a colorful balloon bouquet.

Eden is waiting next to Macy with a bowl of backup confetti.

As for Jaxon, he's standing next to Hudson's library and blowing a noisemaker like his life depends on it.

And Hudson…Hudson is in the center of the room with a hot-pink and silver party hat on his head and a giant cake in his hands that reads, GARGOYLES RULE AND DRAGONS DROOL. Because of course that's what he had them write on it.

"How did you know?" I ask the room at large, but it's Macy who answers with a roll of her eyes.

"I'm your cousin. You think I don't know when you were born?" she asks. "Besides, I marked it on my calendar the week you got here so I wouldn't forget."

It's definitely not what I expect her to say, and I have to look down and blink the tears out of my eyes. Because sometimes when I'm sad about my parents, I focus only on what I've lost and forget how much I've gained. And how lucky I am, after everything, to have been able to land at a place that has given me friends—and a family—like this.

"Are you just going to stand there staring at us all night or are we going to throw some axes?" Flint teases.

"Is that what you want to do?" I ask. "Throw axes?"

"Umm, yeah." He glances at Luca. "Unwind me, will you?"

Luca shakes his head and takes a more direct approach, simply shredding through the streamers with a hand. Hudson sets the cake down on his desk and turns on Rihanna's "Birthday Cake" and cranks it up, while Macy makes a run for the axes, spilling confetti and glitter in a trail behind her.

I follow her at a more sedate pace, but I can't keep the grin off my face. This is so not the way I've spent any birthday before this one, and maybe that's what makes it so perfect.

"The birthday girl goes first," Flint says as he shoves an ax in my hand. "Do you know how to throw these?"

"Are you kidding me? I have absolutely no idea how to even hold one."

He laughs. "Yeah, me neither. Guess we'll have to learn how to do it together."

"And here I thought I wanted to play pin the tail on the donkey," I tease as Hudson comes up to give us a few pointers.

He gives me a mild look. "How about you play throw the ax at the dragon instead?"

"Hey now," Flint yelps. "No need to get violent. I mean, I know Eden is a lot, but she's still a person."

"Yeah, because I'm the one he's talking about there, Fire Boy," she says as she shoulder-checks him. But she grins as she turns to Hudson. "I say we go for it. I think he'd look great with a target painted right over his mouth."

Flint gives her a mock-wounded look. "You know what, Grace? I'm totally ready to play pin the ax on the dragon ass. Turn around, will you, Eden?"

She flips him off but gives her hips a little wiggle for good measure.

I start laughing, and I don't think I stop the entire rest of the night. I can't. My friends are entirely too ridiculous, and I'm having entirely too good of a time.

Hudson apparently made a whole birthday playlist for Macy and me, and I spend half the night dancing around to everything from Jeremih's "Birthday Sex" to "Best Day of My Life" by American Authors. The rest of the time we spend ax throwing, playing Cards Against Humanity, and falling all over ourselves and one another in a supernatural game of Twister that ends up with all of us in a giant heap in the middle of Hudson's floor...with him on top, which is absolutely no surprise to anyone.

I also introduce them to Heads Up! which no one here has ever played. Jaxon—"we used to call this game charades"—ends up kicking everybody's ass, so Flint decides it's time to sing "Happy Birthday."

It's the best night I've had in a really long time, maybe ever, and as my friends finally gather round to cut my birthday cake, I can't help thinking that I don't want this to end. Not just this night—though I'm okay with it going on forever despite my earlier thoughts—but all of this. We graduate in a couple of weeks, and yeah, we've got a prison to go to (and get out of) and maybe even a war to fight, but after we leave Katmere, all of that will be different. All of this will be different.

We'll scatter all over the world, and this perfect-for-me blend of people will be no more. Maybe that's why not a single person has ever mentioned what they plan to do after graduation. I think we all know we're living on borrowed time. The rest of our lives is coming for us, whether we're ready for it or not.

It's an awful thought, one I shove down deep—at least for tonight. And then I make the most important wish of my life right before I blow my candles out.

We eat the cake—or at least four of us do—while I open up my presents. Sparkly earrings from Macy, nunchucks along with a promise to teach me how to use them from Eden, a giant bouquet of flowers from Mekhi, and a Harry Styles body pillow from Flint and Luca.

Hudson gives me a book of poetry from Pablo Neruda, which is incredibly sweet. I start to get up to thank him, but he shakes his head.

"That's just the socially acceptable public gift." He winks at me. "There's another gift I'll give you when we're alone."

Everyone in the room starts teasing him, shouting out guesses, everything from Victoria's Secret (Mekhi) to handcuffs (Flint) to a gag for him (Eden).

I can't help the blush creeping up my cheeks, nor my heart pounding in my chest, imagining what gift Hudson would want to give me...*privately.* Sure, we both know there is a furnace of heat between us every time we get within touching distance, but what no one else knows is that besides a little hand-holding, Hudson and I haven't even kissed yet. So that takes every gift my friends are suggesting off the table, thank God. But what does that leave?

My eyebrows shoot up as I ask him with my eyes what it could possibly be, but he just chuckles and tells me I'll have to wait to see.

I'm about to start begging for a hint when Jaxon walks up to me, a small square present wrapped in delicate pink tissue paper in his hands.

I open his present and gasp in shock. Our gazes collide, and for a moment—just a moment—I see a flare of warmth in the depths of his black-ice eyes. But then he blinks, and it's gone, and in its place is nothing but the same emptiness I've seen from him for days. The same emptiness that is echoing inside me.

"I can't—" I look down at the Klimt sketch I saw in his room that very first day. "I can't take this," I tell him, shoving it back toward him as my stomach begins to churn.

"Why not?" he answers with a shrug. "It's not like I've got a use for it anymore."

His words cut like knives. It feels like he's trying to exorcise *us*, what we had, from his life. Yes, it's painful to think of everything we lost, but I wouldn't trade a single memory for all the money in the world—even knowing it would all end. Usually he seems to have moved on, found peace with what happened and that I've moved on, too, but it's moments like this, I wonder if he really has.

"What is it?" Macy asks, leaning forward to see. "Oh my gosh! It's beautiful, Jaxon!"

"And you should totally accept it," Mekhi says. "It's not like it fits in Jaxon's room anymore—have you seen the dungeon he's turned it into lately?"

I have, and I hate it so, so much. "I just don't—"

"Take it," Jaxon tells me. "It's a gift. And it was always meant for you anyway."

I don't know what to say to that—don't know if there's even anything to say. Besides, things are starting to get awkward, our friends looking between us like they know this is about more than an expensive sketch. Plus, Hudson has moved away completely, looking at anything and everything but Jaxon or me.

"Okay," I whisper, because it's all I can do. "Thank you."

He nods, but like Hudson, he's not looking at me when he answers, "You're welcome."

An awkward silence starts to descend, but God bless Macy, because she says, "Come on, Hudson. Put on one more birthday song before we go."

He shrugs but walks over to his sound system. And seconds later, "Birthday" by The Beatles blasts through the room, complete with all the warm pops and crackles that come from listening to it on vinyl.

And fuck it. Just fuck it. I drop my presents next to my backpack, grab Macy, and dance around the room with her like it's the end of the fucking world.

It isn't until much later, back in my own room with Macy, that I realize Hudson never gave me my second present.

65

A Little Less Talk,
a Lot More Action

The first two days of finals go better than expected—at least by me. I get an A on my case defense in Ethics of Power and a B on my Physics of Flight test, so I'm feeling pretty good about this whole graduation thing after all. Or at least I would be if my history test didn't loom over me like a too-full snowbank, just waiting for something to kick off an avalanche and bury me alive.

To combat the whole death-by-history-final thing, I've arranged for one last study session with Hudson. Jaxon promised he'd tutor me, but I haven't felt like asking him for anything lately.

It's not even about the sketch he gave me, either—or at least not exclusively about the sketch. I can see why he might want to get rid of it, I guess—I don't even have his history with it. And yet, every time I open my desk drawer and see it staring at me, it reminds me of what we've lost and makes me wonder for the hundredth time if he's really been able to move on.

I'd totally get it if he wasn't as good with Hudson and me as he seems, too.

He doesn't know what I know—that we were manipulated by the Bloodletter. That Hudson is my true mate. So for the thousandth time, I wonder if I made the right decision not telling him. But like every other time, I decide it would only do more harm than good.

Besides, it's not just our breakup going on. I sense it. Something feels off with him, and it has for a while. Jaxon has always been a little aloof, a little cold, a little hard to reach. Just because he let me in doesn't mean I didn't see how he was with others. What's going on now, though, is very different. I don't like it, and I don't think the members of the Order do, either. I just don't think any of us knows what to do about it, especially when he's closed himself off so completely.

I text Hudson that I'm on my way to his room, and he immediately texts back that I should meet him by the front steps instead. Which is weird, but he's the one doing me a favor, so I'm not going to question it.

He's waiting by the door when I make it down the main steps. "Hey, what's up?" I ask when he turns around to smile at me. "Do you want to go to one of the study rooms instead?"

"Actually, I thought we might go outside," he says, and the British is heavy in his voice again—which means he's upset or nervous. "It's a right gorgeous day."

"It is," I agree, searching his face for some clue about what's going on in his head. There's no reason for him to be nervous, so I ask, "Everything okay?"

"Sure, why?"

I shake my head. "Just checking. And yes, I'd love to study outside. I just need to run upstairs and get a coat real fast."

"You can have mine," he says as he slips out of his wool Armani jacket. "It's not like I need it anyway."

"Are you sure?" I ask, even as I slide my backpack off my shoulder.

"Yeah, absolutely." He holds it up, and I start to take it before I realize that he's waiting for me to slide an arm into one of the sleeves...because he's a total gentleman, apparently.

When I was in San Diego, I probably would have thought it was strange if a guy did that, but there's something about Hudson that makes the move so smooth, so debonair, so sexy, that I just kind of go along with it. And then sigh with delight when the ginger and sandalwood scent of him envelops me from all sides.

Nobody smells quite as good as Hudson does.

"How do I look?" I ask, giggling as I hold out my arms to show the sleeves falling way past my fingertips. It's a blatant effort to hide the fact that I'm still sniffing his coat like a weirdo, but hey. Any port in a storm.

"Charming," he answers dryly. But he's smiling as he straightens out the front of the jacket and then rolls up both my sleeves until my hands are once again visible.

"Better?" I ask, doing a little pirouette before I bend to pick up my backpack.

I expect him to laugh, but his eyes are serious when he answers, "I like seeing you in my clothes."

And just like that, my mouth goes dry. Because there's no doubt I like wearing his clothes. Or at least this jacket.

The relaxed atmosphere between us evaporates, replaced by a tension that has nothing to do with our former enmity and everything to do with the attraction that keeps growing between us a little more every day.

It's just the mating bond, I tell myself even as my breath catches in my throat.

It's not organic, not real, I remind myself even as my heart stutters in my chest.

It can vanish as easily as it came, I repeat like a mantra even as he leans closer and turns my whole body to liquid.

At least until I realize he's only leaning in so that he can take my backpack and slide it over his shoulder. "Ready?" he asks as he pushes the front door open.

"As I'll ever be," I answer with a roll of my eyes. "This history class is kicking my butt."

"It's just because you've never heard it before. Once you get the basics memorized, you'll do fine."

"I'm not so sure about that." I turn my head up to soak in the warm rays of the sun. "I can memorize with the best of them, but I think my problems are coming from the fact that I'm having a terrible time wrapping my head around these alternate versions of history."

"Most of history has alternate versions," Hudson tells me as we walk down the steps and take one of the paths on the right. "It just depends who's telling the story."

"I don't think I agree with that," I tell him as we pass by a small path of lawn complete with a couple of tree-stump seats that I had no idea even existed until the snow started to melt. "I mean, yeah, there are two or more sides to every story, but facts don't change. That's why they're facts."

"I agree," he says with a nod. "But I think you need to know the whole story before you can decide what's truth and what's opinion. History makes it easier, not harder, to do that, because it pulls the lens back. Lets us see more of the whole picture."

"Yeah, and if you're lucky, that whole picture won't blow your tiny human brain all the way up."

He grins. "Well, yes, that would be the hope."

We come to a fork in the path, and he puts a hand on my lower back as he steers me toward an area I've never been to before. "Where are we going?" I ask.

"A place I know."

"I never would have guessed." I roll my eyes. "Can you give me a little more of a hint?"

"Where's the fun in that?" he asks.

"Just so you know, I hate surprises," I tell him.

"No, you don't," he answers absently as he concentrates on steering me around a giant mound of snow that has yet to melt. "You just tell people that so you always have the inside scoop. It's not the same thing."

"And the hits from having you in my head for so long just keep on coming..." I make a face at him. "You know, this whole you-knowing-everything-about-me-and-me-knowing-nothing-about-you thing really sucks."

"What do you want to know?" He glances at me out of the corner of his eye. "I have no problem sharing."

"Somehow, I doubt that. Doesn't sharing equal weakness?" I snark.

"It's not like I'm planning on announcing my neuroses to the entire campus," he answers dryly. "But if you want to know something, just ask."

There's so much I want to know that I don't even know where to start. What was he like as a child? Did he have a best friend? Where did he go to school? What was his favorite holiday? But every question seems like a minefield of sadness for him, and I don't want to make him relive anything painful just to satisfy my curiosity. "Can I think about it?" I finally ask.

"Of course. Think away." But his voice is stiff when he says it, and I get the impression I somehow said the wrong thing.

"Hudson—"

"Don't worry about it." He yawns. "Psychopathy isn't that interesting anyway."

"That isn't what I meant." I rest my hand on his arm, trying to get him to look at me, but he isn't going for it. Which isn't frustrating *at all*. "Why do you do that?"

"Do what?" His tone is as smooth as canned frosting—and twice as sickly sweet.

"Shut down!" I all but yell at him. "Every time I say something you don't like, you just shut me out."

"Why should that bother you when you've been shutting me out for months?"

"Seriously? That's what you're going to go with? I thought you were *evil*—because you were so busy keeping me out that you didn't let me see the real you."

He starts walking faster. "I showed you the real me. You just conveniently forgot it."

His words land like blows. "Is that what you think? That I don't *want* to remember?" I narrow my eyes. "That's not fair, Hudson."

"You're going to talk to me about what's fair?" he stops and asks with a laugh that is anything but humorous. "Nice." Then he shakes his head and adds, "This was a bad idea."

He turns around, starts to walk away. But I grab onto his hand, try to hold him in place. "Please don't go."

"Because you need help with your bloody history?" he asks snidely.

"Because I want to talk to you," I tell him.

"What do we have to talk about, Grace? I know everything in the world there is to know about you—even the things you wish no one knew—and yet I still want to know more. But you, you can't even think of *one* question to ask me? I'm just tired of it all. Of being the only one here."

"Don't you mean tired of me?" I throw the words at him like a gauntlet, then freak out when I watch them hit.

"Yeah," he says after a second, his eyes as flat as a frozen lake. "Maybe that's exactly what I mean."

My breath catches. Hudson, who has never once given up on me, is giving up. And why wouldn't he? I'd told him I wanted to take things slowly, but instead of going slowly, I pulled him into the quicksand with me. And then watched him sink.

He starts to walk away again, and this time I scramble until I can get in front of him and block his path.

"Let me go," he says, and his blue eyes aren't calm anymore. They're livid with more emotions than I could ever hope to count.

"Why?" I whisper. "So you can go off and build an even bigger wall between us?"

"Because if you don't, I'm going to do something we both regret."

He won't, though. No matter how mad or hurt he is, Hudson would never do anything I didn't want him to do. Anything I didn't give him permission to do.

But we're stuck, and I can't unstick us. With all that I've lost this year, my defenses are too high. I can't let anyone walk into my heart again—they're going to have to crash in. Maybe that's why Hudson and I have always been more comfortable sparring than speaking. It's like we each recognize how high our walls are and what it will take to eventually tear them down to let the other in. And so I do the only thing I can do—I push him over the edge.

"Oh yeah?" I ask, and it's as much dare as it is question. "And what if I *want* you to? What would you even do?"

I get one moment—one moment—to see all that emotion jump the chain he holds it on. And then he's moving toward me, his hands coming up to cup my cheeks. "This," he snarls, right before he slams his mouth down on mine.

66

It Turns Out Diamonds Might Be a Girl's Best Friend After All

The world, quite literally, implodes.

There's no other way to describe it. No way to pretty it up. No way to downplay it. No way to say it other than this: the moment Hudson's mouth covers mine, everything around us simply ceases to exist.

There's no cold, no sun, no messy past, no uncertain future. For this one perfect moment, there's nothing but the two of us and the inferno raging between us.

Hot.

Overwhelming.

All-encompassing.

It threatens to burn me to a crisp, threatens to swallow us whole. Normally, feeling this much would terrify me, but right now, all I can think is bring. It. On.

And Hudson brings it. Oh my God, does he bring it.

His lips are warm and firm against mine, his body lean and strong. And his kisses, his kisses are everything I've ever thought they would be...and so much more.

Soft and lingering.

Fast and hard.

Featherlight and all-consuming.

They send flames racing down my spine, burning through my body. They melt me from the inside, turn my blood to lava and my knees to ashes and still it's not enough.

Still I want more.

I press myself up against him, tangle my fingers in his hair, and when he gasps for breath—starts to pull his mouth from mine—I yank him right back into the fire.

And then it's my turn to gasp, my turn to burn, as he fists his hands in my curls and scrapes a fang across my lower lip.

He takes instant advantage, licking and stroking, sucking and biting his way inside my mouth. I open for him—of course I do—reveling in the way his arms tighten around me, the way his body presses against me, the way his tongue strokes oh so gently against my own.

This feels good—*he* feels good—in a way I wasn't expecting but that now I can't get enough of.

I'm desperate. Determined. Punch-drunk and nearly lost in the smell, the taste, the very essence of him—ginger and sandalwood and sharp, crisp apples.

I press even more tightly against him now, sliding my hands down his back, wrapping my arms around his waist, twisting my fingers in the soft, silky material of his dress shirt as I pull him closer and closer and closer. Hudson groans, nips at my lower lip, tangles his fingers in my hair as our kiss grows deeper, hotter, more intense.

I have a random thought that I never want this to end—that I never want to let him go—but then he tilts my head back, delves into my mouth, and the ability to think abandons me.

All I can do is burn.

I don't know how long we would have stood there destroying each other—burning each other alive—if a couple of wolves hadn't wandered by and let out long, low whistles.

I'm so caught up in the heat sizzling through me that I barely hear them, but Hudson breaks away with a snarl so dark and threatening that their whistles turn to whines as they hightail it back to the castle.

Hudson turns back to me, but I can see in his eyes the same thing I know is reflected in mine. The moment has passed.

Still, as he backs away and I straighten out my hair, all I can think is that the whole mating bond chemistry thing is not a lie.

And also, when do I get to kiss him again?

It's that thought—and the urgency behind it—that has me backing away from Hudson with wide eyes.

"Are you okay?" he asks, and even though he looks concerned, he makes no move to bridge the gap I've opened between us.

"Of course!" I tell him in a voice that sounds anything but. "It was just a kiss."

Even as I say the words, I know they're a lie. Because if that was just a kiss, then Denali is just a hill. Or, you know, a tiny bump in the road.

"Right," Hudson says, and the British is back. "And the sun is a match."

He just holds my gaze, hands shoved deep in his pockets. And waits. He glances around like he's expecting my uncle to jump out of the bushes and throw him in the dungeon for daring to defile his precious niece. "Do you, um—do you still want to study?"

No, what I really want to do is rush back to my room and dissect every second of what just happened with Macy. And then Eden. And then maybe Macy and Eden together. But none of that is going to get me a passing grade in history, so, "Yeah, I do. If it's still okay with you."

He gives me a look. "I wouldn't have asked if it wasn't good with me."

"Oh, right." I give him the best smile I can muster and pray I don't look deranged. Or like I cook small children in the oven of my gingerbread house. The line between my *I'm nervous* look and my *I'm off the rails; you should hide all your valuables* look is a lot finer than I would like.

Still, I must not be too bad yet, because Hudson doesn't run away in terror.

But before we can move on, there's one thing I have to tell him.

"The reason I wanted to think about what question I would ask you is not because I don't want to know everything about you."

He turns his head like he's expecting a blow and doesn't want to see it coming, but I'm not having it. I was a coward before, but I can't always make Hudson be the one to knock against our walls.

So I step directly in front of him until he has no choice but to look at me again. When I'm absolutely sure I've got his attention, I continue. "I know your childhood was terrible, probably worse than I can imagine just from that one peek I had of it with your father, and I didn't want to ask you a question that would cause you pain, Hudson."

A glimmer of hope sparks to life in his eyes, and his mouth moves like he's about to say something. But in the end, he just nods and slips his palm into mine in what is fast becoming a habit, then leads me down the path and around the bend at the end of it. And no, I'm not ignorant to the symbolism there, but I am trying to ignore it.

Which is pretty easy to do when I see where Hudson has brought me—a small outdoor pavilion, complete with a picnic table, twinkly lights, and the most beautiful view of a mountain lake I have ever seen.

All around the lake, flowers are in bloom in every shade of the rainbow—and in the center of the table is a clear vase loaded to the brim with wildflowers.

"You did all this?" I ask, looking around me in wonder.

"I can take credit for the flowers and the lights, but the view is all Alaska."

"Fair enough," I say with a laugh. "But still, you didn't have to go through this much trouble for a study date."

"It wasn't any trouble," he tells me. "Besides, I wanted to give you your other birthday present."

"Oh. But you already gave me my birthday present. Which I loved, by the way. Pablo Neruda is my favorite poet ever."

"You didn't forget I said I had another present for you, did you?" he asks incredulously.

"I love that book. I was very happy with the one present. I don't need more."

"Oh, well, if that's the case, I don't have to give you anything else." He nods to my backpack. "We could just study instead."

"No! I mean, yes, I want to study. But if you already *have* my second birthday present, I wouldn't mind opening it." I'd be lying if I said I wasn't curious. Hudson may act like nothing matters to him, but the truth is he puts a lot of thought into everything he does—which really makes me wonder what he thought he should get for me and what I should only open when we were alone.

"It's actually one of those gifts that's best given fresh," he tells me.

"Like flowers?" I ask, leaning in to smell the gorgeous wildflower bouquet he's put on the table. "I love them!"

"No, Grace." He's full-on laughing now. "Not like flowers." He gestures to the three black rocks sitting on the corner of the table. One is round with jagged edges, one is more triangular in shape, and one is square. "Which one do you like?"

"Which rock?" I ask, because once again, Hudson never does the expected.

"Yeah." He rolls his eyes. "Which *rock* do you like?"

None of them? I've never exactly been a rock girl...which is odd, I know, 'cause yeah—gargoyle. But I can't tell him that, not when he's gone through so much trouble to set this up.

"I don't know. I guess I like the square one the most," I say, picking it up. I look at it for a few seconds, then plan to slide it into my backpack, but now Hudson is looking at me like he has no idea what he's supposed to do with me right now.

Which is more than fine with me. I *never* know what I'm supposed to do with him.

"Can I see it, please?" he asks, holding out his hand.

"You're the one who said it was for me," I tell him, even as I place the rock in the palm of his hand.

"It is," he answers. "Just not yet."

And then he wraps his fingers around the rock and squeezes as hard as he can. And squeezes. And squeezes. And squeezes.

At first, I think he's lost it, but as seconds turn into minutes, an idea occurs to me that's so outlandish, I can't even believe it. And yet...I pick up another one of the rocks and examine it as I try to remember what my six weeks of geology my freshman year taught me about rocks.

"Oh my God!" I say, eyes wide. "Is this *carbon*?"

He grins, does a little eyebrow wiggle.

"How is this even possible? I know vampires are strong, but wouldn't you need your powers—"

"I don't need my powers for this. I can't *persuade* carbon to do anything it doesn't want to do." He winks at me.

After another minute of squeezing, he opens his hand and, where there once was a chunk of carbon, there is now a diamond—and not just any diamond. This one has to be at least five carats. It's beautiful, stunning, and completely incomprehensible to me.

"I thought... I can't... Don't they need to be polished?" I ask. "They don't normally just come out looking like that, do they?"

He lifts a brow. "Like what?"

"Perfect," I whisper.

He grins. "Yeah, well, giants aren't the only ones with a little earth magic. Besides, you deserve something perfect."

And then he reaches over and drops the most gorgeous, flawless diamond I have ever seen right into my hand.

"Happy birthday, Grace."

"Happy birthday, Hudson."

He grins, and when it registers what I said, I can feel myself blushing.

"I mean— I didn't—" I force myself to stop and take a deep breath. Being this tongue-tied around Hudson is *not* what I'm used to. But it's hard not to be when that kiss—and everything that's come after—has completely blown my mind. "Thank you," I tell him after a bit, then grin up at him. "I feel just like Lois Lane."

When he doesn't appear to get the reference, I remind him, "You know, in the movie. Superman crushes coal to give Lois a diamond."

He raises one brow. "Haven't seen the movie, but I think we can both agree I could definitely kick Superman's ass."

I roll my eyes but giggle anyway. I have the cockiest mate in history. And I wouldn't change a thing about him. "Well, thank you."

"You're very, very welcome." His grin turns softer, more intimate, more... vulnerable than I've ever seen it. At least until he reaches for my backpack and says, "Now, about those Witch Trials..."

67

Who Needs Enchiladas When You Can Have the Whole Chimichanga?

I'm done.

I'm done, I'm done, I'm finally done!

I push back from my desk and barely resist doing a little shimmy right there in the aisle as I carry my dreaded—and now fully completed—history final to the front of the room. I drop it on my teacher's desk with a little wave—no way am I waiting around for her to grade it. I didn't get an A, but I know I passed, and today, that is *all* that matters.

Then I turn and walk out the door of the last high school class I will ever have to take.

It feels amazing and strange at the same time.

At least until I look up and realize Flint is leaning against the wall across from my classroom, arms over his chest and a giant grin on his face. "You look pretty pleased with yourself, New Girl."

"I am pretty pleased with myself, Dragon Boy. Thank you very much!"

"I'm glad to hear that." He pushes off the wall and falls into step beside me as I turn toward the stairs.

We start walking down the hallway, and Flint nods toward the long row of windows—and the bright-blue sky just beyond. "It's another gorgeous day. Want to go for a flight?"

My first instinct is to say no—I'm exhausted from too many all-nighters, and the only thing I really want to do is crawl into my bed, pull the covers over my head, and pray I don't have nightmares about Falia's cries...which has been happening more often than not since we got back from the Firmament.

But a closer look at his face tells me that this isn't just about a celebratory flight around campus. He wants to talk. And the thing about friendship is, it's not always convenient. And it's definitely not always fun. But it is important—and when you find the people who matter, you take the good with the bad.

So instead of begging off, I say, "Let me run my backpack up to my room and get changed. I'll meet you by the front steps in ten minutes."

His relieved smile tells me my instincts were right on. "See you in a few, New Girl."

"You know we're graduating in a week, right?" I tell him. "You're going to have to stop calling me New Girl after I actually get a diploma from this place."

"I'll think about it," he says with a roll of his eyes.

But I just roll my eyes right back. "Yeah, you do that!"

Ten minutes later, I'm back downstairs, feeling a little sick from scarfing down a Pop-Tart so quickly, but fast times at Katmere Academy call for fast measures.

"You ready to do this?" I call to Flint, who is currently cuddled up with Luca on the sofa in the common room. "Or did you change your mind?"

"Definitely didn't change my mind." He gives Luca a quick kiss, then bounds over the back of the sofa. "Let's do this thing."

As soon as we get outside, my tiredness falls away. And as I grab the platinum string and shift, I realize I'm glad Flint talked me into this. Stretching my wings is exactly what I need to do today.

"First one to the top of the castle gets to pick the movie tonight," he says, looking up at Katmere's roof.

"I'm not sure you get to promise that if the others aren't around."

"Hey." He shrugs. "They snooze, they lose."

"Fair point," I agree, even though it isn't...right before I launch myself into the air and race straight for the highest part of the castle—which just happens to be Jaxon's tower.

Below me, Flint shouts in outrage, "If you think I'm watching *Twilight* one more time, New Girl—" Then he shifts in a blink and is shooting straight up into the air, too.

He's about to pass me, so I lay on the speed even as I tell him, "I have never made you watch *Twilight*!" Macy and I do that alone in our room, like civilized Twihards.

We both make it to the top of the castle in a dead heat.

I land swiftly on the edge of the roof, and Flint shifts back into his human form just as he's touching down. It was actually a pretty impressive shift to watch, if I'm being honest. I wonder if I'll ever be as confident in my abilities.

We both sit down on the cold brick, dangling our feet over the edge, and look out across the campus.

"Thirsty?" I ask as I reach into my drawstring backpack and pull out two waters.

"You are a goddess," he insists as I toss him one.

"Maybe not a goddess," I tell him. "But definitely a demigod."

"I don't know." He pretends to consider it. "I think you could totally pull off the whole chimichanga."

I crack up. "I think you mean enchilada."

He looks mystified.

"The saying...it's 'the whole enchilada.'"

"Well, that's weird." He makes a face. "Have you ever seen an enchilada? They're tiny. I totally think you can pull off the whole chimichanga. Maybe even two."

I just shake my head and laugh, because sometimes Flint is so ridiculous, there's nothing else to do.

We sit in companionable silence for a couple of minutes, and I can't help thinking how beautiful the mountains are and how much I've come to love them in my time at Katmere. I don't know what I'm going to do after graduation—besides possibly get imprisoned while also doing my best to stop a paranormal war—but I know it probably means leaving here, and that makes me sad.

When I got here in November, I told myself I could get through anything for six months. And I have. I just didn't realize how much I would come to love that anything.

I almost say something to Flint, but he's looking so pensive that I decide to wait. Then he catches me watching him and says, "Soooooooo..." and I know the talking time has arrived with a vengeance.

"Soooooooo," I repeat back to him, brows raised.

He grins sheepishly, then shoves a hand through his afro in a nervous gesture I don't normally see from Flint. Instead of waiting for him to work his way around to whatever's on his mind, I just ask, flat-out.

"You going to tell me what we're really doing up here or am I supposed to guess?"

His look gets even more sheepish. "That obvious, am I?"

"To someone who just lost a flying race to someone made of stone, yeah."

"Umm, excuse me, but I'm pretty sure I won everything anyway." He looks insulted.

"Flint, come on." I give him an encouraging smile. "What's going on?"

"I need to go home this weekend." He takes a deep breath and lets it out slowly. "And I want you to come with me."

68

Gone Courting

"**H**ome? To the Dragon Court?" I ask. "Aren't your parents coming here next week for graduation?"

"Of course they are." He grimaces. "They can't wait. But this weekend is Wyvernhoard. It's basically the biggest holiday of the year for dragons, and there's absolutely no way I can miss it."

"Wyvernhoard," I repeat, trying the word on for size. "What is it celebrating?"

"It's our Feast of Fortune—a combination of our three favorite things."

"Which are?" I ask, fascinated by the idea of a holiday dedicated to good fortune.

"Feasting, hoarding, and fu— Well, you can guess the last one," he says with a laugh. "We're simple creatures, really."

"Oh yeah? So what do you do?" I ask, pointing to a plane that's just come into view on the horizon. "Do you decorate a pile of jewels or—"

"It's called the hoard," he tells me, kicking his feet idly back and forth. "And we don't *decorate* it, but all the attendees do get to choose something from the hoard on the last night. My parents actually host a festival to celebrate, and everyone who attends gets to pick something from the royal hoard."

"The royal hoard? You mean, like, the crown jewels?"

He grins. "Something like that, yeah. And there's fireworks and shows and amazing food. It's actually a really good time."

"It sounds like a great time," I agree. "So why does it seem like you don't want to go?"

He sighs. "Because it's Court, and that means a whole bunch of..." He waves a hand. "You know."

"I don't, actually."

"That's true." He brightens visibly. "That's another reason you should come. You can get a firsthand look at what Court is like. Maybe it will help you when you have to set up your own."

"My own Court?" Immediately, my pleasure in the day wanes. "What are you talking about?"

"You do remember the Ludares challenge, right?" He looks at me like maybe I hit my head one time too many. "You won a seat on the Circle. Which means, yeah, the Gargoyle Court is going to be a thing."

I laugh. "I don't think so. I mean, I'm essentially the only gargoyle in existence." I pause as I think about there being one more. "Okay, maybe there are two of us, if we manage to free the Unkillable Beast. But that would still be the world's smallest royal court."

"Court isn't just how many of your species you manage to gather around yourself," Flint insists. "It's the seat of your political power. And believe me, Grace, if you want to stay alive in this world, you need some political power. Because right now, you've got a big, shiny target on your back."

"Wow, I'm so glad you asked me to come flying with you," I tell him, tongue totally in cheek.

"I'm sorry! Freaking you out was not supposed to be part of the agenda." He shoves a frustrated hand through his hair. "The whole Gargoyle Court will be fine—we've got your back. And so does Hudson. I'm just talking out of my ass because I'm freaked, too."

"About going home?" I ask, still very much in the dark about what could be so bad about going home for a party where free jewels are involved. From what I saw when the Circle came to Katmere, Flint has a really great relationship with his parents—the total opposite of what Jaxon and Hudson have.

"About bringing Luca home with me," he answers in a rush. "He's always wanted to see a Wyvernhoard, so I don't want to say no. But the whole meeting-the-parents thing..."

"Ohhh." Understanding dawns. "It's a lot. After all, not everyone has my luck with parents-in-law, but..."

He cracks up. "Good point. Why am I even worried, considering you had to face Cyrus and Delilah right out of the gate? This will be a cakewalk compared to that."

"Compared to Cyrus trying to murder me?" I ask, brows raised. "You think?"

"Still, I want you to come. If you say yes, I'm going to invite the others, too, so then it really won't feel awkward. Plus, my mom wants to see you. I asked her about the prison, and she's willing to talk to us about it. So if you and Hudson come, maybe we can figure out if breaking you guys out of prison is even an option. She says she knows more about the dragon who once got out in only a day. That's got to be worth Hudson and you risking the trip, right?"

"You want Hudson to come, too?" I ask, and the sinking in the pit of my stomach only has a little bit to do with the fact that I've been hiding from him since he kissed me yesterday afternoon. Well, since we kissed each other. I know I have to deal with it eventually, but I put everything on pause until I passed that history exam. "Won't that put him at risk for getting arrested?"

"Not if it's for official Circle business. He is your mate, and you are to be the new gargoyle queen. Which makes him the king-to-be as well."

"Doesn't that mean he shouldn't be arrested at all?" I counter. "You really shouldn't be able to put your corulers in prison. Besides, if we're monarchs, aren't we always above the law? I'm pretty sure that was just on my history exam." I don't tell him it was a question I think I missed.

"Typically, yes, but again, you haven't been coronated yet. And if we sneak out and don't let anyone know he's gone, we'll be doubly fine."

"And if *he's* not fine?" I ask as we stand up and get ready to head back down.

"He will be," Flint soothes. "My mom assures it."

"But if he isn't?" I ask again once we're both back on the ground.

"Well, if he's not, then he'll get a direct chance to look for the blacksmith." He pulls open the front door. "And we'll get a chance to stage a prison break."

"Am I supposed to be reassured by that?" I ask.

But Flint just blows me a kiss and saunters away, exactly like the dragon he is.

Fuck my life.

69

Falling From Grace

After Flint walks away, I think seriously about going back to my room and crawling into bed with my Harry Styles body pillow and my Netflix account. But the truth is, our talk got me too wound up to sleep, and if it hadn't, Flint's parting shot about the jailbreak certainly would have.

Graduation is almost here, and that means, more than likely, Hudson and I are going to prison. Hopefully with a scheme to break ourselves and Vander out, but if the last year has taught me anything, it's how important it is to say goodbye when you get the chance.

Which means I have to make one last effort to talk to Jaxon. Even if no one else can see it, I can tell something is wrong with him. Something more than just our breakup, although I wouldn't dream of minimizing that pain to anyone.

No, something else is going on, and I owe it to him as his friend to let him know I'm here for him if he needs me. That he doesn't have to push everyone away—which is exactly what his birthday gift to me suggests he's doing.

I think I remember the Order telling me they had some rehearsal for the graduation ceremony they were doing today, which means now might be a perfect moment to get Jaxon alone.

I take the stairs two at a time.

The front room is still totally empty except for the workout equipment, but this time the door to his bedroom is open and, as I cross the room, I can see that it, too, is barren. Gone are the instruments and the art and the books, and in their place is nothing but emptiness. In fact, the only things in the room now are the bed, the desk, and the desk chair. Even my favorite red blanket is nowhere to be found.

And neither is Jaxon.

I don't understand. I don't understand why he would do this. I don't understand what's happened to him. I don't understand how to help him. I just simply don't understand.

I don't realize I've said the last out loud until Jaxon's face appears in the window—from the outside. He's on the parapet. Of course.

"Hey!" I exclaim with a smile. "How are you?"

He doesn't answer the question, and he doesn't smile back. But he does say, "Come on out," as he steps back.

It feels like the perfect chance to talk to him, so I ignore the open suitcase on his bed and head to the window, wondering the whole time how I'm going to get outside. It's not exactly an easy thing to maneuver...at least, not if you're not a vampire.

But there's one thing I forgot. Jaxon may be acting off lately, but he's still Jaxon. And when I reach the window, he's right there to help me through. Just like always.

"Thanks," I tell him once my feet are firmly planted on the stone floor of the parapet.

He shakes his head in a don't-worry-about-it gesture and moves back toward the crenellation, where he just stands and stares out at the horizon.

For the first time in a long time, I feel nervous with him. But it's not the fun, Pop Rocks kind of jitters that filled me up when we first met. No, this is a whole different kind of nervousness, and I don't like how uncomfortable it makes me. Any more than I like what it says about my relationship with Jaxon and where it's at right now.

I follow his sight line and realize he's staring at the pond with the gazebo. It breaks my heart just a little to realize how far we've come...and how much we've lost.

"Do you remember that day?" I whisper. "When you took me out there and we built the snowman."

He doesn't so much as glance at me. "Yes."

"I've always wondered where you got that vampire hat." I lean against the merlon right next to where he's standing.

"The Bloodletter knitted it for me."

"Really?" The idea of her doing that for Jaxon tickles me, even after everything else she's done. All the messes she's made. Again, I think about telling him everything, but I'm afraid it will only make things worse for him and frankly, I don't think he can handle much more at the moment.

So instead of shattering the very last of his illusions, I focus on the positive as much as I can. "I think that's amazing. I love that hat."

He shrugs. "It's gone now."

"No it isn't!" I look at him in surprise. "Is that what you thought? Someone just took it?"

"That's not what happened?"

"No! Oh my God, I forgot! It's in my closet. I went out and got it the next day because I didn't want anything to happen to it for you. I stored it in my closet to give to you later because I was late to art class. But then, you know...I turned to stone for a while. I'm so sorry; I forgot all about it. I'm sure it's still in there."

He looks at me for the first time, and I can see in his eyes the debate raging inside him. I have no idea what side wins, but I do know that there is just a tiny bit more warmth in his voice when he says, "Thank you."

"Of course." I pause for a second, swallow down my fear. Then ask, "Do you ever wish we could go back to that day? When everything was simple? Perfect?"

"Hudson's ex had just nearly killed you in a diabolical plot to resurrect him," he answers. "How perfect could it be?"

"I wasn't talking about Lia," I tell him.

"I know exactly what you were talking about." He swallows, then shakes his head. "We were children, Grace. We had no idea what was coming."

"That was barely six months ago!" I say with a laugh. "I wouldn't exactly call us children."

"Yeah, well, a lot can happen in six months," he says.

And in that one thing, he's absolutely right. Look at us.

There's so much more I want to say, but maybe Jaxon's approach is right. Maybe I should just keep my mouth shut and let it go.

I don't know.

Which is why I do the only thing I can think of. I glance back at the suitcase on his bed and ask, "Why are you always packing when I come up here? Or did Flint already ask you?"

"Ask me what?"

"He's going to the Dragon Court this weekend and wants us to go with him. There's a festival for his biggest holiday—"

"Wyvernhoard, yeah. Aiden and Nuri host it every year." For the first time in days, his lips curve in a tiny smile. "It's a lot of fun."

"You've been?"

"A long time ago. As part of the Vampire Court contingent, back when relations among the Courts weren't nearly as bad as they are now."

"Well, you should come again, then," I urge. "I bet it's more fun when the dragon prince himself is the one showing you around."

For a second, he looks tempted. But then he shakes his head and answers, "I can't. I've been summoned back to London."

"Again?" I ask. "You were just there."

"Yeah, well, I left rather abruptly." He shrugs. "Delilah wasn't impressed."

Annoyance at his mom flashes through me. "I didn't realize you cared how she felt."

"I don't. But if I want her to use her influence on Cyrus to drop the charges against Hudson, it needs to at least look like I'm falling in line."

"Do you think she'll do that?" To be honest, I'm shocked at the very idea. Delilah doesn't exactly seem like the maternal sort.

"I don't know." For the first time, he drops his guard and looks...exhausted. And I don't think he even realizes that he's rubbing his scar—or that he's reverted to keeping it covered. "Hudson was always her favorite, so...maybe? It's the best chance we've got."

I hate hearing that, because what I know of Delilah doesn't make me very confident that she'll do anything to help her older son, especially if it means inconveniencing herself.

"Be careful," I tell him, because I don't know what else to say.

"Says the girl who goes out of her way to get into trouble," he answers with a shake of his head.

"I don't go out of my way. It just happens."

"Yeah, I've heard that before." He moves to the window. "I need to go."

"Now?" I ask, though I don't know why I'm so shocked.

"I do need to be back for graduation in a few days, so yeah. Now." He climbs back inside his room, then holds out a hand so that he can pull me in behind him.

As I watch him gather up his phone and keys, a bad feeling sweeps over me. I'm not normally one to believe in that stuff, but this time...I just can't ignore the gnawing in the pit of my stomach. Or the fact that we haven't discussed what's going on with him. I need to tell him that he has friends, people who still care about him.

"Don't go," I whisper as I grab on to his hand. "Please. I need to tell you—"

"Stop, Grace." He pulls his hand from mine, then picks up his bag and slings the strap over his shoulder. "It's time for me to go."

Then he climbs back onto the parapet and gives me a little nod right before he jumps over the edge.

I think about climbing back out onto the parapet just to watch him go. But what's the point? By the time I get out there, he'll already be gone.

It's a familiar Vega modus operandi.

So instead of chasing after Jaxon, I slowly walk back down the stairs. As I do, I think a lot about that snowman…and everything else that's melted away in the spring thaw.

Maybe all these years, it's not the coming of winter we've had to fear, but the spring that thrives in its desolate destruction.

70

Home-Port Advantage

"**W**hy do we always have to leave on these trips in the middle of the night?" Macy whines as a knock sounds on the door early Friday morning.

"Umm, maybe because we're always doing shit we're not supposed to?" I respond as I walk over to let in Flint and Luca, leaving the door open for Hudson, who should be here shortly.

"Not this time," she tells me as she pulls a sweatshirt over her head. "This time we are going on a fully sanctioned Circle field trip."

"Maybe so. But we still need to get Hudson there without him being arrested, so it's going to be middle-of-the-night runs for a while now."

"So sorry to be an inconvenience," Hudson drawls as he walks in. "I'll try to work on the whole enemy-of-the-state thing for future endeavors."

"Yeah, we both know that's bullshit," I say as I head back to my bed to triple-check my stuff. Flint wouldn't tell me where the Dragon Court is because he wants it to be a surprise, but he did tell me I could pack whatever kind of clothes I wanted as long as I had a sweatshirt and a fancy dress for the party.

At least after the welcome party my first day at Katmere, when I didn't have a dress to wear, I made it a point to order a couple of party dresses online. But a fancy dress means fancy shoes and a strapless bra and a bunch of other things guys don't need to worry about, and somehow I had to make all that *and* three days' worth of regular clothes all fit into a backpack... without using magic, sigh.

"So I'm *not* an inconvenience?" he challenges, leaning a shoulder against my doorframe.

"Of course you're not," Macy tells him. "I was just being—"

"Umm, yeah you are!" I cut Macy off with an eye roll. "You've been an inconvenience since the first day you showed up in my life, and we both know you have no plans to change that anytime soon."

Hudson yawns. "And here I thought I was on my best behavior."

"You probably were," I agree as I zip up my backpack. "But that's not saying much."

"You only say that because you've never seen me on my worst behavior."

"I'm sorry." I grab my sweatshirt and pull it over my head. "You think that's something to brag about while we're all trying to keep you out of prison?"

"Grace!" Macy admonishes.

But Hudson just laughs. "Perhaps you've got a point."

"Yeah, perhaps." I swing my backpack onto my shoulder with another roll of my eyes, wincing a little at the weight of it.

"Do you have everything?" my cousin asks as she triple-checks her own things.

"I think so. And if I don't, I'm sure I can get whatever I need once we make it to Court."

Hudson laughs. "Yeah, that won't be a problem."

"Wait! Do you know where the Dragon Court is?" I turn to him with wide eyes. "Macy and Flint won't tell me. They keep saying they want to see my face when we arrive."

"I know exactly where it is," he answers. "But now that I know you don't, I think I'm going to keep that info to myself."

"See?" I say as I scooch past him in the doorway. "Totally inconvenient."

"Then it's probably a good thing you like me this way, isn't it?" he retorts with a grin.

"I never said that." I roll my eyes at him again, but his grin only grows wider.

"You two have the weirdest relationship," Macy jokes, but she's not wrong. We do.

But it works for us, so I shrug. "It's my job to make sure my mate's ego's in check so he can always fit his head through the door."

"And it's my job to push her buttons," Hudson fires back, dimple flashing.

Macy looks between us both and then says, "Are you guys talking in some sort of sex code?"

Oh. My. God. I glance at Hudson and yes, he was. I shake my head but laugh. "Definitely an inconvenience."

Macy locks the door, and we once again sneak out through her secret passage.

By the time we make it outside, Eden and Flint are already there, as is Luca—and Uncle Finn. Macy squeals in delight when she realizes her dad is going to create a portal for us so we don't have to freeze on an umpteen-hour flight.

"Hi, Uncle Finn." I smile at him, and he returns the smile, although his eyes look concerned.

"I'm only doing this because Nuri asked me herself. She assured me you all would be treated like royalty during this visit." He looks us over, then motions for each of my friends to step up so he can remove their cuffs. Everyone except Hudson, who just shrugs. "But please, try not to cause an international incident for one weekend, okay?"

Flint grabs his chest in mock offense, and we all laugh. Even Uncle Finn, who shakes his head, then begins waving his wand as though conducting a symphony.

I glance at Hudson, but something feels off. His hands are shoved deep in his pockets, his jaw tight. I raise my brows at him, as if to ask what's up, but he just winks and pulls a hand from his pocket to lace with mine. As our fingers entwine, the familiar warmth replaces the tension in my stomach, and I shake the feeling. I must have imagined it.

"I'm going to leave this side open for you, Macy," Uncle Finn says as he finishes the last of the spell. "If you guys encounter any trouble—or create any—get back to campus immediately. Are we clear?"

We all assure him we want nothing more than a relaxing weekend, and then we step through the portal. Surely the universe will give us one weekend before royally screwing us.

71

If All Hell Breaks Loose, Why Can't We?

All I can say when we finally land on the street outside the Dragon Court is, "Wow." I recognize where we are immediately. We are in New York City, baby, and I *cannot wait* to explore!

It's not my first trip to the Big Apple—my parents brought me here when I was little, but I don't remember much about it besides the Empire State Building and a lot of traffic. This time I'm going to remember *everything*.

I know we only have a few days here—and that we have to spend most of our time at the Dragon Court—but I'm not going to let that stop me. I'll go out in the middle of the night if I have to, but I am going to find some time to explore the city. The fact that Macy is pretty close to jumping up and down in excitement tells me I won't have any trouble finding a partner in crime.

The portal dropped us right in the middle of Tribeca, and we cross the street toward the lobby of the ritziest building on this very ritzy block. Apparently, the Dragon Court is doing very well for itself.

"I can't believe the Dragon Court is in New York City!" I exclaim with excitement. But then a thought occurs to me. "But the Dragon Court is much older than the city. Do Courts move?"

Flint nods. "There are dragons all around the world. But the Court is wherever the king and queen wish to reside at any given time. It's the same with every faction. Well, all species try not to move their Court to a city already claimed—that would be an act of war—but otherwise, yeah, it can move around. Who would want to spend an eternity in the same place?" Flint grins at me, and I guess that makes perfect sense.

For just a moment, I wonder where I would want to place the Gargoyle Court, if I could claim any city in the world. I shake my head at my fanciful thoughts. I don't even know if I plan to go to college yet. I certainly am not ready to make a decision like this for a long, long time. If ever.

Once we're inside the building, I can't stop my eyes from looking at everything. Massive, flowing stained glass chandeliers—I'm almost positive they're Dale Chihuly—dominate the room, and I kind of want to spend an hour or three just staring at them. It's the first time I've seen his work in person, and it's as mesmerizing as I always thought it would be. The shapes and swirls he manages to create with glass are truly awe-inspiring.

The rest of the room is just as impressive. Muted gold wallpaper that I'm pretty sure has some actual gold leaf in it, travertine flooring, oversize and overstuffed furniture, and elaborate fresh-flower arrangements fill the upscale lobby. But there are whimsical touches, too—dragon sculptures and a giant bowl filled with fake gemstones, just to name a few.

"Mr. Montgomery!" The older woman behind the fancy gold front desk hustles out from behind it and all but runs across the lobby to get to us. "Welcome home, sir! The queen is expecting you. She requested that I tell you to go on up to the fifty-fifth floor. She's overseeing the preparations for the banquet tonight, but she left strict orders that she would like to see you and your friends before you show them to their rooms." She leans in and whispers conspiratorially, "I think she just misses you and wants to see your face before all the festivities commence."

"I'll find her, Mrs. Jamieson. Thanks for letting us know." He gives her a big hug. "I missed you."

"Oh, you silly boy." She slaps gently at his shoulder, but her cheeks flush with color, and her smile is filled with joy. "I missed you, too. It seems like just yesterday you and your brother were playing fly-and-seek through this very lobby."

Flint's smile dims just a little. "Yeah, seems like that for me, too, sometimes." He pulls away. "I'll come down tomorrow morning, and we can catch up. I want to hear what those grandbabies of yours are up to."

"I've got the pictures all ready for you," she says. "Such a good boy you are."

"I try, Mrs. Jamieson. I try." He winks at her, then ushers us over to a glossy gold elevator that is separate from the other four in the lobby.

"That was very nice." Luca watches him with adoring eyes. "What you did for her."

"Mrs. Jamieson?" Flint looks surprised. "She's the best, man. She used to keep the most amazing cookies in her desk just for Damien and me—"

"Oh, Flint! I almost forgot." Mrs. Jamieson comes trotting back over, a bakery box in her hand. "I picked these up for you on my way to work this morning."

His whole face lights up. "Oh, man. Are these the black-and-whites?"

"Would I get you any other kind?" She gives him a reproving look.

He bends down and kisses her wrinkled cheek. "I'm going to marry you one day, Mrs. Jamieson. Just see if I don't."

"I'm almost certain there's at least three hundred adoring fans who might object to that." Her voice is dry as she punches the elevator button. "Now, go see your mother."

"Three hundred?" Luca repeats, brows raised.

"She was e-exaggerating," Flint stutters as his cheeks turn a lovely shade of burnt sienna. "A lot."

"Of course she was." The mildness of Luca's answer only seems to exacerbate Flint's blush.

The elevator comes right away, which surprises me—at least until we climb in and I realize there are only four floors the elevator can stop on. And they're the top four floors, of course. Figuring I can help Flint by changing the subject, I ask, "Does the Dragon Court have all four of these floors?"

But Flint just laughs. "We've got the whole building, Grace."

"The whole building?" I don't even try to keep the shock from my voice. Manhattan real estate prices are legendary and this place…I can't even imagine what a penthouse here must cost, let alone the entire building.

"Dragons are good savers, Grace. And we figured out early that real estate was a great addition to the hoard."

"Apparently," I answer, even as my mind boggles.

And Flint thinks I'm going to be able to set up a Gargoyle Court? Is he serious? Sure, my parents left me enough money that I don't have to worry for a while, but that's a far cry from being able to afford an apartment in a building like this, let alone the entire building.

And something tells me the other Courts are just as elaborate, which equates to me being totally screwed. I mean, if I decide I actually want to try to do this Circle thing—which I haven't. At all.

But that's a problem for another day, because the mirrored elevator doors are opening and Nuri is waiting for us…along with six armed guards in full Dragon Court regalia.

"Seize him!" she orders, and I don't even need to turn around to know that she's pointing directly at Hudson.

72

Cuff Me Not

"**M**om!" Flint exclaims, throwing a hand out to stop them as the guards get ready to rush the elevator. "What are you doing?"

Their hesitation is all I need, and I move quickly to put myself squarely in front of Hudson. But he's not having it—one second I'm moving to block him and the next he's directly in front of me.

"Stay back, Grace," he growls.

"I will not!" I snap, already reaching for the platinum string that will at least give me a fighting chance against whatever this ambush is.

But Hudson isn't budging, and for the first time, I understand just how immovable a vampire can be—especially one as powerful as Hudson. Because gargoyle or not, there's no way I'm getting in front of him if he doesn't want me there. And right now, he definitely doesn't.

"What's this about, Nuri?" Hudson demands in a voice as cold as a Arctic snowbank.

"That's Queen Nuri to you," she snarls, "and I think you know exactly what this is about. Or are you naive enough to think that you'd be able to come to my Court, without consequences, after what you did to my Damien?"

"I knew exactly what would happen if I came here. Nice to know you didn't disappoint." He lifts a brow. "Then again, like mother, like son, right? Isn't that how the old adage goes?"

Her face turns crimson with so much rage that her voice is shaking when she pivots to the guards and says, "What are you waiting for?"

They move forward as one, and I freak out, knowing there's no way Hudson is going to let me through to put myself between him and them. But ultimately, I don't have to, because Luca does it for me. And so do Eden and Macy.

"You can't do this," Macy cries. "I know you're sad over Damien—"

"It's already done," Nuri answers coldly. "The only question now is how many of you are going to end up in cells right next to him."

"All of us," Luca growls, but I notice Flint hasn't moved.

"Is that true?" Nuri's eyes go among Macy, Luca, Eden, and me. "Are you really going to risk everything for this *vampire*?" She says it like it's a dirty word. "After what he did?"

"Yeah," Macy says. "We are."

"No, you're not," Hudson tells her, and for the first time, he sounds a little unsteady, like he can't believe this is happening.

Not the threat of imprisonment, I realize as I watch his face in the mirror, but the fact that someone is standing up for him. That someone has his back (in my case, quite literally).

"Can we just be frank here?" Eden asks, then continues before Nuri gives her any kind of leave to do so. "Damien was an asshole. I loved him, Your Majesty, just like I know Flint loved him. But he was still an asshole, and his death was his own fault."

"You dare to come into my house and speak ill of my dead son?" Nuri demands. "Your family line isn't strong enough for that."

"With all due respect, this isn't about my family line," Eden snarls. "This is about your son never being the man you wanted him to be, and everyone here knows it. You can pretend all you want, but I've spent almost my entire life at Court, and it was common knowledge. I've also gotten to know Hudson, and he's turning out to be ten times the man your son was."

Nuri stumbles back like she's been hit, and I hold my breath, waiting to hear what she's going to say. Waiting to find out if this nightmare is going to end or if it's just beginning. For a second, she looks older—much older than she did on the Ludares field—and frail, like a stray thought might knock her over.

But then she tamps down her sorrow right in front of us. She pulls herself up so that she looks every inch of her regal six feet plus, looks down her aquiline nose, and orders, "Take her, too."

"For what, Mom? For speaking her mind?" Flint weighs in for the first time in what feels like forever. "That's what Cyrus does—we're not like that."

She ignores him, choosing instead to stare down the guards as she waits for them to do what she orders. And while they were more than happy to haul Hudson to the dungeon or wherever they put people in buildings like this, they apparently aren't nearly as excited about arresting a young dragon female for doing nothing worse than speaking truth to power.

But Nuri is not budging, and as tense seconds tick by, I think we all come to understand that.

Against the protests of Luca, Macy, and me, Hudson steps out from behind our friends, making sure to cover their bodies with his as he does. "I'll go with the guards if you leave Eden and the rest of them alone."

Nuri quirks one imperious brow. "You'll go with the guards no matter what."

"Maybe I will," he agrees with his own arrogant brow lift. "Or maybe I'll level this entire building instead. Want to try me?"

Her gaze flicks down to the magical bracelet he's wearing, the one that everyone knows grounds his power. He just smirks in response. Then he reaches down and unhooks it, holding it up for everyone to see before dropping it at her feet.

Macy gasps, Eden laughs, and Luca looks around like he's trying to find a support beam to crawl under before remembering he's on an elevator.

I don't even have time to process why his bracelet hasn't worked this entire time. But I send him a look in the mirror that says we most definitely will discuss it later. Right now, I am focused on keeping him out of prison.

Nuri studies him from narrowed eyes, like she's assessing him and trying to decide if she wants to call his bluff. But in the end, she just shrugs and says, "Leave the girl. But take him to the cell I have waiting for him."

"Hudson, no!" I try to grab on to his arm, try to make eye contact in the mirror in front of us again. "You don't have to do this."

"It's fine, Grace," he says dismissively, then peels my hand off him and lets it drop, like I'm nothing more than a gnat.

It's not what I expect from him. The blankness in his eyes when they meet mine is so foreign that I can feel everything inside me shrivel. I tell myself that it's just an act he's putting on for Nuri's benefit, that his father taught him anything he loves can be used as a weapon against him, but that doesn't stop my stomach from clenching or my hands from going clammy with fear.

I don't know where she's taking him. I don't know what she plans to do or what she hopes to accomplish other than avenging her lost son. But as I watch the guards slap chains on Hudson's wrists and ankles, the looks on my friends' faces tell me that whatever it is, it's not going to be good.

73

I'm Not Buying
What You're Celling

We watch in silence as the guards drag Hudson away. He's not fighting them at all, but they're either extra scared of him or extra sadistic, because they've put the chains on extra tight—which makes it really, really hard for him to walk. Of course, maybe that's the point.

Either way, Nuri has a small, pleased smile on her face as she watches them disappear with him around another corner. To the freight elevator, I wonder frantically, or to a prison she set up for him on this floor? My guess is the freight elevator, and I make a note to ask Mrs. Jamieson where it is later, because there is no way he's spending a night in prison. No fucking way.

Once the sound of the chains scraping against the expensive flooring dissipates, Nuri turns to us with a gracious smile. "Let me show you to your rooms now."

It's the most bizarre thing she could possibly have said in this moment, that it takes me a few seconds to even process it. But when I do, I turn on her with all the fear and rage bottled up inside me. "You don't actually think we're going to hide in our rooms like good little boys and girls after what you just did, do you?"

"Grace—" Flint steps forward, puts a hand on my arm, but I shrug him off. I'm not exactly happy with him right now, either. He might not have known what Nuri had planned, but he didn't stand up for Hudson either.

"What I expect," Nuri says, "is for you to do what we all do in times like this, Grace. Whatever is most prudent for you—which, in this case, I believe, is going to your room to unpack and cool off a little bit." Her eyes narrow just slightly. "It is unseasonably warm today."

It's a threat, and not even a very veiled one at that, but I couldn't care less. Not when panic is a living, breathing monster inside me, sucking up all my oxygen and battering at my insides. I take a deep breath, then several more as I count to ten, twenty, *fifty*. I name ten things in the room, try to concentrate on the feel of my toes scraping against the bottom of my shoes, but nothing is working. I keep coming back to Nuri's face, to the look in her eyes, and it destroys me. As does the idea of Hudson locked up and vulnerable and being totally unable to help him.

Maybe that's why I whirl on Flint. "Did you know this was going to happen?"

He shakes his head, but he won't meet my gaze. Instead, he stares straight ahead, eyes blank and jaw working feverishly.

It infuriates me like nothing else could have. This emotionless being isn't the Flint I know, which means what? This whole weekend was just a trap? But by whom—Nuri or Cyrus?

I shoot a panicked look at Macy, who's usually really good at knowing how to calm me down, but the look she sends back shows that she's just as freaked out by all of this as I am. Which only succeeds in freaking me out more.

Still, I manage to hold my tongue—and keep my shit together—as Nuri takes us one floor down and walks us to our rooms. She's right. Not that I need to calm down, but that I need to take a moment and assess the situation. Figure out my next move. And if that means going to my room like a good little gargoyle, so be it.

The hallway we walk down is gorgeous, the ballroom we pass exquisite… and set for what looks like close to a thousand people. Any other time, I know I'd be fascinated, but right now, I barely notice. All my attention, every single part of me, is focused on Hudson and the bright-blue string within me.

I don't know how this works, didn't even know these strings existed until Jaxon's and my mating bond. And I've been too scared to look at Hudson's and mine that closely.

Too scared that it will let me see more than I want of him…or him of me.

Too scared that I'll like it too much.

Too scared that I won't be able to let it—to let him—go.

But now, now I reach for it with all the strength inside me, close my hand over it with the same determination I grab hold of my platinum string. I'm desperate to find him, to feel him, to know that he's safe.

The moment my fingers wrap around our bond, I feel him inside me, squeezing his side of the bond back. So many emotions come slamming into me, I almost stumble. Emotions I'm not ready to examine. Not ready to acknowledge. So I sift through the layers of our relationship until I find the part I need—just Hudson.

I expect him to be scared, frantic, as worried about himself as I am about him. But I don't sense any of that—which would scare me, except for the fact that deep inside him there's warmth instead of worry, calm in place of fear.

Hudson is okay—more than okay—at least for now. I have time to figure out how to get him out of there before Nuri moves on to whatever the next step of this plan is.

For a second, I can't help wishing that she was a made-up villain, getting ready to spill her evil plan so that the hero (or in this case, heroine) could figure out a way to foil her. But this is real life, not fiction, and Nuri doesn't look oafish enough to spill her plans to anyone. Then again, she doesn't look like she's capable of kidnapping and imprisoning anyone, either, and yet here we are.

I squeeze the blue string one more time, once again heartened by the zip of electricity that slices back through me. Hudson is still alive, still strong. That's all that matters.

"This is your room, Grace," Nuri says as she stops in front of a beautiful blue room. It's got another Dale Chihuly chandelier hanging over the bed, beautiful white and silver furniture, and a bedspread that, coincidentally, is only a shade or so lighter than the mating bond I've spent the last five minutes staring at.

I nod and, after giving Macy a look that says *come find me as soon as Nuri is gone*, I step into the room. Nuri pauses a moment outside the door, like she's waiting for me to say thank you or close the door, but hell would have to literally freeze over before I even consider doing either.

She invited us here for a celebration and to help us figure out what to do, then turned around and imprisoned Hudson without a second thought. No way am I thanking her for that. And no way am I closing this door and risking her locking me in, too.

This room might be most people's idea of luxury personified, but once that door locks from the outside, it's a prison like any other. Today is not the day for me to willfully give away my freedom. Not when so many other people's freedom depends on me keeping mine.

So instead of saying anything to Nuri or Flint or the others, I put my backpack down on the luggage rack in the open closet beside the door and start fake riffling through it, my back to her.

I can sense her waiting, hear her breathing, but when it becomes apparent that I have no plan to move, she reaches for the door handle and starts to close it.

"No thank you." I stretch out a stone hand and foot and block the door from being closed.

Nuri doesn't look shocked by my move. Instead, she looks intrigued—and watchful. Very, very watchful.

"I suppose we'll leave this open, then," she says before continuing down the hall, my friends following behind her like little ducks...or faithful servants. I guess the next few days will tell.

74

Past Really Is Prologue

"**O**h my God!" Macy says the second she hits my room.

"I know," I answer, moving from my spot on the bed for the first time since I lay down there half an hour ago.

I've counted every rose in the crown molding at least ten times and am happy to report that there are 227 of them with eight petals each, for a total of 1,816 petals. Not that anyone cares, but it gave me something to do besides obsessively checking on my blue mating bond.

"Just, oh my God, Grace."

"I *know*."

"What are we going to do?"

"I don't know." I reach into my backpack and pull out a Twix, then hand one of the bars to Macy. Nuri had small fruit-and-cheese baskets put in our rooms, but at this point, not only do I not want anything from her, I don't *trust* anything from her. "I mean, besides break Hudson out of prison before he levels the whole damn building? I'm pretty sure he'll go to real prison for that, and not just to find the blacksmith."

"Yeah." She sighs. "I know."

I bite into the Twix for some chocolate courage, then ask what's been on my mind since Nuri showed her true colors. "Do you think Flint knew this was going to happen?"

"What?" Macy asks, genuinely shocked. "He wouldn't do that to you."

I want to believe the same thing, but I've been wrong about him before. And while I'm a big believer in letting the past stay in the past, it's hard to do that when the past keeps punching me in the face. Repeatedly.

"I don't know. I want to believe that he wouldn't deliberately screw us over like that, but what if this was all just an elaborate trick to get Hudson here?"

She looks confused. "They have the festival every year. It's not a trick—"

"Not the festival. The Circle business stuff. And the promise of a dragon who came back from the prison in a day. What if none of that was true? What if this is just a wild goose chase that ends up ruining everything?" My voice breaks, and I take a deep breath, determined to will back the panic that's been plaguing me from the moment those elevator doors opened.

Too bad it's easier said than done.

"What if Flint thinks…" I trail off, not even sure what I want to say. And also, maybe a little too scared to put into words what I fear most.

"What if I think what?" Flint asks from the door, face strained and signature grin long gone.

Luca stands behind him, but not in a good way. There's definite space between them, and even from here, I can feel the ice-cold vibe rolling off the vampire. Apparently, I'm not the only one with some doubts.

"I don't know," I tell him as betrayal washes over me, twisting my stomach into knots. "Maybe if I did, I wouldn't feel so fucked over."

His jaw works. "That's not fair, Grace."

"Not fair?" I tell him. "Seriously? You're going to go there? Hudson is in a cell right now—"

"For killing my brother!" he roars. "He's locked up because he murdered Damien. You keep forgetting that."

"I haven't forgotten a damn thing," I tell him.

"Oh my God. You did know," Macy says, and she sounds sick.

"I didn't." He shakes his head emphatically. "I never would have brought you here if I did. But you've got to see her side of it, too. This is the guy who killed her son."

"Because her son was working with Cyrus to take over the fucking world," I tell him, and I can't believe we are even having this discussion. "He was going to hurt a lot of people. He—"

"He was my brother! And I loved him. Now, it turns out he wasn't a good guy—and I'm sorry for that. I really am. But you don't get to kill people for being assholes. Do you really think Hudson should go unpunished for what he did to Damien? For what he did to my entire family?"

"You mean the way you went unpunished for trying to kill me, over and over again?" I ask. "Or didn't I matter, because Lia had already killed my parents, and there was no one left to miss me?"

"My dad and I would have missed you," Macy says quietly.

"Well, then." I give Flint a bloodless smile. "There you go."

"It's not the same, Grace. I was trying to save—"

"What? The world?" I ask, all wide eyes and saccharin sweet. "From whom? Me?"

I give Macy and Luca my most innocent look. "But that's a little strange by your logic, considering I didn't do a damn thing. I didn't even know what was going on. Lia was the one with the evil plan. Lia was the one trying to 'destroy the world' by bringing big, bad Hudson Vega back. But she was too powerful to take on, so *you* decided *I* had to die. *You* decided I was collateral damage in your plot to save the world. *A reasonable loss.*"

My throat clogs up with emotion, but I take a second to clear it because I'm not done yet. "And what did I do, Flint? Did I press charges? Did I demand that you go to prison for attempted murder? Assault? Accessory to human fucking sacrifice? No, I didn't. I let it go; I moved on. Because I understood that you were stuck, that there were no good options, and you were trying to save whomever you could.

"And I'm good with that decision. I still believe it was the right thing to do. I thought we could leave the past in the past and it would all be okay. But you don't get to be all sanctimonious with me now, you sorry son of a bitch. Because the only difference I can see between what Hudson did and what you did is he succeeded. And his target had it coming.

"So fuck you and your whole Dragon Court. I'm going to find this dungeon or basement or wherever they're holding him on my own, I'm going to get Hudson, and then we're going to get the fuck out of here. And if you and I never talk again, well, that's fine by me. I never could stand hypocrites anyway."

75

Ditto

F lint doesn't say a word, though he has turned a sickly shade of beige that would normally concern me. But right now, I'm too damn mad to care. And his blocking the door—and my path to freedom—only makes me angrier. Maybe that's why I put a whole lot of stone into my shoulder when I shove my way past him.

And run straight into Nuri, because apparently, she's fucking everywhere. Fan-fucking-tastic.

"You done with your little temper tantrum?" she asks mildly.

"I don't know. Did you let my mate go yet?"

"Not yet, no."

"Well, then I guess the tantrum's not over yet." I start to walk right by her, but she grabs my wrist, holds me in place. Which makes me even angrier.

"You're going to want to let go of me," I tell her.

"And you're going to want to calm down," she shoots back, but she releases my wrist. "I'm only willing to give you so much room, Grace."

"Yeah, well, I feel the same way about you, *Nuri*."

Macy gulps audibly, and Luca, who is still in the hallway, takes a large step into my bedroom, I assume because he wants out of the blast zone.

In the meantime, Nuri's eyes narrow. "I think you mean Your Majesty."

It's a low blow, pulling rank on me, but here's the thing. She's not the only one with a title. Which is why I smile sweetly at her and say, "Ditto."

Part of me expects her to slap me back into what she thinks is my place—God knows, Cyrus would have—but that same part is also welcoming it. Because I'm not the same girl I was in November, lost and exhausted and so sad that the path of least resistance seemed like the only road to take.

Jaxon and Hudson and Macy have all helped me in their own way to break through the sadness and the numbness, to find myself again—and not just the old me but a stronger version of me, one who is more than capable of taking care of myself *and* the people I love. I'm not going back to that broken existence, not now and hopefully not ever again.

But Nuri surprises me. Instead of taking a swing at me, she says, "Okay, Grace. If you want to play with the big girls, I say let's play *Let's Make a Deal*."

It's my turn to narrow my eyes at her. "What does that mean?"

She laughs. "Don't go getting cautious on me now. Come on, step into my office." Then she turns and starts walking down the hall.

"Said the spider to the fly," I mutter.

"I think you mean dragon, don't you?" she asks over her shoulder with a brow raised in a regal arch. "So much deadlier than spiders."

It's a threat, pure and simple, but it doesn't scare me. She doesn't scare me, at least not anymore. Because if there's a deal to be had about getting Hudson out of those damn chains, I am all in.

Her office ends up being one floor down, so we take the stairs in silence (I don't think either one of us is cool with getting in a closed elevator with the other right now). My phone goes off the whole time, and it doesn't take a genius to figure out Macy is the one blowing it up.

Part of me wouldn't mind a little advice on how to handle Nuri, but there's no way I'm going to show weakness by pulling it out. Besides, I think I need to trust my own instincts on this.

When we finally get to her office, she throws the door open with a theatrical air, and as soon as I pass through the doorway, I know why. Just like I know why she insisted on having the meeting here and not somewhere else. Her office is as dramatic and elegant and *powerful* as the dragon queen herself.

Her desk itself is quite delicate—a Queen Anne writing desk like my mom used to have, though hers was in dark cherry. But that's where the delicacy ends. The colors of the furniture and fabrics and walls are bold reds, majestic purples, and powerful whites that catch the eye and the imagination.

There's a tall glass case towering in the corner, with what look to be Egyptian artifacts on display. A papyrus, a vase, and some ancient-looking jewelry. I remember Flint mentioning once that his mom was from an Egyptian dragon clan, so these are probably objects of great importance to her.

Along the wall facing massive windows overlooking the city—what a view!—are three pieces of modern art in bold colors that send a powerful message of strength and uniqueness, and the knickknacks, all dragon- or royalty-related in some way, add a further note of authenticity to the whole office. As does the heavily used laptop on the edge of the desk.

"Would you like something to drink?" Nuri asks, gesturing to a small wet bar in the corner—and a silver pitcher sitting on top of it, along with several goblets.

"Hemlock?" I ask, because I wouldn't put it past her at the moment.

"Close," she answers with a laugh. "Pineapple juice. Would you like some?"

"I'm good."

"Please have a seat." She gestures to one of the two chairs in front of her desk. They're upholstered in pure, pristine white, and any other time, I might be terrified to sit in them for fear of a leaky pen or spilling my drink.

I pick the left one and am just petty enough to regret not taking her up on the juice.

She takes the purple chair behind her desk, which looks a lot more like a throne than an ergonomic desk chair.

Once seated, she picks up a pen to twirl between her fingers as she watches me for several seconds, waiting, I'm sure, for my nerves to get the best of me. And, not going to lie, I've got plenty of nerves going on. Plenty of voices in the back of my head telling me that I need to be really careful when it comes to Nuri.

Finally, she breaks the silence. "Would you agree, Grace, that actions have consequences?"

"I would agree to that," I tell her. "*If* we can agree motivation should play a big part in those consequences. And I would also argue that those who live in glass skyscrapers shouldn't throw stones."

She doesn't respond verbally to my last comment, but the velocity with which she twirls her fountain pen increases significantly as she continues. "I don't believe you are so naive as to think that there isn't opposition to you and Hudson claiming a spot on the Circle. Right now, we're evenly split—dragons and witches for, wolves and vampires against." She steeples her hands in front of her, then eyes me over her fingertips. "But that can change at any moment."

It's another not-so-veiled threat, and there's a part of me that wants to tell her to hell with the Circle. It's not like I want to deal with the power plays that are a part of it for the rest of my very long life. But she's right. I'm not that naive, and I know that the only power I have—the only real bargaining chip—comes from all the different factions knowing I've earned my spot on the Circle, whether they like it or not.

So instead of telling her off and walking out the way I so desperately want to, I lean back in my chair and ask, "What do you want, Nuri? Because that's what this is all leading up to, right? The *Let's Make a Deal* portion of the day?"

"Actually," Nuri says, "I don't think we're there yet." She studies me for a moment. "For starters, what do *you* want?"

"Hudson released from your dungeon and my friends and family safe," I respond immediately.

"That's it?" She quirks a dark brow. "No Court? No Circle? If you become gargoyle queen, you need a much wider view. It can't just be about your mate, your friends, and your family. It has to be about what's best for our five factions in general—"

"I respectfully disagree," I say. "Yes, we have to govern for everyone. But I think Cyrus's problem is that he thinks he's doing these things for vampires everywhere, but that's not true. Everything he does, he does for himself."

"Finally, something we agree on," Nuri tells me.

"I think if the whole Circle cared more about the concrete people in their own lives and less about the abstract concept of power, we'd all be better off," I add. "It's why I think motivation is so important when it comes to deciding things like punishment or right and wrong. Do actions have consequences? Of course they do. Every single thing we do in a day has a consequence—at least one. Which shirt I wear determines whether or not I feel confident going into my day. The answer to that question determines whether or not I do well on my English presentation. The answer to that determines whether I get to hang out with my friends tonight or if I have to study.

"I'm talking about simple things, yeah, but that doesn't mean they aren't important. Little things become big things, big things become huge things, and huge things—"

"Kill us all," Nuri finishes.

"Pretty much, yeah." I sigh. "And I get it. I'm not obtuse. I understand how soul-destroying it is that you couldn't save Damien. I feel the same way knowing that my parents died because someone who had never met any of us decided to make it so, because she needed something from me.

"Do you know what that feels like?" I ask. "To know that the two people I loved most in the world are dead because of me? And you think I don't know about actions and consequences? You think I don't know that one decision can change everything?"

I think about Jaxon and Hudson.

About the Bloodletter and the fake mating bond.

About Xavier and the way Hudson begged us not to try to take on the Unkillable Beast.

About Lia and my parents.

I think about them all.

"Actions have consequences," I say again. "Mistakes get made. Hearts get broken. But judging those consequences? Deciding the consequences someone must face? Those are just more actions, and those actions lead to more, often bloody consequences. It becomes a never-ending cycle that we have no hope of breaking unless we choose differently. Unless the consequences we enforce reflect not just what happened but *why* it happened and how we can heal the divide it caused."

It's the longest argument I've ever made in my life, and when I'm done, I slump back in my chair and wait for the verdict. Because I wasn't just blowing smoke up Nuri's butt. I meant every word I said, and not just because I want to free Hudson—although that is definitely part of it.

But it's also because I've learned over the last six months that the things we do matter. The things we say matter. We can't just pretend they don't. But until we figure that out, until we start acting like they do, we're just going to make the same mistakes.

Nuri doesn't say anything for a long time, just watches me and thinks. And thinks. And thinks. I can practically see the wheels turning in her brain, the scales wobbling back and forth as she considers and reconsiders what I've had to say.

It goes on so long that I'm nearly jumping out of my skin when she says, "Ask me what I want again."

This is it. I can feel it. My chance to free Hudson and maybe, possibly fix a little of the damage we've all caused. "What do you want?"

"To make sure I don't lose my second son." She looks me in the eye. "Now ask me how we're going to make that happen."

My mouth goes dry, and for a second, I'm not sure I'm going to be able to get the words out. But then I lick my lips, clear my throat, and ask, "How are we going to do it?"

"By doing whatever it takes to bring down Cyrus Vega and achieve peace for the Circle, the factions, and *our* friends and family."

76

All Keyed Up

H er answer reverberates in my head like a wire that's been strung too tight. "If there's no war, they can't kill Flint. Or anybody else."

"Exactly. Because actions have consequences, even in this dark time."

Nuri studies my face intently—so intently that it makes me uncomfortable, and I think about looking away just to get a break for a second. But this is a test as much as anything else that's happened in this room, so I hold her gaze, let her look her fill.

She must find whatever she's looking for, because she sits up abruptly, then reaches into her desk drawer and pulls out a key. We both stare at it before she holds it out to me.

I'm almost afraid to hope, but I take it anyway, determined not to make any mistakes. At least not now.

"The cells are on zero floor. You need to take one of the main elevators to get there."

"Okay."

She lifts a brow. "No *thank you* for setting your mate free?"

"Thank you," I tell her and almost leave it at that. But I can't, not when this meeting is all about establishing some kind of partnership. Partnerships only work when both parties are on the same footing, and I am determined that this one will work, determined to do whatever I have to do to protect the people I love from Cyrus and Delilah and whatever the Circle has planned.

"Please don't do this again," I say, but both Nuri and I know it's more a demand than a request. "I think we both know—now—that locking Hudson up was your way of creating a bargaining chip. And while I...admire...your no-holds-barred attitude when it comes to saving the world, I don't want the people I care about to be used like that again."

I know I'm pushing it, and am half expecting her to lash out at me, but this needs to be said. She has to know that Hudson and Jaxon and Macy and Eden and Uncle Finn and the Order are off-limits to her. That the next time she uses one of them, it won't end up working out as advantageously for her.

She inclines her head, seems to think about it. "As long as I don't feel like my son is at risk, I believe I can live with that."

That seems fair, considering Nuri and I want the same thing. And no matter how mad I was at Flint earlier, I still don't want anything bad to happen to him. "I've considered Flint one of my closest friends for weeks now," I tell her. "Until today, I would have said I would lay down my life for his."

When she leans back this time, she's smiling. "I believe you would. And just so you know, he had no idea what I had planned for Hudson. He was as shocked as you were."

I don't know if she says it to make me feel bad, but it works—a little bit. There were two reasons I was so mad at Flint. The first was because I thought he'd sold us out, but the second really was because he was trying to blame Hudson for what happened to Damien without ever taking responsibility for what he'd done to me.

I really thought I'd moved on, really thought I had left the past where it belonged. But apparently not.

I should probably work on that...later.

"You know, not all vampires are like Cyrus." The way she'd sneered the word "vampire" at Hudson earlier still stings. "Your son has loved two, after all. I definitely think he has a type, so it would probably make for easier family relations if you learned to like them as well."

Nuri offers me a half smile. It's the first chink in her armor all night, and it exposes just a touch of the worried mother underneath her tough royal exterior. "Yes, I've suspected for a while that he was in love with Jaxon Vega." She shakes her head. "But vampires are such cold creatures, and not a good match for our fiery dragon hearts. We love passionately, and I worry Flint will find out the hard way that they do not."

"You're wrong, Nuri. Vampires aren't cold. Just because they don't always show their love with flowery words doesn't mean it's not there. They don't just love with their hearts. They love with every part of their soul—a soul they would easily sacrifice without a thought for the one they love. It's an honor to be loved by so selfless a *creature*." I throw her word back at her and watch as it hits her where it hurts. "Luca is as kind and loving as they come, and

Flint is a lucky guy to have him in his life."

"Thank you for telling me that," she says.

"Does it make a difference?"

"I don't know yet," she says, but I can see she's considering what I said. "What about what I said about Flint? Does it make a difference that he didn't know my plans? Will you seek his friendship again?"

"I don't know yet," I say with equal honesty. We've both said a lot, and we both have a lot of thinking to do.

"Good. You shouldn't let him off too easily." My surprise must show on my face, because she laughs, then repeats her mantra. "Actions have consequences, Grace. You think because I'm his mother, I can't admit that he screwed up spectacularly with Lia? He didn't ask for help—tried to go it alone—and nearly destroyed everything."

"Including me," I say dryly.

"Including you," she agrees, then hesitates, as though she's not sure she wants to say something else. In the end, she must decide it's worth saying. "Trust no one, Grace. Especially not Cyrus."

"Umm, yeah, no worries there. I'd rather trust wet paint."

"Cyrus tricked me once, and it nearly destroyed my people, nearly toppled my entire kingdom. Before it was done, we had to forfeit almost everything we had—our hoards, our belongings, even our homes—including Katmere Academy itself, which was once *my* family's ancestral estate and our original Dragon Court. All because Aiden and I trusted Cyrus."

Her eyes glow even brighter now, and as I look more closely, I realize it isn't power making them glow. It's anger...and hate. "He used that trust to take out the biggest threat to his domination—the gargoyles—and then, once they were gone, he set his sights on destroying us as well."

"You helped?" I ask, the question bursting out of me in a horrified whisper before I can think twice about the prudence of asking it. "The dragons actually helped him destroy the gargoyles in the Second Great War?"

Just the thought has my stomach revolting, my entire being rejecting the idea. I know that Cyrus is evil, know that the need for power is a sickness deep within him, but is everyone like that in this world? Does no one care about anything but themselves and what they can take?

And if so, am I supposed to be the same? Will I join the Circle and suddenly only care about what I can take? Or what I can *steal*?

If so, I want no part of it—no part of any of this.

It's my turn to get to my feet. I stumble toward the door—overwhelmed by what she's told me and even more overwhelmed by what it all means. But before I can reach for the doorknob, Nuri is there in front of me.

"Now is not the time to behave rashly," she hisses at me. "Our history is a complicated discussion for another day. But suffice it to say that no, we were not directly responsible for the extinction of gargoyles, whether that's how that story is told in the history books or not."

I remain standing, but I don't move to leave.

She continues. "Now is the time to take great care, Grace. Cyrus is devious, and he will stop at nothing to get what he wants. Nothing," she reiterates, "even if that means killing his own sons. Exterminating an entire race. Burning the Circle and our whole world to the ground. And we are the only ones who can stop him."

Her words explode through me like a supernova. Not the fact that Cyrus is devious, because been there, done that, have the nightmares to prove it. But the idea that she and I can stop him? That we can change what one thousand years of planning, of plotting—of murder—have put into motion?

All I did was play a game, and it nearly killed me. How on earth can I stand against this man, who makes enemies of anyone who goes against him… and then destroys them just because he can?

"How?" I ask. "How are we supposed to do that? You've already got Hudson in a cage because he told you to—"

"You know about that?" she asks sharply.

"Like you said, I'm not naive, Nuri. I think you enjoyed putting him in that cage because of Damien. But I don't think you did it for that reason. You did it because Cyrus wants him there, and it will curry favor with him for you. He nearly destroyed you, and you're still willing to do this for him, so why the hell should I believe you when you say that we can stop him?"

"Because I gave you the key to get Hudson out." She ticks the reasons off on her fingers.

"Because if we don't stop Cyrus now, he's going to take everything from us. *Everything.* And lastly, because fear only keeps people in line if they have something left to lose. Cyrus has finally hit the tipping point—he's taken so much from so many people that the thirst for justice is completely overwhelming the fear. All we have to do is harness that thirst, stoke it, and—when it's time—let it loose. He won't stand a chance."

77

Where There's a Witch,
There's a Way

My hands are shaking so badly, I shove them in my pockets so Nuri won't notice. She may think we're on the same side, but I don't doubt for a second that she'd exploit my weakness if she thought it would help keep Flint—or her precious Court—alive.

Looks like Hudson was right on earlier with the whole *like mother, like son* thing.

I don't know how I feel about what she's said, don't know how I feel about any of this, to be honest. But war is coming—we all know that—and I can only imagine that it's better to have allies than enemies.

"What do I need to do?" I ask when the silence becomes uncomfortable.

"You need to let Hudson go to prison," she says. "He can't hide forever. Most of the Circle will be at Katmere for graduation next week."

"They can't touch him as long as he's at Katmere! That's how it works—"

"Because Cyrus has proven himself so good at playing by the rules?" She gives me a pitying look. "Who's going to stop him if he decides he wants to arrest Hudson? Finn Foster? A bunch of kids? The new gargoyle queen?"

"So what would you have me do? Just leave him in your cell so you can hand him over to Cyrus?"

"Not to Cyrus," Nuri says. "To the prison. He's your mate. Surely you think going to prison is better for him than being dead, right?"

"To an inescapable prison, where he can stay for eternity, bound by an unbreakable curse?" I snarl at her, only to pause as surprise registers in her eyes. "You didn't think I knew about that, did you?"

She ignores my question—but I'm learning that Nuri ignores whatever she doesn't want to acknowledge. "Alive in prison is better than dead. Even Hudson can't defy the odds twice."

"You think he should be locked up for an eternity?" I ask. "For defending the world from Cyrus's machinations?"

"It won't be for an eternity." Nuri waves a negligent hand. "We can free him as soon as we defeat Cyrus. And defending his mate or not, he scared people. That's the real reason he has to be locked up. He has too much power, and that scares those who will do anything to hang on to theirs."

"Like Cyrus."

"Yes."

"And you," I whisper.

She doesn't deny it. "You saw what he could do. One wave of his hand, and he destroyed every bone in his father's body. One thought, and he brought down a stadium. That kind of power is unfathomable...and infinitely corruptible. We already saw what he did to Damien. What else will he do if he has the chance? If he actually makes it onto the Circle?"

Nothing, I want to tell her. He won't do anything but try to rule the best way that he can. But she doesn't know Hudson, not the way I do, and even if she did, she wouldn't believe me anyway. Whether doing so saved people or not, Hudson will always be the person responsible for her son's death.

So instead of calling her on it, I focus on the next flaw in her plan. "I thought mates choose to go to prison together?"

"Ah, but you're ignoring the key word. 'Choose.' Mates can choose to go to prison together. But they don't have to."

"I'm not sure it's much of a choice." I think back on poor, mad, desperate Falia.

She waves away my concerns. "You're a strong woman, Grace. Stronger than you ever imagined. Will it be painful? Yes. But you can get through it, and when you do—when you come out on the other side—you will be unbreakable, your strength coveted by everyone who meets you. That girl, that *woman*, is the one who can save us all."

"By destroying my own soul?" I ask incredulously.

"If need be," she answers with a calmness that freezes my insides. "Remember where we started this discussion? Saying we would do whatever it took to keep the people we love safe? This is how we do that."

I make a disbelieving sound deep in my throat. "Have you ever thought that that's Cyrus's grand plan? To put Hudson away so that the one person who actually has the ability to stop him never gets the chance?"

Nuri starts to dismiss my words again, but then she stops. Narrows her eyes. Taps a finger to her lips as she stares into space, deep in thought.

Which makes me decide to press my luck. "You want to defend your kingdom against Cyrus? I agree that you and I will make a formidable force—and maybe, just maybe, we'd survive everything that he's ready to throw at us. But the two of us, with Hudson on our side? That's the only real chance we've got."

Nuri is still lost in thought, but when she goes back to steepling her hands on her lap, I know that I've got her. Even before she says, "Flint mentioned you and Hudson were actually wanting to go to prison. He didn't elaborate why, just that you wanted my help figuring a way to get out. Is that still true?"

Now my heart is beating so fast, I'm certain Nuri can hear it. Was this it? Were we finally going to get the answer we needed? I nod.

"Well, maybe we can both get what we want and come out stronger." She pauses and looks at a small statue of a dragon, its wings curved down to nearly cover a small dragon baby within its protective care. "I can agree to this. If Hudson goes to prison, I can curry favor with Cyrus for now, maybe even give the impression that the Dragon Court may want an alliance again. But I will also help you find a way to escape the prison so you are ready to fight by our side when the time is right."

I'm already leaning forward, willing her to continue. Because the truth is, we need more time to prepare. None of us is ready to stand against Cyrus yet, not when he has had a millennium to prepare for his moment.

"I've heard rumors of a witch, the Crone, who helped build the prison. She lives a hermit's life, and no one is exactly sure of how sane she is anymore. But supposedly, if you can get her to talk to you, you can learn the secrets of the prison. And a way to escape. She once helped a dragon do exactly that—but be forewarned, her price was steep."

Tiny wings of hope flutter against my rib cage for the first time since those elevator doors opened. "What was the price?"

"His dragon heart, which is a fate worse than death for a dragon. We cannot take our dragon form without a dragon heart," Nuri says, and the tragic pain in her eyes says it all. We would need to make a much more favorable bargain or there would be no point. The cost would be too high. "But I have to tell you, Grace, it's not good odds."

True that. And still, "Nothing I've done since I first got to Katmere has had good odds, Nuri. But bad odds are better than none."

"Especially for the girl who keeps beating them." She sighs, then says, "I can give you a week."

"A week?" My eyes go big. "To find the witch?"

"Finding her isn't a problem." She pulls out a piece of paper and writes down an address before handing it to me. "Getting her to talk to you and convincing her to help you? That's going to be a bit hard. But any longer than that and Cyrus will want to know why I haven't taken Hudson prisoner. The Dragon Court will look weak—or like it's making a move against him. I can't afford to have either of those things happen."

I get it. I do. In a lot of ways, Nuri is as stuck as I am. But I add, "Do I get to pick which week I want, or are you talking about this *coming* week, which, I don't know, includes nearly all my friends and I needing to be at Katmere Academy? For *graduation*?"

"Definitely this week."

"That's what I figured you would say," I answer as I seriously contemplate banging my head on the edge of her desk. Maybe if I knock myself out, when I wake up, this will all just be a bad dream.

She grins. "Good thing you're the girl who beats all the odds, then, eh?"

"Yeah, good thing," I answer faintly.

"Don't you have a vampire to liberate?" She looks pointedly at the key in my hands.

"Yeah." It's my turn to sigh. "Yeah, I do."

"Better get to it, then. The banquet starts at eight, and I can't stand it when people are late."

78

Dungeons and Dragons: The Grace-Loses-Her-Shit Edition

I make my way out of Nuri's office and down the hall at close to a run (which is the fastest I feel safe going with guards eyeing me every fifty feet). And considering they look like the type to shoot flames first, ask questions never, I don't feel like antagonizing them is the way to go.

I finally make it to the elevator, but the ride down is excruciating—I swear to God, we stop on all fifty-six floors, which gives me plenty of time to picture Hudson bruised and battered and chained up against some wall. The only thing that keeps me calm is seeing that the mating bond is as strong and blue as ever.

And I know he could use his powers to cause some serious damage. I sigh because I also know he wouldn't want repercussions to come to us if he did. So he won't.

By the time the elevator doors open onto the basement floor, my palms are sweating and my stomach is in knots. I dart out of the elevator into the vestibule and look around wildly, not knowing what to expect but desperate to find Hudson.

I figure I'll run into a guard or a warden or a dungeon master of the very non-*D&D* variety—someone who is in charge down here—but there's no one. Just a dark, echoing, cavernous room that totally puts the creep in creepy.

I step forward tentatively, trying to get my bearings in the dim room. From what I can see, the basement is huge—the same size as an entire floor of this building but its opposite in every other way.

There are no Dale Chihuly lights down here, no overstuffed furniture—almost no lights or furniture at all, in fact. There are a couple of flickering light bulbs placed in a seemingly random order on the ceiling, but all they do is light the room up enough to take it from pitch-black to eerie as fuck. Not exactly my idea of a good decorating choice.

Still, standing here freaking myself out isn't going to do any good, so I step farther into the room, straining to see whatever I can. A few more steps and I realize the entire room is ringed in vertical bars, and every so often, the bars are cross-divided by shorter stone walls, forming squares or...

Cells, I realize as I step out of the elevator vestibule and into the main part of this basement. They've divided the room into *a lot* of cells. Like, *a lot* a lot.

Exactly how many prisoners does the Dragon Court anticipate having here at one time, anyway? It looks like Nuri's got enough cells in here to take half of Tribeca prisoner.

All the cells close to me are empty, so I start running toward the center of the room. I'm far enough away from the other side—and the light is so bad in here—that I can't get a good look in the cells.

There's a strange hissing noise coming from the back left corner of the dungeon, and while I can't see what's making the sound, it's animalistic enough that I'm nervous about getting too close. But a quick running tour of this half of the basement shows me two things. One, all the cells over here really are empty, and two, they are modeled exactly after the ones at Katmere Academy...right down to the arm and leg shackles in the walls.

My stomach churns at the idea of Hudson being chained up like this, and I start moving faster, looking in each of the cells I haven't already checked, getting more and more desperate to find him.

Has Nuri been lying to me this whole time? Did she just call me to her office to keep me busy while she had something horrible done to him? The thought has ice slicing down my spine even as I tell myself not to panic, to stay calm. To ignore the strange slithering sound that is growing louder and louder the closer I get to the back corner of the room.

Hudson is in here somewhere, I tell myself. I texted him in the elevator—a long shot, I know—and of course he didn't answer. Maybe if I scream for him, he'll hear me...or maybe whatever is making that sound will hear me and that will be the end of everything.

Still, I have to do something. If he's not in any of the corner cells, then I'm going to need to—

I freeze as I finally realize what the strange slithering sound is. Two guards are sitting on their butts on the hard cement floor, rolling a plastic playground ball back and forth to each other.

Of all the strange creatures—giant spiders, poisonous snakes, rabid dragons—I had imagined being the source of that noise, two guards playing ball (and completely ignoring my intrusion into their prison) didn't even crack my top ten thousand.

For one out-of-time second, I think I'm being punked, that this is some elaborate show to cover up whatever is really going on. And then I realize destruction isn't Hudson's only power—it's just the one I've focused on the most.

"Hudson!" I yell, my voice echoing in the dim, shadowy room. "Hudson, where are you?"

"Grace? What are you doing down here?"

His voice comes from the very end of the row—the very last cell in the corner—and I take off running for it, key in my trembling hand. Only to have him walk right out of the cell in front of me...because the entire front of the cell is missing.

"You asshole." The word comes out before I even know I'm going to say it, but as it registers, I realize I don't want to take it back.

"Nice to see you, too," he says, and there's just enough bite in the words to remind anyone who's listening that he's a vampire...as if they'd need a reminder when he wears it like a damn trophy.

"Are you kidding me? I've been worried sick about you! I fought with Flint—*Luca* fought with Flint—and then I fought with Nuri, the whole time terrified that they were torturing you, and you're *fine*."

"I'm so sorry to disappoint you. Would you rather they *had* tortured me?"

"That's not the point," I growl at him as I turn around and start flouncing back to the elevator.

"What is the point, then?" he counters as he follows directly behind me.

"The point is you're okay. You persuaded the guards to play ball; you've disintegrated most of your cell..."

"So far not seeing the problem, unless you were hoping to catch me all bound up by those lovely chains in the wall."

"I was terrified that's how I would find you!" I snap back. "But you're fine!"

"You keep saying that. Which means what?" In typical Hudson fashion, he manages to sound befuddled and insulted at the same time. "That you're not happy about it?"

"Of course I'm happy about it! It's not like I enjoyed imagining them cutting small pieces off you or—"

"Please," he says dryly. "Spare me the gory details."

"Why should you be spared? I imagined it in goddamn Technicolor. Several times. But you're fine." I shake my head, trying to clear the last remnants of fear and adrenaline away. "You're fine."

"I'm still failing to understand what's going on here," he says, and oh wow, is the British back in force in his voice. "You want me to be fine, but you're upset that I'm fine." He holds his hands up on either side of himself and moves them up and down like they're a scale.

"I'm upset because you could totally get away from this at any second—and, in fact, did get away from it—and instead of putting us out of our misery, you left Luca and Macy and Eden and me to worry about you. How can you not see that that's beyond awful?"

I expect him to scoff at my words, to tell me that I'm being ridiculous. But instead, he just kind of stands there in the middle of the basement and stares at me with the most bizarre look that I've ever seen on his face.

"What?" I demand when he doesn't say anything. "Why are you staring at me like that?"

"You were worried about me."

It's my turn to give him a look. "Of course I was worried about you! What have I been screaming about this whole time? What did you think would happen? That I would just watch you get arrested and be all, *oh well, it was fun while it lasted*? Nice to know you think so highly of me!"

"I'm sorry. I just figured you'd know I could take care of myself."

"I do know that. But I also know that there are a lot of people in this world who can't be trusted, and most of them are gunning for you."

"I'm...sorry," he says again, then blows out a breath. "No one has ever—"

"Oh, no," I interrupt. "No, no, no. You don't get to do that. You don't get to pull that whole poor-little-rich-boy shit on me. You know you have people who care about you now. You know you have friends. You know you have—" I break off, folding my arms in front of my chest in a weak attempt at self-protection.

"A mate?" he asks, slowly walking toward me.

"That's not what I meant!" I tell him, backing away, my heart in my throat for a whole different reason now.

"I think it's exactly what you meant," he tells me, taking another step closer to me...which makes me take twice as many steps back in response.

"You can think whatever you want," I tell him in my snootiest voice. "That doesn't make it true."

I turn to head to the elevator, but he grabs my hand. Pulls me back around until we're face-to-face. "I'm sorry," he says. "I didn't think about how you must have felt—about how I would feel if it was you they took away in chains.

"They brought me down here, and I saw these cells, and I thought, *Blast it. My whole life has been a prison—this is just one more.* But this time it was going to be my choice, on my terms, and I didn't think about anyone else. It won't happen again."

I nod, because I understand what he's saying. And because there's a lump in my throat—for the little boy who suffered through so many unthinkable things and for the man he's become.

Because I know he'll hate my having so many feelings about what Cyrus put him through, I force the lump back down and change the subject. I motion my head toward the sound of the ball being pushed back and forth, still echoing in the basement. "You going to do something about that?"

He seems to think about it. Then says, "A little more time playing a toddler's game might do them good." I just arch a brow at him, and he sighs, then says, "Fine. But only because you asked so nicely."

Then he walks over and whispers something to the guards, who shake their heads and then get to their feet.

When he heads back over, I say, "While you were down here playing, Nuri told me how we might be able to bust out of prison."

Hudson's eyebrows go up. "Do tell."

And so I relate everything Nuri told me about the Crone. Hudson is especially impressed she also gave us directions for how to find her—and skeptical.

"Could be a trap," he says.

"Oh, I would plan for nothing less," I agree. "But I don't think we have a choice. We need the Crone to beat the prison sentence, with or without the blacksmith helping us free the Unkillable Beast. But if we just break out and don't get the Crown as well...we already know Cyrus is planning something—and we can't stop him without the Crown."

Hudson's gaze narrows on me. "If Cyrus harms anyone I love, I will end his miserable existence."

I ignore the thundering of my heart at his mention of love. Instead, I stop walking and hold his gaze. "In which case, we'd need a way to break you out of prison regardless. I think we have a good plan. Let's go bargain for a get-out-of-jail-free card and save the blacksmith and ultimately the Unkillable Beast. If the Beast won't or can't give us the Crown, at least we will have saved some people who are suffering at Cyrus's hands—and that's better than saving none. We're not helpless without the Crown. We will fight to protect Katmere and the students there another way."

"I don't like it," Hudson says. "Without the Crown, a lot of people are going to die. I could just end him now. Save us all the trouble."

"Again, hello? Prison for murder?" I roll my eyes. "Nuri seems to think we have a chance. Speaking of which, how come you can just remove your cuff?"

He looks down at his feet so long, I think he's not going to answer. "Dear old Dad used to put me in them just before...my lessons. He couldn't even conceive someone with my power wouldn't use it to kill." He shrugs. "It just became second nature to disintegrate one of the locking runes before it was fastened on my wrist, rendering it useless. I didn't even think about it when I did it to Foster, and then everyone seemed so much more comfortable having me around if I was 'locked up,' so I just said nothing."

I know I should respond to what he told me, but there's nothing to say that won't upset him—that won't make him feel like I pity him—so I gloss right over it. "Let's head back," I say, and we start walking to the elevators again.

When the elevator finally arrives, he ushers me inside. Then grins and says, "If I'd known it only took getting thrown in a jail cell for you to show you cared, I'd have locked myself up in the tunnels at Katmere on day one."

I narrow my eyes at him.

"What?" he asks as we head up to my room. "Too soon?"

"Waaaaaay too soon."

79

Ball Gown Blues

So when Flint told Macy and me that we'd need a fancy dress for the first night of Wyvernhoard, I didn't realize he meant we needed *a freaking ball gown*. Not that I would have been able to do anything about it on such short notice anyway, but still. It would have been nice to be mentally prepared, instead of spending all night tugging at the hem of my dress that's way too short for a ball gown event.

The dress Macy's wearing is also a little inappropriate for the banquet, it turns out, but it's better than mine.

"Try something new," she'd urged back when we were packing in our dorm room. "Be bold, shake things up."

So I did, and now I'm wearing a red halter top with almost no back and a skirt made of wide horizontal stripes that hugs every single curve I have and still only makes it to mid-thigh. If I was going clubbing in Manhattan, I'd fit right in. But as yet another woman walks by the open door of my room in a floor-length gown, I'm pretty sure I'm going to stick out like a sore talon once we walk into that ballroom.

In my defense, the dress looked a whole lot more innocuous hanging in my closet than it does covering up my curves.

"Stop pulling at it!" Macy hisses at me as we move into the bathroom to stare at ourselves in the wide mirrors. "You look gorgeous."

"And underdressed," I hiss back.

"Way underdressed," she acknowledges. "But that's not our fault; that's Flint's fault, so he can just own it."

We've got about an hour before we're supposed to meet the guys, but honestly, looking at myself in this definitely inappropriate dress for a formal event, I'm thinking I might just hide in my room instead. I look over at Macy, and I can tell she's considering the same.

I'm about to just say it when there's a knock at my open door.

"I'll see who that is," Macy says and disappears. A few seconds later, she gives a high-pitched squeal, and I go running out of the bathroom to stare slack-jawed as rack after rack of the most beautiful ball gowns I've ever seen are rolled into my room and placed against the far wall.

"Miss?" One of the staff presents me with a small white envelope.

"Thank you," I say and take it, my hands shaking so hard, I fumble the envelope twice before finally pulling out the note card with its masculine scrawl.

I close my eyes and take a deep breath. I already know who this is from—of course I do—and if he put something mushy on the card, I don't know what will happen. Those moments in the dungeon were enough to set my heart pounding into overdrive. I don't know if I'm ready to take things any further emotionally than that.

I know we've been moving toward something ever since our kiss. We both know it. But my walls are still too high for anything more than snark and heat to get through, and I've been hoping that he'll understand that.

If he doesn't, I don't know what's going to happen.

I take another deep breath, then blow it out slowly even as Macy implores, "Just read it already!"

So I do. And then I laugh my ass off. Because this is Hudson at his finest and of course—of *course*—he knows what I need. He always has, even when I don't.

Underwear and glass slippers optional.

—H

"What does it say?" Macy asks excitedly as she tries to peer over my shoulder.

Yeah, no way am I going to read this card out loud. "It's from Hudson. He wants us to feel like Cinderella."

I walk over to my backpack and slide the card into the front pocket—the exact pocket where I'd impulsively stashed my birthday diamond before we left Katmere.

"Oh my God," Macy squeals again, and I look up to see her holding two identical dresses. "He sent every dress in both our sizes!"

Of course he did. Ridiculous vampire prince that he is.

I try to pretend that I'm not melting into a puddle of goo, but it's not working—especially when my knees go weak and I've got to sit on the edge of my bed. How am I supposed to resist Hudson when he does stuff like this? It's one thing to send his mate a dress. I could tell myself it was so I was fittingly attired to accompany the vampire prince. But he sent every dress at Bloomingdale's and got the sizes right for both me *and* Macy, too. My eyes mist despite my best intentions.

The jerk.

But Macy doesn't give me a minute to process. She's already in motion, dashing over to me and yanking me back to my feet.

"Get up! We only have forty-five minutes," she says, "to pick out a dress that's going to knock that vampire's socks off!"

I look over at the racks of dresses and square my jaw. He really thinks he can just give up on creeping past my barriers and do something so thoughtful that it blows them to smithereens? Well, not on my watch, Hudson Vega. Not on my watch.

Two can play this game...

80

Armani Make You Mine

"Let's go find the guys and see if Eden made it back from Brooklyn yet," Macy says as we leave my hotel room.

My stomach jumps nervously as I smooth a hand down my dress. I can't wait to see what Hudson does when he sees it.

I chose this dress for two reasons, the first being that it's absolutely beautiful and fits me like a dream. In the front, the soft scarlet satin hugs my curves perfectly until it reaches my knees and flares out to the floor in a deceptively demure silhouette. It's strapless, but the bodice with its tiny little V is still structured enough that it gives me the support I need without making me feel frumpy or too overtly suggestive. The moment I put it on, I felt like Goldilocks—like I had found the dress that was just right, the dress that makes me feel sexy and powerful and ready to take on the world, even if that world includes the sexiest vampire prince ever born.

The back being a little over-the-top just makes everything better. Hudson decided to come after my heart tonight with this little move, and I've decided the only response I've got is to take no prisoners. And this dress, with its deep, *deep* V back is going to hit him somewhere a little lower than his heart...

The second reason I chose the dress is that of the dozens Hudson had sent to the room, only this one is Armani. It's a dare, pure and simple, considering I am 100 percent positive he'll be in an Armani tux tonight. Some dares are meant to be accepted. And some are meant to be eaten by the person who makes the dare.

This is definitely one of them.

I glance over at Macy, who is wearing a loose-fitting, one-shouldered chiffon dress in every color of the rainbow. It's light and airy and so, so bright that it makes my heart ache just to look at it. To look at her and think that finally—finally—Macy is finding her way back.

Eden wasn't around for my total meltdown with Flint earlier because she'd gone to visit her aunt and cousins in the Brooklyn for the afternoon, after swearing that "a pack of rabid wolves couldn't keep me away from tonight's hoard!" Macy and I had fun picking out a dress for her, though, so she wouldn't feel awkward tonight, either. We left it in her room, but now I'm dying to see how it looks on her.

We round the corner into the ballroom and find ourselves right next to the side door where Flint, Luca, and Hudson are waiting. I freeze, because just as I feared, all three are looking unbelievably good in their very appropriate tuxedos. And all three's eyes pop out of their heads as they take in my red dress and Macy's rainbow one.

Flint's signature grin is gone as his eyes meet mine, and I open my mouth to apologize for what happened earlier. Except the words stick in my throat—there was a lot of truth mixed in with the seething rage—and I basically just end up squeaking.

Flint, in the meantime, nods to Macy and me before turning around and holding the ballroom door open for us. Luca gives a fortified smile and says, "You ladies look gorgeous."

As for Hudson, he hasn't moved since Macy and I arrived, and I've apparently left all my courage back in my hotel room, because I can't bring myself to meet his gaze.

Desperate to flee all the awkward and weird feelings rolling around in the hallway, I keep my head down as I start toward the ballroom door.

Behind me, Hudson's breath whooshes out of him all at once, and I can't help grinning. Looks like my plan was as successful as I'd hoped.

I'm feeling a whole lot more confident as I take another step toward the ballroom, at least until Macy steps forward to block my way. Then she leans in close and whispers (in a voice I swear is loud enough to be heard in the back of the ballroom), "Shouldn't you let your mate escort you in?"

Before I can say anything *or* murder her, she takes Luca's offered arm and walks straight into the ballroom, a bright, excited smile on her face.

"Ready?" I ask Hudson, cheeks flushed at her blatant reminder about the mate thing after what happened earlier between us.

"Damn straight," he growls softly, and instead of taking the arm I offer to him in Macy fashion, he slides his arm around my waist and rests his palm at the small of my totally bare back. Then he leans in close and murmurs, "I was really hoping you'd pick this dress."

His breath brushes against the back of my neck, and shivers of awareness make their way down my spine. I tell myself it's because of everything that's happened in the last few days—especially the kiss and the argument in the basement.

But the truth is, Hudson is gorgeous. His very obviously couture Armani tuxedo, with its shiny lapels and white pocket square, fits his long, lean frame like it was made for him (which it probably was, now that I think about it—hello, vampire prince), and he looks like two million bucks. And also totally freaking hot.

"You look good, too," I murmur softly.

The compliment startles him, has his eyes going wide. But his answering grin is the brightest thing in the room—which is saying something, considering every dragon female here is draped in jewels—and the hand on my back gets a little more proprietary. The feel of his fingers curving around the edge of my waist makes my mouth go dry and my already none-too-steady legs shaky.

Determined to get some of my own back, I glance at him out of the corner of my eye and say, "Glass slippers are so last fairy tale."

"Oh yeah?" He moves even closer, his eyes kindling as they sweep over me from head to toe. "What about underwear?"

I lift a brow in perfect Hudson Vega fashion. "I'm pretty sure that depends on the girl."

And just like that, his eyes darken, the heat in them going from a blaze to an inferno in the space between one heartbeat and the next. "What kind of girl are you?" he whispers, his breath hot against my ear.

I let the question linger in the air for one second, two, before leaning in so that my lips brush along the line of his jaw right before I whisper back, "There's only one way to find out."

Hudson groans low in his throat even as his hold goes from proprietary to full-on caveman. His eyes blaze down at me, and I wait for him to say something that will make my cheeks burn as hotly as his gaze, but after several seconds, he seems to get a hold on whatever slipped the chain inside him.

Because instead of pushing full steam ahead, he blows out a breath, shakes his head, takes a beat to get his brain and other parts back in ballroom order. Then he propels me forward with a gentle pressure on my back. "You ready for this?"

I take my eyes off him for the first time to look at the way the room has been totally transformed and realize… "No. No, I'm really not ready for this."

He grins. "Better get ready, then, because here we go."

81

Turns Out Cupid
Is Packing a Lot
More than Arrows

I'm not sure what he's referring to—and am too busy looking at the room and the city beyond its floor-to-ceiling windows. The ballroom overlooks the Hudson and much of Manhattan, so the view is breathtaking as the bright lights of the city reflect off the river. Flint was right when he said dragons figured out the worth of real estate early—this has to be one of the best views in the whole city.

"Oh my God! It's gorgeous."

"Absolutely gorgeous," Hudson agrees. I turn to smile at him, then realize he's not looking at the view. He's looking at me.

Our gazes catch and hold and I forget how to breathe. At least until I get hit in the head by something hard.

"What is that?" I jerk around to see what just hit me.

"Looks like a ruby flying a little low from the hoard," Hudson says with a laugh. He plucks it out of the air somewhere behind us to show me.

"The hoard?" I ask. "What do you mean?"

He just grins and points up.

And *OH MY GOD*. I was so mesmerized by the view of the city that somehow I missed the fact that the air in the top half of the ballroom—starting about a foot above Hudson's head and going all the way to the ceiling—is filled with treasure. Gemstones, gold, silver, keys, and tiny purple envelopes are individually floating in midair. But they're not just hanging there, they're circling the elegantly decorated room very, very slowly, giving every person here the chance to see as much of what's up there as possible.

"Oh my God! What is *happening*?" I ask. "And is it real?"

Hudson laughs. "Of course it's real. It's a hoard."

"You mean like the dragon treasure pile Flint was telling me about?" I can't take my eyes off the sparkling, airborne jewels. It's not that I covet anything from the hoard; it's just that I'm having a hard time wrapping my head around millions upon millions of dollars just circling the ballroom above our heads, like it's no big deal.

"Not like," Hudson says. "This *is* a dragon treasure pile, just charmed to be a little more showy than normal. Every dragon in here is going to get the chance to take something from it tonight."

Flint told me the same thing, but I was picturing a gold coin for everyone or something. Not a diamond necklace or a sapphire as big as a baby's fist. It's mind-boggling, even before Hudson tosses the ruby back up toward the ceiling.

"What— Why—" I let out a squawk of surprise, expecting it to fall back down. But it doesn't. It just hangs there for a second before rejoining the slow spin of the rest of the hoard.

"Why do you look so surprised?" Hudson murmurs as we follow Luca, Flint, and Macy, all three of whom are basically arm in arm, everyone having made up with him after my talk with Nuri—well, except me. I watch as Flint leads them to a table at the very front of the ballroom where Eden is already standing, nervously shifting from foot to foot.

She'd obviously loved the dress we'd left out for her today. She looks stunning in the floor-length black velvet gown. But she wouldn't be Eden if she hadn't paired it with steel-toed Doc Martens and a saucy nose ring. She flashes Macy a big smile, and they settle down next to each other across the table from where Hudson is leading me.

Hudson continues. "The name of the holiday *is* Wyvernhoard."

"Yeah, I get it *now*. I guess I just thought some holidays become more symbolic over time..."

He laughs. "Not this one."

"Obviously not." I eye the flying treasure once again. "What are the keys for? And the envelopes?"

"If I remember correctly from the last time I was here, the keys are to real estate or vehicles, and the envelopes hold stock certificates to companies like Apple and Facebook or cash."

"Of course they do," I say in the most nonchalant tone I can manage— which is not very. But come on! What kind of wealth do you have to be raised around to be as blasé as Hudson is right now? If he remembers correctly? I promise myself I am never going to forget this moment. It's the coolest and most mind-blowing thing I've ever seen.

And I go to school with dragons and vampires...

Once I finally stop looking at the hoard and focus on the people in the ballroom again, I can't help noticing the way everyone is staring at us as we move to find our seats. Part of it, I know, comes from the fact that we're with Flint, the heir apparent to the dragon throne.

But not all the stares are for him...or the new royal boyfriend, Luca. A lot of them are directed at Hudson and me, too.

And while I've learned that vampires—especially vampire royalty—are a little bit like rock stars in this world, I have no idea why they're staring at me. Nobody knows who I am yet. It's not like there are pictures all over the internet of "that new gargoyle girl" or something.

At least until I realize that most of the women we pass are staring at me and my red dress with open jealousy, and they are literally ogling Hudson. I tell myself it's just because he's the vampire prince, but I've got eyes. I recognize envy when I see it. There are a lot of young women in this room who would do just about anything to take my place.

Not that I blame them. The more time I spend with Hudson, the more I realize that he really is a total catch.

No one seems to be upset at all that the vampire who killed the heir apparent is in their midst, and I can't help but wonder if Eden was right and everyone saw what an asshole Damien was. Everyone except his own mother, of course.

We're among the last ones in the ballroom—everyone must know about Nuri's obsession with timeliness—and once we take our seats at the second head table, Nuri and Aiden head to the microphone on the dais.

Aiden is dressed in a tuxedo, as well, but like his son, his jacket has a little more personality than the average basic black. While Flint's is a black-on-black zebra pattern with leather lapels, his dad has gone full color, with a violet velvet dinner jacket and a matching patterned bow tie that shows off his bright Irish red hair perfectly. He should look out of place among this sea of men in black, but he looks amazing.

Then again, being royalty must give you that ability.

Nuri looks fantastic, too. Her amber eyes are glowing, and her tight black curls are unbound for the first time that I've ever seen. As the ballroom lights catch her dress, I realize it's not the basic black I thought it was but a deep, dark, iridescent violet that sparkles every time she moves. Now Aiden's choice of attire begins to make a lot more sense.

The dragon queen takes the microphone first, welcoming everyone to this year's Wyvernhoard celebration. She sounds as giddy as a little kid, and the smile on Flint's face as he watches his mother signals to me that she's being totally genuine when she tells everyone that this is her favorite holiday.

"It will forever be among the greatest honors of my life," she continues, looking out over the ballroom of almost a thousand people, "to be able to invite you into my home for this holiday. Thousands of years ago, dragons were reviled, homeless, hiding wherever we could in a futile attempt to survive human wrath and detection."

She looks from face to face. "But not anymore. We joined the Circle, were gifted a Dragon Boneyard so our loved ones' remains would not be violated by humans, fought for our rightful place beside the vampires, the witches, and the wolves." She says the last with a little sneer that makes her captive audience laugh. "Through our alliance with the witches, we have combined our magic to create the necessary illusions to live in such a hoard-worthy city and still fly in dragon form undetected.

"And now, here we are!" She throws her arms wide enough to encompass not just the ballroom and the hoard but the entire city glowing right outside the windows. "This world belongs to us now, and we are going to have it all!"

82

The Old Ball Gown and Chain

Towering applause and shrill whistles greet Nuri's passionate words, but I can't help noticing that Macy, Hudson, and Luca aren't applauding. In fact, they're just kind of looking at one another like they're trying to figure out if Nuri is being hyperbolic...or if she just announced that she's planning a Circle coup.

And while I'd like to say that my time in her office today reassured me that it's the former, that would be a lie. Yes, she made a deal with me, one focused on destroying Cyrus's reign so that we can bring peace to the Circle and save the lives of the people we love. But she never said what happened next, what she thought that peace would look like to her.

My mistake for not asking.

And when she wraps up her little "dragons rule" speech by introducing the vampires, witch, and gargoyle in their midst, I can't help wondering if she's honoring us as she says...or painting targets on our backs. The looks on my friends' faces—even Flint's—say they're wondering the same thing.

Still, there's not much time to worry about it now, as Nuri has this banquet choreographed to a T.

Dinner is served right after Nuri and Aiden give their speeches, and it is beyond delicious. How they avoid the curse of the rubber chicken at a gathering of this size, I don't know. But I guess if you have enough money, you can avoid anything.

Flint, Macy, Eden, and I stuff ourselves on a wide variety of fancy appetizers that are served family-style on the table, followed by the most beautiful salad I've ever seen. We have a choice for the main course, and I choose a vegetarian pasta dish that melts in my mouth and a truffle garlic bread that's to die for. By the time dessert rolls around, I'm so full, I can barely move, but I take a couple of bites of the tiramisu anyway. Because it's tiramisu and I have to.

Nuri provides blood for the vamps, too, and from the looks Hudson and

Luca exchange when they drink it, it's definitely not the same old animal blood they usually have at Katmere.

As we eat, a fifteen-person orchestra plays softly in the background, and once plates are cleared, several couples move onto the dance floor in the center of the room.

A handful of dragon girls circles our table, and at first I think all the commotion is about Flint, which makes me chuckle a little, since Luca has all his attention. But then I realize it's for Hudson's benefit, and I totally start to feel like a third wheel—especially when they start moving in to ask him to dance, and he keeps using me as an excuse as to why he can't.

Finally, after one girl tosses me a particularly pissed-off look—one that says she's not just wishing me dead but covered in honey and staked over a fire-ant hill—I tell him, "You really don't have to keep doing that, you know."

"Doing what?" he asks, and once again, he's got that confused look on his face.

"Turning them down. If you want to dance, dance," I clarify with a studied nonchalance that I'm far from feeling.

"Oh yeah?" He glances around the ballroom at several of the younger dragons who are giving him attention...which doesn't seem fair. I mean, I'm glad that the dragons are giving Macy and me a wide berth—I have more men on my hands right now than I can handle—but is it so wrong to want your mate to ask you to dance? Or is there a reason he doesn't want to dance with me in front of a room full of the Dragon Court elite?

I'm so busy arguing with myself in my own head that I almost miss it when he asks, "So who do *you* think I should dance with?"

I swallow. Oh shit, what if he *does* ask me to dance? I'll probably just embarrass him in these shoes. "Umm don't you think that's a question you should answer for yourself?"

"You have a point," he says with a surprisingly bright grin. "Maybe I should ask—"

He was definitely going to ask me to dance. "Flint?" I interrupt.

"You think I should dance with Flint?" he asks, giving me a confused look.

"No, I think I should dance with Flint." I turn to look at the dragon in question and ask, "Will you dance with me?"

No one looks more confused than he does, considering the last conversation we had, but well...tripping around on the dance floor with Flint seems somehow less embarrassing than with Hudson. Plus, I owe Flint an apology. And he owes me one. I should have talked to him earlier, when I returned from the dungeon, but I didn't know what to say...and, admittedly, I was hoping he would come to me. But he didn't, and now it's this huge thing between us, and I have the sick feeling that it's gotten weird enough that if we don't deal with it now, we won't deal with it at all.

And I don't want that to happen.

So if asking him to dance will get us past this weirdness—and save me from having to embarrass myself in front of Hudson—then I'm good with killing two birds with one stone.

"You want to dance with Flint?" Hudson asks, his eyes bouncing back and forth between the two of us.

"I do," I say, holding a hand out to him, and decide not to ask again and instead just tell him. "Let's dance."

"Umm, yeah. Of course." Flint and Luca exchange a what-the-hell look, then Flint stands up and takes my hand. "I'd love to, New Girl."

"Okay, then," Hudson snarks as I push my chair back and climb to my feet, hoping I won't sprain an ankle on these ridiculous shoes Macy talked me into packing. "Careful not to come back with fleas."

"Excuse me?" Flint says.

"You too." I give Hudson my most saccharin smile, then grab Flint's hand and all but pull him out onto the dance floor.

"What was that about?" he asks, looking over his shoulder like he's worried about getting a fang in the back.

"Nothing," I tell him as he takes one of my hands and then presses his other against my lower back. "We were just having words."

"Yeah, well, I know that feeling," he says as we start to move with the other dancers. And can I just say, Flint is an excellent dancer. I have no idea how to do much more than hold on to my partner and sway when it comes to slow dances, but Flint is strong enough at leading that he is actually waltzing me around the dance floor.

"I'm sorry," I tell him after a second. "I went off on you this afternoon, and it was uncalled for."

"I wouldn't say uncalled for," he answers. "There was a lot of validity in what you said."

The cold ball of ice that's been hovering somewhere around the vicinity of my heart ever since we had our fight starts to melt. "I agree," I tell him.

"But I didn't need to hurl insults at you, and I definitely didn't need to tell you off in front of everyone. I was just so worried about Hudson and so mad at you—" I break off, because it's not a very good apology if you start lambasting the person all over again.

"So mad at me for not seeing the parallels. You're right. I didn't." He pulls me in for a hug before moving us back into the waltz. "I apologized to you once, but it wasn't enough. I really am sorry, Grace. I can't believe I ever thought that was even an option. I feel like such an asshole."

"Thank you," I tell him. "I know you wouldn't make the same choice today, so…let's just never talk about it again, okay?"

"Okay," he says, just as the music changes to something that sounds like it's probably a swing song. "Besides, we've got some dancing to do."

He snaps his arm out and sends me spinning, then pulls me back in. I'm so not expecting it that I half laugh, half scream as I grab on to his shoulders for dear life.

"What are you doing?" I giggle.

"Having fun," he answers with another waggle of his brows, right before he sends me flying back out again.

It's the most fun I've ever had on a dance floor in my life—despite being half convinced I'm going to break an ankle at any moment. But Flint's a great partner, and he makes sure I'm solid even as he's flinging me around like a rag doll. At one point, I glance over at our table and realize Hudson is still sitting there, talking to Luca and Macy. I glance around the floor and catch Eden being twirled in another dragon's arms, her smile friendly but not overly interested. I can't help but wonder if she plans to ask Macy to dance tonight, or if I just imagined something growing between them these past few weeks.

Hudson's eyes are burning a brilliant cerulean when our gazes collide, and for a second, I can't breathe. But then Flint swings me away again, and the moment is broken.

The song finally ends about a minute later, and I'm ready to plead for a break when Flint looks behind me and grins. "I think I'm being cut in on," he says, stepping back.

"What do you—" I break off as I follow his gaze and realize Hudson is standing right behind me.

"May I?" he asks, holding out his hand to me just as a slow, sexy ballad starts to play.

83

To Hoard or
Not to Hoard...
Asked Nobody Ever

For a second, I'm so surprised that I don't answer him. But then Flint nudges me gently, and I nod so fast, I nearly give myself whiplash. "Yeah, of course."

Hudson smiles, then takes my hand and pulls me straight into his arms. And he may not be as flashy as Flint is, but the boy has style. He knows how to hold a girl just right, so she feels safe, protected, but also free to move however she wants.

Also, I realize as I pull away just enough to shimmy my shoulders and my hips, that's always been Hudson's way with me—with everything. He always stays just close enough to help me if I need him—whether I'm learning to light candles or trying to pass paranormal ethics or taking on his father.

He lets me fight my own battles—in fact, he insists on it—but he's always there to help me if I need it. I don't know why I never realized that before.

It's a little awkward to realize it now, right after he's pulled me back against him so tightly that I can feel his long, lean muscles pressed against me. So tightly that I'm afraid he'll be able to hear the sudden pounding of my heart.

He looks down at me, his eyes filled with a heat that has my hands shaking and my throat closing up. "Hudson." I whisper his name, because it's the only sound I can make, the only word I can think of.

I can see the way it hits him, the way he has to swallow hard a couple of times before he can smile and whisper my name right back.

He lowers his head slowly, slowly, slowly, and my whole body goes on red alert. Because this is a million times different than what happened in the forest near Katmere. That was fast, brutal, an inferno raging out of control. But this, this is a slow, steady burn, the kind that gets hotter so gradually that you don't even notice it happening...until you're almost at the boiling point.

"Hudson," I say again, and my voice sounds weak and breathy, even to me.

He notices it, too—I can see it in his suddenly blown-out pupils, hear it in the stutter of his own breath, feel it in the way his body is now trembling against my own.

And then, just when he's about to kiss me, just when his lips are nearly touching mine, there's a sudden explosion from right over our heads.

Hudson wraps a protective arm around me even as he jerks away. We both look up to see what's happening, and I gasp when I realize what it is. Sometime in the last few minutes, the chandeliers have retracted into a kind of hollow panel in the ceiling, and now the entire ceiling is retracting, sliding back to reveal the sky above our heads—and the most amazing fireworks display I've ever seen in my life.

Hudson laughs, but I'm awestruck by the dozens of giant fireworks going off at the same time, over and over again.

"Come on," Hudson says, guiding me over to our friends, who are all oohing and aahing, too—even Flint, who has, I assume, seen this many times before. But when Hudson suggests moving over to an empty corner where the two walls of windows meet—right over the river—that's when things get truly spectacular.

Because not only are the fireworks directly above us, they're also all around us. Flashes of red and purple, gold and green, pink and white, over and over again. Then, suddenly, new lights join the fireworks, circles that cut through the flashes and align to make pictures of giant dragons and crowns and burning flames.

It's the most incredible show I've ever seen. It feels enchanted, maybe even a little mystical, and even though Luca explains that it's drones that are making the designs, it doesn't matter. It still feels magical.

Everything about this night does. Especially when the fireworks are over and the orchestra resumes, and my friends and I get to dance underneath the stars for hours.

As the clock strikes midnight, tiny bells start tinkling all around the room, and I look up at Hudson. "What's happening?"

He shrugs but offers a half grin. "I think it's time for the hoard."

People all around the room crowd in front of the flying hoard, lifting the hand to one item each and waiting as it gently drops down. There's laughter and screaming and cries of joy as one after another, a dragon reaches into

the hoard to draw out an envelope or jewelry or a key.

As everyone is shaking with excitement at what they've chosen, a sad thought comes to mind of all the dragons *not* here tonight. I turn to Flint and ask, "Is it only Court families who get to choose from the hoard? What about dragons living elsewhere who may not be wealthy?"

Flint looks affronted. "First of all, a dragon not being wealthy?" He pulls a fake knife from his heart. "Dragons love hoarding. It's in our blood. We can't help it. So no matter what we earn in life, we hoard it. We just naturally accumulate wealth—even if it takes generations."

He turns to Luca and drapes an arm over his shoulders before continuing. "But dragons have huge dragon hearts. As much as we love wealth, we love our families more. Our clans. Our people." He motions with a hand to the excited dragons still pulling items from the hoard in front of us. "This festival is going on in every town and city around the world where there are dragons. Granted, no one does it with quite the same flair as the dragon queen and the Dragon Court, but my mother ensures every clan shares in the royal hoard. We take care of our own."

Eden chimes in. "Each dragon and family has their own personal hoards, but we also all contribute to the royal hoard—which then gets redistributed during the festival. Items from the royal hoard are sent to each festival and joined with their clan hoards."

I nod. "So contributing to the royal hoard is like how you pay taxes?"

Flint rolls his eyes at that. "Sure, except without the political greed or benefits for the wealthiest families. The Montgomerys are the ruling family because we are the strongest, not just the wealthiest. And we believe we are only as strong as our weakest clan."

Luca's face is bright, pride beaming at his boyfriend. "You almost make me wish I were a dragon."

Flint grins down at him, his chest puffed out just a little bit. "Maybe one day we'll have to make you an honorary member."

And just like that, the moment between these two goes from sweet to searing hot. Eden coughs into her hand, suggests there's more dancing to be done tonight, and we all turn to head back to the dance floor.

But Flint calls out, "Wait a minute! Did you pick?"

"Pick what?" Macy asks, looking confused and more than a little bleary-eyed from lack of sleep. We've all been up more than twenty-four hours by

now—and between the tense arrival and the dancing, we are more than ready to crash.

Flint grins and gestures above our head to the much-depleted hoard still floating in the air. "Your treasure."

"Oh, we don't need—" Luca starts, but Flint just shakes his head.

"You can't come to the biggest party of the dragon year and leave empty-handed. It just isn't done. My family has contributed enough personal wealth to share with our guests, dragon or not." He narrows his eyes at us. "So pick something."

"Okay, okay." Eden looks up at the gold and gemstones whirling above our heads. "What do you recommend?"

"Depends on what you want." Flint looks up, too. "But I tend to go for the envelopes." He waits until the one he wants is directly above our heads, then reaches a hand up. Seconds later, it zooms right into his hand.

"What's in it?" Macy asks, crowding close to peer over his shoulder.

He shrugs, then tears open the top. Out comes what looks to be about five thousand dollars in cash. He grins. "Seems like breakfast is on me."

"It's that easy?" Macy asks, shaking her head in bewilderment.

"My mom and dad—and my mom's parents before them—worked really hard building up the Dragon Court into something formidable and independent and rich. It means a lot to her that she can give back to her people like this, means a lot to her that there's even this money to give." He inclines his head. "So yeah. It's that easy...and that important."

"And I thought witch history had a lot of land mines," Macy says. "But dragon history is obviously just as complex."

Then she reaches out a hand and pulls down a gold charm bracelet with several different gemstone charms on it—including a charm in the shape of a wolf.

Luca pulls down a gorgeous Breitling watch with a black crocodile band while Eden goes for a key. "Is there a locker around here somewhere that I open with this?"

Flint just laughs. "It's not that kind of key, Eden."

She narrows her eyes at him. "Well, what kind is it, then? I've never drawn a key before."

He takes it over to the nearest wait table and dunks the key chain in a leftover pitcher of water. We watch in amazement as a gold logo that looks kind of like two lions and kind of like wings appears on the key chain.

"It's an Ecosse?" Eden all but screeches. "You're lying. That's just the key chain, right? It's not actually—"

"Oh, it's an Ecosse," he tells her with a huge grin. "Take this to my mom's secretary tomorrow, and she'll give you a choice of which one you want—depending on which ones have been claimed by that time."

Eden looks like she's about to jump out of her skin with joy, and I feel completely confused. "What's an Ecosse?" I ask.

Macy looks as lost as I do, but the other four turn on me like I've just stabbed them in their backs...and their hearts.

"Only the most kick-ass boutique motorcycle in the world," Eden tells me. "Titanium chassis, carbon-fiber wheels, the most gorgeous, custom paintwork in the business—well, except for the Harley Cosmic Starship, but nobody can ride that. An Ecosse!"

"That's awesome," Macy tells her, giving her a huge hug...even as she makes a *just go along with them* face at me behind her back.

"Totally awesome," I agree.

Eden just rolls her eyes. "I'll take you for a ride on it. You'll understand."

"I can't wait," I tell her sincerely. And yeah, my parents used to have a no-motorcycle rule for me, but I figure if I can fly on a dragon and turn to stone on command, maybe I can handle a motorcycle ride after all.

"Your turn," Luca tells me with a wink.

I look at all the stuff flying around, and then I think of how powerless and panicked I felt when I tried to imagine having the money to start up a Gargoyle Court. So I let all the keys pass me by and pick an envelope.

It comes right to me, like the others' choices did for them, and I open it expecting to find the same five thousand dollars that Flint found. Instead, there's a stock certificate. *For 1,500 shares of Alphabet Inc.*

"Holy shit," Luca says. "Seriously, *holy shit*. That's Google."

"Is that good?" I ask. "I mean, I know it's good—Google is huge, obviously, but..."

"Sure it's good." Hudson shrugs. "If you think three million dollars is good."

I choke, swallowing my own saliva. "I'm sorry. What did you just say?"

"You heard me. Each share is trading at somewhere around eighteen hundred dollars. So yeah, almost three million dollars in your hot little hand."

"I take it back," Flint teases me. "*You're* buying breakfast."

"Umm, yeah I am…as soon as I can feel my face again. Or my hands. Or any other part of my body." I stare at the stock certificate in shock. "This is for real?"

"It's for real, New Girl." Flint picks me up and whirls me around. "You're a millionaire."

"What are you going to spend it on?" Eden asks with a grin.

"Apparently, breakfast," I tell her as I start to believe that maybe this actually is happening. "And the beginnings of a Gargoyle Court?"

"Oh, hell yeah, you are!" Macy squeals.

We all laugh, and then I turn to Hudson. "Your turn."

He shakes his head. "I've got everything I need." The fact that he's staring at me when he says it doesn't make my stomach flip at all.

The others groan, and Eden may or may not make a slight gagging noise.

But Flint just grins. Then says, "Yeah, well, reach up there and grab an envelope for Grace, then. Apparently, we've got a Gargoyle Court to build."

84

Slow Hands Are Good,
But Sometimes Fast
Hands Are Even Better

In the end, Hudson does reach up and snag another envelope for me. The one he chooses has a thousand dollars in it—which makes me super happy but gets him booed by Flint.

Still, middle-of-the-night hot chocolate and snacks are on me when we go up to the roof a little later—after changing into comfy sweats and sweatshirts. We're all exhausted, but none of us wants the night to end yet, and there's something magical about being up here, the city spread out below us.

I've never seen New York at this time before, and it's shocking to me how quiet it is in the middle of the night. It's like a switch gets turned off and the bright cacophony of the day and the neon fervor of the evening fade for just a couple of hours and all that's left is…peace.

I can use a little peace right now, and so can my friends, I think. We've got a lot ahead of us, and this night—this stolen moment in time—feels perfect.

Eventually, though, they all start drifting inside. Flint and Luca head out first with a decidedly intimate look in their eyes. Eden heads down next, and Macy not long after.

And then it's just Hudson and me on the roof—along with my rapidly cooling cup of hot cocoa.

"You ready to go down?" I ask as I dig out the last marshmallow from my cup.

"Are you?" he answers.

I should say yes. I'm cold and only getting colder, but…I don't know. There's something about being on this couch with him, the world at our feet and my favorite singer-songwriters' playlist playing on his phone, that feels too special to give up. At least not yet.

So I shake my head and burrow a little deeper into the blanket…and into him.

"You okay?" he asks.

"I just won three million dollars," I joke. "I think I'm doing all right."

He grins. "More than all right, I'd say."

"This whole weekend has been surreal." I don't know how it started with him being arrested and ended with me on this roof with Hudson, three million dollars richer.

"It's been the best weekend of my life," he says quietly.

I start to make a joke about how being arrested isn't usually a bucket list item, but there's something in his voice—something in his eyes when he turns to look at me—that has the words freezing in my throat.

And when Harry Styles's "Adore You" starts playing (because he always puts one Harry Styles song in the middle of a playlist just for me), I can't help myself. I stand up and hold out a hand to him. "Come on," I whisper. "Let's top off the best weekend of your life with a dance at the top of the world."

He grins and takes my hand. Then he's dancing me across the roof to one of my favorite songs, and I realize that Flint isn't the only one with the fancy moves.

"I don't know where you learned to dance like this," I squeal as he spins me out and then pulls me back in perfectly.

"There's a lot you don't know about me," he answers, and there's something in his voice that has my body aching and my throat closing up.

For a second, I'm afraid to ask the question he's set me up to ask, but as the song comes to an end and he dips me with a flourish, I can't help myself.

"Like what?" I whisper.

He pulls me up and into his arms just as "If the World Was Ending" from JP Saxe and Julia Michaels comes on the playlist. His hand slides down to right above the curve of my butt as he pulls me against him and spins the two of us right up to the edge of the roof, so that the lights of Manhattan glimmer below us.

And when he finally answers my question, his eyes are oceanic. "Like, I really want to kiss you right now."

It's all the invitation I need, my hands sliding up to tangle and tug at his hair as I yank his mouth down to mine.

Hudson groans low in his throat, and then he's kissing me back, his lips and teeth and tongue ravaging mine like it's the end of the world and this is the last kiss any two people will ever share.

And I ravage him right back, biting, licking, sucking, kissing, *exploring* every inch of his mouth until I can barely breathe, barely think. Until all I can do is feel.

His fangs scrape against my lower lip, and I moan. I tighten my fingers in his hair and try to pull him even closer.

It's impossible—we can't get any closer—but it makes him growl low in his throat. And this time when he uses his fangs on my lip, he nicks me...then licks away the tiny drops of blood that well up.

"Oh God!" I tear my mouth from his as every feeling I've ever had in my life wells up inside me all at once.

"Too much?" he asks, and he sounds as breathless as I feel.

"Not enough," I answer, and then I'm diving back into his arms. Into *him*. Into the wild, endless incandescence that is the two of us.

His hands slide under my ass, and I wrap my arms around his neck and my legs around his waist. And then we're fading, straight off the roof, down the three flights of stairs, and up the hallway that gets us to my room.

His mouth never leaves mine once.

85

Of Bites and Bonds

I think there's a part of me that always expected it to be awkward if we ever got this far, that expected it to feel strange to be in the arms of this boy who lived inside my head for so long. This boy who knows everything—good, bad, and indifferent—about me.

But it doesn't feel strange at all. It feels…perfect, like this one moment in time was always meant to be.

We're still in the hallway outside my door, like Hudson's afraid of what it will imply if he takes that one last step and moves us inside. But I don't care where we are, and I sure as hell don't care about rules or social niceties or anything that doesn't involve getting his body on mine. It's nice that he does, though. Nice that he wants me to be sure.

But I am. Oh my God, I am. With a little moan, I slide my hands to the hem of his shirt, skim my fingers across the flat, hard plane of his stomach. Then scrape my teeth across his lip the same way he scraped his against mine.

And the heat takes over, a raging conflagration rising up in both of us until it spills over and sets fire to the world.

I whimper deep in my throat even as I grab on to his broad shoulders. I yank at his shirt, dig my fingers into his hard muscles, try desperately to pull him even closer. And something seems to snap deep inside him—something wild and brutal and all-consuming.

He groans as he fumbles us through my door and somehow manages to get it closed behind us. Then he's backing me straight into the nearest wall, his chest and hips and hands pressing into me so completely that I can't tell where I stop and he begins.

And still I want more. Still I'm imploring him, little gasps and pleas pouring from my lips even as he devours me. Even as we devour each other.

Kiss by kiss, touch by touch.

At one point, he pulls his mouth from mine; sucks in deep, shuddering gulps of air; and grinds out, "Grace. Are you sure? Do you want—"

"Yes," I breathe as I pull his mouth back to mine. "Yes, oh my God, yes." If he doesn't do something soon, I'm going to die. Just self-immolate right here and go up in flames.

Hudson snarls as he sucks my lower lip between his teeth, nipping at it just enough to have me gasping and arching against him. He gasps then, too, and this time when one of his fangs slides against my lip, nicking me just a little, he groans like a man who's tasted heaven...or one who is about to lose it.

And it makes me completely consumed with what I want him to do. What I *need* him to do. I arch my back, pull my mouth away from his, and tilt my head to the side like an offering.

He growls deep in his throat. "You don't know what you're asking for."

"I know exactly what I'm asking for," I tell him as I press his mouth to my skin. "What I'm *begging* for. Please, Hudson," I whisper as the heat inside me threatens to overwhelm me, to pull me down into a raging inferno I might never escape from. "Please, please, please."

He lets out a small moan, his hands clenching in my hair so that he can pull my head even farther to the side.

I expect him to strike right then, to tear through me like the rampaging beast that has us both in its claws. But this is Hudson, steady, deliberate, careful Hudson, and tearing into me is apparently not on his agenda, even though he's right there, his mouth pressed against my jugular.

"Please," I whisper.

His lips slide gently across my shoulder.

"Oh my God," I gasp.

His tongue brushes delicate patterns into my collarbone.

"Do it," I urge as his fangs scrape lightly against the sensitive skin behind my ear. "Do it, do it, do it!"

He roars then. It's deep and harsh and animalistic, and it sets everything inside me on high alert, my entire body stretched taut as a high wire as I wait. And wait. And wait.

"Hudson, please," I beg. "It hurts. It—"

And just like that, he strikes, his fangs sinking deep into my throat.

White-hot pleasure slams through me and I erupt, whimpers tearing from my throat. Hudson freezes, like he's going to pull out, but I grasp at him like a wild woman, my hands holding him tight against me.

He growls in response, his hands clutching at my hips as he starts to drink.

And that's when I scream, not from the pain but from the explosion that rocks me all the way to my core.

And still he doesn't stop. Still, he continues to drink from me as his hands skim over my body. There's no surcease from the heat, no ending to the feelings sweeping along my nerve endings and rioting deep inside me.

There is only fire, only flames. They incinerate every barrier I have, laying waste to every stumbling block I put in our way, taking over everything until I can't think, can't breathe, can't do anything but burn.

Hudson must feel the same way, because even when he stops drinking from me, even when he pulls away, when he licks the wounds and closes them, he doesn't stop touching me. His hands are everywhere, his mouth everywhere, and all I want is to make him feel as good as he makes me feel.

I reach for his shirt, pull it over his head, and then my mouth is everywhere, too.

He groans, his hands cupping my ass again as he moves us to the bed. And as he lays down next to me, his long, lithe body pressed against mine, nothing has ever felt so good.

But even as I think it, it freaks me out a little. Because this *is* Hudson, and every warning bell inside me screams that if I let him in, if I choose him, then losing him will absolutely destroy me.

I pull away for just a second, and Hudson pushes up to his elbow, expression quizzical but eyes watchful.

"It's just the mating bond," I tell him.

He lifts a brow. "What is?"

"This." I move over to straddle him, my knees around his hips. "All of this. It's just the mating bond."

At first, I think he's going to argue, but when I lower my mouth to his, he grins against my lips. And says, "I can totally live with that."

86

Kiss and TED Talk

Hudson groans a little, arches into me, and it's my turn to take over. My turn to press kisses to his neck, his collarbone, the hollow of his throat. He smells good—so good—like sandalwood and sun and warm, inviting amber. I want to burrow into him, to stay right here against him for as long as this moment and this world will let me.

Hudson must feel the same way, because he's in no hurry to move this along *or* to move out from under me. Instead, he tangles his hands in my hair, wrapping the individual curls around his fingertips and knuckles until he's tied up in me in a way that feels right and real and terrifying all at the same time.

It's just the mating bond, I tell myself again as I rock my hips against his.

Just the mating bond as I lean down to kiss him and my hair forms a perfect curtain between us and the rest of the world.

Just the mating bond as he presses against me over and over again until I go spinning through time and space once more.

For long seconds afterward, my whole body feels like stardust. Like little droplets of light, millions of tiny explosions, flying, falling, floating through space.

Hudson holds me the whole time, his mouth soft and tender against mine as he presses kisses to my shoulder. Nuzzles into the hollow of my throat. Skims his lips over the sensitive spot behind my ear.

I'm shaking by the time he finally lifts his mouth from mine.

He's shaking, too, his body tight as a bowstring. But when I slide down and reach for his Armani belt with hands that are suddenly all thumbs, he pulls me back up and rolls us over so that he's stretched out over me now, his hips slotted perfectly between the V of my legs.

"You're so beautiful," he says with an ache in his voice. It's the second time he's ever said it to me, and it makes me ache all over again, too. Makes me tremble even more.

"You're pretty okay to look at yourself."

He shakes his head, makes an amused sound in the back of his throat. "I'm glad you think I'm okay-looking."

"Well, you smell pretty good, too," I tell him like I'm pretending to consider. "So you've got that going for you."

He's full-on laughing now, and it's a good look on him. His eyes crinkle at the corners just a little, and that tiny dimple flashes in his left cheek. "Well, as long as I've got something."

"I'd say you're doing all right." I rub my hands over his back, relishing the strength of him beneath my palms and the way his muscles bunch and stretch. Relishing also how this feels right in a way that few things in my life ever have.

I don't know what it means, and I don't want to know. Tomorrow is soon enough to take that bill out of the drawer. Tonight, I just want to be here with Hudson, just him and me for a little while.

"Oh yeah?" He crooks a brow. "Do tell."

"I think I'll just show you." I grin and push him over onto his back, my hand sliding to his belt again. This time, he doesn't push me away.

Hudson groans, and his eyes are wide, his pupils blown out, as he arches into my touch.

He's trembling now—his breathing shallow, his skin flushed and a little sweaty. And watching him like this is the sexiest thing that's ever happened to me. Even before his fingers clutch the sheets and my name pours from his lips like rain over the desert.

After we both come down, we get ready for bed. I expect him to lay down beside me, maybe go to sleep. But instead, he rolls over until he's settled between the V of my legs again. His face is inches from mine, his fingers playing with my curls as he watches me with eyes gone cloudy with release... and with something more that I'm not ready to think about.

It does strike me, though, how natural this feels, like this isn't the first time we've ever been like this. I know it can't be true, know that I would never have been unfaithful to Jaxon while I was locked in stone.

But it does make me want to know more—if not about that time specifically, then about Hudson. And him currently giving me shivers by pressing a line of kisses down my neck is not going to stop me from finding out.

"Can I ask you something?" I whisper.

He lifts his head to look down at me, brow furrowed. "Of course. Do you really even have to ask?"

"Tell me something I don't know about you."

"What, now?" He looks totally confused. "Am I not doing this right?" He gestures to himself currently lying on top of me, his mouth inches from my skin.

I laugh. "You're doing it great, and you know it."

I take his hand, press a kiss to the palm. And watch his eyes go blurry with want all over again, which makes my stomach do a half dozen backflips even as he asks, "So why now?"

"I don't know." I kiss my way over his knuckles and around his wrist. "I was just thinking—"

"So I *am* doing it wrong, then," he interrupts dryly. "I thought the goal was for you not to think."

"Yeah, well, you covered that portion of the program pretty well, too. But seriously." I push up onto my elbows. "You know so much about me, and I know that I used to know just as much about you.

"But I can't remember, and I hate it so much. Can you..." My voice wavers as I think about how much I've missed—and how much I'm missing. "Can you tell me something about you? Something I used to know but can't remember now?"

"Oh, Grace." He drops his head down until his forehead rests against mine. "Of course. What do you want to know?"

"I don't know. Anything. Everything?"

"That's really broad, but okay." He presses a kiss to my lips, then rolls off me and onto his side.

"I didn't mean you had to go." I clutch at him, try to bring him back.

He laughs. "I'm not going far. But if you want me to be able to have a real, coherent discussion, I need to not be on top of you."

"Maybe we can have the coherent discussion later, then." Once again, I try to pull him back over me, but there's no moving Hudson when he doesn't want to be moved.

"Something about me you used to know." He thinks for a second. "I've read every play Shakespeare ever wrote at least twice."

"Yeah, no shit." I roll my eyes. "I didn't need you to tell me that."

"Seriously? You're going to judge what I decide to share?" He looks offended.

"When it's that obvious, yeah. No offense, but I'm pretty sure you're a living, breathing library. And not just like a regular community library. Like the Library of Alexandria."

"You think I'm like a library that burned to the *ground*?" Now he looks more than offended.

"Turns out it didn't actually burn to the ground," I tell him. "Didn't you listen to the TED Talk?"

"Somehow I must have missed that." He makes an are-you-serious face.

"Your loss," I tell him with a shrug. "It was a good one."

He nods, even makes a fairly decent attempt at not laughing as he answers, "Apparently."

"It went up in flames when Julius Caesar set the ships in the harbor on fire. But I guess there's a ton of evidence showing that a bunch of writers and philosophers continued to use the library years later. It wasn't the fire that got it so much as all the subsequent leaders who were afraid of the knowledge it held."

As I finish, I realize Hudson is staring at me with the most bemused look on his face that I have ever seen. "What?" I ask.

He just shakes his head. "I've got to say, Grace, that is some seriously sexy pillow talk."

He leans in for a kiss, but I stop him by pressing my hand to his mouth. "No. No way. No pillow talk for you, and no kisses until you tell me something I actually don't know."

His eyebrows shoot up. "Are you kidding me? You're cutting off *kissing* now?"

"Umm, yes. Until you follow the rules set down, damn right I am." I reach for the duvet, start to pull it over me for good measure.

But Hudson isn't having it. He yanks the blue silk away again, this time going so far as to drop it on the floor, well out of my reach. "In case you haven't noticed, I'm not very good at following rules. Besides, there are lots of other places I want to kiss you."

And then he starts tugging down my sweats.

87

When All the Feels Are a Few Too Many

I wake up slowly to the feel of sunlight streaming over my face and a long, hard, male body pressed up against my back.

There's no moment of surprise, no wondering what's going on. From the second I'm coherent enough to recognize the feel of his breath on the back of my neck, I know exactly what's happening. I'm in bed with Hudson.

I spent the night with Hudson.

And though we didn't technically have sex last night, we did a lot of other stuff. Stuff that goes a long way toward explaining how loose and relaxed and *happy* I feel this morning. Stuff that also makes me feel anxious, because suddenly this might be a thing.

I mean, yeah, the mating bond has always made it a thing, but there was a part of me that still figured things would go back to normal. Then I would...I don't know. Get a choice?

It's not that I hate the idea of a mating bond between two people. I don't. I just always thought choice should factor into it a lot more. I get the whole thing they taught us in class, about how two people have to be open to it for the mating bond to snap into place, but I'm not sure I buy that, considering it snapped into place with Hudson when I was practically comatose from Cyrus's eternal bite.

Does that mean this is a real mating bond or is it another manufactured one like what I had with Jaxon? And do my feelings just ebb and flow along with who I'm mated to? Or do the feelings I have for Hudson have more to do with that three and a half months we spent together than I ever imagined? Does my heart remember something my conscious mind has forgotten?

The thoughts chase themselves around and around in my head until my happy mood dissipates under the weight of the anxiety building inside me.

I don't like this not being settled, and I like even less that I have so little control over my life—and haven't had any for months. From the moment Lia killed my parents, my life has been out of my hands. I just want a chance to take that control back.

Hudson stirs against me and murmurs something into my hair that has my entire body going rigid in shock.

"What did you say?" I ask as I roll over to look into his sleepy blue eyes.

I expect him to freak out, too, or to at least take it back, but Hudson just wraps an arm around my waist and pulls me closer, until our faces are only inches apart. And sidenote—why is it that vampires never get morning breath? I know they don't eat food. But still. It's not freaking fair, considering I'm sitting here with my mouth closed as tightly as I can manage when what I really want is to screech at him to take it back...or say it again.

"Don't worry about it," he tells me, and though his eyes are heavy-lidded and he's got a crease from the pillow on his cheek, there's something in the way he says the words that has my stomach churning as much as the words themselves.

"You can't tell me not to worry about it! Not if you said what I thought you did."

He sighs, shoves a hand through his sexy, rumpled hair. "Does it really matter?"

I look at him like he's grown three heads. "Of course it matters. We talked about this. We said it was only the mating bond—"

"No, *you* said it was only the mating bond," he tells me, sitting up now. As he does, the sheet falls down to his hips and, fight or no fight, there is no missing how beautiful his body is.

"You agreed!" I tell him. "Your exact words were 'I can totally live with that'!"

"I *can* live with it," he tells me with a shrug. "You're the one who seems to be freaking out here."

"Because you said—" I break off as his eyes narrow, become predatory.

"What?" he goads. "What did I say?"

"You know exactly what you said!" I snap at him. "And it's not fair—"

"Fair?" he shoots back, the British coming on thick. "I was half asleep. No, I take that back. I was three-quarters asleep. I can't be held responsible for what I say when I'm barely conscious."

"It's not that you said it!" I'm almost yelling now, but panic is a wild animal within me. It's clawing at my throat, making my head spin and my lungs close up. "It's that you feel it."

"Excuse me?" he snaps, his eyes going Pacific-during-a-thunderstorm dark. "You don't get to tell me how I feel."

I've never heard him sound more insulted, but that just pisses me off more. "Yeah, well, you don't get to tell me how I feel, either."

Now he's the one looking at me like I've got issues. Which, not going to lie, I totally do. "I have never tried to tell you how you feel." His voice cuts like broken glass. "Last night, you told me it was the mating bond on your side, and I told you I was okay with that."

"On my side? Now it's suddenly that mating bond heat is only on my side?"

For a second, I think Hudson might actually explode, just spontaneously combust right where he's half sitting up now. But then he takes a deep breath and lets it out in slow, ragged increments.

Then he takes another one and another one before he finally looks at me again and asks, "Can we please just talk for a second without throwing accusations at each other?"

I have to admit, I appreciate the way he said that—especially as I'm the one who's been throwing all the accusations this morning.

But that means it's my turn to take a few deep breaths before saying, "You told me that you love me and it freaks me out. A lot."

"I'm sorry," he says, his shoulders slumping forward. "I didn't mean to say it. I *wouldn't* have said it if I had even half my wits about me."

"So it's not true?" I ask, and there's a sinking feeling in my stomach that makes absolutely no sense. "You don't love me."

He shakes his head, his jaw and throat working as he looks anywhere but at me. "What do you want me to say, Grace?"

"I want you to tell me the truth. Is that so much to ask?"

"I love you," he says with no flourish, no fanfare. Just three stark words that change everything, whether we want them to or not.

I shake my head, scramble to the corner of the bed. "You don't mean that."

"You don't get to tell me what I mean," he answers. "Any more than you get to tell me how I feel. I love you, Grace Foster. I've loved you for months, and I'll love you forever. There's nothing you can do about that fact."

He reaches for me then, pulls me across the bed, and settles me on top of him. "But I'm not trying to use my feelings as a weapon, either. Did I plan on telling you? No. Am I sorry you know?" He shakes his head. "No. Do I expect you to tell me that you love me back?"

"Hudson—" I can't help the high, panicked note in my voice.

"No," he says. "I don't. And I don't mean to make you feel pressured to tell me anything you don't want to."

Tears clog up my throat, burn behind my eyes. "I don't want to hurt you."

"That's not on you." He lifts a hand to my face, strokes a tender finger down my cheek. "You're responsible for your feelings, and I'm responsible for mine. That's how this works."

Somehow, hearing him say it like that hurts worse than anything. Because I do have feelings for him, whether I want to or not. Big feelings, huge feelings that scare me so much that I can barely breathe. Barely think.

I loved my parents and they were murdered.

I loved Jaxon and he was ripped away from me.

If I love Hudson—if I let myself love Hudson—what's going to happen to me if I lose him? What's going to happen to me if this new world I find myself in won't let me have him?

I can't do that. I can't go through that again. I just can't.

The panic gets worse, my throat clogging up to the point that I can't breathe. I claw at it, try to force some oxygen in, but Hudson clasps my hands. Holds them tight, even when I try to pull away so I can claw at myself some more.

"It's okay, Grace," he says calmly, his voice warm and reassuring and right, so right. "Let's breathe in."

I shake my head. I can't.

"Yes, you can." He answers the protest I didn't even say out loud. "Come on, in with me. One, two, three, four, five. Hold it. Good. Now out. One, two, three…"

He does this several times with me, and when the panic attack passes, when I can breathe and think again, I know two things.

One, I feel more for Hudson Vega than I ever imagined I would.

And two, I can never, ever tell him.

88

The Same
Kind of Stardust

"You okay?" he asks when my breathing finally returns to normal.

"Yeah, I'm fine."

"Good." He smiles at me, even as he slides me off his lap. "I should probably get—"

I stop him with a kiss. Not one of the sizzling, burning kisses from last night but a sweet kiss. A warm kiss. A kiss that tries to show him all the things I feel inside but can't bring myself to say.

"Hey." He pulls away. "You don't have to do that."

"I want to," I tell him as I scramble back onto his lap. As I straddle his hips with my knees. As I press my body to his own. "I can't tell you what I feel, Hudson."

"It's okay," he says. But his hands are on my hips, and I know he's going to push me away.

"I can't tell you," I say. "But I can show you."

I lean forward and once again press my lips to his.

For a long while, he lets it happen, his lips moving under mine. His mouth touching, teasing, tasting.

And then he pulls back, cups my cheek in his hand, drops several tender kisses on my forehead, my nose, even my chin. "You don't have to prove anything to me," he whispers. "You don't have to do anything—"

"That's not what this is."

"Then what is it?" he asks.

Trust Hudson to ask the hard questions, to lay it all on the line just to make sure that I'm okay. That I'm not doing anything that might hurt me or might not be what I really want to do.

I'm grateful for that part of him, the part that always looks out for me no matter what. But right now, I want to look out for him. For both of us.

"I want this," I tell him, because it's easy to talk about the need that burns so brightly between us. "I want you."

This time, when I kiss him, he's all in.

And so am I, even if I can't tell him. Even if I can't yet tell myself.

This time, when his hands move to my hips, it's nothing—and everything—like I thought it'd be.

His mouth, dark and possessive.

His skin, warm and fragrant.

His hands, firm but tender in all the right places.

And his body, his beautiful, strong, powerful body, protecting me, arching against me, pressing into me, taking all that I'm offering and giving me so much more in return.

Nothing has ever felt so good.

Nothing has ever felt so right.

And when it's over, when my hands have finally stopped shaking and my heart has finally stopped racing, I realize the stardust has yet to settle. All the pieces of me and all the pieces of him mix together until it's impossible to tell where I leave off and he begins.

Until it's impossible to tell what either of us is, was, or will become without the other.

89

Hudson and I woke up, had breakfast in bed, and lolled around watching Netflix as long as we could, but eventually he said he wanted to head back to his room and shower.

He's been gone about an hour when Macy discreetly knocks. I open the door and can tell she's trying not to be obvious—but is totally being obvious—as she checks to see if there's anyone in my bed.

I roll my eyes at her but can't help the slight blush warming my cheeks. "Hudson's in his room taking a shower."

She grins and rubs her hands together. "I am going to want *all* the details."

I turn back to the bed so she can't see my blush has turned into a full-on scarlet burn. "Yeah, that's not going to happen."

She pouts. "Fine. But when I get a mate...mum's the word from me."

"Deal." I chuckle.

She's about to plop on the bed next to me—probably to begin the best friend's rightful interrogation—when there's another knock on the door, followed by Eden calling, "Hurry up! My hands are full!"

Seconds later, Macy opens the door and Eden comes in carrying a bag of the most amazing-smelling food ever.

I jump up to take the bags from her. I have worked up a serious appetite. "Whatever you've got in here—I'll take it all."

She laughs. "It's New York, baby. Shawarma, fries, dolmas, and cheesecake. Everything a dragon needs to go into a food coma. But the vamps are on their own."

I empty out the bags on the dresser and steal a fry. Okay, a bag of fries.

Less than a minute later, Luca and Flint pop their heads in the open doorway. "God, it smells like home in here," Flint says with a happy groan. "You're my favorite, Eden."

He gives her a giant, smacking kiss on the top of her head, but she just rolls her eyes. "Who said I got any for you?"

"The text you sent me less than five minutes ago telling me to get my ass to Grace's room." He holds up his phone as proof.

"I must have had an out-of-body experience," she shoots back—right before she tosses a wrapped sandwich in his general vicinity.

Hudson catches it as he walks in the door, snagging it right out of the air in front of Flint. "Eden, you shouldn't have," he says dryly.

"Bro." Flint narrows his eyes. "Unhand the shawarma and no one gets hurt."

"I am, quite literally, quaking in fear." Hudson holds up the sandwich—in a rock-steady hand.

I toss Flint a giant piece of cheesecake. "Eat dessert first. He'll get bored with tormenting you eventually."

"You think so?" Flint asks doubtfully.

"He always gives up messing with me pretty quickly."

"That's because he doesn't want his mate to hate him," Flint argues, even as he digs his fork into the piece of cheesecake. "He doesn't care if I hate him."

"True story," Hudson agrees, flopping down next to me on the bed.

I start to offer him a bite of cheesecake—I only ever give advice I'm willing to take myself—then blush as I realize what I'm doing. "Sorry. I... forgot."

He shakes his head. "No worries." But there's something in his eyes when he looks at me, and I know that it makes me squirm in the best possible way.

"So what happens tonight?" Macy asks in between popping fries in her mouth. "Like, what do we need to wear? Are we going to be walking around or—"

Flint laughs. "Probably not much walking. But wear something comfortable—just make sure you bring a jacket."

Macy makes a face at him. "That tells me absolutely nothing."

"I know." He looks very happy with himself.

"Luca, will you please do something with your boy?" I whine.

"I've done lots of things with him," he shoots back. "So you're going to have to be more specific."

"Hey!" Flint looks embarrassed but also really pleased, and Macy cracks up...and so does everyone else.

Eden even says, "Niiiiice," then leans over and bumps knuckles with Luca, who looks quite proud of himself, too.

And I just watch the whole thing with a giant grin on my face. Because this is what I was saying to Nuri yesterday. This, right here, is what I'm fighting for. And what I'll die for, if I have to.

90

The Sky's the Limit

"This is unbelievable," Macy says three hours later as we walk through Times Square after dusk, the sun just about to dip completely from the sky so it's lit up in dark purples and blues.

"It is," I agree, because there's something totally surreal about strolling through New York City less than a week before I graduate from high school. And not just New York City but one of the most iconic parts of the city: Times Square and Broadway.

My mom was a huge Broadway musical fan, and she kept telling me that the summer after I graduated, we'd come spend a week in New York and see *Hamilton* and *Kinky Boots* and whatever other shows struck our fancy. My being here now, so close to gradation but without her, breaks my heart just a little.

I managed to ignore it all day yesterday—everything with Hudson and Nuri helped with that—but standing here, right outside the Richard Rodgers Theatre where *Hamilton* is performed, suddenly I can't not think about it.

I can't not think about her, singing show tunes in our kitchen as she spread out her herbs and flowers all over the table and made her tea blends.

I can't not think about the fact that she won't be doing my hair for graduation in a few days.

I can't not think about how much I miss her...and how many things I want to ask her about this new world I'm living in, including *did she know.* And if she did, *why didn't she tell me?*

Most days, I'm learning to live with them being gone. But every once in a while, it creeps up on me, and this is one of those times, when the pain sinks through me like a stone hitting the water, ripples widening until they cover every part of me.

"Have you ever seen it?" Hudson asks, and I realize that I've been staring at the front of the theater for way too long.

"No." I turn away, sweep my eyes across Times Square in an effort to find something, anything else to concentrate on.

"Hey," Hudson asks, concern replacing the lightness of his tone from just a few moments ago. "Are you all right?"

"Yeah," I tell him, because I am.

Because I have to be.

"What happens next?" Macy asks as we look out over the neon cacophony that is Times Square. Billboards stretch up the sides of buildings, flashing colors and pictures the size of small buildings. People and cars are everywhere, the sound of their voices and horns filling the street. It's organized chaos that isn't actually all that organized but somehow works anyway.

But all I can think as I look at the thousands and thousands of people crowding the area is, *How on earth are they going to be able to host a dragon festival* here?

"I think we wait for Flint to get back," Eden says as we squeeze between a hot dog vendor and a taxi driver having an argument with a passenger.

"Yeah, but how is this going to work?" I ask. "There are so many people here."

"So many," Macy echoes.

"I'm sure the dragons have something up their sleeves," Luca says. "They wouldn't bring us up here for nothing."

"I know," Macy agrees. "But where?"

We all stand in the middle of the street and look straight up—at the top of the W and the Marriott Marquis and a bunch of other buildings I haven't bothered to identify. The purples and oranges of dusk have started to descend on the patchwork pieces of sky directly above us, and I can't shake the feeling that the dragons are out there somewhere, waiting for something. I just don't have a clue what it is.

"There he is!" Luca points toward the crowded street area right in front of Junior's restaurant, and sure enough, I can see Flint wading through the crowd, a huge grin on his face.

"Sorry about that," he says as soon as he gets to us. "I got hung up helping the Court organize a few last details, but it's all good now. You ready?"

"So ready," Macy tells him. "But where is it?"

He winks at her. "Come on. I'll show you." And then he walks straight through the door of the Marriott Marquis.

The rest of us look at one another, but in the end, we follow him through the revolving door and into the hotel.

Hudson is walking beside me, his hands shoved in his pockets like he's done this a thousand times. My eyebrows shoot up, and I whisper to him, "Have you been to this festival before?"

He meets my gaze and smiles. "But of course."

The others move ahead of us, and I turn to Hudson and grin. "You can tell me. Is the festival here?"

"Kind of," he answers, and I think he's enjoying the mystery.

"You're not even going to give me a hint?" I plead.

"Nope." He grins.

"You suck, you know that, right?" I tease.

"I've been known to," he answers with a wink.

And I have nothing to say to that. Heat creeps into my cheeks at his meaning, and I'd be lying if I said I didn't notice that things had shifted between us yesterday. In the basement, actually. We were both dancing around this thing between us, but we knew…we were headed for a reckoning soon.

We catch up to the others and take the glass elevators all the way to the forty-fifth floor, and when we get out, the entire hotel is laid out below us. I don't know if it's a money thing or a dragon thing, but they sure do like being high up.

There are no ballrooms here, only rooms, and I'm totally confused now because I have no idea how a festival could take place in a hotel room—even a big hotel room, which this is, I realize as soon as Flint swipes the key card. And when I say big, I mean *BIG*. There's an actual grand piano in the middle of the sitting room, for God's sake. You don't see that in a New York City hotel every day…or any day, really.

The suite is filled with people drinking champagne, eating hors d'oeuvres, laughing, and apparently having a fantastic time. It looks more like a party than a festival, at least until Flint brings us over to one of the huge picture windows that overlooks Times Square and asks, "Do you guys trust me?"

"No," Hudson answers immediately. "Not even a little bit."

We all laugh, and Hudson looks at us like he has no idea what the joke is. But I can see the humor lurking in the back of his eyes despite the deadpan delivery.

"Well, then you're really going to hate this," Flint tells us as he puts a hand up to the glass...and it dissolves right in front of us. And out of nowhere, we're at the edge of the room, forty-five stories above Times Square, with absolutely no barrier to keep us from plunging to our deaths.

And that's before Flint steps right off the edge of the building and straight out into thin air.

91

Up Broadway
Is the New
Off Broadway

Luca makes a grab for him but misses and ends up plunging out the window as well.

Macy screams as he falls, and soon half the room is gathered around us, watching as Luca splays out five hundred feet above Times Square. Because he's not falling. He's just lying there, on the air, at Flint's feet.

"It's okay, babe," Flint says, reaching down to help him to his feet as the guests behind us titter in amusement. Because for no rhyme or reason that I can understand, Flint and Luca are literally walking on air.

And so are a lot of the other guests, who must decide it's time to exit the premises. Twenty or thirty of them are swarming into the air above Times Square, bejeweled champagne glasses still clutched in their hands.

Part of me wants to put it down to them being dragons, but none of their wings are out. Plus, Luca is standing there right next to Flint, and I know he can't fly.

"What is happening?" Macy asks, putting voice to the question all five of us are thinking.

"Come on out and see for yourself," Flint says. And though I'm not altogether sure I buy what he's selling, I decide to do what he says. Worst-case scenario, I start to fall—at least I have wings to keep me from plummeting to my death.

But when I walk off the edge of the hotel, I don't feel air beneath my feet. I feel solid ground.

Which is impossible, as we are literally standing in the middle of the air. When I look down, I can see people wandering Times Square. The billboards, the traffic, the lights of Broadway...they are all right there. We were standing down there just a few minutes ago and there was nothing up here. I was looking straight up at the top of this very building.

And yet, here we are. Hudson, Macy, and Eden join the rest of us on what feels like a giant sheet of glass stretching over Times Square—and all the way down Seventh Avenue and Forty-Fifth Street as well. Because as far as I can see, people—dragons—are lining the sides of the glass streets waiting for the action to start.

It is the most mind-bending thing I have ever seen in a year of mind-bending things. But somehow, *somehow*, the dragons have harnessed enough air magic—at least I'm guessing this is magic—to hold an entire festival in the air right above Times Square and no one down below can see it.

It's genius and diabolical at the same time. And also way, hella cool.

"You've got to admit," Hudson says as he elbows Luca. "This takes balls."

"Major balls," Luca agrees.

"Who even thought of this?" Macy asks. "And how did you guys pull it off?"

Flint just grins. "You didn't actually think witches were the only ones who could harness the air, did you?"

"Actually, yes," she tells him. "I kind of did."

"I've heard the Court did this," Eden says, and it's the first time I've ever heard her awestruck in the entire time I've known her. "But I never actually believed it before now."

Flint holds out his arms. "Surprise!"

"No fucking shit surprise," Luca grumbles, but he's grinning almost as hugely as Flint.

"Want to go find a spot?" Flint asks.

"Don't you have royal duties to perform over there?" I ask, pointing to what looks like the main stage for the whole event.

"Later," he says. "I begged off initial duties so I could entertain our royal guests." He gestures to Hudson and me.

Hudson just laughs. "Sounds like a bunch of bollocks to me."

"Absolutely," Flint agrees. "But it got me out of show pony duty, so I'll take it. Now, come on. The festival is going to start in about five minutes, and I want to be able to see it."

He ushers us away from the hotel and a little farther down the block to a roped-off VIP area. It's still crowded, but not nearly as crowded as some of the other areas along the street, so we duck under the ropes gratefully.

We must make it just in time, because we've barely gotten ourselves arranged behind the rope line when the music starts. At first, it's low, barely noticeable, wind chimes spinning through the air. Then it gets louder, bells and flutes joining in, and then the other woodwinds, and finally light strings as the music rolls and flirts its way through the audience, dancing on the air.

It's gorgeous—some of the most beautiful music I've ever heard—but I don't recognize it at all. "What is this?" I whisper, not wanting to break the spell it's weaving over all of us.

"It's dragon song," Hudson answers solemnly, "just in musical form."

"I didn't know that was a thing."

"It definitely is. Ask Eden or Flint to sing for you sometime. It will blow you away."

As the song grows louder and louder, soaring over us, the first performers burst onto what I'm beginning to realize is a giant parade route. Dragons in human form perform aerial acrobatics, tumbling and flying, twisting and weaving ribbons around themselves as they twirl their way down the street. Elaborate makeup on their faces, dressed in colorful leotards with gauzy skirts and overshirts, they epitomize a delicacy I didn't realize dragons were capable of.

As they move farther down the parade route, the music changes—gets louder, more demanding, more powerful. And just as it reaches a crescendo, dragons launch themselves off the tops of the highest buildings all around us and come hurtling straight toward the center of the street.

Lightning sizzles through the sky while fire and ice shoot out in all directions. The dragons race down the glass street, then soar high, high, high above us, only to perform incredible dives and twists and somersaults as they race back down at death-defying speeds.

They do this over and over again, each dive getting more dangerous than the one before it. Then the music changes again, back to the light, ethereal sound of the very beginning. But I can't place the instruments in this song, and as the dragons come into view, I realize why. They are all female, all in human form, and they are singing…this is the dragon song that Hudson mentioned before, and it is so beautiful that it has tears forming behind my eyes.

"You're right," I whisper to him, and my voice breaks just a little bit.

He smiles at me in return, and it's a soft smile rather than his usual sharp ones. And though I worked hard to bat them away, he must see the remnants of unshed tears in my eyes, because he wraps an arm around my shoulder and pulls me into the shelter of his body.

"This is incredible," Macy says as the dragon singers move farther down the line.

"I know," I tell her. "I've never seen anything like it."

But then more dragons drop down onto the parade route. Big, strong, powerful, they send wind whipping through the audience, fire dancing along the edges of the ropes holding us back from the course.

One dragon shoots a ball of fire in our direction, and I gasp, rear back from it, but Flint just laughs. Right before another dragon scoops it out of the air, turning the fire into a large ring. Soon there are a dozen rings of fire lined up in the center of the street, one right after the other, and the dragons take turns flying through the circles as they get narrower and narrower.

After them come the younger dragons, small boys and girls walking the parade route in human form as they throw handfuls of gems and gold coins at the audience.

I half expect people to rush one another for them—God knows, humans would trample one another trying to get a diamond the size of a baby's fist or a sapphire so blue that it nearly looks black—but the dragons seem to take it all in stride, as if they know that everyone who wants something is going to get it before they leave.

More dragons fly by after them, lightning crackling across the air right above us. It's powerful lightning, loud and bright, and I can't help glancing down to see if the people below us have seen or heard anything. But not one of them is looking up at all—it's like they really are alone down there, with nothing but sky above them.

After the lightning dragons zip by, fireworks start going off above us—as big and bright as the ones last night over the Hudson. I figure they mark the end of the show, but then in the middle of all the exploding fireworks, an array of golden dragons comes racing down Seventh Avenue faster than I ever dreamed it was possible to fly.

They get from one end to the other in what feels like a blink of an eye; then they come back and do it all over again—this time tossing what looks an awful lot like a Ludares comet back and forth between their claws.

They're moving so fast, flying so straight, throwing so hard that I barely see the blur of the comet as it leaves one dragon's claw and is scooped up by the next. Back and forth, back and forth, back and forth they go, whizzing the comet among them like they're in the Ludares game of their lives.

"Who are they?" Macy asks, her voice breathy with excitement as the golden dragons turn around and come back for one more lap over the street.

"Those are the Golden Drakes," Eden says, and it's impossible to miss the awe and respect in her voice as she talks about them. "They're the most highly trained dragons in the world and they travel all over, putting on shows and helping train other dragons."

"The first Golden Drake squad came together more than a thousand years ago," Flint tells me, and there's a similar reverence in his voice. "Back when Ludares was more than a game kids played. Back when playing it decided not just who sat on the Circle but who lived and died. The dragons gave their best flyers to the squad to be trained and, slowly but surely, they helped us come out of hiding and poverty. They helped us regain our status and become the Dragon Court who can do all this."

One more time, the Golden Drakes loop around, and when they shoot straight down Forty-Fifth, they do it so fast that they break the sound barrier—a giant sonic bomb echoing forth from the end of the street, so loud and obvious that even the humans down below jump and start looking around for what possibly could have caused it.

The rest of us burst into cheers and applause that last until a whole new set of fireworks starts exploding over our heads, so fast and intense that they light up the whole street and make it look like the sky itself is raining gold.

92

Everything's
Up in the Air

When the show finally comes to an end, Flint goes to work on the receiving line with his parents—it's an exhausting job, one where he, Nuri, and Aiden stand on the official dais greeting everyone who wants to meet or talk to the royal family. He says it will probably take the rest of the night and encourages us to go out and explore the festival.

Luca goes with him—big surprise—so the rest of us wander down glass Forty-Fifth Street to see what we can find.

The answer is a lot.

The reason the parade route went straight down Seventh Avenue is because Forty-Fifth Street is lined with dragon booths selling everything from claw trimmers to fire enhancement pills. While we have no need for the above-mentioned things, we do find a ton of fun stuff to window shop, try on, and/or buy.

Hudson discovers some old vinyl that he insists he needs for his collection—N.W.A.'s *Straight Outta Compton* and Paul Simon's *Graceland*. Macy picks up some dragon's breath candles, and Eden buys a couple of leather cuffs for her wrists that she totally falls in love with.

I don't find anything that I can't live without until we run across a caricature artist. Then I beg and plead with all three of them to sit with me and finally—finally—they agree. The drawing takes about fifteen minutes, and when it's done, my heart jumps to my throat.

Hudson is portrayed as a kind of paranormal band manager, his hair extra spiky and his fangs extra long, while the three of us are shown as his girl group. Macy's in the front, her eyes big and soulful as she croons into the microphone. Eden is on her right, blowing into a saxophone and staring out of the page with suspicious eyes so much like hers that I can't help but be impressed. I, on the other hand, am shown shaking a tambourine. But instead of looking out at the audience, I'm looking up at Hudson with seductive eyes… and he's looking right back.

Macy and Eden laugh over the caricature, but Hudson is as quiet as I am about it, which makes me even more self-conscious. In the end, I roll it up and stick it in my bag for later. After all, the whole point of it was to have a fun memento of the night—nothing more, nothing less.

Flint texts us after about two hours, telling us that he's still stuck and giving us information about different places along both Forty-Fifth Street and Seventh Avenue where there are access doors back to the street. But we end up following the dragon festival all the way down Broadway to Flint's building, which is about three miles total. We don't mean to go that far, but it's so much fun walking around, checking out the booths, being normal people upon whom the fate of the world doesn't rest, it's impossible to resist.

When we get to the airspace in front of the Dragon Court, we find a DJ and a dance floor of sorts set up right outside of it. It's loud and crowded and colorful, and it looks like a lot of fun. But we're all thirsty after the walk and the snacks we bought along the way, so we grab one of the pop-up high-tops near the building and sit down for a few minutes to grab some water and watch what everyone's up to.

About ten minutes after we get our drinks, I notice that Macy keeps shaking her shoulders and tapping her feet like she wants to dance. The old Macy—before Xavier—would have just jumped up and run out onto the dance floor without thinking twice. The new Macy is more cautious, less adventurous, and though I love her dearly, or maybe because I do, it makes me really sad.

I'm about to get up and ask her to dance when Hudson beats me to the punch. Macy is surprised but happy as she lets him lead her to the dance floor.

They pick a spot not that far from Eden and me, so I can't help watching them. Can't help seeing how good Hudson is with Macy, how careful he is and how warm and genuine. It's amazing to me that even after all he's been through, after everything he's suffered, he's managed to come out of it all a really nice guy.

I mean, yeah, he's acerbic and sarcastic and he's definitely grumpy sometimes, especially when he thinks I've done something to deliberately offend him. But when I see him taking care of Macy, trying to cheer her up just because being sad sucks, I can't help but think how amazing he is. He's had a pretty shit life—I think anyone who knows him can agree to that—but instead of getting hard and heartless, he still remembers what it feels like to hurt, and because of that kind of empathy, he makes sure he doesn't do anything to hurt others if he can avoid it.

It's hard not to respect that, harder still not to fall for it at least a little bit. And when he grins down at her and laughs, I feel it all over my body.

"He's an asshole just on the surface, isn't he?" Eden asks, and I realize she's watching Hudson and Macy nearly as intently as I am.

"Actually, I don't think he's an asshole at all." Especially when he's beaming down at Macy like a proud older brother. Or when he's laughing at himself like right now, when the opening notes of the "Cupid Shuffle" start playing, and she's trying to teach him what to do. "Distant, yeah. An asshole, no."

Now Macy's laughing, too, really laughing, for the first time in a long time. And that's when it hits me. Hudson is as big a pushover as I am for the people he cares about. He just hides it better.

As the whole dance floor lines up and starts doing the Cupid Shuffle, I grab Eden's hand and say, "Come on, let's go."

I figure she'll argue, but she's grinning as largely as I am as we run for the dance floor. Macy and Hudson hold out hands and we line up right next to them, just in time to move "to the right, to the right, to the right…"

We're a mess. An absolute mess. Half the time, Hudson is going in the wrong direction, and when he isn't, Eden's kicking backward instead of toward the front, and it doesn't even matter. Macy and I try to keep them in some semblance of order, but by the end, they're just kind of doing whatever the hell they want to, and it's awesome.

When the song ends and Niall Horan's "Slow Hands" starts to play, we pair off naturally, and suddenly I'm in Hudson's arms. And I realize I have been thinking about it all day, have been thinking about him all day, all week, all month, even though it's the last thing I ever expected to have happen.

And when he looks down at me with those bottomless eyes of his—so deep and blue—there's nothing I can do but melt.

Nothing I can do but burn.

Even before he pulls me closer. Even before he presses his long, lean, hard body against mine. Even before he moves us across the dance floor, and it hits me as I look down…

"We're dancing on air," I whisper as another wave of heat moves through me.

He grins even as he pulls me closer and spins us across the dance floor. "Now you know what it feels like."

"What what feels like?"

"Being next to you."

Everything inside me stills at his admission, and I move even closer, wanting, *needing*, to feel all of him against all of me.

Hudson must feel the same way, because his arms tighten around me and he's lifting me up, up, up, until our faces are on the same level and we're pressed together from shoulder to hip to thigh.

"Hi," I whisper as his mouth hovers inches away from my own.

"Hi," he answers as I instinctively lock my legs around his hips.

He shudders, his eyes darkening—his pupils blown out—until I can barely see the blue at all.

"The whole world disappears when you're near me, Hudson," I whisper on a shaky breath. "Are we alone?"

He growls low in his throat at my question, at the aching need trembling between us. "Not yet."

Everything inside me goes quiet all at once, like my whole being is holding its breath, waiting to see what he'll do next.

And just like that, we start to move, fading through the air, down the access ramp, then up the stairs to my room, in that quiet, perfect space between one breath and the next.

93

Existential Crises Aren't All They're Cracked Up to Be

The next morning, the six of us spend the day in New York out of necessity rather than a desire to hang around and give Nuri a chance to take another swipe at us. But Luca and Hudson have both been imbibing human blood since we got here—Hudson more than Luca, obviously—and that means we can't travel until it gets dark.

Eden and Macy take advantage of the time by riding Eden's new Ecosse all over the city while Flint and Luca have a command performance with Aiden and Nuri—the king and queen want to check out the new boyfriend one-on-one, which seems fair.

That leaves Hudson and me to hang in my room all day, watching movies and talking about anything and everything. In my life before Katmere, I was a huge reader—I haven't had time to read much of anything since half the paranormal world painted a target on my back—but it's nice to lay in bed and argue with Hudson about Hemingway (total misogynist, I don't care what he says), Shelley (Percy, not Mary: it doesn't matter how brilliant you are if you're also a total asshole), and Hudson's undying love for the French existentialists (nothing could possibly be as bad as they think *everything* is).

"Seriously, if nothing matters, why do they have to spend so much time whining about it?"

"I wouldn't exactly call it whining," Hudson tells me, and I can tell I've struck a nerve. This *is* the boy who passive-aggressively read *No Exit* when he was trapped in my head and angry with me for kissing his brother.

But I'm not about to give in on this one. "'Anything, Anything would be better than this agony of mind, this creeping pain that gnaws and fumbles and caresses one and never hurts quite enough,'" I tell him, quoting Sartre with a roll of my eyes.

"Okay, so maybe that one is a little whiny." He laughs. "But they aren't all like that."

"'It is certain that we cannot escape anguish, for we are anguish'?" I shoot back. "Keep defending him. I can do this all day."

Hudson holds his hands up in the universal gesture of surrender. "You win. Maybe I just had a lot to be whiny about before."

"Before what?" I ask.

He doesn't answer, just kind of shakes his head. But he's watching me with soft eyes, and I know exactly what he's not saying. *Before me.*

And I don't know what to say to that, so I don't say anything. I just lean over and kiss him and kiss him and kiss him, until Flint knocks on the door an hour later and says that it's time to go.

My stomach twists, and I feel my familiar anxiety returning. We've been living on borrowed time, and it's finally catching up with us. Hudson and I decided not to ruin anyone's time in New York with discussions of prison or the Crone. We'd finally told everyone what Nuri had shared while eating dinner before heading back to Katmere.

So why did I have a gnawing pit in my stomach, thinking that we'd waited too long?

We've barely walked through the door back at Katmere before Jaxon jumps down four flight of stairs and lands at our feet.

"Dramatic much?" Hudson asks as Mekhi comes down the stairs at a much more sedate pace.

Jaxon just bares his teeth in a not very close facsimile of a smile. "I talked to Delilah for you, but if you'd rather not hear what she has to say, I can go back to my room."

"*I'd* rather not hear," I mutter under my breath.

But there is no *under your breath* when vampires are around, and Hudson gives me a look. "Don't judge her until you know everything."

"What *she's* endured," Jaxon mocks—which is essentially what I'm thinking, but not about to say.

Hudson ignores him, speaking to me instead. "I won't defend her. She made her bed when she chose Cyrus. She couldn't leave, but she protected me as best she could. She's endured a lot more than you'll ever know."

"As have I," Jaxon sneers at him, tilting his head so that his scar stands out in stark relief against his cheek. "And I don't have time to think about everything she's done for *you*. I'm too busy remembering how willing she was to destroy me because of you."

Hudson's eyes go to the scar, but he still looks like he wants to argue more. I put a hand on his elbow, hoping against hope that he won't. In the end, though, all he says is, "What message did she send?"

"'Appear weak when you are strong.'"

"Okay, thanks for that." Hudson sighs as he wipes a tired hand down his face. "Can you just tell me what she wanted me to know so we can get to bed?"

"That's it," Jaxon says, and his eyes are nothing but black pits as he repeats, "that's *all* she said."

"That's it? A quote from *The Art of War* was worth demanding your presence at Court?" Hudson asks.

And I have to laugh because he seems so astonished by the whole thing—not just that his mother sent him an odd quote but also at the very idea of deliberately appearing weak. I don't think he could if he wanted to.

"I'm not impressed." Hudson shrugs. "It seems a lot like a BS message to me." His deliberately avoiding looking at Jaxon makes it obvious he thinks his brother is trolling him.

But I don't believe Jaxon would do something like that. The fact that he's gone to Court twice and dealt with his mother both times says everything about how much he wants to help Hudson, no matter what he says.

"I don't think so," I tell him, stepping between them in an effort to lower the tension emanating from them both. "I think maybe it means that she's trying to look weak at the moment, so your father doesn't realize that we're all working against him—including her."

I choke a little bit saying that last part, but maybe Hudson's right about her. *Maybe.*

Jaxon snorts and Hudson narrows his eyes, but neither of them says anything to the other.

"Besides," I continue, "if nothing else, you can ask her when she comes to graduation in a few days."

As soon as I say the words, I know they're a mistake. Even before Hudson's eyes darken at the idea of his parents coming to Katmere—or, namely, his father.

Jaxon reacts just as badly, saying, "Lucky us," then moves back toward the staircase. "Now that I've delivered the message, I'm going to sleep."

"You can't," Luca pipes up for the first time. "We just came back to shower and get some food. We're heading back out again in an hour—we've got to beat the sun."

Jaxon narrows his eyes at him, like he's thinking about what it would feel like to rip Luca limb from limb. Luca holds his gaze for a couple of seconds, then drops his eyes. I don't blame him.

This Jaxon is impossible to defy.

But Mekhi steps forward after a few seconds and asks, "Where are you going this time?"

Now that the tension between the two brothers has been broken a little bit, the others move closer. "We have to see a witch about the prison," Flint tells him. "My mom thinks she might be able to help Hudson escape." Jaxon seems to not care much about freeing Hudson from prison, if the *and?* look he sends Flint is any indication. "Okay, so forget Hudson. I think we can all agree, we need the Crown now more than ever to stop Cyrus. The vampire queen is sending *coded messages.*" Flint's eyebrows go up in a *can shit get any weirder* look.

Jaxon sighs and turns to me. "A witch? What witch?"

"Nuri called her the Crone," I say. "She said no one had seen her in a really long time but that she helped build the prison and might have some advice for us."

"And what, we're just going to run off and trust some witch because Flint's mom told us to?"

"Hey, it's no more illogical to trust a witch than it is to trust a vampire!" Macy tells him indignantly.

He gives her a dark look. "Are you under some delusion that *I* trust vampires?"

"We've got to trust somebody," I tell him.

"And you think someone called 'the Crone' is the one to start with?"

"You don't have to come," Hudson growls.

"Oh, I'm coming," Jaxon snaps back. "God knows you're going to need someone to save your asses when everything goes south."

"Why do you think it's going to go south?" Eden asks.

"I think the more appropriate question is, how the hell can you possibly think it won't?"

94

All That's Sugar
Is Not Sweet

I 've got to hand it to Nuri—the coordinates she gave us for the Crone's house are right on, even though we all doubted her when we looked them up because according to Google Maps, there's nothing here. Still, we decided to take the risk anyway.

And yeah: Nuri 1, Google 0.

Since Macy had never visited this witch, and we didn't want to risk asking Uncle Finn, we couldn't build a portal and had to ride on the backs of Flint's and Eden's dragons. It was a cold and long flight, but at least it gave me a lot of time to think.

Hudson spent an hour trying to talk us out of going, insisting the Crone was going to ask for a price he would never let us pay to save him. But I couldn't think of any other way. Cyrus was going to get him into that prison one way or another. My guess was that the real reason for the warrant was Hudson was too powerful to be left on the chessboard for what Cyrus had planned next. And even though we hated to admit it—Cyrus *is* planning something. We absolutely cannot afford for him to take Katmere.

So yeah, we need the Crone to save Hudson and me from a lifetime in a torture prison. That's definitely a win in my book. But maybe getting lucky enough to free the blacksmith, then free the beast, and get the Crown to stop a war seems like a win-win-win-win. No matter the cost.

I shiver, and Hudson tightens his arms wrapped around my waist.

He leans forward and says in my ear, over the rushing wind, "It'll be okay."

I nod and briefly squeeze our mating bond.

This is a conversation I can't have with him. For once, Hudson is refusing to face something—which should be my first clue as to how badly he thinks this trip is going to end. But we need to figure out what cost is worth a way to get out of prison. What would I be willing to sacrifice to save him?

Anything. The answer skates along my nerves—which should be *my* first clue as to how bad this is really going to get. I glance around at all my friends, though, and realize my answer would be the same for any of them. This is my family now, and I would protect them no matter the cost.

We circle the island once, just to get the lay of the land. Not that there's a lot to observe, save the giant house smack-dab in the middle of the island. And, to be fair, calling the place a "house" is a little like calling a five-star hotel a Motel 6. It's a full-on mansion out here in the middle of the Pacific Ocean.

I'd like to circle a few more times, try to figure out exactly how we want to approach the house—I'm a little gun-shy after that whole experience with the blacksmith's wife. But we've been racing dawn across the horizon, which means Hudson and Luca are almost out of time. At least Macy can make a portal back to school when we're done here.

Flint and Eden drop down first, while Jaxon pulls up the rear. It's pretty obvious that it annoys Hudson that Jaxon can just "float," while he has to ride on Flint's back. Normally, he would fade, but even Hudson Vega hasn't figured out how to run across the ocean quite yet. I'd offered to ride as well, and that seemed to make it better. Honestly, I just didn't think my upper back muscles were strong enough for a transpacific flight just yet, and I worried I'd slow everyone down.

Hudson doesn't say anything to Jaxon, though, as we stand looking up at the house. But I'm pretty sure that has more to do with the house than any actual restraint on Hudson's part when it comes to his younger brother.

"It's not just me, right?" Eden asks. "You all see it, too?"

"It's hard to miss," Mekhi agrees, and his eyes are wider than I've ever seen them.

"What exactly do you call this kind of architecture?" Flint asks, looking at Macy as he does.

"Why are you asking me?" she says. "Do I look like someone who would live in a house like this?"

"So it's not, like, a witch thing, then? You don't all live in houses like this?" Luca lifts his brows.

"I live in a castle, thank you very much. The same castle that all of you live in, by the way, in case you've forgotten."

"Yeah, but it's a choice, right?" Flint continues, eyes cataloging every detail of the house's exterior. "You don't just accidentally build a house that looks like this."

"Do you think she has an oven?" Mekhi asks. "Should we be worried if she has an oven?"

"I'm pretty sure she has an oven," I tell him. "Most people do."

"Maybe she prefers the grill," Hudson suggests dryly.

"Is that a thing?" Flint queries, looking wildly among us. "Grilling?"

"You're awfully squeamish for a dragon," I tell him.

"What does that mean?" he demands, voice high with obvious insult. "It's not like I fly around campus barbecuing local wildlife with my flames."

"I'm thinking pizza oven myself." Jaxon picks up the previous conversation thread without so much as batting an eye. "I think I saw a big one in the back when we were circling."

"In that case, let's go," Eden says, starting toward the front door. "Those things get really hot, so at least we know it will be quick."

"Like, how hot?" Mekhi asks as he follows her down the flower-lined walk.

"Did anyone ever decide what they call this kind of architecture?" Flint asks again as he gapes at the ribbon-bedecked light poles lining the edges of the lawn, each one with a different colored light bulb shining from the top.

"Gingerbread house?" Eden snarks.

"More like gingerbread mansion," Hudson tells her as he takes the stairs up to the front door.

"Gingerbread villa?" I suggest as I climb up right behind him.

"Gingerbread ski lodge," Luca says definitively. "On a tropical island."

"Which makes her what?" Flint muses.

"Architecturally challenged," I whisper as we finally make it to the front door.

"Is it too early to knock?" Macy asks. "I know we need to get Hudson and Luca out of the sun, but what if she's asleep?"

"I'm not asleep," says a light, melodious voice directly behind us.

We whirl around to find a tall, beautiful woman in a long floral dress watching us. She's carrying a basket filled with flowers and herbs over her forearm.

"The hour before dawn is the best time to gather up ingredients for my potions," she says as she dances up the stairs on her tiptoes even as she looks at each one of us in turn. "But I came back early when I saw you land."

"We're sorry to disturb you," Macy says in her sweetest voice.

"It's nothing. I've been wondering when you would come." She waves one elegant, lavender-fingertipped hand, and the double doors that lead into the house swing open. "Come on in, and I'll make you all a cup of tea."

It's the invitation we've been waiting for, but I can't help wondering if this is actually the woman we came here to meet. This can't be the Crone. I was picturing a stooped old woman and instead...she looks like a Greek goddess. Long, flowing hair, perfect porcelain skin, bright-blue eyes that seem to catalog everything about us.

But there's no way to find out unless we follow her inside. And even then, I'm not sure. What are we supposed to say? *Excuse me, but are you the Crone?* It seems pretty freaking rude, really. Especially when we came to ask for her help.

She leads the way through the door, her long hair blowing behind her in the wind. Flint follows her in, then Eden, Hudson, and me. But when Jaxon starts to walk in, she whirls around and shouts, "No!"

He freezes, nearly bouncing off the invisible barrier her refusal slams down in front of him.

"Is something wrong?" I ask. "That's Jaxon Vega. He's—"

"I know exactly who he is," she tells me. Her gaze slides to Hudson. "And who he's related to here. But I do not allow soulless creatures to enter my abode."

"Soulless?" I repeat, totally confused at this point. "He's not soulless. He's a vampire, just like Hudson—"

"I'm sorry, but those are my rules." Her blue eyes are laser bright when she turns them to me. "You and whichever friends would like to join you may stay inside with me while he stays outside. Or you may all leave. But do hurry and decide. I have flowers to process."

She walks through a living room fit for a European palace and places the flower basket on the coffee table before turning back to me. "What's it going to be, Grace?"

"You know my name?" I ask.

She arches one perfect brow but doesn't answer me.

The truth is there's only one possible answer to her question—we have to accept her choice and leave Jaxon outside, no matter how bizarre and unfounded her accusation is.

"Of course we want to stay," I tell her, even as I shoot Jaxon an *I'm sorry* look. The others still seem confused, but they don't argue. They know just as well as I do how stuck we are.

Jaxon—who doesn't seem outraged at her assessment, merely resigned—walks over to one of the two porch swings and sits down on it, stretching his long legs out in front of him as he starts to glide back and forth. As he does, he makes sure not to look anyone in the eye, and I feel awful for him.

He's got a total poker face, but I know this boy, and it is obvious to me how much her baseless accusation actually bothers him. What surprises me is that he hasn't said a word to defend himself.

The others must feel the same way, because it's clear they're torn whether to stay with Jaxon or with me.

In the end, Mekhi and Eden choose to head outside with him, and I know Luca would choose the same thing if he didn't *have* to be out of the sun. Macy, Flint, Hudson, Luca, and I stay in the house.

Once that's decided, the double doors close behind us, and the witch gestures to the two pearl-gray sofas she has in the middle of her living room. "Take a seat. Please."

Once we do as she "requests," she walks over to the bloodred chair to the right of the sofas and sits down, looking for all the world like a queen holding court.

Seriously, Nuri and Delilah have nothing on this woman in terms of royal affect, and I can tell by the way that the two princes in the room shift in their seats that they recognize it, too.

"Would you like something to drink?" she asks, her melodic voice ringing like bells through the air now that everything about this situation is arranged exactly as she wants it to be.

I'm actually really thirsty—it was a long flight, and I ran out of water bottles somewhere near Hawaii—but I'm not taking anything this woman has to offer until I can get a better read on her. Because to me, her sweetness seems more saccharin than sugar, and I'm really not enjoying the aftertaste.

95

Love, Hate, and All the Grace

"**A**ctually, we're good," Flint tells her after a few awkward moments. "But thank you."

"So be it." She snaps, and a glass of lemonade appears in her hand. She takes a long drink, eyes on us the whole time—whether because she doesn't trust us or because she's mocking us for not trusting her, I don't know. But when she finally lets go of the glass, it hovers next to her in midair.

"So tell me, my darlings. What secret do you come here to uncover?"

"I don't think it's so much a secret as a solution." I shift uncomfortably, trying to gauge whether to jump right in or whether to lay our request out slowly. It's a lot, and she has no reason to help us other than the goodness of her heart…a goodness that is already quite suspect in my own mind.

But before I can decide what I want to say next, she looks me dead in the eye and trills, "Everything's a secret, Grace, whether we know it or not."

Then she takes another sip of her lemonade before once again leaving it to hover right next to her. "You know, I've found myself thinking about an old story several times over the last few weeks. I haven't been able to figure out what brought it to mind or why it's continued to linger in the forefront of my memory. Normally, stories show up for a little while and then flit away on the morning breeze when they realize I have no one to tell them to, save my flowers. We are a little isolated out here, aren't we?"

For just a moment, there's a sharpness to her words, but then it disappears so quickly that I think I must have imagined it, especially when the others have no reaction to it.

"But now you're here, and I realize the story must have been waiting for you all along." She locks eyes with each of us in turn. "So I ask that you indulge me in a trip down memory lane, if you don't mind."

"We don't mind at all," I say and smile. "In fact, I think we'd really like to listen to whatever stories you want to tell us."

"All that power, and diplomacy, too. Aren't you a pleasant surprise, Grace?" Her smile is slow and wide, but it definitely doesn't reach her eyes. Which I guess is fair, considering I'm fairly certain mine doesn't, either.

Hudson doesn't like it, though. I can tell from the way he tenses beside me, his body angling toward mine just a little bit, as if preparing to block anything that comes at me—including the Crone.

But she just settles back against her chair with a satisfied smile and begins. "Once, a long time ago, magic sang in the wind that whistled through the trees. It played tag in the waves that kissed the shore and danced in the flames that burned to make the earth grow richer and even more benevolent. It was beautiful and lonely, and it is into this world of unleashed power—so different from the one we now try so desperately to understand—that two children were born."

Her eyes burn brighter and brighter—*she* burns brighter and brighter—as she lays the groundwork for the story, until her entire being seems lit from within. "The children were sisters, twins in fact, born of two deities, Zamar and Aciel, who loved each other so much that they wanted to have a child. But the universe requires balance, and so they had two daughters, each a different side of the same coin. Unfortunately, on the night of their birth, Zamar died and became the very light and warmth that every creature on this strange new planet would bask itself in. Aciel was devastated at the loss but vowed to raise the girls with all the care and support that the other deity would have given them."

She pauses to shove her heavy curtain of hair away from her eyes, and as she does, the early-morning light catches it, and I realize that it isn't the light brown I assumed it was after all. It's actually every color—red and blond and brown and black and silver and white all mixed together in a waterfall of color that feels infinite in a way I can't describe.

She notices me noticing and preens a little, combing her hands through her hair so that the light catches it at the best angle. And I have to fight a grin, because she may be powerful, but she's also vain as fuck. I make a mental note that this might be able to help us later, then wait patiently for her to continue the story.

"Aciel loved the girls equally and always told them that they were born to bring balance to the universe, that their power was so great that it couldn't and shouldn't be contained in one person. 'Power,' they were told, 'always requires a counterbalance. You cannot have strength without weakness, beauty without ugliness, love without hate.'" She takes another sip of her lemonade before adding, "Good without evil.

"And so the sisters were raised in this world they both loved and hated, this world that took Zamar from the girls but also gave them back every day from the moment the sun came up until the time that it went down. They grew under this sun, learning and loving, failing and flourishing, until one day they were old enough."

She pauses again, lets that sink in as she takes a long, slow sip from her drink. I've never heard any part of this story, but I've read enough to recognize a creation myth when I hear it, and I'm dying to get to the good part. Dying to know who created what and why and how this fits in with what we've come to ask her—or even if it fits in at all.

And I've got to say, the Crone knows how to work a room, because we are literally on the edges of our seats, the others with looks of serious interest in what she's saying on their faces, almost as if parts of this myth aren't as unfamiliar to them as they are to me. Not that that's a surprise—the longer I'm in the paranormal world, the more I realize how many things are different from the human world. Is it really such a stretch that their origin myth—their belief system—would be different, too?

Though I am surprised that I've been here this long without recognizing that fact. Then again, I basically hibernated through my culture's most famous holiday last year...

"Old enough for what?" I ask when it becomes obvious that she is stretching the silence out because she *wants* someone to ask.

"Why, to name themselves, my dear. You see, Aciel couldn't do it. To bestow a name on someone is a sacred ritual and with the other deity's passing, the two girls would not be named until they were old enough to perform the rite themselves.

"And so Cassia and Adria were born."

The sisters' names go through the room like a lightning strike, fast and bright and all-encompassing. And as the others nod like this part, at least, is old hat, I realize I *have* heard parts of this story before—in my history class and my magical laws class, though references were always done in passing.

The Crone not only recognizes our own knowledge of the names but she seems to bask in it, her voice growing more and more animated as the story goes on. Her smile even loses its sharpness, becomes warmer and less guarded.

"Many cultures know of Cassia and Adria—though they call them by different names—and many the universe over love them for their sacrifice and their benevolence. Adria loved order so much that she created laws to govern the universe that the sisters both adored and despised. Then she created humans and declared them the perfect creation."

The Crone snarls a little at this, like she can't believe anyone could have the nerve to call humans perfect. And while I'm a paranormal now versus a regular human, the girl who was raised in the human world for seventeen years of her life bristles a little at the animosity, even as I acknowledge that a lot of it is completely justified. After all, look what we've done to Adria's planet...and to one another.

"Cassia, on the other hand, loved chaos and—not to be outdone by her perfect sister—created paranormal creatures and declared them flawless as well." She smiles kindly at us. "And here you all are, children of Cassia's love and imagination."

She pauses like she expects us to thank her, but no matter who the Crone thinks she is, I have a hard time imagining she's one of the two goddesses in a millennia-old creation myth. Call me skeptical, but it's a little hard to believe—even in a world where vampires and dragons walk the earth.

"But from the moment they were created, humans and paranormals have been at odds," the Crone continues a little abruptly when a wave of adoration doesn't immediately come her way. "And so Cassia and Adria watched as their beautiful creations went to war. Humans, who believed in order, tried to tame the universe. They set rules for everything and gave everything a place in the order of things. Paranormals, on the other hand"—she shakes her head like a benevolent mother who will never understand her children—"have never flourished in order. They like to fight, like to sow discord and havoc wherever they go.

"This angered Adria, who was furious at the way her children were being destroyed by the children of chaos." She looks particularly hard at Hudson, as if vampires—and he in particular—are responsible for everything bad that's ever happened in the world. "Seeing her creation being destroyed broke Adria, and she poisoned the Cup of Life that was meant to nourish her sister and her. It was the cup that would allow them to travel through realms and continue creation in them all."

She shakes her head at Adria's wickedness. "And when Cassia, the goddess of chaos, went to drink from the cup, she was immediately poisoned and fell to earth as a demigod, her powers half of what they once were. Adria felt bad for her sister but felt righteous in her decision to protect her creatures and the order necessary for all to flourish. Except the silly goddess forgot one very important thing."

She pauses dramatically, even goes so far as to drain the rest of her lemonade in one long sip.

Macy is on the edge of her seat now, her hands twisted in her own dress as she all but wills the Crone to continue. "What happened?" she finally asks when the Crone doesn't continue fast enough for her. "What happened to Adria?"

"She forgot the most important advice Aciel had given her. The universe requires balance in all things—and she paid the price."

"What price did she pay?" Flint asks, and he, too, looks like he's dying to know what happened.

"And what happened to Cassia?" Macy asks. "Was she okay?"

"Adria fell to earth, too, as a demigod stripped of some of her most important powers. For what befalls one sister must always befall the other—to maintain balance. It is the oldest magic in the universe." She shakes her head as though sad the sisters had forgotten this lesson and what was to happen next. "And Aciel, who had loved and adored them their entire life, abandoned them. They said it was only until they learned their lesson, that once they learned how to get along—how to balance chaos and order—they would come to get the twins."

Her voice trails off as she looks past us and out the large glass picture windows at the back of the room. "But that was a long time ago," she finally whispers. "And Aciel has never come back for either of them."

"And so, the story goes, Cassia and Adria are trapped on this earth to this day, forced to watch as generation after generation of paranormals hunts generation after generation of humans and vice versa. Both sides constantly fighting, refusing to compromise, unable to live in any kind of harmony or balance—just like the sisters who created them."

Her voice hitches just a little and she pauses, blows out a long, slow breath, as if telling this part of the story physically hurts her. Eventually, though, she continues in little more than a whisper. "As fights continued between the two creations and resulted in the First Great War, both sides pleaded with their creators to choose a side, so that finally they could live in harmony—even if that meant wiping the other side out of existence altogether.

"And so Adria began to help her beloved humans, training them in the way of hunting and destroying paranormals once and for all. They destroyed lives, ravaged whole villages of paranormals, brought some of the species to the brink of extinction, but still the paranormals wouldn't yield. Still they continued to fight the humans until a devastating chaos reigned over the world."

She pauses for a moment, her gaze skimming past everyone else and focusing on me alone.

Her eyes are super freaky now, glowing so brightly that they hardly seem real. Tension grows in the room as she stares at me, and shivers work their way down my spine. Even before she says, "It was into this chaos, this disorder, these extremes of love and hate, that you—that all gargoyles—were born."

96

Balance Beams Aren't Just for Gymnasts... But They Should Be

My whole body flashes from cold to hot to cold again as her words sizzle on my skin and skate along my every nerve ending.

I've tried to remain unaffected by her dramatics, tried to act like the story of Cassia and Adria wasn't nearly as fascinating as it is. But she's got me with this one—and the satisfied smile on her face as her eyes return to semi-normal says she knows it.

This is what I've been looking for in all those books. This is the origin story of gargoyles that I haven't been able to find anywhere.

Hudson must sense my excitement, because he slides his hand across the small amount of couch cushion between us and wraps his pinkie around mine. A whole different kind of nervous energy slams through me at the first brush of his skin against mine.

When he uses his pinkie to gently squeeze mine, I squeeze his right back. And am shocked by the amount of heat that small interaction sends spiraling through my entire being.

As if sensing she's lost my attention, the Crone clears her throat several times. Only when all five of us have refocused our attention on her does she finally begin this latest iteration of her story.

"Though the deity had left Cassia and Adria to suffer alongside their creations, Aciel had not forsaken them completely. And so, upon realizing that the world and creatures created by the daughters might never find balance—which would leave them trapped on earth forever—Aciel gifted them with a creation of their own. Gargoyles."

She gives me an eerie smile, the one that has the hair on the back of my neck standing up straight. In response, I can feel something deep inside me stirring, coming to life. At first I think it's my own gargoyle, responding to the rapid changes in my body as I try to absorb all the information the

Crone is giving us.

But then I hear his voice deep inside me. I haven't heard it for weeks, but I recognize it the moment he starts to talk.

No, he tells me. *No, no, no. You need to go.*

It's okay, I tell the Unkillable Beast, who is somehow managing to talk to me despite the distance between us. *She won't hurt us.*

This is bad, bad, bad, he tells me.

It's okay, I say again. *I need to know how we were created. I need to know what happened to us.*

He doesn't say anything else, just sends me a feeling of foreboding before fading away. I just wish I knew if it was because he's trapped and needs me to come release him or if it's because he knows something I don't and is trying to tell it to me...or trying to keep it from me.

Don't worry, I tell him. *I promise I'll come back for you. I promise I'll free you.*

But he's gone as easily and unexpectedly as he came.

"So this deity, who created the girls, made gargoyles?" Luca asks, eyes narrowed in concentration.

"The deity who created the *goddesses*," she corrects him. "But yes. In order to balance out the forces of order and chaos caused by the humans and paranormals, they made gargoyles. It was Aciel's wish that after a while, gargoyles would balance things out, and then one day their daughters—having learned their lesson—would be freed from this earthly realm. But to make that possibility a reality, they had to create a creature who couldn't be swayed by either side.

"Since gargoyles were created from the source of all magic, instead of from chaos or order, you hold both within you, Grace. A desire to create order, a desire to create chaos. Always at war but also always in harmony. It's this ability that allows you to straddle both worlds, become a beacon of peace for both sisters' creations. It's also what helps you channel magic from both sides.

"That is not to say you are immune to magic," she assures me. "You are a creature born of magic, so you will always be tethered to it in one way or another, but only the most ancient magic will ever work on you."

As if to prove it, she sends a little current of electricity across the room that zaps me hard enough to make me gasp.

"What's wrong?" Hudson asks, looking between the Crone and me with narrowed eyes.

"Just a little demonstration of what true magic can do," she answers placidly. "She's fine."

"I'm fine," I echo, even though every nerve ending I have feels like it's been electrocuted.

I have so many questions I want to ask. Does this mean I really am as different from the others as I feel sometimes? Is it because gargoyles have all but disappeared from the earth that things seem to be spinning so rapidly out of control—in both the human and the paranormal worlds? And if so, am I supposed to find a way to bring balance back?

The idea seems absurd on its face. There used to be thousands upon thousands of gargoyles walking the earth. Now there are only two that I know of, and one is chained up in a cave, driven almost completely mad by the isolation. How can we possibly fix everything that's wrong?

It's a lot to process, a lot to think about and worry about and try to find a way to cope with. And now isn't the time for any of that, not while the Crone is watching me so carefully. And not when everything else seems to be spinning out of my control—Jaxon, Cyrus, my feelings for Hudson...

Right now, it feels a lot like I'm walking a balance beam that's way too high. One wrong move and not only will I fall off, but I'll end up smashed to bits. I can sense my chest tightening, my heart hammering as my stomach sinks. *No, no, not now. Not a panic attack now.*

I take a shaky breath and manage to get the words through my rapidly closing throat. "If I am supposed to be able to straddle both worlds of chaos and order, why does even the hint of conflict steal my breath?"

"That *is* a good question, now, isn't it?" She's smiling again—and again it doesn't reach her eyes. But after a few minutes of watching me struggle to breathe, she waves a hand, and it's as though she released a vise around my chest. My breath comes flooding back into my lungs, the anxiety that had seized me only a moment before gone now.

I want to ask her desperately how she did it, but I know I've already shown too much weakness. So instead, I hold her gaze and ask the other question that's been burning in my chest. "But if gargoyles are meant to bring balance and are immune to both sides, how did they lose so badly in the Second Great War? How did they become nearly extinct?"

The Crone shrugs. "How does anything like that happen? Betrayal."

"Betrayal?" Hudson asks, even as the word rocks me to my core. "By whom?"

"The gargoyle king," she answers. "Who else's betrayal could have such a devastating effect?"

"I don't understand," I whisper. "I thought gargoyles were supposed to bring balance. What could he have possibly done—"

"He sided with the paranormals over the humans, even became mated to one. He broke the balance between them once and for all, and for that, he was swiftly punished. But the punishment ended up affecting everyone, not just him. And so one of his men—eager to stop what he saw as a threat against himself and all gargoyles—went to the vampire king and told him how to kill gargoyles, a secret nobody knows. He thought Cyrus would use it only against the gargoyle king—"

"But he used it on all of them," I whisper in horror. "He killed them all."

"He did," the Crone agrees.

Horror washes through me—through all of us, if the looks on my friends' faces are anything to go by. And I would bet we're all thinking the same thing...

If Cyrus knows the secret to how to easily kill a gargoyle—why didn't he use it on me earlier? Why not take me out before the trials? "Cyrus nearly killed me with his Eternal Bite. Is that a gargoyle's weakness, since they *should* be immune to his magic otherwise?"

"Oh no, dear child. Cyrus's bite isn't magic at all. It's venom." Her eyes are twinkling evilly now. "In fact, Cyrus lost most of his magic a long time ago—which is why he rules with fear and ruthlessness. Better for you to fear him than he fear you, no?"

The vampire queen's words to Hudson flood my mind. *Appear weak when you are strong.* We've been so busy trying to figure out what she meant, we didn't even bother to consider that there is a second part to that saying. I turn to Hudson and say, "Appear strong when you are weak."

Hudson's eyes narrow in understanding. The vampire queen was telling us Cyrus is as desperate as we are to find the Crown. He needs power. What would he do with it if he got the Crown before us? Nothing we'd survive, of that I am sure.

97

My Enemy's Enemy Is Still Sketchy as F*ck

Panic starts to well up inside me, and this time I'm not sure I'm going to be able to beat it back. My heart is pounding out of control, my chest feels like an elephant is sitting right on my solar plexus, and my hands are shaking so badly that I slide them under my thighs in a desperate effort to hide them from the Crone and my friends.

I take a few deep breaths, try to calm down, try to tell myself that it's going to be fine. That it's ridiculous to get this worked up about anything. But if there *is* anything in the world worth getting worked up about, an enemy with a secret that could kill me seems a good place to start. Especially if this knowledge was already successful once. And a Crown out there that would give him the power to do even worse.

I'm trying to keep it together, trying not to let anyone know how bad the panic is. But Hudson must sense it—or maybe he recognizes the symptoms from spending all that time in my head—because he scoots over until the outside of his thigh is pressed against the outside of mine.

It's a far cry from grass under my toes and sun on my face, but he feels safe and warm and secure, so I'll take it. I blow out a long, slow breath and concentrate on the feel of his leg against mine. Hard. Strong.

I take another deep breath and then blow it out slowly. Steady. Unwavering.

One more breath in, one more breath out. Right. He feels right.

"Okay?" Hudson asks under his breath, and I nod even though it's not quite true. "Okay" is a definite stretch from what I'm feeling, but it's better than freaked the fuck out, so I'll take it.

I look up to realize the Crone is staring at me like I'm a bug under a microscope. Because she's never seen a panic attack before? I wonder. Or because she's cataloging my weaknesses—trying to figure out where and how to hit me?

I hate that I think like this now, that I look at everyone—even people we're forced to ask for help—as adversaries who might or might not try to destroy us at any moment. It's a bullshit way to live, a bullshit way to think. But considering the alternative is not living at all...the dilemma is real.

The others must notice the same thing, because Flint leaps into action—and by action I mean throws out his most charming grin. "I know you said you were expecting us, but does that mean you know why we're here?"

Reluctantly, she turns her gaze to him...and then stares him down until his smile wilts and he averts his eyes. Only then does she allow herself to smile a little and say, "There are any number of reasons you could be here. My herbal teas. A particularly strong love potion." She examines her lavender-painted nails. "The Aethereum."

My entire body freezes at the last word she says—there's something about the way she says it, with a reverence that makes it sound special to her. Like *had a hand in building it* special?

Either way, it's obvious she's playing coy. I just wish I knew what she got out of it besides a captive audience.

Then again, maybe that's all she needs. If she's been alone out here as long as she says, then maybe all she wants is someone to talk to for a while. And maybe making us guess is how she guarantees we stick around a little bit longer.

Hudson has obviously had enough, though, because instead of playing her game, he just flat-out asks, "Can you help us get out of the prison or not?"

"Get out?" she asks, brows lifted. "Are you planning on doing something to get yourself put inside the Aethereum? And if so, why?"

"There's an arrest warrant out for my mate," I explain. "He pissed off Cyrus and—"

"Enough said. No one likes to toy with his subjects more than the vampire king." She shakes her head. "What a sad little man he is."

"I was thinking horrible little man," Macy says. "But I guess sad works, too."

The Crone laughs. "I like you," she tells my cousin, who grins back.

"I like you, too. And you have great hair."

That startles a laugh out of the Crone, who flips the hair in question. "It is fun, isn't it?" She turns back to the rest of us. "My best advice to you is to stay out of the prison. Do whatever it takes to not be sent there, even if it means fleeing an arrest warrant. Because once you get in, it's not just that it's hell to get out. It's that in a lot of cases, you lose your will to *want* to get out."

"How is that even possible?" Luca asks. "Who loses their drive to get out of prison?"

"Let's just say it's a very...unique place." The Crone smiles. "The design is terribly clever."

"Does that mean you have an equally clever get-out-of-jail-free card you can offer?" Flint asks hopefully.

She clicks her tongue. "Nothing is free, dragon. Certainly nothing of value." She stands up, and at first I think she's going to order us out the door. "If we were to reach a bargain, how many people would be needing...passage... from the Aethereum?"

I cough. "Umm...we would need three."

The Crone's eyes narrow. "That would be quite expensive, my dear. Are you sure you wish to pay the price for such a request?"

This is it. The question I knew was coming, the one I was dreading, and yet I'm surprised how fast my answer comes. "Yes."

We stare at each other, and I can tell she's weighing her next words carefully. "Very well, Grace. I will provide safe passage for three people from the Aethereum in exchange for a favor. One day I will ask something of you, and you will be unable to refuse. Do you agree?"

"No!" all my friends shout at the same time. Well, except Hudson, who offers a healthy, "Hell fucking no."

But the question is simple. Am I willing to trade my future for that of my friends, my family, the Circle's survival itself? For Hudson? And Jaxon?

"Yes," I reply, and she starts to smile, "with several caveats."

"You're not in a position to bargain, Grace."

The words are delivered with deliberate calm, and that's how I know—I have something she wants. Badly. So just maybe I *am* in a position to bargain...

I shrug, "Well, you're welcome to turn down my offer, and we can leave as we came and find another way."

Her eyes narrow on me again before she finally says, "Very well. What are your terms?"

"I will not do anything that harms my friends, my family, or really anyone on this entire fucking planet, whether directly or indirectly."

"Those are the exact words of your terms?" she asks, and I run what I said through my head several times. What loophole did I leave for this witch to exploit?

I can't think of anything. I nod. "Those are my exact terms."

"I accept," she says and walks over to the basket of flowers she gathered this morning before we arrived.

She sorts through it for a few seconds, and as she shifts them, the flowers release the most heavenly scent into the room. I have no idea what she's looking for—or why she's looking for it now—but when she turns around, she is carrying an armful of green stems with clusters of tiny bright-orange flowers.

"This is the only thing I can think of that will get you free from the prison," she says. "But it demands a steep price." Then she walks straight out of the room.

"Umm, was that an invitation to pay her?" Macy asks, rummaging in her pockets. "Because I think I've got twenty bucks on me."

"I don't think that's the kind of payment she's talking about," Hudson says.

"So do we just kind of hang around here and hope for the best," I ask, "or go find her?"

"Find whom?" the Crone asks as she walks in a totally different door—from a totally different direction—than the one she left by.

"You," I answer, leaving the "obviously" off.

She blinks those super-blue eyes of hers at me. "But I'm already here, dear Grace. Why would you be looking for me?"

I have no idea what I'm supposed to say to that, so I just kind of smile and nod. "You're right."

The flowers have now been snipped of their stems and are sitting in a small bowl of water. "These are for you," she tells me, holding the bowl out to me.

"Thank you," I tell her, though I don't know why she would give me a bunch of chopped-up flowers—especially in the middle of a conversation.

But as I lean down to sniff the fragrant blooms, she stops me with a firm hand to the shoulder. "I wouldn't do that if I were you."

I freeze, because if there's anything I've learned from living in this paranormal world, it's that when a being of power tells you not to do something—especially in that tone—you don't do it.

"Okay," I say, lifting my head.

"That's butterfly weed," she tells me. "The only plant in the world that monarch butterflies will lay their eggs in. It's beautiful and it smells very nice and it is horribly, horribly toxic."

"Oh, well then...thank you for the gift?" I tell her, holding the bowl as far away from me as I can get and still be polite.

She sighs. "It's not a gift, dear. It's your—what did you call it?" she asks Flint. "Your get-out-of-jail-free card? All you have to do to cash it in is die."

98

Hope Blooms Eternal

I drop the flowers on the nearest table. I come close enough to dying on a regular basis that I don't need some weed to help me along.

The Crone just smiles indulgently at me, though there is a dark watchfulness in her eyes that doesn't quite fit the *sugar and spice and everything oh so nice* vibes that she's working so hard to give out.

"You won't die from touching them, Grace. Just from eating them," she tells me.

"So let me get this straight," Luca says, "just because I like everybody to be on the same page. My friends tell you they don't want to go to prison—and they definitely don't want to get stuck there for crimes they didn't commit— and your suggestion is suicide?" He looks as horrified as he sounds.

"What? Of course not! Suicide helps no one, young man." She sighs heavily even as she picks up one of the severed flowers and uses the index finger of one hand to spin it around in the palm of the other. "This is my own specially engineered butterfly weed. It has most of the properties of this species of milkweed—including toxins that cause everything from bloating to hallucinations to death."

"Sounds fun," Flint tells her in obvious disgust.

She ignores him. "With a little something extra added from me."

"And what exactly is that extra something?" Hudson demands, and I only thought he looked skeptical before. Right now he looks like she could tell him that today is Monday and he'd tell her she was full of shit, even though it definitely is.

"Just a little…magical genetic engineering I do on some of my flowers. Call it a hobby."

"Making them less dangerous?" Macy asks, and even she sounds cautious. "Or *more* dangerous?"

The Crone's teeth snap together as she smiles. "What do you think? Dear." The last is tacked on, like she had to remind herself to say it.

"I think we should probably not take those flowers," Macy answers.

"That is, as always, up to you." She glides back to her chair. "But they will solve your problem."

"By killing us?" Hudson asks dryly. "Been there, done that. Not keen on a repeat."

"By making you appear dead long enough to break the prison's hold on you and get you taken outside the walls by the guards."

"Is that a polite way of saying they'll bury us alive?" I ask, just the idea making me sweat.

"No one from the prison gets buried when they die," she says sweetly. "That's just silly."

This is getting sketchier and sketchier.

"So, what you're saying is, we eat the flowers, knowing they are poisonous and they will kill us—" I break off as she shakes her head adamantly.

"Make you *appear* dead," she tells me. "Not the same thing at all."

"Oh right, sorry. They will make us appear dead, and then the guards will—for some reason unknown to us—take us outside the prison walls and not bury us, at which time we can get away."

She smiles. "Exactly. Sounds easy, doesn't it?"

"What it sounds like is some magical, next-gen *Romeo and Juliet* shit," Flint answers. "And I think we all know how that worked out for them."

"I've never read it," she tells him, but her tone is about ten degrees cooler than it was.

"Well, let me ruin it for you," Flint shoots back. "They both die in the end. For real."

"Hmm." It's Flint's turn to be examined like he's a bug—and not just any bug. She looks at him like he's a gigantic cockroach skittering across the rug while she's barefoot—right before she turns back to me. "Just to be clear. You're free to leave anytime. You are the ones who came to me asking for help, not the other way around."

"Of course, you're right," I say, because she is. And also because something tells me this witch doesn't get mad; she gets even...in the worst possible way. "We did come to you for help, and we appreciate everything you've done for us."

I pick the bowl of flowers back up, trying my best not to slosh any of the water over the edges. "If you think these flowers are the way to go, then we will definitely take them with us if we end up getting arrested."

Hudson gives me a look that says *the hell we will*, but I ignore him. He can pretend like we have control over what's going to happen to us, but we don't. At least not right now. If this floral death trap gives us some semblance of that control back, then I say we go for it.

"Not like that, you won't," the Crone tells me.

"I'm sorry?"

She shakes her head. "It is a prison, dear, and you don't even know when—or if—you're going to end up there. If the flowers die before you get arrested, they will be useless to you. Not to mention that the prison would never let you in with them."

"Oh, right." I feel like a child as I look down at the bright-orange flowers floating in the water. "So what are we supposed to do?"

"You," she answers, nodding specifically at me, "need to put your hand in the liquid."

"My hand?" I ask with a whole lot of trepidation. There are two reasons I don't want to do what she asks—one is because the flowers are poisonous and the second is because she called the stuff they're floating in "liquid" instead of "water."

I must not be the only one who picks up on that, either, because Flint puts a hand on my forearm to keep me from doing anything as he asks, "What kind of liquid are we talking about here exactly?"

She just smiles. "It won't hurt you, Grace."

"I'll do it," Hudson says, moving forward to block my access to the bowl.

"No, you won't," the Crone answers, and beneath the sweetness is 100 percent steel.

"And why is that exactly?" he asks.

"Because I say so," she snaps, eyes flashing. "And also because this step won't work on a vampire."

Hudson bares his teeth at her—and I can't help wondering if this is all about to go south…in the worst possible way. A way that includes pulling Hudson out of here in a body bag…after she's shoved him into her pizza oven.

"I'll do it," I tell her, stepping around him.

"Grace—" Hudson shoots me a warning look, which I ignore.

Because of course I know it's a bad idea. But bad ideas are what you have left after you've blown through all the good ones.

Is this a last resort? Abso-freaking-lutely. I'm not going to dispute that. But if we get arrested and stuck in an inescapable prison with an unbreakable curse, then I think we're fucked anyway.

So with options that are basically A, die fast, B, die slow, or C, maybe, possibly have a chance of getting the hell out with the help of these flowers?

I totally choose option D. But something tells me there's no way Cyrus is going to allow that, so C it is.

Without waiting for any more objections—or for Hudson to try to stop me—I plunge my hand straight into the bowl of floral liquid.

Romeo and Juliet, here I come.

99

Blood Isn't Thicker than Water

My hand still hurts several hours later, when we finally make it back to Katmere. I try to ignore the burn that's radiating from the three orange flowers now branded into my palm, but it's basically impossible.

Tylenol, here I come.

"This is a bad idea," Hudson tells me as we climb up the stairs to Katmere.

We're all exhausted—we've done entirely too much flying, partying, and tense negotiating in the last seventy-two hours, and all any of us wants to do is get some sleep. Preferably a lot of sleep before graduation tomorrow. Jaxon and the others got back before us, so odds are they're already curled up in bed. I envy them.

I have no doubt that we're going to need all our wits about us once we have to face Cyrus, who I know is going to be on his game.

"I agree," I tell him. "But I still think we can't rule it out."

"Rule it out? How can we even rule it in?" he hisses. "Tell me you don't actually trust that woman."

"'Trust' is a pretty strong word."

"'Trust' is utter recklessness. She lives in a bloody gingerbread house. I don't know about you, but I believe in truth in advertising, and I have no interest in being Hansel *or* fucking Gretel."

I make a face at him. "I really don't think cannibalism is on the table."

"I wouldn't be too sure about that. Did you see the way she was looking at Luca?"

"Yeah, well, I don't think that had anything to do with cannibalism."

We both laugh, and I don't know. There's something about the way he looks—so happy, despite all the shit we still have to go through—that hits me directly in the feels. And has me giggling long after the joke is over.

"You good?" he asks as we walk through the wide double doors at the top of the steps.

"Yeah." I nod. "I am. How about you?"

His eyes go that fathomless blue that makes everything inside me stand up and take notice. Then he leans down a little, whispers, "I'd be better if you decide to sleep in my room tonight."

I roll my eyes. "If I decide to sleep in your room tonight, I think we'll both look like zombies at graduation."

"I'm okay with that," he tells me with a wicked little lift of his brows that has me thinking that maybe sleep isn't an actual physical requirement.

"Maybe I am, too," I tell him, idly turning my promise ring around and around my finger, and his eyes go wide with a delight that makes me laugh all over again.

"I promise I'll let you get some sleep," he tells me. "Eventually."

Then he's reaching over, brushing one of my many errant curls out of my face. As he does, he lets his fingers linger on my cheek for just a second or two, but it's long enough to have my breath catching in my throat.

Long enough to have electricity zinging along my nerve endings.

More than long enough to have me thinking about how good his mouth feels on mine.

He's thinking it, too. I can tell, and for a moment, everything fades away except Hudson and me and this heat that keeps burning, burning, burning between us.

And then all hell breaks loose.

"Don't you fucking touch her!" Jaxon snarls. "This is all your fault! You and your mating bond are the reason she might die in prison, and you think you've got the right to put your filthy fucking hands on her?"

"Whoa, Jaxon." Mekhi tries to put a restraining palm on his shoulder, but Jaxon just shoves it off as he gets right up in Hudson's face.

Hudson's eyes turn glacial in a way I haven't seen from him in weeks. "Well, at least I'm not the tosser who threw his mating bond in the trash, so maybe you shouldn't be too quick to come at me."

"You know what? Fuck you!" Jaxon roars. "You're a sanctimonious prick, and no one likes you. What the fuck are you even doing here?"

"Apparently pissing you off, so I'll call that a win for the day. And here's a little advice. Keep acting like a bloody wanker, and no one's going to like you, either." Hudson starts to brush past him, but out of nowhere, Jaxon grabs him and slams him against the wall so hard that his head makes a cracking sound when it connects with the ancient stone.

"Jaxon!" I grab on to his arm, try to pull him back. "Jaxon, stop!"

He doesn't move, doesn't blink. Honestly, I don't even think he hears me. It's like he's a stranger, someone I don't even recognize.

"You just going to stand there like a cack-handed bell?" Hudson sneers. "Or are you actually going to do something? I haven't got all bleeding day for you to get your bollocks up."

"Hudson, stop!" I shout, but it's too late. I can see the moment Jaxon snaps. His hand goes to Hudson's throat, and he starts to squeeze.

"Jaxon! Jaxon, no!" I grab on to his hand, try to pull him back, but he's not budging. And neither is Hudson, who is staring at him with contemptuous eyes. I wait for him to stop this, wait for him to pry Jaxon off, but he's not even trying. I don't get it until I realize that Jaxon is using his telekinesis to hold him against the wall. And that's when I go from frightened to terrified.

If I don't stop this, Jaxon might actually kill Hudson—again.

"Please." I duck between them so that Jaxon can't ignore me, then grab on to the hand he's using to hold Hudson against the wall. "Come on, Jaxon," I say, determined not to be ignored any longer. "Don't do this."

The eyes he glances at me with are pitch-black and empty, and they chill me to my very core. Because this isn't my Jaxon. Even that very first day, he didn't look like this.

The others have gotten into the act, yelling at Jaxon, trying to pry him off Hudson, but it's not working. Nothing is.

I'm dimly aware that Macy is calling Uncle Finn, but if I don't do something now, this will be over before he can get here. Sure, Hudson could use his power to bring the ceiling down, but he won't do that. Not with the others and me in here.

Which means I have to find a way to stop this, to get beyond whatever's got him in its thrall and reach the Jaxon I pray is still in there.

I take a deep breath to keep the panic at bay, then let it out slowly as I reach up to cup his cheeks in my palms. "Jaxon," I whisper. "Look at me."

For a few impossibly long seconds, he refuses. But then that empty gaze locks on mine, and I nearly cry out, terrified that I'm already too late.

But he's in there; I know he's in there. I just have to find him. "It's okay," I tell him softly. "I've got you, Jaxon. I'm right here, and I'm not going anywhere.

Whatever this is, whatever's going on. I swear I've got you."

He starts to shake. "Grace," he whispers, and he looks so lost, it breaks my heart. "Something's wrong. Something's—"

"I know." The whole room starts to shake now. Things are falling off the walls, stones are cracking, and behind me, I feel Hudson start to sag.

We're running out of time; I can feel it. Panic is a rabid animal inside me now, but I fight it back, refuse to give in. Because if I do, it's over. And then what am I going to do? What are any of us going to do?

For a second, just a second, I look past him and out the still-open doors... and see the aurora borealis dancing across the sky. It gives me an idea. I just hope it's a good one—I know this is the last chance I've got.

"The Northern Lights just came out, Jaxon. They're right outside."

Our friends make disbelieving sounds, like they can't believe what I'm saying. But I'm betting everything on my belief that the Jaxon I loved is still in there somewhere.

"Do you remember that night?" I whisper. "I was so nervous, but you just held my hand and took me right off the edge of the parapet."

The shaking is worse now, in him and the room. But I know he's in there now, can feel him trying to find his way back to us.

"You danced me across the sky. Remember? We stayed out for hours. I was freezing, but I didn't want to go in. I didn't want to miss a second out there with you."

"Grace." It's an agonized whisper, but as he focuses on me, it's enough. His hold on his power slips for just a second, and Hudson strikes.

100

Humpty Dumpty
Got Nothing on Us

Jaxon roars as he hits the wall next to the door hard enough to leave a full-body imprint in the centuries-old stone. He recovers faster than I imagine possible and starts to charge Hudson again. Meanwhile, Hudson's in the middle of the room trying to get his breath back, but the look on his face says he's had enough.

Jaxon starts to swing at him, but he ducks and manages to evade. When Jaxon whirls and tries to use his telekinesis again, Hudson growls, "Don't you fucking dare!" Seconds later, the marble beneath Jaxon explodes and sends him falling into a two-foot hole.

And no, just no.

Jaxon jumps out in one fluid move, and he's got Hudson in his sights. But Hudson is looking right back, his patience long gone, and I am deathly afraid they are going to murder each other if someone doesn't do something.

I must not be the only one, because Mekhi, Luca, Eden, and Flint literally jump on Jaxon, while I whirl on Hudson. "Stop!" I snarl, and he freezes, eyes wide.

And I get it. I'm almost positive I have never sounded like that in my life, but there is no way I'm going to let these two people I love so much destroy each other on my watch. No fucking way.

"You need to back off," I tell him. And yes, I'm aware of how unfair it is for me to say that to him when Jaxon's the one who attacked him, but he's the one with the clear head. I don't know what's going on inside Jaxon, but whatever it is, it's not okay. "Something's really wrong with him."

Hudson blows out a long, slow breath, but he nods and takes a step back. And I...I turn back to Jaxon and the mess that we've managed to make.

He's calmed down enough that Flint and Eden have dropped their hold on him and stepped back. Luca has also let go of him, but he's positioned himself directly between Jaxon and Hudson while Mekhi still holds on tight.

"I've got him," I tell Mekhi.

He gives me an *I don't think so* look, but I just wait him out, everything that's happened in the last few days playing through my mind like a video on a loop. Eventually Mekhi steps back, giving me some room. And I walk straight up to Jaxon and pull him into my arms.

He resists at first, his body stiff and unyielding against mine. But I'm not letting him go and, as he finally figures that out, he drops his head onto my shoulder and buries his face in the curve between my shoulder and my neck.

I don't say anything at first and neither does he. Instead, we just hold on tight to each other as the seconds tick by. At one point, I feel wetness against my neck and realize that Jaxon is crying. And my heart nearly buckles under the pain of it all.

As seconds turn to minutes, I want to pull away so I can find out what's wrong with him and how I can help. But my mom taught me a long time ago to never be the one who breaks a hug like this first, because you never know what the other person is going through…or what they need.

It's obvious Jaxon is going through something, and if this is all he'll let me do for him, then this is what I'll do for as long as he needs me.

Eventually, though, his silent tears dry up, and he pulls away. For the second time tonight, our eyes lock, and then he whispers, "I'm all fucked up, Grace."

It's so obvious now, when I look at him. He's lost weight again and looks even skinnier now than he did when I made it back from being frozen in stone. His face is sharper, the circles under his eyes so pronounced, he looks like he's got two black eyes. And there's still something very, very wrong with his eyes themselves.

"Tell me," I whisper, my hands clutching his.

But he just shakes his head. "I'm not your problem anymore."

"You listen to me, Jaxon Vega," I order, and this time I don't even try to keep my voice down. "Whatever's happened between us, you will always be my problem. You will always matter to me. And I'm scared. I'm *really* scared, and I need you to tell me what's going on with you."

"It's—" He breaks off. Shakes his head. Looks down.

All of which only scares me more. Jaxon is usually pretty straightforward about what's up with him, and if he's acting like this, it must be even worse than I've imagined.

And that's when I remember. "Why did the Crone say that today?" I whisper. "Why did she say that you don't have a soul?"

He's shaking like a leaf again. "I didn't want you to know. I didn't want *anyone* to know."

"You mean it's true?" I whisper as horror shreds my insides. "How? When? Why?"

He doesn't look at me when he answers, but he doesn't let go of his death grip on my hands, either. "I knew something was wrong—it's been wrong for weeks. So when I was in London this last time, I went to see a healer."

"What did she say?" I ask, and part of me wants to scream at him for taking too long. To beg him to just spit it out so I can determine how badly I need to freak out. Because right now, it feels like I should be doing a lot of freaking out. Like, *a lot* a lot.

"He said—" His voice breaks, so he swallows a couple of times and starts again. "He said that when the mating bond broke, our souls broke, too."

Behind me, Macy gasps, but no one else makes a sound. I'm not sure they're even breathing. I'm pretty sure that I'm not at this point.

"What does that mean?" I ask when I can finally squeeze some oxygen into my lungs, but this time it's my voice that cracks. "How can our souls be broken? How can they—" I force myself to stop talking and to just wait, to listen to what he has to say. He's obviously in worse shape than I am, because my soul—and the rest of me—feels fine.

"It's because it happened against our wills—and so violently that it nearly destroyed us right when it happened. Remember?"

Remember? Is he serious? I'll never forget the agony of those moments or how close I was to giving up forever. I'll never forget the look on Jaxon's face or the way it felt to have Hudson talk me off the snow.

"Of course I remember," I whisper.

"You mated to Hudson right after, so the healer is pretty sure his soul wrapped itself around yours and is holding yours together, so you'll be okay. But I'm..."

"Alone," I fill in for him, my entire body crumbling under the weight of my own fear and guilt and sorrow.

"Yeah. And without anything to hang on to, the pieces of my soul are dying one by one."

Flint makes a terrible sound. Luca shushes him, but it's too late. The sound has pain sparking deep inside Jaxon's eyes, has shivers running up and down my spine.

"What does that mean?" I demand. "What can we do?"

"Nothing," he answers with a shrug I know he's far from feeling. "There's nothing to do, Grace, except wait for my soul to die completely."

"What happens then?" I whisper.

His grin is bitter. "Then I become the monster everyone's always expected me to be."

101

Un-Break My Heart

This can't be happening.

This absolutely, positively can*not* be happening. I've lost track of how many times I've thought that since coming to Katmere, but this time is different. This time I really mean it, because I can't do this.

In the last few months, I've learned that I can handle almost anything. But not this. I can't handle this happening to Jaxon. Not now, when we're so close to maybe, finally finding a way to end Cyrus's evil rule.

Not now, when I was actually beginning to think that things might truly be okay.

Not now, and not to Jaxon. Please God, not to Jaxon. He doesn't deserve this. He doesn't deserve any of this.

"Why didn't you tell me?" I ask.

"Why would I?" he answers. "There's nothing you can do, Grace. There's nothing anyone can do."

"I don't believe that." I look around at our friends, all of whom look as horrified as I feel. "There has to be something."

He shakes his head. "There isn't."

"Don't say that. I don't believe it. There's always something, always some loophole or some magic. Someone who knows something that we don't. The Bloodletter—"

"Has nothing. Do you think she wasn't my first stop when I got back from Court? She has no suggestions, nothing that she thinks we can try. She cried, Grace." He shakes his head. "I figure when the Bloodletter is in tears, it's a pretty good sign that it's game fucking over for me."

Rage explodes through me at the idea that that monster just gave up on him. She caused *all* of this and then, when he needs her, she just throws him away? She just cries a little bit and says *too bad, so sad*?

I don't think so. I don't fucking think so.

"That's not good enough," I tell him.

"Grace—"

"No, don't you *Grace* me. Do you know how many times I've beaten the odds since I've gotten to this school? How many times I should have died and didn't? Jesus, two people in this room alone have tried to kill me, and I'm still here.

"That's not even counting Lia and Cole and fucking Cyrus. We beat them all." I look around, gesture to our friends. "We beat them all, and if you think that now, when you need us, we're all just going to lay down and let this happen to you, then you've got another think coming." I look at Flint, at Mekhi, at *Hudson*. "Right, guys?"

"Of course." Macy is the first one to speak up. "We'll figure it out."

"Damn straight," Mekhi adds. "No offense, but you're scary enough as it is. None of us needs the soulless version, thank you very much."

"Not to mention, it's been a week since anyone tried to kill us," Flint jokes. "I figure that means we're about due, right?"

Jaxon smiles and, for a second, I get a glimpse of the old Jaxon, the one who sent me *Twilight* and used to tell me corny jokes. The one I used to love.

My heart breaks all over again when I realize the truth—that I *used* to love. I try to take it back, try to convince myself that it was just an errant thought. That it doesn't mean anything.

And then I realize that it really doesn't have to mean anything. I can fix this, and I can fix Jaxon. All I have to do is fix what shattered his soul to begin with.

I need to find the Crown, just like Hudson and I planned. And once we do, we can use it to break our mating bond, just like we talked about all those weeks ago.

My heart twinges at the memory of the last few days with Hudson, but I ignore it. Tell myself it doesn't matter, just like the tears burning behind my eyes don't matter.

Maybe it won't come to that. Maybe if we find the Crown, we'll be able to use its magic to put Jaxon's soul back together on its own.

But if that doesn't work, if the choice comes down to staying with the boy who wants me but will be just fine without me and the boy who needs me and who will descend into madness without me, well, there really is no choice. Not for me. And not for Hudson, because if I've learned anything about him, it's that he'll make the exact same choice.

Jaxon is his little brother, the boy he carved a horse for. The boy he spent so much of his life missing. There's no way he'll let him lose his soul if there's anything he can do about it.

It's that thought that has me turning around to find Hudson. And as our eyes meet, I realize he's already there. He's already accepted what I'm just coming around to—that the universe is asking us to choose between our bond and the boy we both love. The boy we'll lose forever if we make the wrong choice.

That in and of itself proves there is no choice. Maybe there never was.

I'm sorry, I mouth to him.

Hudson doesn't say anything back. He just nods before turning and walking away.

As I watch him go, I can't help remembering the day he told me he'd never make me choose between them, because he always knew I wouldn't choose him.

It's not until right this moment—when the choice is well and truly out of my hands—that I realize I had begun to hope that maybe I could prove him wrong. That maybe I could choose him after all.

And as Hudson walks away, as he disappears down the hallway that leads to his room—the room I was supposed to spend the night in with him tonight—I tell myself it doesn't matter. And that the breaking I feel deep inside myself is just my imagination.

102

Hot Pink
Is Hereditary
After All

I don't sleep all night.

I'm exhausted—physically and emotionally—from everything that has happened these last few days, and still I can't sleep. Still I lay awake, staring at the ceiling and going over all the different things that could go wrong at any given moment over the next twenty-four hours.

As if that isn't enough, every time I close my eyes, I see Jaxon's soulless orbs staring at me as he rips out some innocent person's throat. Or Macy's throat. Or my throat.

I used to think it was awful having to relive Xavier's death over and over again, but the ambiguity of this—the not knowing what's going to happen or how or when—is even worse.

So yeah, no sleep, despite my never having needed it more. At some point today, Cyrus and Delilah are going to show up, along with Aiden and Nuri. What happens at that point is going to be an absolute shit show, I have no doubt.

And hanging over it all is the specter of graduation—and what happens once we have our diplomas in our hands. How long can Hudson reasonably stay at Katmere before he's forced to head to his lair? And how long can Cyrus afford to hang around outside Katmere's grounds hoping to catch him?

I'm afraid the answer to the latter is forever, especially since Cyrus doesn't have to hang around personally. He only has to leave a couple of guards here to arrest him.

And what happens then? To both of us? And if we end up in prison for who knows how long before we can break out, what happens to Jaxon?

Is it any wonder I can't sleep? My brain is about to explode.

Macy gets up around nine—she tossed and turned, but at least she slept—to say, "Take a shower and try to clear the fog out of my brain."

I wish her good luck and stay right where I am. Even though I know I should get up, too, and at least make an attempt to decide what I'm going to wear under my cap and gown, I instead spend fifteen minutes trying to harness my anxiety and find the will to move, all at the same time.

The struggle is oh so very real.

I'm about to throw myself out of bed when there's a knock on the door.

My stomach jumps, and I immediately wonder if it's Hudson. But when I finally open the door—after taking way too long to arrange my hair in the nearest mirror—it turns out to be Uncle Finn...and a giant bouquet of wildflowers.

"Oh my gosh! They're gorgeous!" I tell him, scooping them into my arms.

"They are, aren't they?" he says with a grin and a wink.

"Thank you so much," I tell him. "I really—"

"Oh, no, Grace! They're not from me. They were laying outside your door when I got here. My guess is a certain vampire wanted to surprise you."

Tears bloom in my eyes, because...Hudson. Even after everything that's happened, everything that's going to happen, he brings me flowers.

What the hell? I've looked forward to my high school graduation for four years and now that it's here, everything is so messed up, I can't even stand it. It sucks. It just freaking sucks.

"Oh, Grace. Don't cry," my uncle says, pulling me in for a hug. "It's going to be okay."

I'm not so sure about that, but it seems rude to contradict him.

"I was actually hoping I'd get some time to talk to you today," I tell my uncle, crossing back over to sit on my bed.

"Oh yeah?" He grabs my desk chair and pulls it over so he's sitting opposite me. "What about?"

"I wanted to thank you."

"Thank me?" He looks genuinely bewildered, and that right there is the reason my uncle Finn is and always will be the best guardian ever.

"Because you took me in when you didn't have to. Because you moved heaven and earth to help me when I turned into a gargoyle. And most of all, because you and Macy gave me a family again. For that I will always and forever be grateful."

"Oh, Grace." Now it's my uncle's turn to sniffle. "You never have to thank me. Not for any of that. From the moment you showed up at Katmere

Academy, you have been a second daughter to me—one I am so very proud to know. You're a strong, smart, capable, beautiful young woman, and I can't wait to see how far you can fly, even without your wings."

I laugh, because my uncle really is the sweetest man in the whole world. "I know we talked about me staying here at Katmere Academy after graduation until I figure out what to do. I just want to make sure that's still okay with you?"

"Why wouldn't it be okay with me?" He looks confused. "You will *always* have a home with Macy and me, whether it's here at Katmere or somewhere else entirely. You're stuck with us, kid. Got it?"

I give him a tremulous half-smile. "I've got it."

"Good." He reaches into his blazer pocket and pulls out a little box wrapped in hot-pink paper. "Macy picked out what she assures me is a kick-ass graduation present from us, but this one is from me."

"Oh, you didn't have to—"

"Yes, I did. I've actually wanted to give this to you for a while now." He nods to the box. "Go ahead and open it."

I full-on grin at him as I unwrap a small red box and pull the top off it. Nestled inside is a rectangular stone. It's bright pink (big surprise) with a few white-and-maroon-colored lines running through it, and carved on the top is an inscription—two Vs nestled together on their sides.

I haven't had much experience with these since coming to Katmere, but I totally recognize it for what it is. "Which rune is this?" I ask.

He smiles. "The inscription means peace, happiness, hope. The stone it's carved in—rhodochrosite—means the same. Emotional healing and joy." His voice breaks a little bit, and he looks away, blinks rapidly.

"Oh, Uncle Finn!" I throw my arms around him. "Thank you. I love it."

He hugs me back and presses a fatherly kiss to the top of my head. "I actually have the whole set for you down in my rooms, but it's a big one, and I wanted to give you something you could carry with you."

My heart melts, and I hug him again. "I don't think you know how much I needed this today," I whisper.

"There's more, and I hope it makes you happy, not sad." He hesitates for a second, and just as I try to figure out what he means, he says, "They were your father's, Grace. He left them in my safekeeping when he and your mother chose to move away from this life. I always hoped he would come back for them, but once you got here, I knew they were always meant to be yours."

His words catch me off guard, and a sob rises up out of nowhere, lodges in my throat. "I'm sorry. I didn't—"

"Shh, it's okay." He pulls me against him and rocks me as I cry into his shoulder just a little.

Because it's my graduation day, and my parents aren't here.

Because I finally opened myself up to Hudson, and now I have to lose him before I ever really had him.

Because I don't have a clue how this day is going to end, and I am terrified that it's going to end horribly.

"Oh, Grace, you're so brave," Uncle Finn whispers to me. "I'm so sorry about everything you've had to endure this year. I wish I could take it away from you."

I pull back as I shake my head, drying my tears with my hands. "I just miss them, you know?"

"I do know," he says. "I miss them, too. Every single day."

"Thank you for the rune," I tell him, picking it up and rolling it back and forth against my palm. It's surprisingly hot for a stone that wasn't being touched.

"Runes—I'll bring the whole bag up to you after graduation. But, Grace?" His voice turns deadly serious. "No matter what happens, no matter where you are in the next several days and weeks, I want you to keep that rune on you at all times."

"Okay," I tell him, but I can't help being a little confused. "Is there a reason why—"

"You'll know why soon enough," he tells me. "And you'll know when. Just remember to trust yourself and the people who love you. We've got you."

He looks like he's about to say more, but Macy comes bounding out of the shower in a long robe, with her hair up in a towel.

"Trust the people who love you," Uncle Finn says again before getting up to go to Macy. "You'll need them all before this is through."

103

With a Lot of Help From My Friends

"**Y**ou ready for this?" Flint asks several hours later as he picks me up and twirls me around.

"As ready as I'll ever be," I answer once he puts me back on my feet. I give him a once-over. "You look like a giant eggplant."

"Yeah, well, better than a mini eggplant," he says with a definite waggle of his brows. "So who gets the last laugh?"

"Apparently you, you perv."

"Hey, you're the one who brought up eggplants." He glances into the makeshift stands—hastily constructed for graduation by the witches after Hudson leveled the Katmere stadium—and waves. "I just came to give you a hug and make conversation."

"Did your parents get in?" I ask, trying to follow where he's looking, but there are just so many people in the stands that it's hard to pick out any individuals—even the dragon queen and king.

"Oh, yeah. They're here," he says, but then his smile dims at the edges. "And so are Cyrus and Delilah."

"Of course they are." I glance around. "Are Jaxon and Hudson okay?"

He gives me a wide-eyed look. "After last night? I'm not sure any of us are going to be okay ever again."

"True that," I tell him, and I can feel my stomach getting tight.

"Grace—" He starts to say something, then breaks off when Eden and Mekhi come walking up to us.

"There's purple, and then there's too much purple," Eden says with an eye roll. "This"—she gestures to her cap and gown—"is too much purple."

"I think you look cute," Mekhi tells her, and he must be feeling really brave today, because he goes so far as to bop her on the nose.

She narrows her eyes at him. "And I think you look like you want to die."

He laughs. "Where is everybody else?"

"Probably making a break for it," Eden snarks. "Because seriously, can you see Hudson in this getup?"

"I wish I couldn't see me in this getup," Luca says as he walks behind Flint and wraps an arm around his waist.

"Oh my God!" Macy comes running up, phone in her hand. "You guys look so great! I have to get some pics."

We grumble a lot, but in the end, we move into some semblance of photo formation—if you don't count Flint either making faces at the camera or "dragon ears" over our heads.

Hudson joins us about halfway through the impromptu photo session. He's got the hat on, but his robe is draped over his arm.

"You're supposed to be wearing that, you know," Macy teases him.

He gives her a horrified look. "This is Armani," he says, gesturing to the bespoke suit he's wearing.

"What does that have to do with anything?" Mekhi asks.

"It has to do with everything, and I'm not covering it up with that monstrosity one second before I have to."

Macy rolls her eyes. "You're a dork, you know that, right?"

"Says the only other person standing here not in a purple robe," he shoots back.

"Only because I can't be in one." Her chin trembles just a little. "I can't believe I'm going to have to be here next year without you guys. What am I going to do?"

"Come visit us a lot," Eden says, wrapping an arm around her shoulders and hugging her tightly. "We could use a little witch perspective in the Dragon Court."

"So you've decided?" Macy asks, eyes huge. "You're going into guard training."

"Yeah, I think so." She glances at Flint. "Someone's got to keep this guy in line."

"The rest of us will be at the Vampire Court soon enough," Luca says, "hopefully putting it back together once we oust Cyrus once and for all. So feel free to visit us, too. London's great."

"And I'm not going anywhere for a while," I tell her, wrapping my arm around her from the other side. Then I think of the Crown I have to retrieve… and what I have to do to get it. "Except prison, but that doesn't count, right?"

Macy laughs, but before she can say anything else, Jaxon walks up—in a pair of jeans and a black T-shirt, sans cap and gown.

"Where's your stuff?" Macy asks. "The ceremony starts in, like, ten minutes."

"In my room, where it belongs."

"You're not going to wear it at all?" I ask.

"And look like a giant penis?" He eyes the other guys with vague amusement. "I don't think so."

"That's it." Macy throws up her hands. "I'm totally getting Dad to change the gown color before next year's ceremony."

"That's a year too late," Luca mutters.

But Macy just rolls her eyes. "Not for me! Besides, better late than never. Now, come on, you guys, squeeze in. I want to take a pic with all of you."

Jaxon rolls his eyes back at her, but I can't help noticing that when it comes time to snap the pic, he's right in the middle of the group—and he's got a tight-as-fuck hold on both Hudson and me.

I can tell Hudson notices, too, because, despite everything, his hold on his brother is just as strong.

"It's going to be okay," I whisper, and even as I say the words, I don't know if I'm talking to Jaxon or the universe or myself. I only know that when the wind kicks up and swirls the words away, I can't help thinking that maybe—just maybe—we'll make it through this if we can all just hold on to the fact that we really do love one another. And that the only people we need to fight are on the other side.

"Okay! I've got the pic!" Macy shouts excitedly.

"No, you don't," I tell her.

She looks confused. "What do you mean?"

"I mean it's not *the pic* unless you're in it. So get over here and let's do this thing."

Macy blushes in delight, even as she blinks back tears. And then we all crowd in around her as tightly as we can as she holds up the camera.

"When I count to three, say 'Fuck Cyrus' as loud as you can," she tells us. "One, two, three!"

"Fuck Cyrus!" we all shout, and she takes the pic.

And as I open it up a couple of minutes later and stare at the eight smiling faces, I pray to the universe as hard as I can that somehow, someway, we all make it through what's to come in one piece...and together.

104

Carpe Seize-Em

The graduation ceremony is surprisingly...anticlimactic. I don't know what I was expecting—maybe a Golden Drake salute, like we saw at the dragon festival? Or witches lighting the place up?

Instead, it is dignified and orderly and basically like every other graduation in the world. Which I get. How exciting can you make a ceremony that involves walking across the stage to get a fake piece of paper that you later have to turn in to get your real piece of paper? Yeah, ours is printed on two-hundred-year-old papyrus, but other than that, I figure it's pretty close to the ceremony I would have had in San Diego. Except here I have a lot more friends...and a lot more enemies.

After taking another round of pics—this time with most of their families—my friends and I head back to the castle. Since graduation had to take place at dusk to accommodate the vampires, Uncle Finn has a family dinner planned for Macy, him, and me; then tonight is the grad night that everyone says should be freaking fantastic...not to mention filled with all the paranormal spectacle graduation lacked.

I'm planning on checking my troubles at the door and having an *amazing* time, considering none of us has any idea what tomorrow will bring. And considering that, so far, Cyrus and Delilah have been on their best behavior today.

Which means it's just a matter of time before the other shoe drops.

I'm about halfway to the castle when Hudson makes his way over to me. And, not going to lie, there's a part of me that's super excited he sought me out...and another part of me that just wants to run away as fast as I can. After last night, I don't know what to say to him—or even if there is anything to say. I do know that I don't want to fall for him any more than I already have...and I don't want him to fall for me any more, either. This is already going to be hard enough.

The heat from the mating bond is still there, combined with the friendship and respect we've built up over the last few weeks... I don't know. I don't know how this is going to work, how we're supposed to be together but not be together.

It was easier before New York, easier before he'd kissed me and touched me and... So much easier that I almost wish it hadn't happened. Almost. Because the truth is that no matter what happens next, I wouldn't trade those hours in New York for anything. Lying in Hudson's arms, listening to him talk about everything and nothing...knowing it's never going to happen again makes it even harder to look at him.

"Hey," he says after we've walked several feet together in awkward silence.

"Hey," I answer back. "Thank you for the flowers. They were beautiful."

"I'm glad you liked them," he answers, glancing at me out of the corner of his eye.

"I loved them." I clear my throat, searching for the right words to say. In the end, all I can come up with is, "I'm sorry."

"Nothing for you to be sorry about," he tells me.

"That's not true," I say, reaching for his hand—then wishing I hadn't as heat zings back and forth between us like a live wire. "I've made a mess of this from the very beginning. I didn't remember you. I didn't believe you. I didn't..."

"Love me?" he asks with a smile that is more resigned than sad.

That's the thing. I don't know if I do love him yet, but I'm well past the point of realizing that I *could* love him...if things were different. If we were different. If this whole messed-up world were different.

"I'm sorry," I say again, but Hudson just shakes his head.

"I love him, too, you know," Hudson says, "and I need him to be okay as much as you do—despite his disturbing propensity for wanting me dead *and* wanting to be the one to kill me at any given moment."

I laugh because the only other option is to cry, and I've already done that. "How's your throat doing?"

"Vampires heal fast," he tells me.

I glare at him. "That's not an answer."

"Sure it is. In fact—"

He breaks off as Nuri and several of her guards step into our path.

"Hudson Vega," she says, "you're under arrest by order of the Circle."

Surprise flashes over his face, but it's gone between one second and the next. "Seriously, Nuri? Haven't we done this before?" He fakes a yawn.

"We have," she agrees with hard eyes. "But this time I came prepared."

Four of her guards rush him, and seconds later, they slap thick, power-draining cuffs onto both his wrists and his ankles—cuffs that make the bracelets my uncle uses here at Katmere look like a child's toys.

"Nuri!" Uncle Finn comes racing across the grounds. "Let him go immediately."

"This isn't your business, Finn," she tells him.

"He is one of my students, which makes him my business," my uncle growls furiously. And I have to admit, I didn't know Uncle Finn had it in him, but right now he looks like he's ready to take someone apart with his bare hands.

"Correction," she tells him with a gleam in her eye that says she's enjoying this a little too much. "He *was* your student. As of about half an hour ago, he is a regular citizen."

"Yes, but you still can't arrest him on Katmere's grounds," I tell her, outraged at her betrayal...and her breaking of the law.

She won't even look at me when she answers. "The Circle passed a new law late last night. Students who break the law are safe on Katmere Academy grounds only while they are enrolled. The moment that enrollment lapses—through withdrawal or graduation—the school's protection becomes null and void."

"That's bullshit," Uncle Finn snarls, saving me from telling her the exact same thing. "You can't change laws and enforce them before you've even let people know they've changed."

Uncle Finn lifts his wand and points it at Hudson's chains.

"Don't do it, Finn," Nuri warns him, looking over his head. "You'll regret what happens if you do."

I follow her gaze and see Cyrus watching from the edge of the tree line like the bully he is. Nuri gave us a week, but here she is after only three days going back on her word. I know it's for his benefit, whether it's because he threatened her or promised her something, I don't know.

And honestly, I don't care. Not now when she's proven, once again, that she can't be trusted.

"You're pathetic," I spit at her, more furious than I've ever been in my life.

"What did you just say to me?" she snaps back.

"I said, you're pathetic. More, you're a coward. You act like you're so powerful, like you can take on anyone, but the truth is, you can't do shit." I nod toward Cyrus, whose eyes are gleaming as he watches this go down. "You gave in to a vampire—you gave in to Cyrus, who you hate—because you're as weak and power-hungry as the rest of them."

"Grace, stop," Uncle Finn tells me, and there's a warning in his voice—in his eyes—that I'm going too far.

But I don't care. I'm sick of this woman and her lies, sick of this fucking world where everyone in power is just out for what they can get, not caring who they have to fuck or who they have to destroy to get it.

She rounds on me with rage in her eyes. "You are a naive, naive child."

"And you are an even more naive woman." I'm as angry as she is, but my rage is a living, breathing thing inside me, beating against my chest, begging to be set free. Begging me to give in and give up control. And I want to, more than I've ever wanted anything, but I know it will get us nowhere. So I take a deep breath and say with a biting chill, "Which is fine. You do you, Nuri. Protect who you want to protect and be as shortsighted as you want to be. But don't come bitching to me when your little unholy alliance bites you in the ass. Because it will. I may only be eighteen years old—and half human—but I'm smart enough to know that you're already over. You just don't know it yet."

"You've lost any support you might have had from me," she hisses.

"Yeah, well, right back atcha," I snarl. "And something tells me you're going to miss my support more than I'll ever miss yours."

For a second, I think she's going to explode. But then she takes a deep breath and turns to my uncle. "Do you have anything to say about this?"

"Except for telling you that the Circle is going to be hearing from my attorney within the hour?" Uncle Finn asks. "Not really, no."

"What about you?" Nuri demands of Hudson. "Anything you want to say before we take you out of here?"

He pretends to think about it, then shakes his head. "Nah, Grace pretty much covered it and then some." He grins at me. "Good job."

Nuri bares her teeth, looking more like a dragon than I've ever seen her. "Take him away," she grits out to her guards before turning back to Hudson. "You'll be dead before you get out of that prison."

Hudson looks at me then, and for one second there's something in his eyes that rips my fucking heart out. But then he turns to her with a wicked grin and says, "Yeah, well, it wouldn't be the first time."

My heart is racing as the guards start dragging him away because—just like at the Dragon Court—the cuffs on his legs are so tight that it's nearly impossible for him to walk. Nearly impossible for him to do anything.

I turn to follow his progress with my eyes and realize the rest of my friends have joined the ever-growing crowd...and they look as furious as I feel. Except for Jaxon, who just looks empty.

And no matter how much I want to stay here, no matter how much I don't want to do what I'm about to do, I know this is it. It's now or never.

"Wait!" I tell Nuri.

She's back to ignoring me, refusing to so much as glance in my direction. Which I acknowledge is well deserved. But that doesn't mean I'm going to let her get away with it.

"I'm his mate!" I say so loudly and clearly that it echoes off the trees, bouncing around the meadows. "It's my right to go with him, my right to not be separated from him."

She swings around to face me. "You want to go to prison?" Her tone implies that something is very, very wrong with me.

And as terror slides down my spine, I can't say that I disagree. But I'm in too deep to go back now, and I wouldn't change my mind even if I wasn't. Too much is riding on this.

"I want to be with my mate," I tell her.

"Grace, no!" My uncle Finn steps forward, tries to put himself between us. "There are other ways—"

Not to do what I have to do. I don't tell him that, though—I can't without tipping off Cyrus and the rest of his unholy alliance. "It's going to be okay," I tell him, leaning in to give him a fast hug and slip my father's rune into his pocket. And to whisper in his ear, "Give Jaxon my rune. Tell him to hang on, that I'm coming back for him. Macy will explain everything. Listen to her."

"All right, then." Nuri swings around to her guards. "You heard her. Seize the gargoyle."

And just like that, my life changes. Again.

105

If You Lay Down with *ssholes, You'll Wake Up Completely Screwed

Nuri's guards come at me like berserkers. I don't know if it's because they think "the gargoyle" is dangerous or if it's because they're pissed off at me for what I said to their queen. Whatever caused it, it still feels like my arms are going to be yanked out at my shoulder sockets as they pull my arms behind my back and slap thick cuffs on me.

"Hey!" Uncle Finn yells. "You don't have to grab her like that. She hasn't done anything wrong."

"Just standard procedure when transporting people to the Aethereum," Nuri tells him, voice neutral. But it doesn't feel very standard when the guards grind down on my wrists so hard that I see stars.

Hudson, who has been remarkably cool through this entire thing, looks like he's about to lose it for the first time. "Release her!" he snarls. "She's mistaken. She's not coming with me—"

"It's not your choice," Nuri tells him. "In fact, from here on out, nothing is your choice. Think about that while you spend eternity in prison."

His eyes turn deadly then—and so does his voice. "I'll be thinking about a lot of things while I'm in prison," he tells her. "And I promise you, it won't be for an eternity."

"Take them both away!" Nuri grinds out over the shouts and protests of our friends and a bunch of other Katmere Academy students who have gathered.

But again, before we can even make it out of the clearing, the guards are forced to stop. This time by the vampire king himself.

"I'm sorry to interfere with the strict adjudication of justice," Cyrus says, and I can't help enjoying how pissed off he looks that he has to be talking to us while leaning on a cane while he still heals from Hudson's attack—even one as impressive as the silver and black one he's currently wielding. The rest of him is just as dapper as usual, however, in a patterned bespoke suit. "But the Circle issued one more writ of arrest during its special meeting this past weekend."

"Meeting?" Nuri asks, eyes narrowed. "I wasn't informed of any Circle business this past weekend."

"It seemed inappropriate to disturb you during the most important dragon holiday of the year." Cyrus is all benevolent, *I have the right to make decisions like that* dictator, and I can tell it's hitting Nuri exactly as it should: in all the wrong ways.

"Next time, please don't make a decision like that for me, Cyrus." She glances down at the writ in his hand. "Who else has the Circle decided to arrest?"

"Who else is guilty of a crime, you mean?" he answers silkily.

"Yes, of course." She shoots my uncle a steely look. "Apparently, Katmere Academy has become a hotbed of crime over the past several months."

Uncle Finn doesn't react, but he does look like he wants to turn her into a toad.

"The writ of arrest is for Flint Montgomery, and the charge is attempted murder of the last gargoyle in existence."

For one brief second, no one responds. We just stand there, stunned at the charge—and at his audacity. Part of me wants to scream at him that he's been trying to kill "the last gargoyle," who he knows very well isn't the last gargoyle, for a while now, so why the hell isn't there a writ out for his arrest as well?

But before I can reconcile how I would say that—or even if I should mention the Unkillable Beast—Nuri loses her shit completely. She goes for Cyrus's throat, her guards falling right into line behind her.

At first, I'm certain that we're about to see who wins in a vampire vs. dragon fight to the death, but as Cyrus draws himself up for the fight—his silver cane now a seriously wicked knife—Uncle Finn uses magic to spin an unbreachable wall between them.

It's the most magic I've ever seen him do—sometimes I actually forget he's a warlock—but watching him do this is seriously badass. I guess I always figured he didn't have much magic because he seems so...sweet, but the man in front of me has all the power. More than enough to keep Nuri and Cyrus exactly where he wants them.

"You can't attack him, Nuri," Finn tells her softly. "It's what he wants—a chance to get you kicked off the Circle or put in prison."

"He's my son, Finn." She looks devastated. "I've given Cyrus everything he wants. Why would he do this?"

Because he can. Because you *have* given him everything he wants. The answers are right there on the tip of my tongue, but now's not the time to say them. I've never been an I-told-you-so kind of person...and I've definitely never been a fan of kicking people when they're down.

Besides, she already knows. It's written all over her face. As is the determination to pay him back for this somehow, someway.

Of course, that could just be me projecting. God knows, I've never wanted to kick someone's ass more in my entire life. Not a team of surrogates for him this time but his actual ass.

She waves a hand at Uncle Finn, telling him without words to lower the wall. And while I'm not so sure that she's chill enough to hold herself back, he obviously sees something in her face that he believes.

The wall comes down, and we all hold our breath as we expect Nuri to at least walk over to Cyrus and say something to him. Instead, she ignores him in favor of approaching her son.

Flint looks more somber than I've ever seen him, but he doesn't look afraid. And he doesn't look defiant. In fact, if it makes any sense at all—which it doesn't—a part of me would say he looks almost...relieved.

She reaches for his hands, but they're already cuffed. So she puts a hand on his shoulder instead and waits for him to look at her. "You need to atone," she tells him.

"I don't know— I can't—"

"Listen to me," she says, her voice low and urgent as she leans forward. "You didn't kill Grace, so the price you have to pay isn't to forfeit your life. The prison only holds the guilty until it deems you've paid your debt. If you want to get out, you need to atone for what you've done."

It's the most anyone has ever talked to us about what goes on in the prison, and my mind is whirling as I try to figure out what it means. I understand the concept of paying your debt, but how does a prison—which is still a building, no matter how enchanted it is—decide that you have atoned enough? Or worse, that you haven't?

I can't wrap my head around it as they walk us into the forest—and straight into a portal that Cyrus obviously had opened for just this occasion. Then again, I realize I don't have to imagine it. I'll be seeing it firsthand soon enough.

106

There's Never a Pair
of Ruby Slippers Around
When You Need Them

This portal isn't like the ones at the Ludares tournament. There's no stretching, no pain, no quick dive in or even faster roll out. There's nothing but a free fall through darkness that goes on and on and on.

I strain my ears, trying to orient myself. Trying to find Hudson or Flint in the middle of this never-ending blackness, but I can't. I'm completely isolated, completely alone, and it's as terrifying as it is disorienting.

A scream wells up inside me, and I reach out a hand, certain that if I can just find Hudson or Flint—if I can just touch one of them—it will make all this bearable. But I can't reach them, can't touch them. It's like they've vanished, and I really am all alone in this.

I don't know how long the portal takes—probably only a couple of minutes. But it's the longest couple of minutes of my life, and all I want is for it to end.

Until it does.

The portal vomits me out in the middle of an obscenely bright room, the lights like giant needles being shoved into my eyes after the absolute darkness of the last few minutes. I'm disoriented, can barely see, and am more scared than I want to admit when I land on my knees with a hard *thud* that sends pain ricocheting through me.

My first instinct is to stay where I am until I can get my bearings, but it's not like they don't know where I am. Plus, being unable to see and on my knees makes me feel way too vulnerable—I'd rather be on my feet when I meet whatever comes next.

It turns out that whatever comes next is a woman in a severe black business suit and black sunglasses, her black hair tamed into a ruthlessly precise bun. She's standing a few feet from me, and though I can't see her eyes, the tilt of her head says she is very much watching me, like I'm an animal in a cage.

Though I guess that's precisely what I am. Precisely what Cyrus has turned all three of us into.

My instincts tell me to duck my head, not to look at her even as she studies me. But that feels too much like defeat to me—too much like giving up at a time when I'm going to have to fight harder than I ever have in my life. So I stare right back at her, the blankest look on my face that I can manage. After all, she's going to do what she's going to do. My refusing to cower isn't going to change that.

I wish she'd take off the glasses, but something tells me they might be there for my protection, not hers. I can feel the magic in her, but I have no idea what she is—definitely not a vamp or any of the other paranormals I'm used to running into at Katmere Academy. But as I'm learning, there are a ton of other creatures in this world that I don't know about yet, and she is definitely one of them.

"Welcome to the Aethereum, Miss Foster," she hisses, her *S*'s extremely exaggerated as she walks around me in a circle that has the hair on the back of my neck standing straight up.

I turn with her, everything inside me screaming not to give this woman my back. The cold smile on her face tells me she's amused by my reluctance, but all her body language shouts that she's not going to put up with it for long.

Even before she says, "Turn around, please." Again with the long *S* sound.

It takes every ounce of strength I have to do as she orders, but I manage it. Then nearly sob in relief as she loosens the punishing cuffs. At least until I feel two sharp pricks in my wrist.

I start to jerk my hand away, but she stops me.

"You belong to the prison now, Miss Foster. You do what I say and nothing else."

"What did you do to me?" I ask, the sting in my wrist getting worse instead of better.

"Ensured that your powers belong to us now. Nothing more, nothing less."

"What does that mean?" I demand even as I reach inside me to find my gargoyle. Not because I want to shift but because I need the reassurance. Need to know that she's still there. Except she isn't...I can't even find the platinum string, let alone reach for it.

I quickly check for my other strings, and I'm a little dizzy as I find my mating bond string, still shimmery and beautiful. But my gargoyle string is…gone.

Panic races through me, and I want to scream at her, want to beg her to tell me what she's done. But I already know that she won't tell me—this is prison, after all, and she doesn't have to tell me anything.

And that's before I feel something cold encircle the same wrist she pricked, before I feel a snug metal bracelet snap into place.

"You may turn back around now," she says. "And follow me." Without the *S*'s, her syllables are sharp, bitten off.

I do as she says, rubbing at my wrist as we walk out of the brightness into a shadowy hallway. I keep trying to get a look at what she did to me, but the bracelet is covering it up.

As for the bracelet itself, there are strange etchings on it that look a lot like runes—similar to the one my uncle gave me this morning, in fact.

In the center of the bracelet—directly over the pricks to my skin that are finally starting to calm down—is a glowing red dot. I assume the red light has something to do with my gargoyle going missing, and everything inside me wants to claw at this bracelet. To tear it off. To rip it to pieces, anything to get my powers back.

It's ridiculous, I know, to be this upset about my gargoyle being bound—especially considering I didn't even know she existed before a few months ago. And it's not like I didn't know they were going to bind my powers in prison. They have to if they want to have any hope at all of controlling the prison population.

But knowing it and feeling it are two very different things, and now that my gargoyle is gone, I feel so empty. Like a giant part of me is missing and I'll never find her again.

Intellectually, I know that's not true. I know that once Hudson, Flint, and I make it out of here, my gargoyle will come back…and so will all the other strings. I just have to hold on to that, just have to remember that this isn't forever.

That everything is going to be okay.

Of course, that might be easier to remember if we hadn't just stopped in front of a Plexiglas cubicle about five feet by five feet. The woman holds open the door and says, "Step inside, please."

I don't want to step inside, but it's not like I have a choice. And not like fighting is going to do me any good. So I take a deep breath and pretend that I'm not completely freaked out at the thought of being locked inside a small, see-through box.

For a second, I think it might be a shower, which is horrifying, even though I know it happens in regular human prisons. But this one has no showerhead, which I hope is a good thing, even though I'm definitely not willing to bet on it...

I walk through the door and try not to wince at the sound of her closing—and locking—it behind me. "Stand in the center of the room, arms at your sides. And don't move."

"What is this place?" I do as she says but keep looking around, hoping to find some hint of what's about to happen.

"I said not to move."

I freeze in place. "Okay, but can you at least tell me—"

"Close your mouth."

I snap my jaw shut so fast that my teeth clack together. Just in time, it seems, because a huge wind kicks up out of nowhere. It buffets me from all sides, making it nearly impossible for me to follow her repeated warning to "stand still."

Just when I think I'm about to blow away, the wind dies down, and fire takes its place.

"Do not get off the X," the woman orders.

I do what she says, forcing my feet to stay on the black painted X even as smokeless flames dance across the floor just out of reach of me before licking up the walls to the ceiling. It's like no fire I've ever seen before, the individual flames so hot, they're burning blue, and I know that one slip, one wrong move, and I'll end up incinerated.

It seems to go on forever, until I'm terrified I'm going to burn just from the heat in the room alone. But then, all of a sudden, the heat just disappears.

"Follow me," she instructs again, and I do on wobbly legs.

I still want to know what just happened to me, but to be honest, I'm too scared to ask. Every time I open my mouth in here, something worse happens.

The next station requires a clothing change—out of the cute sundress I wore to graduation and into the black jumpsuit that's going to be my prison uniform until I finally manage to get out of here. My phone and earrings are taken now and put into a bag along with my dress.

I expect her to take my promise ring, and my chest tightens. But she just turns to me and asks, "Do you wish to keep the ring?"

I know I'm not supposed to ask questions, but I can't stop the words that rush out. "I can keep my ring? But I thought no jewelry?"

She stares at me hard, and I think she's not going to answer, but then she says, "We make exceptions for promise rings to prevent people from having someone incarcerated to cancel a promise. The Aethereum is not a personal escape clause."

My heart is pounding in my chest, and I stare at the ring, twisting it around and around my finger. I still don't know what Hudson promised me. Do I want to hold him to his promise? And what about when we escape and I go back to Jaxon? Is it fair to hold him to his promise then?

Twist, twist, twist.

"Choose quickly, Miss Foster."

I take a deep breath and reach for the ring...and can't do it. Removing it now would be like giving up on Hudson. On us. And I know I will have to eventually to save Jaxon, but I can't do it today. I'm not ready to lose him yet.

"I'll keep it."

107

Un-Solitary
Confinement

We stop at two more stations, both of them as scary in their own way as the first one, before she leads me down one more dark hallway. This is the longest we've had to walk, and I'm beginning to hope that all the intake procedures are finally done, but then she leads me into one more room.

My stomach clenches as I pass through the door after her, terrified of what might be coming next.

It turns out that what's next is the bureaucratic part of intake, considering this room is filled with desks and filing cabinets. I should probably be reassured, considering that part, at least, looks like every other government bureaucratic room in the world. And maybe I would, except for the fact that the entire room looks like something out of a Transylvania horror movie… and the creatures sitting behind the desks look even creepier.

Eight black desks are lined up in two rows running the length of the room. The laptops and file folder holders on each one should have lent an air of normalcy to the space, but the pointy black nightmare chairs behind each desk—and the occupants of said chairs—take even that away.

The intake guards, or whatever you call them, are the creepiest-looking people I have ever seen. Zombies? I wonder as I eye their grayish, nearly translucent skin and yellow eyes. Or something even more menacing?

Their cheeks are sunken, their long hair gray and greasy looking, and their fingers tipped with two-inch-long razor-sharp talons that click ominously every time they make contact with the keyboards.

"Have a seat." The whisper is paper thin and directed at me, though I'm not sure where it came from—at least not until the woman who has escorted me this far orders, "Go to the first desk on your right. This is the last step."

"Last step of what?" I ask, hoping to stall a little. Everything inside me is screaming at the idea of sitting in front of one of those things, whatever they are.

"Intake," she answers through narrowed eyes, and it's the first question of mine other than the promise ring that she's answered. And, her look says, it's going to be the last.

When I don't immediately start moving, she walks toward me with narrowed eyes. And this time when she tells me to move, her tongue comes out in warning. I nearly scream when I realize it's forked...and black.

I start walking, not sure which is worse at this point—dead-looking desk guy or snake lady—but deathly afraid I'm about to find out.

But I'm barely halfway to my assigned desk when the door opens and Hudson walks in, escorted by a man in a black suit and sunglasses who looks remarkably like the woman I've been stuck with all this time.

"Grace!" he says, relief practically dripping from the word.

He's dressed in the same black jumpsuit that I am—and looks better in it than I do, I'm sure—but his normally perfect pompadour is currently sticking straight up. There's also a line of soot running down his left cheek, and his knuckles are all scraped up.

"I'm okay," I tell him, starting toward him instinctively.

But the woman is there between us, tongue out in warning as she orders me to "ssssit," in a tone that brooks no more disobedience.

So I do, hightailing it over to the super-creepy-looking guy manning the first desk to the right.

Hudson ends up sitting directly across from me, and he looks a lot more composed than I feel, despite the disheveled hair. When I finally manage to catch his eye, he gives me a reassuring smile and a little nod, and it works...a bit. And when Flint walks in a couple of minutes later, his afro blown out bigger than I've ever seen it, courtesy of the wind/fire room from hell, we both breathe giant sighs of relief.

The woman, whoever she is, disappears once Flint is seated—and so do the two men who obviously escorted Hudson and Flint through their own hellish intake procedures.

The moment they're gone, we all relax a little, because while these guards are really creepy to look at, they don't seem overly motivated to do anything but their jobs.

"Are you okay?" Hudson asks Flint once the door shuts behind the scary woman and her two compatriots.

"Yeah. You?"

He nods, and so does Flint.

"What just happened to us?" I whisper. "And, Hudson, were you able to… you know…*take care of* your cuffs?"

Hudson shakes his head, looking down at his hands. "I've never seen cuffs like these before. I didn't know which rune to remove."

"This whole place is ridiculous," Flint adds. "I've been thinking about it. I'm pretty sure the flames were magical delousing, making sure we had no extra magic hitchhiking on us that the bracelet couldn't neutralize."

"And the imaging in the last room was to map us for identification," Hudson says. "In case something happens to us."

"Yeah, that's what I figured, too," Flint says after clearing his throat a few different times. "I don't know what any of the rest was."

"Silence, please," the intake officer checking in Flint demands, his raspy voice sending shivers all the way through me.

We shut up for a few minutes, but I can tell Flint and Hudson are worked up about something, because they keep exchanging looks. Which only manages to freak me out more, which I definitely don't need at the moment.

"What were those people?" I ask, almost afraid to hear the answer. "Her tongue—"

"Basilisks," Flint answers grimly.

"Basilisks?" I repeat, horror moving through me.

"Silence!" a second prison intake officer growls in a way that makes even Flint close his mouth.

Long minutes pass with no sound but the eerie clicking of those nails on the keyboard. The not-silent silence grates on my nerves, and I can tell I'm not the only one by the way Flint's leg is bouncing up and down and the way Hudson keeps tapping his thumb and middle finger together.

Finally, when the silence has stretched all of us near to our breaking point, Flint asks his intake officer, "So what happens now?"

He doesn't look away from his laptop screen as he rasps, "Now we assign you to a cell."

"With Remy?" Flint asks.

The officers exchange a long look—which Hudson definitely notices.

His eyes grow watchful even as he kicks his legs out in front of him and leans back in the chair. "I want to bunk with Remy, too. It's more my style, don't you think?"

I shoot Flint a confused look, but he just shrugs—which seems strange considering he's the one who brought up remies, whatever they are, to begin with.

"Oh, and since you're in the middle of assigning a cell, we were hoping we could get one by the sea?" Hudson jokes. "That's how Remy likes it, right?"

"You better watch your mouth," the officer doing my paperwork whispers, his long nails making a screeching noise as they scrape against the desk. "Remy's got a quick temper."

Hudson's brows go up at the confirmation that Remy exists. And obviously this is a scary person if the guards feel the need to warn us against him.

"He's been expecting her," a huge voice from the shadows at the back of the room booms.

I jump, even before he steps into the light, because I had no idea anyone was even back there. Once he does step forward, though, everything inside me freezes. Because this creature makes everyone who's come before him seem like a fuzzy monster from a child's Halloween show.

He is seriously and completely terrifying. It's not just the weird-ass antlers on his head, because I have nothing against moose normally. But his face is also filled with all kinds of sharp angles that aren't human and aren't moose but something in between that is vaguely demonic-looking.

More, his gray skin is almost completely translucent, his veins and arteries much more visible than they are on a normal person—or even the rest of the creatures in this room. When he sees me looking, he gives me a grim facsimile of a smile—one that reveals double rows of razor-sharp teeth.

He takes a couple of steps toward me, and I yank my gaze away, back to Hudson, who looks like he's about one second from jumping in between us. And while I am firmly aware that Hudson is the biggest badass around even without his powers, I'm also pretty sure that this guy would give him some stiff competition.

So I force a smile I am far from feeling and mouth *I'm okay*, even though I feel anything but.

Hudson watches me for several seconds, but eventually he sinks back against his chair and starts that silent tapping of his thumb and finger again.

A few minutes later, they finish our intake paperwork. Then they scan our bracelets and run a scanner over us one more time to check to make sure all our personal items have been removed. Then the giant guard from the back of the room lumbers forward and orders us to follow him.

He leads us out the door and back down the shadowy hallway until we get to a high-tech portcullis. The metal door is crisscrossed, just like the gates in old castles, but from what I can tell, each strip of metal is lined with motion- and heat-detecting sensors.

The portcullis reminds me of Katmere, and not for the first time, I wonder how my friends are doing. I hope Uncle Finn didn't get into too much trouble when he went off on Nuri and Cyrus. And I really, really hope Jaxon got my father's rune and Macy and the others aren't totally freaking out. I just hope we can get through this quickly. I don't know how much longer Jaxon has.

"Which cell?" the guard working the gate asks. He looks an awful lot like the guard who is leading us, except one of his antlers is half broken.

"They're with Remy," the guard leading us answers.

The other one nods and plugs a bunch of numbers into the fancy electronic dashboard he's got sitting behind him. "They're parked in cellblock A, spot 68 today," he tells him, and our guard nods.

I'm a little intrigued by the idea of cells being parked like cars, but that's something to worry about another time. Right now I have a more pressing question.

"Who's Remy? And how did you know to mention him?" I ask Flint under my breath as the portcullis starts lifting with a loud clang.

"My mom whispered to me right before Cyrus took me away. She told me to find Remy. I don't know why."

"Let's go," the guard says as he begins lumbering down this new hallway.

We follow him, sticking close together because the farther we walk down the hallway, the narrower and shorter it gets.

We pause outside another gate, and the two guards have basically the same conversation we just went through. But instead of ignoring us, this guard looks at us as he opens the portcullis. And says, "You'd better hope that he's in a good mood. Remy hates surprises."

"Yeah, he does," agrees the guard who's been leading us here. "How many guards did it take to collect the pieces of the last person to ask for Remy?"

"Four," the gate guard answers. "And they had to make multiple trips."

Suddenly a room without a sea view—and without Remy—seems like the way to go, no matter what Nuri said.

But just as I'm reaching that conclusion—along with Flint and Hudson,

I'm pretty sure—the guard presses a bunch of numbers on his control pad. But this time, instead of the portcullis going up, I can hear the sound of metal rubbing together, like massive gears grinding against each other.

As the gears move, both guards step a little closer to the metal gate. I'm about to ask what's going on when the floor we're standing on drops into a steep slant.

"What the hell?" Flint squawks, trying to grab on to something. But it's too late. We're already sliding down, down, down...and right into a giant metal tube slide.

I hit the slide first, and I claw at the sides, trying to find something, *anything* to hold on to. But it's completely smooth, no ragged edges, no handles, nothing to grab. Which might be a blessing, considering I can hear Hudson and Flint sliding hot on my heels, and I really don't want to be crashed into by either of them.

It takes nearly a minute before I reach the end of the slide, and then I fall about five feet through the air onto a pristine metal floor.

This time I hit ass first, because apparently landing on my feet with a little bit of dignity is too much to ask. It hurts, but I've got no time to absorb the pain because I've got to scramble backward to avoid being hit by a falling Hudson who, of course, sticks his landing like a gymnast at the Olympics. Seconds later, Flint does the same thing.

The jerks.

"Where do you think we are?" Hudson asks as he reaches down to pull me to my feet. I take the help because both my ass and knees hurt now, and we haven't even been in this place two hours.

"Cell block 68?" I answer as I look around the room, which is nearly as shadowy as the hallway. Still, there's enough light for me to register that we're standing in a cell made completely of a perfectly smooth, perfectly polished metal. It's old metal—a little discolored in some places, a little dull in others—but metal just the same.

I run a hand over the wall, but there are no ridges or seams at all. From what I can see, the whole thing is one continuous piece—walls, ceiling, floor. I've never seen anything like it, and the artist in me is fascinated, even as the rest of me is terrified that we've just landed in a perfect metal coffin.

And that's before a low, terrifying growl comes from seemingly nowhere and makes every hair on my body stand straight up.

108

War-Locked Up

I whirl around, trying to figure out where the sound is coming from, but Hudson and Flint have already stepped in front of me—blocking whatever it is from getting to me but also blocking my view of whatever it is.

Another, deeper growl sounds, and I can't help wondering if Remy is a T. rex, because I can't imagine what else could possibly make a sound like that.

I try to push Hudson aside a little bit, but he's not budging. And when I try a second time, he lets loose a warning growl of his own. Too bad I don't have a clue whether it's directed at me or the terrifying creature that has now taken to snarling at us basically nonstop.

I finally figure out that if I angle just right, I can peer between Hudson and Flint and see what they see—which at the moment appears to be a pair of glowing red eyes.

"Now, Calder, keep your drawers on," says a low, deep voice that's as hot as cayenne pepper and as smooth as the pecan pralines my mother used to love. "Don't you recognize company when you see it?"

Apparently not, because—drawers not withstanding—the only thing Calder does is let loose another long, slow growl.

"Who are you?" Hudson demands.

"I should probably be asking you that question, don't you think?" comes the easy answer. "Since you came uninvited into *my* home and all."

"Uninvited?" I squawk. "It's not like we had a choice."

"Sure you did, *cher.*" He takes a couple of steps forward now, and though he's not out of the shadows yet, he is close enough to the light that I get the impression of shaggy dark hair, broad shoulders, and a strong jaw.

"Not exactly," I whisper. Okay, maybe we did, but I'm not telling *him* that. At least not until we figure out which answer might get us eaten by whatever is still growling in the corner.

"Hmm," he answers. "In my experience, 'not exactly' sounds an awful lot like 'yes.'"

"Not exactly," I say again, and this time he laughs—big and bold, but it only ratchets up the tension in the room.

"You've got gumption," he says in a slow, New Orleans drawl that wraps around each word and drags it out, and I wonder if that's where this prison is. "I'll give you that."

"And you've got issues, at least according to the guards," I shoot back. "Do you tear everyone to pieces or just the ones who aren't afraid of you?"

Flint makes a choked sound, and Hudson inhales a little too fast, but neither tries to convince me to stop talking. They do, however, brace for whatever it is he's going to do.

But he does nothing, save shake his head as he finally, finally steps out of the shadows. And as I get my first real glimpse of him, I realize he's nothing like what I expected.

To begin with, he's young—like about my age or a year younger. Admittedly, that doesn't necessarily mean anything in this paranormal world, as Hudson is more than two hundred and looks about nineteen.

But I don't get a vampire vibe from this guy, with his shaggy hair and forest-green eyes, nor do I get a vibe that says he's been around a long time. And he's huge and heavily muscled—at least six foot four, with shoulders almost as wide as the door. He'd definitely give Flint a run for his money. And unlike the rest of us, he's not dressed in prison black.

Instead, he's wearing a pair of well-worn jeans, ripped at the knees, and a white T-shirt that makes his warm brown complexion look even warmer, richer.

I'm about to decide this kid's not so bad—and then our gazes collide, and a shiver of fear skitters down my spine.

There might be a rabid beast in the corner of this cell, dying to rip us limb from limb, but one look at those eyes and I know Remy is the real danger here.

I don't know what he did to get thrown in this prison, but I can guess one thing: he definitely did it. And probably smiled the whole time.

"Good question. What do you think?" he asks as he strolls over to us like he's at a Sunday picnic on the banks of the Mississippi.

It's hard to tell if his words are an implied threat, since he says them so casually, but Hudson must think so because he snarls, "Get away from her," in a voice so low and controlled that it has shivers tearing down my spine.

Remy, on the other hand, just kind of looks at him, dark eyebrows raised. "Nice little attack dog there, darlin'. You might tell him to stand down...if you want him to leave here with all his pieces attached."

Hudson steps forward to meet him and gives me the opportunity I've been looking for. I dart out between him and Flint and throw myself bodily in front of him. "Stop it," I hiss at Hudson and Flint. "This isn't helping."

"Like he is?" Hudson asks, offended.

"I don't know what he's doing yet, but let's at least try to find out before the two of you beat the hell out of each other."

"I'm not sure that's how this is going to go," Remy says. "Though I do enjoy a challenge."

"I'm happy to show you exactly how this is going to go," Hudson growls back, fangs on full display.

"Okay, that's it." It's my turn to snarl. "Can we please tamp down the level of testosterone in this room before it poisons us all?"

"Not to interrupt what is obviously a champion pissing contest," Flint says in his most pious voice. "But I'd like it noted that my testosterone is completely tamped down."

And in the span of a second, Remy and Hudson go from snarling at each other like two junkyard dogs to staring at Flint like he's the interloper.

I, on the other hand, am about ready to kiss him. Trust the charming dragon to figure out how to lower the tension in the room when everything I do only seems to escalate it.

After giving Flint a sketchy once-over, Remy turns back to me. "Quite the companions you have there, Grace."

Everyone stills. "How—how did you know my name?"

But he just holds my gaze until I feel a jolt of electricity go through me. It's not the same kind of heat I feel with Hudson, obviously—in fact, it's not sexual in the slightest. But it is a powerful jolt nonetheless. Almost like he's looking inside me, sorting through the blood and organs, cells and molecules, to find who I really am under all the trappings.

It's an odd feeling, one that only increases the longer our gazes are connected. And then his eyes turn dark and swirly, like a storm-tossed sky, and I can feel the power inside him, tugging at me, trying to latch on to something and pull me forward. And I almost go. At least until Hudson wraps an arm around my waist and pulls me into him so that his front is pressed against my back.

"Don't look him in the eyes," Hudson whispers, and though we currently have bigger fish to fry, the warmth of his breath against the sensitive skin of my ear and neck has a tiny frisson of heat uncurling deep within me.

Then he looks straight at Remy and orders, "Stop with the tricks, witch. Or I'll stop them for you."

109

A Charmer, a Bad Boy, and a Lost Soul All Walk into a Cell...

Tense silence ensues while Remy studies us like we're bugs under a microscope.

"All in due time, Grace," he eventually says in answer to my question about how he knows my name. Then he makes a little clicking noise with the corner of his mouth. "Why don't you come on over here, *cher*, and tell me a little bit about yourself."

I can't decide if that was meant as an invitation or a command. In fact, I'm having trouble figuring out exactly what Remy is all about, in general. Yes, he looks scary and cold and intimidating, but you know, we *are* standing in a prison. Also, how the hell did he know my name? That might be the scariest thing about all this, despite something inside telling me I don't have to be afraid. That he feels familiar. And more, that he feels safe.

Which makes absolutely no sense.

Everything about him screams *run scared*—except his eyes. His eyes are too watchful. Too careful. Too...*needy*.

And that's when it hits me. I know exactly why he feels familiar.

He's not the first guy I've met who pretends to be a psychopath so no one looks closer and sees his pain... Been there, done that, currently mated to him.

And that's it; I can't help it. I burst out laughing. Men. They really are simple creatures sometimes.

"Why don't you come on over here and tell us a little bit about *yourself*," I shoot back. "Starting with how you managed to get your bracelet off." I stare pointedly at his bare, unmarked wrist.

There's a moment's hesitation before he tells me, "I like you." And now I see it—his eyes are positively dancing with merriment. This whole thing has been a joke to him.

"Yeah, that's obvious," Hudson mutters, but Remy ignores him.

Instead, Remy follows my gaze and stares at his bracelet-less wrist like he's going to answer. But then he kind of shrugs and says, "Guess I'm just special like that."

"'Special' is one way to put it," Hudson mocks, and if his hold on me got any tighter, I'm pretty sure it would cut off my circulation. "Narcissistic is another. But hey. Potato, po-tah-to, right?"

Remy looks so surprised—and disgruntled—at the comeback that I can't help giggling.

And apparently, I'm not the only one because the beast from the shadows laughs—a deep, rollicking sound that fills up the whole cell with joy. And like that, Remy's laughing, too.

"Well, hell, Calder. You've gone and ruined the whole game. You might as well stop hiding in the shadows."

"I was wondering when you were going to let me out to play," a light female voice answers, which has Hudson, Flint, and me exchanging *what the fuck* looks.

Because how the hell could someone who sounds like *that* make the growls we just heard? At least until Calder steps out of the shadows, and we realize she is a giant of a girl. An Amazon who stands as tall as Flint and has biceps as big as Remy's and looks to be about seventeen herself.

She's also gorgeous—no doubt about that. Long red hair, big brown eyes, boobs that make even mine look small, and an infectious smile that lights up the whole room as much as her laugh did.

I start to step forward, hand extended, to say hello, but Hudson mutters, "Jesus," as he pulls me tighter into his side.

In the meantime, Flint sniffs the air and then asks with wide eyes, "Holy fuck. Is that a manticore?"

"Damn straight I am," Calder replies. "And so you know, I prefer it when men talk *to* me, not about me."

"Oh, yeah, right. Sorry." Flint's cheeks turn ruddy.

And I'm not trying to be rude here, especially since this girl looks like she could tear any one of us limb from limb with her bare hands, but I also have no idea what's going on. "I'm sorry," I say. "I'm kind of new to the whole paranormal world. What's a manticore?"

Remy laughs again, but Calder lifts her head proudly, red hair streaming down her back and announces, "Only the fiercest and most beautiful creature ever created."

It doesn't tell me much, but it's one hell of a description. And, looking at her, I can't help thinking that it is right freaking on.

110

The Big Not-So-Easy

"**M**anticores are part human and part lion, with eagle wings and a scorpion's tail," Hudson tells me softly.

"That is totally badass!" I exclaim.

"I know." Calder grins, pretending to buff her nails on her shirt. "We're the best."

"Definitely the most modest," Hudson interjects dryly.

Flint makes a choking sound, but Calder waves an airy hand. "It's okay. I don't believe in hiding my light under a bushel."

It's, like, the most perfect answer ever—at least from this glorious creature, which is probably why I crack up the second Remy's eyes meet mine. He laughs, too, but Calder just fluffs up her hair and swishes it back and forth.

"So why don't you pull up some metal floor," Remy suggests. "Get comfortable, and tell me what made you ask for me."

"You mean get uncomfortable, right?" Flint asks as he looks at the scarred and dented floor. I look closely, too, pretty sure that some of these scars are actually...claw marks? The thought makes my stomach sink.

What happens in here that someone would have to do something like that? And how do we keep it from happening to us?

Remy grins. "Comfort's relative after a life in prison. But I guess you'll find that out soon enough."

"Actually, that's kind of what we were hoping you could help us with," I tell him. "Flint's mom is the dragon queen, and she told us to find you. We need to locate someone else in the prison and then break out, preferably as soon as possible."

"Is that right?" Remy asks, brows raised. "You're gonna break four of you out of this place like it's nothing, huh?" He snaps, and sparks explode from the ends of his fingertips. They hang in the air between us for a moment or two before slowly fading away.

"That's the plan, yeah," Flint tells him.

"You know this place is governed by an unbreakable curse, right?"

"We do," I say.

"So, what?" he asks. "You think you might be the ones to actually beat that?"

"We *are* going to be the ones to beat it," Hudson tells him, and for a second he sounds just as arrogant as Calder. And, like with her, the confidence works on him.

Like really, really works on him. His blue eyes are gleaming as he squares off against Remy, his dark hair falling over his forehead since the wind/ fire thing destroyed his normal style. Plus, the prison jumpsuit that looks ridiculous on me actually looks pretty damn good on him, especially with its open collar leaving his very kissable throat on display while also molding to the rest of the muscles on his upper body pretty damn well.

I know we're in prison, just like I know that things don't get much worse than this.

I also know if we succeed in actually finding the blacksmith, we're going to use him to find the Crown, defeat Cyrus, and break our mating bond so that we can save Jaxon's soul.

But right now, right at this very moment, when my mate has his arm around me and is preparing to wheel and deal with a warlock and a manticore, it's pretty hard to remember all that. Honestly, it's pretty hard to remember anything *except* that. For some reason I can't begin to understand, the universe made this gorgeous, sexy, brilliant guy my mate. *Mine.*

I'm trying not to draw attention to myself, but something of what I'm feeling must be showing on my face because Hudson keeps shooting me weird little looks. And when our gazes actually meet for a second or two, he squirms uncomfortably and—I'm pretty sure—forgets how to breathe.

It's only proximity, I tell myself. *Only biology.* But when Hudson lifts a sardonic brow in response to Remy's "no one breaks out of this prison," all of a sudden he's not the only one squirming.

"So how do we get out, then?" Flint asks. "Because we *are* getting out."

I don't know if Remy is humoring us or if he believes us, but after he studies each of our faces in turn, he says, "First? We barter."

"What does that mean?" I ask. "You think we can buy our way out of prison?"

"*Cher.*" He gives me a look like he's disappointed in me. "Haven't you figured out by now that anything can be bought with the right price?"

"Yeah, so name your price," Hudson tells him. "We'll get it for you."

"Well, well. Aren't you the big man?" Calder says, and I can't tell if she approves or if she's being sarcastic. At least not until she looks Hudson over from head to toe...and licks her lips.

Which is just...fantastic. Apparently, we're supposed to put our fate in the hands of a depraved Amazon and a warlock who feels an awful lot like a con man. Lucky, lucky us.

"It's not quite so simple," Remy says, and I swear his accent has gotten even heavier.

"What does that mean?" Hudson responds.

"It means you need to slow your roll. Getting to where you *might* be able to bust out of this place is a process, and it doesn't matter how impatient you are; some things can't be rushed."

"I understand that," Hudson counters. "But is there any way we can maybe speed it along a little?"

Remy shakes his head, like he pities Hudson. "You're in N'Awlins now, baby. That's not how things work down here."

A prison for paranormal creatures is in New Orleans. Everything about that sentence makes total sense.

"So how exactly do they work, then?" Hudson eyes him like he's wondering what size bucket he'd need for Remy if he decides to go full Bloodletter on his ass.

"Nice and slow. Just like all the best things in life," he answers, even as he sends me a cheeky little wink. "They don't call it The Big Easy for nothing."

Flint bursts out laughing—which he hastily turns into a cough when Hudson turns to stare at him with narrowed eyes.

"Sorry," he murmurs.

Hudson sighs and rubs his eyes like he's got the world's biggest headache... which seems fair, to be honest. Remy is...a lot.

"So what *do* we need to do?" I ask, hoping to give him a chance to regroup.

"I've been waiting for this moment since the day I was born," Remy replies. "So the first thing you need to do? Listen to me."

"You remember the day you were born?" I ask, which is, admittedly, the most inane of the questions racing around in my brain. But it's the one that somehow comes out, partly because it seems ridiculous and partly, I think, because the paranormal world is just bizarre enough that that could actually be a thing, especially considering I am currently sitting with a dragon, a vampire, a warlock, and a manticore. Anything is possible.

Remy doesn't answer right away, and after a few seconds, I decide he's not going to answer at all. But then he says, "When you're born in a prison, you tend to remember it."

"You were born here?" Flint asks. "That's…"

"What it is," Remy finishes with a warning look. It's obvious he doesn't want any sympathy from us, but that seems impossible when my heart is breaking for him.

Still, I clear my throat in an effort to sound normal and *not* all choked up. "So you've never been outside these walls?"

"It's not so bad." He shrugs. "Once you learn how the prison works, you do okay. It's not like I'm lacking for anything."

Except freedom. And fresh air. And the choice of what to do with any and every part of his life.

He's right. It's not so bad. It's horrible. Especially when I think about the fact that he did nothing to get here. He's spent his entire life locked up in this prison simply for the crime of being born.

Actually, it's beyond horrible.

"I'm—" I break off, not sure what to say.

But Remy just shakes his head. "Please don't tell me you're sorry."

"It's hard not to," I respond.

"It shouldn't be. Not for you."

I don't understand. "Why not?"

"Because, *cher.* You're the only thing I've been living for for the last couple of years. And hearing you say you're sorry about that would plain break my heart."

111

I Never Asked to Be
Your Saving Grace...But
Someone's Got to Do It

"What exactly does that mean?" Hudson's voice cuts like broken glass through the silence.

"It means I've been waiting for her for a long time." Remy smiles at me. "You disappeared for a little while there, but you came back a few weeks ago. And I, for one, have to say that I am intensely grateful for whatever put you back on the path of debauchery and mayhem that landed you in this fine establishment."

"No debauchery or mayhem," I tell him.

He *tsk*s at me. "Now, I have a hard time believing that, Grace. I have seen you in my dreams for a lot of years, and if I know anything, it's that you're a wild one."

"What did you just say about her?" Hudson demands.

"In your dreams?" I ask, confused. "You mean your dreams..."

"Come true? Yes. My mom was a witch, but not a very strong one—even before they slapped a bracelet on her. She died when I was five. My father, on the other hand...I know nothing about him because she never said a word, but he did give me one little present. I can see the future. And I have seen that you are my key to escaping this shithole prison."

He grins. "And like I said, Grace, I've seen you coming for a long time. I'm merely glad you finally got here." He reaches over and pats my knee, which has Hudson giving him an evil look all over again.

But I get it. I can't imagine seeing someone coming your whole life who you think can play a role in freeing you, only to have her disappear on you, just when it's almost time.

I know those weeks he was talking about—and I can tell Hudson knows them, too. It must have been the time I was mated to Jaxon. When I was with him, it must have taken me off the path of following Hudson to prison.

I glance at him out of the corner of my eye, and he looks devastated. I know he's blaming himself, know that he thinks it's his fault that I'm here. But if Remy's seen me all along, doesn't that prove that Hudson and I were always meant to be mates?

The thought breaks my heart way more than being in this prison ever could. Because this is the real thing. Hudson is the mate the universe gave me, and I'm the mate the universe gave him. But we still can't be together… If we are, we'll lose Jaxon. And I know neither of us would ever be able to live with ourselves if that happened.

Still, I reach over and squeeze Hudson's hand. Because whatever happens between us—whether we find the Crown and break the mating bond or not—there's a part of me that will never forget that Hudson loves me, warts and all.

Remy is watching us closely, and there's something in his eyes that makes my heart hurt for him even more. But the second he notices me watching, it disappears and the smart-ass grin is back in place.

"I do have to say one thing, though, Grace. I think you should have held out a little in the mate department."

"Oh, really?" I ask, keeping a firm grip on Hudson's hand when I see the fangs come out.

"Yeah." He gives Hudson another smug once-over. "You totally could have snagged someone with a cheerier personality."

"Someone like you, you mean?" I ask dryly.

"Me? I'm flattered." He gives me a faux-shocked look that we both know is total bullshit. "But now that you ask, I do have an opening."

"Am I sitting here right now or am I fucking invisible?" Hudson asks. "For a guy who wants our help, you sure have a fuckton of nerve."

Remy looks him straight in the eye. "I've been living in this shithole my whole life. Nerve is the only thing I've got to my name."

"Maybe that's because you're an asshole who drives everyone away," Hudson shoots back.

"Hey!" Calder stops braiding her hair long enough to glare at Hudson. "That's not nice. You should apologize." She fluffs her bangs. "I'm somebody."

For a while, Hudson just stares at her, nonplussed, and it takes every ounce of self-control I have not to laugh. Because the truth is, my mate is a lot of things. Brilliant, funny, self-deprecating, sexy as fuck.

But he is also used to being the biggest diva in any room. And now he's up against Remy, who uses his appeal like a weapon, and Calder, who is so completely self-absorbed that Hudson's sarcasm doesn't have a chance of getting through.

Frankly, I'm amazed he hasn't started pulling out his hair yet. Then again, that would cause an unsightly bald spot...

"What are you laughing at?" Hudson asks quietly.

"I don't know what you're talking about." I give him my best deadpan look. "I'm not laughing at all."

He rolls his eyes. "You are on the inside. I can feel it."

"Sorry, I was just..." I lower my voice to a whisper. "Imagining you with a bald spot."

The look he gives me is so affronted that both Flint and Remy burst out laughing. Calder doesn't even notice.

"Vampires don't go bald," he hisses.

"Which is why it was such a funny thought." I widen my eyes, going for the innocent look. But the downside of having Hudson live in my head for so long is that he doesn't believe it for a second.

"Can we focus, please?" he asks. "The sooner we figure this shit out, the better. We need to get home." He turns back to Remy. "How fast do you think we can make that happen?"

"That depends on the three of you," he answers. "I want out of this shithole more than anybody here, but there's no cheating the system."

"We know the curse is supposed to be unbreakable," Flint says. "But there's got to be a loophole, right?"

"There's no loophole," Remy says. "But the flowers will—"

"Wait." Hudson's eyes narrow. "You know about the flowers?"

Remy sighs. "Which part of 'seeing the future' do you not understand?"

"The part where you're an asshole. Oh, wait, that's the present *and* the future. My bad."

The two of them look like they're about to get started on another pissing contest, but frankly, I don't have the energy for it.

Besides, there's a bigger problem. "I have the flowers, but I have no idea how to use them."

112

Warlocks Spell
It Like It Is

"I do," Hudson says.

"What? How? When?" I ask. "I thought you didn't even believe the flowers would work!"

"I don't have a clue if they'll work," he tells me. "But I've seen this kind of magic before. You just press your fingers against the tattoo as though picking the flowers out of thin air, and they'll come to you. It's a spell of need."

"More like desperation." Flint snorts. And he's not wrong. Still...

"You. Are. Brilliant!" I tell Hudson. And to hell with our audience and us basically living a soap opera. I lean over and give him one quick but perfect kiss.

Hudson's brows go up, but he's totally on board. "There are three flowers," he murmurs against my lips. "You know, in case you want to show your appreciation for each flower."

I laugh but give him two more quick kisses, because I want them as much as he apparently does.

"This is awesome!" I say once I'm settled in a spot on the ground. "I've spent the last umpteen hours worried to death that we wouldn't be able to get them."

"Umm, Grace?" Flint interrupts. "I hate to be the one to burst your very happy bubble, but we still have a problem."

"What's that?" I ask.

"There are three flowers. Counting the blacksmith, there are four of us—"

"Five," Remy interrupts.

"Umm, six," Calder reminds us sweetly.

"Okay, *fine*," Flint says. "Counting the blacksmith, there are *six* of us who need to escape and only three flowers to help us do it. Can we use half a flower per person instead, you think?"

"Yeah, and only end up looking half dead?" Remy says skeptically. "That gets us a trip to Bianca's infirmary, and there ain't nobody who wants to go there.

"Besides, they're really small flowers." He looks at my tattoos doubtfully. "And if it's the same blacksmith I think you're referring to, he's a really big guy. Half might kill his welding hand, but that's about it."

"Vander Bracka, a giant who makes magical cuffs?" I ask, just so we're clear what blacksmith we need—'cause it wouldn't be awkward to break out the wrong one or anything.

Remy nods. "Yup. That's him."

"Well then, we're back to where we started," I say. "We've got nothing."

"Not nothing," Hudson tells me. "You and Flint can still find the blacksmith, and the three of you can escape."

"I'm not okay with that," I tell him.

"Umm, me neither," Calder says. "What makes her so special?"

Hudson lifts a brow. "She brought the flowers?"

"Yes, but we've been waiting for the girl with the flowers *forever*. I don't think it's fair that we're not even in the running to leave with her—especially since we all know they'll look best on me."

"Who cares who they'll look best on?" Flint asks. "We're going to eat them."

She fluffs her hair, shrugs. "I'm just saying, aesthetics are important. And mine are obviously the best."

Flint stares at her for a second, like he can't quite decide if she's real. Then he shakes his head as if to clear it and says, "Here's an idea, aesthetics aside. How about we come up with a plan that gets *everybody* free? What's the point of having all this awesomeness in one group if we can't figure this out?"

"Aww, you're so sweet," Calder tells him, then stage-whispers to Remy. "Flint called me awesome."

Flint, Hudson, and I exchange looks that ask pretty clearly if this girl is for real, but Remy nods like she's said the most logical thing in the world.

Then he turns to us. "Look, for all I know, the rest of you ride a rainbow-tailed unicorn out of here. But Grace gives me a flower. I've seen it a million times. It's my only way out."

"Unicorns don't like manticores," Calder says matter-of-factly. "Probably because we have cooler tails. Besides, you wouldn't leave me here, so one of the flowers must be for me, too." She shrugs as if to say, *Logic*.

So now we're down two flowers, and we haven't even found the blacksmith yet? This is beginning to sound a little fishy to me. It must sound that way to Hudson, too, because he asks the question that's been on the tip of my tongue since I got here. "*How* do you two know each other?"

The obvious answer is prison, but there has to be more to it than that. It's such an odd friendship. They clearly love each other, but it's not the least bit sexual. More like brother and sister.

Which makes me wonder—how far would Remy go to get Calder out of here? Far enough to trick us and try to steal a flower?

"Calder and I go way back, don't we?" Remy gives her a slow grin. "And I've seen her end—and it's not in this shithole. As for how we met... That's her story, not mine."

"Some stories aren't meant to be shared," she answers with a little shrug. "It makes them lose their magic."

This is getting us nowhere, so I turn to Remy. I'm beginning to think I need to make one thing clear. "*No one* gets a flower unless we have another way out—*with* the blacksmith."

Calder tilts her head as she studies me appraisingly. "I think I like this one, Remy."

Remy just grins. "I'm sure we can come up with a way to get you guys out. If you're lucky enough *and* can survive long enough *and* do exactly what I tell you." His grin turns to a grimace. "But the blacksmith, well, he's a prize down here, and not exactly small enough to hide if we plan on sneaking him out."

Something must occur to him, because his eyes narrow as he looks each one of us over before asking, "Exactly what did you guys do to end up in here, anyway?"

"I had a disagreement with my father." Hudson says it casually, like it's no big deal. But his eyes are watchful as he waits to see what they do.

"A disagreement landed you in here?" Calder says skeptically. "What did you do? Turn him into a dancing chicken?"

"I turned his bones to dust." The words are flat and obviously a challenge.

"Dust?" Calder asks. "Like ashes to ashes, dust to dust? That's brutal." She doesn't seem put off by the fact.

"He's not dead, if that's what you're asking," Hudson answers, deadpan. "I *just* turned his bones to dust."

An avaricious gleam enters Calder's eyes as she looks him up and down. "You and I are going to be really good friends."

I think we're both okay with that proclamation *until* she licks her lips again and adds an eyebrow wiggle.

Hudson scooches a little closer to me on the floor, and I can't say I blame him. So I wrap my arm around his shoulders and say, "Mine." Simple, to the point, hard to misunderstand.

Of course, it also makes Hudson lean over and give me the goofiest smile imaginable, because ugh. Men.

Calder bats her eyes innocently before turning to Flint. "What about you, big guy?"

Flint looks a little shame-faced as he nods toward me and admits, "I tried to kill Grace."

"Only *tried* to kill her?" Calder looks a little disappointed, which…thanks. It only takes her a second to bounce back, though. "I'll tell you what," she says with an excited squeal. "The next time you try to kill her, I'll give you pointers. I'm really good at it. Then I'll take Hudson, and the three of us can be best friends."

"Tossed me over already?" Remy asks, even as I roll my eyes. Hard.

"Anyone care why I'm here? Because the answer is I'm his *mate.*"

"Well, that's no fun." Calder looks nonplussed. "Of course, that's why the big guy's gonna kill you, silly. Then it will all work out."

Remy laughs and winks at me. "Ignore her, *cher.* She's just trying to see what you're made of, but she's harmless."

I start to reply *stone, I'm made of badass stone,* but then I remember this prison took my gargoyle, and my shoulders sink a little. What *am* I made of without my gargoyle? I honestly don't know.

"Do you mind if I ask what the big deal is about the blacksmith?" Remy asks. "Like I said, he's a favorite down here, so getting him out is going to be a little rough."

We don't answer right away. Flint, Hudson, and I exchange glances, none of us sure how much to share with our cellmates. What if Remy plans on using what we tell him to get himself out?

Then again, he seems pretty convinced he uses a flower to get out. Besides, he doesn't know the real reason why we're here yet, so he has no motive to lie. And Nuri specifically told Flint to find Remy. What did she know about him that would help us?

My stomach is in knots trying to figure out our next move, but one thing I do know for certain...we're going to have to trust someone down here if we hope to get out alive. And since Remy's the only one lining up for the job, the choice is an easy one.

I take a deep breath and pray to God I'm not wrong. "We need the blacksmith to defeat Cyrus."

Remy's and Calder's eyebrows both shoot up so fast, it's almost comical. Almost. You know, if we weren't sitting on the floor of a prison trying to plan an escape, that is.

"So let me get this straight," Remy says in his smooth Cajun drawl. "You three are just hanging out, planning a coup to defeat the vampire king... from *prison*?"

Hudson shrugs. "Ultimately, he didn't like it much when I turned his bones to dust."

Remy's eyebrows are practically in his hairline now—well, what I can see of his hairline around his long, shaggy hair. "Your dad is the *vampire king*?"

"What's wrong?" Hudson asks, tongue very much in cheek. "Didn't see that one coming?"

Remy shakes his head. "Not even a little bit."

"Oh, I am so in," Calder says, her face positively lit from the inside with excitement as she turns to Hudson. "Like one thousand percent in. I'll hold him down while you fuck his shit up, pretty boy."

Flint lets out a snort-laugh and Hudson glares at him. And me? I'm grinning ear to ear. Because Calder's eyes never sparkled when she flirted with Hudson like they are now at the thought of killing Cyrus. That's what *real* interest looks like.

"What exactly did Cyrus do to you?" Flint asks Calder, and I notice Remy's gaze softens on her.

"Oh, nothing to me," she says while tossing a nod over at Remy. "But Cyrus is the reason my boy has been in this prison his whole life. That's not okay."

Remy inclines his head. "Family is everything to a manticore." It's as much a warning as it is a statement.

"I didn't realize you two were related," I answer, surprised.

"Family doesn't have to be blood," Calder says, like it's the most obvious thing in the world.

I think of Xavier, of Flint and Eden, Jaxon and Hudson, Mekhi and Luca, and I couldn't agree more. "You know what, Calder? I think I like you, too. So much that I'll even let you flirt with my mate."

"Wait, what?" Hudson whispers as he throws me a desperate look.

But now I'm grinning right along with Calder. "No touching, though."

"See, I knew we were going to be friends," Calder says. "Wasn't I just saying that, Remy?"

"Does that mean you'll help us?" I ask Remy.

"If it means making Cyrus pay for what he did to my mother? Oh, *cher*, you needn't even ask," he says, then tacks on, "but I will be taking one of those flowers as payment."

113

Come On, Baby, Cuff Me One More Time

"**L**et's assume we agree to your terms," Hudson begins. "What's your other idea for how to get out without the flowers? And more importantly, why didn't you try it for you and Calder?"

Remy shrugs. "Seeing the future isn't all it's cracked up to be. The future is constantly changing. Just because I see one path doesn't mean it'll happen. Look at how I saw Grace giving me a flower, then she disappeared from my dreams for weeks."

I have no idea what point he's trying to make. "And?"

"I knew I was going to get out with a flower. I knew roughly *when* Calder would get out," he says. "At least there was hope for us. To risk trying to get out another way could have failed *and* changed the future—meaning we might never get out." He must see that I'm still not understanding, because he holds my gaze as he says, "What's a better bet, *cher*? The sure thing that you'll get to leave this shithole one day, even if you have to wait years, or a chance at freedom that could mean you never get out? I decided to bet on the sure thing."

I think about his words, chew on them. What would I have done? I honestly don't know. I can't imagine spending one extra day imprisoned if there was even a chance of getting out—but then I haven't spent seventeen years in here. Yet. I might just want a sure thing myself by then.

"But you think there's a way out for us?" Flint asks.

Remy nods. "Like I said, it's going to take a whole lot of luck and even more money…and that's only if we survive the trip. But there's a chance. It's happened before."

That last comment perks up all our ears. We only knew about the dragon who got out—and he'd made a deal with the Crone for a flower. There was another way that didn't require me signing a devil's pact with a witch and her pizza oven? Well, super awesome that we're only learning about it now.

"Okay, so what's the big escape plan?" I ask.

But before they can say anything, there's a scraping sound on the floor across the room.

"What's that?" I ask, even as Hudson moves so that I'm once again behind him.

"Dinner," Calder answers, and though she doesn't sound happy at the prospect, she also doesn't sound traumatized. Which is something, at least, especially since my stomach has decided to let me know that it is well aware that it has been many hours since I've eaten.

"They feed us through a hole in the floor?" Flint sounds horrified.

"That floor panel is the only access in or out of this room," Remy explains. "There's no door, no window, nothing. Just the tube that dropped you in and this tiny door the guards have to move us to unblock. Oh, and the fold-down staircase right below it that they have to activate."

"Move us?" Flint asks. "What does that mean?"

"You'll see," Remy answers.

His matter-of-fact tone should reassure me—he's pretty blasé about the situation, after all—but instead, it freaks me out. So far I've done what I think is a pretty good job of keeping my panic at bay, but the idea that there is literally no way out of this place except waiting for the guards to not only open our cell but to unblock the entrance completely... Well, let's say it makes me want out of here right freaking now.

I mean, does this place not answer to a fire marshal?

Calder walks over to the now-open hole in the floor and pulls out a triple-stacked tray. "You came on a good day," she tells us. "It's chicken and mashed potatoes."

Not going to lie. The food choice kind of blows my mind. I don't know what I expected to eat at the most diabolical prison ever created, but it definitely wasn't my mother's favorite comfort meal.

As she's handing out the covered trays to Flint and me—and a cup of what I assume is blood to Hudson—we all settle on the floor again and dig in.

After we take a few bites, Hudson puts aside his distrust of Remy long enough to ask, "Can you tell us a little more about how this place works? Our powers feel like they're gone."

"That's because they're blocked," Calder says. "Like, really blocked."

"By the cuffs on our wrists?" Hudson asks. "I've worn a cuff like this before—it's never really cut me off from my power, though. Not like this."

"Because it's not just that cuff." Remy takes a bite of a dinner roll and motions with it at the room. "Look around. The cuffs block all your magic, even shifting magic, but let's say we break those…"

Calder shakes her head. "You'd still have no abilities. The cell itself is a cuff."

"Oh, shit. That's brilliant," Flint says, and the look on his face is half respect and half horror as he glances around the room. "That's why the cell is all metal."

"The whole outside prison wall is a giant cuff," Remy tells us. "Then each cell is a cuff in a long chain of cuffs that, when locked together, make another cuff. And then, of course, there's the cuffs on your wrists."

"Four cuffs?" Flint asks, and for once, he seems totally cowed. "There are four separate cuffs between me and my magic?" He shakes his head. "No wonder I can't feel it at all."

That's why my gargoyle string has completely disappeared. It's locked away, hidden under one layer of metal after another, until there really is nothing left. I push my food around on my plate, my appetite suddenly gone.

The cruelty seems unfathomable. I understand that this is prison. I understand that powerful beings have to be contained. But they're using safeguards upon safeguards upon safeguards upon safeguards to ensure that people can't access something that is as much a part of them as their heart or their blood… It's beyond horrible. It's an actual violation.

"And just think," Remy says grimly. "We're the lucky ones. At least without a cuff, I have access to *some* of my magic. I can't imagine how the rest of you lot get by with none. It's a plain tragedy."

"Lucky?" I ask. "How so?"

"We're in the East Wheel, which is the political prisoner and petty-crime side. If you go over to the West Wheel—where the real criminals are—there are even more layers of protection."

I don't even want to think about it. But then, I realize, I don't have a choice. We didn't plan for the prison layout because we didn't know about it—it's a tightly held secret. But that means… "Do you know where the blacksmith is?" I ask. "On the East Wheel or the West one? Because if he's in the West Wheel…"

"We are totally screwed," Flint finishes for me.

"And then some," Hudson agrees.

"He's somewhere else entirely," Remy tells us. And maybe I would be relieved if he didn't have such a wary look on his face.

"So where is he, then?" I ask as my stomach cramps in dread.

Remy and Calder exchange a look. "He's in the Pit, Grace," he answers reluctantly.

114

How A Prison Cell Became the Room Where It Happens

"The Pit?" I look at Hudson and Flint, but they both seem as lost as I feel. "What's that?"

Remy lifts a brow. "Ever read Dante's 'Inferno'? I'm thinking he took inspiration from this place, because someone had some fun with the idea."

"I haven't, no."

"I have," Hudson says grimly, and his arm goes around my waist again. "And I would sincerely prefer not to be frozen in ice...or anything else."

I have no idea what he's talking about, but I'm totally willing to agree with it.

Calder stands up and puts her tray back in the hole in the floor, and we all do the same. I look around the cell, wondering if we're going to have to piss in a different hole next. Calder must catch my expression and guess what I'm thinking, because she smiles and says, "Bathroom's at the other end, in the shadows hidden behind a wall."

I mouth *thank you* to her and catalog that info away for later.

Remy moves over to the tube we fell down and pulls on the chain attached to the end of it. He slides it through a pulley attached to the ceiling and slowly, slowly, slowly, beds start to crank down from the walls at the twelve, two, four, six, and eight positions on a clock.

"In case you don't want to sleep on the floor," he says and winks at me. "That bed opposite the tube is mine. Calder sleeps in the one to the right of it."

"Oh, thank God," I whisper, dropping down on the bed next to Calder's. Hudson takes the one next to me, which leaves the last one in the circle for Flint, but he perches on the end of mine for now.

"But we have to get the blacksmith," Flint says, and I know he's thinking about how Luca is the firstborn at Katmere and what that could mean if Cyrus has his way. "Otherwise all of this is for nothing."

"You're right," I agree before turning to Remy and Calder. No way are we staying in this prison. And no way are we leaving Jaxon high and dry or Katmere vulnerable to Cyrus's plans. "So how do we do that?"

Remy and Calder exchange a look that's more serious than anything I've seen from either one of them. "We run the gauntlet and reach the Pit," they both say in unison.

"Why exactly do they keep him in the Pit?" I ask, choosing to ignore the gauntlet comment entirely for now. "I thought he was here as a political prisoner, not because he was an actual criminal."

"He's not in the Pit because he's a bad guy, *cher*. He's in the Pit because that's where the forge is."

"The forge?" Hudson asks. "He's still a blacksmith?"

"He's the best blacksmith in the world," Calder says as she starts undoing the braid she just put in earlier. "Do you think they'd leave him sitting around in a cell all day?"

"He makes the bracelets," Remy says, nodding at our wrists. "It's why they're so effective."

"And that's why you said he's a favorite down here," Hudson says. "He's useful, which means they're not going to want to let him go."

"Yeah, well, I say that's their problem. Did you see that poor man's wife and what this has done to her?" I focus on Remy and take a deep breath. "So what's this gauntlet? And how long does it take?"

He blinks at me with those eyes of his that see way too much. "I've got to say, darlin', I really like your get-shit-done attitude. It's refreshing."

"I'm glad to hear that. Now, can we actually try to get shit done?"

"By all means." He reaches into a drawer under his bed and pulls out a small notebook and pen. He makes a couple of quick drawings, then moves over to sit next to me on the bed. With him on my left and Flint on my right, it's a tight fit, so I angle my shoulders to give us all a little more room on my tiny bed.

Hudson moves to sit on Remy's bed directly across from me and flashes the warlock a little fang. I'm pretty sure it's on account of me—a quick reminder of whose mate I am—and I can't help it: I giggle because the whole thing is so ridiculous. Which makes Hudson smile sheepishly at me for a second before going back to glaring at Remy. It's total caveman behavior, and it doesn't bother me in the slightest. I mean, there were a few moments earlier when Calder was licking her lips that I had to warn her off as well. Turns out, we're quite the possessive pair.

"So this is our cellblock, right?" he says, pointing to the rough chain of cells he drew.

"And this right here is something they like to call the Chamber." He points to an oval he drew directly between the two ends of the chain.

"And what does the Chamber do?" Flint asks.

"Makes you wish you were never born." Calder is stretched out on her bed now, braid gone and hair fanned around her head like a crown. The fact that her tone is so mild, she could have been talking about lunch or the weather or a million other topics, only makes what she said sound worse and resonate more.

"Could you maybe be a little more specific?" Flint asks, and he looks really nervous.

Not that I blame him. I'm pretty sure I look nervous, too. Hudson's face having gone completely blank says he's feeling the stress as well.

"The Chamber was built for rehabilitation purposes," Remy tells us.

"Rehabilitation as in learn a trade?" I ask. "Or as in the Spanish Inquisition?"

Remy thinks about it for a second. "I'd say a little more painful than the Spanish Inquisition."

"By a little, he means *so* much more painful," Calder translates. "Like so, so, sooooo much more painful."

"And we have to go into the Chamber to get to the Pit?" I ask, my stomach churning wildly now.

Calder sighs. "It's because the prison is judge, jury, and executioner. I'm sure you know how hard it is to have a real trial in the paranormal world— people use magic to game the system or use their power to topple the Court. All kind of things. So this prison was built with an unbreakable curse—no one in here could game the system. And once you're in, the only way out is to prove that you're rehabilitated."

Remy laughs, but there's no amusement in the sound. "Of course, that means the prison itself gets to judge *when* you're rehabilitated. It provides your punishment in increments via the Chamber, and when it thinks you've atoned enough, it decides to let you go."

Calder nods to Remy. "And if you're unlucky enough to be born inside, well, being born is apparently your crime—and there's no way to atone for that sin."

I gasp and stare at Remy. No wonder he's so certain a flower is his only way out.

"The prison decides," Hudson says, totally blank-faced. "And who runs the prison?"

"That's the kicker," Remy says. "No one does. Supposedly, the prison is governed by ancient magic. It makes its own decisions, does its own thing, and because it has no human emotion or drive, it can't be bribed or get angry or anything. Although I have my suspicions."

"My mom said something when I was being arrested about atoning," Flint tells us. "I didn't know what she meant, but she must have been telling me to go to the Chamber."

"She couldn't have known what she was asking," Calder says. "Nobody would wish that on someone they care about."

"And yet you do it every month just so I can get to the Pit." Remy smiles at her.

For the first time since we've met her, Calder seems a little flustered. But she recovers quickly. "Well, I have to go get my nail polish anyway. Beauty has its costs."

Flint looks from her nails to Remy to me, and I shrug. I would be the last person to go through a little light torture for a new nail polish color.

"So how do we get to the Chamber?" I ask, terrified but also resolved. We need to get to the blacksmith, and then we need to get the hell out of here. If the Chamber is the way to do it, then sign me up. "And how long does it take to get from where we are to the Pit?"

"Do you know, Calder?" Remy asks. "I can't remember where in the cycle we are. I think we're six or seven days out—"

"Six," Calder says, and now she's sitting up, painting her toenails black. I have no idea where she pulled the polish from, but I have to say, she's really, really good at it.

"So in six days, we'll be in the Pit?" Hudson asks.

"If you choose to risk the Chamber every night."

"What do you mean, 'risk it'?" Flint asks, and he, too, is watching Calder paint her nails.

"It's like playing Russian roulette," Remy explains, standing up and heading back to his bed as Hudson moves over next to me, "and the Chamber is the bullet. If we decide we want to play, that night we'll join the rotation. We may land in the Chamber; we may not. If we don't, we still drop a level and we get a good night's sleep, then play again the next day. If we do land in it, we go through hell and then—if we're up for it—we play again the next day. Six days out means six spins of the Chamber, six possible nights of torture, but then we arrive at the Pit."

"We'll be up for it," Hudson assures him. "How badly could they hurt us in one night?"

"Oh, it's not physical," Calder says. "The Chamber never harms a hair on your head. But you'll be begging for mercy by the end." She puts her nail polish away, pulls her knees into her chest, and rocks a little.

"What does it do?" I ask, terrified to hear the answer.

"It makes you face the worst things you've ever done, over and over and over again, until it's sure that you've atoned for them *all*. Days, weeks, years." Remy's face is grim. "People go crazy from it—sometimes the first night, sometimes several months in. It simply depends on the person."

"And the crimes," Calder reminds him.

"And the crimes," Remy agrees. "So I guess you have to ask yourselves. What's the worst thing you've ever done?"

115

How Can You Tell the Future if There's No Future to Tell?

The question hangs in the air for what feels like forever after Remy asks it, growing bigger and bigger and bigger until it's all I can think about. All any of us can think about.

Flint is the first to move. He stands up and starts pacing, the look on his face telling everyone that he's already in a dark place.

Hudson doesn't react at all. His face stays blank, and he doesn't so much as move a muscle. But I'm holding his hand, and I can feel him trembling.

I try to catch his eye, but he's staring straight ahead, and I know he's going over and over and over those last days and weeks at Katmere before Jaxon killed him. I know at the time he thought he was doing the right thing, but I also know how much his mistakes hurt him now, in retrospect. The idea of having them shoved in his face all night—every night—seems beyond cruel.

"What if you don't want to play?" I ask abruptly. "What if you don't want to risk ending up in the Chamber?"

"The prison isn't completely cruel," Remy answers. "You simply don't slot yourself in for the spin. You stay exactly where you are. You can take six months to get to the Pit. Or you can take a year. Or you can take forever. But if you don't atone in the Chamber..."

"Then you never get the chance to leave," I fill in for him.

"Exactly."

"Fan-fucking-tastic," Flint growls from where he is still pacing, showing no sign of settling—or sitting—down.

"So we already know we don't have enough flowers to get all of us out of here, and we're six days from reaching the blacksmith," I say, ticking off the information that we have in an effort to make a plan—and to avoid my own stress about my own "crimes." I may not have used my mind to force people to kill themselves, but not standing up harder against Jaxon about the Unkillable Beast and then getting Xavier killed is not something I even like to think about, let alone relive again and again and again.

But if we do this thing, I am going to have to relive it. Until the prison thinks I've atoned enough and lets me go...or until we find a way to escape anyway.

Like Flint said. Fan-fucking-tastic.

"Out of curiosity," I say as I go over in my head everything Remy and Calder have told me. "What are the odds that we get to the Pit in six days and the prison decides we've atoned enough and just lets us go?"

"Zero," they both answer at once.

"Really?" I ask. "Even if we get the Chamber every night? There's still no way the prison will let us out?"

"We won't get the Chamber every night," Remy tells me. "It never happens like that. I heard a guard say once that everyone used to have to choose Chamber or pause. But over the centuries, the prison became overcrowded, so now we spin for who gets the Chamber each night. And I don't know if it's that or simply the way this fucked-up prison was built—but atonement is a joke. In seventeen years, I've never seen anyone rehabilitated by torture."

That's a chilling thought, and I can tell everyone is letting those words sink in.

Calder eventually breaks the silence. "Also, if we did end up getting the Chamber every night... No one can withstand what the Chamber does over and over and over again—especially if it's that close together."

"So we won't get it six times," I say, trying to sound upbeat. "We can do it two or three times, right?"

"Once is enough for a lifetime," Calder tells me, and she already sounds... empty. Like she, too, is in a dark place, and she's merely trying to figure out how to get through it.

"But I thought Remy said you two make this trip once a month?" I ask.

"We do," Remy agrees and winks at Calder. "Of course, Calder *is* particularly fond of nail polish."

I want to ask if she sniffs it, because who would voluntarily choose torture over no torture? But then my stomach starts to pitch as another reason comes to mind. Is what happens while on "pause" even worse than the Chamber?

My anxiety shifts into overdrive. Panic wells up inside me, and I bend over, start to take off my shoes, but then I realize the only thing I have to feel is cool, smooth metal, which will do nothing to calm me down.

I can't pull a breath into my lungs, can't think. I try to name things in the room to ground myself, but there's nothing here—and the room itself is built to make me anxious as hell. I grab on to my bedcovers, scrunch them in my hands, and try to concentrate on the feel of the fibers. But they're thin and again just reinforce where we are.

I start to count backward as my heart feels like it's going to explode, but then Hudson is there. Letting me feel the strength in his hand, feel our fingers brush against each other's, letting me ground myself...in him.

It's rough going for a couple of minutes, but he seems to know instinctively what to do to make me feel better. He doesn't crowd me, doesn't try to talk, doesn't do anything but be there with me. And eventually, I am able to breathe again.

"I'm sorry," I tell him when I finally feel normal—or as normal as I can feel in this situation.

His laugh is dark and painful to listen to. "Don't apologize to me. Not for this. Not for anything." He shakes his head, his jaw working. "I can't believe I did this to you."

"You didn't do this to me," I whisper fiercely. "I chose to come. We have a plan—"

"You chose to come because the alternative was just as bad. That's not a choice!"

"Don't do this, Hudson. We've been in this together from the beginning—don't change that now. And don't take my agency in this away from me. I make decisions for my life, not you. Not anybody else."

At first, he doesn't answer. But then he grabs me and pulls me to him until our bodies are only inches apart. "I don't want you to suffer any more because of me," he whispers. "I can't—" He breaks off, throat working.

"And I don't want you suffering because of me," I shoot back. "I don't want anyone in this room suffering. But we're in this together, right?" I look around to everyone else, who are all trying studiously not to listen...and failing.

"We're in this together, right?" I repeat. "Whatever happens, we're going to find the blacksmith and somehow, we're going to get out of this prison. I swear it."

I turn to Remy. "You see the future, so tell me, what do you see? You use the flower to get out, but what do the rest of us do?"

"I don't know," he admits.

"What do you mean, you don't know?" Flint demands.

His green eyes are swirling eerily, but then he shakes his head and they're back to normal. "It means, all I know is that I use the flower. So either you give it to me to use, or I kill you and take it, or you find another way out."

"Well, that's a hell of a lot of *or*s," Hudson growls, looking like he once again wants to rip him limb from limb.

"I can't see the future unless it's decided," Remy answers. "And right now, what happens to you is entirely up in the air."

116

The Price Is Fright

"Y̶ou're just the bearer of all the good news, aren't you?" Flint asks as he plops down on his bed.

"It's not my job to make you feel better about your choices in life," Remy tells him, and though the rolling syllables of his New Orleans accent are still readily apparent, there's an edge to his tone that hasn't been there since the very beginning.

"Yeah, well, I'm taking a nap. Wake me up when we need to do this Chamber thing." Flint closes his eyes, and it only takes a couple of minutes before his breathing evens out.

"Must be nice," Hudson mutters under his breath, and—not going to lie—I had the same thought. Sure, Flint was stressed out earlier about whatever he thinks the Chamber is going to throw at him, but apparently he's conquered the fear. Which is great for him, but I wish I could conquer my fear of the Chamber half as easily. The idea of seeing Xavier die again and again and again... I fight the urge to dive under my bedcovers and never come out.

"All right, guess we're going to play," Remy says, then presses a large button near the bed pulleys.

"Three hours before the spin," Calder says as she stretches out on top of her bed, too.

"How do you know?" Hudson asks.

She points to a series of small dots on the wall behind the tunnel chute. Three of them are lit a pale fluorescent blue.

"Are you sure you want to do this?" I ask her.

She shrugs. "You won't get out if we don't, so..."

"Yeah, but it doesn't seem fair to you," I say as it really sinks in what we're about to put Remy and Calder through.

She makes a *whatever* sound deep in her throat. "Nothing about this place is fair, Grace. The sooner you figure that out, the sooner you find a way to accept your time here." She shrugs. "Besides, I want out as much as the rest of you do. I'm willing to do whatever it takes to make that happen. Killing Cyrus once we get out—well, that's just icing on the cake."

It's the most thoughtful I've heard her since we met, which only makes me more concerned about what's coming. If it can do this to Calder...

Hudson stands up and then motions for me to do the same so he can pull back the covers. Once he does, I climb into bed and scoot all the way to the edge to make room for him.

He hesitates for a second, but I am not having it. "If all hell ends up breaking loose, I want to have spent these last three hours with your arms around me," I tell him softly.

He makes an agonized sound low in his throat but then scoots in behind me. He slides an arm under my head for me to use as a pillow, then wraps his other arm around my waist and pulls me into his body so that I can feel him completely enveloping me.

It feels so good. He feels so good. I melt into him, pressing myself even more tightly against him, so that all I can feel is him.

"No biting," Flint says sleepily, which probably means he isn't asleep after all. "Unless I get to watch, I mean. Then feel free to bite away, Hudson."

"You are such a perv," I tease.

"Only way to be," he jokes back. "Besides, that's the way you like me."

Hudson growls a little, but it's without heat and, judging by the little chuckle he gives, Flint knows it.

"We're going to get out of here," Hudson whispers against my ear, and the way he says it sounds like a vow. "And when we do, I'm going to do a hell of a lot more than disintegrate Cyrus's bones."

He doesn't say anything after that and neither do I. Instead, I snuggle closer and finally give in to the exhaustion that's been overwhelming me for days.

I don't know how long we sleep, but I do know that I don't wake up until I hit the ground. Hard.

Earthquake is my first thought, because you can take the girl out of California, but you can't take California out of the girl.

But the shaking is actually worse than an earthquake—which I realize when Calder yells, "Beds up!" like her life depends on it.

"We overslept," Remy shouts as he races for the chain behind the tube and yanks on it so hard that Flint almost doesn't make it out of bed in time.

"What's going on?" I ask, pushing to my knees. But the floor is still violently shaking, which makes it nearly impossible to climb to my feet.

The beds snap into their spot in the wall as Hudson barks, "Give me your hand."

He's got one foot braced against the wall as he reaches for me, but before I can grab on to him, the room starts to spin. For about three seconds, it's not so bad, and then it's like a switch is flipped and it goes from zero to three hundred in no time flat.

I get picked up and slammed against the wall like I'm on one of those carnival rides, the centrifugal force holding me pinned there as the room spins and spins and spins. Faster and faster we go until the simple act of lifting my hand off the wall becomes impossible.

Next to me, Calder is laughing like she's on a ride at Disneyland. My stomach didn't get that memo, though, and it twists and churns as the chicken from earlier threatens to make a very unpleasant reappearance.

Just when I'm sure I'm going to turn this into a real-life version of the Vomitron, we grind to a stop.

I slide back down the wall, never more grateful in my life for my feet to be touching solid ground. But as the cell settles back into place, all twenty-four dots on the countdown clock turn red at the same time—and so do the recessed ceiling lights.

Calder stops laughing and murmurs, "Well, fuck."

And that's when I know.

We got the Chamber.

117

Hell Hath No Fury
Like a Prison Scorned

Remy reaches for my hand.

"What happens now?" I ask, but I get my answer before Remy even says a word.

Across from me, Hudson's eyes roll back in his head, and he crumples to the ground.

I scream, then easily pull free of Remy's hold and make a mad dash across the cell.

"Oh my God, Hudson! Hudson!" I turn to Remy, start to ask what the hell is going on. And realize that Calder and Flint are also passed out on the ground.

My blood turns cold.

"Is this what the Chamber does?" I whisper.

"It is, yeah." He shrugs. "No worries, though. They're fine."

"They're *passed out*. How fine could they be?" I check Hudson's pulse to be sure.

"Better asleep than awake." He walks back over to the chain and unrolls the beds from the wall again. "No one needs to be conscious when going through what's happening to them right now."

"Is it really that bad?" I ask as I smooth a hand down Hudson's face before moving on to check on Flint, then Calder.

Remy's right. They're both breathing fine.

"Worse," he answers, even as he picks up Calder and carries her to her bed.

"What can we do to help them?"

"Nothing to do but wait," he answers, even as he tucks Calder under her sheet and blanket. "The Chamber will let them go…when it's ready."

I watch in silence as he carries first Hudson and then Flint to their beds, too, all without so much as breaking a sweat. Once all three of them are settled—and I've checked a second time to assure myself that they really are okay—I ask Remy the question that's been on my mind since the minute I realized what was happening to everyone else.

"I don't understand," I say as he stretches out on his bed, a well-worn book in his hand.

"Why didn't the Chamber take me?" I think about how Hudson, Flint, and Calder are suffering God only knows what and here I am, hanging out and feeling just fine, as guilt swamps me. It's not right. "Why Calder? Or Flint? Or—"

"Hudson?" Remy lifts a brow. "That's who you really want to know about, right?"

"He's had a rough time," I tell him. "What he has to face—"

"He'll face or he won't. There's nothing either of us can do about that."

"But there is," I tell him. "Obviously there is. Somehow the Chamber skipped me, so maybe it could skip them one night."

"It didn't skip you. I kept you out."

My eyes widen in shock. "If you can keep people out, why not the others?"

"That's just it," Remy tells me with a shake of his head. "I can't keep anyone else out. Only you."

"What do you mean, you can't? Why not?"

"Don't you think I've tried to keep Calder out before? Every time. It doesn't work. But I knew the minute we met that I would keep you out, simply by touching your hand. I don't know why—I just saw it, so I did it when the time came."

"Why didn't you say something before we got the Chamber?"

"Seemed no point in upsetting anyone else over me already knowing we were getting the Chamber tonight." He shrugs. "And before you ask again, I have no idea how I can keep you out but no one else. There's something about you that lets my limited magic work."

What he's saying makes a horrible kind of sense. It's probably my gargoyle. She's hidden under layers of metal, but she's still a part of me. And the one thing she's very good at is channeling magic.

Which doesn't make me feel remotely less guilty.

Hudson was so afraid of the Chamber. He never said a word to me, never let on about anything but that tremor he couldn't hide. But I know he was afraid, know he couldn't stand the idea of facing what he'd done in his past.

There must be something more Remy can do, but his face is closed. There's no way I'll get anything else out of him now.

But that doesn't mean I won't be able to try again later...and to maybe convince him to give holding on to Hudson a bigger try if we ever hit the Chamber again.

It's not that I'm anxious for another turn at whatever is doing this to two of the strongest guys I know. If things go the way I'm really, really hoping, we'll never hit the Chamber again. But if we do...if we do, it's only fair that I take a turn going through hell.

I settle onto my bed and just stare at Hudson next to me, ready to go to him if he needs me. I don't know how long I sit there watching him. I don't have any idea what time it is, either—they took my phone from me, and it's not like they have a clock in here other than those horrible lit dots on the wall that count down every hour—but I'm dying to know how much longer this is going to go on. It feels like I've been waiting an eternity for the three of them to wake up. But all twelve lights are still lit, which means this hasn't been going on for even an hour.

"How much longer?" I ask Remy, because if this is going to last all night, I need to prepare myself for it.

He glance at the lights on the wall, then shrugs. "It usually takes about an hour and a half, so maybe an hour more."

"An hour and a half," I repeat, relieved. "That's not so bad."

Remy snorts. "Maybe not for you, *cher*, but for them?" He shakes his head. "It's like dreaming. You know how when you're having a really elaborate dream, a ten-minute nap can feel like eight hours of sleep? That's what it's like in there for them right now. This shit is assaulting them from every angle, and they feel like hours are passing."

"I'm really beginning to hate this place," I tell him, hands clenched at my sides.

"And you haven't even been here twenty-four hours. Think about how the rest of us feel."

"I'm curious. If you've been in prison your whole life, why do you have a Cajun drawl like a native from New Orleans?" I turn my head to stare at him. He's got one leg crossed at the knee, a book leaning against it while he's lying down. "Have you really never been out?"

He doesn't answer at first, but eventually he sighs and admits, "The prison guards and creatures in the Pit raised me. Most of them are from N'Awlins, so I just sort of picked it up."

"I can't even imagine. I—"

It's Hudson's turn to scream now, over and over again. It's eerie, because he's not actually making much noise at all. Though his mouth is fully open, stretched wide, the only thing that comes out is an agonized whisper so awful that it chills me to my bones.

I go to him then. I can't *not* go to him when he sounds like that, looks like that. He's still asleep, still totally out of it, but when I brush my fingers over his hair, he grabs on to my hand and holds it for long seconds as he screams and screams and screams.

It breaks something inside me to see him like this, and I sink onto my knees even as I bring my other hand up to cup his cheek, brush against his hair, rub over his arm and shoulder and back.

Eventually, the screaming stops, but his grip on my hand never does. So I stay with him the whole time, watching every flicker of horror cross his face. Feeling every twitch of his body, hearing every silent scream and plea.

It's the longest ninety minutes of my life, and that's coming from someone who's been tied up on a human-sacrifice altar waiting for death. But being here, witnessing Hudson's and Flint's and Calder's pain and shame, is by far the worst thing I've ever experienced. And all I'm doing is watching. I can't imagine what it feels like for them.

Hudson whimpers again, and I lean over him, whisper that I'm here, that everything is going to be okay, but I don't know if that's true. I would take his pain if I could, go through watching Xavier die a million times if it meant sparing Hudson this. But I can't, so I do the only thing I can do right now—sit here holding on to him and praying for it to be over soon.

Eventually the red lights click back to normal.

The dots on the wall reset themselves to green.

And Hudson's lashes finally flutter open.

I've never been more relieved to see someone wake up in my life. At least until he looks at me and whispers, "I don't deserve to ever leave."

118

Long Time
Gone From Grace

"**O**h, Hudson." I reach for him, but he turns away, tucks himself into a ball like he's trying to protect himself. From what? I wonder. The Chamber...or me?

It doesn't make any sense that it would be me, but every time I try to touch him, he shudders a little, like he can't stand it. Which ends up freaking me out, because that's definitely not a problem Hudson and I usually have. Normally, he can't wait to have my hands on him.

He's shuddering now, his whole body trembling like he's freezing cold. I want to go to him, want to hold him until he can warm up—another problem he usually doesn't have—but I'm afraid of what will happen if I try to touch him. Because every time I try to get near him, he shrinks away.

But he's shivering so badly that I can't just do nothing—especially when his teeth start to chatter.

Not knowing what else to do, I go back to my bed and strip the thin blanket off it. It's not much, but it's better than nothing. I place it over Hudson, on top of the sheet and blanket he's already got on him. I'm tempted to tuck it in around him, but I hold back.

He's already so freaked out that I don't want to do anything to make it worse.

My stomach is pitching and rolling like we're still spinning around, and for a second, I think I'm going to be sick.

I take a couple of deep breaths, breathing in through my nose so I can keep my jaw firmly locked against the nausea churning deep inside me. But when Flint lets out a low scream and jerks so hard that he slams onto the floor next to his bed, I know I'm going to lose the fight.

I race to the bathroom and throw up everything in my stomach, then deal with several rounds of dry heaves as well. I know Remy said the Chamber was bad—he and Calder both did—but I didn't expect anything like this.

Not when Hudson and Flint have both proven that they are more than happy to walk into hell if they have to—and come out the other side making jokes. For them to be acting like this?

Another wave of sickness hits me.

When it's finally over, I make myself stand up. Make myself brush my teeth with one of the brand-new toothbrushes that came through the hole with our dinner.

Make myself rinse off my face and take several deep breaths to try to calm down.

There's no mirror in here, but I don't need one to know what I look like right now. Limp hair, ashen skin, eyes wide and bruised-looking.

I feel like I've been run over by a herd of rampaging elephants, followed by half a dozen city buses and an eighteen-wheeler or two. And I didn't even have to go in the Chamber.

I walk back through the bathroom door when all I really want to do is hide in here forever and move to Flint, who is awake now but still lying on the ground, curled full-on into the fetal position.

I struggle and help him back into his bed despite the way he flinches away from me, too. And the way he looks at me with horror-drenched eyes.

After Flint is taken care of, I glance at Calder and realize that Remy must have taken care of her when I was in the bathroom. She, too, is tucked under the covers, and while she's not curled up like Hudson and Flint, her fists are clenched and her mouth is stretched open in a silent scream.

I move back to check on Hudson. Unlike Flint and Calder, he's still awake. Even worse, he pushes himself all the way back against the head of the bed when he sees me walking toward him—like he can't get far enough away from me.

It hurts, but I have no idea what he suffered in the Chamber. I have no right to judge—or be hurt by—him wanting nothing to do with me. Or, more, that he seems scared of me.

I stand near the end of his bed for a while, trying to decide what to do. He looks like he needs comfort—more comfort than I think it might be possible to give—but he's also made it clear that he doesn't want any of that comfort to come from me.

In the end, I walk back to my bed and sit down in the center of it. Then

I pull my knees to my chest and prepare for a never-ending night.

It isn't long before Calder lets out a guttural scream, and Flint rolls over and presses shaking hands to his ears.

"Is it happening again?" I ask Remy, and even I can hear the fear in my voice.

But Remy shakes his head. "It usually happens like this. Calder can sleep for up to ten hours after she's been in the Chamber."

"Ten hours?" I ask, horrified. I can't take ten more hours of not being able to reach Hudson, of not being able to talk to him, to see his eyes, to make sure he's okay.

"Consider it a blessing. The nightmares only last for a few minutes, and then they'll settle back down."

I hope he's right, but the way they're tossing and turning makes the theory sound pretty far-fetched. "This is awful."

Remy shrugs. "It is what it is."

He sounds callous as he goes back to reading the book he must have pulled out of his underbed drawer, but then I realize two things at once. One, he's had to go through this who knows how many times with Calder, and the only way for him to survive without losing it is to put some distance between him and the process. And two? The book he's "reading" is upside down, which means he's nowhere near as untouched by all of this as he wants me to believe.

I think about calling him on it, but before I can say anything, Flint shoots up out of bed with a hoarse scream.

"It's okay," I tell him, rushing over to sit on the bed next to him. "You're okay."

He's shaking so badly that I'm afraid he's going to end up falling off the bed again. I take his hand, try to calm him. At least until he opens his eyes and realizes I'm the one holding his hand. He flinches, instinctively holding a palm up in front of his face, like he thinks I'm going to hit him.

"It's okay, Flint," I tell him soothingly. "Whatever you dreamed, it wasn't real. It was—"

"It was real," he tells me hoarsely, and he's pulling his covers up like he wants to hide underneath them.

Like he wants to hide from me.

Which freaks me out enough that I stand up, hands in the air to show him that I'm not going to hurt him...or even touch him. It doesn't seem to make much of an impression through the fear, though, so I back away, tears in my own eyes.

As Flint settles into an exhausted sleep, I turn to look at Calder. And realize she's finally settled down, too, though her cheeks are still wet with tears.

And fuck this, just fuck it. The Chamber and its aftermath are truly the most horrible things I've ever witnessed. Whoever devised this prison was a monster. And so is anyone who sentences people here.

Fuck them all.

Seven hours later—at least according to the ridiculous dots on the wall that are back to counting down to tonight's Chamber—breakfast comes through the slot in the floor. Remy and I don't even glance at it. If I try to eat now, I'm positive that I'll throw up again.

Instead, I cuddle on Hudson's bed behind him, curling my body against his. He's still trembling badly as I wrap my arm around his waist, but at least he's asleep. And not trying to get away from me anymore.

But as I lay here listening to the too-fast beating of his heart, I can't help thinking that there has to be another way.

Can't help thinking that we can't go through this for five or six more nights.

Because if we do...if we do, the question won't be about how we get out anymore.

It will be about who we are when we finally do.

119

Big Stick Energy

Hudson wakes up about an hour later, though he looks like he hasn't slept at all. His hair is disheveled, yes, but not in the sexy way I'm used to. It's more like a been-to-hell-and-I'm-still-living-there look. The fact that Flint and Calder are sporting the afro and prom queen versions of his not-so-pompadour look only makes everything feel so much worse.

He sits up, and I try to reach for him, but he evades my hands, and I end up clutching at air.

He walks straight to the bathroom and turns on the shower. It runs and runs and runs for what feels like forever.

Remy, on the other hand, has pulled a couple of wrapped packages out of the drawer under his bed—apparently he's got an entire convenience store in there. "Get ready," he tells me over his shoulder.

"For what?"

Calder smiles and tosses her long red hair like she's in a fifties movie set and she's the main pinup girl. Only the fine tremor in her hands betrays that she's as shaken up as Hudson in her own way. "To channel your inner badass, of course."

I have no idea what that means, but I glance over at Flint to share a grin. And also because I expect him to have all sorts of questions—that's the kind of proclamation that usually has him intrigued. But he's just sitting on his bed, arms wrapped around himself as he stares off into space.

I cross the cell with some vague idea of offering comfort and whisper, "Hey." I don't bother to ask if he's okay. It's clear he's very, very far from okay.

But Flint pulls away, wraps his arms even more tightly around himself, and stares anywhere and everywhere but at me. When our gazes do glance off each other's by sheer luck, I can't help but notice that the bags under his eyes could take up half the cargo area on a 747.

It's terrifying, and it makes me wonder exactly what happens in the Chamber if it did this to two of the strongest guys I know. I want to give Flint a hug, want to wrap myself around Hudson and hold him until he can look at me again, but neither of them seems like they want to be touched... or even spoken to.

"Not sure any of our inner badasses are functioning today," I finally tell Calder as I sink back down onto my bed to wait for Hudson to get out of the shower.

"Well, you'd better find them, *cher*," Remy tells me. "Because we've only got fifteen minutes before it starts."

Now I'm getting alarmed. "What's *it*?" I ask warily.

"Hex time," Calder answers. "And unless you want to be thought of as new meat, you and your friends had better pull things together."

I've watched enough prison movies to know what "new meat" means, and the thought has my stomach churning. Not because I don't think we can take care of ourselves in a situation like this, but because I don't want to have *to be* in a situation like this. I don't want to have to fight anyone, and I sure as hell don't want to pick a fight with someone. Isn't having to deal with the Chamber bad enough for Flint and Hudson? Do they really have to beat people down, too? During something called Hex time, of all things?

"What exactly is Hex time?" Flint asks. And though he doesn't crack a joke like he normally would, at least he's asking questions. That's something, right?

"Time in the Hex," Calder answers...which tells us absolutely nothing.

"And the Hex is..." I give her an I-have-no-idea-what-you're-saying look.

"It's the yard," Remy answers. When I still look at him blankly, he rolls his eyes and continues. "We get two hours a day out of our cells. Most of the time is spent in the Hex, though once you've been here a few weeks and earned privileges, you can go to the library and a few other places."

"How exactly do you earn privileges?" I ask warily.

"By not getting into fights with the people who want to get into fights with you," Remy tells me like it's the most obvious thing in the world.

"Except you have to get into fights," Calder says. "And win. Or they'll eat you alive."

"Me?" I squeak, because there's still a part of me that can't believe this is happening, That can't believe I am actually having this conversation right now. In prison.

I mean, yeah, we've all seen the movies where they say pick the biggest guy in the prison and show no fear, but I never thought it would be advice that applied to me. It's all fun and games when Groot picks up the guy by the nose in *Guardians of the Galaxy*. Here, it seems like a nightmare instead.

"Can we just stay in our rooms? And not go out there at all?" I suggest nervously.

"It's required," Calder says as Remy goes to knock on the bathroom door and tell Hudson to shake a leg. "And if you hide in here, it'd be like saying you're easy pickings anyway."

Of course it would. "So basically there's no winning, is what you're saying?"

"I'm not saying that at all." Calder fluffs her hair again. "What I'm saying is go out there and be your beautiful, badass self. Walk the Hex like you mean it—and carry a big stick."

I recognize the Teddy Roosevelt quote but still, I can't resist responding, "I don't have a big stick."

She rolls her eyes. "Sure you do. You've got Remy and me. We're pretty much the biggest stick there is in this place."

"Speak for yourself," Remy says in his slowest drawl. "I'm a lover, not a fighter."

Calder laughs like he's said the funniest thing ever, and I can't help thinking back to what the guards said earlier—about how the last person to get dropped into Remy's cell was taken out in pieces. Once we met Calder, I kind of figured that was because of her—I mean, that growl was enough to make me tear *myself* into pieces preemptively, just to avoid whatever she's got planned for me.

But maybe it's Remy after all. There is something about him that screams he can handle himself and everyone and everything else that comes along. Kind of like Hudson, now that I think about it. But in a totally different package.

"Okay, then." I swallow past the lump in my throat. "Anything else we need to know about how to survive in this place?"

"Don't take shite from anyone," Hudson says as he walks out of the bathroom. His hair is still wet, which means it's down and falling over his forehead. It's the first time I've seen him like this, and despite his tough words, it makes him look...vulnerable. Then again, that could be the look in his eyes. Guarded, distant, vacant.

Despite all that, he still looks sexy as all get out. Of course, this is Hudson Vega we're talking about. I'm pretty sure the method to take away from his sexiness hasn't been invented yet.

"Exactly." Calder grins and bats her eyes. "Hudson gets what I'm saying."

I glance at Hudson, hoping to catch his eye to share a little smile about how ridiculous—and ridiculously adorable—Calder is. But he's deliberately not looking at me, so there's nothing for me to do but share a grin with Remy, who shakes his head in a gotta-love-her kind of way.

I start to say more, but before I can, all the lights in the room turn blue.

"Hex time?" I ask nervously.

"Hex time," Remy answers, right before the small trapdoor in the floor slides open.

120

Why Turn the Other Cheek When You Can Smack It?

"**W**hat do we do first?" Flint asks as we wait for the steepest, narrowest staircase I've ever seen to descend at a painfully glacial pace. It's going so slowly that I'm pretty sure I could rappel down faster, and I am terrible at rock climbing.

"I've got some rounds to make—a couple of packages to deliver," Remy says. "You can come along if you like."

"Or you can come with me," Calder says. "I'm way more fun than Remy anyway."

Remy doesn't argue, just gives a rueful tilt of his head that seems to say, *Yeah she is.*

"What are you going to do?" I ask her, because I'm not sure Calder and I have the same definition of "fun." Like, at all.

Her teeth glisten in the bright lights of our room. "Find a game, of course."

"A game?" Flint asks, like it's the last answer he expected.

"We're going to be at the Pit in a few days," she explains. "Which means we're going to need money. Which means..."

"We need to find a game to bet on?" I finish for her.

"Exactly," she answers.

"What kind of games are we talking about here?" Hudson asks.

"Don't worry. There's a game for every appetite," Calder tells him, looking him up and down like he's a prize horse...of the stallion variety.

"Lucky us," he answers, even as he wraps an arm around my shoulders. I'm pretty sure it's in self-defense—Calder is getting more and more brazen—but that's okay. I'm more than happy to run a little interference for him.

Plus, I like the way he feels against me. And the way he finally looks at me as I snuggle even closer beneath his arm. Like I'm everything he wants all rolled into one.

And I know—I know—this is a bad idea, playing at being mates when we know how this has to end. But it's hard to ignore the pull between us now that we're locked up in such close quarters. Even harder to ignore the way he feels about me when it's written all over his face...and also harder to ignore my suspicion that I'm falling for him, too. Or worse, that I've fallen for him already. And that the idea of giving him up hurts way more than I want it to—way more than I can stand right now.

But what else am I supposed to do? Let Jaxon lose his soul—let him become what he fears most—when I have a chance of preventing it? I can't do that. More, I won't do that. But the pain is already there, waiting for me—waiting for us. What will it hurt if, just for a little while, I pretend that Hudson is mine? And let him pretend that I am his?

"About time!" Flint says, and I realize the ladder has hit the ground. "Let's go."

"Ready?" Hudson asks me, brow raised.

"Not even a little bit."

"Aww, come on. It'll be fun," Calder tells me with a huge grin. "There's a bunch of new inmates recently—I know we can hustle some of them into arm wrestling."

"Umm..." I look from her gigantic biceps to my very-much-not-gigantic one and suggest, "Maybe I should sit that game out."

"Well, obviously, Curls." She rolls her eyes in a friendly way. "I was talking to the vamp."

"My mistake," I say with a laugh as I duck out from under Hudson's arm. "By all means, hustle away."

"I intend to," she says with a waggle of her brows. Just before she slaps Hudson right on the ass. "Move it or lose it, partner."

And then she dives down the steps.

"Did she..." Hudson looks at me with bemused eyes.

"She did," I tell him. "I think it was a teammate thing. You know, like how football players smack each other on the ass right before they go into battle."

"I know. But I think that's the first time anyone has smacked my bum since I was..." He pauses to think about it, then shakes his head. "No, that's the first time anyone has *ever* smacked my bum."

He doesn't sound upset so much as contemplative.

"Look at you," Flint teases as he follows Calder down. "All kinds of new experiences in prison."

"If it makes you feel better, I can slap the other cheek," Remy deadpans. "Even you out."

Hudson rolls his eyes. "I think I'm good. Thanks, though."

Remy shrugs philosophically. "Your loss, *teammate*." And then he, too, disappears down the stairs.

I start after him, but Hudson grabs my hand and pulls me back into his arms.

"Oh yeah?" I ask with a flirty grin as I wrap my arms around his waist. "You want me to slap you on the ass instead of Remy?"

He pretends to think about it, then grins and says, "Anytime." Right before he lowers his mouth to mine.

It's a sweet kiss, a quick kiss, and still it has me going all soft and melty inside. Maybe that's why I slide my hand a little lower and slap the other ass cheek, just like Remy suggested.

Hudson laughs—like, full-on cracks up—and I know I did it because nothing in the world makes me happier than seeing Hudson laugh.

"Let's go," I tell him as I head for the stairs. "Last one down has to arm wrestle Calder."

The fact that he doesn't even try to beat me to the bottom shows what a gentleman Hudson truly is.

121

It's Only a Food Fight
if the Food Fights Back

It appears the Hex comes by its name legitimately.

Partly because it's a huge room, at least two football fields wide, with six sides, and partly because everyone in it is trying to pull some kind of magic to screw everyone else over—without any actual magic, of course, thanks to the bracelets.

The room itself is lit up as brightly as Times Square on a Saturday night. But that's where the light ends, because everything about this place is dark.

Dark and deadly and devastating—that's basically how I'd sum it up, and not only because I'm a whore for alliteration.

Guards are stationed every ten feet along the stained and scarred walls— and can I just say that in daylight, the really creepy moose-like things with translucent skin are a thousand times scarier than at night. And I didn't think that was possible.

"What are those things?" I whisper to Hudson as we pass by the biggest one in the room. He guards the main entrance to the place, and though he's dressed in a relatively plain olive-green uniform, I can still see the veins and muscles and, in some cases, *bone* directly under his skin. Add in the really scary teeth and the even scarier claws and I can see why he doesn't need a weapon. He *is* the weapon.

"Windigos," Hudson replies quietly. "You don't want to mess with them."

"Yeah, no shit," I say.

"Seriously. They're vicious and they eat humans, so don't get on their radar."

"They're not so bad," Remy says. "I mean, don't piss them off, but as long as you're cool, I can almost guarantee they won't eat you."

"You know, that 'almost guarantee' thing of yours is super effective in calming nerves," Flint tells him as he side-eyes another guard.

"That's Bertha," Remy says. "She definitely won't hurt you...unless you mess with me."

"So what you're saying is that I shouldn't slap you on the ass, then?" Hudson deadpans.

"That would depend," Remy says after he stops laughing, "on whether or not you want to have a hand left when you're done. She's particularly fond of barbecued finger bones."

"Everyone's got a favorite," Flint agrees, and I can tell he's forcing it, but I appreciate the effort. "Mine's chocolate cake, but who am I to judge? I mean, barbecue's good, too."

"You really are ridiculous," I tell him. "You know that, right?"

"How could I not when you keep telling me?" he answers with a wink.

"So what do we do now?" Hudson asks.

"Now we find some people to relieve of their funds," Calder tells him as she nods toward a group of misfit paranormals sitting together at a couple of tables in the center of the room. Unlike most of the other groups in the cavernous Hex, this one doesn't seem to be made up predominantly of one kind of paranormal. Instead, there is a mix of species—fairies, dragons, witches, vampires, and a bunch of others I can't identify in their human forms.

"You're really going to arm wrestle?" Remy asks, shooting her an amused look as we pass a group of what I'm pretty sure are warlocks, covered from head to toe in runic and other ancient magical tattoos.

Drawn on the ground in front of them is a black pentagram, and inside it they're rolling dice. I look closer, expecting to see magical symbols on the dice, but instead they're just the regular, six-sided dice with dots on them that most of the world plays with.

"What's going on over there?" I ask as a paranormal type I don't recognize rolls inside the pentagram. She comes up with a one and a two. The warlock running the game laughs and holds out a hand. She rolls her eyes, but she slaps a gold coin into his palm before reaching for the dice again.

"Can't load magic dice." Calder sneers. "So unless the person playing demands otherwise, those necrolytes use regular dice and get the gullible and the unsuspecting."

"Do a lot of people demand otherwise?" I ask.

"Are you kidding? It's the Hex. No one trusts anyone," she answers. "Even the good guys."

"Are there any good guys down here?" I ask while eyeing a bunch of different paranormals I am in no way equipped to identify yet.

"We're here, aren't we?" Remy asks.

"And yet Calder is planning on using Hudson to sucker in new bets," I remind him.

"That doesn't make me evil," Calder says with assurance.

"What does it make you, then?" I ask.

"Hey, I simply play on vanity. Those guys cheat—it's not the same thing," she tells him, even as she stares at Hudson and says, "Look more pathetic."

"Excuse me?" He lifts a brow.

"Channel some of that *just got out of the Chamber* shit you had going on earlier. No one's gonna believe you can't kick their ass when you walk around looking like that." She bats her eyes at him. "Honestly, right now you look almost as good as I do."

"So why would they believe you can't kick their ass?" Hudson asks, and though his face is serious, I can tell he's completely amused.

"Because." She makes an *obviously* face at him even as she holds her arms out wide. "Feminine wiles, baby. Feminine wiles."

"Grace has feminine wiles, too," Flint says as he nudges me with his shoulder.

"Yeah, but that's all she has." She makes a *pfft* noise. "What's she going to do? Strangle them with her curls?"

"I didn't realize I needed to strangle anyone," I answer mildly.

"Exactly!" she says triumphantly, which leaves me wondering how and why she plans to strangle her arm-wrestling victims. And why she thinks doing so would help her collect her winnings.

It also makes me determined to prove my worth somehow—even if it isn't in the arm-wrestling arena. If I had my gargoyle, I'd be able to do a lot of things. Without her, I'm merely regular old Grace. But these people are without their powers, too, which means at least I've got a shot.

We pass another group of paranormals—fairies, I think, judging by the small wings and multicolored hair. They're running a shell game with a gold coin, and I watch with interest as they take their mark for way more than what that gold coin he's chasing is worth.

In the corner is a group of wolves running a blackjack game, and though I don't wait around to see what they're doing—or how they're doing it—it's obvious they tried something, if the pissed-off player is any indication. In fact, he's pissed enough that I hurry my group along before—

A chair goes flying, crashing into the dealer, as the player screams about cheating. He barely gets a few words in edgewise, though, before another wolf is on him, strong fist around a neck. And that's when all hell breaks loose. The player was obviously a troll, because a mess of trolls descend on the wolves' game en masse, which leads to a bunch of wolves doing the same thing.

Blood and bodies are flying as Remy hustles us along, but the commotion doesn't last long, because two of the guards hit the game running. The biggest one skewers a wolf through the shoulder with one of his long nails and then holds him up so everyone can see, while the second one grabs the troll who started everything and rips his leg clean off…right before he starts to eat it.

The troll is screaming, blood is flowing freely, and the other guards are circling with their teeth bared and their claws at the ready. My stomach roils at the carnage, and I almost vomit but just manage to swallow it down. I can only imagine what weakness that would have shown in a place like this. I'm terrified to see what happens next but even more terrified when I realize that most of the people in this place barely even notice.

Remy and Calder do little more than give the bleeding troll a look before moving on with their agenda. I, on the other hand, can't stop seeing the windigo start to eat the troll's leg, even though Hudson has his arms around me and my face pressed into his chest.

"We need to get out of here," I whisper to him as my stomach twists and turns in a desperate effort to throw up what's left of the chicken from earlier.

"It's only two hours," he tells me. "It'll be over—"

"No, not the Hex. This prison. We can't stay here. We can't—"

"Not so loud, Curls," Calder says, her mouth inches from my ear. "The last thing you want to do is broadcast our agenda in this place. We'll end up in solitary confinement in three minutes flat…and probably missing a limb or two while we're at it."

After what we just saw, I believe it. What kind of a prison employs guards who actually like to eat the inmates? I mean, yeah, it probably does away with that pesky prison overcrowding problem, but it's also murder. Why put people here to punish them—and make them atone—for violent crimes if you're then going to let the people who run it commit as many violent crimes as they want?

It makes no sense, but even more than that, it's wrong. Just plain wrong.

"Keep walking," Remy says, and for once there is an urgency in his voice that refuses to be ignored.

So we do, stepping one foot in front of the other, even though all three of us are shaken.

Hudson seems the most unaffected by what we just witnessed, but he did spend a huge part of his life in Cyrus and Delilah's Court. Who knows what he saw there?

We don't stop moving until the commotion has died down and we're right in the center of the Hex, standing in front of a table of "infergins," or marks, as Calder calls them.

They all look a little lost, a little confused, and a little scared, but none of them runs away when Calder plops herself down on the tabletop they are all sitting around and asks, "Who wants to play a game?"

122

What the Hex?

"Are you going to eat us if we do?" asks the lone demon from his spot at the end of the table.

Calder blows him a kiss. "Only if you ask nicely."

"Does that work in reverse?" calls one of the two vampires who have been eyeing her ever since we got here.

"Only if you ask nicely," she says again, and this time the whole table laughs. "I will tell you one thing, though. To the victor go the spoils. Right, Hudson?"

My mate doesn't say anything to that, simply inclines his head in a whatever-you-say-goes kind of way.

But he looks adorable when he does it—which is not lost on much of his audience. That and the eyebrow wiggle Calder gives the group of them is all it takes to set off a stampede.

I don't know if it's because one of the regulars is finally acknowledging their existence or if it's because they're just that taken with Calder and Hudson, but the infergins nearly trample themselves in their enthusiasm to get to the front of the line. Before I know it, every single one of them has put up a gold coin for the privilege of wrestling either Calder or Hudson.

Calder puts up money for each of them as well, and I wonder how many coins she's got with her. Both of them have long lines—nearly twenty-five people deep for each of them—surely they won't win them all. Some of their competition is huge. There are also other vampires, and while I'm sure Hudson can take care of them, I'm not so sure about Calder.

I know she's really strong—that's obvious—but is she strong enough to take on a fully grown vampire in his prime? Especially if she can't access her manticore side?

My stomach clenches nervously as the first two people come up to wrestle them. Each slaps his coin on the table next to Hudson's and Calder's and then slides into their chairs, arms up.

Hudson and Calder lean forward as one and lock hands with their competition. And then Flint—who has somehow been roped into acting as referee—announces the rules. "Butts in chairs at all times, one arm only, winner takes the bet, and the ref calls all ties. Those are the rules. If you don't like them, hit the road now."

No one moves or complains, so Flint continues. "We go on three. One, two, three!"

It's over before he even finishes the word, Calder and Hudson slamming their oppositions' arms down on the table so hard that I can't help wondering if they're going to leave dents.

They don't, but I'm pretty sure at least one wrist got sprained.

The second and third matches go essentially the same way, but the fourth match pits Hudson against an actual giant. Calder wins her match against the demon, but Hudson gets his ass handed to him.

He takes the loss with a grin and a joke, and soon the tense atmosphere that's invaded the competition goes away and everyone's having a good time—unlike most of the other games in this place.

Soon after, Remy heads off with his two mysterious packages, and I decide to wander a little bit, as the other three are still all wrapped up in their arm-wrestling game. Normally I'd stick close, but I'm smarting a little over Calder's comments about my feminine wiles being the only thing of value I've got.

At the same time, I don't go too far—that seems like a bad move, considering what I just saw happen with the wolves and the troll. I like my limbs exactly where they are, thank you very much.

So instead of wandering toward one of the guards, I stick close to the tables at the center of the Hex, looking for something to catch my interest.

The first thing I come to are a bunch of dragons in human form who are running some kind of card game. They're in bad shape, their human skin scraped up and full of sores that makes me feel horrible for them. The prison's fault, I wonder, or maybe the Chamber's?

I wander past a group of small paranormals with wings, multicolored hair, and rows upon rows of sharp teeth. Fairies, I wonder? Pixies? Or something else entirely? I don't know, but one of them smiles at me and tries to suck me into buying some kind of iridescent powder from them. Near them are selkies who are selling vials of some kind of water...seawater, maybe? I end up watching a game of Razzle-Dazzle run by two witches—the younger of whom reminds me a lot of my friend Gwen, with her sleek black hair and shy grin.

Except the longer I stand here, the more I realize she uses that smile to her advantage, to convince people that there's nothing shady about her game. But I've played this a bunch of times—Heather's dad is a math professor and he loved nothing more than demonstrating to us how different games were sucker games...and also how to beat them.

When the last player gives up in disgust—but without throwing a fit to attract the guards' attention, thankfully—I slide into the open seat.

"You're new here," says the old witch who runs the game.

"I am," I agree.

"Who are you with?"

I don't know what she means, and it must show on my face, because she laughs and says, "Who brought you here?"

"Oh, Remy and Calder. They're—"

"Everyone knows Remy," she tells me, and there's a softness in her voice when she speaks of him that is unexpected...but also not. She must be one of the longtimers here, who's known Remy since he was very little. "But I do have to say, I'm surprised he let you out of his sight."

"He's busy," I tell her with a shrug. "And I thought your game looked like fun."

The witches exchange a look. "Oh, it's definitely that," says the youngest one. "Want to play?"

"I do, actually." I look at the familiar board, with its seemingly random arrangement of numbers between one and six, and try to figure out if there's a pattern. Like Heather's dad teaches his advanced math students, this one has a lot of fours, a lot of ones, and not very many fives or sixes. The big numbers are concentrated mostly in the center of the board, which very few people notice is slanted a little bit higher than the rest of the board, so the marbles I roll will fall away from the center.

"But I don't have any money on me to bet with."

"None?" the witch asks, and she is obviously astonished.

"None," I reiterate, and I feel like a jerk. The whole point of these games is money. How did I think to sit down without so much as a dollar to my name?

The truth is, I've been so annoyed at Calder's comments about me that I just didn't think. "I'm sorry. I'll leave."

"Not so fast." The witch's wizened old claw grasps on to my arm, keeps me in place. "Do you have nothing of value on you at all?"

I start to say no but then stick my hand in my pockets—and find one gold coin. I have no idea how it got there, but it had to be Calder or Remy. I'll have to remember to thank them later.

"How many games does this buy me?"

Quick as lightning, her hand flashes out and grabs it as avarice burns in her eyes. "One game," she tells me. "If you win—"

"One?" I ask, incredulous. "No thank you." I reach to take it back, and she snarls—literally snarls—as she yanks it out of my reach.

"How about ten games?" the younger witch suggests. "You can play five. If, at any time, your numbers add up to win one of the prizes"—she gestures to the various pile of coins behind the winning combinations of twenty-six, eighteen, forty-one, and thirty-two—"you take the coin and the prize. If you lose the game, the coin is ours."

The older witch is grinning now, and though I know the deal favors them— or so they think—I decide to go for it. All of Heather's dad's instructions are running through my head as I take the handful of marbles and roll them near the bottom of the board.

They land all over the place, and when we add them up, they equal nineteen. No prize.

The old witch hisses in delight.

"Four more," the young witch tells me as she hands me back the marbles to roll.

I shake them a little more this time and roll them again. They end up totaling twenty-three—still no winner.

The older witch leans forward, a macabre grin on her face. "Three more turns, my pretty."

I nod and then take my time shaking the marbles as I try to decide what to do. I threw the first two rolls, so do I throw a third to lull them into a false sense of complacency? Or do I start winning now, so they can't call the last roll lucky?

There's no easy answer, considering if they kick up a fit, I could end up like that poor troll with one less leg. Considering I like my legs—and my arms—it's a real dilemma.

I throw the marbles one more time, and they add up to eighteen.

Both witches rear back in shock as I grin and hold out my hand for the eighteen coins that come with my win.

"How'd you do that?" the younger witch demands, her hand hovering over the bag of coins.

"What do you mean?" I ask, all wide-eyed innocence. "I thought the goal was to get one of the numbers on the board?"

"It is. You did well," says the older witch as she puts a restraining hand on the younger one's arm. "Before you receive your payout, shall we play double or nothing?"

"I don't have another coin to put up," I tell her, even though I know that's not the plan.

"Of course you don't. We'll play for the same coin and double the money. If you win again, you get the coin back and double the winnings you would normally earn. If you lose, I keep everything."

I pretend to consider. "That sounds fair, I guess."

"Of course it's fair. That many gold coins is a lot in the Pit." She grins slyly. "That is where you are going, isn't it?"

I don't ask her how she knows. Instead, I smile at her as I roll the marbles...and they come up with thirty-two. Eighty-two coins—which I'm pretty sure is more than Calder has made arm wrestling at this point. Not that I'm counting or anything.

"May I collect my winnings, please?" I ask, using the most pleasant voice possible.

"You cheated!" the younger witch whispers to me, eyes narrowed and voice livid.

"I was just playing your game," I tell her even as I hold my hand out for my winnings.

"There's no way you won fair and square. No way at all," she hisses at me.

"Why wouldn't I have?" I ask quietly. "Unless you're saying that *you're* cheating?"

She doesn't answer, but her fingers curl like she's simply dying to rake them down my face. Instead, she shakes her head. "That's not the deal we had. You don't get to collect your money until you take your last turn."

"But I'm good. I don't want any more turns."

She leans forward then, slides one razor-sharp nail down the side of my face. "Then you forfeit your winnings, my pretty. A deal is a deal, after all."

I start to argue with her—our deal said nothing about combined winnings, so technically I should get paid for these two turns and then take the fifth, free and clear. But one of the guards is circling this way, and there's no chance I'm about to get caught arguing.

So I just nod when she says, "Double or nothing," again, and I take the marbles she hands me.

Then the younger witch shakes the board: "For luck, nothing more."

But I can tell a difference in the board, can see how it's listing to one side a little so that the stones will roll down and away from the higher numbers. Heather and I spent hours practicing when we were kids, determined to show up her dad. And after literally tens of thousands of throws, I know that the trick is to throw half from the low side and then twist my hand so that the other half come out near the top where the lowest numbers are grouped.

But that was on her dad's board, which was so minutely slanted that you couldn't even tell—kind of like this one was before she shook it. I'm not sure I'll be able to make the same thing work when the board's not flat, but I tell myself it doesn't matter. I put a coin up at the beginning, knowing I could lose it. Worst-case scenario, I come out of this with nothing to show for it and all my limbs, because I'm not about to fight.

Best-case scenario? Calder learns my feminine wiles aren't the only things I have going for me.

With that thought in mind—and with a growing crush of people shooting covetous looks my way—I take my time shaking the marbles in my hand before finally letting them fly.

123

Hex This

I hold my breath as the marbles roll around the board more than I like and will them to land in my favor. I thought my throw was right on, but as they bounce from side to corner to board and back again, I can't help wondering if I made a mistake and overthrew.

Eventually the throw winds down, the marbles start to land, and I add them up—three, nine, fifteen, eighteen, twenty-two, twenty-three, twenty-seven, thirty-two.

I blink my eyes, double-check. The number is still the same. Thirty-two. It's a winning number.

I look up from the board at the same time the witch does, and suddenly she's in my face, an athame to my throat. I don't know how she got it in prison—and at the moment I don't care. All that matters is that she not slice my throat open.

And that the damn windigo guards don't show up and tear either of us limb from limb.

"You don't honestly think I'm going to pay you, do you?"

"You're going to pay her, Esmerelda," the slow, southern drawl comes from behind me. "And you're going to get that knife away from her throat, or we're going to have a real problem, you and I."

Esmerelda snarls at Remy, who doesn't say anything else as she glares over my head at him. But she must know about the last person taken out of his cell in pieces, too, because it only takes a few seconds before she lowers the knife and I take my first real, throat-expanding breath since she grabbed me.

"Thank you," Remy says in his mild way, but when I glance over my head, I can see that his eyes are swirling in that strange, smoky gray-green way they have. And, not going to lie, out here in the middle of all this—it's freaky as hell. Even before he looks at me and asks, "How much does she owe you?"

"One hundred and sixty-four gold coins," I tell him and watch his eyes go big.

"She cheated," Esmerelda snarls. "I shouldn't have to pay her."

Behind me, I can hear people moving restlessly, and I don't know if it's because of the argument or if it's because a guard is coming. But if it's the latter, I don't care what Calder and Remy say about the Pit. I don't need money badly enough to risk getting on some windigo's bad side.

"We could forget the double-or-nothing bet," I tell her. "You could just pay half—"

"A bet's a bet," Remy contradicts me. "Pay her, Esmerelda, or I will, and then you and I are going to have words. You don't really want that, do you?"

Apparently not, because two sacks of gold coins hit the table pretty damn fast after that.

"Thank you," I say as I reach for the money.

"Don't thank me yet, little girl," she says, her voice loaded with rage... and promise. "I'll be coming for it."

I don't know what to say to that, so I don't say anything at all. Just gather up my winnings and let Remy guide me away—which he does, very quickly.

It turns out Hudson is right behind Remy, and he's the other reason no one tried to interrupt the game—or steal the gold I won. The only other time I've seen him look like this is right before he disintegrated Cyrus's bones and, magic-tamping bracelets or not, he does not look like someone to mess with right now. And that's before he flat-out stares down one of the guards who starts to intercept us.

After that, people don't merely step back as we pass—they literally scramble to get out of our way. Flint and Calder—who were cleaning up in the arm-wrestling ring—meet up with us halfway across the Hex. And then I feel like I'm walking in some kind of paranormal cage, with Remy in front of me, Hudson behind me, and Calder and Flint on either side of me.

"Where are we going?" I whisper as I scramble to keep up with Remy's long-legged strides. And can I just say how much it sucks to be the only short person in the middle of a group of tall people, who are all hell-bent on getting somewhere really damn fast?

"Back to our room," Hudson tells me. "Between what you won and the arm wrestling, we're carrying enough gold to have half the floor coming for us."

And sure enough, when I glance around, I realize that every person in the place is staring at us now. And what I see in their expressions isn't good.

Fear, avarice, curiosity, rage. It's all right there, and I can't help wondering how long before everything blows up.

We have six more days to reach the Pit—which means five more days of visiting the Hex. I thought the Chamber was the worst thing we had to go through in this place, and now I can't help wondering if it's really just a matter of going from the frying pan into the fire and back again.

We make it to our room in what I'm pretty sure must be record time, but none of us relaxes until the staircase retracts and the trapdoor slides shut behind us.

The second it does, Calder lets out a huge whoop. "I take it back, Grace. That was one hell of a show. Looks like you've got way more going for you than I thought."

It's the most backhanded compliment I've ever received, but Calder seems sincere, so I smile and say, "Thanks?" Although it doesn't seem exactly fair to take the compliment, considering Remy had to rescue me. If he hadn't, I'm pretty sure one of the witches or I would have ended up losing a limb—or more—at the hands of a pissed-off windigo.

"I agree, that was one hell of a show," Remy says.

"They were great, weren't they?" I ask, grinning at Hudson. "I couldn't believe how long you lasted against that giant."

"I don't think the arm wrestling was the show he was talking about," Hudson tells me with a grin. "You were spectacular."

"Me? All I did was roll some marbles."

"Against two members of the evilest coven in the place," Remy tells me. "And you practically had them in tears before you were through."

"All I did was play the game—"

"No one ever wins their game. Ever." Remy gives a little disbelieving shake of his head. "It's kind of a thing around these parts."

"What made you choose them, anyway?" Flint asks.

"I know the game—my friend Heather's dad used to have a board like that. And I just wanted to make some money to help everyone." I leave out my desire to show Calder that I'm good for something, but the look in Hudson's eyes says he already knows. And is highly amused by the competition.

"I think you made almost as much as Hudson and Calder combined,"

Remy says, and it's obvious he's amused, too. "Looks like you're the biggest badass of the day."

"I'm not so sure about that," I answer. "Hudson did stare down a windigo like it was nothing."

"What can I say?" He shoots me a tiny grin that gives me all the feels in all the places. "I like you with all your pieces attached."

"Yeah, me too," I agree fervently.

His eyes darken at my tone, and just like that I'm back in that hotel room in New York, my arms and legs wrapped around Hudson while he does all the right things to those pieces he likes so much.

124

Is It Still Russian Roulette if the Gun Is Fully Loaded?

I don't know how long we stand there staring at each other with way too much heat in our eyes, but it's long enough for Calder to start fanning herself and for Flint to head to the bathroom, commenting that, "I strangely feel the need for a cold shower."

Remy, on the other hand, simply laughs and goes over to his bunk.

It's not long after that the rest of us do the same.

Lunch comes through the trapdoor—turkey sandwiches this time—and I eat like it's been a year since I've seen food. Who knew that nearly getting murdered would give a girl such an appetite?

Afterward, I figure we'll sit around talking—there's not much else to do—but Calder, Flint, and Hudson fall asleep pretty quickly. Which seems normal, at least until each of them starts to shake or whimper.

I've never felt more pathetic—or more useless—in my entire life.

I hate that they're suffering, hate even more that there's nothing I can do to take it away. Still, Remy says he'll keep me out again tonight—and if he can't keep any of the others out, I'm going to let him.

My only hope for the others is that we don't get the Chamber again tonight. Remy and Calder say it never happens simultaneously. That maybe, maybe you'll get the Chamber twice on your trip to the Pit—if you're unlucky.

I have my fingers, my toes, and everything else I can think of crossed, praying that they don't have to go through that again. That Hudson and Flint and Calder don't have to face whatever it is the Chamber gives them—especially since tonight's will be worse, as we're one level closer to the Pit.

Part of me wishes I had read Dante's "Inferno," just so I understood how this whole layers-of-hell/prison thing works. But the other part is grateful that I don't know. Hudson and Macy make comments about me burying my head too much—and they're right. I do. But when it comes to this, the last thing I need is images of what's to come emblazoned on my brain.

Besides, it's not going to come if we don't get the Chamber again, I remind myself. And we're not going to get the Chamber. We're not. Surely we can't be that unlucky.

Except we are. Over and over again.

Every night, the cell circles around as we wait to find out if we hit the Chamber. And every single night, we end up in hell.

"This isn't fair!" I rage to Remy on the third night. "Why does this keep happening to them?"

"Life's not fair, *cher*," is his laconic reply. But his knuckles are white as he clutches his book like a lifeline.

"They can't keep going through this!" I yell when we hit it again on the fourth night. Guilt and desperation eat me up. But all I can do is sit out here and watch as they go through hell.

That night, their screams are louder and more frequent. And the following morning, none of them even tries to pretend to recover.

Flint looks like hell. I haven't seen his grin in two days, his eyes are sunken pits from lack of sleep brought on by nightmares, and his hands tremble now almost all the time.

Calder's skin has lost its shine, and she has dark bags under her eyes. Even her glorious hair has gone dull, and at least half the time she's holding back tears.

As for Hudson…Hudson is wasting away right in front of me. He doesn't touch the blood they send for meals—in fact, he doesn't even look at it. He barely talks, barely sleeps, and every day he seems to be slipping more and more away from me.

"It's going to be okay," Remy reassures me, but I can see the doubt creeping into his eyes.

On the fifth day, we don't even make it through half of our allotted Hex time. Everyone else on our level is in a great mood, as none of them has gotten the Chamber even once, except the few others in our cellblock (who look like they would beat us down if they weren't so beaten themselves from the Chamber). The games of chance are growing more and more daring, and Remy cleans up at a shell game. He tries to talk the others into arm wrestling again, but it becomes apparent pretty quickly that none of them is in any shape for it.

Flint loses his first three matches and quits.

Calder can't sit still long enough to even get into position.

And Hudson flat-out refuses to touch anyone. He also doesn't stop by to browse at even one of the stalls bartering books, which he's done almost every other day.

We end up back in our room in less than an hour.

Later that night, after Calder starts crying hysterically the second the light clicks down to one hour before the Chamber spin, I beg Remy to try to let me take one of their places.

"I can't do this!" I tell him. "I can't watch them suffer like this another night and not do something to try to help them."

"It won't work," he answers me through gritted teeth.

"But how do you know until you try?"

The look he pins me with is as dark and desperate as I feel. "How do you know I haven't already tried? Every night, I've tried to take one of their places myself, to keep one of them out. It doesn't work, Grace. For whatever reason, it only works for you."

By the sixth day, we're all shells of our former selves. Flint stopped eating and drinking yesterday, too. He doesn't talk, he doesn't move, and when Hex time came around, Remy had to make an excuse to the guards because there was no way we were getting Flint off his bed. He's spent nearly every hour of the last twenty-four sitting on his bed, arms wrapped around his knees as he rocks and rocks and rocks.

I try to talk to him, to comfort him or make him laugh, but every time I come near him, he looks like I've hit him. I don't know what he's going through in the Chamber, but whatever it is is killing him. And I can't stand it.

Hudson is almost as terrible now, the black circles under his eyes so bad that he looks like he's been hit...repeatedly. He doesn't run from me, but he doesn't talk to me much, either. Whenever I get too close, he stiffens up, and whenever I try to dig into what went on in the Chamber the night before, he tells me not to worry about it. That he's got it. That he deserves what's coming his way but that it will take more than this to bring down his vampire ass.

I wish I could be so sure.

I know this won't kill them—Flint and Hudson are way too physically strong to be felled by a week of barely eating. But mentally and emotionally are a whole different ball game, and I don't know how much more they can take.

Even Calder, who's been through this before, looks ready to break. She's spent most of the day in the shadows, and every time Remy and I make a noise, she cowers and begs us not to hurt her. Her normally sparkling brown eyes are dull and lifeless, and she hasn't even bothered to brush her hair. For a girl who is normally an obsessive self-groomer, the change is startling. And disturbing.

As night descends and the lights on the wall get closer and closer to go time, tension ratchets up inside our cell.

Flint has finally moved and is now lying on his stomach, head buried under his pillow and entire body stiff.

Calder is still in the shadows, but she's talking nonstop, her voice high and tight as the words come faster and faster.

And Hudson... Hudson spends most of the evening in the shower, and I don't know if that's because he wants to scream without us hearing him or if he's just trying to make himself feel clean.

By the time the last light flickers off, I can barely breathe, barely think. All I can do is close my eyes and pray as we spin round and round and round.

125

At the End of My String

As soon as we stop, I know we're fucked. The lights turn red and once again, Hudson, Flint, and Calder collapse.

I think I scream—I can't be sure because the horror inside me is all-consuming now, panic lighting me up in all the wrong ways. My stomach is twisting, my heart feels like it's going to explode, and all I can think is *not again. Not again, not again, not again.*

"It's the last time," Remy says, but he sounds as exhausted and defeated as I feel. "They can get through it."

"They shouldn't have to," I snap back at him, and for the first time I realize I'm on my knees, even though I have no recollection of how I got here.

I try to push myself up, but my legs are shaking so badly, they can barely hold me. I can't do this. I can't watch them go through this again. I can't.

A scream echoes through the chamber, and I'm sure that it's mine, except it's not. It's Calder, who's screaming and begging whatever is happening in her head to, "Stop. Please, God. Just stop."

Flint is crying, tears running down his face, as he sobs like his heart is breaking.

And Hudson—Hudson is shaking so badly that his teeth are chattering, and he keeps banging his head against the wall he collapsed next to.

"We need to get them into their beds before they hurt themselves," I say, and Remy nods.

"They'll be okay," he tells me for what feels like the millionth time.

But as he carries them to their beds and I pull the covers over them, he doesn't seem so sure. All three of them look like they're full-on being tortured and standing here powerless while it happens may be the worst experience of my life.

When Hudson starts to cry, too, I can't take it anymore. I whirl on Remy and beg, "Help him. Please, you have to help him."

Remy shakes his head, but for the first time since we've gotten here, he looks helpless…and as crushed as I am. "I can't, Grace. It doesn't work that way."

"Fuck how it works! He can't take any more!"

But Remy is adamant. "He's going to have to. They all are, because they have to find their own ways out."

"But what if they can't?" I point to Hudson, who is curled into an even tighter ball than the others…and is still shaking so badly that he's making the metal frame of his bed bang against the wall. "What if he can't get beyond whatever's in his mind?"

Remy doesn't answer, simply goes to his own bed and pulls a sketchbook out of the drawer under his bed.

"Remy?" I prompt, and when he still doesn't say anything, I push again. "What do you think we should—"

"I don't know!" he explodes. "I have no fucking idea what happens now. I've never even heard of anyone getting the Chamber six days in a row. It just doesn't happen."

"Doesn't that make you wonder why it's happening now?" I ask.

"They must have done something pretty awful and the prison is demanding atonement," he answers. "How else does it assure people have made up for what they've done?"

"This isn't atonement!" I shout at him. "This is revenge, pure and simple."

"No." His voice is adamant. "The prison doesn't feel. It can't want vengeance."

"Maybe not. But the people who built it can. And so can the people who fill it with prisoners." I turn back to look at Hudson and Flint. "Do you know who they are?"

"A vamp and a dragon," he says with a shrug.

"Not just any vamp or any dragon," I remind him. "That's the crown vampire prince over there, and that is the crown dragon prince. Their parents sit on the Circle."

Remy knows who they are, of course—we talked about it before—but I can see a dawning look as *who they are* enters his expression. "What *are* they doing here?"

"They tried to change things, tried to fight an unjust system where power skews toward the most brutal and the most ambitious. They took on the vampire king, and the establishment absolutely fucked them."

"Yeah, it did." His drawl is out in full force.

"Now you see why I don't think us getting the Chamber every night is an accident?"

"I don't know." He tosses his sketchbook on the bed, giving up any pretense of being unaffected. "I've lived here my whole life. I know this prison inside and out. And I had no idea it was even possible to control the Chamber spin." He looks over to where Calder is curled around her blanket, whimpering. "It's not okay to do this to people."

"None of this is okay," I tell him. "It's barbaric and a total abuse of power. It has to stop. Not just the repeated nights in a row but the whole practice altogether. No one should have to go through this simply to leave a prison, especially if they don't even belong in it to begin with."

Remy nods his agreement. "But I still can't help them. I would if I could, Grace, but there's literally nothing I can do. If there was, I'd be doing it already."

It's not the answer I want to hear, but looking at him now—seeing the outrage on his face—makes me believe him in a way I didn't before. There really is nothing he can do to save them.

"I don't think they—" I break off as Hudson screams.

Whatever grip I have on my emotions shatters. And that's it. That's just it. I can't do this for one second longer. I can't sit here and watch him suffer.

Rage rips through me, and with it comes an idea. It's a long shot, but it's the only shot I've got. So I reach deep inside myself and start looking for one string in particular—the shining blue one that I've tried so hard to ignore—that's blazing as brightly as ever. I grab it and close my eyes before squeezing as hard as I can.

126

I Love You to Death (Whether I Want To or Not)

When I open my eyes, I'm back at Katmere—in Hudson's room. I can see the big red-and-black bed that I've had so many fantasies about, can feel the warmth of the spring sunshine filtering through his windows. And I can hear Lewis Capaldi's "Grace" coming through the speakers.

But those are the only things that feel familiar. Everything else is wrong.

The furniture is smashed to bits, his vinyl is scattered and broken all over the floor, and his bookshelves have been ripped straight out of the wall. Books are lying in destroyed piles underneath them, torn pages floating through the air.

And in the corner, right behind his audio equipment, is another version of me. I'm dressed in my Katmere uniform, but instead of sitting on the bed (as I've imagined more times than I want to admit, even to myself), I'm cowering in the corner, crying and begging for someone to, "Stop! Please, please, please stop!"

Someone is snarling loudly enough to be heard over the music, and when I turn to try to figure out who it is—and what's going on—I find Hudson standing right there. His fangs are extended and dripping blood, and there's a look in his eyes that warns me that my time has run out. There's nowhere to go, no place to escape to.

"I can't stop, Grace." He's screaming at me. "I can't stop. I can't stop." He reaches up and grabs handfuls of his hair in his fists. "It hurts. It hurts. I'm trying to—" He breaks off with a growl, his entire body convulsing as he fights against the urge to lunge for me.

"Please, no. Please don't make me. Please, please, please." He seems to plead with someone I can't see. "Don't make me do it. I don't want to hurt her. I don't want—" He breaks off, another shudder running through him. And then he yells, "Run, Grace, run!"

And the other Grace tries. She does. She springs into action, racing for the door, but even as she runs, I know it's too late.

He's on her in a second, leaping the length of the room in one bound. She screams for one long moment, the sound hanging in the air as he rips her throat out and starts to drink.

The moment she dies, the compulsion ends and Hudson is left, covered in her blood—in *my* blood—as he sinks to the ground. He cradles me to his chest as blood continues to spill out of my severed carotid artery, and though there are silent tears running down his cheeks, he doesn't make a sound. Instead, he just holds me in his arms and rocks and rocks and rocks as my blood spills all over the both of us and onto the floor around us.

His hand is on my neck, and it's obvious he's trying to stop the blood flow, but nothing can stop it. It keeps pouring out until we're both drenched in it, until it coats his floor, soaks the pages of his favorite books, covers his entire room—so much more blood than my body could ever hold.

But that doesn't matter in this hellscape.

Nothing does but torturing, breaking, *destroying* Hudson.

And when he throws his head back and screams like everything inside him is shattering, I can't help but think it's succeeded.

Then, in the space between one blink and the next, the blood is gone, and Hudson is sitting on his couch reading *The Stranger* by Albert Camus (of course). JP Saxe and Julia Michaels's "If the World Was Ending" is playing as a knock sounds on his door, which breaks my heart all over again.

It's the other Grace, and she throws her arms around him as soon as he opens the door. He drops his book and picks her up. Her legs go around his waist the same way mine did that night in New York, and they're kissing like it's the only thing that matters in the world.

Finally, she pulls her mouth from his and gasps for air.

He grins and whispers, "You smell so good," as he nuzzles his way along her throat.

"Oh yeah?" The other Grace tilts her head to the side a little and whispers, "Maybe you should take a little bite. See if I taste as good as I smell."

He groans low in his throat before scraping his fangs along the sensitive column of her neck.

She shivers, her hand clutching at his hair as she tries to pull him closer. "Please, Hudson," she whispers. "I need you."

But he just shakes his head and whispers, "I can't. If I bite you now, I won't be able to stop. I'll drink you all up."

That's when it hits me. Hudson's crime—the thing he has to atone for—is compelling everything that happened at Katmere before Jaxon killed him. Whether it was for the greater good or not, whether they were secret supremacists working with Cyrus, he took their choice from them and turned them into murderers.

And now the prison is doing the same thing to him, compelling him to murder his mate again and again and again.

The Hudson in the vision must realize it at the same time I do, because he sets her back on the floor and whispers, "Run," right before his fangs explode in full force.

The other Grace heeds the warning, but he's blocking the door, so she runs deeper into the room. She trips on the corner of his rug and goes flying, though, and that's how she ends up cowering near the audio equipment. As he walks toward her and the music switches to Lewis Capaldi's "Grace," I realize that this is it. This is where he kills her. And as horror registers on Hudson's face, I can tell that he knows it, too.

I also realize at the same instant that the real Hudson—the one shaking and pleading on the bed next to me—is so far gone that if he has to spend another hour killing me, even if it is only in his nightmares, it just might shatter him forever.

127

If You Can't Stand the Heat, Stay out of the Hellscape

I don't know what to do for him, don't know how to stop this from happening—how to stop any of this from happening.

As I stand here, watching the prison compel him to do this, I finally understand—really understand—what he meant when he told me his power was the nuclear option. And why he's refused, over and over again, to compel anyone to do anything.

I thought he would do it at the Firmament when the Watch surrounded us. Later wondered why he hadn't in New York when Nuri went to arrest him. But he never did—and now I know why. He's never forgiven himself for what he did last year, never forgiven himself for what he caused. He did it because he felt he had no choice, and those boys died. Which was tragic.

Were they planning horrible things? Yes, absolutely.

Would they have killed people of their own volition? Probably.

But we'll never know.

And now, watching this—watching him—I realize it's not them being dead that is eating him up so completely. Yes, the deaths obviously bother him, but what is destroying him is him having taken away their choice. He compelled them to do something so appalling, so soul-crushing, that he can never forgive himself. Disintegrating them would have been more humane, but he couldn't let his father know that ability still existed. So instead, he was cruel and forced those boys to play bystander in their own bodies while they killed their classmates—killed their friends.

And now he's suffering the same thing, over and over and over again.

No wonder he looks like hell. No wonder he can barely stand to be near me. Every time he looks at me, all he sees is what he did. And what he is capable of doing.

Right in front of me, the other Grace is looking for someplace to run. Someplace to hide. She tries to make it back to the front door, but he cuts her off. When she rushes toward the library, he leans over and catches her in the shoulder with his fangs. And when she darts toward the bed, he follows her, fangs dripping blood even as he begs her to run. To get away. To not let him hurt her.

And then, there she is, cowering behind the audio equipment, exactly as she was when I first entered this hellscape, and I know we've all run out of time.

Desperate to stop him, desperate to spare him the terror and the agony of murdering me again, I call out to him. "Hudson! Hudson, stop! I'm right here."

For one second, two, he freezes, head tilted a little as if he could hear me.

"Hudson, please! Hudson, it's okay. You don't have to do it! You're okay. You're—"

I break off when I realize that, not only isn't he listening any longer, but my shouting is actually making things worse. Because there is a part of him that can hear me, and it's adding to his desperation to stop even as the compulsion pushes him forward. Now, he hears not just the compulsion in his head but my voice, too, and as agonized tears roll down his face, I can't help thinking that I'm only torturing him even more.

The idea traumatizes me, and when he grabs the other Grace again, when he tears her throat out again, I can feel his terror as clearly as I can feel my own. And when he drops to his knees, the other Grace in his arms, I can feel something deep inside me break into a million pieces. Because the look on Hudson's face as he tilts his head back—the tears, the anguish, the soul-deep guilt—is more than I can bear.

Because this boy, this beautiful, beautiful boy whom I love so much, doesn't deserve this.

He doesn't deserve to suffer like this.

He doesn't deserve to be broken like this.

He's already learned his lesson, has already repented for the things he did. He's changed, he's *really* changed, and this forced atonement is destroying the person he's working so hard to be.

I have to stop this. I have to fix this.

But I've only got one shot at it.

As the scene resets to Hudson reading on the couch, I take a deep breath and force myself to let go of our mating bond. It's harder than it should be, even knowing it's the only chance I have of stopping this.

I drop back into the cell just in time to hear Hudson scream. Which makes me wonder if he was more aware of me along the mating bond than I thought. He's at the early part of the nightmare—before anything bad happens—so he shouldn't be this freaked out yet. But he's convulsing on the bed, his entire body shaking as he groans in distress.

I drop to my knees next to the bed and put an arm around him. "I've got you," I whisper into his ear, hoping against hope that somehow he'll hear me in the middle of that hellscape. "I'm going to get you out."

I turn to Remy then and ask, "Can you help me? I need to hold him down."

"Of course," he answers, all but leaping off his bed and running across the cell to us. "What happened in there?" he asks as he drops to his knees beside me.

I don't take the time to answer him. I can't afford to, not knowing what's coming next for Hudson. Instead, I wrap one hand around Remy's wrist and whisper, "I'm sorry."

Then, praying this works, I close my eyes one more time and use my other hand to grab on to the mating bond.

It takes a few more seconds than it did the first time, but when I open my eyes, Remy and I are both in Hudson's nightmare.

"What the fuck did you do?" Remy yells. He doesn't seem angry, more astonished. Which I get, considering I'm a little shocked that it worked, too.

"Channeling magic is one of my powers," I tell him. "And even though my powers are currently locked up, yours aren't. So I took a really big chance, hoping that the magic used to channel comes from the source—you—and not me, which would make it immune to the whole prison-cell/grounding situation we've got going on here." I give a slight grin. "Apparently, it's a chance that paid off."

"Apparently," he agrees. "Nice job, Amazing Grace."

"How about we save the superlative nicknames until we know whether my plan works or not?" I look down at where my hand is still wrapped around his wrist. "Do you mind?"

"For you, *cher*?" He gives me a playful wink. "Not even a little bit."

I'd roll my eyes at him, but I'm too busy using every ounce of strength

I have inside me to focus on every ounce of magic I can sense inside him. There's more than I thought, but not as much as I'd hoped—or as much as I think we'll need. But I don't care. I have to try.

Drawing as much of that magic into me as I possibly can, I focus on Hudson—who is currently stalking the other Grace across his room—and shout, "Stop!" as loud as I can.

128

Now You Kill Me,
Now You Don't

A t first, I don't think he hears me. He doesn't move, doesn't falter, doesn't so much as look my way. But I'm not about to give up now. Not when I'm so close to getting his attention…and he's so close to self-destructing.

"Hudson! Stop!" I shout again.

This time, he does more than pause. He turns to me and slowly, slowly registers that I'm inside the dream with him.

"Grace?" he whispers. "What are you doing here?"

"It's okay," I tell him, walking toward him. "I've got—"

"No!" he yells, throwing a hand out as if to ward me off. "Don't come any closer."

He sounds so anguished, so panicked that I freeze about halfway across the room.

"Hudson, please. Let me touch you."

"I can't." He holds up his hands, and suddenly they are drenched in blood, even though he hasn't so much as touched the other Grace. "I'll hurt you."

"No." I shake my head even as I take another step toward him. "You won't. That's just a nightmare. It's not real."

"It *is* real," he says, and his voice is shaking in a way it so rarely does. "I hurt everyone. It's what I do. It's all I know how to do."

"Is that what you really think? Or is that what this place is telling you?"

"It's the truth. I killed those people. Worse, I made them kill themselves."

"You did," I agree. "And it was a terrible thing. But it wasn't all on you, Hudson. It was on them, too."

"It was all on me. I took away their choices. I made them do what they did—"

"Because you felt like *you* didn't have a choice," I remind him. "They were going to do something awful. They were going to hurt, maybe kill, all those kids. Destroy all those families. You didn't know who you could trust, so you did what you thought you had to do to stop them."

"I made them kill their friends, all the while as they screamed in their heads to stop," he whispers, then continues on a ragged sob, "but they couldn't. They couldn't stop. They couldn't stop. They couldn't."

Before I can think of anything else to say, the Grace cowering on the floor starts to scream. "Stop! Please stop, Hudson. Please don't hurt me. Don't—"

"Get out now!" he growls at me. "Before it's too late."

Then he turns and advances toward the kneeling Grace, and I know he's going to kill her again. But I also know that this is the time that's going to break him—I can see it in his eyes, can hear it in the agony he doesn't even try to hide.

Can feel it in the misery stretching between us, like a mating bond on the brink of unraveling.

And I know I can't let him do it. Not this time. Not ever again.

So I do the only thing I can think of, the only thing that might be able to reach him. I drop my hold on Remy's wrist and let him fall back out of the hellscape—I don't need him now that Hudson knows I'm here—then leap across the room, throwing myself between that other Grace and him.

"Get out of here!" he yells again, and now the bloodlust is in his eyes, the compulsion raging through him like a forest fire. "I can't hold back any longer."

"Then don't hold back," I tell him, moving so that my body is pressed up against his. "Do whatever you need to, Hudson. Because I'm not walking away—from this or from you."

"Grace," he growls, even as the fire burns in his eyes. "Grace, no."

"It's okay, Hudson." I thread my fingers through his hair, press myself even closer against him.

"I can't—" he chokes out, and I can see his fangs gleaming in the light. "I won't be able to—" He breaks off, buries his face in the sensitive space where my neck and my shoulder meet. I can feel him fighting himself, can feel him trying to pull back, to move away. But I can also feel the heat in him, the need, and the bloodlust. And I know if I let him go now, he'll be on the other Grace—the Grace this hellscape is wielding like a weapon against him—and there's no way he'll survive.

No way either of them will survive.

And I'm not about to let that happen. This shithole has been using me to hurt him from the first day we arrived...

But that ends here and now.

"Nobody lives their lives without regrets, Hudson," I say, looking intently into his eyes. "Everyone makes shitty decisions at some point, tough decisions, ones we'll spend the rest of our lives regretting." For just a second, I think of my parents. "The key isn't to try to live life regret-free. It's to always try to make the best decision you can in that moment, because the regret's going to come whether you like it or not. But if you tried your best, well, that's the most anyone can ask of you."

I pause, take a deep breath. "It's okay," I whisper to him again, even as I tilt my head back and to the side. "I want you to."

He tries one more time. "Grace—"

"I've got you, Hudson. I've got you."

He groans low in his throat and then, with a flash of teeth, he's on me.

He bites me right over the pulse point at the base of my throat, his fangs slicing cleanly through skin and sinking deep into my veins.

I cry out at the sudden movement, the quick flash of pain, but it fades as rapidly as it started. Then he starts to drink, and everything fades but Hudson and me and this one moment...

He shifts against me, looking for more, and I tilt my head back to give him better access. I press myself even more tightly against him so that I can feel every part of him against every part of me. Then revel in the way his hands tighten on my hips, in the way his mouth grows slower as he drinks and drinks and drinks from me.

For what feels like an eternity, I forget where we are, forget why we're doing this, forget anything and everything but Hudson and how if I don't break through to him, I might never get him back.

He shifts against me, pulls away, and I moan. With a ragged voice, I whisper, "Hudson, I trust you—"

He strikes again, deeper this time, and I gasp. Shudder. Try to wrap myself around him as he continues to take. As he takes whatever I have to give and then demands more. Demands everything until my knees go shaky, my breath goes shallow, and my hands and feet turn ice-cold despite the heat blazing deep inside me.

And even as the pleasure swamps me, engulfs me, there's a tiny part of me that understands: Hudson has taken too much blood.

129

Some Days Life's a Bowl of Cherries; Some Days It's Just the Pits

For one brief moment, I think of protesting, of pulling away.

But my mind is cloudy, my body weak, my will to resist nonexistent. Because this is Hudson.

My mate.

My best friend.

My partner.

And because he is all those things, I know something he doesn't. Something this hellscape can't imagine and something he will never let himself believe. He made the best choice he could make with those boys... and I would never blame him for it. Regret? Yes. But also forgiveness.

And so I say again, stronger this time, "I trust you, Hudson."

Hudson pulls off me with a strangled groan, his eyes confused but clear as he looks between me and the Grace on the floor. As he realizes that it really is just a nightmare.

It's his turn to bury his hands in my hair as he whispers, "Are you all right? Did I hurt you?"

"That's the whole point," I murmur, turning my head so I can kiss the sensitive skin on the inside of his wrist. "What I've known all along and what I need you to believe, too. You will never hurt me, Hudson. At least not like that. You would never hurt anyone if you could help it."

He shakes his head, starts to speak, but I stop him with a soft finger over his lips. "Never," I reiterate.

We both glance down then, toward the other Grace who should be cowering on the floor near Hudson's desk. But she's gone, and when I look toward the door, I see her disappearing out of it, backpack over her shoulder and curls streaming behind her.

"It was wrong," he tells me, and I realize he's watching the other Grace walk away, too. "What I did to them."

"Yes," I agree, because it was. "But, baby. War turns everyone into villains. There's never been a way to get around that fact."

He doesn't answer, just closes his eyes with a sigh and nods.

And he looks so tired, so worn out, that I wrap my arm around his waist and pull him into me so I can help support his weight. "How many times have you killed me so far?" I ask.

He swallows hard, his throat working overtime. "Too many. Thousands." He sighs again. "Maybe tens of thousands."

"It's enough," I tell him. "More than enough."

He might have only suffered this punishment for a few days, but it's a pretty fucking terrible punishment. And he suffered it over and over and over again. At some point, enough is enough.

He shakes his head. "It's only been a few days."

"No," I tell him, and this time it's my turn to shake my head as I quote his favorite movie back to him. "'It's not the years, honey. It's the mileage.'"

And for the first time in days, he smiles. Because he finally gets it.

"It's time to forgive yourself, Hudson. It's time to let it go."

He doesn't say anything, and at first I think he's not ready. But then he smiles and bends to kiss me again.

This time when he pulls away, we're back in the cell.

"What the hell?" Remy stops pacing the second we wake up. "You can't do that to me, Grace! I've been freaking out for the last twenty minutes. I thought he was going to kill you!"

"Is that how long we've been in there?" I ask. "It felt like only a couple of minutes."

"Yeah, well, I told you time passes differently in there. Sometimes it feels longer; sometimes it feels shorter." He makes a sound low in his throat, and it's obvious he's pissed as hell. "Next time you want to hitch a ride on someone else's magic, pick anybody else, *cher*. Because that was some real bullshit."

"I'm sorry," I tell him. "I never meant to freak you out. And I do appreciate the help. More than I can say."

"That's how you got in?" Hudson asks, glancing from Remy to me.

"Yeah. Your girl pretty much dragged me into that hellscape." Remy rolls his eyes. "Though, I gotta say, respect, man. I don't know how long I'd be able to handle what you did."

Hudson looks discomfited for a second, like he doesn't know what to do with someone besides me having seen what was going on in his head. And I get that. I know how weird it felt to me to know that Hudson was in my head back when I didn't trust him. I can only imagine how it feels to him to have some warlock he barely knows have access to his deepest fears—and by reflection, his greatest shame.

At first, I think he's going to retreat behind his shell and pull out something obnoxious to say. But in the end, he must decide to roll with it, because instead of being an ass, he offers his hand to Remy and says, "Thanks for the help."

Remy looks surprised, too, but he takes the offered hand and nods an obvious *you're welcome.*

I settle down on my bed, and Hudson lies down next to me, his arm around my shoulders. Flint and Calder are still out, and it's awful to watch them twitch and shudder on the bed—especially now that I have an idea of what they're going through. But the only way I was able to reach Hudson is through our mating bond. I have no "in" with them, and it's an awful realization.

"This is it, right?" I ask as the minutes slowly tick away. "We're at the Pit now?"

"Yeah," Remy says. "And if we're lucky, we won't have to do this again."

"Let's be really lucky, then, shall we?" Hudson's accent is thick, his expression totally dry.

"The luckiest," I add, even as I try to imagine what the Pit will be like if this was just the trip *to* it.

I mean, Hudson made a joke earlier that in Dante's "Inferno," the Pit was where Satan himself was, so a part of me is absolutely terrified of what's going to happen when the doors open in the morning. What we've seen in the regular levels during Hex time has been terrible enough. If it wasn't our only chance of finding the blacksmith so we can get out of here and save our friends from Cyrus, I'm pretty sure nothing would make me leave this room.

I start to ask Remy about it, but if he says it's as bad as I think he will, I'll only freak out about it until the doors open. Besides, he and I haven't talked any other night during the Chamber because it seems disrespectful when people we care about are suffering.

Tonight is no different, despite Hudson having finally managed to beat his hellscape. So instead of talking, Hudson and I curl up on my bed and hold each other in silence.

As the last few minutes of the Chamber draw to a close, I can't help thinking about Flint. About what his punishment is. He was arrested for trying to kill the last gargoyle, which makes me think that his punishment must have something to do with me—especially considering how he's been acting every time I try to talk to him these last few days.

Having seen how I was used against Hudson in his punishment—and what that punishment did to him—I'm sick to my stomach about what might be happening to Flint. And this place having spent the last week using me against both my mate and one of my closest friends.

This place is evil, and if I get half a chance, I'll do whatever I can to see it leveled. Rehabilitation is one thing. Torture is another. And what the Aethereum does is torture, pure and simple. I don't care what its purpose is, I don't care what it was built for, that's not what it does. And that is not okay.

The minutes finally tick down, the red lights overhead slowly fading back to their normal cool white as Flint and Calder start to stir.

He looks so defenseless lying there, curled up in the fetal position, shivering under the blanket I draped over him an hour ago. I've known he's suffered, have seen the dark circles and the shaking and the way he's stopped smiling and eating. But I guess I've been so preoccupied with Hudson when the Chamber first ends each night that I haven't realized just what bad shape Flint is in when he first comes out of it.

Or maybe it's because today's was the worst one yet. I don't know and I don't care. The moment Flint sits up, I'm across the room, kneeling next to his bed.

He flinches away from me the second I reach for his hand, though, and I consider walking away. I definitely don't want to make this harder for him when he's already suffering so much. At the same time, though, if I can find a way to help him—I want to.

"I'm sorry," I tell him softly, knowing the others are probably listening but still trying to keep this as much between us as I can. "I'm so sorry you're going through this."

He shrugs and stares at the wall beyond my head. "I deserve it."

"Nobody deserves this." I try to reach for his hand again, and this time he lets me.

"That's not true," he tells me. "I nearly killed you, Grace. I nearly *killed* you. And for what? To stop Hudson coming back?" He glances over at my mate and deliberately raises his voice when he adds in an abysmal British accent, "I still think he's a bit of a wanker," to which Hudson flips him off without even bothering to look up from the book he borrowed from Remy.

"But he shouldn't have died for it. And you definitely shouldn't have nearly died because of it. I was so blinded by fear and rage and hate that I nearly destroyed one of the best people I've ever met." He clears his throat, swallows. "Which makes me no better than the brother I was trying to avenge. Damien was a monster; I just didn't want to see it. And I nearly killed an innocent girl because of it. I deserve every day I have to spend in here and then some."

"Why? Because you need to suffer?" He looks away, and I squeeze his hand. "No. You've suffered enough, Flint. It's time for you to forgive yourself."

"I don't—" He breaks off, then starts again. "I don't know if I can do that."

"I forgave you. I know I yelled at you about it when we were in New York, but I forgave you a long time ago. And I think if you want to beat this prison, then you have to do what you just did. You have to acknowledge your actions and why you did them. But you also have to forgive yourself. If you do that, this shithole can't torture you anymore."

Flint doesn't say anything, but he is listening. I can tell. And for the first time in almost a week, he manages to smile at me. It's not his usual charming grin, but it's a smile, and I'll take it.

I don't know what to say to Calder, who is hugging her knees to her chest and rocking, but I know she was listening to what I was saying to Flint, too. And as the knowledge sinks in that she made it through—that they all did—I can see her finally start to really breathe.

"You should paint your nails again, for the Pit," I suggest, holding her gaze. I know if Calder is grooming, she's going to be okay. And so I wait. And wait.

It seems to take her forever, but eventually she nods and reaches under her bed for a bottle of blue nail polish with glitter, and I breathe a sigh of relief. Calder is going to be okay. They all are. We made it through the gauntlet, a little worse for wear maybe, but we made it.

Eventually, we all head to our beds to grab a little rest. Even Hudson, though he first spends what I sincerely hope is his last hour in a shower trying to scrub my imaginary blood from his skin. But we all try to sleep at least a little. Because we know what's up next...

I can't stop the pounding of my heart a few hours later when we start moving again—though at a much more sedate pace than the Chamber roulette. It only lasts about fifteen seconds, and then every light in the room turns bright purple.

"What's going on?" Hudson asks, eyeing the purple lights with amused trepidation.

Remy grins as he slides open the door in the floor that our food normally comes through. "Hold on to your money and your magic, boys and girls, because we have finally made it. Welcome to the Pit."

130

Fortune Favors the Trolled

My stomach is in knots as we make our way down the steps. I've grown used to the Hex—I hate it, but I've grown used to it. Yet I can't even imagine what the Pit must be like. I know we have to go, know we have to face whatever's down here, but there's a part of me that wants to stay right here.

I glance at my group and realize, not for the first time, how small I am compared to them.

Flint and Hudson don't seem to have any such reservations about heading down, judging by the way they're crowding around the opening trying to get a look at whatever the Pit has to offer.

Calder starts to head down, but Remy stops her with a hand on her shoulder. "If there's anything you want from here, you need to get it now," he tells her.

The look that flashes across her face is scarier than any I've ever seen from her, and for a second, I think she's going to shrug him off. But then she goes back to her bed and opens the drawer underneath it. I'm not sure what she grabs, but it must be small, because she hides it somewhere on her person.

"Remember," Remy says. "We've got twelve hours to get the hell out of this prison. If we don't escape by then, we've got to head back to our cell and start the whole process all over again. Only this time, we'll have to do the full nine spins of the Chamber." He looks between us. "None of us wants that. But if it's coming up on twelve hours and we're not out… You need to make sure you're back here, even though it sucks. Any cell that's late coming back from the Pit draws the Chamber for a month straight. Obviously nobody's ever late. Let's not be the first."

"We're going to find a way out," Hudson says, and I wish I felt as confident. Maybe Hudson beat it today and he won't have to go back in, but I don't trust anything about this place—I'm not going to take that assumption or any other for granted.

"I really hope you're right," Remy replies. And then he gestures for us to precede him down the stairs, and my stomach sinks.

I really don't want to be one of the first down. What if someone from the Hex is waiting for us? Or worse, someone who *lives* in the Pit? I shudder and am about to suggest I go down last, but then I glance at Calder fluffing her hair, Flint rubbing his hands together, and the smile in Hudson's eyes to see me finally leave this cell, and I realize I can't show anyone how scared I really am. I might be the weakest link in our group, but there's no reason I have to show it.

I walk up to the hole and watch Calder go down first, and then I follow her while the guys pull up the rear. But the second I make it to the bottom, I realize that something is very, very wrong.

Because the place I'm staring at is nothing like I was expecting the Pit to be. In fact, it's like nothing I've ever seen before. Whether that's good or bad, I don't know yet.

All around us, other people are descending from their cells, hitting the ground running…and heading for the maze of merchants and stalls that line the long road we've descended upon. Hundreds of people running for dozens of little booths, where they can buy clothes, food, beer, and any number of other things, if the bright, colorful signs above the shops are any indication of the wares inside.

It's the last thing I ever expected to be here, but now I know why Remy was so adamant about us making money every time we went into the Hex these last several days. There's no way to survive down here without it.

I might not know much about this place, but I'm definitely smart enough to know that much. And if we want help, we're going to have to pay for it.

"This is the Pit?" Hudson asks. He looks as astonished as I feel.

"I thought it was going to be…" Flint trails off, and I get it. He's trying to find the least offensive way to say it. I know, because I've been doing the same thing for the last five minutes.

"A share-the-adventure version of your own private hellscape?" Remy asks.

Flint shrugs. "Maybe something like that."

"Why would anyone try to get to the Pit, then? The whole point is to make people want to atone for what they've done. If you risk the Chamber—and especially if you get it—this is your reward." Calder holds her hands out and spins around like one of those old-time game-show girls showing off the merchandise.

"Where do we go first?" I ask as we start weaving our way through the throngs of prisoners. Everyone from our level is here tonight, which means all the familiar faces from the Hex.

A coven of witches passes, giving me what I'm sure is the literal evil eye for the first time in my life, but I ignore them. Which is easy to do when Hudson places a hand on my back in obvious support.

"I've got a couple of packages to pick up," Remy says. "Then I say we find the blacksmith."

"Always with the packages," I tease.

Calder does her patented hair fluff and head toss. "How do you think he got to be the richest guy in prison? I mean, if it was just based on good looks, I'd be loaded."

"You absolutely would be," Remy agrees with a grin, even as Flint rolls his eyes.

"If you're the richest guy in prison," I muse aloud, "why did we need more money to get out?"

"*Cher*, if I had enough money to get out, don't you think I'd have done it by now?" He raises one brow at me as he steps to the left to avoid a huge metal trash bin on the side of the road. "And now we need to get *six* people out. Like I said, it's going to take even more money and a whole lot of luck."

The streets continue to fill up as we walk through them, the crowds growing thicker and more boisterous as the last of the cells empty. By the time we make it to the corner, the five of us are so tightly packed together that I end up stepping on Hudson's feet more than once. Eventually, we stop at a beer-merchant/drinking stall with a sign proudly calling it PARADISO—and I sincerely hope this isn't the owner's definition of paradise, 'cause no.

A ton of elves (pointy ears) and goblins (nuff said) look like they're already on their second or third drinks. "Is the merch ready?" Remy asks the creepy-looking bartender with the dead eyes and sallow skin, who I'm pretty sure is a merman based on the Triton tattoos he's got all over his currently naked upper body.

The bartender finishes pulling a pint of some kind of dark beer and slides it down the polished plywood bar to an elf sitting on a stool at the end. Then he wipes his hands on a towel before reaching beneath the makeshift bar and pulling out a brown-wrapped package.

Remy takes it with a nod and fist bump, then turns and walks away.

The third time this happens, we end up at a sketchy fortune-telling place, complete with dirty tarot cards and a wizened old troll dressed in a shiny orange-and-purple blazer with sequins on the collar and wrists. Apparently, being born with magic doesn't also mean you're born with taste.

We wait outside while Remy runs in and delivers one of the packages he picked up earlier, and as we watch the guy doing card tricks with his tarot, Hudson asks Calder, "How does he tell fortunes with his magic bound?"

"It's not bound," she answers. "None of the people working the Pit are inmates. They're merchants who come in every day to ply their trade."

"And they're okay with what goes on here?" I ask, horrified. "Just because they can make some money off it?"

"Maybe they don't know," Flint suggests. "If this is all they ever see—"

"Maybe they don't *want* to know," I shoot back. "I mean, look around at these people. Everyone has their magic bound; a bunch of people are missing body parts courtesy of psychotic, cannibalistic guards; a lot of the prisoners are skating the edges of sanity themselves because of time in the Chamber. How could they *not* notice?"

"Yeah, well, people tend to think those who are in prison deserve whatever punishment they get," Hudson comments. "You're only in prison because you did something wrong. You chose to commit a crime. Of course, if *they* break a law, it was situational. They had no choice. They were a victim of circumstance."

Remy shrugs. "Only criminals are behind bars. Victims aren't. That's how you tell them apart, I figure."

"That's horrible," I reply.

"It is what it is."

I cross my arms over my chest and lean back against the pole holding up this ramshackle booth. "Yeah, well, it sucks."

"If these people come in," Hudson says, "then there must be a way for them to leave."

Remy grins as he joins us again. "Bingo."

The breath I didn't know I was holding slowly eases from my chest as I glance at Flint and Hudson, and we all smile together. This. This is a chance.

And Remy seems tight with the merchants—maybe that's been his plan all along. To see if we could escape with them at the end of the day. No wonder he's concerned about hiding the blacksmith, though.

Remy turns to leave, but the troll follows us out, his tarot cards in hand. "Let me tell your fortune, pretty girl."

"Not today, Lester," Calder tells him. "We have stuff to do."

"I wasn't talking to you," he answers as he fans out his deck of cards. "Pick one," he directs me.

"Oh, I don't think—"

"It's on the house," he says with a wave of his hand. "You look just like my favorite granddaughter."

I have no idea how to take that, considering he's a troll, but I merely smile and say, "Thank you. But we need to go."

"What's your hurry?" He glances at his watch. "You've got eleven and a half hours left before you've got to be back in your cell. You can give ol' Lester three minutes."

I start to say no again—with everything we're about to attempt, it seems really rash to let some fortune-teller get a look inside my future.

But Remy gives me a little go-ahead nod, and it's obvious he's got a soft spot for Lester. So even though I know I'm going to regret it, I give in and pull out a card. Then jump a little as everyone around me tenses—including Lester.

"What is it?" I ask, since I don't exactly know tarot cards that much.

"Trouble," Hudson answers as he studies the card that looks like a tower being struck by lightning.

"Big trouble," Lester tells me as he grabs my hand with his free one and brings it to his lips. But then he sniffs me for one long breath, and his eyes go big. "You didn't tell me who she was," he reprimands Remy.

Remy doesn't answer, just kind of smiles a little even as I wonder if it's so obvious that I'm a gargoyle.

Lester must figure out that Remy's not going to answer, because eventually he turns back to me and says, "There is only one path for you, my queen."

131

Lost and Bound

Despite myself, my heart speeds up, and I lean forward a little. Because if this guy can tell me what my one, true path is, I am all in. God knows I haven't been able to find it myself.

He must notice he's got my undivided attention, because he shoves his cards in his pocket, then covers our joined hands with his other hand. "You must find this path and follow it, my beauty, before it's too late."

I wait for more, but then he steps back and grins. "See, I told you it would only take a couple of minutes." He winks at me. "Go find that path, girl."

Remy flips him a coin as we all wave and walk away, but as soon as we turn a corner, he cracks up. "Your face was the most priceless thing I've ever seen," he tells me. "Worth every cent of that coin I gave him."

"Well, how was I supposed to know he was full of it? We're surrounded by paranormals."

"Oh, I don't know," Flint says with a grin. "Maybe because he was a literal troll?"

"Fair point," I say as we turn down another corner and get hit by the most amazing smell. "Tacos?" I ask, because if there is one thing I can recognize at a hundred paces, it's the scent of tacos. "You didn't tell me there were tacos in the Pit."

"Tacos and pizza," Remy says.

"I don't care about pizza, but I would do just about anything for some tacos right now."

"Anything?" Remy asks and tosses Calder a wink.

"I'll get you some tacos, Grace." Hudson moves ahead of the group. "How many do you want? Five? Ten?"

I laugh, because Hudson is being ridiculous. Whatever Remy is thinking he might extort from me for tacos, it is definitely *not* what Hudson is thinking.

"How about three?" I tell him as I hurry to catch up with him.

It takes a few minutes—apparently paranormals love tacos as much as girls from Southern California do—but eventually we're crowded around a picnic table devouring some of the best carne asada tacos I have ever eaten. And even Hudson is eating again; he has a full thermos of blood from a nearby stand.

But Hudson isn't focused on his own meal. Instead, he's watching me eat with a huge grin on his face—for someone who doesn't consume food, he sure enjoys feeding me. As the lunch finally runs out, he turns to Remy. "Since your troll friend wasn't much help, I've got to ask. Have you seen it yet?"

Remy shakes his head. "Just enough to know that it all hinges on Grace."

I swallow down the fear bubbling up in my chest, threatening to make me lose my tacos. If this plan was counting on me to save everyone…we're doomed.

"What *do* you see?" Hudson asks, reaching down to entwine our hands.

Remy leans back, his hands crossed over his chest. "Like I've said, we're going to need money and a lot of luck."

"That's not much of a plan," Calder says, and for the first time, she sounds like she's really in the conversation. Like she's thinking about something other than herself. "Considering we've got six people to get out of here."

"I know." Remy shakes his head. "But we've got three flowers, which means we only have to figure out how to get three of us out. The blacksmith gets one of the flowers, obviously. No way is the prison ever letting him go unless it doesn't have a choice. My visions keep telling me that the only way I can get out is with a flower. But there must be another way for everyone else."

His eyes are swirling smoke again. "Sometimes I see you getting out. Sometimes it disappears." His eyes settle back into their usual forest green as he continues. "So clearly there are things we need to do that are still undecided."

"Maybe they've atoned enough," Calder says. "Maybe that's how you get Flint and Hudson out. And Grace takes the last flower."

"That still leaves you," I tell her.

"Maybe that was just a pipe dream. Maybe the prison can't stand for me to go anywhere." She forces a wide grin, then does a truly impressive hair toss—so impressive that someone actually whistles from the table behind us. "I mean, would you give this up if you didn't have to?"

"We're not leaving without you," I tell her, something Remy quickly seconds.

"Well then, let's do what we can," Hudson suggests. "We've got ten and a half hours before everything goes to hell, so let's work the problem. What's the next step?"

"The blacksmith," Flint answers. "Right? Our options change based on if we can convince him to leave with us or not. So let's get him on board before we worry about the rest."

He's right. It is the obvious next step. Which is why, after throwing our trash away, we follow Remy back into the crowded street.

It isn't long before he turns us down a narrow, dark alley and then past two massive windigos. I expect them to stop us, but one nods while the other pats Remy on the head. And I'm reminded, once again, that these people— these creatures—raised Remy after his mother died when he was five years old. That this place is as much a home for him as it is a prison.

I can't help wondering what that feels like, what it does to him to know that once he leaves, he'll never see any of these people again—even though some of them are the closest he's ever had to a family.

The other day, Calder mentioned something I learned when I got to Katmere—that it's not only the family you have that makes you who you are but also the family you make. Often it's the latter who helps you catch the wind on sunny days and who anchors you when seas get rough.

How terrible to have to give that up just for the chance to finally truly live.

We take two more turns as a sound like thunder booms all around us. I want to ask Remy what it is, but he's moving fast, and I figure I shouldn't distract him. Also, I'm honestly not sure I want to know.

We take one last turn, and it lands us on a building-lined path so dark, I have to hold on to Hudson to make sure I don't trip in the pitch-black. And for a creature who's supposed to be "of the dark," it's total bullshit that I don't have better night vision.

On the plus side, the path lightens up a little the longer we're on it, but it's not until we almost reach the end that I realize why.

The light—and the heat—we're feeling is coming from the hugest furnace I have ever seen. A furnace that is currently being manned by a giant with a massive welding mask over his forehead. A giant who, upon seeing Remy, lifts his mask...

And I gasp.

His face is crisscrossed from forehead to chin with the most brutal scars I have ever seen.

132

Chains Aren't the Only Things Getting Broken

Cyrus did this. I know it. Everything inside me screams it. He tormented this man—just like he's tormented the Unkillable Beast for a millennia—simply because he could.

It's disgusting. Unthinkable. And yet here it is, more proof that Cyrus is vile, inhumane, evil. And that he must be stopped, no matter what the cost. Because anyone who can do this, anyone who hurts someone like this because they can, anyone who spends centuries using and destroying their own son, is capable of anything.

When I consider what he's sentenced us to prison for while he runs free, it makes me even more determined to stop him. More determined to make sure he can never hurt anyone again. When we break out and I get my gargoyle back, I promise myself Cyrus will pay for this.

"What do you want, kid?" the blacksmith asks Remy in a voice so low and rumbly that it rattles the windows in the buildings around us. Which makes sense, considering he's gigantic. Not Unkillable Beast gigantic, but not regular-giant gigantic, either. He's big, really big, but it's not until Remy walks closer to him that I realize just how big. Remy, at about six foot four, barely makes a third of this guy, who must be almost twenty feet tall. A giant among giants.

No wonder he has such a huge furnace.

"We have a proposition for you," Remy says, speaking loudly.

"I don't have time for any propositions. I've got cells to make." He turns around and grabs a massive curved mold from the stack behind him, then brings it over to lay on his workbench.

I recognize the shape and curve of it—I've been staring at a fully realized version of this for days now in our cell. It's part of the cell wall that makes up the cage we're in, and he's hauling the thing around like it weighs nothing.

Cells, I mouth to Hudson, whose face has gone grim. The bracelet within a bracelet within a bracelet that we're all trapped in? No wonder he's all but enslaved down here—the prison will eventually cease to exist without him... which, not going to lie, feels like a win-win to me.

"Why are you making cells?" Remy asks. "Mavica says we have some empties for the first time in years."

"Calm before the storm," the blacksmith tells him as he slides his helmet back into place and opens the huge doors of the furnace. The blast of heat that comes out is so hot that I don't have a clue how Remy could stand being so close to it. I feel like I'm half melted, and I'm at least twenty feet away.

"What does that mean?" Flint yells to be heard over the roar of the giant fire.

"It means someone is planning on sending a shit ton more prisoners here," Hudson answers grimly. His tone suggests Cyrus is the someone in question.

"From Katmere?" I ask, feeling sick.

"From wherever, I would imagine," Remy answers caustically.

The blacksmith slowly fills the mold with molten metal, then sets it aside before laying a massive piece of hot metal on his workbench and starting to pound on it with a sledgehammer that's almost bigger than Flint. He pounds and pounds at it—each slam of the sledgehammer echoing like thunder—until a very distinctive, very recognizable curve starts to form.

But by the time the curve shows up, the metal has started to cool, so he opens the furnace back up and thrusts it inside again. Which is good with me, considering his banging is so loud, it makes it nearly impossible to think.

"You need to go," the blacksmith tells us as he reaches for a ten-gallon jug of water and takes a quick drink.

"I think you're going to want to hear what we have to say," Remy says, matter-of-fact.

The blacksmith looks like he's going to refuse, but in the end he grabs a seat on a massive rock and eyes us with annoyance. "Fine, tell me what you want so I can turn you down and you can be on your way."

It's not the most open invitation I've ever heard, but it's more than I was beginning to think we would get from him, so I'm trying to be optimistic.

"We need you to make us a key," Flint tells him, starting off slowly—I think to see if he'll nibble.

Thankfully, he does. "What kind of key?"

Hudson steps in and explains about the Unkillable Beast, who has been chained up for a thousand years with a cuff he made.

But as soon as the giant hears about the beast—and the cuff—he starts shaking his head. "I can't do that," he tells us. "There's no way."

"Why not?" I ask. "Don't you think a thousand years is long enough for anyone to be chained up?" I use the argument purposefully, considering he's been enslaved for just as long.

"A thousand seconds is too long for someone to be enslaved," he snaps back. "But my believing that doesn't mean I can help you."

"But it's your work. You're the blacksmith who made the cuffs to lock him up."

"Yes, and I'm also the blacksmith who's an indentured servant to this prison. For the most part, they leave me alone as long as I make the cells and the bracelets. I like it that way, and I'm not about to risk the life I've got to try to make things better for some creature who pissed Cyrus off for all eternity. Some creature I don't even know."

But you do know him, I want to say. *In so many ways, he's just like you.* But I know it won't matter. People rarely commiserate when in pain.

"If you won't do it for a stranger," I ask, "what about for someone you do know, Vander? Someone you love?"

"How do you know my name?" he demands. "No one here knows my name."

"Because I know Falia," I tell him. "And she wants you to come home to her."

"Lies!" he booms. "What trickery is this? My Falia is thousands of miles away from here—"

"In a redwood forest, I know. I was there with her a few weeks ago." I gesture to Hudson and Flint. "All three of us were."

"I don't believe you. Why would you go to see Falia? And how?" His voice is scornful. "You're in prison."

"We've only been in prison a few days," Flint tells him.

"And we came here, at least in part, for you," Hudson adds. "To convince you to make us a key and to help get you out so you can return to Falia."

"Lies!" he bellows again as he turns and picks Hudson up in one of his meaty fists. He shakes him. "No one ever gets out of this place. No one. Which means I will make you pay if you are telling me lies about my Falia."

"No lies!" Hudson's face is straining with the effort to pull his arms free of the giant's hand, but I can tell he's not going to break the hold before he's crushed. I rush to his side, place one hand on the giant's free arm. "I swear it. She told me to tell you, 'Still I recall.'"

He drops Hudson so fast and hard that Hudson almost doesn't land in a crouch. "What did you say?" Vander whispers, and the eyes he turns to me are filled with tears.

"She said you would know what that meant," I tell him.

"She still remembers the poem." His breathing is shaky now. "She still remembers me?"

"She loves you, Vander," Hudson tells him. "She's never stopped loving you. She suffers for it."

The last is like a body blow to the giant, knocking him back down on his boulder even as his hands shake. "And our children?"

"We didn't get to meet them," I tell him softly. "Only Falia, who is filled with grief at your absence. Who holds on to the promise you made her—the ring you gave her."

His gaze fills with anguish, with such naked pain that it's almost too painful to witness.

But I press on. "You made her a promise...and I promised her I would help you see it through. That I would free you and send you home to her." I pause, consider Vander might need a bit more convincing. "And that's not just an ordinary promise. I'm the future gargoyle queen, and my promises become law." I pause, studying his face to see if my hyperbole landed.

He still looks skeptical.

"We have a plan to escape," Remy says quickly.

"But we'll be needing that key first," Hudson adds.

At first, the blacksmith doesn't say anything. He just stares into space, tears the size of my fist rolling slowly down his face. Finally, when I'm beginning to think that we didn't reach him—that there's nothing left to reach—he whispers, "This key. When do you need it by?"

The five of us exchange a quick look. "Tonight," Remy says. "If you think you can manage."

The blacksmith glances at the exposed metal beams in the warehouse, then stares back down at us. "I need six hours."

"Six hours to make it?" Hudson asks, to clarify. "If we come back in six hours, you'll have the key?"

"If you come back in six hours, you'll have the key. And you'll have me." His gaze glides over all the others to lock with mine. "You'll take me out with you when you go?"

"I promise," I tell him. "We have a way to free you."

He nods, then says again, "Six hours. I'll be ready."

I smile up at him softly and say, "Thank you."

He nods. "Thank *you*."

I want to bask in the win for a minute—and the fact that we might actually get out of here and find a way to free the Unkillable Beast—but apparently Remy has bigger fish to fry.

I've barely taken two steps away from the giant when Remy claps his hands and says, "If we've only got six hours, we had better get busy."

133

Everyone's Got
a Little Skin
in the Game

"**W**hat do we need to do?" Flint asks as we head back into the darkened alley that led to the blacksmith, and I can tell from the way he's bouncing on the balls of his feet that he's ready to get going.

Not that I blame him. I'm so excited that the blacksmith agreed to help us that I'm ready to jump out of my skin. I've been so afraid that he would say no, so afraid that he would have forgotten about his wife and children and want to stay here, where he thinks he belongs.

But that didn't happen. He's making the key to free the Unkillable Beast, and he's coming with us. I couldn't think of anything more badass than that if I tried.

"I need you and Calder to find Bellamy. He's here in the Pit today, but he's hard to find. Tell him I need a number. He's the only one who knows the right one."

Flint looks confused. "A number? Like any number, or are you talking about a specific one? Because I can give you a number right now. I can give you lots of numbers—"

"It's a specific number, and he'll know what I need," Remy tells Flint with a shake of his head. "And before you start in about not knowing who Bellamy is—"

"I don't."

"Calder does. That's why I put you two together." He looks to his friend. "Check the gaming shops first. See if you can pick up his trail there."

"I was planning on it. This isn't my first rodeo." She loops an arm through Flint's. "Let's go, big guy."

As the two walk away, with Calder trying to lead Flint in a song none of us has ever heard of, Remy turns to me. "I need you to come with me, Grace. We have somewhere to be and not a minute to waste."

"Where are we going?" Hudson asks.

"Not we," Remy shoots back. "Only Grace and I are going. We have something else we need to do. I've seen it. But I've got a different job for you."

"Yeah, well, I'm not leaving Grace's side."

"I know I'm only human, but I'll be okay," I assure him. I try to focus on how sweet it is that my mate wants to protect me, instead of that he doesn't think I can protect myself.

His eyebrows shoot up. "Of course you'll be okay, Grace." He shakes his head. "You're right. You'll be fine without me. Where do you need me to go, Remy?"

"To the rings. If we're going to get out of here, we're going to need a lot of money. Only way to make that much money in this short of time? Fight for it." He shrugs. "That is, if you think you got it in you."

"Where do I start?" Hudson grins, even as he wraps an arm around my waist and pulls me into him.

"There are four different rings two streets over. Pick one and get started." He tosses Hudson a couple of gold coins. "These should get you bought in."

Hudson catches them with his free hand and slides them in his pocket. "I've got my own, but thanks." Then he turns his head and presses soft kisses to my cheek and ear. "I've got this, babe."

"You're going off to beat the shit out of people and let them beat the shit out of you. Sounds delightful. You better come back in one piece," I insist.

"Guess you'll just have to wait and see." He gives me one more kiss—a real one this time—then pulls away. And gives Remy a warning look. "I want her in exactly this condition when you get back from whatever errand you need to run."

I roll my eyes. "I could say the same for you."

But he merely laughs and promises, "I'll try," before heading back the way we came.

"That's not very reassuring!" I call after him, but he simply laughs again and fades away.

"He better not get hurt," I tell Remy as he herds me in the other direction.

"Yeah, well, hurry up." Remy really starts to hustle me along. "Or you're going to miss your shot at proving your own badassery."

I narrow my eyes. "I don't do fight clubs."

"You won't have to." He laughs. "It's not that kind of place."

"What kind of place is it?" I ask.

"Far more exciting."

134

I'm Wearing a Lot
More than a Heart
on My Sleeve

Ten minutes later, I'm staring at the window of the shop Remy wants to take me into. Hard.

"I'd rather do the fight clubs," I tell him, eyes wide.

"Yeah, well, that's Hudson's job. This is yours."

I shake my head. "I say we switch."

He laughs, the jerk. He actually laughs. Even as he starts guiding me straight for the door. "I'm afraid it doesn't work that way."

"Dude, I'm not getting inked."

"You have to."

"Excuse me?" I glare at him. "You don't get to make that decision for me."

He sighs. "I'm not trying to force you into anything. Except if we want to get all of us out of this place, this is the only way I know to do it."

"With a tattoo?" I ask skeptically.

"With one of Vikram's tattoos," he answers as he holds the door for me. "I have a theory."

"I'm about to get inked for a theory?"

"You're about to get inked by one of the most powerful warlocks in the Pit for a theory." He winks. "It's not the same thing."

"So what is it, then?" I ask him.

"I've been thinking about this ever since you pulled me into Hudson's hellscape. You can channel magic, right?"

"You know I can." I glance around the place, which looks more like an upscale hair salon than any tattoo parlor I've ever seen. Not that I've seen a lot of them, but unless every movie ever is lying—not to mention every tattoo parlor I've ever driven by—this is a really chichi one. Which isn't a bad thing, I decide, as the green-and-gold-haired receptionist offers us cucumber water as we wait. "But I can't use your magic like you can. I can only channel it."

He nods. "I noticed that. I think it's because you're not built to hold magic—so it leaves you as soon as you receive it. You're a conduit."

Well, who doesn't love being compared to an electrical cord? Although, I have to admit, I'm curious where he's going with this. "Let's say I agree with that. What does a tattoo have to do with it?"

"Vikram's tattoos can do all sorts of things. So what I think is, with the right tattoo, you can pull my magic from me, including magic I've never been able to access, and hold it in the tattoo—then send it back to me, freed from the prison's magical locks." He pauses while I absorb this idea, then leans forward, and I don't know if it's me he's trying to convince of his next statement or himself. "I don't know who my dad was, but my mom used to tell me a bedtime story that he gave me enough power to tear a hole in this prison. To level it—when I was ready."

I think back to that minute when I first wrapped my hand around his wrist—he had power, but not very much. Was it simply hidden from me? "Is that how we get out?"

He shakes his head. "I don't know. But I know when you give me the flower, you have a tattoo on your arm. And since you don't have a tattoo on your arm now...you must get one in the Pit. And why else but to help free my magic to break us out?"

"So this tattoo might be necessary to get us out or it might not. All you know is that I get it?" I think about this and then sigh. I want to tell him *no way* on the tattoo, but what if he's right and it's our only way out? I'd hate to blow everything because I didn't keep an open mind. "Can it be small, at least? And somewhere that my uncle Finn won't see it?"

He just laughs. "It can be anywhere you want, Grace. I don't think the location I saw it in matters."

Except that turns out not to be true, because when Remy gives his name to the receptionist, her eyes go wide. She excuses herself and hurries to the back of the shop. Seconds later, the tattoo artist comes out to greet us, and she is totally kick-ass. She's probably about fifty or sixty, and she's got short white-gray hair that she wears in two pigtails that are dipped in shades of blue so that they look like dripping icicles. She's wearing a black tank that shows off both her sleeves of tattoos—one a full waterscape, one a full earthscape—and they are absolutely beautiful.

"Remy?" she asks. "Is it you?"

"Yeah?" He seems confused. "I'm sorry. Have we met?"

"Your mom brought you here when you were a little boy, too young to remember, I imagine." She holds out a hand. "I'm Eliza."

He takes it and shakes. "I'm…" His cheeks flush as he realizes he's about to introduce himself again, and I note it's the first time I've ever seen him discomfited. I wonder if it's because she knew his mom or because—for the first time since I've been here—someone knows more about a situation than he does.

He gestures to me. "This is Grace."

"Grace?" she says, eyes widening. "So this is the girl who took on the Nightbloom coven…and lived to tell the tale. I've been hearing good things about you, Grace."

It's my turn to be uncomfortable. "Oh, um, thanks. It was more chance than anything else."

She laughs. "So much of life is." She waves us to the back of the shop. "Come on, let's get started."

"But we haven't picked a design yet," I protest. She's cool-looking and all and I love her ink, but I do not want a full sleeve covering all the skin on my arm. At least not right now.

Eliza seems confused. "But I've already created the design. Remy's mom paid me to do it twelve years ago and said you would show up when you needed it. I just assumed, when you came today—"

"My mom did all that?" Remy asks, and he sounds astonished…but also touched in a way he doesn't seem able to process.

"I think she always knew that one day you would need her to have done so," Eliza says as she reaches over and squeezes his shoulder. "I knew your mom—did ink on her a few times through the years. And if I know anything, it's that she loved you, kid."

Remy swallows. Then whispers, "Thank you."

"You're welcome." She nods brusquely, like she's used up her quota of emotion for the day and then some. "Now, who's ready to get inked?"

"I am," I tell her, even though my stomach feels a little hollow. "Can I at least see the design first?" *Since I'm the one who will be wearing it for the rest of her life*, my tone implies.

"Nah." Eliza grins. "I think this one should be a surprise."

135

Punch Drunk

"**A**re you going to stare at that all day?" Remy asks, amused. We're winding our way back to meet the others at the taco place near the blacksmith's forge, but we're running late because the tattoo took almost the full six hours the blacksmith gave us.

But even though my arm is sore, I can't stop looking at it. Eliza knows what she's talking about—and so, apparently, did Remy's mom—because it's the most beautiful tattoo I've ever seen. Which is a good thing, I suppose, considering it's *on my body*.

Eliza cutting the arm out of my jumpsuit concerned me at the time, but now I'm thrilled. I wouldn't be able to see the tattoo if she hadn't, and honestly, I can't take my eyes off the thing.

It starts at the outside edge of my left wrist and wraps around my arm in a widely spaced, sloping design that goes all the way up my arm until the tattoo ends on the inside of my upper arm, where it meets my body. From a distance, it looks like a drawing of a delicate vine with flower blossoms and drops of dew, but when you get closer, there are no actual lines in the entire piece. Instead, it's made up of millions of tiny different colored dots placed so close together that they form an incredible picture—like pixels on a TV screen. If that TV *shimmered*.

From a distance, it's beautiful. Up close, it's absolutely breathtaking—and impossible to imagine how it all came together. I was there, watching the whole thing, and I still have no idea how or when it went from a bunch of dots to this gorgeous, delicate, feminine tattoo that I love entirely too much.

Now the only thing to worry about is if it actually works. It's a tattoo I'll wear with pride my whole life, of course, but it would be so much better if it manages to do what we need it to do. Which seems far-fetched, I admit, but no more far-fetched than anything and everything else that happens in this place.

But when we get there, I forget all about my tattoo because Hudson is sitting at a table (though "sitting" might be a bit of a stretch as a descriptor of what he's currently doing), looking like he got run over by an eighteen-wheeler...or three.

I take inventory as I race through the maze of picnic tables to get to him.

Both of his eyes are black, his nose is a shade crooked in a way it wasn't before, the skin under his left eye is split open, and so is his bottom lip. His knuckles are raw, his neck has been clawed, and nearly every ounce of skin he's got showing is black-and-blue. Then again, judging from the way he's slumped over the table holding his side, I'm betting whatever injuries are under his jumpsuit are worse.

"Wow," I say as I get closer and realize just how beaten up he is. I'm freaking out a little bit, but there's no way I can show it here. Not in front of Remy and definitely not in front of all the other inmates at this prison, who are watching him like they want another shot. "I'd hate to see the other guy. Or should I say guys?"

"You're the best," he tells me with a loopy smile that concerns me even more than the bruises. "See, Remy. This is why you need a mate! Didn't even consider I'd lose, did you, honey baby?"

Honey baby? Just how many times did he get hit in the head, anyway? He's grinning at me now, his smile lopsided and swollen but so, so happy.

"Not even for a second," I tell him, while I try to get a good look in his eyes to measure his pupil size.

"How much did you win?" Remy asks, but before Hudson can answer, Calder comes striding through the tables with Flint over her shoulder. He's singing Billie Eilish's "bad guy" at the top of his lungs, and he is completely wasted.

"What the hell did you do to him?" Remy asks, exasperated, as Calder slings him down on top of the table.

Flint simply lays there singing until he gets to the chorus; then he grins up at me with a smile even loopier than Hudson's. "Hi there, pretty lady," he tells me in the worst version of a southern accent I have ever heard.

"Hi, Flint."

"You have pretty hair. Did I ever tell you that you have pretty hair?" He reaches out and grabs a curl.

"You haven't, no."

"She does have pretty hair, doesn't she?" Hudson agrees as he picks up a curl from the other side of my head.

"Is this seriously happening?" Remy asks, glancing around like he's waiting for someone to tell him this is one big cosmic joke. "Are two of the five of us completely out of their minds right now? At the worst possible time?"

"Sorry," Hudson says. "But the cyclops hit hard."

Remy shoots me a *what is even happening here* look. "You took on a *cyclops*?"

"He wanted to fight," Hudson says. "You told me I had to fight. So I did."

"I didn't tell you to fight a *cyclops*!" Remy growls.

Flint finishes with Billie Eilish and moves on to BTS's "Dynamite." And oh my God. Listening to him belt out one of the boy band's biggest hits has me all but suffocating as I try not to laugh.

"What. The. Fuck. Did. You. Do. To. Him?" Remy grinds out through his teeth as he stares between Flint and Calder.

"You told us to get a number from Bellamy. We got the number. But we had to drink with him until he was drunk enough to spill." She gives Flint an affectionate smile. "Apparently, he looks a lot tougher than he is."

Flint responds by waving goofily at her and changing to Miley Cyrus's "Wrecking Ball."

"Apparently," Remy says as he turns to me. "Can you do something to help them?"

I stare between Flint and Hudson, who is currently sniffing my hair and telling me how good I smell, and ask, "What exactly do you suggest I do? Keeping in mind that this mess was all your idea."

Remy blows out a long breath, then sinks down on the bench across from Hudson. "What was the number Bellamy gave you?"

Calder's amusement disappears as quickly as it came. "He said it needed to be at least a hundred thou."

"Per person?"

"Yeah."

Remy does a little shrug, as if to say, *The hits just keep on coming.* Then he sighs and asks Hudson, "So how much did you win?"

Hudson stops sniffing my hair long enough to reach under the table and pull out a sack of money, which he drops on the table next to Flint's head. It's filled with gold coins—so many that I'm a little dizzy—but Remy looks disappointed.

"If that's all, then we are fucked," he tells Hudson.

But Hudson just laughs—and then groans and holds his ribs. "It hurts," he wheezes to me.

"Oh, baby." I press a superlight kiss on his shoulder. "I'm so sorry. What can I do?"

"Don't let him make me laugh," he answers. Then bends down and pulls out another sack of money. And another. And another.

And another.

"Holy shit," Calder says, her eyes huge. "How many people did you fight?"

"All of them."

"All of them?" Remy asks. "Everyone in the arena?"

"Everyone in all the arenas," Hudson clarifies. "They just kept lining up, so I just kept knocking them back down. You told me we needed a lot."

"Yeah, I did. No wonder you're so fucking loopy." Remy shakes his head, then shoots me a grin. "I've been reserving judgment up until now, *cher*, but your mate's a stand-up guy."

Hudson is back to sniffing my hair, so I laugh and say, "Yeah. Yeah, he is."

"I do have one question, though," Remy adds.

"What's that?"

"If things go to shit in the next couple of hours, what the hell are we supposed to do with them?"

136

Talk About a Giant
Temper Tantrum

I don't have an answer for that question except to say, "Vampires heal fast."

"That fast?" Calder asks.

"I have no idea."

Remy stands up again. "Let's see if we can't get the dragon and Golden Gloves over here on their feet enough to head back to the blacksmith."

"Can you walk, baby?" I ask Hudson.

"For you?" He sighs. "Anything." And then nearly falls backward as he stands up.

I quickly reach an arm around his waist and let him lean against me. He pushes his face into my hair and sniffs. "I love the way you smell." Which, okay. He smells pretty good himself. But then he adds, "You taste better, though," and my cheeks heat.

I glance around to see if anyone heard him, but Calder is trying to coax a glass of water down Flint. "Come on, big guy. Drink up. I'll sing 'YMCA' with you if you can walk on your own."

Flint sits up like someone gave him an IV of coffee, then grins goofily at Calder. "Really?"

She rolls her eyes. "If I must..."

Flint staggers to his feet. "A deal's a deal. But you gotta do the arm movements, too." And then he starts belting out the first line of the iconic song.

"I've got the funds," Remy says as he starts hoisting the sacks of gold coins into his arms.

"How much time do we have?" I ask, glancing at Hudson again, who is still none too steady on his feet.

"Not a lot. Why?"

"I thought maybe we could catch up to you in a few." I try to sound casual, but even I know it fails—even before his eyes narrow.

"What's going on, Grace?" Remy asks suspiciously.

"I was hoping maybe I could..." I don't know why I'm so embarrassed to admit this out loud. It's a normal biological function.

"Maybe you could ...?" Now he's beginning to look pissed.

"I thought I could give Hudson a few minutes to drink from me," I finally blurt out. "The blood will help him recover faster."

"Oh!" Remy goes from suspicious to amused in two seconds flat. "I've got to admit, *cher*, I didn't know you had it in you."

"Had what in me?" Now I'm a little insulted. Do I not seem like the kind of girl who would take care of her mate?

"It's okay," Hudson says, and though his words are still a little slurred, his eyes are sincere. "You don't need to do that."

"Yeah, but you're hurt—"

He wraps an arm around my neck and pulls me close. "Grace, there's no way I'm going to take blood from you in the middle of a bunch of criminals. Who knows what kind of lowlifes that will attract?" He kisses my nose—which would be weird except for the fact that I think he was aiming for my mouth. "Besides," he whispers kind of close to my ear, "once I get to bite you again, I don't think I'm going to want to stop anytime soon."

His words make me flush a little, but before I can respond with something a little bit sexy, Calder calls back to us that she's going to come do the "YMCA" dance on our asses if we don't shake a leg.

"We really don't have time anyway," Remy says and turns away to catch up with Flint and Calder.

Hudson smiles at me, then leans in for another kiss. This time he gets the bottom of my chin. "I'm going to take you up on that offer when we get out of here," he tells me groggily.

"*If* we get out of here," I answer grimly even as we catch up to the others and start making our way back to the blacksmith and his furnace.

It only takes us a few minutes to make it to the forge again, even though half the group is staggering. Partly because Flint's dragon metabolism is sobering him up in record time, and partly because when no one was watching, I let Hudson take a few pulls of blood from my wrist. I couldn't stand the idea of him suffering, even if he was starting to heal. He's certainly nowhere near 100 percent with such a small amount of blood, but I can already see his eyes and lips are clearing up and mending and he's walking on his own power again.

As we near the blacksmith, Vander says, "I have the key." Then he checks us over, taking in that we look a little worse for wear since he saw us last, and pats the large pocket on his shirt. "I'll keep it safe until we *all* get out."

"I have a flower to give you that will simulate your death," I say, pointing to one of my flower tattoos. "Once they think you're dead, they'll remove your body from the prison and you will be free. We don't have enough flowers for everyone, though, so we need the key so we can exit in a different way."

"Give me one of the flowers now," the giant says.

I glance at Hudson, who just nods; then I think about how badly I need the flowers. After that, I reach toward my tattoo... And then nearly screech in surprise when one of the flowers floats off my palm like it was waiting for me to call for it.

The Crone assured me it would work no matter what. At the time, I wasn't sure why she was so insistent, but now I know what she meant. Or at least I hope I do. She was insisting that her flowers' magic would work here, even though nobody else's does.

I hope she's right.

"Right good job!" Hudson whispers to me, and I grin at him, because the British always makes me smile. And also because his eyes appear a bit clearer than they did, and that makes me happy.

"Give me that!" the giant growls and grabs at the flower, then tosses it into his mouth. It's so small, he can swallow it without chewing, and we all step way back in an effort to keep a twenty-foot giant from falling on us.

Except...nothing happens.

He doesn't fall over. He doesn't die. He doesn't even look sleepy, actually. Just pissed off. "You tricked me."

"We didn't!" I tell him. "The flowers are supposed to work."

"You're going to pay for this," Vander says. "Nobody lies to me."

"Don't threaten my mate," Hudson says coldly, and for the first time since the fight debacle, he sounds like the old Hudson. "We *didn't* lie to you. Maybe you're, I don't know, immune," he tells him.

"Why would I be immune?"

"I don't know. Maybe because you're twenty feet tall and a thousand pounds and it's one little flower?" Hudson shoots back. "Or maybe giants don't respond to this. How are we supposed to know?"

At first, it looks like the giant might be thinking about it, but then he yells, "Lies!" and lifts his hand like he's going to hit me.

I quickly reach back into my tattoo and pull out a second flower. Maybe because Vander is so big, he requires more than one flower. I don't remember telling the Crone that the person we were trying to break out was a giant.

Which turns Hudson's eyes to blue fire. He starts to move in front of me, but Calder springs into action and gets there first. She lands right in front of me, then grabs one of the other flowers from my hand. "Want proof we didn't cheat you, old man?" She shoves the flower in her mouth and eats it.

"Calder!" Remy yells, rushing over to her. "What have you done?"

"What I always do," she says with a cocky grin. "I saved your ass...and looked damn fine doing it."

"Yes, but—"

He breaks off as her eyes close, and she pitches forward.

I grab on to her, swaying under her weight even as I refuse to let her hit the ground. Hudson starts to take her from me, but he's banged up so badly that he hisses through his teeth the second her weight lands against his injured side.

"Give her to me," Flint says. "I'll take her."

"You're drunk," Remy snarls.

"Not that drunk," Flint tells him. "Not anymore."

He picks her up and shifts her weight until she's lying over his right shoulder, imitating the fireman's carry she used on him earlier.

"Well, that was...unexpected." Hudson gives me a *what the fuck* look, but I just shrug.

"What do we do now?" I ask the group at large.

"Leave her here for the guards to find?" Vander suggests.

"She goes where we go," Remy tells us, his voice brooking no room for argument. "We're not leaving her."

"Of course we're not leaving her," I say.

Hudson nods, even as he shoots a warning look at Vander. "That's not even a question."

"You were going to leave me," Vander says, and I'm pretty sure he's pouting.

"You're twenty feet tall and went off half cocked," Hudson snaps. "You caused all of this, so stop your bitching."

Vander goes slack in shock, and I don't blame him. I'm pretty sure no one has ever talked to him like that in his life.

"We still need to figure out what to do," Flint says.

"I know what we need to do." Remy sighs.

"Which is?" I ask.

"Plan B." He turns to Flint. "And pass me a couple of those sacks of money. At this point, we're going to need every penny to pull this off."

"What about me?" Vander asks. "Should I come, too?"

Remy eyes him, then gestures to Hudson and says, "Maybe pass me all the sacks."

137

The River
Stick-It-to-Ya?

To my surprise, Remy takes us back toward the cellblocks.

I thought the goal was to get thrown over the fence out of the prison, so going backward doesn't make much sense to me. Then again, we have five people to get out and one flower to do it in, so I guess it's not exactly surprising that Plan B involves something totally different after all.

I can't help but be curious if my tattoo is part of this new plan, and I ask as much. "Are we going to try to use the tattoo?"

"Not yet, *cher*," Remy replies. "That one's an even bigger long shot. Besides, I still see myself leaving this shithole with a flower. If I leveled the prison with my magic, why didn't I just use that to leave?"

"But I don't understand," I start. "Who cares how you get out as long as you are free?"

Remy pauses long enough to hold my gaze while he says, "Because, like I said, I'm not screwing up my sure thing. I get out with a flower. So that's how I'm going to get out. And you don't give me a flower unless you're freed, so there is obviously another way to get you out."

He doesn't wait for me to respond to that. Just turns and starts heading down the road, his long strides eating up the distance between us.

Fine. I can sort of understand why he doesn't want to risk his chance at getting out. If I were born here, maybe I'd feel the same.

I sure wish his Plan B didn't involve going into the scariest, sketchiest area of the Pit yet. A quick glance at Hudson tells me he's thinking the same thing—at least if the way his gaze is constantly scanning the alley is any indication. Not to mention how he's studiously avoiding meeting my eyes, like he doesn't want me to see how concerned he is.

"We're almost there," Remy tosses over his shoulder, and I hope he knows what he's talking about because I can't see anything. Most of the shops in the

Pit have started to close up, as time is running out for prisoners, many of them already heading back to their cells early—probably not to risk accidentally being late and getting a month in the Chamber. If we weren't hell-bent on our plan to escape, I know I'd be doing the same.

As the streetlights don't seem to run this far south, I'm trying not to totally freak out. I comfort myself with the reminder that Hudson and Flint can see, but considering neither of them is in tip-top shape, I'm really hoping that Remy knows what he's doing.

We finally make it to the end of the alley, and Remy punches the buttons on a control pad—the only lighted thing in this whole place. Which seems weird in and of itself, considering we're standing in front of a brick wall. No doors, no windows, nothing but this bizarre-ass intercom hanging out in the middle of it all.

"State your name and business," comes through the speaker loud and clear.

"You know who it is, and unless your network has broken down, I'm pretty sure you know why we're here."

There's a laugh at the other end. "Do you have enough?"

"You mean you haven't heard about our recent windfall?" There's definite mockery in his tone, but the guard—or whoever it is—on the other end of the exchange just snickers.

Which reminds me again of how different Remy is treated here. I've seen enough in the six days we've been in this prison to know that anyone else would be missing a throat—or at least a limb—for mocking one of the windigos that way. But Remy simply gets a laugh. It's strange to realize that they really do love him in their own way.

"He's busy right now," the guard tells him. "Come back later."

"I've got four hours left, and he knows it. There is no *later*. Just now. So open the door and let me see Charon."

Charon? I glance at Hudson to see what he thinks of the name, and in the dim light, he looks as puzzled as I feel.

"Like the River Styx Charon?" I ask. I mean, normally Greek mythology would be a huge stretch of the imagination, but I am currently standing in an alley with a vampire, a dragon, a warlock, a giant, and a manticore. Reality as I knew it fled the building a long time ago.

"Hell no," Remy answers with a laugh. "He gave himself that name, which basically tells you everything you need to know about him."

Right. If you're going to make up a name for yourself, shouldn't it be something a little less grim than Hades's ferryman?

For several interminable seconds, nothing happens. No response, no crackling of the intercom, nothing. And then, when I'm least expecting it, a massive rumbling sound fills the air.

"What is that?" I ask, instinctively tucking myself a little closer to Hudson. He grins at me like I just gave him the best Christmas present on the planet and wraps an arm around my shoulders—the one that isn't still lugging several sacks of money.

"It's okay," he tells me as he nods straight ahead. "Look."

I follow his gaze and watch in shock as the brick wall in front of us splits in half to reveal a long, well-lit corridor patrolled by three very large windigos.

Remy moves forward to speak to the guards, the bags of money clutched in his hands. Behind me, the blacksmith rumbles almost as loudly as the cogs moving the wall, and honestly, I don't blame him. I've been here six days, and I want nothing to do with those windigos. He's been here a thousand years.

"It's okay," Flint reassures him...and the rest of us. "Remy's got this."

"He does," Hudson agrees, and as the bags of money change hands, I can feel him relax against me.

He even goes so far as to glance over at me—and my uncovered arm. "I like what you did to the jumpsuit," he teases.

Normally I'd pay him back with a soft elbow to the ribs, but he's so banged up that I'm afraid to do anything but roll my eyes at him.

His grin softens, and he leans down and softly whispers in my ear, "I like the new ink even more."

A shiver works its way down my spine courtesy of the whisper and the words. "Oh yeah?"

"Yeah." His mouth is even closer to my ear this time, his lips brushing against the sensitive skin of my lobe while his warm breath lights up every single nerve ending I've got. "It's really sexy."

"You're really sexy," I tell him, the words slipping out before I even know I'm going to say them.

But I don't regret them, not when his poor, abused face lights up like the Fourth of July.

He slides his arm down around my waist, then moves behind me so that he's holding my back flush against his front. He feels good, so good. Warm and safe and definitely sexy. Even before his laugh tickles my ear and he murmurs, "You didn't happen to get any other tattoos I should know about, did you?"

"Other tattoos?" I twist around enough to see the wicked glint in the swollen eyes that are already beginning to heal. "Such as?"

"I don't know. A flower on your hip, maybe?" His hands skim the body part in question, and heat flares along my skin.

"A pair of wings on your shoulders?" He moves his hands up and rubs muscles I didn't even know were sore. I melt against him in response.

"A heart with my name on it on your ass?" There's a hint of humor in his voice as he moves his hand down my back to—

"If you slap my ass," I warn, "I'm going to make you suffer."

He laughs, then holds his hurt ribs with a groan. "It might be worth it. Especially since you didn't deny having the heart."

"Why should I deny it? Where else would an ass like you belong?"

Hudson chuckles, but Flint groans. "Jesus. Could you two just do it and get it over with already? Some of us are sick of suffering through your sexual frustration."

"That's not frustration, dragon," Hudson growls, but there's no heat behind the words. "It's foreplay. Do I need to give Luca a little direction in that area?"

"Luca's doing just fine in that department," Flint tells him. "But thanks for the offer."

Hudson starts to say something else, but Remy beckons us forward into the corridor before he can bust Flint's balls any more. "We've been granted an audience."

"By Charon?" Vander asks. He sounds astonished.

"By Charon," Remy confirms.

"I hope you've got an escape route."

Remy's smile is grim. "This *is* my escape route."

"Yeah." Vander sighs. "That's what I was afraid you were going to say."

138

Déjà Doomed

I expect the windigos to lead us down the hallway, but they just let Remy go—like he's got the run of the place or something. Then again, maybe he does.

Either way, we walk down a really, really, really long corridor until we get to a pair of gold double doors. At first, I think they're simply painted that way, but as Remy holds one open for the rest of us, I realize it's not paint. It's real gold...which is really, really gross.

Because who's got the money to do that? And who chooses to spend their money on solid-gold doors inside a prison instead of helping someone with it?

It gets worse when we walk in the door. The room itself is royal purple and gold, loaded with plush furniture, the most expensive electronics, all the bells and whistles anyone could possibly imagine.

But the pièce de résistance, in the center of the room, is a solid-gold throne covered in purple pillows. And sitting on that throne is a kid, no more than ten or eleven.

He's decked out in a fancy suit, with rings on every finger and a big, fat Rolex on his wrist. I've never seen anything like it. Part of me thinks he must be a prisoner like the rest of us, a young kid stuck in this hellhole through no fault of his own.

But nothing here speaks of him being a prisoner, not even the two giants on either side of him who I'm pretty sure are his guards. Still, he's a kid, and I have to ask.

"Is he okay?"

"Am I okay?" he repeats in what might be the snottiest prepubescent voice I've ever heard.

"Meet Charon," Remy says, his tone as ironic as I've ever heard it. "When people are finally granted their freedom from the Aethereum, Charon is the one who carries them across."

"So he works for the prison?" Flint asks, and I can't tell if he really thinks that or if he's just trying to piss this kid off. If it's the latter, it definitely works.

"Excuse you, dragon. I *own* this prison, and no one does anything in it without my say-so. And they definitely, definitely don't leave unless I. Let. Them. Go."

"Which you don't," Hudson says, and I'll hand it to him. When he puts on the bored-prince voice that used to get so far under my skin, he can go head-to-head with this guy for who's the biggest douche.

"Why should I?" Charon counters.

"Because it's supposed to be the whole point of the prison?" I suggest. "Complete your punishment, atone for what you've done, and be set free."

"Yes, but who can actually tell when someone has been adequately punished? Been truly repentant?" Charon says with a shitty little shrug that looks particularly awful coming from a ten-year-old. "One can't be too careful."

"Especially if *one* wants to rule his own kingdom," Hudson comments. "Rules are so boring and unnecessary."

Charon's eyes narrow, as if trying to figure out if he's being made fun of or if he's found a kindred spirit. "Who are you again?" he finally asks.

"This is Hudson Vega, my liege," Remy says with a false obsequiousness that practically screams that we're not in Kansas anymore.

Charon chooses to ignore the impertinence and instead focuses on my mate. "Ah yes, the vampire prince back from the dead. Welcome to my humble abode."

Hudson glances around, and I'm pretty sure he's thinking the same thing I am. That there's nothing humble—or tasteful—about this place.

Charon pauses the conversation, waiting for him to answer, but Hudson isn't giving him the satisfaction. After more than a minute of awkward silence has passed with the prison owner getting angrier and angrier, Remy asks, "Can we talk about the price now, *Charles*?"

"Charon!" he rebukes. "How many times do I have to tell you? My name is *Charon*!" The only way he could sound more obnoxious is if he threw himself on the floor and had a full-on tantrum.

"Excuse me. *Charon*, can we please talk about the price now?"

"We could," he says with a gleeful yawn. "But you don't have enough."

"Bellamy set the price today at one hundred thousand per person. We have enough." He gestures to the bags full of gold coins that Hudson is carrying.

"That *was* the price. The new price is much higher." Charon gives him an *oops* look.

"Since when?" Remy presses. "It was the price an hour ago."

Charon shrugs. "A lot can happen in an hour."

"Such as?"

"An additional wire transfer from the vampire king, assuring that his son remains in prison, for one." Charon flicks a speck of imaginary dust off his shoulder. "He already paid a king's ransom to get him here. But today's payment... Let's just say it's enough to keep him housed for at least a hundred years—or three."

He glances at Vander for the first time. "And can you imagine what would happen if we lost his favorite blacksmith? And our little gargoyle queen?" He mock shudders. "There wouldn't be enough people for him to kill in the world if you slipped through his fingers."

"You're really that afraid of him?" Remy asks.

"I'm afraid of no one!" comes the immediate response. "I am an addonexus, and we fear no one!"

"An addonexus?" I whisper to Hudson, who mutters back under his breath, "An immortal tween with a god complex." Sure. That explains it all. Is it really too much to ask that someone might want to share with me if this child is capable of smiting us all with a sneeze?

"Then what are we bickering about? We all know you love money. We have a lot of money." Remy motions to Hudson, who dumps one of the sacks on the ground. Thousands of coins pour out. "Let's make a deal."

Charon's eyes light up with greed, and for a second, I think it's going to work. But then the kid tears his eyes away from the money and shrugs. "It would cause a mutiny. My men have been complaining for the last hour that the young vampire prince fleeced them."

"Every fight I was in tonight was a fair one," Hudson tells him coldly.

"I guess there's only one way to find out for sure, isn't there?" His smile is evil. "I think it's only right that you give my men a chance to win back what you took from them. Double or nothing. If you can beat Mazur and Ephes, you walk away with double the money—enough to buy your freedom."

"And if I don't?" Hudson raises a brow.

"I get you and the money, obviously."

"Obviously," is Hudson's snide response. "I'm o—"

"That's a sucker bet, and you know it." I jump in before Hudson can do something ridiculous—like actually agree to this plan. The guy can barely stand as it is, and he thinks he's going to fight two giants? There's no way. "Look at him. You could never call it a fair fight."

Charon sighs. "Of course it's the gargoyle causing trouble. You've always been such troublesome creatures."

"I wouldn't say sticking up for someone is troublesome," I tell him.

"Yes, well, everyone is entitled to their opinion, I suppose." He focuses his cold gray eyes back on Hudson. "Do we have a deal?"

Hudson starts to agree, but I talk over him again. The vampire has absolutely no sense of self-preservation. "You do not have a deal."

"Keep it up and you're going in the dungeon!" he snaps.

"Wouldn't be the first time," I snap back.

"That's it! You want the fight to be more fair? Fine, you can fight with him."

"What?" Hudson roars. "No!"

"You just lost your chance to vote," Charon sneers. "You want your freedom? You two can fight my giants for it. If you don't, you can feel free to leave the money and head back to your cells right now. But this discussion is over."

He starts to stand, but Remy holds up a hand to stop him. "Give us a second, please."

Remy pulls us aside, and Hudson and I both round on him, fire in our eyes. "No way is she going in an arena with Frick and Frack," Hudson snarls at him.

"Yeah, well, neither are you," I snarl back. "They'll kill you in two minutes flat."

"Thanks for the faith, mate."

I roll my eyes. "I'm sorry, but have you looked in a mirror since you got your everything bashed in?"

"It's the only way," Remy tells us. "We won't get another chance like this one again. He'll make sure of it."

"I've got this," Hudson tells him…and me. "The day two giants can take me out is the day I let them remove my fangs."

"This is a bad idea," I tell them.

"A very bad idea," Flint chimes in for the first time.

"Yeah, well, at this point, there's no good ideas, so..." Remy moves back to Charon. "Give me your word, and we'll agree on this."

To which Charon replies, "My bond is my word."

The two of them shake, and I blow out a long breath as I close my eyes. I just need a minute to regroup, to try to get my head together, and then Hudson and I can figure out what to do.

Except now I can hear people yelling and shouting, can smell meat roasting and popcorn popping.

And then someone yanks on the back of my prison uniform. When I open my eyes, I'm dropping down, down, down into the center of a giant arena.

139

There's Never a Slingshot Around When You Need It

I've never wanted to be able to shift into a gargoyle so much in my entire life. Not only because of all the cool things I could do right now to help get me out of this mess, but because wings are pretty much a necessity at this exact moment in time...considering I'm about to break every bone in my freaking body.

Every. Single. Bone.

And there is absolutely nothing I can do about it—except close my eyes and wait to die.

I remember reading once that it's not the fall that kills you; it's the bounce. If your parachute ever fails and you end up slamming into the ground, you're supposed to try to dig in. You'll break everything, but if you don't bounce, you just might live.

I can't believe I'm going to die by bounce—at the hands of a snotty immortal ten-year-old, no less. Not quite the way I'd hoped to end this little seven-day soiree to prison, but it is what it is.

I start to close my eyes and pray that it's fast...

Except Hudson fades over faster than he's ever faded and, before I'm about to hit the ground, he's there to catch me.

"Parachutes are overrated," he says with a cocky grin. But the words are a little slurred, and he's shaking as he sets me on the ground.

The fade took a lot out of him, but he's rallying fast.

"I think you tore your spleen on that Superman move." I slide an arm around his waist to help support his body weight while he catches his breath. I know I should say thank you, but I'm too busy trembling with fear that he might have wasted too much energy catching me.

"Spleens are overrated, too." He winks at me.

"What are we going to do now?" I ask.

But before he can answer, the two giants—Mazur and Ephes—vault over the fence. When they hit the ground, the whole arena shakes.

And I...I kind of wish Hudson had let me fall. It would have been a painful death, but at least it would have been a quick one. At this point, I think that's all either of us can hope for. Because this? This is going to be bad.

"Should we go for the quick death or the slow, agonizing one?" I ask Hudson, and it's clear by his we-got-this-grin that he thinks I was kidding. I was not.

"We need to tire them out," he says, and okay, that could be a plan. If Hudson hadn't just beat the entire prison population and I weren't a short human.

I glance around the arena, looking for somewhere to hide until we can figure out a better plan, and realize that there is no such place. Everything is wide open.

I also realize that we're not in a real arena—yes, there are spectators watching the show from bleachers roped off on either side of the room, popcorn and beer at the ready, but that's where the resemblance ends. This room is pure ballroom—from the ornate drapes to the baroque carpet to the fancy white chandeliers tied back to keep the center of the room clear for the giant fights.

I don't understand what's happening—how did these people know to be here? How did Charon know to have this ballroom set up for a fight he had no idea was even going to happen?

Unless he did?

Maybe he knew this was going to happen all along. But if he did, how?

Before I can work out the answer to that question, Charon's voice booms overhead, welcoming the audience to today's installment of the Colossus Clash.

The giants stand in the middle of the room, flexing for the crowd and waving their arms around as Charon reads off their stats. Apparently, Mazur is twenty-two feet tall and a little over a thousand pounds while Ephes is twenty feet tall and a trim seven hundred and fifty pounds.

"It's like we're at a boxing match," Hudson says to me out of the corner of his mouth.

"This isn't a boxing match," I shoot back as the truth finally dawns on me. "This is the Colosseum, and we're the gladiators being fed to the lions."

"No way this is a one-shot thing," he grits out, and I can see a kernel of rage burning deep in his eyes.

It's a perfect match for the fury kindling inside me as I realize this is all just a racket. That no one actually goes free. All those people Remy thought atoned and bought their freedom really ended up here, in the arena. The newest victims of the Colossus Clash.

"This is bullshit," Hudson growls as the truth occurs to him, too. That everything the prisoners have been promised, everything they torture themselves to obtain, is just another lie so that Charon can get richer.

The bastard.

I want to think about this more, to figure out how abuse of power of this magnitude manages to go on right under the noses of the entire paranormal community. But that's not going to happen right now. Not when the crowd has grown tired of the parading giants and is obviously ready for some action—action that involves Hudson and me being torn limb from limb, most likely.

"You ready?" Hudson asks.

I shoot him an *are you kidding* look. "Not even close."

"Yeah, me neither." And then he looks me straight in the eye, and his poor, lopsided grin has gotten even worse as the swelling has set in. "Let's do it anyway."

"You act like it's a choice," I tell him as Charon goes through a quick list of match rules—all of which seem to favor the giants. Big surprise.

I'm leaning forward a little, weight balanced on my toes as I get ready to run.

"Deciding on a vacation house in Tahiti or Bora Bora is a choice," he tells me. "This—"

"Is what we have to get through to be able to make that choice," I finish for him.

"Okay, then," he answers with a laugh. "You take Tahiti"—he nods toward Ephes—"and I'll take Bora Bora." Another nod, this time toward Mazur. "Sound good?"

"No," I tell him.

But when the whistle blows, I do the only thing I can do. I take off running and send a prayer out to the universe that Tahiti doesn't catch me.

140

The Bigger They Are, the Harder I Bawl

Who knew? The universe is a fickle, fickle bitch.

Or she just flat-out hates me, which I'm beginning to think is a more reasonable explanation for this current nightmare.

I dart toward Ephes, like Hudson and I decided, and it only takes about three seconds for me to figure out that his reach is longer than I thought. Of course, by the time I realize that, I'm airborne, soaring across the ballroom and crashing against the side wall, shoulder first.

Pain radiates through me, but I stumble to my feet—just in time to watch Hudson go flying in the other direction. But he does a flip in midair and lands in a crouch, his gaze immediately sizing up the giant's location as well as mine.

I tear my gaze away from Hudson as Ephes bears down on me again, murder in his mismatched eyes. I stay where I am, though not by choice. I'm frozen. Fear is a living, breathing thing inside me, and that bitch has taken control of my legs.

Ephes is completely focused on me, and he reaches back with a giant fist—and swings like a batter in a cage and I'm the poor ball.

Out of nowhere, Hudson grabs me, and we fade halfway across the ballroom—and Ephes turns on a dime to watch us. Damn it.

"Why'd you do that?" I demand. Hudson's brilliant blue eyes are dim, but he's still on his feet. "You can't keep wasting your energy like that!"

But he's already gone before I finish my sentence, running as fast as he can toward Ephes. Just as Ephes swings an arm toward Hudson, he fades left, then left again, then left one more time—until the giant is spinning in a circle. It was a good plan, and it would have worked if Mazur didn't take advantage of Hudson's distraction and aim a well-placed kick in Hudson's side.

Hudson goes flying through the arena, and I let out an ear-piercing scream as his body crashes into the wall, then falls to the ground like a rag doll. The crowd goes wild.

Ephes must have heard my scream, though, because he turns toward me and takes off running again. I have a brief thought of, *What if I run toward him...*

Either he'll catch me and this nightmare will be over, or, if I'm lucky, he'll have too much momentum to turn quickly and I'll make it to the other side of the arena before he can catch me. It's a good plan...if I didn't have the shortest fucking legs in existence.

I'm running full-out, and Ephes just slows down and watches me race by. He *watches* me—then swings a huge hand down to scoop me up.

But before he can close his fist around my shoulders, Hudson fades out of nowhere and grabs me, and then we're halfway across the arena again. But this time, Hudson leans forward and presses his hands into his knees, dragging huge gulps of air into his lungs.

"Nice—*breath, breath*—try." He squeezes my hand. "Just—*breath, breath*—run closer—*breath, breath*—to his legs."

My eyes widen. Is he kidding right now? I could have run close enough to trim his toenails, and I didn't have a shot in hell. But I don't have time to explain the physics of my short, human legs to him because both giants are heading right for us again—and so Hudson takes off to draw them away from me.

What if I run close to the wall? Surely I might at least be fast enough to roll out of the way then, with less space for a giant to maneuver. It's a plan, so I take off for the nearest wall. Ephes is all about my wall idea, too, if the speed with which he chases after me is any indication.

My heart is pounding in my chest as I run as fast as I can. I see his hand start to swing toward me and at the last minute, I roll out of the way. And he misses. But there's no point in celebrating because I have neglected to consider a very important detail. He has *two* hands.

He grabs me around the waist with his other hand and shakes me until my brain feels like it's rattled loose inside my skull. Then he spikes me at the ground like I'm a football and he got the game-winning touchdown.

It hurts. A lot. Then again, everything in my body hurts at this point. Even before he lifts his colossal foot and starts to stomp down on me.

I manage to roll away from him before he can grind me into dust, but it's a close call. And it's only getting closer as he stomps another foot down, this one barely grazing my hair. I roll one more time, but I have to admit, my rolling days are limited. I'm sucking wind right now, and I might just throw up if I roll one more time.

I look up as Ephes's disgusting foot is about to slam down on me—and this time there's nothing I can do. I close my eyes and curl my body into itself, but then I feel myself being lifted on a breeze, cradled against Hudson's hard chest, as once again he fades me out of danger.

Before my feet are even fully on the ground, he's fading away again, drawing the giants to the center of the arena. I can't understand why he wouldn't draw them all the way to the other end of the arena where he'd have more room to fade away again, when I realize something very bad. He faded to the middle of the arena because that was as far as he *could* fade.

I only have about a second to process that information before Mazur slams a fist into Hudson's stomach—and sends him flying. He skids across the floor face-first, and the fact that he didn't fade to get out of the situation tells me everything I need to know about how drained he is.

And how fucked we are.

I'm so busy trying to will Hudson to get up, I don't even realize Ephes is only twenty feet from me until it's almost too late. I take off running, but he easily backhands me a hundred feet through the air, and I hit the ground. Hard. I can't even pretend to have the energy to pick myself back up.

As if in a fog, I realize I've landed only about ten feet from where Hudson is sprawled on the ground, facedown. The ground is shaking as one of the giants races toward him, and I force myself to roll to my knees. I don't know what I plan to do—*drag Hudson out of the way* is at the top of my thoughts—but I can't do it. I don't have the energy to get to my feet, and I instead watch in horror as Mazur aims a foot for Hudson's broken body.

I scream as loud as I can, which admittedly isn't very loud given I can barely pull air into my lungs without passing out from pain. But before Mazur's kick lands, Hudson rolls to his feet at the last minute. Then he jumps twenty feet in the air and hits Mazur right in the nose.

Mazur roars his displeasure as blood squirts everywhere. But instead of grabbing his nose, he snatches Hudson right out of thin air and sends him spinning across the ballroom. Again. Hudson crashes headfirst into a pile of cheering, stomping crowd members, who roll his limp body right back down onto the ballroom floor.

I struggle to get to my feet. I can't just let him lay there and get trampled, but Ephes has me in his sights. I race (if someone's definition of "race" is running in quicksand) in the other direction, trying to flee from him and run straight into the still-bleeding, still-furious Mazur. He snatches me up by the hair, and it's my turn to go spinning across the ballroom.

I don't stop until I hit the wall.

Hudson, who, in the meantime, has managed to get to his feet, fades over to me and tries to help me up. But my head is throbbing, my ears are ringing, and I'm seeing three of him instead of one. Plus, I'm pretty sure Hudson isn't the only one with a broken rib anymore. My side burns like hell every time I try to take a breath.

And that's before Ephes pulls back his foot and punts us both across the ballroom, straight at Mazur.

Mazur lets loose a shout and jumps into the air, stretching himself out in the most bizarre imitation of a pro-wrestling move I've ever seen in my life. Especially when he starts to belly flop down right on top of us.

I freeze, screaming, but Hudson wraps his arms around us and rolls us away. Then, with what has to be the last of his strength, he fades us as far away from the giants as he can.

Unfortunately, it's not far enough.

If he'd faded only himself, he would have made it. But with the extra weight of me, I realize, with cold precision, that *neither* of us is going to make it.

Ephes laughs and picks Hudson up by one foot. He twirls around, holding Hudson straight out from his body like a dirty sock as he builds up speed and momentum.

When he finally lets him go, Hudson soars shoulder first into the wall at the bottom of the bleachers.

And just like that, I'm done. I'm just…done.

Not that it matters. I wouldn't be able to do anything to stop this even if I wasn't.

I'm *useless* without my powers. Absolutely useless. I can't fly. I can't fight. I can't do anything but get hurt over and over again. Or, worse, get Hudson hurt, since he's so hell-bent on trying to save me.

If he keeps this up, he's going to end up dead, too, and it's going to be my fault. He's already so broken and battered. There's no way he can fight these giants off if he also has to worry about me. No way he can find a way to defeat them if he's too busy running cleanup on the poor, pathetic human.

Across the ballroom, Hudson rolls over with a groan. The spectators are on their feet now, yelling and jeering. They're throwing popcorn and cups down onto the ballroom floor as I struggle to my feet, and I get hit in the back with a full can of beer.

It douses me, but worse, it makes the floor so slippery that I end up on my ass again—just as Mazur turns to bear down on me.

"Get up!" Hudson yells from across the ballroom as he, too, tries to struggle to his feet. "Grace, get up!"

When he doesn't see me climbing to my feet, he fades to me, but it takes so much out of him that he ends up on his knees by my head. I brace myself, expecting Mazur and Ephes to finish us off while they have the chance—or at least to finish *me* off, because I need Hudson to move away from me. I need him to live. But they pause for a second in the middle of the ballroom and show off for the crowd, waving their arms and getting everyone even more excited.

And maybe I should be insulted, since the giants obviously don't think we're any threat or they wouldn't be showing off like that. But realistically, I'm grateful for the reprieve. I may not be afraid of death after everything that's happened these last six months, but I'm not exactly looking forward to it, either.

"We need to move, Grace." Hudson's voice is low and urgent in my ear.

But I shake my head. "You go."

"I will. We just need to get you up."

"No," I whisper.

"What do you mean, no?" He sounds totally confused.

"I can't do this," I tell him. "There's no way I can beat them, and I'm causing you more trouble than I'm worth. Leave me."

"Leave you?" Now he sounds totally insulted. And utterly pissed.

I sigh, tears trembling behind my lashes. "I'm tired, Hudson, and I hurt so much. Besides, the only chance we've got—the only chance any of us has got—is for you to make it out of this and finally stop Cyrus. You're not going to do that if you're trying to take care of me. I don't have my gargoyle. I'm just a weak human, and I'm going to get you killed. So yeah, leave me. Get the key, free the beast, and end Cyrus once and for all. I know you can do it.

You just need to let me go."

Already, the room is spinning so badly that I'm half afraid I'm going to throw up. I drop my head down onto Hudson's knee and wait for him to kiss me, to tell me that he loves me, to say goodbye.

Finally, I see why Jaxon was always trying to protect me. He must have been petrified every day of all the different ways I could easily die. All this time, I just wanted him to treat me as an equal—never once considering that I *wasn't* his equal. Nor am I Hudson's. What a horrible universal joke that these two amazing, powerful boys both ended up mated to *me*.

I thought with my gargoyle, I was a badass. I never once considered that that's *all* that made me a badass worthy of Jaxon...or Hudson. Beautiful, amazing, selfless Hudson. He would lay down his life to save mine without a moment's hesitation. It's time that I do the same for him. So with the last of my strength, I look into his beautiful blue eyes and whisper, "Save yourself."

Tears are nearly clogging my vision entirely, so much so that I can't see his expression, but I know this is going to be hard for him. He loves me so much; I can see that now. But I know he also loves Jaxon, and without freeing the blacksmith and then the beast, without the Crown, Jaxon's soul will be lost forever. Our friends will be facing Cyrus powerless. Hudson loves me, and I know he will save the people I love *for* me. I just want to feel his lips brush against my hair one more time. Hear him say he loves me one more time...

I close my eyes and wait.

Instead, he jerks away and lets my head bounce against the cold hardwood floor. And then his voice is *full* of British as he yells at me, "Have you lost your bloody fucking mind?"

141

Not-So-Amazing Grace

Well, that's not how I expected this to go. I thought, maybe, I'd get an *I love you*, a kiss goodbye, an *I'll miss you*. Not an, "Are you fucking kidding me right now, Grace? Are you *fucking* kidding me?"

Behind us, the giants are strutting their stuff, loud music sweeping through the ballroom as they do a little previctory victory dance.

Which only makes Hudson yell louder as he continues. "I've been with you when we were frozen in stone. When you lost your mate. When you had to win a Ludares championship on your own and when you survived my arsehole father's fucking eternal bite. And this?"

He sweeps an arm around the ballroom before squatting down next to me again. "This is what you want to let take you down? Two giants barely smart enough not to drool on themselves and a sociopathic ten-year-old with a God complex?"

Well, when he puts it like that…

I sigh. When he puts it like that, it still doesn't matter. "I'm tired, Hudson." I sigh again. "I'm tired and I'm going to end up getting you killed," I tell him, lifting a trembling hand to his cheek. "I couldn't live with myself if something happened to you."

"Jesus, how the fuck hard did you hit your head anyway?" he growls, and through all our bickering, all our fights, I've never seen him look so mad. Or so disappointed. "Where's the girl who never gives an inch? The girl who always digs in when things get bad? The girl who always argues with me?"

"I don't always—"

"That's shite and you know it." He narrows his eyes at me. "From the day we met, you have done nothing but fight with me. Over everything from *The Empire Strikes Back* being the best movie ever made to whiny existential authors to whether or not I'm allowed to tell you I love you. Hell, we once had a fight *over the color black*."

"It's not the same—" I start, but he cuts me off.

"You're damn right it's not. You can fucking lecture me on a toothpaste cap—and how not screwing it back on wastes thirty percent of the tube—and somehow turn that into a *dissertation* on personal space. But this, this comes along and you're like, 'Sorry, I'm out'?"

"Toothpaste doesn't matter," I tell him. "It can't kill you."

"Maybe not, but the Unkillable Beast sure as hell could. Where's the girl who faced him down and tamed him in the end? Who took on Jaxon Vega when the entire world was scared of him?" His voice goes soft. "Who gave me the courage to fight my own nightmares and win—even when the threat that she might die saving me was very, very real?"

"That Grace is gone," I say. "The only Grace here now is a weak human—and I'm going to fucking get you killed!"

He studies me for several long seconds, those blue eyes of his memorizing every inch of my face. And then he leans back and snarls, "Get your arse up."

"Excuse me?" I have to strain to hear him over the loud music and the celebratory stomping of the giants, but he's never talked to me like that, no matter how heated our fights got.

He raises his voice. "You heard me. You will get up right this minute and use that big, beautiful brain of yours to find a way for us to *win*. Do you hear me? I cannot fight two giants *and* take care of you—just because you've decided to have a goddamn pity party today."

I wince, but he doesn't understand. I reach for his hand, my eyes pleading with him. "You can take both of them if you don't have to worry about me."

He stares at me incredulously. "You think I'm worried about two fucking giants? I couldn't give two shites about them. Once you get your shite together, we'll go out there and kick both their arses. Of that I have no doubt."

His voice breaks. "But what happens to me if you give up, Grace? What happens to me if I lose the mate I've waited almost two hundred years to find? You think you can't make it if you lose me? What the fuck do you think happens to *me* if I lose *you*?"

Everything inside me goes still at the agony in his voice. "Hudson—"

"Don't you *Hudson* me, Grace. I've had to share you from the very first day you came into my life. And I have done it. I have shared you with Jaxon and I have shared you with the whole fucking world that needs you. And I have never complained because I know who you are. I know what your heart looks like. I know the baggage you come with, and I am okay with all of it.

"But I am not okay with you just checking yourself out, with you walking away and leaving me here alone because you're tired. Because you're scared. Because you don't want to hurt anymore.

"That's not how this works. That's not how the world works, and that's definitely not how you and I work. I have waited every miserable day of my whole miserable fucking life for you, and you are not giving up now."

He drags a shaky breath into his lungs, but it doesn't lessen the fury burning in his eyes. "Now, you listen to me, Grace Foster. I am in love with *you*. Not a human. Not a gargoyle. *You*. I am in love with the girl who has a heart bigger than the entire world and the fucking gumption to demand it *kneel* at her feet if it harms someone she loves."

His voice catches at the end, and I reach up to wipe the tears flowing unchecked down my face so I can look into his blue eyes again—and I am devastated by what I see. I did this to him. I broke this beautiful boy's heart, not by not loving him back as I always feared—but by not loving myself as much as he does.

But he dashes a quick hand across his face, wipes the wetness aside as though his pain is unimportant. He's in my face now, and I have never seen such rage and such love on one face at the same time in my entire life. "But I can't do this alone. I need you more than you will *ever* need me. And I swear to God, if you give up on yourself when you refused to ever give up on me...I will follow you to the afterlife and drag your stone ass back one painful mile at a time. So stop whatever this bullshit is you've got going on right now and. Get. The. Fuck. Up."

142

A Little Fight
Left in Me

Hudson's words reverberate through me as I lay on the ground looking up at him, trying to decide what to do.

At one point, he asked if I'd lost my mind, and though he was harsh—and more than a little rude—there's a part of me that can't help wondering if he was right.

If maybe I am being a coward.

If maybe I am making a mistake.

He's definitely wrong on one thing—I'm not afraid of the giants or of Charon. I'm not afraid of dying at their hands, and I'm not afraid of any other creature this whole ridiculous paranormal world can throw at me. After all, you can only die once (unless you're Hudson) and how it happens doesn't really matter.

So no. I'm not afraid of dying. But I am terrified of living...with or without Hudson.

I'm terrified of being mated to Hudson. Of really, truly being mated to a man who thinks of me as an equal in every way and who is willing to take me exactly as I am. But I'm just as terrified of living without him.

Nobody in my whole life has ever been willing to take me as I am. As I *really* am.

My parents spent their lives hiding from what I am.

Heather spent years trying to make me more extroverted, more bold, more like her.

Jaxon wanted me to be the girl he could keep on a shelf and protect.

Even Macy, in her own helpful way, wants me to be the Grace she used to know, the cousin she made up in her head, instead of the Grace I've become.

Only Hudson takes me as I am.

Only Hudson knows every single thing about me—the good and the bad—and wants me anyway.

Only Hudson doesn't expect me to be anybody but who I am.

Only Hudson thinks that Grace—the real Grace—is more than good enough.

Is it any wonder that I'm terrified of him?

How could I not be? It nearly destroyed me when Cole broke my mating bond with Jaxon—and that was only a manufactured bond. What's going to happen to me if my bond with Hudson breaks? What's going to happen to me if I lose him?

I don't think I'll survive. And if I do...will I be like Falia, a shell of my former self, dying a little more each day but without the ending that comes with death?

I can't do that. I won't do that.

But what's the alternative? I wonder as I take Hudson's hand. Giving up without even trying? Letting him go instead of fighting for the life that we could have together? Depriving us both of the happiness we could find, just because I'm too scared of what might go wrong?

That's so much worse.

Hudson has been to hell and back. He's lived with two parents who used him as a pawn, who isolated him and hurt him and only wanted him when they could use him as a weapon—against each other and the rest of the world. He lost his brother, and then, when he thought he would get him back, he ended up losing him again. He literally died so that Jaxon could live.

And still he's willing to try. Still he's standing right here in front of me, loving me despite everything he's been through and everything I've put him through.

He doesn't expect more from me than I can give.

He doesn't even expect me to fight these giants as well as he can.

He just wants me to be in it, with him.

He just wants me to believe in myself—and believe in us—as much as he does, no matter what the future holds.

And damn it, he's right.

I run my thumb over Hudson's promise ring—over my ring—as the truth sweeps through me. I've had a metric shit ton thrown at me since getting to Katmere, and I've made it through every single thing with the help of the people who care about me. I've done whatever I had to do to survive without also losing myself, and there is no way I am going to quit now just because having someone who sees me—really sees me—scared the hell out of me for a little while.

Those two giants don't scare me and neither does Hudson. He's one hell of a guy, and he deserves a girl as strong as he is. I guess it's time I prove I'm that girl.

"You forgot your ex-girlfriend's human-sacrifice plot," I tell him as I finally pull myself to my feet.

He looks baffled. "What does that even mean?"

"When you were listing the things that I've survived, you forgot Lia's little shop of horrors. And I figure if I can get through that, I can get through anything. Even you."

"Oh yeah?" He lifts a brow, but his eyes are brighter, more intense, than I have ever seen them.

"Yeah." I take a deep breath. "So let's go kick some giant ass, shall we?"

"Pretty sure that's what I've been saying all along," he answers. "Now duck."

I do, rolling under Mazur just as he launches another flying-body tackle straight at me.

Hudson laughs, then fades to right behind the giant—a surefire sign that he really is reaching the end of his strength. He's only fading short distances now, the energy it takes to go from one end of the ballroom to the other too much for him.

Which means I'm going to have to figure something out. Because no way am I disappointing Hudson or myself. Not like this and not ever again.

Ephes is still racing toward me, and as I stop, drop, and roll right through his legs, I catch sight of something that just might help me end this ridiculousness once and for all.

Game. Fucking. On.

143

Hit Them with
My Best Shot

There are no weapons in this damn ballroom, nothing I can use to bring down a giant—which is basically the point. Charon stripped the room of everything that might be of use to Hudson and me...or so he thought.

But there's one thing he forgot to take, one thing my months at Katmere definitely taught me could be one hell of a weapon. The chandeliers. And these aren't just any chandeliers.

At first, I thought they were made of bones, like the ones in the tunnels at Katmere. But as I look at them closer, I realize they're made of animal teeth and tusks. Which is awful and horrible—what the fuck was Charon thinking?—but also not unhelpful in my present situation.

Because there are a couple of narwhal tusks up there that could do the job. And if not, well, concussions are good, too.

Mazur is back and he is *pissed*, so I dodge one huge foot and take off running toward the other end of the ballroom with him on my tail.

He's even angrier now that he missed me, and he starts smashing the ground with his fists like he's playing a game of Whac-a-Mole. Or, more likely, Whac-a-Grace. It's not that hard to dodge when he's just using one fist, but when he starts using both, I end up having to hop around like a frog on speed to avoid getting pancaked.

But then Hudson fades over to me, Ephes hot on his heels. I give him a *what the hell* look—I'm a little busy trying not to get squished by one giant right now—but then he does something genius. He starts fading in little back-and-forth movements around the giants—next to one's foot, then the other's, zigging and zagging. Between that and me continuing to jump to avoid slamming fists, it doesn't take long before the giants are totally confused—and hitting and kicking each other in their effort to get to us.

Which pisses them off—and at each other—and gives Hudson and me a little leeway to get to the other end of the ballroom without having to worry about getting squished.

I'm breathless by the time we make it over there—even if he's not fading, I can't keep up with Hudson—and I brace my hands on my thighs and gesture Hudson closer to me.

"I know you're having trouble fading, but do you think you can do it two more times?" I ask as I drag deep breaths into my lungs, every one more painful than the last. "I've got a plan."

"I'll do whatever you need me to. You know that." He bends down a little until his face is right next to mine. Then he steals a quick kiss before asking, "What's the plan?"

The part of the crowd that isn't currently booing the giants for fighting each other goes wild at the kiss, but I ignore them. What kind of jerks show up to a gladiator match anyway, let alone show up and want a little romance with their blood and gore? Assholes.

"I'm going to use myself as bait," I tell him, "and get them both in the center of the arena. If I can keep them there for a few seconds without getting ripped limb from limb, do you think you can release the rope on one of the chandeliers before fading to the other end of the ballroom and releasing the other chandelier right after?"

His eyes light up. "You're going to try to knock them out with the chandeliers? I love it."

"Yeah, well, it's not exactly an original idea," I tell him with a grimace. "You forgot one other thing I survived at Katmere—death by chandelier. But if we're lucky, it might work today."

"Tell me when you're ready and I'm on it," he says, and he sounds like the same cocky Hudson I'm used to. But his eyes are shadowed, and his breathing is a little shallower than usual.

"You sure you're okay?" I ask as the giants stop trying to hit each other and start smashing the ground again—because apparently, they haven't figured out that we're already gone.

Hudson was right. There's absolutely no way it's okay to die by these two bumbling assholes.

My mate gives me a cocky grin, because he might be down, but Hudson Vega doesn't know the meaning of out. Then he says, "Don't worry, I'm good. I got this, love."

And there's something about the way he says it, something about his total willingness to just trust that I know what I'm talking about, that gets me right in the feels. Well, that and the way he called me "love," the way it rolled right off his tongue and sounded so freaking perfect.

And just like that, I know.

I love Jaxon—a part of me will always love Jaxon. How could I not, when I'm one of the lucky ones? My first love is a really great guy, and we found each other when I was lost and alone and needed him most.

But that girl? The Grace who was wildly in love with him and whom he wildly loved? She's gone and has been for a while. That girl was scared and lonely and naive. She needed protecting. More, she *wanted* protecting as much as he wanted to protect her.

But that's kind of how young love is, isn't it? It's idealistic and explosive and perfect...until it's not anymore. Until it blows up or fades away or you just move on.

I moved on during those three and a half months I don't remember. I changed, and Jaxon didn't. It's nobody's fault. It's simply how it is.

And I know that in the end, it's all going to be okay. That Jaxon and I are going to have a wonderful life together once we manage to get the Crown and our mating bond is restored. He will be fine, his soul no longer in tatters, and we'll be good for each other. He'll learn to respect me more as an equal, and I'll learn to let him take care of the small things that don't matter so much. He's an amazing guy, and we'll be amazing rulers together.

I take a deep breath, then blow it out as slowly as I can manage. Because it's pointless to be sad. It's pointless to want something more when I already have so much.

It's pointless to regret what has to be—especially when what has to be saves someone you love.

But the truth is, I want Hudson. I *love* Hudson. I think I have from the moment I walked onto that Ludares practice field and saw him reading *No Exit*. He was pouting because I'd gone to see Jaxon—I didn't know it at the time, of course—so when he teased me about my undies, I was easy pickings.

But right from the beginning, things have been different with Hudson. He saw every part of me, even the parts I'm not proud of. He took me on my good days and teased me out of my bad moods on my most obnoxious days, and he loved me through it all. He believed in me through it all. He protects me—of course he does—but he does it so differently from Jaxon. He pushes me, believes in me, wants me to be the strongest and best that I can be.

He's got my back—he'll always have my back—but he likes me to be powerful, too. He likes me to stand on my own. He likes the kick-ass gargoyle as much as he likes the not quite so kick-ass human.

He's smart and funny and sarcastic and sweet and strong and kind and hot. He's everything I could ever ask for in a guy, everything I could ever want, all rolled into one unbelievably sexy package.

And I've never told him. Not even when he told me. I just shoved it down, refused to acknowledge it, never even admitted it to myself. And now we're stuck in this arena, and I can make all the disparaging comments about giants that I want, but we both know if we make one wrong move—if we're off by one second—then we're totally screwed. There would be no Crown, no emotional declarations, nothing but pain, death, loss.

And that's not fair—to either of us. I can't risk what we have to risk here, can't go on to the rest of our lives, and not let him know how I feel.

He starts to move past me—to get ready to run—but I grab on to his wrist. Rest my trembling hand against his beautiful, beloved face. And say the only thing worth saying at a time like this. The only thing worth saying to a man like this. "I love you."

For one second, he looks startled, his blue eyes going wide and wild as they search my face for I don't know what. But then that damn dimple of his comes out to play as he grins and grins and grins. But all he says is, "I know."

"Seriously? You're going to be Han fucking Solo right now?" I ask, even though I have to bite the inside of my cheek to stop myself from laughing. Because, oh my God, do I love this man.

"Excuse me." Both brows go up at the insult. "But there's never a bad time to be Han *fucking* Solo. Besides—" He grins. "I *did* know all along. I was just waiting for you to catch up."

"Yeah, well, I'm all caught up," I tell him as I lean in and kiss him one more time. "Now, let's do this thing, shall we? I'm more than ready to get the hell out of this place."

He reaches for me, but I take off running, yelling and clapping and making as much noise as I possibly can to make sure Big and Bigger follow me.

And it works. Mazur comes running straight for me like he's on fire and I'm the only hydrant around. I wave, then blow him a little kiss to piss him off. But when I turn around to do the same to Ephes, I realize that we've got a problem. Because he is headed straight for Hudson with an intensity that says nothing, and no one, is going to get in his way.

144

In One Ear and Out the Other

Hudson's all the way on the other end of the ballroom now, with Ephes hot on his heels. If I try to help him, and Mazur follows me, there's no guarantee I'll be able to get them both back in the middle again anytime soon. I'm finding giants are more than a little distractible.

Thankfully, Hudson figures out there's a problem right away, and while I play ring-around-the-very-big-rosies with Mazur, he fades right back to the center of the arena. Seconds later, Ephes whirls around to chase him.

"You still got this?" I ask, because I know that last fade used up a bunch of energy and now he's got to do the whole fade again to get back to where he started.

Hudson is breathing hard, really fucking hard—maybe for the first time in his life—but he gives me that ridiculous grin of his that makes me feel way too many things. "My girl just told me she loves me," he says. "I've got enough energy in me right now to fade to Katmere Academy and back. Don't worry, Grace. I've got this."

Even the idea is absurd. He's listing to one side, for God's sake. But I know he's got it. In my opinion, there's nothing Hudson can't do if he puts his mind to it—including this.

So I nod and hold his gaze for a few extra seconds as I say, "I've got this, too."

"Never doubted it. Go on three?"

I nod again. "One, two, three—"

Hudson explodes toward the end of the ballroom, and I let out a shriek loud enough to have people in the stands groaning.

Mazur screams back at a lower octave and swings a fist toward me to shut me up. But I'm already moving, darting between them as fast as I can go, grunting through the pain of my broken ribs and everything else that hurts right now. Ephes bends over and tries to grab me, but I dart between his legs and punch up as hard as I can.

He bellows in rage and tries to grab me again, but he misses.

Mazur's closing in, though, and he's always been a better aim than Ephes, so instead of trying to dart around him, I drop to the floor and roll just out of reach.

Ephes has recovered from my sucker punch, though, and he's out for blood. As I roll by, he slams a foot down on the floor so hard, the wood buckles and I go flying up—right within his reach. But Mazur wants me, too, and he dives for me. The giants collide, and I tuck and roll through a tight alley created by how close their parallel feet are to each other.

Mazur screams at my evasion, and I scream back as I notice one chandelier and then the other swinging free within seconds of each other.

And this is it, right here, the only chance we've got—the crowd gasps, screams, and fucking Mazur turns to see what they're yelling about...

"Hey, you!" I shout at him as loudly as I can, then drop right at his feet—the easiest prey he's had all night.

And it works. He turns back around and scoops me up and—bam!

The chandeliers meet. The sheer weight of them knocks the two giants together—and then physics takes over. Unstoppable force, immovable object... The narwhal tusks sticking out from the chandeliers slam right into the giants' heads.

One tusk goes straight in Mazur's left ear and out his right, while a tusk on the other chandelier drives clear into Ephes's right eye.

Blood and I don't even want to know what else sprays all over me, and then his muscles go lax and he drops me. Hudson plucks me out of the air, and we scramble back as the two giants fall to the ground, dead.

The crowd goes wild.

145

Never Bet Against the Louse

"**H**oly shit!" Hudson yells as he hugs me so tightly that I can barely breathe. "We did it!"

And yay! I'm all for celebrating not dying at the hands of the giants. But I've got a more urgent problem. "Get it off, get it off, get it off!" I wipe the sleeve of my black prison jumpsuit across my face before I start yanking at the front zipper. Just because I'm a badass doesn't mean I want to be covered in giant blood and body parts—so these clothes *have to go.*

"It's okay," Hudson soothes as he tries to wipe away whatever he can with the sleeves of his uniform. For obvious reasons, he does not have the same objection to blood that I do—even if it means being covered with it instead of drinking it.

Pandemonium reigns all around us—the house lights come up, confetti pours down from the ceiling, and people from the stands try to rush the field to meet us. But I don't want to meet any of these horrible people, and I definitely don't want to celebrate my having a whole lot to do with two people getting dead.

Yeah, they would have killed Hudson and me without a second thought, but that doesn't mean I don't feel remorse that things had to go down this way. In a perfect world, all four of us would have walked out of this ballroom.

Then again, in a perfect world, we wouldn't have been in this ballroom to begin with. And there sure as hell wouldn't have been a crowd full of spectators chomping at the bit to see us kill each other.

"Get it off!" I tell Hudson again, but he pulls me close and whispers calming sounds in my ear as he strokes my hair.

"I promise we'll get you cleaned up as soon as we can," he tells me. "But I've got nothing right now and—"

"Here," Remy says as he comes up behind us. He's got a wet towel in his hand. "You can use this to clean yourself up."

Hudson shoots him a grateful look, but I'm too busy squealing with delight to say anything. I reach for the towel, but Hudson takes it instead and starts cleaning me off while Remy, Vander, and Flint—still carrying Calder over his shoulder—keep the epic pandemonium away from us. Thankfully, it only takes Hudson a few minutes to get me as clean as he can with one damp towel.

It's not perfect, but my hair, face, and hands are clean, and I can't feel anything sticky on my uniform, so I'm going to go with it. I shove the image of myself covered in someone else's blood for the second time this year back into my bill drawer, and I don't regret it even a little. Late payment or not, I'm perfectly okay with never taking it back out again.

"We need to go," Remy says out of nowhere, and just like that, he's hustling Hudson and me toward one of the ballroom's side doors that no spectator is going out of. Flint and Vander pull up the rear.

"Where are we going?" Flint asks, but Remy's too busy hauling ass to answer.

And as we make it through the door and into one of the back hallways, I know why. Charon is trying to sneak away. The jerk.

"I know it's past your bedtime," Remy calls out as we catch up with him, "but we've got some business to take care of."

Charon turns around, annoyance in his eyes. "I have to say, that was unexpected."

"So was getting tossed into a ring with two giants out for blood," I shoot back. "But I guess we all have to adapt."

He looks me over from top to toe. "Apparently there's a lot more to you than meets the eye." The obvious disgust on his face says that's not a good thing.

"A deal's a deal," Remy tells him.

"Yes, I know a deal's a deal." He mocks Remy's accent. "I was simply going to my office to make arrangements."

"Exactly what arrangements need to be made?" Vander asks, his voice rumbling through the hallway. "Our people won, fair and square. You need to let us go."

"I don't need to do anything," Charon snaps back. "I run this prison, not you. I make the decisions about who goes and who leaves, not you."

"But that's exactly it, right?" I tell him, arms crossed over my chest. "No one ever gets to leave, do they? You make them go through the whole Chamber facade because that keeps them docile for a long time. Then, when they finally realize no one atones, they have to make enough money to buy their freedom from you—which feels like serious bullshit to me, but hey. Your prison."

I hold up my hands like it's no big deal, like the entire situation—and his obvious exploitation of the people under his care—isn't one of the most hideous things I have ever seen or heard of. "And then, once you get the money from them, you make them fight to the death with giants they can't beat—all while taking money from Cyrus and God only knows who else to keep people in prison who don't even belong here."

"Your point?" he snarls.

"My point is you can pretend your word is your bond, but the truth is, your word doesn't mean shit."

"That's not true!" he tells me, and for a second I think he's going to have a temper tantrum right here in the middle of the hallway. He's actually stomping his foot and everything. "My word is my bond! It has always been my bond."

"Because you say so?" I mock. And I know I should shut up. I know I'm probably making everything worse. But I am beyond angry that my fate and the fate of my friends—that the fate of everyone in this place—is at the mercy of a little boy-man without a conscience or a shred of actual decency to his name.

"Because it's true!" he howls.

"Then keep the deal you made," Hudson says.

He doesn't want to. It's written all over his face that he had planned to keep us in here where he can torture us some more, make us pay for what we did to his carefully laid plan. Because if he lets us go, he has to deal with Cyrus and who knows who else.

"You do realize if you keep us here, we won't be silent, right?" Flint adds. "I'll tell everybody in the Hex what we've learned. What are you going to do? Send the windigos after the crown dragon prince because he's telling everyone your rules are bullshit? Good luck with that."

Charon holds our gaze, a muscle in his jaw ticking the seconds down. "Fine! I'll take you across. Let me message my guards, let them know that we're coming. And then we'll head out."

The idea of finally getting away from this place has relief flowing through me. I'm still angry, will be angry for a very long time, but I'm ready to be gone. Ready to get the Crown and take care of Cyrus once and for all.

Thinking about him and the inevitable war that will be coming our way has me itching to get moving. But it's also got me itching for something else.

"You need to take off our bracelets before we go," I tell Charon, holding out my hand for easy access. Already, joy is seeping into the emptiness inside me caused by the choking of my powers. I knew I missed them, knew an important part of me was gone, but until I opened myself up to the idea of getting them back, I had no idea just how much I've missed being a gargoyle.

For a girl who was a little traumatized at the idea a few months ago, I've grown awfully used to being able to fly and access the elements and channel magic. I can't wait to feel my wings—I'll never complain about them giving me a backache again.

Charon laughs, just full-on laughs. "Sorry," he answers in a voice that lets us know he very definitely isn't. "You didn't negotiate for that."

"We negotiated to be let free!" Flint exclaims.

"Yes, and I will set you free from the prison." Charon's smile is evil now. "But that's all I'm responsible for."

"You put these cuffs on us," Hudson said.

"No, one of the intake officers put the cuffs on you. I don't really get involved in that side of the prison, so again. I'm sorry. Now, the deal was for five of you, so let's go."

"No!" I tell him. "The deal was for six of us!" I look around and do a quick mental count again, in case I've gone delirious. Flint, Calder, Remy, Vander, Hudson and me. No, that's definitely six.

"The deal was for five," Charon informs me, eyes narrowed. "If you don't like it, take it up with your magician friend. He's the one who negotiated."

"Remy?" I ask, turning to him. "What's going on?"

"Why does he think there's only five of us?" Vander asks. "So help me, if you betrayed me—"

"You're going," Remy cuts him off. "You're all going. I'm the one who's staying."

146

Hide-and-Sneak

"W hat the hell?" squawks Flint. "Why would you—"

I hold up a hand, and for once, Flint actually listens to me and quiets down. "You didn't include yourself in the deal?" I ask. I keep my voice calm even as I struggle to understand.

He shrugs. "I told you, *cher.* I was always meant to take the last flower."

"Yeah, but wouldn't this just be easier? You could come with us now—" I start to turn back to Charon to try to negotiate. I know it's a lost cause, but I have to do something. We can't leave him in this hellhole.

"I know what I see, Grace. And this isn't the way for me."

"Because you won't let it be," Hudson tells him. "What if your vision is wrong? You said yourself that sometimes things are blurry—"

"Not this. This has been crystal clear for years." He smiles at me, even chucks me on the chin. "Don't be sad, *cher.* It'll be okay."

Then he glances down at the bracelet on my wrist. "Besides, we're not done quite yet."

"What does that mean?" Charon demands. "I need to go to bed. I need—"

"Your pacifier?" Remy asks, even as he winks at me. "Keep your diaper on, Charles. This'll only take a couple of minutes."

Charon's face goes from pasty white to bright pink to red to nearly purple, which is one hell of a journey to watch. I'm actually fairly certain that if he keeps this up, Charon is going to explode. Although that wouldn't exactly be a bad thing.

But Remy ignores him, choosing to focus on me instead. "I didn't negotiate for the cuff removal because I still need something from you."

"Well, that was a pretty shite move, wasn't it?" Hudson asks mildly.

"I had to make sure you still needed me, too," Remy says. "And now you do. Free my magic, and I'll remove your bracelets, and your magic will be free, too."

"I don't know if I can do that—"

"You mean you *won't* do it," he says, and he doesn't sound angry. Just disappointed—in himself, in the situation, and most of all, in me.

"No, I mean I don't know if I can. Without my powers—"

"That's what the tattoo is for," he tells me. "You need to trust it."

"The way you trusted me?" I ask, because his lack of trust hurts. I thought we were friends.

"It's not the same thing at all." He sighs, drums his fingers on his thigh as he searches for what he wants to say. "I couldn't afford to trust you guys and be wrong, Grace."

"I know," I tell him, because I do.

He's spent his whole life in prison, his whole life under the thumb of people like Charon and the windigos, who will as soon rip you apart as talk to you. Is it any wonder the boy has trust issues? Maybe instead of being disappointed that he doesn't trust me, maybe I should be thrilled that he's trusted me as much as he has.

"So what do you want us to do?" Flint asks as he shifts a still-deadweight Calder from one shoulder to the other. I can't imagine how tired he must be after carrying her for this long, but he doesn't falter. Doesn't show by even the flicker of an expression that he's annoyed—if he even is.

"I need Grace," Remy answers. "She's the only one who can do this."

I step back and brush my hand against Hudson's. It's a small reassurance, one I know he doesn't even need, but it's one I want to give anyway. And one I can tell he appreciates when his smile turns soft.

He takes my hand, tangles his fingers in mine for just a few moments before letting me go. But I feel the heat of his touch for much, much longer.

"I'm ready," I tell Remy as I step back to him.

He takes my hands and holds them faceup, my arms extended out from the elbow. Then he softly, carefully presses his palms to mine. "You need to dig deep, Grace. I've been imprisoned my whole life. My magic is buried far below the surface."

I nod. Close my eyes. Take a deep breath. And reach for him with the furthest recesses of my mind.

At first, I don't feel anything, just a blank canvas across from me. But after a minute, I know he's there. I can feel him—little pieces of Remy squeaking through the wall.

A wink. A laugh. A slow smile.

Knowledge. So much knowledge.

Kindness.

Wariness.

And then, when I start to despair of ever finding it, a thin, wispy tendril of power.

It's elusive, darting this way and that as I chase after it. I try to catch it, but my hand reaches right through it again and again and again.

Frustrated, I open my eyes and take a deep breath. My arm is burning, and when I look down, I realize that the bottom of my tattoo—the part that wraps around my wrist—is glimmering a little. I look closer, try to encourage the warmth to spread.

When I go back in, I find the slippery tendril of magic again, and this time I reach for it with my tattooed arm. It slips past me twice, but third time's the charm, and I catch hold of it.

As I do, it zips along my fingers, kindles to life inside me, and then burns out just as quickly. I dig deeper, search for another tendril, a bigger flare of power, but there's nothing there, and my heart drops to my toes.

How do I tell him that? How do I tell this boy with the infinite eyes and even more infinite heart that there's nothing there? That whatever well of magic his mother said was inside him is actually little more than a puddle?

I know what that feels like, know how it empties you out—how it hollows you—to know that the people you trusted most in the world betrayed you. Bargained away your freedom like it was little more than a trading card.

My parents knew, they *knew* that I was a gargoyle, and they never told me. They knew there was magic in this world—magic my father could even wield himself—and they told me nothing. They kept me ignorant, did whatever they could to obfuscate the situation so that I felt odd, out of place, a fish out of water in my own body...and in my own life.

To have to explain that to Remy, this boy who was born in a prison, who lost his mother when he was five and never knew his father, who was raised by prison guards and inmates who came and went...how do I tell him that the one constant in his life, the magic he's counted so heavily on, is just one more ephemeral thing? Just one more shit circumstance he'll never be able to get out from under?

Because no matter how much Remy might wish it otherwise...he doesn't have a hidden well of power. His mother lied to him.

147

Totally Lit

I take a deep breath, try desperately to find the words not to break his confidence and shatter his heart, but when I open my eyes, Remy is already watching me. His green eyes swirl with mist as he holds my gaze and drawls, "I told you you'd have to go deep, *cher*. You may not have found it yet, but it's in there."

"I'm not so sure, Remy. I can't—"

"My mama wouldn't have lied to me, not about this. She knew it was my only chance to get out of here, and she wouldn't have given me false hope."

I don't know if I agree with him—not when I would have said the same thing a year ago. I would have laughed at anyone who tried to tell me my parents were liars. Who tried to tell me that the whole reason I existed was because my parents went to the Bloodletter and basically sold me to her before I even existed.

"It's in there, Grace," Remy says again, and there's so much confidence in the statement that a part of me wants to yell at him, to tell him that he doesn't know. That parents do bizarre and terrible things every day, tell bizarre and terrible lies. Sometimes we never find out, but sometimes we do, and when that happens, hiding from it isn't going to change anything. But his belief in his mother is absolute. "You just have to dig until you find where she put it."

"How do you know she didn't lie?" I ask.

"Because she was my mother," he answers. "She may have made mistakes in her life, but she wouldn't have left me unprotected as long as there was breath in her body. This is how she protected me."

And there's something in his words, so simple and yet so profound, that takes me right back to the days before my parents died. To the whispered fights, the tense meals, the way they clammed up whenever I walked into a room.

How could I have forgotten that? I wonder, even as I go searching for

Remy's magic again. In the aftermath of their deaths, how could I have forgotten how tense things had become around the house?

How every time I turned around, my mother was handing me a cup of tea to drink. Insisting on me finishing it even when I'd rather have a sparkling water or a Dr Pepper.

How my father kept trying to talk to me, but my mother would interrupt, her face alive with a fear I didn't understand.

How they'd asked me to spend Sunday with them so we could talk about some stuff, but how I told them I couldn't because I had to finish up a set of volunteer hours before I did my college apps.

It all seems so silly now—that I missed out on my last chance to talk to my parents, to see them alive, because I was trying to pad my college applications. Which I ended up never going back in and filling out. What a damn waste.

I can't help wondering now, as tiny glimpses of Remy's magic slide in and around my searching grasp, what it is they were going to talk to me about and how I could have forgotten that they wanted to.

Had they decided I was finally old enough?

Were they going to tell me what they'd done?

Were they going to tell me *everything*?

I'll never know—they died before we could have the conversation. The brakes failed, their car went over the cliff, and Lia got her way.

Just like that.

And now that I've got the benefit of knowledge, the benefit of hindsight and many months to look back on everything, I realize that maybe I can't hold the secrecy against them after all.

Does it suck? Yeah, absolutely.

I hate that I'll never have the chance to talk to my father about his runes or my gargoyle or this damn mating bond debacle they helped set into motion.

I hate that my mother will never know how much fun it is for me to fly or how much I miss her tea or how much I miss her.

But as I stand here, combing through Remy's soul for his magic, I can't help thinking that they did the best they could to protect me. Like when I chose not to tell Jaxon about what the Bloodletter did to us—nothing would come of that but pain, so why hurt him more if I didn't have to? Why tell Flint when it would just make him relive the pain of Jaxon's rejection all over again?

Sometimes there are no right and wrong answers in life. Sometimes you have a sucky hand and you do the best you can with what you've got and pray it all works out—and that you don't hurt anyone along the way.

Sometimes, that's all you've got.

Like Remy, as he did his best to get us to this point, even when he didn't trust us.

Like me, right now, trying to find his magic, though I don't have a clue how to do it.

It's that thought that pulls me back, that has me refocusing on Remy. And believing that he's right. His magic is too important for his mother to have lied about, not if she ever wanted her son to find his way out of prison.

"You're right," I tell him. "Your mother wouldn't lie to you."

And so I do another deep dive, send my senses out wide as I try to find a trace of his magic, a trace of something that will save him.

His eyes are swirling again, smoky green and gray, and I know I'm on the right track. And then, there it is right in front of me. Not his magic but a gigantic wall.

Everything inside me screams that it's there, walled off, hidden from him and me and everyone—a protection left by his mother for all those years he had to spend in the prison. If she hid his magic deep enough, then no one could get it. Not Charon, not anyone.

But Remy's not a kid anymore and his magic—this magic—is the only thing that can save him now.

And so I put my head down and burrow through the wall, digging and digging and digging—

My whole hand catches fire.

"Oh my God!" I gasp as the flame wraps itself around me, starts creeping up my forearm with a strength I barely know how to withstand.

Tendrils of his magic are all around me now, slipping and sliding through my grasp. Wrapping themselves around me, climbing over my hand and through my fingers, playing hide-and-seek and catch me if you can.

My whole arm is aflame now, and a quick glance down shows me the tattoo is glowing with the magic pouring through me, every dot from my wrist to my shoulder lit up like Mardi Gras, until my entire arm is incandescent with heat. With power. With the very essence of Remy's magic.

I take it all, every single drop I can find. Every tendril. Every spell. Until the swirling magic in his eyes is gone, and he looks completely normal again.

"You steady?" I ask as he sways on his feet.

He shrugs, and for a second I think he's going to crumple. I know how he feels. I know how empty and strange it is to be missing magic where there once was some. Even just the little bit that he had access to must make him feel awful when it's gone.

I glance down at the bracelet on my wrist with the same intense rage and dislike I usually reserve for Cyrus and Cole. Once we bust out of here and get these damn things off—I swear, I'll rip to shreds anyone who ever tries to put one on me again.

Remy sways, and I reach for him. But Hudson is already there, holding him up, lending Remy as much of his remaining strength as he can.

"You ready for this?" I ask, because if losing it was a lot, I can't imagine what it will feel like to have it returned to him all at once—especially since he's never felt this much magic before.

But Remy simply winks at me. Then he braces himself—grounded feet, tucked chin—and says, "You know me, *cher*. I was born ready."

148

Every Little Thing
He Does Is Magic

"**Y**eah, me too," I say with a laugh.

Remy gives me that wicked grin of his and says, "Well then, let's do this thing, shall we?"

"Definitely." I take a deep breath to calm the raptors going wild in my stomach, then instinctively find Hudson's gaze with my own.

He's right there next to Remy, wearing his own wicked smile—dimple definitely included. I focus on his eyes. His oceanic eyes that see so much, encompass so much, and promise to give it all to me.

"You've got this," he says, and I nod. Because I do. This is what I was made for.

I hold on to that thought—hold on to Hudson's support—and focus on the burning in my arm. Holding Remy's magic is very different than when I held Hudson's during the Ludares challenge. Hudson's I could feel all the way through me, warming me up in every nook and cranny as I found a way to wield it.

Remy's exists only in my arm—captured by the tattoo that's so bright now, it's practically blinding as it swirls and dances up and down my biceps and forearm.

"Okay, here we go," I say. And then I breathe in. Hold it for several long seconds. And when I breathe out, I channel his magic out with the air. I send it spinning across the space between us, arcing it straight into him like an arrow.

He must feel it, because his head falls forward, his entire body bowing as he absorbs and absorbs and absorbs.

There's so much of it—so much magic, so much power—that I'm a little astonished my tattoo could hold it all. That Remy's body can contain it all. I feel it spread out, leaking into his arms and hands, his legs and back, and

I make sure to keep it on this side of the wall this time so that he can access it whenever he wants.

I'm almost done, and I can see the power in him now, those wild eyes of his growing smokier and smokier even as they begin to swirl faster and faster. His whole body is shaking now, the wealth of unleashed power so strong that it threatens to knock us both off our feet, threatens to burn us both alive.

But I reach forward, grab on to his hand, and we hold tight to each other as the magic overwhelms us both. Lightning blasts through the room around us, and the ground shakes. But we hold tight, tight, tight and then—just like a lightning strike—it's done.

My tattoo stops looping around my arm, the flames stop dancing along my nerve endings, and the strength leaves my knees all at once—even as I feel the last of the magic leaving me knitting my ribs back together and healing my broken body.

I cry out, certain I'm going to hit the floor, but Hudson is right there, catching me. Pulling me against him. Murmuring, "You were amazing," against my temple.

"Yeah?" I ask him.

"Oh yeah." His lips brush against my ear as he whispers, "Also sexy as fuck, so definitely feel free to try that again. Maybe with my power next time."

I laugh, smack out at his stomach gently, but he bites his lip as he stares at me with eyes that are completely blown out. And suddenly, it's just the two of us. No Charon. No Remy. No dead giants in the next room. No prison to escape from. No Crown waiting for us.

Just Hudson and me and the feelings that flow between us like the purest and best magic.

At least until Flint groans and says, "Come on. I swear, when we get back to Katmere, I'm going to spend weeks making goo-goo eyes at Luca in front of you to make up for this."

I laugh, as he intends, and don't bother to mention that there are no weeks left. We've graduated. We've done everything at Katmere Academy that we can. Everything except save it.

Hudson doesn't say anything, either. Just looks at Remy and asks, "What next?"

Remy grins. "A promise is a promise." He holds his hand out, and a red ball of power glows right in the center of his palm. He throws it straight up in the air before lifting his arm above his head and circling his hand.

The ball loosens up, becomes a bigger and bigger spiral above all our heads until it covers the whole ceiling. Once it does, Remy stares straight at me and winks.

And the red spiral whirls around Flint, Calder, Hudson, and me, spinning like a top for several beats. And out of nowhere, the bracelets fall right off our wrists and land at our feet. Flint whoops and hollers the second he realizes he's free, then shoots a stream of fire straight down the hallway.

"Hey!" Charon squawks as he dives to the side just in time to keep from being barbecued. "What was that for?"

"Because I can," Flint answers.

And God, do I feel him. Part of me wants to shift to make sure that I can. But I settle for looking deep inside myself and finding my platinum string right where it belongs, like it was never gone.

"Finding your stone legs again?" Hudson asks, like he knows exactly what I'm doing.

"Found them," I tell him with a grin. And then I put a hand on the bright-blue string and love the way Hudson freezes, his breath catching as a shiver works its way through his body. "How about you?"

"I'm doing just fine," he says, wrapping an arm around my waist. "Now let's get the hell out of here before that changes."

Vander, Flint, and I echo the sentiment, and I start to follow Charon...at least until I remember that Remy can't come with us. This is as far as he goes.

I turn and run back to him, throwing my arms around him in a giant hug. At first, he's completely stiff, but then he hugs me back so tightly, I can barely breathe.

"Thank you," I tell him as tears burn the backs of my eyes. "For everything."

"It's all good." He starts to pull away, but I hold him tight, not ready to let go of this ridiculous boy who somehow worked himself as far into my heart as Flint and Macy and the others.

"You're going to be okay, right?" I whisper into his ear.

"I'm going to be great," he whispers back. "And so are you."

Now I'm the one who pulls away. "Is that a friendly comment or a you-see-the-future-type comment?"

"Maybe it's both," he answers before pulling me into another hug. "But if you want another prophecy, here's one. This isn't the last time we'll see each other, Grace. But it's going to be a rocky road for both of us before we do."

This time when he pulls away, he takes a few steps back.

Worry for him churns in my stomach. "Remy—"

"Go," he tells me with his patented wicked grin. When I don't move, he flips his hand again, and smoke fills the room between us. When it clears, he's gone.

I close my eyes and whisper a quick prayer to the universe for that brash, beautiful boy. Then I turn back to Hudson, who smiles as he holds out a hand for me. I smile back as I move to take it.

And then we're racing down the corridor after Charon and his guards as we finally make our way back to the surface...and the light.

149

The Fragile and the Sweet

Charon leads us down several hallways, each one sloping up until we finally make it to a large circular iron gate.

"This is it," Charon tells us reluctantly.

"How does it open?" Vander asks.

Charon walks to the wall to the right of the gate and uses a key to open a small door. Inside is a keypad into which he punches several numbers.

The gate makes a loud clicking sound, and then Charon inserts another key—this one into the keypad itself—and the gate spins around several times before the eight triangles that make up the circle start to retract, leaving a circular opening wide enough for even Vander to walk through.

"That's it?" Flint asks. "No magic? Just a key and some numbers?"

Charon narrows his eyes at him. "If you'd like, you can stay on this side of the gate until I make it more of a challenge for you."

"Was there *ever* an unbreakable curse in this prison?" I can't help but ask. He hadn't performed any big spells or magic to set us free. "Or is the whole thing a scam?"

Charon lifts his chin. "Hey, don't judge me. I give the people what they want. A place to hide away their monsters and an idea it's for their own good." He glares at each of us one by one. "Unless you feel maybe you shouldn't get out before people who've been here longer…"

"No, we're good," Hudson says. Then he turns to me. "Ladies first."

I think about arguing with him, but fuck it. The sooner I get through that door, the sooner everyone else does, too. So I squeeze his hand and, when his guard is down, send a huge rush of energy straight at him.

"Grace!"

"We don't know what's out there, and I figure it's smart to have you in fighting form."

He looks like he wants to argue some more, but I'm not up for that. So I just blow him a kiss and disappear through the gate. Vander comes right after me, followed by Flint and Calder, and finally Hudson—who looks half amused and half like he still wants to fight when he takes hold of my hand.

Behind us, the gate thwumps closed, and that's when it hits us. We're free. We're actually free.

I turn to Vander, and tears are pouring down his face as he glances around at dawn breaking over the grass and the trees and the...sepulchres all around us?

"We're in a cemetery?" Flint asks, and he sounds as confused as I feel.

"I guess?" I reply as I notice row after row of headstones.

"It's definitely a cemetery," Hudson says.

Vander walks over to me and pulls a key out of his pocket. "You did it," he tells me. "You freed us."

"We all did it," I answer.

"You truly are worthy of wearing the gargoyle crown," he tells me, ignoring my protests as he falls to his knees in front of me. "I can never thank you enough for what you've done, Queen."

"I just held up my end of the deal," I tell him quietly. I'm completely overwhelmed—and more than a little traumatized—to have someone kneeling in front of me as he calls me "Queen." To be honest, I don't think I'll ever be okay with it.

Which is why the words nearly trip over each other as I tell him, "Please get up. Please. You don't need to do that."

But Vander refuses to be moved as he proffers the key to me. "I never should have made those shackles," he tells me. "I don't know how I can ever look my Falia in the eye again."

"You can look her in the eye because she loves you. Any mistakes you made millennia ago have long since been forgiven," I tell him as I take the key and put it in my pocket. "Just go home and see her. Fix up your garden. Eat your daughter's chocolate chip cookies—they're very good, by the way. Right, Hudson?"

"Sure, they're...delicious," he tells me, but he doesn't come any closer. Instead, he stays where he is and watches me with such pride on his face that I'm afraid I might start sniffling right along with Vander.

"My daughters," he breathes as his face crumples. "Thank you."

"You're welcome," I tell him. "From the bottom of our hearts. But how are you going to get home?" I ask as the logistics of the giant problem come to me in a rush. We can travel via Flint, but Vander is bigger than the dragon. No way can we give him a ride.

"Don't worry about me," Vander says, and he walks over to the nearest tree—a giant magnolia—and puts his hands on the roots.

Right in front of us, the ground around the tree starts to shift and move as the roots rise to the surface.

"Earth magic," Flint says, wonder in his voice as the roots wrap themselves around a kneeling Vander, totally encompassing him.

The whole process takes a minute, maybe a little more, and then the roots start to right themselves, digging a path back into the soil.

As they finish unwinding, it becomes clear that Vander is gone.

"That was—" Hudson blows out a breath. "I've got to tell you, Grace. Hanging with you is never boring."

"Right?" Flint laughs. "Though I do have one more question."

"What's that?" I ask.

"Any ideas if that earth magic works on manticores, too?"

And that's when it hits me. He's still got Calder draped over his shoulder.

"Well, shite," Hudson says. And then all three of us start to laugh, because what else can we do?

We're thousands of miles away from home, we're hauling one stray manticore, and we just watched a tree absorb a giant. And that's not even the weirdest thing to happen this *hour*...

Suddenly, a scream sounds behind us, followed by a familiar voice yelling, "I told you I felt magic over here!"

I whirl around in time to catch Macy as she throws herself into my arms.

150

I've Got Friends in Eerie Places

"Grace! Thank God we found you!" my cousin squeals as she hugs me so tightly, I'm pretty sure I'll have bruises. "We've been in this spooky cemetery for *days* just waiting for you to make your way out."

"Yeah, but how did you even know this is where the prison leads?" I ask as I hug her back.

"Nuri told us after they took you from graduation," Luca answers as he grabs Flint—and the still unconscious Calder—and lifts them both off the ground in a huge bear hug.

"You've been here all week?" I ask, shocked and touched.

"Damn straight," Eden says as Macy finally lets me go long enough to throw herself onto Hudson. "You didn't think we were going to leave you here alone, did you?" She gives me a very uncharacteristic hug, which I return.

"I...I don't know what I thought," I tell her.

"We've been trying to figure out how to break in for days," Mekhi tells us once the hugs and fist bumps have all been dispensed. "But that place is more heavily guarded than the Vampire Court, which I didn't know was possible."

"Right?" Luca says with a laugh. "So eventually we decided we were going to have to wait for you to break out."

"What if we didn't make it?" Flint asks as Luca helps him lower Calder to lay on a patch of grass.

The others exchange a look. "Yeah, well, we weren't ready to talk about that eventuality yet," Jaxon answers, speaking for the first time. He moves closer, out of the shade cast by the early-morning sun and one of sepulchres, and I can't help but notice that he looks even worse than he did at graduation.

He's lost weight—again—so that his cheekbones seem like they'll punch through his skin at any moment. The circles under his eyes are worse, and the coldness I've felt radiating from him for weeks has grown to arctic levels.

"Thank you for coming for us," I tell him as I pull him into a hug.

He hugs me back, and as he does, I can feel the desperation and the fear coming off him in waves. "It's okay," I whisper as I hold him close. "I've got the key. We can save you."

He blows out a long breath, buries his face against my neck, and my heart breaks wide open. Even before I turn and find Hudson staring at us with eyes—and a heart—that are just as shattered.

When Jaxon finally pulls back, he stumbles a little. And Hudson is right there to slide an arm around his shoulders, to hold his little brother up even as his own world is crashing down around him.

"I'm sorry," Jaxon whispers.

Hudson shakes his head. "You've got *nothing* to be sorry about."

An awkward silence descends as our friends look anywhere but at the three of us. At least until Calder moans and starts twitching on the ground.

"Is she all right?" Macy asks, eyes wide as she moves to crouch next to the manticore.

"She took one of the Crone's flowers," Flint answers as he stretches his back. "She's been out for hours."

"But she's not the blacksmith," Eden says matter-of-factly.

"No, the giant left before you showed up," Hudson says. "His magic is what Macy felt."

"So you just happened to bring someone else along for the ride?" Mekhi asks skeptically.

"It's a long story," I answer. "We'll tell you someday when it's not so..."

"Fresh," Hudson finishes for me. "It's been one hell of a day."

"Apparently," Eden tells him. "You look like—" She breaks off, shakes her head. "I don't think I've even got a word for that." She gestures up and down, from his head to his waist, with a disbelieving shake of her head.

"She's right, man," Luca agrees. "You look rough."

"I feel rough," Hudson answers with a laugh.

Calder groans again, but this time her bright brown eyes pop wide open. "I'm not dead," is the first thing she says.

"Definitely not," Flint tells her with a grin. "Considering I've been carrying you around for the last two hours."

"You lucky boy," she purrs.

Luca looks shocked, but Flint just laughs as he reaches a hand down to help her up. "You're right. I am." And then he wraps his hand around Luca's waist and pulls him close, whispering something that has his boyfriend's jaw relaxing.

Once standing, Calder pats him on the head and says, "Thank you for getting me out of there." Then she smiles her sexy grin at Luca. "You've got yourself a good one here."

It's the most sincere I've ever seen her—except when she's talking about herself, of course—and Hudson and I exchange surprised looks. Right up until she spots Mekhi and says, "Well, hello there." She tosses her hair and focuses her gaze on him like she's achieved missile lock. "How are you this fine morning?"

Mekhi seems completely overwhelmed under the onslaught. Not that I blame him. Calder is a lot in regular mode. Now that she's in spotted-a-hot-vampire mode, she truly is something to see.

"I'm good, thanks," Mekhi says after clearing his throat about five times. "How are you?"

"I'm fabulous," she tells him with another flip of her hair. "But I guess you already know that, don't you?"

"I'm, uh—" He glances to us for help, but we're too busy trying not to laugh to give him any.

Except Macy, who slides her arm through Calder's and spins her slightly away from Mekhi, just enough that he can break away from Calder's mesmerizing eye contact. "You are fabulous," Macy tells her with a bright smile that maybe doesn't quite reach her eyes. "Your hair is beautiful."

"It is one of my best features," Calder agrees. "But then all my features are my best features, you know?"

Eden cracks up, just full-on cracks up.

I start to interrupt Calder's litany on her own beauty—after six days, I've learned how to work with her—but before I can, she looks around and asks, "Where's Remy?"

My look must say it all, because her face falls.

"He didn't make it out?"

I shake my head. "No. He's okay, but he stayed behind—at least for now. He does have a flower, though."

She presses her lips together, and for a second I think she might cry. But in the end, she smiles and says, "Sounds like I have something to look forward to, then."

I want to say something else, something that might make her feel better. But nothing comes to mind, and before I can figure anything else out, Liam, Rafael, and Byron come fading through the cemetery like their everything is on fire.

"We've got a problem," Liam says, which—judging from the looks on all three of their faces—is the biggest understatement ever.

"Is it Cyrus?" Hudson urges.

"He's marching on the Unkillable Beast tonight," Byron answers. "With a whole battalion."

"That's fast," Mekhi whispers. "How did he even know we would be going for the beast?"

"Charon," Hudson and I say at the same time. The little bastard knows everything that goes on in his prison, which means he knows why we needed Vander. Nice to know he wasted no time in running to Cyrus with news of our release...and the intel that we've now got a key to free the Unkillable Beast.

"The river guy?" Eden asks, confused.

"Different Charon. His name is actually Charles," I tell her before turning to the group. "We need to go. We have to get there now, which means—"

"No riding us dragons," Eden finishes for me.

"Exactly."

"Honestly, I'm pretty freaking glad to hear that," Flint says. "I'm tired."

"Okay then," Macy says, dropping Calder's arm and stepping away to rummage in her ever-present backpack. "Portal it is."

"Do you need help?" Eden asks as she follows Macy over to a small clearing beneath the magnolia trees.

"Nuri and Aiden are leading the dragons to meet him," Byron continues. "But it's going to take time for them to get there and amass their troops."

"Yeah," Hudson agrees grimly. "We need to figure out a way to hold Cyrus off until the dragon army can get there."

"Yeah, but how?" Luca asks.

We start to talk strategy, but then I realize we have another problem.

"Calder?" I loop my arm through hers and pull her a little bit away from the group as Hudson and Liam start arguing about the best way to approach the Unkillable Beast's cave.

"Yeah, Grace. What's up?"

"We have to go."

She nods. "I know."

"We're going off to fight Cyrus. I know you wanted a piece of that, but I think Remy would be disappointed if you weren't here when he walks out."

She nods again. "I know."

"I...I guess it feels wrong, leaving you here alone. Are you going to be okay?"

She laughs. "Oh, you're so sweet. I'm going to be fine." She tosses her hair.

Okay. Not quite the response I was expecting. Then again, maybe she hasn't been in prison very long. Maybe she has family close. "So, umm, what are you going to do?"

"I don't know," she answers. "But I'll figure something out. I always do."

She's probably right. But I'm still not okay with that. "Can you wait here for a second?"

"I should probably say goodbye to Hudson and Flint and then take off—"

"Just give me a minute, okay?"

I'm afraid I've made her uncomfortable and that she's going to take off the first chance she gets, so I hurry over to Jaxon and whisper, "Do you have any money?"

"Yeah, of course." He lifts his brows as he reaches for his wallet. "How much do you need?"

"Everything you've got," I tell him.

It's a testament to who he is—and, maybe, the relationship we have even after everything—that he doesn't hesitate as he pulls five hundred dollars out of his wallet and hands it all to me. "Is that enough?"

I stare at it and try to think. "I actually don't know." How long will it last if Calder needs to get a hotel room or pay for new identification or simply find a way home? "It's for Calder," I tell him. "I don't think she has anywhere to go."

Luca hears me and pulls out his wallet, too. And so do the other members of the Order. When I head back over to Calder, I have about $1,200 to hand her.

"Oh, no, I can't take that, Grace." She tries to push my hand away.

"Please, I can't just leave you here. Not after everything you've done for us."

"But I don't know when I'll see you again to pay it back."

"It's a gift," I tell her. "So you can get a hotel room and some food for a few days."

She still looks like she wants to refuse, but in the end, she nods and whispers, "Thank you."

I give her a hug. "Thanks for everything," I tell her.

"Thanks for getting me out of there. You saved my life." She hugs me again. "Bye, Grace."

"Bye, Calder."

"Okay, I'm ready," Macy calls. "Let's move!"

Calder backs up, blowing kisses to Flint and Hudson and even a few at Mekhi as Macy performs the spell to open the portal. The last thing I see as we dive through it is Calder pulling a magnolia bloom off the tree and tucking it in her hair.

It makes me smile, despite everything we've got waiting for us. Maybe she really is going to be okay on her own after all.

151

Not Every Island
Is a Fantasy

Macy opens up a portal to the same beach we left from before, and I can tell by the stiff set of her shoulders that she's thinking about what happened the last time we were here. I think we all are. It's hard to walk out onto this beach without thinking about Xavier's body lying only a few feet away from where we are now, hard to walk toward the cave where he died.

But there's no other way to free the beast. No other way to get the Crown before Cyrus. No other way to save Jaxon. No other way to stop Cyrus from attacking Katmere. And no other way to stop the coming war. So into the belly of the beast we go.

But we soon realize that Nuri and her troops have gotten here before us. They're circling the air all around the island, guarding it and performing aerial surveillance. They're watching for Cyrus and his army, determined to cut him off before he has a chance at the Unkillable Beast...or the Crown.

I know they've got the surveillance down, but I'm still worried enough that I look around for any sign that Cyrus has beaten us here. So do the vampires—Hudson, Jaxon, and the rest of the Order fan out over the entire beach area, looking for any sign that the dragons might have missed.

But there's nothing. The beach is clear, the sand completely undisturbed. To be honest, it looks like no one has been here since we were, all those weeks ago.

When Hudson is convinced we haven't missed anything, he fades across the beach to me. "Hey," he says, wrapping an arm around my shoulder as I shiver in the chilly arctic air. "You ready for this?"

"Of course," I tell him, even though I'm anything but. Because now that we know the beach is clear, it's time to breach the rock formation separating the beast's cave from the rest of the island. It's time to go free him and get the Crown.

And it's time to sever our mating bond once and for all.

"How about you?" I ask, leaning in so close that we're breathing the same air.

He smiles that cocky grin of us—the one I used to hate but now love so much—and says, "Not even close."

This time when I breathe out, the air is choked with tears.

"Hey, none of that," Hudson tells me, like his voice doesn't sound a lot thicker than usual. "It's okay."

"It's not okay," I tell him. "None of this is okay."

"Oh, Grace." He pulls me close, strokes a hand down my cheek as he presses kisses to my temple. "I told you a long time ago that I'd never ask you to choose. Nothing's changed."

"Everything's changed!" I tell him, and for the girl who used to never be able to cry in front of anyone, I've sure changed my tune. "You wouldn't ask because you thought I wouldn't pick you. But I would. I would pick you, Hudson. If there was any other way, I would choose you. I love you."

"Well, shite," he says, looking away—but not before I can see tears glistening on his own cheeks. "I always knew you were going to crush me one day, Grace. I just didn't know that..."

"You were going to crush me, too?"

"Don't say that." He shakes his head, pulls me even closer, and his voice nearly breaks as he says, "I can let you go. I can watch you build a life with my brother. I can even come by every once in a while and be fun Uncle Hudson. But don't tell me that you hurt the way I do, Grace. Don't tell me that. Because I wouldn't wish this on anyone, and I would never, never wish it on—"

He breaks off as an explosion rips across the island.

And then all hell breaks loose.

152

Armageddon Me
Out of Here

For one second, two, Hudson and I stare at each other in shock as we try to figure out what's happening.

But as the screaming starts, we jump up and race toward the rock formation that leads to the cave. I leap on the rocks, start to race right through the opening, but Hudson grabs me by the waist and yanks me down behind one of the huge boulders just as a stream of lightning shoots over our heads.

"What's going on?" I shout at him. "Cyrus?"

"And witches," he says grimly, nodding toward a warlock racing across the top of the boulders, firing shots of lightning from his athame.

Macy peeks her head up from a boulder several yards away from us and shoots him with some kind of spell right in the ass. He falls into the hot spring with a screech.

All around us, vampires and witches are popping out from everywhere. They were in the water, in the trees, on top of the very rock formation we've been searching for the past fifteen minutes. How could the dragons have missed them? How could *we* have missed them?

"Vanishing spell," Hudson says, and I realize I asked the last question out loud. "We were looking for the vamps. We didn't know Cyrus had the witches with him. Charon probably tipped them off hours ago—as soon as I started earning money in the Pit. And he knew we were freeing the blacksmith. They've had plenty of time to scout out the island for the best positions, plenty of time to cast the spells to hide themselves." The last is little more than a growl.

"What do we do?" I ask as a dragon grabs a vampire in his mouth and flies straight up into the sky with him. "How can we help? And how do we—"

"Get to the Unkillable Beast?" He shoves me down with one hand, reaches up with the other, and yanks a made vampire off the rock right above us. The vampire falls, fangs flashing, and Hudson snaps his neck without blinking. Then he reaches in his mouth and yanks out one of his fangs, flinging it across the sand.

"We need to get moving," I tell him as I ready myself to run for the Unkillable Beast's cave. "Others saw him disappear. It's only a matter of time before they swarm this area."

He nods, and we run for the cave, doing our best to take cover from the various trees and boulders along the way.

All around us, war is being waged, dragons against vamps and witches. Paranormals are being ripped in half, set on fire, skewered by spears of ice, and screaming in agony as their still-beating hearts are ripped from their chests. And in the middle of it are my friends—some are trying to get to the cave, while others are trying to help the dragons who would have been a match for the vampires but are horribly outnumbered now that the witches are involved, too.

A spell flashes right above our heads, and I drag Hudson to the ground. We crawl behind some bushes, and I measure the distance between where we are and the mouth of the cave. It's about one hundred yards, the length of a football field, but right now it feels so much longer.

And even if we do manage to get there, we have no idea what's waiting for us in the cave itself. My gut says Cyrus—he knows that's where Hudson, Jaxon, and I are going to go, which means it's his very best shot at us. Especially if he's been set up inside the cave waiting for us for hours.

But what's the alternative? Run away? Flee this island and head back where? To Katmere? Maybe that *is* our best bet, now that I think about it.

Yeah, Cyrus is here with the Unkillable Beast—which feels like a major crisis to the safety of the Crown. But he doesn't have the key. He can't open the cuffs. And if he doesn't open the cuffs, the beast will never be human enough—cognizant enough—to be able to tell him where the Crown is.

It's not a long-term plan, at least not with Vander and the key in the world. But if we leave now, we can save a lot of bloodshed. Why fight Cyrus here when he's got the advantage? Why not leave and make him come to us?

"We need to go," I tell Hudson.

"What do you mean?" He looks at me like I said the absolute last thing he was expecting. "Go where?"

"We have the key," I tell him. "If he fights us and wins, he gets the key."

He gets the Crown. He gets everything. But without it—"

"He has to work a lot harder. You're right. Let's—"

He breaks off as another scream rends the air, only this one sounds really, really familiar and sends a chill down my spine.

"Flint?" I turn, and I don't even think. I just run. I dash around a boulder and over a fallen tree…and then I see him—lying at the opening to the cave about thirty yards away. He's not screaming anymore, and I try to tell myself that's a good thing.

But it's not, because it only takes one look to realize that something is very, very wrong.

He's completely motionless, and he's surrounded by a growing puddle of blood.

He's not dead—I know he's not dead, or his bones would have been called back to the Dragon Boneyard. But he's not okay, either. This isn't some flesh wound he'll get back up from.

"We need to be *there*," I tell Hudson, who picks me up and fades us straight across the distance. He doesn't stop until we're next to Flint's head, and once I look down at his body, it's all I can do not to give in to the terror trying to claw its way out of my chest. The nausea rising in my throat. The dizziness that steals the strength from my legs as I collapse on my knees beside his body.

Thunderous explosions are going off all around us—I know they are because I can see rocks and trees and dirt flying through the air—but I can't hear anything above the sound of my own screaming in my head. Because what I'm looking at is the most horrific thing I have ever seen. And it's Flint.

His leg is sliced open from ankle to past the knee, all the way to the bone. His foot is barely attached to his leg, and blood is pumping out from a severed artery in his leg so fast, it can't even soak into the sand. Instead, his life is pooling all around him in a sticky, sandy, bloody mess and I know—I know I can't save him. No one can.

I can heal, but not this. Never anything like this. It's too much. It's just too much.

I turn to Hudson, who looks as shaken as I feel, but he grabs my arm and says, "Take whatever you need."

I don't know what I need, don't know how much power I'd have to find to possibly counteract this. But I'm running out of time to think. I have to do something, or Flint is going to die. My heart is pounding in my chest and my hands are shaking so badly, I can barely hold on to Hudson. But I do. For Flint.

Closing my eyes, I reach deep inside Hudson and pull out as much of his power as I can take. He's still weak from the Pit, but I gave him enough energy earlier to start the healing process, and he's a lot better off than he was even a few hours ago.

My tattoo burns as the magic lights each tiny needle prick in incandescent light, starting at my wrist and winding, winding, winding around my arm. By the time the tattoo is lit halfway up my arm, I decide I've taken enough. "Go!" I yell to Hudson as I turn toward Flint and set to work trying to heal him.

I close my eyes again and channel as much of my energy into Flint as I can, as fast as I can.

All around us, witches and vampires are attacking with fangs and spells and paranormal powers. But I don't pay attention to any of it. I can't. Flint has lost so much blood, he's in such bad shape, that any break in my concentration might end up harming him irreparably.

It's not like I'm an expert at this, not like I know what I'm doing. Like with Mekhi back before we came here the first time, I just follow the pain, follow the injury, and do whatever I can to bind what's been broken back together again.

Besides, Hudson has my back. I can hear him throwing vamps and witches away from Flint and me, know he's fading around and around to keep us safe, and I've never been more grateful that I have such a badass mate in my life.

I might not have enough confidence to trust anyone else like this, to just give my life and Flint's life up to them so completely. But this is Hudson, and if there's one thing I know, it's that as long as he has a breath in his body, nothing will touch us again.

So I focus on Flint and start with the artery, because if I don't get that stopped, fixing the rest doesn't matter. He's already lost so much blood. His breathing is shallow, his heartbeat too slow, and I know he doesn't have a chance if I don't hurry.

I'm not exactly a biology major, but I'm going to go with the small, slippery thing gushing blood as being the artery. I grab on to it—thankful it hasn't rolled back up his leg like I've seen in a few war movies—and get to work healing the opening.

It's harder than I expected it to be, and I don't know if that's because

I've never had to heal something this serious before or if it's because Flint is so far gone.

I don't like the thought of it being the second reason, so I block out the fear and concentrate only on what I know, on what I can figure out.

"Don't you die on me, Flint," I order as I squeeze the artery together and try to mend it by envisioning hundreds and hundreds of little stitches closing the severed pieces of tissue, holding them together.

I don't know if that's right, don't know if anything I'm doing is right, but the longer I hold the artery and stitch, the slower the blood flows. And in the middle of all this epic disaster, I'm going to consider that a win.

Heat burns through my hand, up my arm, and I nearly weep with relief at the proof that my healing powers have finally kicked in, are able to draw energy from my tattoo. And so I keep doing what I'm doing, imagining the stitches, imagining the artery weaving itself back together slowly, slowly, slowly.

But it doesn't take long before the heat starts to go away, and I know it's because I'm running out of power. I open my eyes, look around for the first time in several minutes, and realize Hudson is taking no prisoners. He's fading all over the area around us, and more than one vampire body hits the ground in the next few seconds.

I want to call to him, want to tell him that I need more, but I don't want to distract him. Not when people are dying out there and, with one distraction, he could just as easily be next.

He must feel me staring at him, though, because less than a minute passes before he's back, sitting down next to me. His face and hands are streaked with blood, he's breathing hard—a surefire sign that his energy reserves are running as low as mine are. But his cobalt eyes are as bright as ever as he offers his hand to me.

"I'm sorry," I tell him, hating what I need to do even though I have no other choice.

But Hudson just shakes his head, as if to ask, *What for?* And even manages a grin as he says, "Take whatever you need, baby. I'll be fine."

153

With Grace Power Comes Grace Responsibility

I take as little as possible from Hudson. I know it's not enough to even begin to heal what I'm dealing with from Flint, but I also know there's nothing I can say to keep Hudson from going back out there. I can't send him off with nothing, no matter what he says.

"You sure that's all you need?" Hudson asks as I turn back to Flint, and I nod, making sure he can't see my face as I do.

"Okay," he says, brushing a gentle hand over my hair. "Good luck." And then he's gone again, fading straight back into the fray.

I know it's bad out there. I can hear the screams and the growls, the sounds of bodies hitting bodies and bodies hitting the ground or the water. I still don't look, though. I don't want to know, not when Flint is still so close to death. And not when there's a chance I can save him.

I finally have the artery closed to my satisfaction, but there's so much more to repair. To begin with, if we don't get the muscle at least somewhat pieced back together, I am afraid the artery is going to roll all the way back up his leg. Plus, if I don't get the artery that's in his calf repaired, he's going to lose his leg—and that's *if* I can keep him alive.

I dig down deep, try to find more energy to do this next step, but there's almost nothing left. I'm exhausted, worn down, my power completely drained. But if I can't find something soon, I'll lose Flint, and I can't let that happen.

So I reach out for earth magic, let it flow up my legs and into my tattoo—but nothing happens. I glance down at the delicate pattern of flowers and leaves, but I can't seem to get earth magic to store inside my tattoo. I only spare a moment to wonder if the ink doesn't work with elemental magic before I decide that's a question for another day and instead try to just channel the earth magic to heal Flint.

But where Hudson's magic in my tattoo was strong and enabled me to quickly close an artery, earth magic is clearly only good for healing more minor injuries. I can't draw in enough power to heal Flint faster than he's losing blood. I'm about to give up and call out for Hudson to give me a little more juice when I glance left and spot Jaxon standing ten feet away, staring at Flint's mangled body.

"I'm here," Jaxon says as he fades to the mouth of the cave. And oh my God. I thought Jaxon looked bad before? As he stares down at Flint, the agony etched in his hollowed features grows exponentially. He thrusts his arm at me, shaken, his gaze never leaving Flint's leg. "Take whatever you need."

I don't think twice. I just grab on to him and channel and channel and channel, even as I keep my other hand on Flint's leg, sending some into Flint, filling my tattoo with the rest.

"Is it too much?" I ask after a minute, because Jaxon's looking mighty gray.

But he merely shakes his head. "Do what you need to do."

And so I keep taking energy from Jaxon with one hand, turning it into power within me and using that power to slowly start putting Flint's leg back together enough that I'll be able to attach the two pieces of the next section of severed artery together.

But can I just say that before I try anything like this again, I need some training, because instinct, high school biology, and emergency room dramas can only get me so far. They're not enough to teach me what I need to know to do this. And I'm so scared. My hands are coated in so much blood, and as fast as I'm trying to work, I can feel his heart slowing, can feel Flint slipping away.

I lift my hand from Jaxon's arm to let him know there's no point in killing them both, but he clasps his other hand over mine. "Don't give up," he begs me. "Please. I've got more."

I don't know if he does or not, but I choose to take him at his word. Because I can't give up on Flint. It would be like giving up on Jaxon, too. And so I grab his arm again, and I draw his power into me, seek out more tears in Flint's blood vessels, and I knit.

I'm working as fast as I can, sweat dripping down my face as I turn my attention from one mangled area of his body to another, careful to take some of Jaxon's power and store it in my tattoo for later as well as heal, and for the first time, I think I might actually be making progress. Flint's heartbeat is still dangerously slow, but I've almost got the blood flow stanched. I need a little more and—

Luca fades right up to us. "Hudson says—" He breaks off as he sees Flint for the first time.

"What—" His voice breaks. "What do we— What can we—"

"She's doing it," Jaxon tells him, voice blank but eyes absolutely livid.

Luca falls to his knees beside Flint, picks up his hand, and presses it to his face. "Please," he whispers to me. "Please."

"I've got him," I tell Luca, even as I pray that it's true. "I'm not letting him go."

He nods, looks at Jaxon. "What do I do?"

"Use it," Jaxon snarls, and Luca nods.

Seconds later, he's gone, and screams split the sky as witch and vampire alike fall to the rocks below us.

I don't bother to ask if it's Luca doing the killing. I already know that it is.

"Go," I tell Jaxon, and he takes off as I turn to Flint and continue to heal. I think about changing to my gargoyle form, about taking a small piece of myself and using it to heal Flint the way I did Mekhi. But every instinct I have is urging me to stay the course, screaming at me that it's not time for that yet, that this is the only way to save Flint.

And so I do, pouring everything I have inside me into him until my tattoo grows dull again. Each time it happens, I grow weaker, more exhausted, but it only makes sense. Power is a gift and a responsibility, but no matter how much you have—or how much you can borrow—there's still a price for cheating death.

I've learned it from Jaxon, from Hudson, from Mekhi, and even from Xavier in his own way. There is only so much power can do, but here, now, for Flint, I'm determined to do whatever that is. Whatever it takes.

Hudson and Jaxon pop back around, and they're even bloodier, even more beat up this time. Still, they hold their wrists out to me, and I don't hesitate as I grab on to both. I take energy to do the next round of healing, and then they're fading right back out.

Luca stops in a couple of minutes later to check on Flint. He's shaky, not steady on his feet, but still insists I siphon as much as I can from him. The moment I touch him, I realize he's nowhere near as powerful as Hudson or Jaxon, but he's got some power, and I do my best to tap into it. It's harder with him than it is with the two of them, and I don't know if it's because he just doesn't have the same strength or if it's because my life has been irrevocably connected to the Vega brothers.

I guess it doesn't matter in the long run, especially since Luca jerks away from me the second a witch pops up next to us. She sends a bolt straight at Flint but it misses, and Luca takes off after her. He almost catches her, but at the last second she turns around and sends a spell careening straight toward him.

He tries to dodge, but it's too late. The bolt slams straight into the center of his chest.

154

Till Death Do Us Part

I scream as the sickening scent of charred flesh fills the air. It makes me gag, nearly makes me vomit, but I swallow down the bile...until Luca's lifeless body lands a few inches from where I'm kneeling.

I knew he was gone before he hit the ground, but it doesn't stop me from reaching for him, from telling myself it's not true. From trying to take it all back.

But it's too late. There's nothing left for me to do, nothing left for me to heal. He's gone. He's really gone.

And Flint is likely to follow.

Grief and fear and rage consume me. How can this be happening? He sends us to jail for trying to stop a war and now he's *starting* one? He's killing people, destroying them, because he's greedy—and because he can. But *we're* the criminals?

I look out at what was once one of the most peaceful, beautiful places I'd ever seen. Hot springs and trees against the backdrop of mountains and an arctic sea. Now, it's littered with bodies, with blood and gore and broken hearts, and I want to be out there. I need to be out there.

The wolves are here, too, now, fighting with the vampires and the witches. There are so many of them—too many. There's no way the dragon guard can hold them off, even with so many of my friends fighting alongside them.

I think about shifting. About going out there to fight with Hudson and Jaxon and Macy and Mekhi. But if I do, Flint will die. It's true they need more fighters, but I have to trust them to pull this off. Trust them the way that they're trusting me to take care of Flint.

It's a lose-lose situation, but maybe—just maybe—I can save Flint. Maybe. And if I can, maybe they can find a way to save the rest of us.

I scramble back to Flint's body, wishing I had something to cover Luca with out of respect. But there's nothing, so I empty myself in an effort to save the boy who Luca gave his life for. The boy who Luca loved.

Tears are flowing down my face, sobs racking my body, and I know that I need to stop. I need to take a minute and just get my shit together. But I can feel Flint's spirit flickering inside him, and I know that this is it. This is when things go right or they go very, very wrong.

And so I keep my hands where they are, emptying every single speck of power that I can find inside him. A werewolf bounds across the rocks at us, and I brace myself for the attack. I've left myself open. In draining myself this much, I don't even have enough energy left to shift.

But at the last second, Macy drops down in front of me, and she sends a spell at the werewolf that petrifies him where he stands, his body sliding straight off the rocky edge into the hot springs.

"Jaxon told me what happened," she says. "I've got you." And then she performs another spell, one that slaps up a magical barrier between us and the rest of the world.

Hudson basically squeaks in before the barrier closes. He takes one look at me and holds a hand out so that I can siphon more power. But then his eyes fall on Luca's body, and everything inside him withers right in front of me.

"He was trying to protect Flint," I tell him even as I take his hand and channel more power from him. Not too much, because I know why he's here this time, and it has nothing to do with giving me power and everything to do with putting an end to this once and for all.

"Who was?" Macy asks, turning around for the first time.

She gasps as she catches sight of Luca's body, her eyes filling with tears as she looks between him and Flint's injury. "Oh no," she whispers, and I know a part of her is thinking about Xavier.

I brace myself, expecting her barrier to falter—it's hard to control magic when your emotions are volatile, I'm learning the hard way—but Macy's magic never wavers. Instead, she locks her jaw, keeps her wand pointed at the barrier, and stretches her other hand out to me.

"Use me this time," she says. "Hudson needs his energy more."

Which means that she, too, knows why he's here.

I switch to channeling her energy. It's so different from Hudson's or Jaxon's or Remy's that at first I'm not sure I'm even doing anything. But then I feel it, feel her—light and feminine and powerful in a very different way—and I start pulling in as much of her as I think she can stand.

More screams echo outside our barrier, and Hudson seems to crumble right in front of me. "Grace," he whispers, and I nod. Because I know what he's here to ask. I know what he needs me to say.

He is the one who can save us. He is the one who can bring all of this to an end. But at the same time, what will it cost him to do it?

Everyone is afraid of him, of what he can do. But that's only because they don't know how much he hates his powers. How he would trade them in an instant.

I saw his eyes in the Chamber, saw how tortured he was by what he'd done and what he could do. He's used his powers only once in all the time I've known him—the day of the Ludares challenge. And even then, even furious at his father and enraged at the idea of me dying, he'd made sure everyone was safe. Made sure that when he brought that stadium down, no one was inside it.

But here, now, it's the opposite. If he uses his powers—if he takes off the leash he keeps tied so tightly around them—it would be the nuclear option.

He doesn't say a word, but he looks at me with eyes that have seen too much and a heart that has been broken too many times to bear. At first, I think he's asking for my permission, but the longer I gaze back at him, the more I know that that's not it at all. He's seeking forgiveness, not for the past but for what he's already decided to do.

Not because he's a murderer like his father or an opportunist like his mother but because he loves the people who might very well die in this fight if he doesn't stop it. Jaxon. Macy. The rest of our friends.

Me.

That's the real rub, the one thing he could not bear. It's written all over his face—he would disintegrate anyone—everyone—if it means saving me. He would literally set fire to the world.

The girl I used to be, the girl who once judged him so harshly, would be horrified by that thought. But the woman I've become—the woman who has fought alongside him for her friends, for her family, and for the men she loves understands more than he would ever think she could.

Because I would burn down the world for him, too, if I had to.

And so I do the only thing I can do for him. I nod.

He closes his eyes, blows out a breath. He opens his eyes again and holds me transfixed. Then murmurs, "I love you."

I smile, because I know what he means. I know that he loves me, not because I forgive him but because I gave him permission to forgive himself. For someone who has spent two centuries torturing himself over things that he's done and things that he hasn't done, it's a powerful gift.

I whisper back, "I know," and his eyes crinkle slightly at the corners at our inside joke.

Then he closes his eyes...and lets me go.

He squares his shoulders, prepares himself for what he has to do. And even though it could very well crush his soul, he's going to save us all. He's going to go out there and be the person he needs to be. Not for me. *Because* of me. The same way he makes me want to be the best version of myself because of him.

And that's why I know what I have to do.

I can't break our bond just because Jaxon needs me. Yes, I hate the idea of him suffering for something that wasn't his fault, for losing his soul over something he never had any control over. But we'll find another way.

Because this beautiful boy standing in front of me has never asked anything of me for himself. And he deserves the best of me now. Just as I deserve the boy I love.

I reach deep inside myself and grab on to our blue string. I squeeze it as hard as I can and watch Hudson's eyes widen. And I say, "I choose you."

I can see the indecision on his face, read it in his every breath. A beautiful symphony of agony and ecstasy playing across his features. He wants me, but not at the cost of killing his brother. And I love him even more for that.

"It's okay." I smile at him gently. "I chose so you don't have to. Now go kick some ass so I can focus on Flint and then come back to me where you belong. We'll find another way to save Jaxon's soul. If Cyrus wants the Crown this badly, I'm betting fixing a soul is the least it can do."

Hudson's face goes blank for one second, two, and I start to ask him what's wrong. But then I realize it's not blank at all. There are tears in his eyes, and he's trying not to let them fall before he heads out to deliver the ass-kicking Cyrus and his allies so richly deserve.

Before he turns away, he squeezes the mating bond right back and finally opens himself up to me. And oh, what I see—as he reveals what's really inside him—I learn what I've been missing. Learn that my fears have been groundless.

Because for me, Hudson's love is endless.

155

I Never Promised
You Forever

Hudson starts to move back through the barrier, but before he can, Jaxon lands on the cliff right outside the cave entrance. He grabs on to the wall, and Macy drops her magic enough for him to stumble inside.

"Jaxon?" Macy gasps, reaching out.

But Hudson gets there first, catching him with an arm around his waist just as Jaxon's legs give out. In a grim voice, Jaxon mutters, "Fucking Cyrus."

"What's wrong?" I ask, straining to see…and then wish I hadn't. Because there are two massive bites on the side of his neck.

"No," I whimper as I look at Hudson. "Don't tell me that. Please don't tell me he bit him." But he did. The evidence is literally all over Jaxon. The eternal bite.

"What do we do?" Macy gasps as her gaze darts among the three of us. "How do we fix it?"

"We can't fix it," Hudson growls, and he's shaking almost as badly as Jaxon now. "I'm going to kill him. I swear to God, I'm going to kill that son of a bitch."

"Maybe I can—" I freeze, looking back and forth between Jaxon and Flint as my worst nightmare comes true.

"Save him," Jaxon tells me, his voice already broken and shocked from the pain.

I remember that pain, remember every second of agony as Cyrus's venom spread through me. I want to hold Jaxon, want to wrap myself around him and take the pain away, but I can't even do that. I can't do anything but watch him die.

"Did you hear me, Grace?" Jaxon reaches out, grabs hold of my hand. "Take it all. Take everything inside me and *save Flint*."

"No." I shake my head as tears I didn't even realize I had left to cry spill down my cheeks. "No, Jaxon. No. Don't ask me do that. I can't. I—"

"Listen to me," he grinds out. "We both know I'm dead already. My body just hasn't hit the ground yet. Take whatever's left in me, whatever you can get, and use it to save Flint."

"Jaxon, I—"

"Please, Grace." He squeezes my hand as tightly as he can manage. "I'm begging you. Do this for me. *Please*."

My stomach revolts, and for a second I think I'm going to vomit.

How many times can one heart shatter?

How many times can I break wide open?

I'd do anything Jaxon asks of me, but I can't do this. I can't kill him. Not Jaxon. Please, God. Not Jaxon.

He must see it on my face, must know that I'm going to refuse, because now there are tears in his eyes, too. Hudson moves to lay him down, but he grabs on to me with his left hand. "Grace," he says, and for that one moment, it's as clear and commanding as anything he's ever said to me. "If I ever meant anything to you, if you ever loved me at all, you'll do this one last thing for me."

My gaze finds Hudson, and he looks as devastated—as decimated—as I feel. But when our eyes meet, he nods.

And I know it's the right thing to do, but still. It makes me so mad—at him, at Jaxon, at the whole fucking universe—because they aren't the ones who have to do this. They aren't the ones who will have to live with this for the rest of their lives.

"Okay," I whisper, and I take one second—just one precious second—to smooth Jaxon's hair back from his face. "I'll do it."

"Thank you," he whispers, his hands dropping away from me.

"Lay him next to Flint," I instruct, kneeling between them as Hudson does as I ask.

Once he's settled, I put my hand around his wrist and ask, "Are you ready?"

He nods, even as he stares at me with pleading eyes. "Don't leave me, okay?"

"What?"

"When it's done, when Flint is healed... I know I don't have the right to ask anything else of you, Grace. But please, I don't want..." He closes his eyes, as if ashamed. "I don't want to die alone."

I only thought my heart was broken before because, just like that, it cracks straight down the middle. "You don't have to worry about that," I promise him. "I'm not going anywhere."

Behind me, Macy is sobbing full-out, and Hudson looks like he's ready to rip his father limb from fucking limb—a plan I am more than on board with.

I close my eyes, take a deep breath, and prepare to kill the first boy I ever loved.

156

Talk About a Dustup

It only takes a second before his energy starts pouring into me, his power lighting up my tattoo so bright that I can barely look at it. There's so much power—so much heart—inside him, it only takes a few seconds before the tattoo starts to undulate on my arm, snaking up and down and around as it glows more and more brightly.

My other hand is on Flint, and I'm pouring Jaxon's unchecked power into him in a way I couldn't do before. Normally, when I channel power from Hudson or Jaxon, I skim the surface, take only what's on the very top layer. But now, with Jaxon, I dig deeper so that the energy rolling out of him, rolling through me, rolling into Flint is more powerful than anything I've ever tried to harness before—except maybe for Remy.

I can feel Jaxon weakening, can feel the spark deep inside him starting to grow dim, and it makes me want to scream. Makes me want to break the whole fucking world. But a promise is a promise, so I stay the course.

Already, I can see Flint's wounds getting better in a way they weren't before. The muscles are building up enough at this point that I might even be able to try to repair his leg.

Jaxon must feel himself fading, too, because he looks at Hudson and says, "You better take good care of her, or I'll haunt your ass for an eternity."

Hudson's eyes say he's screaming inside right along with me, but his voice is droll when he answers, "I don't think vampire ghosts are actually a thing."

Jaxon chuckles. "Yeah, well. You know me. Always wanting to be an original."

"That's for sure," I tell him, even as his words to Hudson register. Is that why he went after Cyrus alone? Because he had heard what I said to Hudson?

"I'm sorry," I whisper, and this time I can't keep the sobs at bay. "I'm so sorry."

"Nothing to be sorry for," he tells me. "I love you, Grace. Too much to ever let you choose me." He squeezes my hand. "This is how it was always supposed to go."

"Jaxon—" My voice breaks.

"No more," he tells me, eyes glittering with a million different emotions. "Now, hurry up and finish it. Pull out what you can get before that bastard's bite takes it all."

Hudson reaches over and puts a hand on Jaxon's shoulder. "I love you, brother," he murmurs, but Jaxon is too far gone to answer.

Then, with the fury of a thousand suns burning in his eyes, he gets up and walks to the edge of the rock formation we're balanced on.

"Drop the protection," he tells Macy, and there's something in his voice—in his demeanor—that has her letting go of the spell without so much as a word of protest.

He strolls all the way out onto the ledge, hands at his sides as he surveys the havoc and the damage his father continues to wreak.

A witch comes flying at him, wand at the ready. But just as she is about to launch her spell, Hudson glances her way. And she turns to dust in an instant.

He moves to look the other way at a small pack of wolves making their way up a boulder to ambush Mekhi from behind. With a flick of his wrist, not only are the wolves gone but so is the giant boulder Mekhi was standing upon. Dust fills the air around him as he falls harmlessly to the sand.

A pack of made vampires—under Cyrus's direction, I'm sure—makes a beeline for him, and Hudson disintegrates the whole group of them in the space between one breath and the next, the dust of what they used to be hanging in the air like a dream.

And still he's scanning the area, his gaze moving from tree to tree, boulder to boulder, for any sign of enemies—for any sign of Cyrus.

He's here; I know he's here. I can sense the evil in him. Can feel his malevolence infecting the whole area, and I can tell that Hudson can feel him, too.

In the meantime, Jaxon can't even keep his eyes open anymore, his energy so low that I know I won't be able to hold on to him much longer. Even if I don't let him go, even if I try to hold on, the eternal bite is closing in. Shutting down his organs and his systems. Turning him into petrified stone from the inside.

Death is too good for Cyrus, but I'll take it. I'll take anything that gets that bastard out of our lives for good.

Jaxon moans, shudders, and I know the pain must be excruciating by now. "It's okay," I whisper to him as I smooth a hand over his hair. "I'm right here."

He's too far gone to answer, but I keep stroking him even as I drain him of more power.

Outside, Hudson is still under fire...and still kicking ass. A rogue dragon sends a dagger of ice straight for him, but with a flick of his finger, the dagger disintegrates. And so do the dragon's wings.

In the blink of an eye, ten to twelve vampires swarm him—and then melt into nothingness with only a look. This is Hudson Vega, the most badass vampire in existence, and he is beyond livid.

He's walking along the edge of the cliffs now, decimating anyone who crosses his path. Two werewolves, teeth gleaming as they lunge for him, become dust. So does a witch lucky enough to land a spell on his shoulder.

Hudson staggers as the bolt slides through muscles, but the witch doesn't get a chance to touch him again. And neither does anyone else, because Hudson has had enough. He's made it to the edge of the rock formation, hands raised high above his head.

I brace myself, expecting anything—expecting *everything*—and when he lowers them in a powerful whoosh, I am not disappointed. Because out of nowhere, it all disappears. The hot springs, the surrounding cliffs, the dozens upon dozens of trees, all gone in the blink of an eye.

For several beats, everything comes to a stop. The fighting, the skulking, the flying spells. They stop as every single person in the entire area focuses on my mate. On Hudson.

He's drained—I can tell that last move took everything out of him. The energy he's given me, the fading, the fighting in the Pit, it's all caught up to him, and that last blast took everything he had in reserve. I can feel through the mating bond that there really is nothing left.

And yet he chose this path anyway. He could have killed everyone with that blast, could have melted their bones and turned every person in the whole area to dust if he'd wanted to.

Instead, he'd chosen mercy—and left himself vulnerable because of it.

There's a part of me that admires the move, that knows there's no forgiveness needed for what he's done here. But the rest of me—the mate part that loves him more than my own life—is livid. Because he's left himself wide open to attack at a time when he needs to be as invulnerable as possible.

But this is Hudson, and if there's one thing he's better at than razing things to nothing, it's bluffing. And as he stands up there, surveying everyone who has fought with him and against him, he raises his hands up again and bellows, "I will only show mercy once. Leave now or you. Are. Next."

No one moves, and I feel my stomach tighten as I realize that the bluff didn't work. That they are going to call him on it. But then I realize the witches are spinning portals as fast as they can make them, then diving through just as quickly.

And as they all flee—Cyrus at the forefront, I'm sure—I can't not think of Delilah's message from all those weeks ago. *Appear weak when you are strong.* And the second half she didn't say: *Appear strong when you are weak.*

He bluffed and, in doing so, saved us all.

157

All the Broken Pieces

As Hudson watches Cyrus's allies turn tail and run, I focus on Jaxon. And realize that I've taken all that he has to give. There's nothing left for him and, truthfully, barely anything left *of* him, either.

I hold his hand still, but I stop siphoning any energy from him. I direct the last little bit of power housed in my tattoo into Flint. Then smooth a hand down Jaxon's ashen face. His breathing is shallow now, his body shivering so much that Macy has shrugged out of her hoodie and draped it over him. But it's still not enough to stop the drastic shaking as his entire body prepares to enter the death throes.

"Was it enough?" Jaxon seems to gather some new reserves of energy, enough to choke the words out as I continue to stroke his face. Because there's no chance that I'll let Jaxon die alone as he feared. No chance he is going to die any other way than surrounded by love. Flint and me on one side of him, Macy on the other.

We owe him so much more than that, but here, now, it is all that I can give him.

"More than enough," I tell him, and he smiles, even as his eyes drift closed one last time.

"God, have I got a headache," Flint groans from the other side of me as he struggles to sit up. "What the fuck happened? What did Jaxon do? Did we miss the whole fight?"

Jaxon groans, though he's not strong enough anymore to open his eyes. "Leave it to you to bitch at me for saving your sorry ass," he says so quietly, I have to strain to hear him.

"The day you need to save me," Flint starts to joke, then freezes when he gets his first good look at Jaxon. "What's—" His voice breaks. "What's wrong with him, Grace?"

"Cyrus bit him," I answer softly. "And you were badly wounded. He didn't want to die with all his power inside him if he could save you, so I..." I let the words drift away, barely able to think them myself, let alone say them to Flint.

"Don't tell me that." Flint's eyes well up. "Don't you fucking tell me that, Grace."

He rolls over, tries to reach for him. "It's okay, Jaxon. You're going to be okay."

Jaxon laughs a little at that, which causes a massive coughing fit. "I think—" He starts when he can finally breathe again, then breaks off because he's too winded and it takes too much energy. "I think you've pretty much run out of time on that prediction," he finally manages to gasp out. "This is as good as it's going to get."

"No," Flint says, and there's an agony in his eyes I wouldn't wish on anyone. Then again, it's the same agony burning a hole deep inside me at this very moment. "Don't do this, man." He turns to me. "Don't let him do this."

"I can't stop it," I whisper, and I've never felt like more of a failure in my life.

"You're going to be okay," Jaxon gasps out.

It's the last thing he says as Hudson, Mekhi, and the rest of the Order come racing across the ledge with the dragon army right behind them. Once they reach us, as many of them as can fit crowd into the entrance of the cave. Hudson and the Order all look as broken as I feel. Even Eden is crushed.

Flint searches their faces with wild eyes, and at first I don't know what he's hoping to see—until the moment it dawns on me. "Luca?" he whispers, hunching in on himself like he can't bear to hear the answer.

I shake my head, whisper, "I'm sorry."

"What happened here?" Flint almost screams. "What the fuck happened here?"

No one answers as Jaxon's chest rattles, his breath growing more and more shallow.

Hudson falls to his knees beside his little brother, dropping his head onto Jaxon's shoulder as he grabs hold of his hand.

"Somebody please tell me what the fuck I missed," Flint begs as Jaxon exhales again. Long seconds pass as we wait for him to inhale. And wait. And wait. And wait.

But it never comes.

"He's gone," Macy whispers as she pulls her hoodie up to drape over Jaxon's face. "How can he be gone?" She's not crying now. She just sounds... bewildered.

"How did we let this happen?" Mekhi whispers, shrugging out of his own hoodie so he can do the same for Luca's body.

"It happened because I failed you," Nuri says, dropping to her knees beside her son and pulling him into a hug. "This is my fault. From the first time I aligned myself with Cyrus, I knew that this could happen...and still I did nothing. Still I let him run roughshod over every important law we had. And now we're here."

"They're gone, Mom," Flint whispers, tears streaming down his face, and he sounds more broken than I've ever heard him.

"I know, my love. I know." She looks away from his face to the terrible wound at the bottom of his right leg, and when she turns back to me, she has steel in her voice. "There was no other choice? Only..."

"I tried," I tell her, even as shame burns inside me. "But either I'm not strong enough or it couldn't be healed. Not if I wanted to save his life."

For the first time, Flint seems to notice that the pain he's in is from more than an injury. It's because he's missing his right leg from the knee down.

"I'm sorry," I tell him. "I'm so sorry."

But he just shakes his head. "I've lost Luca and Jaxon," he tells me through a throat thick with fear. "What do I care about my fucking leg when I've lost them both?"

"No, son," Nuri says with a shake of her head. "You haven't. I won't let that happen."

"It's already done." Mekhi speaks up. "There's nothing to stop."

But Nuri squares her shoulders. "This is my fault. And I will set things to right." She moves to her husband. "Aiden, darling—"

"I'm here," he tells her, wrapping an arm around her waist like he needs to hold her up. "And I'll be right here no matter what."

She nods regally and then steps back.

158

Cross My Heartstone

My heart is in my throat as I watch Nuri move to the front of the cave entrance. I don't know what she's going to do, but I know it'll be something big. The way Aiden is looking at her like she's the bravest, most wonderful woman in the world tells me that much.

Flint isn't watching. He's got his head in his hands sobbing, and his grief is a wild thing tearing through the room, biting and clawing at all of us who are already in such bad shape.

Nuri holds one bejeweled hand up and changes into the most beautiful, elegant golden-brown dragon I have ever seen. She's proud and huge and regal, so regal, as she gazes down at her son.

Flint watches the shift, and his eyes go wide as his face drains of color. "No!" he screams. "Mom, no!"

He pushes up, tries to get to her, but he's still weak from everything he has lost, and one of his legs is still useless.

It's over in the space of one beautiful heartbeat. Nuri uses a talon to slice her chest open, then reaches inside and pulls out a glowing red jewel so big, it barely fits in her hand.

Her dragon makes one long, low, keening cry of sorrow, so heavy and profound that it has all of us falling to our knees in front of this woman and her sacrifice.

In a blink, she's human again.

Tears are pouring down Aiden's and Flint's faces and even Eden's cheeks, as they watch her walk to Jaxon. A sweep of her hand has Macy's hoodie on the ground, and then she's placing the jewel right in the center of Jaxon's chest.

As soon as it touches him, it starts to pulse, the light it casts diffusing through the room until every single one of us is touched by it. Only then does it begin to spin, slowly at first and then faster and faster as it seems to drill itself right into Jaxon's pale, still chest.

"Oh my God," Hudson breathes, his tone more reverent than any I have ever heard from him. "She gave him her dragon's heart."

The moment the stone finishes sinking into his chest, we all wait. One beat, then two. And then Jaxon gasps. His body arches off the ground where it's been lying, and he jackknifes into a sitting position as he draws loud gulps of air into his chest.

It's a good thing I'm still kneeling, because every bone in my body has just gone weak. Hudson grabs me and holds on tight, but he's shaking so badly that I'm not sure if it's because he wants to support me or because he needs me to support him.

Either way, we're holding on to each other now, and I figure that's the way it's supposed to be.

"Your dragon heart," I breathe. I remember the story she told me of the price a dragon paid to the Crone in order to leave the Aethereum: his dragon heart. *A fate worse than death*, she'd said.

"I've only heard rumors," Hudson says as Nuri's dragon guard surrounds her. "I didn't think it was possible."

She emerges cloaked in one of the dragon guard's capes, and her eyes zero in on Hudson's. "Yes, we can give our dragon heart if all the circumstances are right."

"It's rare, though," Eden murmurs. "Because once you gift it—" She breaks off, has to clear her throat as tears continue to slide down her cheeks.

"Once you gift it, you lose your dragon forever," Flint finishes. "You can never shift again."

My hands fly to my mouth as the pain of her sacrifice reverberates through me. I lost my gargoyle for a week, and I could barely stand it. Nuri just gave away her heart—and her dragon—to Jaxon for the rest of her life.

The sacrifice is unimaginable.

"Nuri." I call her name because this is the bravest, most beautiful act of love I have ever seen.

She just smiles at me. It's a sad smile but a smile nonetheless. "Whatever it takes," she whispers, and it brings me right back to that moment in her office and what we promised—to ourselves and to each other.

Whatever it takes to defeat Cyrus. Whatever it takes to keep the people we love safe.

I nod, and she shifts her gaze to Jaxon, who is staring at her, at all of us with wide, confused eyes. "You owe me a life debt, vampire. And I am claiming it here. Protect my son."

Jaxon nods, and the look on his face slowly morphs from shock to understanding. "Thank you," he whispers.

She inclines her head, then turns to her husband, who still has tears streaming down his face. "It is time to go home, my love."

He nods and shifts into a bright-green dragon that looks so much like Flint, it makes my heart ache. Nuri climbs on like she was born to ride a dragon—nothing like my awkward ascent onto Flint's back all those weeks ago.

We watch, silent and overwhelmed, as Aiden takes to the skies, the dragon army right behind him, carrying their wounded in their talons.

And as they stretch their wings, as they fly out to sea, the bodies of the slain dragons slowly rise from the ground beneath us, the last of their magic bearing them across the ocean to the Boneyard where they will rest for an eternity.

And as I watch them go, I think again of the vow Nuri and I made to each other.

These are still early days. The war is coming, the world we live in changing as incessantly as the seasons by which we mark our lives. But now, as I stand here, surrounded by the people I love most in the world, I finally understand what it means to rule with compassion. With dignity. With love.

159

On a Wing
and a Prayer

Silence reigns after the dragons disappear into the horizon. Until Macy whispers, "What. The. Fuck. Just happened?"

The words open a floodgate of emotion—astonishment, joy, despair, anger, fear, resolution. I think we all run the gamut as we stare at one another with wide and wild eyes.

Hudson collapses on the ground next to his brother, arm braced on Jaxon's shoulder as he keeps staring at him like he can't believe he's real.

Jaxon blinks at his brother. "My soul. I can feel my soul again."

As I watch Hudson pull Jaxon into his arms, a few tiny pieces of my broken heart start to mend themselves together. Because this is how Jaxon and Hudson should always have been, how they would have been had their parents and a grotesque promise not ripped them apart all those years ago.

With Mekhi's help, Flint manages to stand, then hobbles over to Luca's lifeless body.

Macy and Eden hold each other, faces pale with the ordeal we have all suffered through while Liam, Rafael, and Byron don't seem to know how to feel any more than they know what to do. They end up moving back and forth between Jaxon, who is alive again, and Luca, who I never even had the chance to try to save.

As for me, I stay exactly where I am—on the ground between them all as conversation and emotions ebb and flow around me.

"What does it mean for a vampire to have a dragon heart?" Macy whispers to Eden.

Eden gives her an *I have no idea* look and whispers back, "What does it mean to have a dragon queen who has given away her dragon?"

Macy shakes her head.

Flint kneels down beside Luca, jaw locked and eyes broken as he pulls

Mekhi's hoodie down enough to see his boyfriend's face. "I'm sorry," he whispers. "I'm so sorry."

It hurts worse when I remember the way he and Hudson were teasing each other just the other day, and the promises he made about what was going to happen when he saw Luca again.

"We need to take him home," Jaxon says hoarsely as he pushes to his feet. He's still a little wobbly, but Hudson reaches out to steady him.

Jaxon walks over and squats down next to Flint, his hand heavy on the dragon's back as he reaches out and takes Luca's hand for the last time. He murmurs something over the dead vampire, then turns to Flint, who hasn't relaxed his death grip on Luca's body one iota.

"It's time to let him go," Jaxon whispers to Flint. "You've got to let him go."

Flint nods even as his shoulders begin to shake. As he lets go of Luca, he seems to collapse in on himself, but Jaxon is right there, holding him up. Flint wraps himself around Jaxon, burying his head against his shoulder as he sobs.

Jaxon holds him through it, deep pain etched on his own face—for Flint *and* for Luca.

Tears roll down my own cheeks—I didn't know I could cry this much—and Hudson finds me. Of course he does. He pulls me up from the floor, wraps his arms around me, and holds me as I try to find the energy to keep going.

He's drained himself, his energy left on the field of battle. But somehow just holding each other—my arms wrapped around his middle as his lips skim across my hair—makes us both feel a little bit better.

"We need to take him home," Jaxon says again, his voice thick with his own grief when Flint finally stops crying.

Flint nods, jaw working but eyes finally dry. The Order nods as they move in to pick up the body. Seconds later, they've faded away.

Only then does Flint grab Jaxon and me in a hug and whisper, "Thank you. From the bottom of my heart, thank you."

I don't say anything back—there's nothing to say at a time like this except what's already been said—so I hug them both as tightly as I can. Then Jaxon and I step back as Flint shifts, his dragon form much better at balancing his missing leg than his human form is yet. And then he takes to the air to help the Order bring Luca home.

When they're gone, those of us who are left—Jaxon, Hudson, Macy, Eden, and me—all kind of collapse, the emotions of the last few hours catching up with us.

I don't know how long we sit there.

Long enough for my hands to finally stop shaking.

Long enough for my shoulders, and my soul, to finally relax just a little.

More than long enough for Hudson to pull me into his lap and hold me like I'm the most precious thing in his world.

Eventually, though, I'm ready to do what we came here to do, and I push myself to my feet. "I think it's time," I say, holding up the key I've managed to hang on to through everything.

"Damn straight!" Eden says, hopping to her feet right alongside me. "Let's go get this Crown and shove it up Cyrus's ass."

"I can totally get behind that," Macy agrees, holding out a hand so I can pull her to her feet.

Jaxon and Hudson nod, too, and then the five of us make our way along the rocky ledge until we get to the entrance that leads us to the Unkillable Beast.

160

Ill-Gotten Chains

The cave is exactly as I remember it, circular in shape with a giant, rocky wall against the back. As we get closer, the wall starts to move like it did last time, and the beast slowly lowers himself to his feet.

He's even bigger than last time, his shoulders wider, his chest broader. But his face looks the same, sad and a little macabre at the same time.

Please, no, he says, and I hear him in my head like I have for so many months. *Leave. You have to leave.*

It's okay, I tell him as I walk slowly but steadily toward him. *I came back to free you. Just like I promised.*

Free? he asks.

I take the key from my pocket to show him, and it becomes a kind of mantra in his head…and in mine. *Free. Free. Free. Free. Free.* Over and over again.

"Be careful," Jaxon tells me, his body poised to intervene.

"She's got this," Hudson tells him as he grins at me.

And I grin back at both of them, because some things will never change.

There are four cuffs—two for his wrists and two for his ankles—and after I undo the bottom two, I grab my platinum string and shift, flying up so I can unlock his arm cuffs as well.

As the last one falls away, the beast throws back his head and bellows like his life depends on it. The roar bounces off the rocky walls and ceilings, echoing throughout the cavern for several seconds.

And then he shifts, and a man is standing in front of me dressed in a royal-blue tunic, gold leggings with laces, and a gold and royal blue cloak tied over one shoulder and fastened with a large sapphire broach.

He's tall, with smoke-gray eyes and blond hair fastened into a braid. He's also got a short, pointed goatee and seems to be in his late thirties.

I shift back but don't try to approach him. "Are you all right?" I ask this man who has suffered so much and who, in his own way, has helped me through so many of my own troubles.

He looks at me like he doesn't understand what I'm saying, but eventually it must sink in because he nods. "Th-th-thank you," he finally manages to say.

I approach him slowly, but he shrinks away from me. And I get it. It's been a thousand years since he's been human, and the last people he saw did this to him.

My eyes narrow at the thought. Just one more atrocity Cyrus has to answer for.

"It's okay," I murmur to him—out loud and with my mind. "I'm a friend."

He stops, tilting his head like that last word gets through to him.

"Friend," I say again, placing my hand on my chest. "Friend. I'm a friend."

He studies me for a while, then puts a hand to his own chest. "Friend," he says as well.

I smile at him, then glance at Macy, about to ask if she brought some of the granola bars I practically live on when we go on trips like this. But she's already walking forward, a bottle of water in one hand and a pack of cookies in the other.

He won't touch them when she offers them to him, so I take them and try. I even open the bottle of water and take a sip to show him that it's okay. His eyes follow the water bottle like a starving man, and this time when I hand it to him, he practically snatches it away from me.

He drinks it down in a few long swallows. By the time he's done, Macy has another one for him. He drinks this one much more slowly, and I open his bag of cookies for him while Macy stashes the empty bottle in her backpack.

After he's had his fill of water and cookies, he bows toward Macy and me both, then says, "Thank you." This time his voice is a little stronger, more confident.

Which means it's time to ask him about what I came here for all along. "Crown?" I ask.

He looks confused, this poor man who is more instinct than human at this point. Who understands bare necessities like food and water more than he understands anything else.

"Do you know how to find the Crown?" I ask, and this time I hold my hands right above my head, mimicking the act of putting on a crown.

The confusion only grows worse as he starts to babble. "No crown. No crown. No crown."

It's not the answer I'm expecting—not the answer any of us is expecting—and I glance back to see worry on Hudson's and Jaxon's faces. Because if he doesn't have the Crown, where is it? And does that mean Cyrus can find it first?

But before I can ask him about the Crown one more time—just to be certain—he starts to babble again. "Her crown. Her crown. Her. Must give Crown to her. Must protect her. Must protect Crown. Her."

Now I really do rear back in shock, because who is *her*? And why does she need to be protected if she's already got the Crown?

161

Crown Your Sorrows

"I t's okay," I tell him, stepping closer so I can put a soothing hand on his shoulder. He freezes at my touch and I realize—like with the water—this is the first real human contact this poor man has had in more than a millennia.

The knowledge hits me deep inside, makes me want to hug him and punch Cyrus at the same time. I settle for patting his shoulder and saying, "I will protect her. If you tell me who she is, I will protect her."

His eyes narrow and he looks at me, half hopeful and half suspicious. "You will protect her?"

"I will. If you tell me how to get the Crown, I will give it to her, as soon as I save my friends."

Again that look, as if he's trying to assess me even through the jumbled mess of his mind. "You give her Crown?" he asks.

"After I save my friends, yes," I tell him. "But do you know where it is?"

He nods quickly. "You promise. Give her Crown. Protect her. Agree?"

I have no idea who "her" is, but if it gets me the Crown, I'm totally willing to try to figure it out. It's not like I want the Crown longer than it takes to defeat Cyrus.

But before I can agree, Hudson makes his way closer. "Be careful what you promise, Grace. It's not the same in our world. What if 'her' is Delilah? Or someone worse?"

I nod, because I know he's right. Look at Charon, who let us out of that prison against every instinct and desire he had, simply because he'd made a promise. What if I promise this Crown to the vampire queen or the Crone or someone equally as horrible who I don't even know exists yet?

And so I turn back to the man/gargoyle and ask again, "Who is 'her'?"

But he just shakes his head and says, "Crown give her," over and over and over again.

I don't know what to do, don't know what to say to get him to trust me with the whereabouts of the Crown or the identity of "her."

He's growing as frustrated as I am, maybe more, and this time when he starts to babble, he says something else. Something more important. "Give mate Crown."

I whirl around to look at Hudson, and he has the same thunderstruck expression on his face that I am sure I have on mine. "She's your mate?" I ask. "You want your mate to have the Crown?"

He nods.

"You want to protect your mate?"

He nods again. And I'm reminded of Falia and Vander, both of whom had to go a thousand years without their mates. It devastated them, nearly destroyed them, and I wonder what must have happened to this man's poor mate all these years. He was frozen in stone, but if she's still alive, she's suffered through all the agony of not having a mate, completely alone, unable to even communicate the most basic things to him.

I glance at Hudson again as something else occurs to me. If he has a mate, does that mean there's another gargoyle out there somewhere? That maybe the two of us aren't the only ones in existence? I mean, yeah, he could be mated to someone non-gargoyle—look at Hudson and me—but there's a chance she's a gargoyle. And that is the most wonderful and amazing thing I've heard in a really long time.

Hudson must feel my excitement, because he nods at me and even grins a little. I love that he reads me so easily and that—despite the bickering—we're so often on the same page when it really matters.

And so I turn back around and say in a loud, clear voice, "Yes. If you give me the Crown to save my friends, afterward, I promise to search for your mate and give it to her."

For the longest time, the gargoyle doesn't move. He just studies me with eyes that grow older with every second that passes—eyes that seem to hold eternity in their pewter-gray depths.

I'm about to say it again, to ask if he's okay, but then quick as a striking snake, he grabs my hand and says, "Agree. "

His palm slides against mine, and then he takes off running toward the entrance of the cave.

"What the—" Jaxon tries to race after him, but I stop him.

"Wait! Let him go. It's okay. There's nowhere to run, and we can chase after him in a minute."

"But the Crown," Macy says.

"He gave me something," I answer, scratching at my palm because it's suddenly burning and itching.

I turn it over, and tattooed right in the center of my hand, taking up almost my entire palm, is a series of seven concentric circles in the shape of a wreath...or a crown.

I hold my hand up for my friends to see, and as they all crowd around, I can't help asking, "Now what?"

You Really Can't Go Home Again
—Hudson—

"**R**eady to go home?" I ask Grace as Macy prepares to open one last portal.

She turns to me, and the wind is blowing her curls across her face, so it takes me a few seconds to realize she's been crying.

"Hey." I pull her into my chest, and she comes—which, honestly, feels a little like a miracle in and of itself in a morning that's been full of miracles already. "You okay?"

She nods even as she buries her head against me.

"Does it still hurt?" I take her hand, gently turning it over so that I can see the Crown emblazoned there. It's glowing eerily, something her other tattoo only does when it's actively channeling magic, which makes me wonder all kinds of things about this one. None of them good.

"It's not too bad," she answers. "More annoying than anything else. Not…"

"Not like the rest of the day, which has hurt like hell?" I fill in the blanks for her.

She nods. "Something like that, yeah."

"Macy's almost got the portal ready," I tell her, nodding to where Macy and Eden are laying stones on the beach.

"Good. If I never see this place again, it'll be too soon."

I know what she means. First Xavier, then Luca. Yeah, we managed to hang on to Jaxon and Flint, but only because of those aforementioned miracles. "I'm beginning to think this island is cursed."

"Or we are." Now it's Grace's turn to look down at her palm. "What am I supposed to do with this thing?"

"We'll figure it out," I promise. "Maybe Foster or Amka have some ideas about it. And if they don't, we'll find someone who does."

"Someone who won't chop off my hand just to try to possess it for themselves?" She lifts a brow.

"Good point. Surely there's someone who can—" I break off as she looks back toward the area that used to house the hot springs and trees and beautiful rock formations, an area that is now mostly dust.

Because of me.

I try not to panic as she stares at it for several silent seconds. I've spent the last hour waiting for the other shoe to drop, for her to realize that she doesn't love me after all. Or worse, that she doesn't love me enough to stand up to her feelings for Jaxon, feelings she couldn't help but realize as he lay dying right in front of her.

I wouldn't even blame her. Those moments when Jaxon was dead... I would have done anything to take his place again. Anything for it not to have been my brother lying there cold and lifeless.

Anything, that is, but give up Grace. Maybe she had the same thought about me, without the caveat.

But then she turns to me and smiles, and it takes my breath away all over again. And when she joins her non-tattooed hand with mine, hope trembles inside me like a bird just beginning to stretch its wings.

Even before she whispers, "I love you. I think I've always loved you."

And just like that, the bird takes flight.

Still, I don't throw myself at her feet and gush the way I'm desperate to—a man needs some dignity, after all. Instead, I smile and whisper, "I know," right before I take her mouth with mine.

It's a brief kiss—soft and sweet and perfect—but she pulls away laughing after only a few seconds. "Are you always going to say that?"

"If it's good enough for Han Solo and Princess Leia..."

She grins. "Then it's good enough for us?"

"Something like that." I pull her into my arms one more time just because I can. She melts against me, and I whisper what's been burning inside me for nearly six long months. "I love you. I love you, I love you, I love you."

This time she kisses me, and there's nothing brief about it. We don't pull away until we're breathless, our lips swollen and our bodies gasping for air.

"I love you," I tell her one more time. As I do, I slide a finger over her ring—the promise I made to her before I ever had a clue that we were going to end up here.

"I know." She smiles before holding her hand up between us. "So are you ever going to tell me what you promised me with this beautiful ring I'm never taking off?"

My chest feels tight in all the best ways—and so does the rest of me—at the idea of Grace wearing my ring for an eternity.

I think about telling her. It's not that I'm worried she'll freak out—I know now that she loves me and she isn't going anywhere. But still, I gave her this ring before I'd ever told her I loved her. Before I'd ever even kissed her. Maybe she needs a little more time to get used to us before I tell her what I promised her before we were even an official couple.

"I'll tell you," I finally say as I drop one more kiss on her too-sexy-for-my-own-good lips. "If you guess it correctly."

She narrows her eyes at me. "That doesn't exactly seem fair."

"I thought you figured out by now that I don't play fair."

She rolls her eyes. "Big, bad Hudson Vega?"

"I don't know about *bad*," I answer. "As for big..."

She pretends to think about it for a second, then says, "I think you promised to never let your ego get in the way." She gives me a mock-innocent look. "Oh, wait. Too late for that."

"Next guess?" I ask, grinning right along with her now.

"Hmm, how about you promised to never leave the toilet seat up. Which I would really appreciate, by the way."

If there's one thing I can say about Grace, it's that eternity will never be boring with her. Lucky, lucky me. "We're going to live a very long time, Grace. I can't be making rash promises like that."

"Okay, then how about—" She breaks off as Eden yells to us to get the lead out, that she has places to be.

Grace rolls her eyes. "Dragons always think the world revolves around them." But her voice is teasing as she starts pulling me up the beach to where Macy and her portal await.

On the way, we catch up to the other gargoyle, who hasn't spoken another word to us after he gave Grace the Crown. Part of me expected him to run somewhere we couldn't find him after we freed him, but he *has* been chained up for a thousand years. It's hard to imagine there was anywhere he'd really want to go.

And since there's no way Grace is going to leave him here on this island alone—she doesn't have it in her to abandon anyone—he's making the trip back to Katmere, too. At least I think he is. He didn't say anything, but he nodded when she asked if he wanted to come with us.

Macy's grin is fierce as we approach the spinning portal and so is Jaxon's, even as he says, "Don't rush on our accounts."

"Believe me, we won't," I shoot back, but I'm smiling just as big. Because he's not dead and neither is his soul, thanks to Nuri. Despite everything, I owe her a debt I can never repay.

"Ladies first," Jaxon says as he waves Grace toward the portal. She elbows him a little on her way but then turns and blows me a kiss before diving headfirst into it.

And she wonders why she never lands on her feet on the other side...

I make a mental note to give her a heads-up on the problem as I wait for Eden, the gargoyle, and Jaxon to go through. Then, after checking to make sure Macy's got everything she needs to follow us through, I step into the portal and fall, fall, fall through it.

And can I just say how much better Macy's portals are than the average? The girl's got a gift.

After about a minute, the portal ends, and I step through, expecting to find Grace and the others waiting for me. Instead, they're racing toward the school like the hounds of hell are after them. And maybe they are, considering the forest all around me is burning.

Macy tumbles onto the ground behind me, and she screams as she gets her first look at the devastation burning around us. "What's happening?" she demands.

"I don't have a fucking clue." I pick her up and throw her on my back before fading straight for Katmere's gates.

Jaxon is already inside, but I get there just as Grace and Eden land. "What's going on?" I demand as Eden slides the other gargoyle onto the floor, then shifts back to her human form.

"I don't know," Grace answers as the gargoyle settles on the entry steps and the four of us race up the stairs.

Macy lets out another little scream as we burst through the front doors to find that the common room on the first floor is completely wrecked. Couches are ripped to hell and back, chairs and tables smashed to bits. Both TVs are broken, and everything else is in pieces. Even the chess table near the stairs is shattered.

Jaxon races back into the room, a wild look in his eyes.

"Where's my dad?" Macy asks, her voice loud and shrill.

"Gone," he answers hoarsely. "Everyone's gone."

"You mean the students?" Grace asks. "Maybe they went home for break—"

"They don't go home," Macy says as she starts running down the hall, screaming for Foster. "Not en masse. Only the seniors leave."

Grace heads after her cousin, but Jaxon and I exchange a look before racing toward the stairs at a dead fade. We make it to the fourth floor at the same time. He turns left and I turn right, but it takes less than a minute for me to make it down the dorm hallway and back. The doors are all broken or hanging off the hinges, and there's no one around. No one.

"They're gone," Jaxon says grimly. "They're all gone."

"Yeah."

He shoves a hand through his hair. "What the fuck happened? Macy talked to her dad a few hours ago, and everything was fine."

But my mind is already working, a terrifying scenario playing itself out in my head. "What if everything that just happened was the distraction?"

Jaxon's eyes narrow as he looks around, arms up. "But what is this supposed to be distracting us from?"

"No, not this. I meant on the island, with the Crown. I wondered why the wolves never joined the fight until the very end, and now I think we know why. What if the island was the distraction and this..." I look around at the claw marks in the walls, the broken lights and torn-up banisters.

"This was the main event?" he asks, horror coloring his tone.

I get what he's feeling, what he's thinking. People died on that island today. A lot of people. Jaxon himself is only alive because Nuri sacrificed her dragon for him. For that kind of carnage, that loss of life, to be nothing more than a distraction?

Eden comes racing up the stairs. "We found Marise."

"What?"

"Grace and Macy are with her in the infirmary. She's the only one we've found so far—"

I take off, jumping down the stairs and landing on the foyer floor. I'm about to fade to the infirmary when the front door bursts open again.

I whirl, prepared to fight, but it's just the Order and Flint finally arriving.

"What the fuck?" Mekhi demands as they lay Luca's body on the floor and cover him with a fallen blanket. "What happened here?"

"Where is everyone?" Byron asks.

"We're about to find out. Marise is in the infirmary."

We fade to the infirmary, where we find more destruction. Grace and Macy have turned one of the beds back over and have Marise on it, but the vampire looks weaker than I've ever seen her.

"It was your father," she tells Jaxon and me.

"That's impossible," Jaxon tells her. "We were just fighting him—"

"His troops with an army of wolves," Grace interrupts. "They stormed the school, took all the students and teachers. Exactly as we feared."

"All of them?" Byron demands, looking around like he thinks a bunch of students are going to pop out of the fucking woodwork.

"Yeah, all of them," Jaxon grinds out. "There's no one upstairs, and everything's broken all to hell."

"You mean we're it?" Macy whispers, looking us over one by one.

And I get what she's thinking. There are ten of us—eleven, if you count Marise. Against all of Cyrus's considerable forces. Yes, we have the Crown, but that's *all* we have.

How the fuck are we going to fix this?

"This is an act of war," Flint says, and he's looking more than a little rough around the edges. Mekhi had faded with him here, but now he's leaning against a wall, his weight on his only good leg.

"The second act of war today," Byron adds grimly.

They're right. It is. Rage boils inside me, but I tamp it down, try to think through this whole fucked-up mess. No wonder he wanted Grace, Flint, and me in prison. No wonder he had everyone challenging us for the last few weeks, knocking the shit out of us, getting us grounded.

Of course this was his endgame all along, just as they'd feared. Kidnap the kids of the most prominent members of the Circle. Hold them until you get what you want—total and absolute control of everything. And who's going to fight you? The parents whose kids you are holding hostage?

I don't think so.

"If he wants a war," I say, looking around at our friends, all of whom look like they've been to hell and back, "then we'll bloody well give him a war."

"With eleven of us?" Liam asks incredulously.

"Yeah, with eleven of us," I tell him.

"We've beat bad odds before," Mekhi says.

"There are bad odds, and then there are everyone's-going-to-die odds." Rafael speaks up for the first time.

"Maybe that's true. But dear old Dad miscalculated this time," I say.

"And how's that exactly?" Macy asks.

"He didn't kill us on that island," Jaxon finishes for me as he, too, looks everyone in the eye individually. "And now we're coming for him."

"So, what?" Eden asks. "We're just going to bring this fight to him?"

"We're going to bring it to his motherfucking door," Jaxon says. "And then we're going to burn his shit to the ground."

"You need her."

I turn at the tremulous voice to find the guy who used to be the Unkillable Beast staring at us with anxious eyes. "She can save us. You need her."

"Who?" Macy asks, walking toward him slowly so as not to scare him.

"She can save us," he repeats.

"Who?" Macy asks again.

He points to Grace, or more specifically, Grace's hand. "Her. Her. Her." And then he turns to stone. And, not going to lie, didn't see that coming. Just great.

As everyone mills around, trying to figure out who "her" is and if there's another gargoyle around, I can't help thinking that I need to talk to Grace. Because if this is going the way I think it is—which is straight to hell—it's probably time I tell her what I saw that night in the laundry room all those weeks ago.

I think it's time I tell her about her emerald-green string.

END OF BOOK THREE

But wait—there's more!

Read on for an exclusive look at two
chapters from Hudson's
point of view.

Nothing is as it seems...

Blood Really Is
Thicker than Water
—Hudson—

Grace looks so knackered when we get back to Katmere from visiting the Crone that I want to wrap my arms around her and carry her to my room, but I have no idea if she'll let me or not. Or how awkward of a position that will put her in with Jaxon if she does.

Though, to be honest, I've about reached my capacity to care about awkwardness when it comes to Jaxon. Do I feel bad that the Bloodletter fucked him over? Fuck yeah, I do.

Do I feel bad that he lost his mate? In theory, absolutely. In practice, not so much, considering how things landed.

And finally, do I feel bad that I've somehow ended up with the kindest, most beautiful, take-none-of-my-shite mate a bloke could hope for? Not in the bloody slightest.

Grace is a fucking gift, one I'll be thankful for for the rest of my days.

Still, as we climb the stairs back to school, I can't help saying one more thing about this whole shite plan. "This is a bad idea."

"I agree," she says, shooting me an *obviously* look. "But I still think we can't rule it out."

"Rule it out?" I ask, incredulous. "How can we even rule it in? Tell me you don't actually trust that woman."

"'Trust' is a pretty strong word." She makes a face, and I love her. I do. But she is way too calm about this whole situation.

"'Trust' is utter recklessness," I tell her. "She lives in a bloody gingerbread house. I don't know about you, but I believe in truth in advertising, and I have no interest in being Hansel *or* fucking Gretel." Or Snow White, for that matter. Or any of the other eponymous characters in fairy tales with wicked fucking witches. The woman has issues wide enough to fly a dragon through.

But Grace just pulls a face at me. "I really don't think cannibalism is on the table."

"I wouldn't be too sure about that. Did you see the way she was looking at Luca?" I lift a brow.

"Yeah, well, I don't think that had anything to do with cannibalism."

We both laugh, and I know I'm grinning like a total tosser right now, and I don't even care. Being with her, making her laugh, it reminds me of the way things used to be. I knew I missed it—I just didn't know how much until this moment.

"You good?" I ask after a second, just to check in with her.

"Yeah." She nods. "I am. How about you?"

Fucking ridiculous to get a little moony-eyed about such a throwaway question, but when Grace asks me, it doesn't feel throwaway. Especially since she's the only one who's ever asked and then actually waited around to hear the answer.

Maybe that's why I say what's on my mind for once, instead of weighing my options. "I'd be better if you decide to sleep in my room tonight." Then try to pretend I'm not holding my breath like a lad with his first crush as I wait for an answer.

She rolls her soft brown eyes. "If I decide to sleep in your room tonight, I think we'll both look like zombies at graduation."

"I'm okay with that," I answer with a lift of my brows to let her know just how little sleep actually means to me. Especially if it's a choice between sleep and having her in my bed.

She tilts her head down so her glorious curls fall in her face. But then she grins and gives me a sexy little side-eye as she says, "Maybe I am, too."

The fact that she's twirling her promise ring around her finger as she says it only makes her words that much sweeter. She said yes. The words reverberate in my head. *She said yes.*

I reach over and brush one of her gorgeous curls out of her face, letting my fingers linger just a little. Her skin is so soft and warm, and it feels so good to be touching her that I think about pulling her against me right here and now and to hell with what anyone else thinks. Instead, I pull back and whisper, "I promise I'll let you get some sleep. Eventually."

And then all hell breaks loose.

"Don't you fucking touch her!" my bloody wanker of a brother snarls.

"This is all your fault! You and your mating bond are the reason she might die in prison, and you think you've got the right to put your filthy fucking hands on her?"

"Whoa, Jaxon." Mekhi fades over to him, tries to grab his shoulder, but Jaxon isn't having it.

Big surprise. The boy always was a drama queen.

But then he's right up in my face, so close I can smell the blood he had for dinner. It makes me want to punch him in the throat, but I settle for giving him a scathing look as I answer, "Well, at least I'm not the tosser who threw his mating bond in the trash, so maybe you shouldn't be too quick to come at me."

"You know what? Fuck you!" Jaxon roars. "You're a sanctimonious prick, and no one likes you. What the fuck are you even doing here?"

His words are a direct hit, but it's not like I'm going to cry about it. Two Vegas acting like babies are two Vegas too many. Instead, I snarl, "Apparently pissing you off, so I'll call that a win for the day. And here's a little advice. Keep acting like a bloody wanker, and no one's going to like you, either."

I start to brush past him, livid at the fact that he's such a fucking child, but then he grabs me and slams me against the wall so hard, my head bounces against the stone. And I lose another notch on my temper.

"Jaxon!" Grace grabs on to him, and the sight of her small hand on his arm makes me see red in a whole new way. "Jaxon, stop!"

"You just going to stand there like a cack-handed bell?" I sneer when he doesn't even acknowledge her. I'd give anything to have Grace look at me like she looks at him, and he just pisses it away. "Or are you actually going to do something? I haven't got all bleeding day for you to get your bollocks up."

"Hudson, stop!" Grace shouts at me. Like this is my fucking fault? He's the arsehole who can't get his shite together.

But it's too late. Captain Pouty-Pants has got his mad on, and out of nowhere, he snaps. He goes for my throat, and then he starts to squeeze just because he's a total fucking blighter.

"Jaxon! Jaxon, no!" Grace reaches for his hand, and I try to get her attention, to tell her to back off because my little brother is truly in a snit and I don't want her to get hurt. But she's not even looking at me—big shock— because she's too busy trying to placate the baby. I want to suggest she try a pacifier next time, but he's starting to dig in.

I'm so pissed off at the little prick that part of me wants to slap the shite out of him right here, but there's another part of me that wants to see how far he'll go. At least until he starts to use his telekinesis to hold me against the wall.

The little fuck.

"Please." Grace ducks between us and gets right up in Jaxon's face with her big brown eyes and sweet smile, even though I'm the one currently being choked.

For a second, I think about blasting out and using my power to persuade him to back the hell off, but I don't want to do that to him unless I actually think he's going to kill me. And if we get to that point, then we're all fucked. But for now, he's really more about causing pain and humiliation than actually trying to murder me, so I'll bide my time.

Grace doesn't seem to know that, though, considering she's now got her fingers wrapped around his hand and is trying to pry him off me. I'd say something, but he is cutting into my windpipe, so there's not a lot there to use to vocalize.

"Come on, Jaxon," she says in a voice that won't be ignored. "Don't do this."

He barely even looks at her. But the others are all up in the mess now, yelling at Jaxon, trying to pry him off me, and it's still not working. I'm thinking I'm going to have to do something soon or everyone is going to be totally freaked out. Apparently, they just don't do sibling rivalry over here in America the same way we do it in Britain.

And then Grace does something that makes me think twice about letting this go on. My *mate* reaches up and cups my brother's cheeks in her hands. Then she whispers, "Jaxon, look at me."

It's a bloody gut punch after she spent the weekend at the Dragon Court looking at me just like that. Holding me just like that.

He finally looks at her—of course he does. This is Grace, and how could he not? I'd do anything—everything—to have her look at me like that, just for an instant.

"It's okay," she whispers to him. "I've got you, Jaxon. I'm right here, and I'm not going anywhere. Whatever this is, whatever's going on. I swear I've got you."

The words make me bleed, but as Jaxon starts to shake, I actually do wonder if there's something more going on than my brother being a whiny arse.

And when he whispers, "Grace, something's wrong. Something's—" I can't help growing worried.

"I know," she answers as the whole room starts to shake. Things are falling off the walls, stones are cracking, and Jaxon's hand tightens on my throat enough that I start to feel light-headed. The room spins, and things start to go dim.

Thirty more seconds, I tell myself. Thirty more seconds and I'll do something to end this. But if I do that, if I break into his mind, that's a move I can't take back.

"The Northern Lights just came out, Jaxon," Grace whispers to him, her voice sweet and light. "They're right outside."

All around us, her friends make noises like she's doing something wrong. But I lived in her head long enough to know exactly where she's going. And while it hurts a lot to think of her like that—to think of them like that—I just let it roll over me. I can take the pain. I'm not sure Jaxon can.

"Do you remember that night?" she asks. "I was so nervous, but you just held my hand and took me right off the edge of the parapet."

The whole room shakes like a never-ending explosion is rocking its foundations. But still Grace doesn't give up.

"You danced me across the sky. Remember? We stayed out for hours. I was freezing, but I didn't want to go in. I didn't want to miss a second out there with you."

"Grace." His voice is agonized, his eyes broken as he focuses fully on her for the first time. It's the opening I've been waiting for, the chance to resolve this without crossing any more lines, but as Grace snuggles into him a little more, I strike out with perhaps a touch too much strength, and Jaxon goes flying.

My little brother roars as he hits the wall next to the door hard enough to leave a full-body imprint in the centuries-old stone. He recovers fast, though, and comes right at me as I bend over and suck a full breath in for the first time in long minutes.

Jaxon takes a swing at me—big surprise—and I dodge it. But when he whirls around and tries to use his telekinesis on me again, I've had enough.

"Don't you fucking dare," I growl and direct just enough power at him to make the marble beneath his feet explode, opening up a hole that Jaxon falls in.

It only takes him a second to jump out and come straight at me again. Which is fine. I've put up with a hell of a lot from this arse for the past few weeks, and right now, I'm done. I'm bleeding done.

Everyone must know it, too, because the others grab on to Jaxon with everything they have while Grace whirls on me.

"Stop!" she yells, and I freeze, even before she continues. "You need to back off. Something's really wrong with him."

She's right. I know she's right—I can feel it in him myself. But I can't help being pissed off that she's taking his side *again*.

Nothing to be done, though, short of acting like a tosser myself, so I nod and take a step back. Just in time to watch her turn back to Jaxon...as always.

Jaxon's calmed down enough that Flint and Eden feel comfortable letting him go. Luca gets between him and me—it's a little laughable that he thinks he's going to stop another confrontation, but I don't say anything.

Especially since it's Grace who convinces Mekhi to drop his hold on my brother with a whispered, "I've got him."

And then she walks right to him—right fucking to him—and pulls him into her arms.

It hurts more than I thought possible, even though I understand. There is something really wrong with my brother, and Grace is the only one he trusts to deal with it.

Fine, whatever. It doesn't make it any easier for me to see her holding him, his face buried against her neck and their bodies curving together.

And fuck, I don't want to do this. I just don't want to do this anymore. I'm sick of coming in second to my brother with my own mate over and over again.

I get it. I do. They've got history. They love each other. And I love them both. If something is wrong with my brother, of course I want him to get the help he needs. I just wish that help wasn't always from Grace.

They whisper between themselves for a couple of minutes, and I don't even try to hear. Whatever it is, it's between them. And once I know she's safe, that Jaxon isn't going to lash out at anyone else, I'll leave. Give them both the space they need.

And, selfishly I know, to give myself the space *I* need. Because it's hard not to need space when Grace starts talking this time, loud enough for the entire room to hear.

"You listen to me, Jaxon Vega," she orders loudly. "Whatever's happened between us, you will always be my problem. You will always matter to me. And I'm scared. I'm *really* scared, and I need you to tell me what's going on with you."

He starts to speak, then just shakes his head until she whispers, "Why did the Crone say that today? Why did she say that you don't have a soul?"

Everything inside me freezes even before Jaxon answers, "I didn't want you to know. I didn't want *anyone* to know."

"You mean it's true?" she asks. "How? When? Why?"

Like everyone else in the room, I lean forward to catch his answer, even as terror rips through me. Because no matter how pissed off I am at him and this situation right now, he's still the kid I used to protect from Cyrus. Still the kid I did my best to hide from Delilah's wrath. Still the kid I chose to die for when the only alternative was killing him.

"I knew something was wrong—it's been wrong for weeks. So when I was in London this last time, I went to see a healer," he tells Grace, even as he keeps a death grip on her hand.

"What did she say?" Grace answers.

"He said—" Jaxon's voice breaks. "He said that when the mating bond broke, our souls broke, too."

And fuck. Just fuck. I want to howl as rage and horror and fear tear through me in equal measures.

"What does that mean?" Grace asks. "How can our souls be broken? How can they—" Her voice breaks, too.

"It's because it happened against our wills—and so violently that it nearly destroyed us right when it happened. Remember?"

"Of course I remember," she whispers.

"You mated to Hudson right after, so the healer is pretty sure his soul wrapped itself around yours and is holding yours together, so you'll be okay. But I'm..."

"Alone," she says.

"Yeah. And without anything to hang on to, the pieces of my soul are dying one by one."

"What does that mean?" she demands. "What can we do?"

"Nothing," he answers with a shrug. "There's nothing to do, Grace, except wait for my soul to die completely."

"What happens then?" Grace whispers.

His grin is bitter. "Then I become the monster everyone's always expected me to be."

There's a lot more talking, a lot more horrible news to wade through, but I barely listen to any of it. Because there's nothing more to say that matters. Nothing more to say that will change anything.

There's no way either Grace or I could live with ourselves if we let Jaxon lose his soul. No way we could ever be together if we knew that doing so meant destroying Jaxon forever. Not when we both love him as much as we do, and not when we've both sacrificed so much for him already.

Grace turns around to meet my gaze, but I already know. I've known from the moment the words left Jaxon's mouth. So when she mouths, *I'm sorry*, it doesn't even hit.

How could it when the body blow came five minutes ago?

And so I do the only thing I can. I leave.

There's no place to go, no one to be with. The closest people I have to friends are in the foyer comforting my brother. Which is how it should be.

But my night has taken quite a turn from where I thought it was going to go, so it's not like I've got anything to keep my mind busy as I make my way down the stairs to my room.

I asked Grace to come back here with me earlier because I'd wanted to be with her. But I also did it because I wanted to see what she'd say. I wanted to know if what happened in New York mattered to her as much as it did to me or if it was just something that stayed there.

When she said yes...when she said yes, I don't think I've ever been happier in my life. And now, half an hour later, it's gone completely to hell. And all I have to show for it is a bruised throat and a long, mate-less existence.

Fate really is a fickle, fickle bitch.

But what's the alternative?

The truth is, there is none. And there never has been, despite the hope that's beaten like feathered wings deep inside me for months now.

Grace and Jaxon belong together. Even if the universe hasn't decreed it, the Bloodletter and some dark magic has. There's no getting around that now. Maybe there never was. I was just too naive to realize it.

When I get back to my room, there's nothing to do. Graduation is tomorrow, so there's no schoolwork. No late-night study session. No one to talk to.

And though I've spent my life alone, after these last few weeks with Grace and the others, solitude suddenly feels like punishment.

The silence gets to me—which is ridiculous, but there it is—so I put on some Dermot Kennedy just for the noise. Then I take a quick shower.

When I get out, I resist the urge to check my phone to see if Grace has texted me. It's harder than it should be.

It's okay, I tell myself as I drink down a bottle of water in a few gulps.

Everything's fine, I say to myself as I turn on the fireplace and get it burning hot.

It wouldn't have worked anyway, I reassure myself as I sit down on the couch.

I'm all right. Everything is all right.

I say it like a mantra, say it until I believe it. Say it until I can finally pick up my phone and text Grace in response to what turns out to be a half dozen texts she's sent me.

Grace: Hey

Grace: You okay?

Grace: I'm so sorry

Grace: I don't know what else to do

Grace: You there?

Grace: I wish it was different

Hudson: I'm good

Hudson: Hope you're good, too

Grace: Hudson, please

Hudson: Night

I put the phone down on the end table next to the couch.

See, that wasn't so awful.

None of this is actually good or bad.

It just is what it is.

Easy peasy, like Macy always says to me when we're playing chess. Easy peasy.

There's nothing else to say.

Convinced I've got my shit under control, I pick up the book lying next to me on the couch, the one I was reading before we went to the Dragon Court. I open it to the page I bookmarked and start to read. I even make it through two pages before I realize what I'm reading.

And as Dermot Kennedy switches over to JP Saxe and Julia Michaels's "If the World Was Ending," the words swimming before my eyes finally register.

And that's when I do the only thing yet another tosser who throws away his mating bond can do.

I go to the front of the book and rip out the first page of Pablo Neruda's *Twenty Love Poems and a Song of Despair*—the same book I gave to Grace on her birthday—and toss it into the fire.

I do the same with the second page. And the third. And the fourth and the fifth and the sixth.

Before I know it, I've burned the entire book.

And I'm still not okay. More, I'm pretty sure I never will be again.

Blood Brothers

—Hudson—

This is a bad idea.

A very bad idea. But since the alternative is staring at the ceiling in my room and pretending to be asleep while the clock moves at a bloody snail's pace, I figure a bad idea is better than no idea at all.

I put on a pair of running shoes and grab a hoodie; then I take the stairs three at a time.

All the way up to my baby brother's tower...because apparently he needs one to feel like a prince.

I figure he'll be asleep, but catching him with his defenses down might not be a bad thing.

But Jaxon must not be getting any more sleep than I do these days, because when I get to his room, he's not in bed. Instead, he's lying on a weight bench in the center of the room, bench-pressing a truly impressive amount of weight while Linkin Park blasts from his phone.

"What do you want?" he demands the second he sees me, his voice extra loud so I can hear him over the pounding music.

"Quality time," I tell him, deadpan. His only response is a roll of his eyes as he lifts and lowers the weights.

"So if quality time isn't on the table, I thought maybe you'd like to join me for a run?"

I know it's a strange invitation—our entire relationship is off and has been for a very long time—but I figure if one of us doesn't try to take a step, whatever fucked-up shite this is between us will go on for another century or ten, and I don't want that. Especially not with what's coming our way in the not-so-distant future. And especially not when Jaxon's been so fucking decent about Grace lately—something that's hard to believe but definitely appreciated on my part.

A long silence follows my invitation—too long if you ask me. But eventually Jaxon raises a sardonic brow and asks, "What? Are we bonding now?"

"Bonding seems a little extreme. I thought we'd start with talking and running. Preferably at the same time, if you think you can handle it." It's a deliberate goad, one that must hit its mark because the next thing I know, Jaxon is off the bench.

"Let me grab my shoes," he tosses over his shoulder as he walks toward his bedroom. "Then you can tell me what this visit is actually about."

Oh, I don't know. How about the fact that we've been at each other's throats for more than a century and I don't even know why? Besides the whole *born vampire supremacy misunderstanding* nightmare. And the *him killing me* nightmare. And the *mated to and in love with the same girl* nightmare...

Jesus. Is it any wonder our relationship is so completely fucked? The deck's been stacked against us from the very beginning.

Except I remember when it wasn't, probably a lot better than Jaxon does.

I remember when we were little and used to play hide-and-seek all over the Vampire Court. It used to make Cyrus so pissed, especially when Jaxon would use his powers to flush me out of hiding. At least a quarter of the fun of the game was seeing how mad our father would get when Jaxon's earthquakes disrupted his meetings. But Cyrus was already locking me up at that point, pushing me into losing my temper so he could test my powers, and any payback I could deliver was totally worth it to me.

Except when they took Jaxon away. Nothing was worth that.

I didn't get to see him for more than a hundred years, no matter how much I pleaded or how much my father used him as a carrot to dangle over my head to get me to do things I didn't want to do. At least it didn't take long to figure out that it didn't matter how well I controlled my powers or how well I performed in whatever destructive task he set for me, I would never get to see Jaxon.

I don't want that to happen again. And with graduation looming, I definitely don't want to go another hundred years without seeing my baby brother.

As he ties his running shoes, I walk around his room and try to find something I can "pretend" to look at to keep myself busy. To be fair, there isn't much. He's taken everything out of the sitting room since the last time I was up here, until the only things left are the weight-lifting equipment and a couple of stray books stacked on the windowsill. Next to a small carved horse.

It's not even a surprise—I saw it the last time I was here—but I end up stiffening anyway. Because I don't know how I feel about the fact that he still has it. And he probably has no idea why it matters.

I start to turn away, but in the end, I can't resist picking it up. I spent days carving it for him when we were kids, and while it's not a perfect model of his own horse, it's pretty good. Even the mane and tail look about right. I can't help being impressed with young Hudson's skills.

I hold it up to get a better look at the defined swirls in the mane and tail. Yeah, not too shabby at all.

Except when Jaxon comes back from his bedroom, a bigger scowl than usual flits across his face. "Why are you touching that?" he demands, striding across the room to get to me.

"Why do you care?" I shoot back, even as I put the horse back down gently.

He doesn't answer, just walks out the door.

"Where do you want to run?" Jaxon asks as we make our way down the stairs to the front door.

"Down the other side of Denali?" I query. "Near the resorts?"

"Sure." Once we're outside, he takes off at a full-on fade, not quite what I'd had in mind.

I catch up to him, and we fade alongside each other for a while, but it's not exactly conducive to talking.

He finally slows down for a second at the bottom of the mountain and I stop, determined to have my say before he takes off again.

"Hey." I grab his arm.

Jaxon turns around with his fist clenched and, for a second, I think he's going to punch me. Instead of fighting back, I decide to let him.

But the swing never comes.

He drops his fist. Shakes his head. And asks, "What are we doing here, Hudson?"

My skin starts to feel too tight. "I thought we were running?" I say as casually as I can manage.

"Not what I mean, and you know it." He walks a little bit away, leans against the trunk of one of the big trees that fill up so much of the wilderness around here.

I do know. I clear my throat. Shift my weight back and forth. Stare off into the distance. Then finally manage to get out, "I wanted to say thank you."

"For Grace?" he demands hoarsely. "Don't thank me for that. The mate thing was all her—"

"I'm not thanking you for the fact that she's my mate," I tell him. "I'm thanking you for…"

"What?" he demands, and suddenly my baby brother looks tired. Really, really tired.

I blow out a long breath. "For what you did the other night," I finally say.

He shrugs, jaw working. "It didn't mean anything."

"It meant everything—to me and, I think, to Grace. You didn't have to do that—"

"Yeah, I did," he tells me. "Watching Grace walk around like a whipped puppy may not bother you, but I couldn't take it anymore."

It's bait, no doubt about it, and I know he threw it out there like that just to see if I would take it. But even knowing that, it's hard to walk away when I've spent weeks trying to get out of their way, despite Grace's and my bond.

Still I manage it, nodding and speaking through gritted teeth as I answer, "That's fair."

"That's *fair*?" he mocks, and his black eyes are narrowed dangerously. "Nothing about this is fair, Hudson. You'd know that if you weren't so busy being magnanimous."

"Is that what you think I'm doing?" I ask him.

"Isn't it?" he shoots right back.

"Not even a little bit. I'm trying—" Again, I break off, because it's not easy to talk to him at the best of times. Right now, when he's determined to mess everything up? He's impossible.

"What?" he snarls.

But I don't answer him. I can't. Instead, I just shake my head and turn back toward school. I knew going in that this was a bad idea. I just hadn't realized how bad.

"So you're just going to walk away?" he mocks. "You get me out here, and now you're just going to walk away without telling me what you want? Real mature, Hudson—"

Something inside me snaps.

"I want my brother back!" I hurl the words at him like knives.

He freezes. "What did you say?" he finally asks hoarsely after a few seconds pass.

"You asked what I wanted." I bite out the words. "That's what I want. I *want* my brother back. I miss him." I swallow. "I miss you."

He stumbles back. "It's hard to miss what you've never had," he tells me.

"Is that what you think?" I whisper. "That we never had a relationship?"

"We didn't." He sounds so sure. "I got shipped to the Bloodletter when I was young. You stayed at home with dear old Mom and Dad and that was that. We're just two strangers who happen to share the same blood. It doesn't mean shit."

"You don't really believe that," I tell him, even as something breaks inside me—something I didn't even know was there.

"I do believe it. It's not our fault. It just is what it is. Trying to change it after nearly two centuries—" He shakes his head. "There's no point. Especially now."

"The point is you're my brother."

"So what?" He shrugs. "It's not like our family tree means shit to either of us. There's nothing I got from either of them—from any of you—that I want to keep."

The words hit like actual punches, and before I can stop myself, I'm snarling back, "Then why do you keep it? If you want nothing to do with any of us, why do you keep it?"

"Keep what?" he asks impatiently.

"The horse. I made it for you more than a hundred and fifty years ago, and I gave it to you the day Delilah took you away. If we're two people who just share the same blood, if family doesn't mean anything, why do you still have it?"

"*You* made it?" he whispers.

"Yeah. I still have the scar to prove it." It's a small, wicked-looking hook across my left index finger. "Where did you think it came from?"

"I don't know. It's just always been there..." He trails off as he realizes what he's saying.

"You were crying the day they took you away. The only thing that made you stop was that damn horse. Thunder—"

"Thunder."

We both say the name at the same time.

"I'm sorry," I tell him. "I never meant to hurt you. I never meant for any of this to happen."

"I know." He looks down, shuffles his feet. "And I'm sorry I... killed you. It was a shit move."

For a while, neither of us moves as the words hang there between us. And then we both crack up. Just full-on, rollicking guffaws. Because seriously, that's one hell of a thing to apologize to someone for.

"You think they make Hallmark cards for that?" I ask when we finally stop laughing. But just imagining it sets us off again, and for long minutes, we do nothing but stand there in the middle of the wilderness and laugh and laugh and laugh.

We don't stop until an alarm goes off on Jaxon's phone. "I need to go," he says. "I'm helping Grace study for history in half an hour."

Those words would have stung an hour ago. Hell, they would have stung fifteen minutes ago. But now, I don't know. They seem...if not right, then at least okay.

Kind of like Jaxon and me.

We're not right yet. We may never be right. But we're better than we were, and maybe that's enough for now.

Maybe it's a start.

I can't help grinning at the thought, even before Jaxon narrows his eyes at me and says, "Race you back?"

And as we take off fading back up Denali, I can't help thinking that sometimes you get lucky. Sometimes the family you're born with and the family you make coincide. And that makes all the difference.

Pulse-pounding romance, epic world-building, and plenty of twists and turns. Turn the page to start reading your next book obsession!

Prologue

Draven

Even from our position on the roof, the alleyway reeks of cured meats and rain-soaked garbage, the stench curling upward like it's as desperate to leave this place as I am.

A metallic groan splits the silence in the alleyway below us, and my gaze sharpens as a fainter scent penetrates the rotten odor, almost hidden beneath it—something *different*.

The door swings open, and a thick streak of yellow light darts across the cracked pavement. A girl shoulders a bag of garbage into the alley, striding quickly toward the dumpster still in the shadows. My heart kicks up a beat.

"She doesn't look like much," Cassiel says from my left, his obsidian wings tucked in tightly behind him. His eyes are as sharp as mine, piercing through the night without difficulty. The girl wrestles the garbage over the lip of the dumpster like the bag's filled with bricks. "Certainly not enough to tear a hole through the world."

I cut a glance at Cassiel. "That's exactly what the lion says to the honey badger right before getting his ass handed to him."

Cassiel arches a brow but then returns his attention to the girl.

She wipes some of the misty rain from her forehead, lingering by the dumpster like it's the only quiet break she's had all day. Then her gaze snaps down the alley.

Her spine straightens, and my heightened senses prickle as she effortlessly shifts into a defensive stance.

"Two of them," Cassiel says, his voice low and cold.

"Humans," I say, scenting them on the air.

A woman cries out, and the girl rushes toward the sound in a blink. It's like her instincts push her *toward* the danger instead of away from it.

Cassiel and I move silently along the deli's roof, keeping her in our sights.

"Todd, stop!" the woman cries out. "This isn't funny anymore. Stop," she pleads again as she struggles against a much larger man's hold.

"Hey!" The girl skids to a stop before the struggling pair, and the man

Chapter One

Harley

"Are you sure you don't want to bail after..." Kai—my best friend and total worrier—motions to my split lip and bruised cheek as we hustle down the crowded sidewalk toward Bottom Lounge.

"It's nothing," I say, shaking off his concerned stare. I told Nathan the same thing—the guy in the alley earlier? That was nothing compared to what I'm used to. "You've been planning this for months, Kai," I continue, allowing real excitement to chase away the grittiness from earlier.

Adrenaline still sizzles in my blood, but the buzzed sensation isn't anything new to me. At least the girl got away. Rather me than her.

"Besides," I say, forcing myself out of my head, "Nathan is watching Ray." My boss is my absolute second favorite person on this planet, right behind my baby sister. With her safely taken care of tonight, it's my one chance to pretend to be someone else...*anyone* else. "My dad thinks I'm working a double shift," I add. "I'm ready to have fun." I loop my arm through his.

Kai looks like he wants to argue, those blue eyes searching my face and lingering on what will be a hell of a bruise tomorrow. But we've been friends for almost a decade, so he knows not to push me on this.

"Be honest," he says as we round a corner and the small bar comes into view. The brick building's black lettering is illuminated by a single backlight, and a few concertgoers hurry through the doors. "How excited are you?"

I grin up at him, one of the few unhindered smiles I've mustered lately. I've had a countdown for this concert since he snagged the tickets—a rare escape. Any nights away from Ray are a struggle because the distance feels like a physical strain on my soul. But I know Nathan will keep her safe, and in the end, that's all that matters.

Tonight—and *only* tonight—I get to act like a normal girl headed to a concert with her best friend.

Not the real me—a girl who has worked tirelessly to survive her home life and graduate high school, raise her baby sister, and soon, hopefully, help her escape.

But tonight? Tonight, I want to be someone else entirely.

"Beyond pumped," I finally answer Kai, dropping his arm as we show the bouncer our tickets and head through the doors.

Instantly we're hit with the opening act's music—loud bass filtering through the small space. Dim lighting illuminates the stage and half of the dance floor, the rest of the place covered in a faint darkness that sets the electric mood—which is exactly what I'm looking for tonight.

"Dance floor or bar?" Kai asks, his voice barely heard above the music and chatter.

I bite my lip, torn between my craving for a strawberry lemonade and my need to move. My muscles itch to sway, to lose myself to the music and simply *be* for a few blissful hours.

"Dance floor," I answer, tugging him through the crowd of people covering the floor.

The opening act finishes up, and after a small break, my favorite artist takes the stage. Bishop Briggs isn't just a phenomenal singer—she writes songs I can relate to. Pain, secrets, having a dark side—they're fire.

"Happy early birthday, Harley," Kai says after I've stopped cheering at the sight of her.

"You're seriously the best," I say as we dance in the small space we've claimed—well, *I* dance, while Kai sort of shuffles side to side a foot away. He's never hidden his distaste of dancing from me before, but he indulges me on special occasions. Something I'm forever grateful *and* guilty for. I'll never be able to repay him, even when he says I don't need to. All the money I earn from the deli, I save to keep Ray and myself fed, clothed, and, hopefully soon, free.

Once I have enough saved for an apartment—

Stop.

I clench my eyes shut, focusing on the music. I'm not going down that road now. Not tonight, the one night of the year I've allowed myself to be the version of Harley I wish I could be—fun, baggage-free, maybe even a little wild.

I laugh at myself then, and Kai tilts his head, but I wave him off. Even if I can explain it, he won't be able to understand. And why would he? Kai has the perfect life—loving family, wealthy, smart as hell. He'll never need to pretend to be anyone else.

The band transitions to a slower, sultry song, and I adjust my pace, escaping in the notes that tumble over one another like honey dripping from a bottle. Sweat beads on the back of my neck, and I lift my long red hair up, gathering it in a knot atop my head.

"You need a drink?" Kai asks, hunching down a bit awkwardly for me to hear him over the music.

"Please?" I nod without stopping my moves.

He flashes me a thumbs-up, then slips through the crowd at a slow pace, heading toward the bar.

A rough shove and a quick *sorry!* has me tumbling backward—another overzealous dancer knocking into my space.

Warm, strong hands steady my shoulders from behind, but I quickly right myself and shake them off.

I whirl around, ready to apologize for the domino effect, but the words die in my throat.

I look up and *up* to lock gazes with a pair of amber eyes that stare at me with such intensity, the hairs on the back of my neck stand on end. His skin is a rich golden brown, his hair a mess of black curls atop his head. A black shirt cinches tightly over tons of corded muscle.

I suck in a sharp breath—not from how hot he is, because, *yeah*—but because of his eyes. There is something there, a churning sense of emotion I can't put my finger on. It stirs up my insides, anticipation and curiosity and just the hint of fear.

"You're welcome," he says before I can get a word out.

"Excuse me?" I gape at him. "I didn't need your help."

A smirk shapes his full lips, a grin equal parts mischief and danger. He raises his hands in defense. "I guess next time, I'll let you fall."

I blow out a breath, calming my instincts to argue. "Thank you," I say a bit begrudgingly. *Who the hell is this guy?*

"Of course," he says, his eyes practically gold in the flickering lights bouncing off the stage. The music swells to a new song, the concert still going full swing despite everything in my world narrowing to him. "Now that we've got *that* out of the way," he says, arching a brow at me. "Should we dance? Or do you not need help with that, either?"

A laugh rips from my lips. "You want to dance?" I ask, rolling my eyes. "Is that your game? Rescue girls *not* in need and then ask them to dance?"

"For one," he says, shock coloring his eyes, "you couldn't handle the games I play. Two—"

"There isn't *anything* I can't handle," I cut him off, my heart racing from the back-and-forth. I can't deny the electricity buzzing in my blood from the verbal battle, or the fact that I could've left him in the dust a half dozen times now.

But here I stand, unable to resist hearing what he'll say next.

"I think you truly believe that," he says, then shakes his head. "Two," he continues. "It was a friendly question, not a marriage proposal. You don't have spit fire over it."

My lips part open, a tiny gasp escaping. He's pinned me—my default setting is defensive, but I have my reasons.

He flashes me a questioning glance, muscled arms outstretched in an offer.

And I'm almost as shocked as he looks when I step into his space and start to move.

Maybe it's because he's a stranger. Maybe it's those eyes or maybe it's because I want so desperately to be a different Harley tonight. One who can laugh and flirt and dance with a dark stranger.

Either way, I purse my lips. And *move.* "Can you keep up?"

"Try me," he says, his hands falling lightly to my hips.

And his touch is *searing.*

I sway back and forth, watching as he matches me dip for dip. Instantly, like a magnet, he falls into my dance, that grin lighting up the sharp angles of his face.

This is the Harley I want to be—fun and flirty and adventurous. I force myself out of my own head and dive into the music, the dance, the way this stranger laughs with each roll or sway or dip.

"You like this song?" I ask when the band shifts to a new tune.

"It's...enjoyable," he says, the words low and rough.

A warm shiver skates over my skin, my heart racing against my chest. "From the way you're smiling, I'd say you're *more* than enjoying it."

"It's not the song," he says, his breath warm from where he leans down to speak into my ear.

The fingers on my hips flex, and I whirl out at his gentle nudge. Another laugh escapes my lips as he draws me back in, and I can't help it—I love the way he dances. Love the way he dives in headfirst, matching my moves and upping the game with some of his own.

"What is it, then?" I ask once I've caught my breath.

"It's you. You're a bit reckless when you dance." My heart stutters at his words, at the way he's watching my every move. "You consume the space."

My stomach dips, a bubbly sensation filling my lungs so much, I can't breathe. Reality sets in, and I shake my head as I step out of his touch. He stays close but doesn't reach for me. I can't decide if I like that or hate it. "Do lines like that *ever* work?" I ask.

"Depends on the girl," he says, shrugging.

"Not this one."

"Definitely not." He smirks. "Give me time," he says. "I've been told I'm an acquired taste."

A warm ripple races down my spine as I'm suddenly thinking about what he tastes like. From the smell of him—all citrus and cedar and amber—I'm guessing pretty damn great.

"I don't have time," I say, the truth in that statement catching up with me. I have tonight—this one night of freedom I'm allowing myself. The rest?

Take care of Ray at all costs.

All the wild adrenaline wears off, leaving me slightly cold inside.

He leans down, his full lips at the shell of my ear. "That's the first true thing you've said all night."

"And it's the last," I say, stepping out of his touch as the band shifts to another tune. "Thanks for the dance." I back up another foot, both relieved and disappointed when he doesn't protest.

"Harley!" I hear Kai call from behind me. I glance over my shoulder and spot him at the edge of the dance floor, two drinks in his hands as he motions me over. I turn back around, my hand prepped for a wave goodbye, but the boy is gone.

I scan the area around me, almost desperate to lock onto those amber eyes.

Nothing but dancers laughing and cheering.

I ignore the hollow disappointment that sucks at the bottom of my stomach.

I already stopped the dance. Of course he left after my obvious shutdown.

I start toward Kai, forcing myself to smile.

Forcing myself to forget the searing heat I feel lingering on my skin from the stranger's touch.

Tonight isn't over, but I can't help but feel like I've lost something.

A pair of golden eyes flash behind my lids and a thrill shoots straight through the center of me.

I continue to give the place furtive glances, but even after an hour, the dark stranger never shows up again.

For the best, I think.

Because I've never allowed myself to *want* anything before, and I sure as hell can't afford to start now.

Acknowledgments

Writing a book with as many moving parts as this one takes a whole village, so I have to start by thanking the two women who even made it possible: Liz Pelletier and Emily Sylvan Kim.

Liz, I know this was the roughest one yet, but I loved (almost) every second of it. Thank you for continuing to push me past what I think I can do as a writer, for dragging me out of my comfort zone, and for helping me create a story I will be proud of for the rest of my life. You are a truly brilliant editor and an even more incredible person and friend. I can't wait for our next adventure.

Emily, I hit the agent jackpot. Sincerely. We're sixty-six books in, and I couldn't be more grateful to have you in my corner. Your support, encouragement, friendship, and joy for this series has kept me going when I wasn't sure I'd be able to make it. Thank you for everything you do for me. I am so, so, so lucky that you were willing to take me on all those years ago.

Stacy Cantor Abrams, it is a joy to be working with you on the biggest YA series of my career. You gave me my first break in YA all those years ago, and the fact that we still get to work together is such a bright spot in my career and my life. Thank you for all you've taught me through the years and for all your enthusiasm and late-night help with the Crave series. I feel so lucky to have you in my life.

Jessica Turner, thank you so much for making the magic happen. You are the most amazing associate publisher I've ever had the pleasure to work with. Thank you, from the bottom of my heart, for all you've done for this series. I am blessed to have you on my side.

To everyone else at Entangled who has played a part in the success of the Crave series, thank you, thank you, thank you, from the bottom of my heart. Bree Archer for making me ALL the beautiful covers and art all the time, and for always being so amazing when I need help with something. Meredith Johnson for all your help with this book in all the different capacities and for talking me through a few meltdowns. You're the best! To the fantastic proofreading team of Judi, Jessica, and Greta, thank you for making my words shine! Toni Kerr for the incredible care you took with my baby. It looks amazing!!!!! Curtis Svehlak for making miracles happen on the production side with such grace and humor and for putting up with me (still) being late on everything—you are a godsend! Katie Clapsadl for putting up with all the questions as I learn this brave new world, Riki Cleveland for being so lovely always, Heather Riccio for your attention to detail and your help with coordinating the million different things that happen on the business side of book publishing.

Eden Kim, for being the best reader a writer could ever ask for. And for putting up with your mom's and my badgering of you ALL the time. ☺

In Koo, Avery, and Phoebe Kim, thank you for lending me your wife and mom for all the late nights, early mornings, and breakfast/lunch/dinner conversations that went into making this book possible.

Emily McKay, for all these years of friendship and for the support and safety blanket you have always offered me. You are one of the very best things that this career has given me. I love you lots.

Megan Beatie, for all your help and enthusiasm with getting this series into the world. Thank you so much for everything!!!

Stephanie Marquez, you are the best thing to ever happen to me. Thank you so much for all the excitement, love, kindness, support, and help you give me every day. And most of all, thank you for finding me.

For my three boys, who I love with my whole heart and soul. Thank you for understanding all the evenings I had to shut myself up in my room and work instead of hanging out, for pitching in when I needed you most, for sticking with me through all the difficult years, and for being the best kids I could ever ask for.

And finally, for fans of Jaxon, Grace, Hudson, and the whole crew. Thank you, thank you, thank you for your unflagging support and enthusiasm for the Crave series. I can't tell you how much your emails and DMs and posts mean to me. I am so grateful that you've taken us into your hearts and chosen to go on this journey with me. I hope you enjoy Covet as much as I enjoyed writing it. I love and am grateful for every single one of you. xoxoxoxo

Let's be friends!

🐦 @EntangledTeen

📷 @EntangledTeen

📘 @EntangledTeen

📰 bit.ly/TeenNewsletter

entangled teen

an imprint of Entangled Publishing LLC